the quest for the trilogy

THE ROVER SERIES FROM TOR BOOKS

The Rover

The Destruction of the Books

Lord of the Libraries

The Quest for the Trilogy

The Quest for the Trilogy

A Rover Novel of Three Adventures

mel odom

TOR®

A TOM DOHERTY ASSOCIATES BOOK
NEW YORK

This is a work of fiction. All the characters and events portrayed in this novel are either fictitious or are used fictitiously.

THE QUEST FOR THE TRILOGY: A ROVER NOVEL OF THREE ADVENTURES

This book is printed on acid-free paper.

A Tor Book
Published by Tom Doherty Associates, LLC
175 Fifth Avenue
New York, NY 10010

www.tor.com

Library of Congress Cataloging-in-Publication Data

Odom, Mel.
The quest for the trilogy : a rover novel of three adventures / Mel Odom. —1st ed.
p. cm.
"A Tom Doherty Associates book."
ISBN-13: 978-0-765-31517-5 (acid-free paper)
ISBN-10: 0-765-31517-3 (acid-free paper)
1. Historians—Fiction. 2. Librarians—Fiction. I. Title.
PS3565.D53Q47 2007
813'. 54—dc22 2006039658

First Edition: March 2007

Printed in the United States of America

0 9 8 7 6 5 4 3 2 1

For my son, Jeremy Johnson,
who has always been in my heart.
The world can be a dark place, but you've always
been one of the lights in mine.

Love,
Dad

Acknowledgments

To Brian Thomsen, who always keeps an eye peeled for shoals and reefs, and is always good for a tale or two.

To Lawrance Bernabo, who keeps a light out for traveling literary characters, and whose opinions are valued.

To Janet Adair, who supports the Rover series with her patronage, enthusiasm, and by sharing her books.

To Kathleen Doherty, who has always been the perfect hostess and a charming conversationalist.

To Tom Doherty, whose vision and love of literature allow countless worlds and stories to be born.

And to Amy, Joe, and Lauren, faithful readers all. Enjoy the adventure!

BOOK ONE

Boneslicer

Foreword

"Education Is Overrated, Grandmagister Juhg!"

"Having second thoughts, Grandmagister?" a deep voice asked from behind Juhg.

Startled, Juhg turned and faced the speaker. He hadn't even heard him approach. But that was usual for the man. Craugh had spent much of the last thousand years skulking in shadows.

He stood on the loose cobblestones of the street. Dressed in dust-stained russet-colored homespun garments, he didn't look like a wizard. Instead, six and a half feet tall and skinny as a rake, he looked like a weary traveler, days from his last meal.

A wide-brimmed, peaked hat shadowed his face from the noonday sun, but it didn't completely smooth out the crags years had left stamped upon him. Scars lay there too, from knife and sword and arrow. Still, his hawk's beak of a nose and his bright green eyes implied power and a relentless nature. He leaned upon the rough staff he carried, hand resting idly on the crook at the end of it. He drew his other hand through the tangled mess of his long gray beard.

In all the years past that Juhg had known the wizard, Craugh had only referred to him as "apprentice," as if he were the only Novice Librarian that Grandmagister Lamplighter had ever taken on to train at the Vault of All Known Knowledge. Now, with the Grandmagister's departure and Juhg's naming to the position of Grandmagister, Craugh addressed him by his title. Most of the time.

(Sometimes the wizard still referred to Juhg as *idiot* and *buffoon*, and those weren't meant as terms of endearment. They both missed Edgewick Lamplighter, for reasons each their own, but that didn't mean they agreed how to proceed without their friend.)

"I'm long past second thoughts," Juhg muttered. He drew himself to his full height, still only a little more than three and a half feet tall. He was a dweller, much thinner and more wiry than most. Dwellers tended to be short and stout, and fat in their later years when they could afford to succumb to their innate selfishness. Juhg was pale at present, with fair hair and a youthful appearance. Today, instead of Librarian robes, he wore finery that he felt uncomfortable in.

"Eh?" Craugh said, holding a hand to his ear.

Juhg sighed. He hated it when the wizard pretended not to hear him because he couldn't speak *tall* enough.

"I'm long past second thoughts," Juhg said more loudly, curbing at least three—no, *four*—sharp retorts that came to mind to address Craugh's hearing ability as well as his advancing years.

At the moment, though, he didn't wish to lose Craugh's support and—perhaps it would stretch the very nature of the definition to call it such—friendship. As the new Grandmagister negotiating with the important leaders of the dwarves, humans, and elves along the Shattered Coast, Juhg felt inept and very much alone these past few days.

"Good," Craugh said, and smiled grimly. "You should be of a more positive mind."

"I'm probably on forty-sixth or forty-seventh thoughts," Juhg admitted. "And that's just today. After lunch." In truth, he felt sick. Even so, he felt driven to at least attempt to accomplish the goal he'd set for himself. "I just don't want to botch this."

"Nonsense." Craugh gazed up at the town meeting hall. "You'll do fine."

Making himself breathe out so he wouldn't hyperventilate, Juhg checked his journal to make certain it was the right one and he hadn't forgotten his notes. "I'm afraid they don't like me."

"Poppycock," Craugh said.

Juhg felt a little relieved at that.

"They don't know *you* well enough not to like you," Craugh went on. "It's your ideas they hate."

Those are exactly the words of confidence I was looking to for inspiration. But Craugh's assessment of the situation, however true it might be, stung Juhg's pride. He stood a little straighter and looked into the wizard's insolent gaze.

"They don't know my ideas well enough to hate them," Juhg insisted. "I've barely begun speaking."

"Then perhaps," Craugh said, "we should go inside and finish what you have begun." Without another word, he stepped toward the town meeting hall.

Sighing again, taking one last look at the ship in the harbor, Juhg followed the wizard. *Craugh will lead you to your doom*, he warned himself. *How many times did Grandmagister Lamplighter tell you about adventures he went on because of Craugh? Dozens! At least that many. And how many times did those adventures nearly get him killed? At least nearly every time. At one point or another.*

In the main hallway, dwarven and human guards dressed in heavily armored leather stood watch over the door to the meeting room. They held axes and swords naked in their fists. All of them were sworn to provide security for the important people they represented. Atop the building, elven warders stood at the ready, their hawks and falcons skirling high in the sky to keep an eye on the countryside and the sea.

One of the human guards challenged Craugh, swinging the long handle of his axe to block the way. The guard was younger, taller, and broader, and evidently full of himself concerning his fighting prowess.

"Who are you?" the guard demanded.

Drawing himself up to his full height, Craugh fixed the man with his stare. Displeasure and anger clouded the wizard's face. Lambent green sparks jumped and swirled at the end of his staff.

"I am Craugh," he declared. And his voice filled the space in front of the door like a blow.

Immediately, the guard paled and took a step back, clearing the way. He broke eye contact. His hand shook on his axe. "Forgive me. Please don't turn me into a toad."

The reputation the wizard had for turning people into toads when they irritated him was known far and wide around the mainland. It was rumored that he had increased the toad populations in some areas by whole communities.

Craugh passed on without another word.

Juhg started forward as well, but was blocked instantly by the guardsman's axe. Looking up at the guard, who had seen him both days before when he'd gone into the meeting hall, Juhg blinked in disbelief.

"Who are you?" the guard challenged, sounding fiercer than ever. Evidently he felt he had to regain his status with his companions.

"You know me," Juhg said, exasperated.

"Show me your bracelet," the guard ordered. Copper bracelets stamped with trees, ships, and mountains had been issued to those who were allowed into the meeting.

"I'm the Grandmagister," Juhg began, starting to push back his sleeve to reveal the bracelet. His wrist was bare. Feeling stupid, he remembered that he'd left the bracelet in his room aboard the ship.

"Well?" the guard demanded, as if sensing weakness on Juhg's part.

"I'm the *Grandmagister*," Juhg said again. "I don't look any different today than I did yesterday or the day before."

The guard leaned in more closely, obviously wanting to intimidate Juhg with his greater size.

Juhg, who had grown up as a slave in a goblinkin mine, who had carried the left legs of fellow slaves who had died in the mines back to the harsh overseers to prove the hapless individuals had indeed perished, was not intimidated. He had fought wizards (though not because he wished to), battled goblinkin (only because running hadn't been an option at the time), and faced incredible monsters (drat the luck he sometimes had when he thought about it). Juhg was not impressed.

Although Grandmagister Lamplighter had freed Juhg from the goblinkin slaves and taken him back to Greydawn Moors during one of his adventures, the Grandmagister hadn't ever been able to free him from his anger. Two days of being largely ignored and sometimes ridiculed hadn't set well with him.

Before Juhg could stop himself, he caught the human's big nose in a Torellian troll nerve pinch and squeezed. Torellian trolls had at one time been known for their torture techniques. Lord Kharrion had made extensive use of them during the Cataclysm.

The guard yelped in stunned and pained surprise. Paralyzed by the grip the Grandmagister had on his snout, the burly human dropped to his hands and knees and quickly begged for mercy.

Shocked at what he had done, aware that the guard's companions were closing in on him with edged steel, Juhg released his hold and stepped back. "I am the Grandmagister," he said again.

"I don't care who you are, bub," one of the other human guards growled, "no one lays a finger on one of Lord Zagobar's personal—"

Craugh raised his staff and brought it down sharply. Green lightning flew from the bottom end of the staff and shot along the hallway floor. Several of the armored guards cried out or cursed. Many of them jumped and rattled their armor. A few of them fell—*splat!*—on their backsides.

"He's with me," Craugh declared, glaring at the guards. "Does anyone have a problem with that?"

"Of course not," the guards all replied in quaking voices. "Go right inside. Sorry to be any trouble."

Juhg heaved out a disgusted breath as he trailed in the wizard's wake. *A wizard should not get more respect than a Librarian.* But that was the way it had always been. After all, Librarians couldn't turn malcontents into toads.

Behind him, one of the dwarven guards took off his hat and enthusiastically smacked the fallen human guard with it. "You stupid miscreant! You could have gotten the lot of us turned to toads!"

Juhg had to hurry to keep up with the wizard. They passed through the rows of seats, most of them filled with those who had come to the meeting. They still glared at Juhg with a mixture of awe, disbelief, and resentment. Several were openly hostile. After all, during the thousand years that had followed the Cataclysm, most of them had thought all books were destroyed.

Lord Kharrion's campaign, besides taking over the world, had been directed toward the destruction of every book that had been written. During the war with the goblinkin, none of the elves, dwarves, or humans had known Lord Kharrion was searching for *The Book of Time*, which had been lost. *The Book of Time* was indestructible.

The fact that Kharrion had also been Craugh's only son remained unknown by all except Juhg.

Craugh stopped so suddenly that Juhg nearly tripped over his own feet while trying to stop. The wizard turned around and gestured Juhg to the front of the great hall.

Juhg stood for a moment. "I thought perhaps," he said quietly, "you might like to say a few words."

"No," Craugh replied.

"But you came such a long way."

"To hear *you*."

After two days of arguing and attempting to justify his existence, Juhg felt hollowed out. *I should have run for the ship*, he told himself.

Impatiently, Craugh waved him to the front of the room. Lamps lit the stage there, filled with lummin juice, which the glimmerworms of Greydawn Moors produced, and which burned more cleanly and efficiently than whale oil or tallow. That fuel had interested several of the merchants among the crowd and lent proof to Juhg's statement that he was from another place.

But a *Library*? When Juhg had first told them that, even though most of them had heard the rumors that had spread when the Vault of All Known Knowledge had been destroyed almost eight years ago, they had looked upon him with derision.

He was a dweller. By their standards, since dwellers couldn't or wouldn't fight, didn't produce anything worthwhile, and on the whole were known for their greedy and selfish ways, he couldn't possibly be in charge of such a great thing as the Vault of All Known Knowledge. In fact, Grandmagister Lamplighter had been the first to ever hold that office who wasn't human.

"Go," Craugh admonished, shooing Juhg along as he would a child.

Reluctantly, Juhg walked to the front of the assembly. He felt the cruel stares boring into his back. His feet felt leaden and everything in him screamed, *Run!* But he didn't. He was following in Edgewick Lamplighter's footsteps and forging a path of his own.

Grumbles and curses arose all around him, sounding as unforgiving and throaty as the Lost Sea, which had been trapped in an underground cave in the Krelmayne Jungles. Even though the lake and the surrounding cave systems had been filled with savage predators that had no eyes and hunted by vibration, Juhg thought he would rather be there again at Grandmagister Lamplighter's side in the sinking dinghy once more than facing the hostile crowd.

At the stage, Juhg climbed the stairs, then walked over to the lectern, which hadn't been cut to dweller specifications. He had to climb up on two wooden boxes to reach the proper height.

The audience laughed *at* Juhg, not *with* him. A few disparaging comments about short people and dwellers reached his sensitive ears. His face flamed slightly, but it was as much from anger as from embarrassment.

"Greetings," Juhg said bravely. And he smiled just the way Barndal Krunk had suggested in his book, *Oratories of Those Who Would Be Listened To*. It didn't work and he felt stupid standing there grinning like a loon. He also tried imagining the audience was sitting there in their underwear, but that didn't work either. He was fairly certain several of the poor sailors of the nearby Twisted Eel River didn't own underwear. And imagining the fierce Blade Works Forge dwarves in their underwear was just too horrible to contemplate.

Now, for the first time, utter silence filled the great hall.

Juhg tried to find Craugh out in the audience, hoping to find a friendly face to focus on. *If that's the friendliest face you can hope to find*, he told himself, *you might just as well hang yourself on this stage*.

"As many of you have come to know these past two days," Juhg ventured on, knowing that there were some among the assembly now who had only arrived, "I am Grandmagister of the Vault of All Known Knowledge, the Great Library that was built near the end of the Cataclysm to save the books from Lord Kharrion's goblinkin horde."

"Dwellers is worthless!" someone roared from the back. A chorus of boos followed.

Patiently, Juhg waited for the remonstrations to die away. He gripped the edges of the too-wide lectern. "I sent heralds to gather you all here," he went on, "in the hope of presenting my vision of schools along the Shattered Coast."

"Schools!" someone yelled. "Fish got schools! We ain't fish!"

"Your children and their children need educations," Juhg said. "With Lord Kharrion defeated, with the goblinkin horde in abeyance—"

"They ain't in abeyance!" someone shouted. "They's down to the south! Where they always been! We need to go down there an' burn 'em all out rather than sittin' here on our duffs listenin' to a halfer tryin' to convince us he's important!"

Cheering broke out immediately.

Thoughts of war bring these people together, but peacetime divides them. Juhg couldn't believe it.

"We should all get us an ale down at Keelhauler's Tavern an' head on out down there."

And more wars have started with tankards of foaming ale. Juhg raised his voice. "You'll have your chance at the goblinkin soon enough. But if you aren't ready for them, they'll destroy you."

That declaration set off another wave of hostility.

An elf stood up in the front row. His two great wolves roused with him, growling fiercely as they stood with their forelegs on the arms of his chair and rose nearly to their master's shoulders.

He was an elven warder, marked by his green leathers, bow, and pointed ears as well as the animal companions he kept. His long hair was the color of poplar bark and stood out against the golden skin. Amethyst eyes glinted like stone. Thin and beautiful and arrogant, the elf leaned on his unstrung bow and gazed at the assembly.

"Quiet," he said. "I wish to hear what the halfer has to say."

A group of rough-hewn sailors stood up in the back. "We don't take no orders 'cept from our cap'n, *elf*," one of their number said. He made the word a curse.

The elf smiled lazily. "You'll do well to take orders from me, human. Or at least not feel so emboldened in my presence. Your continued survival could count on that."

A dwarf stood up only a few feet from the elf. His gnarled hand held a battle-axe that was taller than he was. Scars marked his face and arms, offering testimony to a warrior's life and not a miner's. His fierce beard looked like the hide ripped from a bear but was stippled through with gray. "That'll be enough threats, Oryn."

Still smiling casually, the elf turned to face the dwarf. "Really, Faldraak? You should know me well enough to know that I don't make threats. I make promises."

"An' you don't have sense enough to come in from the rain," Faldraak accused. "Are you prepared to fight a crew of humans?"

"I am," Oryn replied. "The only question is whether or not I have to fight a dwarf as well."

Several other elves stood up. "Oryn won't fight alone," one of them promised.

Armor clanking, a dozen dwarves flanked Faldraak.

"Fight!" someone in the back yelled. "There's gonna be a fight between the elves and the dwarves!"

Unable to bear it any longer, Juhg gave in to his anger. "*Stop!*" Amplified by the construction of the stage, his voice rang out over the assembly hall with shocking loudness. Before he knew it, he'd abandoned the lectern and stood at the stage's edge.

The crowd turned on Juhg at once, as if suddenly realizing their presence and the discomfort between them there was his entire fault.

Too late, Juhg realized that he should have stayed behind the lectern. At least it would have offered some shelter against arrows and throwing knives. Still, his fear wasn't enough to quiet the anger that moved within him.

"Look at you!" he accused. "Ready to fight each other over a few harsh words!" He stood on trembling legs but found he couldn't back away from his own fight with them. "Is this the kind of world you want to give each other? One where you have to fight each other instead of the goblinkin?"

No one said anything. All eyes were upon him.

"Because that's how it was before Lord Kharrion gathered the goblinkin tribes, you know," Juhg said. "Before he came among them, they were wary and distrustful of each other. They preyed on each other, thieving and murdering among themselves because they didn't like fighting humans, dwarves, or elves. But Kharrion taught them to work together. *And they very nearly destroyed the world.*"

The audience stood quietly listening to Juhg for the first time in three days.

"Now that the goblinkin aren't the threat they used to be," Juhg said, "maybe you can go back to killing each other over territory nobody wants or needs. Or to feel secure. Or over harsh words. Or any of other reasons people have found to go to war over since groups first gathered."

"Make your point, halfer," a human merchant said. He was dressed in finery and accompanied by a dozen armed guards. Age and success had turned him plump and soft. His hair was black but the color looked false. Jeweled rings glinted on his fingers. "For two days, you've stood up there and ranted and raved about the Library's existence, which"—he turned to address the crowd—"I think nobody really cares about."

A few in the audience agreed with him.

"I'd heard the Library existed only a few years ago," the human continued. "There was some mention of a battle against a man named Aldhran Khempus. Supposedly, there are *two* libraries, in fact."

"Yes," Juhg said, "there are." He had discovered the second while rescuing Grandmagister Lamplighter and searching for *The Book of Time*.

"In the past," the merchant said, "simply owning a book was enough to get you killed not only by the goblinkin, but generally by anyone who found you with one."

"The times are changing," Juhg said.

"You're only here," the merchant continued, "because you want the people here to help aid in your defense from the goblinkin. I've heard they've sent raiding parties out to your little island."

"They have," Juhg admitted. "Those goblinkin raiding parties haven't succeeded in reaching Greydawn Moors. They never will. The island's defenders will never allow that to happen."

"How many dwellers are among those defenders?" the human taunted.

"Dwellers," Juhg said, "aren't warriors. We were charged by the Old Ones to become the keepers of the Great Library."

"That's what you do?"

"Yes."

The human held up his hands in fake supplication. "Then why did you call us here, telling us that the fate of the world rested in our hands?"

"Because it does," Juhg said.

"How?"

Leaping from the stage, Juhg opened his backpack, took several books from it, and walked to the elven warder and surveyed him. "You're a Fire Lily elf from the Joksdam Still Waters."

Oryn was unimpressed. "A number of those present know who I am."

Opening the book, Juhg flipped to one of the illustrations that showed the wide river that wound through what had once been Teldane's Bounty but was now the Shattered Coast. "But I know the history of your people. I know what Joksdam Still Waters looked like when it was whole, when it was a place of beauty and not a place of dead trees and cities."

The picture was in color, elaborately inked and designed to catch the eye. It showed an elven warder on a leaf boat sculling the waters and battling a sea troll three times his size.

Reverently, Oryn took the book. "Kaece the Swift," he marveled. The other elven warders crowded in around him to peer over his shoulder.

"Yes." Juhg had deliberately ordered the story of Kaece the Swift copied. "This is his story, Oryn. His *true* story. Before Lord Kharrion came among the Fire Lily elves and destroyed them." He changed his language to the elven tongue. "And it's written in the language of your people."

Cautiously, Oryn flipped through the book, stopping at several other pictures. All of them were in color, which had drawn a lot of complaints from Juhg's overworked Library staff, but he'd wanted to make a good impression.

"You know his story?" Oryn asked.

"I've read it," Juhg said.

"There have been few like him."

"I know."

Oryn looked at Juhg with new respect. "You have read this?"

"Yes."

"Could you"—he hesitated, because elves were haughty beings and didn't like being beholden to another—"read this to me?"

"I will."

Oryn's hands closed tightly around the book. "What do you want for such a book?"

"The book is yours," Juhg said. "It's the Library's gift to you."

"I can't just accept such a gift." Nor did Oryn seem especially desirous of returning the book. "There must be something I can give you in return."

"There is," Juhg said.

Wariness entered the amethyst eyes.

"Give me your promise that you will let me teach you to read this book," Juhg said. "And others like it. Whether at the Vault of All Known Knowledge, your home, or someplace else you might wish to meet. And promise me too that you will teach at least two others to read this book, and that they will each teach two more, and that the teaching will continue."

"I have two sons and a daughter," Oryn said. "I give you my word that I will do as you ask."

"Thank you," Juhg said. He turned to Faldraak and took out another book. "You're of the Ringing Anvil dwarves."

"I am," Faldraak replied proudly. "Ringing Anvil steel is like no other. We're known for it."

"Your people once built armor for kings," Juhg said. "And you constructed iron figureheads and rams for ships that were magically made so they wouldn't rust."

Faldraak shook his shaggy head. "A myth, nothing more."

Dwarves and magic didn't get along well. Everyone knew that. Humans and elves were more open to it, though elves held more with nature and humans tended to be more destructive.

Juhg opened the book. "The secret of that magically imbued iron was the Ringing Anvil clan's alone. They wrested the process from a dragon named Kallenmarsdak who lived long ago and high up in the Boar's Snout Mountains."

The dwarf's eyes widened. "Not many know that tale."

"I know more than the tale," Juhg said quietly. "I know the secret of how magic was put into that iron."

"No," Faldraak whispered hoarsely.

Juhg opened the book to a picture of a dwarf grabbing hold of the toe of a dragon swooping over a mountaintop with the setting sun in the background. "Drathnon the Bold. The Ringing Anvil dwarf who bearded Kallenmarsdak in his lair."

Faldraak snatched the book from Juhg's hands. "The secret of the magical iron lies in here?"

"It does."

"And you would give it to me?"

"It's yours."

"You will read this to me?"

"I will. But only at the same price that Oryn's paying."

Without warning, Faldraak gave a cry of gladness, tossed his battle-axe to one of his companions, and wrapped his arms around Juhg, lifting the dweller from his feet like a puppy. "Ah, now you are a surprise, you are! You done filled this old dwarf 's heart with gladness! I'd thought that secret lost an' gone forever!"

Juhg almost couldn't breathe. He felt certain his ribs would be bruised for days. A moment later, Faldraak placed him back upon his feet.

During the next several minutes, Juhg passed out twenty-seven other books to people who had come to the gathering. Only five histories didn't have descendants to give them to, and several others were disappointed that they didn't have anything. Juhg got all their names and promised to get them each books upon his return to the Vault of All Known Knowledge. He could only imagine the protests of his poor staff, who were dividing their time between getting the Library back into shape, teaching Novices, and carrying on their own works and studies.

In the end, he returned to the stage, though he didn't humiliate himself by crawling up to the lectern again. He spoke to them from the stage's edge.

"These books represent the worlds that existed before the Cataclysm," Juhg said.

Amazingly, the audience was quiet now, hanging onto his words. He couldn't believe how much giving them the books had impressed them.

"They also represent the worlds your children and your children's children can return to," Juhg went on. "As the goblinkin are driven back, and I believe they will be, the world will grow smaller, not larger. Our lives will become larger. We won't exist as little communities. But as we grow, we'll develop the same problems we had that Lord Kharrion was able to take advantage of in the early part of the Cataclysm."

"What are you talking about?" the human merchant demanded.

"Sit down, Dooly!" someone yelled. "I want to hear the halfer speak!"

"Don't you know what he's talking about?" Dooly demanded. "Truly?" He hurried on before anyone answered. "This halfer is intending to pick your pockets! Who do you think is going to pay for these schools he intends to build?"

That started another ripple of speculative conversation. Obviously, the merchant could smell a plea for donations a mile away.

"Tell them," Dooly snarled at Juhg. "Tell them that's why you gathered them here. To fleece them of money."

Honesty is the best policy, Juhg told himself. He tried desperately not to remember how many times he knew of that such a practice had gotten the practitioner killed.

"The establishment of schools will require help," Juhg said.

Immediately some of the good will of the book presentation evaporated. No one liked the idea of giving away gold.

"Some of that help," Juhg said, speaking over the noise, "will, of necessity, be of a financial nature. To feed and clothe the students and teachers while they are at their studies for the first year. Then they can garden, hunt, or fish to get what they need or the goods to trade for what they need. But most of the help needed will be only labor to build the schools."

"For what purpose?" Dooly asked. "To deprive farmers of their helpers? Artisans of their apprentices? To make every man and woman work two and three times as hard as he or she should have to, while their sons and daughters sit in some schoolhouse and do nothing?"

"To get an education," Juhg replied, trying to control the damage of the merchant's words. "In order to learn to do things and teach others. In order to better live with one another. We will someday live in one world again. We should live in it better than we have in the past. The children need education to do that."

"Education is overrated, Grandmagister," Dooly accused. "You stand up there today, offering your gifts and your promises, and you want only to make our lives harder. I've had just about enough of this foolishness and your empty words."

A single green spark danced from the back of the room, drawing the attention of several attendees. As Dooly continued haranguing Juhg, the spark sailed over and attached itself to the back of the merchant's head. As Dooly talked, his tongue got longer and longer, and his face broadened and shortened, till he soon showed the wide face of a toad atop human shoulders. His hair became bumps and warts.

Several of the people around Dooly started laughing. Even Juhg couldn't help smiling.

Abruptly, Dooly stopped speaking and glared at the people around him. "What?" he demanded. His tongue flicked out like a whip. Evidently he saw that movement for the first time. Experimentally, he flicked his tongue out several times. Then he raised his hands and felt his head.

"Oh no!" he cried. "Oh no! Oh—*ribbit*!" Holding onto his head, he fled the room. Before he reached the door, his gait changed from a run into bounding hops. The door closed after his retreat.

"Perhaps," a deep voice from the back of the room suggested, "we could do the Grandmagister the courtesy of listening to his plans."

"It'd be better than being a toad," someone grunted irritably.

"Continue, Grandmagister," Oryn said.

And Juhg did.

"Coercion wasn't part of my presentation," Juhg said.

"No, I claim credit for that," Craugh responded. "Once I used it, things seemed to go more smoothly."

Juhg looked around Keelhauler's Tavern, which was a waterfront dive not too far from *Moonsdreamer*, the ship that had brought him from Greydawn Moors. That also meant the ship was only a short distance away if things turned ugly locally and they had to run for it.

Over the years, the tavern's owners had enlarged the building three or possibly four times, simply hauling over other structures and attaching them, then laying in a floor. As a result, the floors were of varying heights and weren't always level. The furniture consisted of a hodgepodge of whatever had showed up at the door.

Although the tavern was filled near to bursting with all the extra people in for the meeting, no one sat close to Craugh and Juhg. It was, under the toad circumstances, understandable.

"They're afraid of you," Juhg said.

Craugh preened in self-satisfaction. "They should be."

Juhg sighed. "It's difficult to get anyone to do anything charitable when they feel threatened."

"I beg to differ. After the possibility of being turned into toads was presented, they sat and listened while you droned on and on about schools and education."

"I didn't drone."

Craugh frowned. "Your elocution lacks. 'We must build for the future. We must ensure our children know about the past before they step into the future.' " The wizard shook his head. "The toad threat? That was eloquent. Short, punchy, attention-getting." He took another cream-filled bitter blueberry tort from the plate he'd ordered and dug in. For all his leanness, the wizard was a bottomless pit when it came to food. "You don't *ask* people for help. You *tell* them to help you."

"Or you turn them into toads."

Craugh shrugged. "If I threatened that, then yes, I turn them into toads. Threats don't carry much weight if you don't occasionally carry them out."

Despair weighed heavily on Juhg. "Toads can't build schools."

"Actually, toads can't do much of anything. Except eat flies." Craugh brushed cookie crumbs from his beard. "I believe that was the point."

"We need these people's goodwill."

"Over the years, Grandmagister, I have found that people demonstrate an overall lack of enthusiastic goodwill without being properly motivated. Especially when it comes to public projects. I merely provided the motivation. Had I been here two days ago, doubtless you would have already been finished."

One way or another, Juhg silently agreed.

"Now if Wick had addressed those people today—" Craugh caught himself and shook his head. "Alas, but that's not to be, is it?" He smiled a little, but sadness touched his green eyes.

"I regret that I'm not Grandmagister Lamplighter," Juhg said, feeling the old pain stir inside him as well. Although he understood Grandmagister Lamplighter's decision to explore the realms opened up to him by *The Book of Time*, Juhg hadn't quite forgiven his mentor for leaving.

"No," Craugh said forcefully. "Never regret that. You are you, Grandmagister Juhg, and were it not for you, the possibility of giving back all the lost knowledge to the people of the world would never have come this far."

Pain tightened Juhg's throat. For all that they argued and disagreed, he and Craugh had shared a love and deep respect for Edgewick Lamplighter. They were the only two who knew most of the Grandmagister's life. They had shared his adventures outside Greydawn Moors and had gotten to see him work. None of the Grandmagister's acquaintances on the Shattered Coast had ever come to Greydawn Moors.

"Thank you," Juhg whispered.

"Your friendship these days," the wizard said, "means a lot to me."

That admission from Craugh was both surprising and touching. Juhg didn't know what to say. The silence stretched between them, crowded by the conversations throughout the rest of the tavern.

"You didn't come here today for the presentation, did you?" Juhg asked. He'd asked earlier, but Craugh had never answered him. The wizard didn't answer any questions until he was ready. But that didn't mean he couldn't be asked again.

"No, I didn't." Craugh took another tort and nibbled at the edge. "Something else brought me to you."

Silently, Juhg waited. Only trouble would bring Craugh to him. He didn't want to ask what *that* was. So he didn't.

"Tell me," Craugh said almost conversationally, as if the potential fate of the world didn't hang in his words, "have you ever heard of Lord Kharrion's Wrath?"

Juhg reflected for a moment. "No. Not really. There was some mention of it in Troffin's *Legacy of the Cataclysm*."

"I'm not familiar with that."

"Most people aren't. The Grandmagister had me read it one day, but he never explained why."

"Ah. What did the book say about Lord Kharrion's Wrath?"

"Only that it was a weapon the Goblin Lord had been building toward the end of the Cataclysm. I think the legend was eventually dismissed as a fabrication."

Craugh took out his pipe and filled it. He snapped his fingers and a green flame sprang to life on his thumb. In short order, he had the pipe going merrily and a cloud of smoke wreathed his hat.

"What," the wizard asked, "if I told you the story of Lord Kharrion's Wrath was true?"

Juhg thought about that. "Then I'd say it was over a thousand years too late."

"Perhaps not."

Disturbing images took shape in Craugh's pipe smoke. Wars were fought in those small clouds. Juhg didn't know if the smoke revealed things yet to come or were drawn from the wizard's memory.

"Wick, at one time, was on the trail of Lord Kharrion's Wrath," Craugh said. "Quite by accident, though. He'd ended up in the Cinder Clouds Islands as a result of an argument between Hallekk and another ship's crew one night in the Yondering Docks."

"The Grandmagister wouldn't get involved in an argument," Juhg said automatically. "Besides, there'd be nothing to argue over. The Grandmagister would know the answers."

"No one believed him."

"And he went to prove them wrong?" Juhg shook his head. "That still doesn't sound like the Grandmagister."

Craugh coughed delicately. "Actually, Wick wasn't given a choice."

Juhg lifted a suspicious eyebrow.

"We waited until Wick was deep into his cups, then we took him back to the ship."

"You shanghaied him? Again?" Juhg could't believe it.

"It was Hallekk's idea, actually."

At the time, Hallekk had probably been first mate on *One-Eyed Peggie*, Greydawn Moors' only dwarven pirate ship. The crew had shanghaied Grandmagister Lamplighter from the Yondering Docks all those years ago to fill their crew, so deep in their cups they hadn't realized then that he was a Librarian.

Juhg wondered why the Grandmagister would have gone adventuring again just to satisfy Hallekk's need to win a wager.

"Did the Grandmagister believe in Lord Kharrion's Wrath?" Juhg asked.

"He did. He saw it."

That announcement took Juhg by surprise. "He never mentioned it to me."

"Wick has lived . . . an *adventurous* life. Quite contrary to a normal dweller's desires." Craugh puffed on his pipe and a dreadful dragon sailed in full attack in the clouds dappling the tavern ceiling. Several nearby patrons sat in frozen astonishment, then carefully—quietly—left their seats and departed. "I'm sure he didn't tell you everything."

"I've read everything he wrote."

"Perhaps he didn't write about everything he witnessed."

Juhg shook his head immediately. "That wasn't his way. He taught me the importance of keeping a journal." Reaching into his robes, he took out a journal he'd made himself.

After placing the journal on the table, he flipped through the pages and revealed the images and words he'd wrought over the last few days. Images of Shark's Maw Cove, the meeting hall, the principal attendees he'd met, as well as plants, structures, and animals that had caught his curious eye all filled the pages amid notes and monographs.

"This is just the bare beginning of this book, though," Juhg said. "I've been working on a more finished one on board *Moonsdreamer*." He closed the book and put it away. "The Grandmagister kept a record of *everything*."

"So he did. Which leads us to the conclusion that you *haven't* read everything Wick wrote."

"Impossible."

Saying nothing, the wizard reached inside his traveling cloak, took out a fat book, and dropped it with a *thump* onto the table. "Have you read this?"

Juhg recognized Grandmagister Lamplighter's handiwork immediately. The Grandmagister had always been very exact when he built a journal to record his adventures. This one had a lacquered finish over maple stained deep red that would be proof against impact and water.

Opening the book, Juhg found the Grandmagister's hand upon the pages. Juhg knew his mentor's style instantly from the Qs. Grandmagister Lamplighter had the most beautiful Qs of any Librarian.

Several of the pages, though, showed charring. Other pages showed where pinholes had burned through.

The frontispiece showed an exquisite drawing of *One-Eyed Peggie* sitting at anchor at the Yondering Docks. Dwarves, one of them barrel-chested Hallekk, stood on the deck working at their chores.

"Where did you get this?" Juhg asked, astounded.

"At the Vault. I just came from there."

"Impossible."

"You didn't know where all Wick's hiding places were," Craugh said.

"He would have told me."

"That book that you hold in your hand proves that he didn't."

Juhg couldn't argue that and didn't, though he sorely wanted to. "Why wouldn't he tell me?"

"Maybe he just never got around to it," the wizard gently suggested.

Looking at the opening pages, Juhg discovered that he couldn't read them. "It's written in code."

"Wick was very careful."

Let's only hope the Grandmagister still is, Juhg fervently hoped. *Wherever* The Book of Time *has taken him*.

"Can you read it?" Craugh asked.

Quickly, Juhg took out his own journal and tried some of the various codes he and the Grandmagister had devised over the years of their adventuring. In short order, the strange symbols became perfectly understandable words.

"Yes. It's written in one of the first codes the Grandmagister taught me." Excitement filled Juhg at the discovery.

"Good. That proves that he intended to let you know about this book at some date," Craugh said.

Relief flooded Juhg. "Why did you bring this book to me?"

Craugh was silent for a moment, contemplating his response. "Because I can't read it. I need it translated."

"You want me to translate this?"

"Can you name another more suited to the task?"

"No," he replied.

"Neither could I."

"Don't you already know what this book contains?"

Hesitantly, Craugh shook his head. "I don't know. Though Wick and I trusted each other and would have laid down our lives for each other—and almost had occasion to do so now and again—we still maintained our own counsel in some areas." He sighed and a lightning storm manifested in the smoke over his peaked hat. Green sparks danced within the storm. "I think it was because Wick knew—*knows*—that I have my own secrets from him."

Chief among those secrets had been Craugh's own early villainy and search for power through *The Book of Time*. And the fact that Craugh had fathered Lord Kharrion. Only Juhg knew that, and it had been the first secret he had kept from Grandmagister Lamplighter.

"But I was with Wick when he found Lord Kharrion's Wrath," Craugh said.

"It *is* a weapon?"

"Yes."

"What kind of weapon?"

"Read the book," Craugh directed. "I don't want to risk influencing translations or interpretations of what you find there. When you have the book decoded, we'll compare what we know."

Suddenly a thump sounded on the tavern's roof. Then more thumps followed, as if a giant were walking across the split wood shingles. Other thumps sounded in different spots, indicating that more than one thing now walked atop the building.

Craugh stood immediately and took up his staff. His eyes narrowed in consternation. "Quickly, Grandmagister. It appears my arrival here hasn't gone unnoticed."

"Unnoticed?" Juhg got to his feet. "You were trying to arrive *unnoticed*?" That could only bode the gravest trouble.

Striding to the center of the big room, Craugh glared up at the ceiling.

"Unnoticed by whom?" Juhg asked, remaining by the table. He peered through the window. Outside, night had come to Shark's Maw Cove. Lanterns lit the crooked boardwalks that led through the boggy marshland to the docks and dilapidated warehouses.

"Those who would prevent me from learning anything further of Lord Kharrion's Wrath, of course." Craugh took his staff in both hands. Green sparks whirled around both ends of it.

The magic was so intense in the room that Juhg felt the hairs on his arms standing to attention. He reached down and slipped out the long fighting knife his friend Raisho had given him years ago when they had entered a trade partnership. That had been when Juhg had tried to leave the Vault of All Known Knowledge because he and Grandmagister Lamplighter had been of different views on how to proceed with the Library.

Juhg said, "Who—"

Then the roof splintered and caved in, scattering shingles in all directions. Three impossible figures dropped to the tavern floor and stood on clawed feet with toes as big as tree roots.

They were vaguely human in shape, possessing two arms and two legs, and had vaguely human features that looked like ridged skulls with flat brown eyes the size of saucers. No nose and a ragged slit for a mouth completed their features. Warped ears twisted like conch shells stuck out on the sides of their heads. They had four fingers and four toes at the ends of their extremities, but those were each as large as a man's wrist. Their skin looked like cypress bark streaked with moss. When they stood, Juhg realized they very nearly reached the ceiling beams, making them at least thirteen or fourteen feet tall. Pungent and strong, the stink of a fecund swamp clung to them.

As one, they turned their gazes on Craugh.

"Get behind me," the wizard ordered.

Juhg did as he was bade, but he was thinking that since the creatures seemed interested in Craugh, maybe that was the *last* place he wanted to be. Still, he couldn't desert the wizard and leave him to face his foes alone. He shoved Grandmagister Lamplighter's coded book into his backpack, took a fresh grip on his fighting knife, and peered around Craugh's leg.

"Dark magic!" someone cried in warning.

"Bog beasts!" another shouted.

The Keelhauler's Tavern emptied in short order. Several of the patrons simply threw chairs through the windows and followed them outside. Only a few elven, dwarven, and human warriors remained. Most of those who had been bending their elbows were sailors and merchants, not versed in the arts of combat.

"Wizard," one of the bog beasts growled in a deep voice that seemed to erupt from within him. It threw a hand forward and a vine leaped from it like a fisherman's line. Thick and fibrous, the vine streaked straight for Craugh.

Hardly moving, the wizard attempted to block the vine with his staff. The vine reacted like a live thing, curling around the staff and tightening. The bog beast fisted the vine and yanked.

Incredibly, Craugh stood against the creature's immense strength, once again demonstrating that he was more than human. He spoke a Word in a harsh tongue. With a *bamf!*, green flames spread along the staff. The vine crackled, burning to ash in the space of a heartbeat.

The bog beast screamed in pain and drew back its hand.

"Get back, foul swamp spawn!" Craugh commanded.

The bog beasts surged forward. Their feet hammered against the wooden floor, shattering thick planks that had withstood the test of time till that night.

"Axes!" one of the dwarves yelled. "Don't let them black-hearted beasties tear up *our* tavern!"

At once, the dwarves broke up into three groups of four, standing one by two by one deep. As needed, they rotated the leader in case he grew tired from attacking their enemies or was wounded, moving into the defensive anvil formation—two by two, with shields raised—to wear through an opponent's attack, then back into the axe formation.

The elven warders had nocked their bows. Arrows sped across the short distance of the room and feathered the bog beasts. The creatures roared in anger and pain but showed no sign of turning from Craugh.

Roaring, unleashing Words of power, Craugh raised his flaming staff and brought it crashing down on the floor. In response, Juhg thought the earth had shivered free of its moorings. He toppled and fell, striving desperately to push himself back to his feet.

Everyone in the tavern fell, including the elves, dwarves, and humans. Even the bog beasts toppled. Then what was left of the roof dropped as well, crashing down around Juhg. None of it hit him. When he peered fearfully up from under his folded arm, he saw that a green bubble surrounded Craugh and him. Sparks shimmered along the surface of the bubble. Then it disappeared.

Juhg stood. Tremors continued through the ground and he felt certain the earth would open up and swallow them at any moment.

Bellowing angrily, the bog beasts surged up from under the debris that had fallen on them. One of them threw a vine at Craugh, catching the wizard around the lower right leg. Obviously drained by the spell he had cast, Craugh was slow to react. The bog beast yanked, pulling the wizard from his feet.

Moving by instinct, Juhg scrambled after Craugh, leaping to the top of a broken table and slashing his knife across the vine. The fibrous length parted with only passing resistance. Another bog beast cast its line, but Juhg stomped on an abandoned serving platter and caused it to leap into the air. The vine pierced the platter and was deflected from its target enough to miss, though it was only a matter of inches.

Craugh regained his feet and clapped his hat back on. He took a firmer grip on his staff.

"Scribbler!" a familiar voice yelled.

Turning, Juhg saw Raisho standing in the crooked doorway. The young sailor had become Juhg's best friend during recent years. They had become trading partners when Juhg had been determined to abandon the Vault of All Known Knowledge eight years ago; Raisho had only been twenty.

(Eight years meant a lot to a human. Now Raisho had found his true family, married a mermaid, and had one child and another on the way, and captained *Moonsdreamer*, the ship he'd named after his daughter. At six feet two inches tall, he had filled out over the years, becoming thicker and more powerful, but still went smooth-shaven because his wife preferred him that way.)

Blue tattoos showed on his ebony skin, marred here and there by scars from men and beasts he'd battled while sailing the Blood-Soaked Sea and adventuring with Juhg. A headband of fire opals, made by his beautiful wife, held his thick, unruly black hair back from his handsome face. Silver hoops dangled in his ears. He carried a dwarven smithed cutlass in his hard right hand. He wore only sailor's breeches, soft leather boots, and a chain mail shirt over his bare chest.

"Scribbler!" Concern etched on his face, eyes straining against the darkness inside the tavern, Raisho strode into the tavern.

"I'm here," Juhg called.

"Thank the Old Ones," Raisho said, striding over to join him and Craugh. "I thought ye'd 'ad yer gullet slit for sure this time. Especially after I'd 'eard Craugh was about an' I saw the dragon flyin' around."

"Dragon?" Juhg echoed.

Raisho nodded. "I was told it was the dragon what dropped them creatures onto the tavern. Didn't know what they was lookin' for. Till I 'eard Craugh was 'ere with ye."

"Dragon?" Juhg repeated, stuck on the possibility that one of those monsters might even now be lurking about outside awaiting them.

"Of course there's a dragon," Craugh growled. "I was going to tell you about the dragon."

"You might have mentioned it before now," Juhg grumbled.

Roaring war cries, the dwarves and humans took up the attack once more, chopping into the backsides of the bog beasts with unrelenting zeal. Shooting with their incredible skill, the elven warders put more arrows into their targets around their fellow combatants. The two back bog beasts had to turn to deal with their opponents.

The bog beast facing Craugh rushed forward, flinging both hands out so that vines shot toward him.

The wizard ducked, whipped his hat off with one hand, spoke a Word, and sent his hat spinning toward the bog beast. Inches from the creature, the hat turned into a flaming fireball nearly two feet in diameter that slammed into the bog beast's chest with a *boom!* louder than thunder.

The creature rocked back on its tree root toes. Dry cracks spread across its chest where the fireball had struck. Craugh pressed his advantage, ducking in and driving the end of his staff into his opponent's chest. Startled, the bog beast glanced down and started to close a hand around Craugh's staff, then the dryness spread through the creature and it fell to pieces.

One of the dwarves grabbed an unbroken lantern from one of the wall sconces. The wick remained aflame inside the glass. Yelling a warning to his fellow warriors, the dwarf heaved the lantern at the bog beast. The lantern shattered against the creature, spreading oil that quickly caught fire. Dry patches showed on the bog beast and it began struggling to move. A moment later, spreading fires throughout the wreckage of the bar, the bog beast broke into pieces.

Taking note of what was going on, the elven warders dipped their arrows in oil and loosed flaming shafts into the remaining bog beast, quickly reducing it to chunks of dry earth that tumbled across the shattered tavern floor. The combatants cheered at once, no longer divided in their goals while facing a common foe.

"Go," Craugh said, "quickly. We may yet face more opposition." He waved his arms to usher Juhg and Raisho into motion.

"Mayhap if we were to split up," Raisho suggested to the wizard. "Ye can go one way. Me an' Juhg, we'll go another."

"No," Craugh said.

Raisho gave a disappointed frown. "I thought not. But I'm tellin' ye now, if 'n ye get me ship busted up somewheres, ye're gonna be responsible for replacin' 'er."

Together, they ran out of the building as the flames leaped higher.

"Too bad about your hat," Juhg told Craugh.

"Eh?" the wizard said. Then nodded. "Right. My hat." He snapped his fingers and suddenly the hat was sailing through the air toward them. Effortlessly, Craugh caught the hat and clapped it onto his head. He smiled and wiggled his eyebrows. "This hat has gotten me out of several tight spots over the years. One day, mayhap, I'll tell you the story of how I acquired it."

Intrigued as he was by the story of the wizard's hat, Juhg glanced overhead, spotting the two moons that circled the world. Bright red and speeding on the first of his trips across the night sky, Jhurjan the Swift and Bold was full and close now, occupying fully a tenth of the sky. Farther to the south, glowing a demure pale blue, Gesa the Fair made her way more sedately, with grace and self-control.

There were, thankfully, no dragons in sight.

They ran on, racing down the hill toward the harbor, then down the steep, crooked steps, and—finally—across the swaying bridges that connected the decrepit docks. When they reached *Moonsdreamer*, Raisho hailed his crew, who were already crowded at the railing with weapons to hand.

In minutes, they cast off and *Moonsdreamer*'s sails scaled the masts and belled out from the 'yards. Juhg stood in the bow. Before he knew it, his personal journal and a piece of charcoal were in his hands. By Jhurjan's light, he quickly blocked out the shapes of the bog beasts. Despite the danger, it was what Grandmagister Lamplighter had trained him to do. He wrote his questions for Craugh in the margins while Raisho got his ship into the wind with all due haste.

Unfortunately, Craugh didn't intend to answer many questions.

Seated in the galley with a hot cup of spiced choma at the table before him, Juhg looked at the wizard. "Who sent the bog beasts?"

Craugh scowled. "I told you I wouldn't influence your reading of Wick's book. I meant that."

"Those were bog beasts," Juhg said. "I've never seen creatures like them."

"See? Even more reason I shouldn't answer your idle curiosities."

Not believing what he was hearing, Juhg said, "They tried to kill us. I'd say that I'm motivated by more than idle curiosity."

"Still," Craugh said, "your neutrality in the matter of decoding the book is important, Grandmagister. You have a duty to do the best that you can."

Using his title as he did, Juhg knew that Craugh sought to motivate him. However, knowing the wizard was a manipulator negated that maneuver. Unfortunately, Juhg also saw the truth in Craugh's words, so it may well have been that the pronouncement wasn't a manipulation. Thinking like that made Juhg's head hurt.

In the end, he knew what Grandmagister Lamplighter would have done: seek out the mysteries the book held.

"All right, all right." Juhg sighed. "I understand all that, and mayhap I even agree that you might be correct in your assessment of how things should be handled."

"Thank the Old Ones," Craugh replied with a small smile that he didn't truly mean.

"That said," Juhg went on, "what *can* you tell me?"

Craugh counted off answers on his fingers. "That we are arrayed against a powerful enemy. That Lord Kharrion's Wrath truly exists. That Wick was on the trail of it all these years ago. That there are secrets that no one was meant to know all those years ago that we must surely find out now." He paused for a moment. "Oh, and one other thing: The stakes are high."

Juhg waited.

"What you may find out in that book," Craugh said, "might well affect the futures of three different communities. One or all will prove guilty of some of the vilest villainies perpetrated during the Cataclysm. When others find out, old enmities might well be re-established and result in hundreds or thousands of deaths." He regarded Juhg. "Is that enough?"

More than enough, Juhg thought, suddenly feeling glum and overwhelmed.

"Scribbler."

Juhg looked back to see Raisho standing in the doorway to the stairs that led up the deck. The familiar roll of the ship across the waves rocked them.

"There's no sign of pursuit," Raisho said. "We escaped clean enough."

"Good." Juhg felt a little relief. He picked up Grandmagister Lamplighter's book and ran a finger along the charred pages. Curiosity nagged at him as it always did.

"Doesn't mean there won't be any," Raisho went on, and the statement was more of a question.

"I've laid enchantments on the ship," Craugh said. "We're protected better than most."

Raisho nodded. "I'll keep double guards posted in any case. But what 'eading should we take?"

"You've stores packed away?" Craugh asked.

"Aye."

"Then stay at sea."

Raisho frowned. "I've got perishable goods aboardship."

"Continue the trade route we planned on," Juhg said. "We don't want to draw any more attention than we have to. A trade ship not trading will trigger prying interests."

"We may need to travel once you have the book deciphered," Craugh pointed out. "It would be better if we knew from where."

"We'll deal with that when—and *if*—it happens," Juhg replied. He looked at the wizard, expecting an argument.

Instead, Craugh quietly agreed.

That let Juhg know how serious the situation was. And how dangerous. He sipped the choma and turned his attention to the book that contained one of Grandmagister Lamplighter's adventures he hadn't known anything about. In a short time, the coded entries turned into words in his mind and he wrote them down in a new book.

1

The Tavern Brawl

"Wick."

Placing his finger inside the book to hold his place, Second Level Librarian Edgewick Lamplighter sighed and glanced up at the speaker. He tried not to show his displeasure at being interrupted at his reading, but it was difficult.

"What is it?" Wick asked.

"Your friends," Paunsel whispered. He was a dweller like Wick, only grossly rotund with slicked-back hair and a thin mustache. He wiped his hands nervously on a bar towel.

"What friends?" Wick was immediately interested, for as a Librarian he had few friends among the sailors and merchants that lined the Yondering Docks in Greydawn Moors.

Paunsel jerked a hesitant thumb over his shoulder.

For the first time, Wick heard the raucous laughter and ribald poetry coming from the tavern's main room. Choosing to be alone with his book (and only a nonreader would call it alone because those poor unfortunates couldn't truly trigger the magic captured in the pages of a book!), Wick had retreated to one of the small side rooms and refused to acknowledge the baleful glances the cleaning crews had given him.

Peering cautiously around the tavern owner, keenly aware that one of the back doors out of the buildings was close at hand just as he'd planned, Wick stared into the main room. Of course, since the Wheelhouse Tavern served all who had coin to pay for it, the place was packed with dwarves come to slake their prodigious thirst.

"The dwarven . . . *pirates*," Paunsel whispered.

Glee touched Wick's heart then. There was only one ship that came to the Yondering Docks carrying *dwarven* pirates. Many months had passed since he'd last seen the crew of *One-Eyed Peggie*. He looked forward to seeing Cap'n Farok, Hallekk, Zeddar, Naght, Jurral, Cook, and even Critter, the foul-tempered rhowdor ship's mascot.

But Wick also knew what the ship's crew was like when they were in their cups. He looked at Paunsel. "Are they fighting someone?"

"Not yet."

"But the likelihood is there?"

Paunsel looked aggrieved. "Yes. Otherwise I wouldn't have bothered you at your studies, Librarian." The tavern owner was one of the few in Greydawn Moors who talked respectfully with Librarians.

Over the years, most of the townsfolk had come to resent the Grandmagister and the Librarians, insisting that the food sent up to the Vault of All Known Knowledge was a burden the rest of the population shouldn't have to bear. Of course, it was mostly the dwellers that said that. The elven warders who guarded the island's forests and mountains, the humans who pretended to be pirates out in the Blood-Soaked Sea, and the dwarven guards and craftsmen were more generous.

Hmmm, Wick thought, for roving across to the Shattered Coast and beyond had taught him to always carefully examine his options. *Renewing acquaintances at the cost of becoming embroiled in a battle isn't all that appetizing. Especially on a full stomach.*

Despite Hallekk and Cobner's attempts to turn him into a pirate or a warrior, Wick was very much satisfied with being a Librarian. He preferred to do his adventuring in the stacks of romances in Hralbomm's Wing while avoiding Grandmagister Frollo's wrath. The Grandmagister was of the opinion that Wick should use his personal reading time more wisely.

"Well?" Paunsel prompted.

"I'm thinking," Wick replied. He tried drumming his fingers on the tabletop the way Grandmagister Frollo did, but evidently the task wasn't as easy as he'd believed. Also, the cadence of Taurak Bleiyz's brave war song was stuck in his head from the book and his fingers kept finding that beat.

"They're going to tear up my tavern," Paunsel said.

The angry voices in the next room rose to a new, and even more threatening, level. Wick's ears pricked, listening with more experience than he'd ever intended for the hiss of swords clearing leather.

"Who are they arguing with?" Wick asked. *Perhaps if it's someone Hallekk and the others can easily frighten off, I could go meet them. After all, if they win an argument, their purses will open and the wine will flow.* It was a pleasing prospect. But he longed to get Taurak Bleiyz across the spiderweb and safely away from his enemies.

"Humans," Paunsel sneered. "The crew of *Stormrider*."

Wick knew of the ship and the crew. If ever there were warriors that could evenly meet dwarven warriors, it was *Stormrider*'s crew.

"What are they arguing about?"

Paunsel sighed, obviously on the verge of giving up asking for help. "Something that happened long ago. An alliance or something that met Lord Kharrion's goblinkin army in the Painted Canyon."

"Ah." Although Wick didn't know the story of the battle well, he was a Librarian. A recently promoted *Second* Level Librarian at that. He thought he could settle an argument between ships' crews and probably earn himself a few more cups of sparkleberry wine for his troubles. "I can handle this."

"Thank the Old Ones," Paunsel said, though with far more sarcasm than Wick would have wanted to hear. The tavern keeper waved the Librarian to the main room.

Wick placed his bookmark within the romance and glanced at the page number to memorize it just in case before putting it into his book bag. The memorization was a practice he'd made a habit of when he'd first gone to the Great Library as a Novice. Then he slid out of the booth, straightened the lines of his Librarian's robe—now gray with dark blue fringe, changed from white to denote his promotion—grabbed the straps of his book bag, and headed for the main room.

The room was packed with sailors and cargo handlers. Lanterns filled with glimmerworm juice glowed softly blue in sconces. Several others hung from ships' wheels suspended from the ceiling. A number of patrons gathered around the fireplace at the other end of the room. Humans and dwarves sometimes mixed, but the five elven warders in from the forest to trade for goods they couldn't get on their own in the wild sat by themselves.

"—'Twas Oskarr what betrayed the alliance at Painted Canyon," a human at one of the tables declared. He was easily six and a half feet tall, almost a giant. His shaggy blond hair trailed down to his shoulders and matched the full beard he sported.

"No!" Hallekk bellowed, standing at the bar with his fellow pirates from *One-Eyed Peggie*. He was tall for a dwarf, and an axe handle would be challenged to span his shoulders. His dark brown beard was braided with yellowed bone carved into fish shapes. A bright kerchief bound his head and gold hoops danced in his ears. He wore a seaman's breeches and shirt, and held his great battle-axe casually at his side.

In Wick's opinion, *One-Eyed Peggie*'s first mate didn't look like a dwarf anyone would want to rile. *Unless, of course*, he amended, *you're a human giant and you've had too much to drink*. Wick could see at once that the situation could easily get out of control.

"Now I've kept a civil tongue in me head while ye've been blatherin' on about what happened back then," Hallekk roared loud enough to earn the attention of everyone in the tavern, "but I'll not have ye besmirchin' the name of Oskarr."

"Don't let him talk to you like that, Verdin," one of the other human sailors piped up. "Stupid dwarf is thick everywhere else, ye know he's gotta be thick in the head, too."

Hallekk bristled at the insult.

Verdin's eyes narrowed as he strived to look even more fierce and threatening.

"Ye better not be a-glowerin' at me," Hallekk growled in warning. "I don't take kindly to such intimidation."

"Go on, Hallekk!" a shrill voice called out. "Poke him in the eyes! Tweak his nose! Pull his hair! Thump him till he rings like a drum!"

The voice drew everyone's attention to the rafters above the counter, for the moment silencing the verbal sparring between Verdin and Hallekk. A rhowdor stood on the rafter, dressed in bright plumage that began with an explosion of red on its chest and wings with a few scattered patches of yellow. The ends of the wings and the tail feathers turned green that was so dark it looked blue and black. The bird flailed his wings, shadowboxing unsteadily on the rafter and breathing in short gusts through its curved beak.

Little more than a foot tall with twin pink horns jutting from above its hatchet face, the avian peered down with its one good emerald eye. A black leather patch that bore a skull and crossbones made of studs covered the other eye. A golden hoop earring dangled from one ear tuft.

The rhowdor was intelligent, capable of speaking the common language as well as any others it learned. There were few of the creatures in the world these days. This one was named Critter and crewed aboard *One-Eyed Peggie*.

"What are ye a-lookin' at, ye daft idiot?" Critter called out, taking a break from matching skills with its imaginary opponent. "Ain't ye ever seen a talkin' bird before?"

It was obvious that Verdin hadn't.

"Why, ye're a pantywaist, ye are," the rhowdor crowed fiercely. It walked along the rafter, and from the stumbling steps it took, Wick knew the bird had drunk far too much for its own good. "I could take ye with one wing tied behind me an' me tail feathers on fire." The bird held one wing behind its back and fluttered the other one, nearly knocking itself from the rafter. "I'll show ye. Somebody get me a rope an' tie me wing up behind me back."

"Somebody get me a *stewpot*," Verdin replied, and several of the tavern's patrons—including members of *One-Eyed Peggie*'s crew—laughed uproariously.

"I'll keelhaul ye!" Critter swore. "I'll turn ye inside out an' hang ye with yer own tripe!" The rhowdor launched itself from the rafter, spreading its multicolored wings out in a three-foot span that suddenly made it look huge. It flew straight at Verdin, claws raking the air.

The human sailor ducked beneath the claws, eyes wide with surprise.

Critter sailed above the heads of the other patrons, wobbling drunkenly like a floundering ship, and managed to swing around for another pass. It screeched at the top of its voice.

Verdin stood suddenly and snatched a serving platter from a nearby table. The young sailor held the platter up like a shield.

Spotting the obstruction, Critter tried to stop the attack. Instead, all the rhowdor managed was an ungainly and panicked wing flapping. It hit the wooden serving platter with a pronounced *thump!* that scattered feathers in all directions.

The crowd all groaned, "Oooooooh!" in sympathy.

Even though he didn't especially like the rhowdor, Wick winced a little himself. The bird would be lucky if something wasn't broken by the impact.

Off balance, Critter sailed on, flapping weakly and somehow gliding back toward Hallekk and the dwarven pirate crew. The front row of human sailors had to duck to let the rhowdor go by. It landed on its back, wings spread across the sawdust-covered floor, feathers wafting through the air in its wake, and came to a stop at Hallekk's boots.

"That's gonna leave a mark," someone promised.

"*Awwwwwwrrrrrkkkkk!*" Critter cried out. The rhowdor lifted its head uncertainly, bobbing at the end of its long neck, and fastened its beady eye on Hallekk. "He sucker-punched me, Hallekk! Struck me while I wasn't lookin'!" Its head wobbled one last time, then thudded against the floor. The rhowdor lay still.

Wick stood in frozen awe. Even though he didn't like Critter, he'd never wished the rhowdor harm. Well, maybe that wasn't quite as truthful as it could have been. He actually *had* wished Critter harm; he'd just never wanted to be there when it happened.

The silence held for a moment as everyone stared at the fallen rhowdor.

Finally, someone asked, "Is it dead?"

"We should be so lucky," someone else (and Wick truly believed it was one of *One-Eyed Peggie*'s crew that said this) unkindly added.

Hallekk knelt down and picked up the rhowdor by the feet. The bird dangled limply, a scrawny shadow of its former self. The dwarf squinted at it and smelled its beak.

"Oh, it's dead all right," the big dwarf growled. "Dead *drunk*." He shook his shaggy head. "It's still breathin'."

"Be careful with him!" Slops shouldered his way out of the crowd of dwarven pirates. Old and flinty-eyed, he was the ship's cook. When Wick had been shanghaied and first crewed aboard *One-Eyed Peggie*, Slops had been a cruel taskmaster in the galley.

Twisting slightly and flipping his wrist, Hallekk tossed the unconscious rhowdor to Slops. The cook caught Critter tenderly, and held the bird in his arms like a newborn babe.

"Ye gonna let that loudmouth get away with harmin' the ship's mascot?" Slops demanded. "If 'n ye ask me, if 'n ye do, why ye ain't much of a—"

Hallekk shoved his big face into the cook's, stopping Slops's tirade at once.

Slops backed away meekly. For all his bluster and loud voice, the ship's cook knew the first mate would pound him into a Lantessian pretzel. "I'm just gonna take Critter back to the ship. Tend to him a little."

"Good," Hallekk said, " 'cause I've had me fill of him tonight, I have." Then he shifted his attention back to Verdin, who still held the serving platter. "Now ye, ye're gonna take back everythin' ye said about Master Blacksmith Oskarr."

"Over me dead body," Verdin said. "Or do ye let yer ship's mascot fight all yer battles for ye?"

Grim faced, Hallekk started forward, lifting his battle-axe easily in one hand. *One-Eyed Peggie*'s crew fell in behind him.

Verdin and his crew stood up as well and advanced a line.

That was when Wick decided that discretion was once again the better part of valor. He started to turn to head back for the exit in the other room. At that same time, though, Paunsel acted in the only way he knew to prevent damage to his tavern: He shoved Wick in between the two groups.

Stumbling and flailing, realizing that he very probably looked like a good imitation of Critter flying through the air after he'd struck the serving platter, Wick caught himself against a table and managed to stay upright. Unfortunately, he was between the two groups of combatants, both of whom had braced with drawn weapons against the unexpected attack.

Cowering, Wick closed his eyes, dropped to his knees, and covered his head with his arms. He waited to be pierced and smited.

"Wick," Hallekk growled.

Cautiously, Wick opened one eye, marveling at his survival. The humans and dwarves still stood poised. *I'm not dead*. Then he looked at the weapons ringing him, some of them only inches away, and decided that his present predicament hadn't appreciably improved. He swallowed hard and his Adam's apple bobbed past a sailor's cutlass blade both ways, though hanging slightly on the way up.

"What're ye a-doin' here, little feller?" Hallekk asked. There was some sincere warmth in his eyes. He even had a trace of a smile.

"I'm attempting to keep you from killing these sailors," Wick said, still on his knees and both hands wrapped around his head, though he had managed to open both eyes now.

The humans snorted and addressed him with threats regarding their skill and his assumption of who would lose the coming fight.

Sensing the sudden shifting of the tide of animosity in the room, Wick quickly added, "These *brave*, *brave* sailors without whom Greydawn Moors would never have enough trade goods." *Surely that will appease them*, the little Librarian hoped. He stopped himself from swallowing again because he didn't think his Adam's apple would survive a second trip.

"Get yer hands off him," Hallekk ordered. "He's a Librarian. Ain't no one a-gonna harm ye." He knotted a big fist in Wick's robes and yanked him into a fierce hug that left his feet dangling. "I've missed ye somethin' awful, little man. No one tells a story quite the way ye do."

"Hallekk?" Wick wheezed, certain he'd never draw another breath through the cracked rib cage he must have.

"Aye," the big dwarf said, his ugly face only inches from Wick's.

"Could you put me down?"

"Well, sure." Hallekk did with surprising gentleness.

Straightening himself with as much aplomb as he could muster on knees that rattled with fear, Wick nodded at the dwarf. "It's good to see you again, Hallekk."

"I wish it were under better circumstances," Hallekk replied. Straightening his kerchief, he waved at Wick. "An' if 'n ye'll shove off for a bit, it'll get better really soon. We got some business here needs tendin', a bar what needs a-clearin' of the riff-raff."

"Ha!" Verdin exclaimed. "Ye ain't dwarf enough to get that job done!"

"About that business," Wick began, trying to interrupt before they closed ranks with him in the middle, "I really think we should talk."

"Ain't no time for talkin'." Hallekk glared fiercely across the top of Wick's head. "Gotta smash the knobs of these here bilge rats."

"Gonna *be* smashed, ye mean," Verdin said.

"Maybe I can help," Wick said.

The human and the dwarf looked at him.

And maybe I can die right here, Wick thought, shrinking inside like new-fallen snow under a gentle rain.

"How can ye help?" Verdin asked.

Hoping that his weak knees didn't desert him entirely, Wick stood erect as Grandmagister Frollo always told him to when he addressed assemblies at the Vault of All Known Knowledge. "I'm a Second Level Librarian at the Great Library," he said. "You're obviously in a war of wits."

"An' they didn't come armed," Hallekk said.

Verdin scowled at the big dwarf. "Mayhap he's come to take yer final words." He turned to Wick. "That'd be somethin' along the lines of 'Ow! Ouch! By the Old Ones, he was too fast an' too strong fer me!' "

"Why you—" Hallekk began, starting forward.

Wick shoved his hand against the big dwarf 's chest, but he might as well have been seeking to stop a warship under full sail with a good wind behind her. In seconds, he was smashed between the bodies of the two combatants.

"Enough!" Wick cried in a voice too shrill to be his. But it was the best he could manage under the circumstances with the wind left to him. "Don't make me tell Grandmagister Frollo!"

Surprisingly, that threat stopped the two crews in their tracks. Hallekk and Verdin separated and Wick plopped to the ground.

"Ye'd do that, ye little halfer?" Verdin asked, eyes round with surprise.

"Over a tavern brawl?" Hallekk asked, surprised as well.

Then Wick remembered the power the Grandmagister had over the ships' crews. They all operated by charter with the Vault of All Known Knowledge. Although Grandmagister Frollo hadn't taken much of an interest in the affairs of Greydawn Moors, the previous Grandmagister, Ludaan, had spent a lot of time among the Greydawn Moors townsfolk, including the elven warders, dwarven guards, and human sailors. Ludaan was even friends with Craugh the wizard, which seemed a most unlikely and unthankful task.

At any time, the Grandmagister could revoke a ship's charter and order the crew landlocked. With as much anger and consternation as he'd drawn, Wick was certain he'd threatened far beyond his intentions. He stuck out a foot and started to ease away.

Paunsel blocked the path, folding his arms and shaking his head.

"Well," Wick tried in a less threatening tone, "perhaps it needn't come to anything as dire as that."

"C'mon, little man," Hallekk beseeched. "A good fight clears the air an' invigorates the blood. I'm just gonna thump him a little. Teach him the wrongness of his arrogant ways. It's a lesson his da shoulda taught him."

"Gonna get thumped, ye mean," Verdin replied.

Sensing that everything was about to get out of hand once more, Wick said, "Maybe I could help."

"Who?" Hallekk and Verdin demanded at once, shoving their faces into his.

"Eeep!" Wick cried, suddenly startled again. Embarrassed, cheeks burning, he clapped his hands over his mouth.

Verdin turned to Hallekk. "Seems a mite sheepish."

Hallekk shrugged. "Ol' Wick's better at adventurin' when things gets impossible."

"Humph!" the sailor snorted. "Sounds about as threatening as a hissing Kardalvian dung beetle!"

"Still," Hallekk sighed, "he does have the ear of the Grandmagister. Perhaps 'twould be better if 'n we heard him out. Then we can get back to the thumpin'."

Wick stood on shaking knees. *I faced the dragon Shengharck in his lair in the Broken Forge Mountains. I slew him there. Well, perhaps that was by accident, but I did it*. He made himself take a breath because he'd suddenly realized he wasn't breathing, and turning blue while trying to make a point didn't seem very inspiring.

"You're arguing over the events of the Painted Canyon," Wick said in what he hoped was a reasonable and not fearful tone of voice.

"Aye," both potential combatants replied.

"Everybody knows they was betrayed there," Hallekk said. "Thousands of warriors lost their lives in that battle."

"By Oskarr the dwarven leader," Verdin said. "He was the one what sold out the human an' the elven warriors what was gathered there against Lord Kharrion's armies."

Instantly a quiet fell over the crowd. No one spoke the Goblin Lord's name out loud for fear it might trigger ill luck. Only a few years ago, on the night when Wick had first been shanghaied by *One-Eyed Peggie*'s crew, Boneblights had descended upon Greydawn Moors and very nearly been the end of him. But they had been after the book Warder Kestin had taken to Craugh.

"Master Blacksmith Oskarr of the Cinder Clouds Islands was a good an' fair dwarf," Hallekk insisted.

"No one," Wick said, before he had time to truly think about what he was saying or remember why he should keep his mouth shut, "knows who betrayed those warriors. I've studied the Battle of Fell's Keep, which is what that engagement in the Cataclysm was called."

Verdin fixed Wick with a glaring eye. "Ye know about that battle?"

"I do," Wick said. It had been mentioned in one of the books he'd read. He didn't forget anything he read, which was partly due to his training and partly because that's just the way he was.

"Then who was the traitor?" Hallekk asked.

And the whole tavern leaned in closer to listen to the tale.

2

A Tale of Betrayal

"The Battle of Fell's Keep took place near the end of the Cataclysm," Wick said in a good strong voice that he used for training Novices at the Vault of All Known Knowledge. He sat on the counter in front of the tavern, which didn't please Paunsel, but at least none of the crockery seemed at risk. "At that time, as you may recall, the Goblin Lord—"

"Was thumpin' melons an' takin' names," Hallekk scowled. "Aye, we know all of that. 'Twas a hard time for the Unity."

"Goblinkin tribes had laid aside their old rivalries," Wick said, "and they'd gathered beneath the Goblin Lord's banner. Everywhere an honest dwarf, human, or elf looked in those days, they saw the banner bearing the crimson mailed fist clenched on a field of sky blue. Those were the Days of Darkness."

Enamored of the attention he was getting from the previously raucous crowd—and perhaps a little emboldened by the sparkleberry wine and the tale of Taurak Bleiyz he'd been enjoying, Wick pushed himself to his feet. Although he often spoke in front of groups within the walls of the Vault of All Known Knowledge, those instances paled in comparison to how he'd felt while speaking in front of *One-Eyed Peggie*'s crew or the Brandt's Circle of Thieves. They'd been audiences who had appreciated his skills as a raconteur. He'd come alive then in ways he knew Grandmagister Frollo would never have approved of.

"Teldane's Bounty had fallen by that time," Wick continued. "Lord Kharrion's evil spell had wreaked havoc on the mainland. He'd sent a plague of locusts, followed by a killing blight that stripped the orchards and farms that grew there.

Ships had gone down to watery graves with thousands of men, women, and children aboard, most of them freezing in the wintry waters of the Gentlewind Sea after Lord Kharrion had summoned mountains up from the sea to break apart the land."

A sad quietness held sway over the tavern crowd. Wick knew that Paunsel would hold him accountable for slowing the flow of wine and ale in the tavern. But Wick was consumed by the tale, as were his listeners.

"Those deaths were not in vain," Wick said. "For the first time since the beginning of the Cataclysm, dwarves, humans, and elves set aside their differences and came together for one purpose. Though there had been talk of working together to make the world a better place, that course had never taken root. But they could agree to save the world. And they set about that task."

"But it was almost too late," someone said.

"Silverleaves Glen fell in the next year," Wick said, remembering the poor, cursed creature he had met on his first voyage aboard *One-Eyed Peggie*. "Lord Kharrion destroyed the elven tree village, Cloud Heights, and killed King Amalryn and his beautiful queen, N'riya."

The elven warders in the back room lowered their proud heads in sympathy. All the elves had known about Silverleaves Glen.

"Furthermore," Wick said, "the Goblin Lord put to death the three princes. He reserved a far harsher fate for the nine princesses, breaking them and warping them into creatures he could use. They became Embyrs, beings of flame who lived only to destroy, and who had no memory of what they had been or what they had done."

"Aye," a human sailor said. "I've heard tell of 'em, all right. They're still out there, still killin' an' destroyin'. Made all of fire, they are, an' terrible vengeful. They find a ship at sea, like as not they'll burn her to the waterline just outta spite."

The crew of *One-Eyed Peggie* said nothing. They had seen an Embyr up close and been some of those fortunate enough to have survived such an encounter. Wick had managed to save them all by touching, if only briefly, the Embyr's angry heart.

Wick strode along the countertop, knowing that he held captive every eye in the room. "The goblinkin came roaring up out of the Western Empire, destroying everything in their path. Lord Kharrion designed a pincer movement, one that would trap those retreating overland from the south in the narrow confines of the Painted Canyon as it passed through the Unmerciful Shards, that range of the Misty Mountains where the dragonkind spawn."

Hallekk handed Wick a tankard of sparkleberry wine and he quaffed it down, warming to the story.

"For those of you who don't know, the goblinkin first took over the south," Wick continued. "They came up from Gaheral's Wastelands, where vile things were said to run rampant after the wizard unwittingly unleashed bloodthirsty creatures from other worlds." He shrugged. "Or mayhap they were created when Gaheral's Wild Magic finally turned on him as everyone believed would happen."

"They had driven them goblinkin there over the years," Hallekk said. "Beat 'em back until they had no place to go but the Wastelands."

"Before Lord Kharrion showed up in their midst, yes," Wick agreed. "But the

Wastelands turned out to be a boon to the goblinkin. The harsh territory killed off all the weaker ones, leaving only those strong enough to survive the unforgiving climate and the bloodthirsty predators. When the Goblin Lord gathered them to his cause, they were ready to kill everything in their path."

"An' they did," Verdin said.

"Yes," Wick echoed as he watched Hallekk pour him another tankard of wine. He drank it down gratefully, surprised at the way his head felt as if it were floating. "They did. After Teldane's Bounty was destroyed and the ships dragged down to the bottom of the Gentlewind Sea, after Cloud Heights was ripped asunder and torn from the trees at Silverleaves Glen, humans, dwarves, and elves began a mass exodus from the south, driven unmercifully by the combined might of the goblinkin tribes."

Despite the time spent in the Wastelands, the goblinkin population hadn't dwindled. They had no equal when it came to bearing offspring then, and still didn't. Even the humans came in at a distant second, followed by the dwarves and elves, but the goblinkin far outlived the humans.

Unless they were killed, Wick remembered. And that had been an accepted solution to the goblinkin problem for a long time.

Moving quickly, Wick lined up several tankards on the countertop, fashioning a replica of the Painted Canyon to better illustrate his story. He tiptoed through the tankards as he continued.

"The fugitives from the south were desperate," Wick said. "The number of warriors among them had drastically been cut, split off in the effort to hold Teldane's Bounty, and falling to goblinkin weapons. They needed an escape route. But the Goblin Lord was determined not to let them have it."

"He was waitin' on 'em in the Painted Canyon," someone said.

"He was," Wick agreed. "He harried the escapees from behind with one army, while he worked around to their flank with another. He planned to ambush them there in the Unmerciful Shards."

"How did Lord Kharrion get through the dragons?" someone asked.

Wick paced along the countertop. "Foul being that he was, the Goblin Lord had established a treaty with the dragons through the Dragon King Shengharck. Several of those the goblinkin captured were delivered to the spawning dragons in the Unmerciful Shards. And other places. The dragons didn't have to hunt anymore, and they didn't have to worry about being destroyed. All they had to do was not attack the goblinkin."

The horror of the thing washed over the crowd. Wick doubted that any among them had ever seen a great dragon feed on bound prisoners, but he had while in Shengharck's lair in the Broken Forge Mountains. It was a terrible sight and sound that he would never forget.

"Fortunately, the Unity found out about Lord Kharrion's ambush," Wick said. "They were able to muster three armies, though none of them at full strength, and get them to the Painted Canyon. Each of those armies represented the humans, dwarves, and elves who had taken up arms against Lord Kharrion."

"But there wasn't a dweller army, was there?" someone asked snidely.

"Noooooo. The halfers were hidin' out here in Greydawn Moors, puttin' their little Library together, protectin' the books."

"Quiet!" a voice thundered.

Every head in the tavern snapped in the direction of the voice. Hands reached for swords and axes. Then, when they recognized Craugh standing in the doorway, the dwarves and humans quickly looked away and were silent.

The wizard walked into the room and a threatening chill seemed to follow him. "Continue your tale, Second Level Librarian Lamplighter." He paused and looked around the room. "And just for clarification, there'll be no fighting here tonight."

"Thank the Old Ones." Paunsel sighed.

Wick was grateful to see that Craugh had put in an appearance, but he was worried as well. Since the very first time he'd gone with the wizard to the mainland on one journey or another, his life had been at risk constantly. He didn't think Craugh had shown up at Paunsel's for the sparkleberry wine.

"Okay," Wick said. But some of the drama had gone out of the presentation. Craugh was the only person he'd known who had actually lived through the Cataclysm and knew many of the key events firsthand. "Where was I?"

"The Unity forces sent three armies to the Painted Canyon to head off Lord Kharrion's forces." Craugh sat at a table near the front whose previous tenants had rapidly evacuated at his approach. He placed his staff across the table and stretched his long legs under it. "One of dwarves, one of elves, and one of humans. Carry on."

"Right." Wick tried to marshal his thoughts, but the sparkleberry wine was interfering almost as much as his nerves. "So there they were. Three armies headed for Painted Canyon and the goblinkin hordes. Master Blacksmith Oskarr of the Cinder Clouds Islands led the dwarves. The elves were marshaled by King Faeyn of the Tangletree Glen. And General Crisstun of Promise Wharf commanded the humans. The reached the pass at the Unmerciful Shards under the cover of night before the fugitives and were able to set up defensive positions at Fell's Keep, an old human trading post that had been abandoned after the dragons had started nesting there."

The tavern crowd hung on every word. Although none of them had experienced war on quite the level of the Cataclysm, all of them had probably fought for their lives against men or beasts at one time or another. They knew what those armies faced.

"The defenders let the fugitives through," Wick said, "and settled in to fight. Then came the goblinkin, marching in double-time, their ranks swelled with monsters and dire creatures Lord Kharrion had lured to their dark cause. Confronted with so many goblinkin, the three armies knew they were fated to die. If they tried to fall back, their resistance would fall apart and they would leave the rearguard of the fugitives open to attack."

Silence rang throughout the tavern.

"They'd already lost so much at Teldane's Bounty," Wick said, "that no one could bear to lose women and children again. So it was decided among the warriors of those three armies that they would sell their lives as dearly as possible and hope to slow the encroaching goblinkin horde enough that the fugitives might be able to escape."

“ ’Twas a brave an’ selfless thing they did,” Hallekk stated.

“ ’Twas,” Verdin agreed. “Too bad they had to go an’ get betrayed the way they was. Mayhap more of ’em might have survived.”

“For nine days,” Wick went on, hurrying so the argument wouldn’t begin again, “the defenders of Fell’s Keep kept the goblinkin at bay. They fought till the Painted Canyon ran red with blood. At night, when the goblinkin made camp and slept, elven warders went quietly among them and stole supplies and arrows, and killed goblinkin where they found them—strung up the bodies from the cliff sides, tossed their ugly heads into the campfires, and put horse droppings into the soup the goblinkin had made of fallen enemies—as testimony to the fate that awaited those who continued to fight.”

The crowd listened in rapt attention.

“Goblins know of the Battle of Fell’s Keep,” Wick whispered, pitching his voice to roll over the crowd. “Stories of those days are still told around goblinkin campfires, and they’re whispered among the young to scare each other.” He knew that because he’d sat as captive around those campfires a time or two.

“Who betrayed them?” someone asked.

“No one knows,” Wick said. “Although many tried to guess afterward.” He sat heavily, no longer as sure-footed as he’d been. He didn’t know if it was the sadness of the story or the potent sparkleberry wine that did him in. “On the morning of the tenth day, nearly all of the Unity army took sick and couldn’t even stand to defend themselves. The goblinkin came among them like butchers in the slaughterhouse. No one was spared.”

“It was the dwarven leader,” Verdin insisted. “He spread the sickness among the surviving troops so that his own life might be spared.”

“Watch yer blasphemous tongue there, swab,” Hallekk growled.

“Then ye explain to me how it was Oskarr managed to escape the sickness an’ make it back to the Cinder Clouds Islands.”

“He were a warrior!” Hallekk roared. “He managed to evade that sickness, an’ he got what he could of his troops outta the Painted Canyon an’ retreated.”

“After they’d made a pact to stay an’ die together.”

“Doesn’t make no sense to die when it ain’t gonna help nothin’. They knew if they’d bolted from Fell’s Keep that most of ’em woulda died. The sickness did ’em in afore that. The only thing Oskarr could do was lead them what was healthy enough to run for their lives an’ take ’em outta that death trap. He did it.”

“He went back home and stayed away from the fighting.”

“But Oskarr didn’t leave the war,” Wick said. “Oskarr returned to the Cinder Clouds Islands and worked on the side of the Unity until Lord Kharrion was finally killed.”

“Hammerin’ out swords an’ armor from the safety of his forge,” Verdin accused.

“It’s powerful hard for an army to fight when it ain’t got the tools it needs to see the job finished,” Hallekk said. “When it come to a-buildin’ them tools, wasn’t none finer than Master Blacksmith Oskarr. He hammered out a lot of armor an’ weapons them Unity troops needed over them years.”

"Faugh!" Verdin said. " 'Twas fightin' that were needed! An' after that, Oskarr lived himself out a life that was fat an' happy."

"No," Wick said. "Oskarr died there in the Cinder Clouds Islands. For six years, Master Blacksmith Oskarr and his chief armorers supplied the Unity army. The forges never ran cold and the dwarves worked in shifts every hour of the day, hammering out swords and armor and arrowheads. During that time, it is said, the Cinder Clouds Islands were never silent, and the ringing of hammers filled all of the forges. In time, their work there drew the ire of the Goblin Lord because the supplies Master Blacksmith Oskarr and his people made started to turn the tide of the war."

"Lord Kharrion attacked the Cinder Clouds Islands," a dwarf said.

"He did," Wick agreed. "The Goblin Lord's spies discovered that Oskarr was preparing another large shipment of equipment in one month. Lord Kharrion put goblinkin ships in the water and went on the attack. He lay siege to Oskarr's city and waited to starve them out. As everyone knows, there wasn't much else in the Cinder Clouds Islands but veins of iron ore. It was a hardscrabble place even then. Only lizards and scrub brush lived there. Oskarr and his people depended on trade to keep food on the table."

"There was fish," someone suggested.

"The water was fouled by the forges," Craugh said. "The Cinder Clouds Islands dwarves used forges tapped directly into the volcanoes that spewed forth the island archipelago. Sulfur, soot, and ash clouded the waters around the island and chased away all living things on land and in the sea. It's impressive that the dwarves were strong enough to survive there. Volcanoes are very hard to tame."

Wick felt certain the wizard spoke from experience.

"There's no truer heat than that of a volcano," a dwarf stated. "Makes metal easy to work with, then leaves it hard as can be. The Cinder Clouds Islands dwarves weren't the only ones who learned that trick."

"And they could have only fished out to sea if they had access to the harbor," Wick said. "With Lord Kharrion's forces sitting in the Rusting Sea, that wasn't going to happen. But the Goblin Lord was too impatient to simply wait Oskarr and his people out. Instead, he worked his evil magic and turned the volcanoes the Cinder Clouds Islands dwarves had tapped into against them." He paused to let the dramatic tension increase. "The Goblin Lord's spell struck deeply into the heart of the volcano and wreaked havoc with the forges. In seconds, several of the islands—including the one where Oskarr and his hand-picked blacksmiths worked—sank beneath the waves of the Rusting Sea."

"Oskarr died?" Verdin asked.

Wick nodded. "He did. And nearly every man, woman, and child of his village died with him." Shuddering at the memory, he tried to forget about the accounts he'd read of the horrifying incident. It was no use. His imagination, in addition to being wild and vivid, also knew no rest. "Throughout the rest of the war against Lord Kharrion, no weapons or armor came from the Cinder Clouds Islands forges."

"Pity he didn't die before he betrayed the others at Painted Canyon," Verdin said.

"Why do you think Oskarr betrayed them forces?" Hallekk demanded.

"He was the only one of the leaders that didn't succumb to the sickness," Verdin said.

"That's because he was a dwarf!" Hallekk exploded. "Dwarves don't get overly sick!"

"Plenty of other dwarves got sick durin' that time." Verdin stuck out his jaw defiantly.

"Is that true?" one of the other humans asked Wick.

The little Librarian hesitated, but he knew he couldn't lie to those gathered there. "Many of the dwarves did get sick," he answered.

"But not Oskarr?"

"Not Oskarr."

"Why not?"

"No one knows." Wick listened anxiously as silence created a pall over the room. *Perhaps that telling lacked something*, he told himself. At least they weren't threatening to kill each other anymore.

Later, when the tavern had cleared out and most of the patrons had returned to their ships, Wick sat drinking quietly at a table with Craugh and Hallekk. Paunsel didn't dare chase the wizard off because he had no designs on becoming a toad.

Talk was small, generally anecdotes about things they'd seen or done, bits and pieces Wick had read of late, and a few choice comments about the ongoing chess game the Librarian and the wizard conducted through a series of letters through shipboard mail.

Wick could see that Hallekk was mightily disturbed over the argument that had cropped up during the night. He hated to see his friend so troubled.

"For what it's worth," Wick said, "I don't think Oskarr betrayed those men at the Battle of Fell's Keep."

Hallekk sighed, and the candle flame on the table between them danced between life and death, then finally stood tall once more. "I know, little man."

"I tried the best I could to express the situation."

"I saw that." Hallekk frowned. "The problem is that that battle is still talked about, even a thousand years later." He waved at the tavern. "Not just here. But all along the mainland as well. Ever'where ye go, sooner or later, the talk'll turn to the Battle of Fell's Keep."

Wick knew that was true. He'd been in taverns along the Shattered Coast that had turned into great battles themselves between humans, dwarves, and elves over what had transpired in the Painted Canyon at the end of those ten days of siege.

"What happened there," Hallekk said, "it's a sore spot that most just can't keep from pickin' at. Ye don't see it come up so much here on Greydawn Moors, but out in the rest of the world?" He shook his big head.

"It's a serious problem," Craugh said. "One that will have to be dealt with sooner or later."

Wick studied the wizard. Although he hadn't yet said what had drawn him to Greydawn Moors, Craugh had come in looking slightly bedraggled, with half-healed cuts on his face and hands. Obviously he'd been somewhere dangerous doing something dangerous against someone who had been . . . dangerous.

Wick was unhappy with his limited mental word choice. Finding new words was somehow beyond him. *You've got to slow down on the sparkleberry wine*, he told himself. *It's making your head as thick as Slops's mashed potatoes. And they could be used for mortar.*

Cleaning the mess those potatoes made on plates after they'd gotten cold had been one of Wick's greatest struggles while he served as dishwasher aboard *One-Eyed Peggie*. He hadn't known how the dwarven pirates had gotten it through their systems. It had to have been a gastronomical feat.

But he didn't say a word when Hallekk filled his tankard again. Trying to match a dwarf in drinking was usually a strategy bound for painful failure and serious regret, but Wick thought himself equal to the task that night. If only the room would occasionally stop spinning.

"Even with Lord Kharrion out of the way," Craugh said, "the goblinkin have continued to hold sway in the south, and they look to be turning an avaricious eye to the north. Their numbers are on the increase again, and they'll soon be back up to fighting strength."

Hallekk looked at the wizard. "Do ye think they'll take another run at her? Killin' out all the other races, I mean?"

Wick hadn't thought about that. He'd been to the mainland a few times, and he'd seen how the goblinkin empire had fragmented somewhat, but they'd remained particularly strong in the south. Thinking that they might someday unite and take up the genocidal war once more was frightening. Even the magical fog and enchanted sea monsters in the Blood-Soaked Sea couldn't protect the Vault of All Known Knowledge forever.

"If they do, humans, dwarves, and elves will have to find the strength to once more stand united," Craugh said. "If they don't, they will all fall." He sipped his wine. "It would be better if they were able to put the Battle of Fell's Keep behind them."

"They're still different races," Wick pointed out. "There's some natural discord between them anyway."

"Yes, but it's been my experience that those dislikes can be worked through. Prejudice is an ugly thing that feeds on its own energies. It doesn't bring anything with it; the perceived hatred of others that are different drains and limits." Craugh tugged at his beard. "But it would be better if the questions over the Battle of Fell's Keep were resolved."

"There has to be an answer somewheres." Hallekk fixed Wick with a curious look. "Mayhap in them books of yers."

"They're not mine." Wick had to work a little harder to make the words come out.

"Haven't ye got someplace where ye can look up the battle?"

Wick shook his head and felt it sway sickeningly, thinking just for a moment that it had somehow come loose from his shoulders. “We’re still sorting out all the journals, memoirs, and histories. If anything was written by anyone who was there, it hasn’t turned up yet.”

“Perhaps,” Craugh suggested, “those manuscripts never made it to the Vault of All Known Knowledge.”

“But why wouldn’t they?” Wick asked.

“Perhaps,” Craugh said slowly, as if warming to the possibility himself, “those memoirs weren’t yet written at the time the different cities and towns surrendered their libraries.” He took out his pipe and lit up. “It is something to think about.”

Personally, Wick thought he’d be better off thinking about it in the morning. For the moment, he was sleepier than he’d ever been.

When he felt himself swaying, Wick believed at first that he was still asleep. During the night, he’d dreamed of being Taurak Bleiyz rescuing the fair Princess Lissamae from the evil clutches of the cunning wolf’s head, Mamjor Dornthoth in the Gulches of Fiery Doom. He thought the swaying was just his imagination taking him out over the spiderweb spanning the Rushing River.

The dream had been an enjoyable time spent in slumber. In fact, he was already thinking of how he’d like to render a second, fresher version of the tale with color illustrations.

Opening his eyes, something he wasn’t always able to do while held captive in a dream, Wick stared at the low ceiling overhead and the end of the hammock he was lying in.

“No!” he croaked.

Panicked, he tried to turn over in the hammock to take in the small room and promptly fell out onto the hardwood floor. His head slammed into the solid surface. Stars spun behind his eyes. That was further proof he wasn’t dreaming: He never hit bottom when he fell in his dreams.

The impact ignited a headache that seemed on the verge of shattering his skull. A nasty, bitter taste filled his mouth. That definitely wasn’t normal. Suspicion darkened his thoughts.

Moaning a little with the effort, Wick levered himself up and stumbled to the porthole. He peered out at the curling waves of plum-colored ocean.

I’m on the Blood-Soaked Sea! he thought in disbelief. *I’ve been shanghaied! Again!*

3

"We Have a Mission for You, Librarian Lamplighter"

Angry and hurting, Wick headed for the door. Then he noticed the small hammock hanging above the one he'd fallen out of. Inside the hammock, Critter slept with its wings flared out to its sides.

Remembering how Critter had unmercifully awakened him the first time he'd been taken aboard *One-Eyed Peggie*, Wick yelled, "Wake up, ye goldbrickin' feather duster!" and gave the small hammock a spin, looping it over and over from its ties.

The rhowdor spun in the hammock, then fell out and tumbled toward the ground. Critter fluttered and landed on its bottom on the floor with its legs flared out. For a moment, its head bobbed like a yo-yo on a string. It blinked its eye quickly, then focused on Wick with a narrowed, baleful gaze.

"Why ye sawed-off sorry excuse fer a pirate!" Critter exploded. It kicked its claws and got its legs under it. "Ye slime-suckin' bilge rat! Ye're gonna pay fer that, ye are!" It came at Wick, barely weaving as its sticklike legs churned.

Still, Wick moved quickly and let himself out the door. He closed it behind him just in time to hear a satisfying *thud!* that warmed his heart and alleviated some of the misery he felt.

Critter cursed Wick thoroughly through the door and kicked it.

Ignoring the rhowdor, knowing the bird couldn't open the door and trusting that it would be some time before Critter could fly through the porthole, Wick turned his attention to the ship's deck. If waking up in a hammock in the same room as Critter wasn't proof enough, all the familiar faces of the crew told him immediately he was on *One-Eyed Peggie*.

They all called out to him in greeting, but most of them were moving slowly after shore leave. Sail filled the 'yards and popped in the strong breeze. The sun hung high in the eastern sky, and he noticed they were headed toward it. The mainland lay in that direction, but he judged that they were headed too far south to be making for the Shattered Coast. Somewhere south of there then, but he hadn't yet been in that direction.

Why? Wick wondered. But he knew asking himself that question wouldn't do any good. So he went looking for Hallekk, going up the stairs to the stern castle.

The big first mate was on the stern deck, just as Wick thought he would be. Surprisingly, Cap'n Farok was there as well. Even Craugh stood there with them, brimmed hat shadowing his eyes as he gazed out to sea.

That can't be good, Wick thought, but his anger grew inside him. He strode over to them and they all looked at him.

"A fair mornin' to ye, Librarian," Cap'n Farok greeted in his creaky voice.

Cap'n Farok was the oldest dwarf Wick had ever seen outside of an illustration in one of the books in Hralbomm's Wing in the vault. Almost a head shorter than Hallekk, Farok had silvery gray hair so aged that it was turning alabaster. The years had robbed his face of its firmness, so wrinkled that it looked like it had been hollowed out and was falling in on itself. He wore a fine suit and a decorated hat that set him apart from his crew.

Some of Wick's anger evaporated at seeing the old ship's captain. Farok's health hadn't been good for the last few years. Much of the time he was bedridden. On occasion, he'd talked of stepping down from his post and letting Hallekk take over as captain, but his crew had refused. Everyone knew that the only family Farok had was aboard *One-Eyed Peggie*. If he returned to Greydawn Moors, or any other place, for that matter, he'd only die among strangers.

"A fair morning to you, too, Cap'n," Wick said respectfully. "I—"

"I 'spect ye got questions," Farok interrupted.

"Aye, I do. Also, I need to ask you to turn around and take me back to Greydawn Moors. I've work to do at the Vault of All Known Knowledge. I don't know whose grand idea it was to kidnap me—" Here he glared at Craugh and Hallekk, both of whom he knew well enough to trust that they wouldn't turn him into a toad or beat him to a pulp respectively. Although the kidnapping had been a total surprise. "—but someone here deserves a swift—"

Farok held up a quavering hand. "It were me idea, Librarian."

Over Farok's shoulder, Craugh and Hallekk grinned at Wick and raised their eyebrows, waiting to see how he was going to finish the threat he'd started.

"—*chance* to let me know what's going on," Wick fumbled. He couldn't believe Farok had given the order to take him from Greydawn Moors. They traveled well aboard the ship when Wick was about tracking books down on the mainland, often playing chess and talking over nautical stories—which were a treasure trove for Wick because he took notes in his journals, but both of them knew he wasn't exactly pirate material.

"Over the mornin' meal then," Farok agreed. "I 'spect ye've got an appetite?"

Wick's stomach rumbled for all to hear.

"Well then," Farok said, laughing, "that's answer enough." He turned to the first mate. "Hallekk, the table if ye please. We'll be after takin' our meal here on the stern deck."

Hallekk went to the stern railing and bawled out the orders.

"An' when we finish the morning meal," Farok went on, "then we'll talk about why ye're here."

In short order, ship's crew brought out the captain's table and covered it with food. The sea was calm enough for them to eat, and being outside in the open was better than being closed up in the captain's cramped quarters or sharing mess with the crew down in the galley.

"Tuck in, Librarian, tuck in," Farok invited as he shoved a napkin down the front of his blouse. "We've just come from shore leave, an' them good people of Greydawn Moors has been mightily generous."

Hallekk passed plates around.

They were fired pottery, robin's-egg blue with gold-leaf trim showing beautifully rendered images of fantastic forest beasts. The luster of the plates was so shiny Wick could see himself in it.

"Oh my," he gasped. "Have you seen this?"

Farok leaned over and peered at the plate. "What is it? Did Slops not get them plates clean again? I've already had a talk to him about that."

"No. The plates are fine. But it's the plates themselves." Wick turned the plate to face the dwarven captain. "Do you know what they are?"

"Why, they's plates," Farok said.

"I believe Wick is referring to the fact that these plates are Delothian warder plates." Craugh sawed through a plump sausage with a knife, then forked up a chunk and popped it into his mouth.

Wick gazed at the wizard in disbelief. "You knew that?"

"Yes. I'm not uneducated."

"But you're eating off them!"

"That's what they were made for." Craugh sectioned a firepear and forked a bit of it as well. "To be eaten off of."

"But not by a bunch of dwarven pirates!" Wick was suddenly aware of how quiet the stern deck had gotten. Had the wind died down? He tried to recover. "Dwarven pirates who are actually heroes in disguise." *There. That sounds better, doesn't it?*

Hallekk looked grudgingly at his plate, then a little ashamed. "I ain't fit to be eatin' off this plate, is that what ye're a-sayin'?"

"No," Wick replied, feeling bad and wishing he had a way out of the hole he'd dug for himself. "What I'm saying is that these plates have a unique history." He turned the plate in his hands, finding the beginning of the story rendered there in the images. "This tale is about Noosif, the beaver companion of Warder Riantap, who was a great champion and cared for the Cealoch River from the Sparkling Falls to the Moons-kissed Deltalands where the Haidon lumberjack settlement lived."

Leaning close to his plate, scraping away a piece of egg from the edge, Hallekk said, "This one's about an eagle."

"That's probably an owl," Wick said automatically. "The Band of Fur, Feather, and Fin didn't include an eagle. There were twelve animals in all, creatures of the Delothian warders—humans, not elves—who fought the Mad Empress Maligna during the Zenoffran Troll War."

"I weren't aware there were any trolls in Zenoffra," Hallekk said.

"There weren't," Wick agreed, "after the Delothian warders finished with them. Until that time, the Mad Empress had employed them to build engines of destruction in the Skytrees Forest. Then the Haidon lumberjacks were able to move in and start harvesting trees for the ships made down in Cogsdale, where so many cargo ships were built. That war was important to the human sailors because it gave them resources to build fleets of trading and war vessels." He shrugged. "Of course, they immediately started competitions for trade goods and sank many of those ships."

"Are ye a-gonna eat, Librarian?" Farok asked. "While it's still hot? Would ye rather have another plate if that one doesn't suit ye?"

Wick sighed. None of them understood. "These were built for the Delothian warders, to commemorate their victory over the Mad Empress. Most of them died or lost their animal companions. They're works of art."

Craugh scooped up a big spoonful of hash browns fried with sweet onions, and plopped it into the center of the plate Wick held. "And today they hold food provided by generous hosts." His eyebrows arched in mild rebuke over his green eyes.

Giving up, Wick quickly filled his plate with sausages, fresh baked biscuits, firepears, corn pancakes that he covered in sweet sparkleberry syrup and tart limemelon wedges.

"Well," Hallekk said, eyeing Wick's burgeoning plate, "one thing ye got to say for them potters what made these plates: They certainly made big ones. Ye ought to be grateful 'bout that."

Wick was, but he ate carefully and didn't drag his fork over the plate.

After the table and the remnants were packed away, Farok and Craugh filled their pipes and lounged in their chairs to smoke. Hallekk went to see to his rounds.

One-Eyed Peggie continued to slice through the Blood-Soaked Sea. The eternal fogs, kept in place through the magical glamours that protected Greydawn Moors, ghosted across the deck and limited vision in all directions. But the sun felt warm.

"Awwwwwwrrrrrrrkkkkk!" Critter moaned below. The rhowdor sounded as if it were dying.

For a moment, Wick felt sorry for the bird. But not too much. Critter would live; it just wouldn't enjoy the experience for a while.

"Awwwwwrrrrrrrkkkkk!" Critter cried again. A moment later, it stumbled across the deck. Its pinkish horned face looked decidedly green. Its brilliant tail feathers, now tangled and some of them broken, trailed on the deck after it.

Struggling mightily, the rhowdor climbed the side, hooked its claws in under the top rail, and hung its head over. It used its wings to steady itself, then heaved again and again, sounding like it was strangling.

Mercilessly, the crew guffawed and hurled insults at the poor bird, making fun of his condition. "That'll teach ye to drink that rotgut, ye bone-headed bird!" someone yelled.

"Just keep throwin' up," someone else said. "When ye see yer claws an' tail feathers comin' up, ye'll know ye're almost done."

Critter tried to hurl an insult back, but ended up hurling over the side halfway through. Trapped with no way to respond, the bird had no choice but to take every scathing insult the crew could think of. And they could think of a lot because they spent a lot of time at sea with nothing to do.

Wick chuckled at the rhowdor's plight in spite of his mood. No one aboard the ship would see any true harm come to the rhowdor, but the bird was not well liked by anyone.

"I'd come to Greydawn Moors on another matter," Craugh said, "when I found you lecturing in Paunsel's."

"I wasn't lecturing," Wick said. "I was merely trying to forestall a brawl. If I'd had any sense, I'd have left out the back way."

"It's probably a good thing you didn't. Tempers seemed high last night." Craugh puffed on his pipe.

"What other matter brought you to Greydawn Moors?" Unable to simply sit and listen, used to having his hands busy all day, Wick reached down into his rucksack and took out one of the journals he kept on hand. A brief check inside assured him that it was blank.

He had a habit of carrying several different journals with him at all times because his attention constantly jumped from subject to subject. Grandmagister Frollo faulted him for that on a regular basis. Wick just had a hard time staying still—unless he had a truly good book in his hands. Thankfully, the Taurak Bleiyz book was in the rucksack as well, though he didn't know when he would ever get the dweller hero across the spiderweb above the Rushing River.

"The Cryptkeeper of Houngal," Craugh said.

Wick glanced sharply at the wizard. "I thought the Cryptkeeper was a myth."

Craugh puffed solemnly on his pipe. "I'd hoped." Something dark and dreadful flickered in his eyes. "But I think I met it."

"Where?" Unbidden, Wick's hands removed a stick of charcoal from the rolled leather pouch that held his writing utensils. Quickly, he sketched out the tall, lean frame of the Cryptkeeper, shrouding the crocodile's skull he reportedly wore in the hood of a tattered cloak.

"Near Moiturl," Craugh answered. "There are ruins there—"

"Tumbledown City," Wick said, nodding, watching with growing interest as the Cryptkeeper took shape on the blank page. "It wasn't always called Tumbledown City. From the geographic references I've been able to piece together,

Tumbledown City was once a human settlement called Arrod. It was a meeting place for the humans of Northern Javisham."

"Correct," Craugh said, looking more than slightly impressed. "Truly, Second Level Librarian Wick, your knowledge of the world before the Cataclysm sometimes astounds me."

"You have to remember that all the books I read are pre-Cataclysm," Wick said. "But I listen to the travelers' tales down at the Yondering Docks, and I can sometimes put today's places with what they were all those years ago. During that time, Arrod was a large town—for a human settlement, which wasn't common given that humans tend to wander—and the center of three different trade routes." He started to name them, but Craugh held up his hand in irritation.

I guess, at the moment, he isn't prepared to be astounded anymore, Wick thought.

"We need to talk about why you're aboard *One-Eyed Peggie*," Craugh said.

"What happened to the Cryptkeeper of Houngar?" Wick asked. He hated mysteries. Well, truth to tell, he actually enjoyed them. But not if they weren't properly finished.

"All those years ago? Or when I met him?"

"Both."

"All those years ago, he was a graveyard attendant who stole from the dead. As a result, he was cursed to eternally guard the dead but he couldn't leave the graveyard."

"And if he did?"

"He turned to dust."

"Oh. So you lured him away from the graveyard."

"No," Craugh said, frowning, "I turned him into a toad. When I left, he was hopping around the crypt. If he didn't hop away from the graveyard, he's still there." He smiled a little. "It's a rather fascinating experiment, actually, to see if my spell or the curse gives out first."

"You turned him into a toad. Haven't you ever thought about turning those who vex you into . . . I don't know, *something* else?"

"No," Craugh said flatly. "It works. Why fix it?"

"It's not very creative."

Craugh shifted irritably in his seat and came close to glaring. "Do you think I stole you away from Greydawn Moors to critique my choice of transformations?"

Wick was suddenly aware that he was out on thin ice. "Uh . . . *noooo?*"

"I did not."

Then, before he could stop himself, Wick said, "I thought Cap'n Farok made the decision to shanghai me."

Craugh's face colored darkly with anger.

"I did," Farok said. "After Craugh put the sleeping powder in yer drink an' Hallekk carried ye back to the ship."

"You?" Wick exploded. "Put sleeping powder in my drink?"

"You wouldn't have agreed to come if I'd asked," Craugh said.

"Of course not!" Wick couldn't believe it. The wizard had betrayed him in the past, but nothing like—Then he stopped himself. *Actually, this is exactly like that time in Cormorthal*. He groaned. He couldn't believe he'd been made the fool. *Again*.

"I made the decision for ye," Farok said. "So if 'n yer after a-placin' blame, let it be on me head."

Wick gazed at the captain's rheumy old eyes. Even though he struggled valiantly to hang onto his anger, he couldn't. Farok had never betrayed him, never once deserted him to deal with razor-tusked melanoths in a dead-end alley, never abandoned him to explain the theft of an ensorcelled skull in a temple of Thurdamon the Cursed, never—well, all things considered, there was a lot Craugh had to answer for over the years.

Sighing, Wick said, "I'm not going to blame you, Cap'n Farok."

"Good," Craugh said. "Then we can be about this bit of business."

"I *am* going to blame you," Wick declared fiercely.

With an acutely threatening air, Craugh leaned forward and gave Wick the hairy eyeball. "Are you auditioning to be a toad, Librarian?" the wizard asked in a cold, hard voice.

Striving to control his bladder, hoping his voice didn't squeak when he spoke, knowing his first clue would be when the chair he was sitting in suddenly seemed too big, Wick leaned back at the wizard. "I don't know. Can a t-t-toad do whatever it is y-y-you've set your c-c-cap for me to d-d-do?"

For a moment longer, Craugh glared at him. Then he started laughing. "By the Old Ones! Do you know when the last time was that someone stood toe-to-toe with me?"

No, Wick thought.

"Well, actually," Craugh went on, "it was more like toe-to-toad, but there you have it." He looked away and swirled his staff through the air, scattering green embers upon the wind. "We have a mission for you, Librarian Lamplighter. Captain Farok and I."

"I didn't volunteer for this," Wick said.

"Ain't no one more suited to the task," Cap'n Farok said. "I knowed that after Craugh laid it out afore me." He looked at Wick. "We need ye to do it, lad. *I* need ye to do it."

If it had been anyone else who asked me, or threatened *me*, Wick thought, *I wouldn't do it*. But over the years and the journeys to the mainland, he'd developed a strong affection for the crusty old dwarven sea captain. He took a deep breath and let it out.

"What is it?" Wick asked.

"We need ye to go among the Cinder Clouds dwarves an' find Master Blacksmith Oskarr's magic battle-axe, Boneslicer."

"But the Cinder Clouds Islands *sank*!"

"Mayhap not," Cap'n Farok said. " 'Tis true them islands got mightily shaken up, but some of 'em's still there."

"If the battle-axe was still there, someone would have found it."

"Not necessarily," Craugh said. "There were many things lost during the

Cataclysm." A great scowl darkened his face. "The problem with lost things is that they don't always stay so."

Wick silently agreed. Cursed objects had a habit of turning up again and again to cause new problems. "Okay, let's assume it's still there. Wonder of wonders, let's assume I even find it. What good will it do?" Though he didn't want to admit it, he was intrigued.

"Magical items, especially ones forged for their bearer, as Boneslicer was for Master Blacksmith Oskarr, have a tendency to absorb something of their respective owners," Craugh said.

"What good will that do?"

"One day, Librarian," Cap'n Farok said, "not in my lifetime, of course, but perhaps in yours, the world will become closer. Dwarves, humans, an' elves will need to know how to live with each other again. If there's to be any peace at all betwixt 'em, them questions about the Battle of Fell's Keep need to be answered. Mayhap, the Old Ones willin', we can get some of them answers ready."

"By going to the Cinder Clouds Islands and finding Master Blacksmith Oskarr's battle-axe?" Wick asked.

"Aye." The old captain nodded.

Wick sighed. "How are we going to do it?"

" 'We'?" Craugh shook his head. "There's no 'we' to this, Librarian Lamplighter. There's only you."

"*Me?*" Wick couldn't believe it. "You're going to plunk me down on an island and expect me to survive? *And* find a mystical battle-axe no one has seen in a thousand years in an island group that was disrupted by volcanoes?"

Craugh looked at him. "No one said this was going to be easy." He was silent for a moment. "But there is an added attraction."

To getting killed and eaten by goblinkin? To being put to death by suspicious dwarves who don't take to strangers? To getting burned to a crisp by a sudden volcanic eruption? Wick couldn't wait to hear how the wizard was going to *attempt* to entice him. If he wasn't sure they'd put him ashore anyway, he'd have argued and demanded, maybe even begged and—

"Master Blacksmith Oskarr believed in the power of books," Craugh said. "The rumor goes that he kept a few personal favorites—and his journals—with him even after he sent everything else he had with Unity ships."

Wick knew they had him then. No one else aboard *One-Eyed Peggie* would lay his life on the line for books. Not the way he would.

He sighed. "All right. But I'm not going to like it."

4

Marooned in the Cinder Clouds Islands

One-Eyed Peggie sailed slowly through the islands, most of her sails furled and crew lining the railing with weighted lines to call out the depths as they went forward. There were hundreds of islands scattered over the Rusting Sea, which got its name—Wick discovered—from the tiny flecks of oxidized iron ore that fluttered through the depths. As a result, the sea looked dark orange and murky. He doubted anything could live in those waters, but every now and again he saw something huge and monstrous slide through the sea.

Or maybe it was only the churning of the sea, caused by underwater volcanic vents.

The islands came in all sizes. Some of them were no bigger than a foot or two across, looking like a flagstone footpath that had been scattered across the sea. But they were attached to spires of rock firmly attached to the ocean bottom that could rip out an unwary ship's hull. Several others were scarcely large enough for a hut.

Then there were some that soared three and four hundred feet straight up, broken and craggy things devoid of vegetation except for a few gnarly trees and ugly brush that had peculiar reddish-gold blossoms Wick had never before seen.

"What are those blossoms?" Diligently, Wick captured the shape and relative size of the blossoms in his journal. He mixed the color with the pigments he brought with him, but only put a dab of the color on the page to extend his supply. Although, with the ore seemingly in goodly supply on the islands, it was possible he could make more paint by mixing ore in powder form with animal fat. He'd been working quickly, blocking out first impressions of the Cinder Clouds Islands.

Hallekk stood only a short distance away. He looked alert and ready, but he was uneasy about sailing into waters that were unknown to them. Especially a sea that presented such dangers to ships' crews new to the area.

"Them are goldengreed weeds," the big dwarf answered. "Ye'll want to stay away from 'em."

"Why?"

" 'Cause they bite."

" 'Bite'? Like with teeth?" Wick had seen flesh-eating plants before, but they didn't bite. They usually had a tendency to swallow prey whole, asphyxiate it or poison it, then digest it at their leisure. Brandt had once cut him out of a crest-hearted gulper they'd found in a wizard's enchanted greenhouse up in the Thundering Hills while looking for a treasure.

"They bite," Hallekk said, "but not with teeth. Don't know how they do it, an' I've no wish to find out. They got a workin' relationship with a uniquely loathsome weevil what feeds on human flesh."

"You mean they're symbiotic?"

Hallekk glanced at him for a moment. " 'Course I do. How could I mean anything else? Once a goldengreed bites ye, they deposit a weevil what's about to lay eggs—"

"You mean she's gravid," Wick said automatically.

"If 'n ye say so. Anyways, the weevil burrows up in yer skin, then digs in deep an' tight. After a few days, she ups an' lays her eggs in ye an' she dies. Only a short while later, them little weevils hatches an' eats ye from the inside out."

"That's disgusting," Wick said. He thought the whole process unnatural and needlessly morbid.

"Aye. Goblinkin in these parts use goldengreed as torture sometimes. Stake a prisoner out, then make bets on how much of him gets eaten afore he croaks." Hallekk looked at Wick with concern in his eyes. "I've heard tell that if 'n them newborn weevils are left to their own business, they can eat a man down to skin an' bones in a few weeks. Usually he dies somewheres in there, but it ain't an easy way to go."

"No," Wick agreed, his throat tight and dry. *And they're going to put me off in the middle of that?* "So . . . if I get bitten, what should I do?"

"Burn it out if 'n ye can. Dig it out with a knife." Hallekk shrugged. "If 'n ye think ye're still infested an' ye can live without that part of yerself, if 'n it's only a finger or a toe—or even a hand or a foot—cut it off."

"Oh."

"It's best if ye doesn't get bitten."

"I'll keep that in mind."

"Oh, an' don't go to sleep within driftin' distance of a goldengreed plant. Sometimes them blasted things gets desperate an' takes their chances by jumpin' out of the plant in hopes of landin' on something close by. They get the chance to crawl into yer ear, they'll do it. Then ye'll be keepin' a weevil in mind." Hallekk showed him a callous grin.

Never sleep with your ears open. Wick wrote that in his journal and underlined it. In case he forgot. But he didn't see how that would happen.

"Are you afraid, Wick?"

Startled, Wick looked up from his journal. Actually, while he'd been working, he didn't feel anything at all. But now that the thought of dying was suddenly thrust into his mind again, he was terrified.

Craugh stood at his side, gazing out at the sea. With the sun setting in the west behind him, Wick could only see the wizard mostly in silhouette. As a result, Craugh looked almost insubstantial, while at the same time shot through with darkness.

"More than I've ever been," Wick said, hoping that Craugh might relent. He knew if he could get the wizard to change his mind, Cap'n Farok would change his, too.

"Well," Craugh said, looking out over the Rusting Sea, "it's always good to be a little afraid, but don't let that fear rule your thinking. Use it to keep you alive."

"Why don't you go," Wick asked, "and I'll stay on the ship and give *you* advice?"

"Do you think the Cinder Clouds dwarves would talk to a wizard?"

No. Nobody wants to talk to a wizard. But Wick didn't say that. Instead, he pointed out, "You don't have to tell them you're a wizard."

Craugh frowned at Wick. "Do I have to ever tell anyone I'm a wizard?"

Wick thought long and hard about that, seeking any avenue of escape. No matter where they went, no one made the mistake of thinking Craugh was just an old human. When someone looked at him, they just saw . . . *wizardly*.

"No," Wick grumped. Then in a lower voice, he mumbled, "But a lot of people think you're an *evil* wizard."

"I heard that."

"You were meant to."

"I know you're not happy about this, Wick," Craugh said, "but it's for the best." He pointed.

Following the bony finger, Wick spotted a seagull flying low over the water on *One-Eyed Peggie*'s port side. The bird cruised easily, no more than ten feet above the placid, orange-tinted surface.

"Let's say that seagull represents the present," Craugh said. "It sails through life blithely, but one day the past will rear up its ugly snout—"

The water under the seagull suddenly erupted and a wart-covered red snout led a reptilian body up from the sea. Massive jaws opened and closed swiftly with a *snap!* of teeth that sounded like a tree trunk splitting. In the next instant, the seagull was gone and only a few white feathers drifted on the air.

"—and the present will be ripped away," Craugh said.

Listening to the wizard, Wick detected a deeper level of meaning to Craugh's words. The warning scraped against something personal inside Craugh.

"You have to pay attention to the past, Wick," Craugh said quietly. "You read books and look for the old science and history that has been lost or forgotten. But you have to understand that people—humans, dwarves, and elves, and even dwellers—lived in that science and history. They had lives in addition to discoveries and explorations, and some of those lives weren't quite as heroic as the authors of those books would have readers believe. People—" The wizard took a deep breath. "—well, they have a tendency to fail and disappoint. Especially when you view them as strong figures."

The anger and fear drained from Wick when he regarded the wizard. For the first time after all the adventures they had been through, Wick thought Craugh looked somehow vulnerable and lost.

How can you go through a thousand years of living? he wondered. *How many friends, how much* family, *did you lose over those centuries, Craugh?*

But he knew he dared not ask.

"Those warriors that died at the Battle of Fell's Keep need to be remembered," Craugh said. "But they need to be remembered as a whole, not disparate groups." He looked at the islands before them. "If we can find Oskarr's battle-axe—"

"Boneslicer," Wick put in.

"Just so," the wizard said. "Once you find Boneslicer, we can begin healing that old wound."

Wick thought that all sounded well and good, but he kept remembering how easily the snouted beast—*a giant crocodile?*—leaped from the water and snatched the unsuspecting seagull. How could Craugh and Cap'n Farok possibly believe he was going to succeed at this insane quest?

At dusk, *One-Eyed Peggie* dropped anchor less than a hundred paces from one of the islands. The lookouts had kept careful watch and didn't think any goblins were in the area, but they had heard the clangor of dwarven hammers in the distance and knew they had to be close to a dwarven village.

Dressed in a modest traveling cloak, his journal hidden under his shirt in a waterproof oilskin along with a quill and ink bottle and a few sticks of charcoal to work with, Wick stood ready to leave.

Wheezing with effort, Cap'n Farok joined Wick beside the longboat the crew had prepared to lower over the side. The sulfurous air hadn't agreed with the dwarven captain the whole day. Now he looked pale and wan.

"Ye keep yer head about ye while out there," Cap'n Farok said in a no-nonsense tone. "I don't like losin' crew, an' I won't stand for it outta stupidity."

"Aye, Cap'n." Unconsciously, Wick stood a little taller and puffed out his chest. There was something innately noble about the old captain, something that reminded Wick of Grandmagister Ludaan, who had accepted him as a Novice and shown him the secrets of the Vault of All Known Knowledge.

"Ye come back to us when ye've finished yer quest, Librarian Lamplighter," Cap'n Farok said. "We'll see ye through the monster's eye an' come to fetch ye when ye've got Oskarr's battle-axe."

The monster's eye Cap'n Farok referred to occupied a large bottle kept under the captain's bed. The ship's captain could use the eyeball (which still lived inside the jar) to see any past or present crewman that yet survived, no matter where they were.

Unfortunately, the sea monster could also keep watch over the ship and—every now and again—track it. *One-Eyed Peggie* had been attacked a number of times so far.

"I will, Cap'n Farok," Wick promised. "We've still got your memoirs to write."

"In due time," the old captain said. "In due time." With that, he ducked in for a quick, fierce hug that touched Wick's heart. "Fair weather an' followin' seas to ye, Librarian."

"And you, Cap'n."

Wick stepped into the longboat, joined by Hallekk and Craugh. The wizard's decision to risk stepping ashore surprised Wick, but he didn't say anything. Three more crewmen joined them, filling out the longboat crew.

Luckily, the ocean was calm. Wick took up one of the oars and pulled with a trained stroke, falling easily into the silent rhythm with Hallekk and the dwarves. They had to make an adjustment because Craugh didn't pull an oar, but the wizard kept watch.

Wick knew his hands were the roughest of any Librarian. They were even rougher than those Librarians who made most of the paper at the Vault of All Known Knowledge. That process involved harsh chemicals.

Grandmagister Frollo faulted him for his worker's hands on several occasions, but Wick took a curious pride in them. There were several scars in with the calluses, from knife and rope and other sharp edges and fires, and looking at them was almost like studying a table of contents in a book. Each of those scars told a story.

Only a short time later, with the moonslight blunted by the thick smoke that shrouded the islands, the longboat ran up on the shore. Hallekk and the others got out, shipped the oars, and pulled the boat up so the retreating tide wouldn't carry it back out.

After a brief search of the coastline by torchlight, they found a cave where Wick could weather the night. With the area heated by the volcanic activity, it was warm enough that he didn't worry about being cold. He had precious little supplies.

Besides his hidden journal and writing utensils, he had only ragged clothes and a patched traveling cloak. All of it was clothing an escaping slave—if he were fortunate enough—could have stolen.

"Well then, little man," Hallekk said a little uneasily, "we've put ye up as best as we can with what we've got to give ye."

"I know," Wick said.

"I'll be askin' the Old Ones to keep an eye on ye."

"Just make sure the cap'n does the same," Wick said. "If he sees me running ahead of a goblinkin horde, or the dwarves are intending to chop me up, it's probably time to come get me."

Despite his anxiety, Hallekk grinned. "We'll come get ye straightaway. Ye got me word." He held out a big paw, and when Wick took it, he pulled the little Librarian in close and held onto him for a moment. "Ye just take care of yerself.

I 'spect to hear all ye stories when ye come aboard again. Make sure yer knob stays attached properlike."

"I will."

Hallekk turned away, leaving Craugh standing there to say his good-byes.

"This is uncomfortable," the wizard said after a moment.

Wick silently agreed. Although he and Craugh had journeyed together in the past and had shared meals, stories, and hardships in their adventures, they weren't close friends.

"You're not making it any easier to leave," Craugh growled.

"If you ask me, the easy part is getting back in that longboat to return to the ship. Not staying here," Wick said.

Craugh grinned at him then. "I guess you're right. Well, we've seen harder times than these. You haven't gotten yourself killed before, so just keep doing that." Without another word, Craugh turned and walked away.

An empty feeling opened up in Wick's middle and spread quickly outward.

"Oh." Craugh turned around. "There is one other thing."

"Another warning?" Wick asked.

"No. I see no reason not to believe you've been given a sufficient number of those." Craugh reached inside his travel cloak. "You'll need a guide of sorts while you're here."

"I thought no one was staying."

"No one is. This guide will blend into the surroundings, but he's not very noticeable." Taking out his hand, Craugh held a foot-long skink by the tail. He opened his fingers and dropped the lizard with a *plop* to the ground.

The skink immediately slithered away and raced over to a clutch of rocks. It sat there looking at them with big, unblinking eyes.

"You're leaving me a lizard to act as a guide?" Wick asked in disbelief. *Maybe I could use it as bait for fishing.*

"Yes. I think you'll find him useful. His name is Rohoh. There's more to him than meets the eye."

Good, Wick thought, *because what meets the eye isn't even worth throwing into a kettle and using as soup stock.* "Sure," he said.

Quietly, with a few last-minute well wishes, the ship's crew—including Craugh—was back in the longboat and pulling for the ship. *One-Eyed Peggie* sat at anchor, riding the ocean's gentle swells. A few lanterns used as running lights marked her for Wick to see.

He stood there on the shore, listening to the slap of the waves, and watched as the pirate ship unfurled part of her sails and got underway again. Getting seen by an incoming ship or by dwarves looking for new ore wasn't a good idea. It would be easy to guess that perhaps Wick wasn't an escaped slave.

After a while, *One-Eyed Peggie* disappeared over the horizon.

"Hey," the skink said.

Wick glanced at the lizard in surprise. "You talk."

"Sure I talk." The skink whipped his tail around as if taking pride in his accomplishment, or maybe it was to show disdain.

"It figures. Don't tell me, you're here to tell me what Craugh would do whenever there's a problem."

"Actually," the skink said, rising on his two hind legs to address Wick from the rocks, "I'm not any happier about this than you are."

"Getting stranded on this lump of rock in the middle of the Rusting Sea?"

The skink looked around. Moonslight gleamed over the small scales. "This is actually a pretty good place. Warm and cozy." He took a deep sniff. "And it has a certain . . . aroma about it that seems fascinating." He glanced back at Wick and sniffed. "Craugh lied to me."

"Craugh lies to everybody. It's one of those dependable things in life."

"He told me you were a bonafide hero."

"I'm a Librarian," Wick said because he was tired and he wasn't thinking straight what with all the worry and fear clamoring inside his head.

"Oh," Rohoh said disdainfully. "A *book* person."

"You know about book people?"

"Mold, mildew, and dust. Those are terrible smells. Yes, I know books." He inhaled again. "Not like this."

"How do you know about books?"

"I've traveled with Craugh to different places. I've been to the Vault of All Known Knowledge. There was a man there. Grandmagister Ludaan. I played chess with him."

Wick *was* surprised. "You knew Grandmagister Ludaan?"

"Yes. A fascinating man. For a human with no wizardly abilities." The skink rubbed his light green stomach. "He was always generous with his food."

Suspicion darkened Wick's thoughts. "Were you something else before you met Craugh?"

The skink blinked. "Yes, I was. I was much safer. And I was happy."

"You weren't a human? Or an elf? Or a dwarf? Or a dweller? Or something else?"

"Please." Rohoh crossed his skinny arms over his narrow chest. "Why would I want to be *anything* else than what I am now? Being a skink is perfect for me."

"Then why are you here?"

"I owed Craugh a favor. He told me I'd be working with a hero who had dunderheaded tendencies."

" 'Dunderheaded tendencies'?"

"Yes. But I wouldn't take it personal. Craugh doesn't have a high opinion of anybody." The skink used his thin, pointed tail to pick his teeth. "Except for Grandmagister Ludaan, of course. I think Craugh likes his food, too."

Sighing, Wick marched back to the small cave they'd chosen for him to spend the night in.

"That reminds me, I'm hungry," the lizard said. It scurried after him, its lightning quick skills easily making up for Wick's longer stride.

"So?" Taking off his traveling cloak, Wick folded it into a rough pillow at the back of the cave and laid down. "Go catch a bug."

"Have you ever tried to clean bug legs out from between your teeth?"

"You don't have teeth." Wick struggled in his bed on the hard rock and succeeded in finding an almost comfortable position.

"I was trying to put it in perspective for you. And if you swallow them whole, you end up swallowing them again and again. All night long. It's not worth the bother, I tell you."

Wick turned away from the skink and ignored him. *What have I gotten myself into?* Something scurried across the cave ceiling above him. When he looked up, the lizard hung upside down by its hind feet, regarding him with unblinking eyes.

"Don't you have anything to eat?" Rohoh asked.

"No," Wick said. "Craugh and the others took it away from me. I'm supposed to be an escaped slave."

"You don't have *anything*?"

"No."

"Can I search your pockets for crumbs?"

"No."

"You might have missed something."

"If you crawl inside my clothing," Wick promised, "I'm going to feed you to the first goblinkin I find."

Just then, light flared into the tunnel, chasing away the darkness. The skink hung frozen for a moment, his mouth wide in surprise. Then he bolted for the back recesses of the cave.

"Now an' why would I want to eat a skinny ol' lizard what's probably tough as leather when I could fetch me a nice plump halfer fer me stewpot?" a rough voice demanded. "Lookee here. I told ye I thought I smelt me a halfer."

Putting a hand up to block the torchlight, Wick spotted three horrible shapes standing in the cave mouth. Goblinkin! He was doomed even before his task got underway!

5

On the Menu

Springing to his feet, Wick tried to run for his life. The skink had managed to escape. But the cave ceiling was low. Wick didn't see the overhang that caught him across the forehead and knocked him from his feet. Nearly senseless, he landed flat on his back and couldn't move.

I'm paralyzed! he thought. Panic coursed through him.

The light from the goblinkin's torch came on into the cave, trailing the rude laughter from the approaching goblinkin.

"Stupid halfer," one of the goblinkin snarled. "Goin' a-runnin' through a dark cave like that when ye can't see. Ain't got no sense."

"Well," another said, "we ain't gonna eat him 'cause he's smart. We're gonna eat him 'cause he tastes good. Leastways, he'll taste good once we get him all stewed up."

"Maybe ye don't care for 'em none," a third commented, "but I like halfer brains. They's soft. I can swallow 'em down without even chewin'."

Wick discovered that he wasn't totally paralyzed because his stomach turned queasy at that revelation. He'd never made a study of what goblinkin ate. The information he had came as a result of misfortune. And he surely didn't want to learn about the culinary delights of goblinkin firsthand.

Bats fluttered on the ceiling, hanging upside down like dried figs. Several of them turned loose their holds and dropped, then spread their tiny wings and flew toward the cave mouth.

"Look out!" one of the goblinkin shouted.

The torchlight danced crazily as the goblinkin dodged the bats. Then the bats were gone from the cave.

Wick suddenly discovered that he wasn't paralyzed anymore. He tried to get to his feet. Only then a clawed goblinkin foot came crashing down on his chest and knocked the breath from him as it pinned him against the cave floor.

"Good thing ye didn't let him run," one of the goblinkin said. "Halfers is almighty quick. I hate fast food."

"Where do ye a-think ye're a-goin'?" The goblinkin leaned down, thrusting his ugly face into Wick's.

"N-n-nowhere," Wick stuttered, wishing he wasn't so afraid. But even after years of trekking around the mainland chasing after books and legends and seeing goblinkin many of those times, he still wasn't used to them.

Goblinkin were particularly ugly. Baby goblinkin were even more so, which was why they started out in the world unloved and pretty much on their own. Besides that, there was always another goblinkin that came along in case the first was eaten by something larger than him, killed while on a battlefield or falling from a mountain, or beneath the tusks of a wild Borhovian skurulta (which, for some odd reason no one knew, fancied goblinkin flesh), or was butchered and eaten by siblings who had grown tired of him.

The goblinkin's face was a triangle shape, with the narrowest point being the chin. Using the allotted space for features, nature had spread the piggy eyes apart so there was plenty of room for the bulbous nose to take root over the narrow mouth jammed with crooked, yellow fangs. The hair was tied back in a ponytail festooned with rocks and gems and bones that told the story of the goblinkin's tribe and accomplishments.

A sparse sprinkling of bushy black hair on the chin formed something of a beard. The ears were huge sails as big as the bats that had fled the cave, and both were punctured several times over with earrings fashioned from victims' bones. In proper daylight, the skin was splotchy gray-green that maintained an unhealthy pallor.

"That's right," the goblinkin taunted, "you ain't a-goin' nowhere."

"Uh, Sebble," the smallest goblinkin said hesitantly.

"What, Droos?" Sebble snarled.

"The halfer." Droos nodded at Wick. "He's gotta go somewhere."

"No, he ain't," Sebble said, " 'cause I said he ain't a-goin' nowhere. An' I'm the chief of this here patrol."

"Okay," the younger goblinkin said, looking around. "We can eat him here, I suppose. But he's gonna be cold an' tough if 'n we don't cook him up proper."

"Oh." Sebble appeared to give that some thought. He scratched his head with a black talon. "We need to cook him, don't we?"

"We could eat him raw," the third goblinkin suggested. "Just open him up like a melon an' he can be his own bowl. After we scoop him clean, we can eat the rind. We've done it afore." He kicked Wick with a big toe. "That way we don't have to share him. Ain't enough meat on his bones to share with the others anyway."

"You don't want to eat him raw," a voice called from the back of the cave. Wick recognized the skink's voice but apparently the goblinkin didn't.

"Right," Sebble said. "We don't want to eat him raw, Kuuch."

"Why not?" Kuuch asked.

"Well," Sebble said, evidently thinking it over again.

Some chief, Wick thought.

"Because if you eat him raw, you'll get a bad belly and . . . and . . . a case of the spoilt meat trots," Rohoh called from the back of the cave.

Sebble slapped Kuuch with an open hand. "We doesn't want to eat the halfer raw, ye idjit. It'd give us the spoilt meat trots, is what it'd do."

"Take him back to the camp and put him in a stewpot," Rohoh suggested.

If I ever *see that turncoat again*, Wick thought, *it's going to be too soon!*

"We have a stewpot back at the camp," Droos said.

"Yeah." Sebble nodded. "We'll cook him up there. Let's go. We gotta find some potatoes."

"An' some carrots," Droos said. "I like carrots. But we don't wanna cook 'em too long. I like 'em crunchy."

"That's 'cause ye still got all yer teeth," Kuuch snarled, slapping the back of the younger goblinkin's head. "I like me carrots mushy. Otherwise I have to pick 'em out."

"Ain't my fault ye lost yer teeth," Droos sniveled, backing away from the others. "Told ye eatin' that many carrion rats at one time wasn't good for ye. Give ye gas an' rotted out yer teeth. Ye shoulda mixed 'em better with them slimeweed greens."

"I hate slimeweed greens," Kuuch moped.

"You'll want some salt and pepper, too," Rohoh called from the back of the cave.

"An' salt," Sebble said.

"An' pepper," Kuuch added.

Sebble glared at the other goblinkin. "I was gonna say that."

"And onions," Rohoh said.

Sebble turned to Droos. "Are ye rememberin' all this?"

Droos shrank back. "Maaaaybeee."

Sebble slapped the younger goblinkin again, making Droos yelp. "Remember it, ye worthless gullet. Potatoes an' carrots an'—"

"Salt an' pepper," Kuuch said.

"I was gettin' to that," Sebble whined. "I wasn't gonna forget salt an' pepper."

"I think maybe we used up all the pepper," Droos said.

"We got pepper," Kuuch said. "Banna still has some he's hid up an' I know where he hid it."

"There was somethin' else," Sebble said. He'd been counting ingredients on his fingers and had nearly a full hand.

"*Onions*," Rohoh said.

"Oh yeah," Sebble said. "Onions. There's them wild onions what grows on the hill."

"I don't want them wild onions," Kuuch whined. "They gives me gas."

"Ever'thin' ye eats gives ye gas," Droos said. "I tell ye, ye shouldn't got a sweet tooth fer them carrion rats."

"Well, I like them wild onions," Sebble said. "But ye're a-sleepin' downwind of us after we eat."

Wick lay still under the goblinkin's foot. He couldn't believe he was fated to become indigestion after years of serving as a Novice and a Third Level Librarian. He'd practically only gotten promoted to Second Level Librarian. Maybe First Level Librarian wasn't going to happen any time soon, but it was a possibility he was looking forward to. Everything happened eventually.

But not if he ended up as a repast for goblinkin.

"Firepears would be nice," Rohoh said.

Sebble nodded. "They would at that. I like firepears." He looked for another finger on his first hand and discovered that he was all out. He turned up a finger on his other hand like it was something he'd never seen before.

"C'mon," Sebble said. "We ain't got all night if we're gonna have the halfer stewed by mornin'."

Wick knew pleading for his life wasn't going to do any good. But he still felt inclined.

Together, the three goblinkin turned and walked away, arguing among themselves how best to prepare a dweller stew. Wick lay on the ground unnoticed. They were so involved in planning their meal they'd forgotten the main ingredient. Cautiously, head aching from the impact, Wick got to his feet.

"Wait," Droos said from outside the cave. "We left the halfer."

Seeing the torch hurrying back toward him, Wick turned to run again. Perhaps he could lose himself in the back of the cave. All he needed was—

"Look out!" Rohoh yelled.

The familiar impact slammed across Wick's forehead again. He was lying on his back, seeing stars, when Sebble returned for him.

Grinning, the goblinkin fisted Wick's clothes and lifted him from the ground. "Ye're really stupid, halfer. I hope I don't catch it from eatin' ye."

A short while later, Wick trudged up the mountain in the darkness. The rope around his neck chafed something fierce. Tied behind his back, his hands had gone numb. He fell again and again, bruising his face and cutting his lips and chin.

Every now and then, when he didn't fall fast enough to suit Sebble, who held the rope around Wick's neck, the goblinkin yanked the line and caused him to fall. Sebble and Kuuch hooted with laughter at the sport.

"Mayhap we could walk closer to him with the torch so he could see," Droos suggested. For a goblinkin, he seemed to have a more tender heart.

"Nah," Sebble replied. "All that fallin' down he's a-doin' is just tenderizin' him some."

"Well, if 'n ye keep a-playin' with our food like that," Droos said, "ye're liable to lose him over the side in one of them firepits."

So much for the tender heart theory, Wick thought. Then, *Firepits!* He peered over the side of the trail and noticed that, indeed, he felt an occasional wafting of heat from that direction. Evidently the island still had vent tubes that ran to the heart of the smoldering volcano on the ocean floor.

Up and up and up, Wick went, following a narrow path that had been worn into the stone. Since there wasn't any game on the island that he knew of, Wick felt certain goblinkin or dwarves had made the trail.

Without warning, something ran up Wick's leg. Tiny claws bit into his flesh. Memory of Hallekk's description of the goldengreed weed ran through his mind and he couldn't help thinking that he'd stumbled against one of the plants in the dark and was now infested with flesh-eating insects. He halted in the middle of the trail and howled helplessly, jumping up and down. The claws just bit in more fiercely.

Concerned by their prisoner's antics, the goblinkin halted. Sebble raised his torch and looked at Wick. "What are ye about, halfer?"

"Something's on me!" Wick cried, jumping and flopping his elbows—which was all he could manage with his hands bound behind him. "I think I was bitten by a goldengreed weed!"

Anxiously, the goblinkin stepped back. That didn't help because Sebble kept a firm grip on the rope and yanked Wick off balance. He hopped and skipped a short distance back down the trail. Instantly, the goblinkin retreated farther and started yelling threats, but that tactic didn't do any good because Sebble kept hold of the rope and kept pulling Wick after them. Down and down they skipped, till finally the little Librarian lost his balance and fell with a thud.

Frantic, Wick rolled and accidentally tumbled into one of the craters. Suddenly the only thing keeping him from plunging into one of the volcanic vents was the hateful rope around his neck. Thankfully the goblinkin had tied it well and it was a strong rope.

But he was strangling.

"Quick!" one of the goblinkin cried. "Pull him up afore we lose our dinner!"

"Maybe we should let him go," another suggested. "I don't want to eat any of those weevil eggs."

"Or we could just let him dangle a bit until he's properly steamed. Likely as not, the meat would fall right offa the bone in a little bit."

Wick felt like his eyes were about to pop from his head. He couldn't breathe and hot air from the vent came close to scalding his legs. It didn't take much for him to imagine the red-hot lava waiting only a short—or long—distance below.

Whatever was on Wick ran up his back, hooking claws into his shirt, then clung in his hair by his right ear. "Shhhhh!" Rohoh hissed. "It's me. I came to help."

Help? Wick thought. *How is a skink going to help me? Especially since it's the same skink that gave the goblinkin the stew recipe?*

Rohoh crawled along Wick's shoulder and hid behind his hair. "Just keep quiet," the skink whispered. "I'll get you out of the mess you got yourself into soon enough."

Mess I got myself *into!* Wick tried to speak but couldn't. He kicked against the side of the crater wall, trying in vain to find some kind of purchase. At the same time, he was afraid his struggles would yank the rope from the hands of the goblinkin.

"If he's got weevils in him," Kuuch said as if he'd given the matter grave consideration, "we could just lop off that part. Would mean we'd have less to share, but I'd still like to have me dinner. I worked up an appetite just bringin' it this far."

"Gggggghhhhhh!" Wick managed. Even he didn't know what he was trying to say, but he felt certain something *had* to be said.

"I wasn't bitten," Rohoh called up. "It was a mosquito."

"All that noise over a mosquito?" Sebble pushed his ugly face over the crater's edge and peered down with the torch in hand. "Ye've got mighty sensitive skin, halfer."

"Yes," Rohoh said. "It just means I'll be more tender."

"Tender is good."

Strength drained from Wick. He thought this was the end after all. In Hanged Elf 's Point, he'd escaped the slave market (he'd had help, of course, but that was beside the point) and here in the Cinder Clouds Islands, he couldn't even make it into a goblinkin stewpot.

"Pull me up," Rohoh cried again.

"All right," Sebble told his companions, "heave ho."

Wick thought his head was going to separate from his shoulders when they started pulling him up, but it didn't. By the time he reached the top of the crater and solid ground again, his tongue was protruding from his mouth.

The goblinkin loosened the rope around his neck and peered down at him.

"Is he dead?" Kuuch asked. "If he's dead, maybe we could just eat him here. Doesn't make much sense to cook him if he's dead. Now I can work me up an appetite watchin' him flop around in the stewpot when the water gets hot."

"He was talkin'," Sebble argued. He kicked Wick in the head. "Are ye alive, halfer?"

"Yes," Wick croaked, even though he couldn't believe it. "I'm . . . alive."

"Good. Now get up an' walk. We got a stewpot waitin' on ye."

6

The Goblinkin Chef

Weak and hurting, Wick finally stumbled to the goblinkin lair in a cave formed from a large vent hole at the top of the island. Ten other goblinkin sat around a large fire made of timbers that looked like they'd once belonged to a ship.

"What's that ye got, Sebble?" one of the other goblinkin asked. The foul creature stood up and hitched up the belt around his bulging waistline that held up his ragged breeches.

"Dinner," Sebble said. "Thought I smelt me a halfer, an' I did."

"Bring him over here."

Barely able to stand, Wick walked over to the fire and stood while the goblinkin poked and prodded him with callused fingers.

"Ye got a scrawny little thing," one of the goblinkin said. "Couldn't ye a-taken a better one?"

"This 'un was the only one there was." Sebble pulled Wick back, then stepped in front of him. The goblinkin's hand tightened around his club. "He's ours, Hesst. We foun' him an' we catched him."

"You a-gonna roast him?" another goblinkin asked.

"Thought we'd make stew," Kuuch answered.

"Well then," a particularly loutish goblinkin said with a grin, "if ye're a-gonna be makin' stew, ye'll be wantin' to use me stewpot." He tapped a foot lazily against the heavy iron cauldron sitting crookedly against the wall.

"We do," Sebble said.

"I can let ye use the stewpot," the goblinkin offered, "but it's gonna cost ye."

"What's it gonna cost?"

"A few bowls o' stew, 'course."

Angrily, Sebble pinched one of Wick's arms. "Ye can see for yerself there ain't much here, Ookool. We'll be lucky to have enough for ourselves."

"If'n ye roast him, ye're gonna lose a lot of the fat to the fire," Ookool pointed out. "The fat's some of the most flavorful. That's why makin' a stew out of him is such a good idea."

Wick couldn't believe he was standing there listening to the goblinkin figuring out how best to serve him. And where was Cap'n Farok and the crew of *One-Eyed Peggie*? Shouldn't they be putting in an appearance about now?

"I'd really like a nice stew," Droos said. "I kinda had me heart set on it."

Sebble sighed as if put upon. "All right. We'll make stew. Ookool, we'll use yer stewpot an' ye can have a bowlful or two. We'll be needin' some vegetables, too. Some potatoes an' carrots . . ."

"Salt an' pepper," Droos added.

"An' onions an' firepears," Kuuch put in.

Sebble tied Wick to the kettle and went searching for ingredients. The goblinkin set about their savage scavenger hunt. There were a number of ale kegs, proof they'd taken cargo from ships.

As they sorted out the vegetables, Wick spotted the broken bones piled against one of the cave walls. Evidently the goblinkin had been getting by on fish, turtles, dwellers, and dwarves.

"Get a grip," the skink said from his hiding place beneath Wick's hair. "I've got a plan."

"If they put me in that stewpot," Wick promised, "I'm taking you with me."

Rohoh snorted derisively at that.

"What's the plan?" Wick asked.

"They're not going to cook you with the rope around your neck and wrists," Rohoh said. "When they take it off—*run*!"

Wick shook his head. The goblinkin were more successful in their hunt for side dishes than he'd thought. The vegetables were piling up in front of the stewpot, which Ookool was filling with fresh water from the barrel they had.

"That's it?" Wick asked in disgust. "*That's* your big plan? *Run for it?*"

"If you get a better idea," the skink said, sounding miffed, "maybe you should let me know."

Watching the goblinkin bring up the vegetables, Wick suddenly remembered a story he'd read in Hralbomm's Wing. Actually, the tale had gotten handed down through several different cultures that had written it up.

Thinking quickly, Wick latched hold of a desperate idea. He tried to be calm and rational, but it was hard to when presented with becoming the main course for goblinkin gluttony.

"Wait!" Wick yelled.

The goblinkin all frowned at him.

"I hate food that talks," Ookool grumped.

Several of the other goblinkin agreed.

"Have you ever eaten dweller surprise?" As soon as the words were out of his mouth, Wick wished he'd remembered the name of another dish. He needed something more exotic if he was going to get their interest. But smoked dweller, dweller al fresco, and—especially—shredded dweller or blackened dweller sounded worse.

The goblinkin looked at each other.

"Have ye ever had dweller surprise?" one asked.

"No, not me. But I've *surprised* a few now an' again."

"I can fix dweller surprise!" Wick yelled.

"Ye can?" a goblinkin asked. He turned and nudged the fellow next to him. "Hey, the dweller says he can fix dweller surprise."

A large goblinkin with a prodigious belly shoved through the others till he stood in front of Wick. Judging from the finger and toe on his necklace, he was the chief of the goblinkin tribe. "Ye can make dweller surprise?"

Wick swallowed hard. His legs trembled. "I can. I've fixed it before."

"Have you?" Rohoh whispered in his ear. "Well, now that's just disgusting. Craugh really left me in the dark on this one. I bet you're a real favorite at all the goblinkin parties."

Wick shook his head, trying in vain to dislodge the skink.

"Well," the chief said, scratching the tuft of hair that grew on his bony chin.

"C'mon, chief," Droos said, rubbing his belly in anticipation. "Let him fix the dweller surprise. Ye can' have the first servin'."

The chief slapped Droos and made him yelp. "I get the first servin' anyway," the chief snorted.

But the other goblinkin joined in, all clamoring for dweller surprise.

"Okay then," the chief grudgingly gave in. "Ye can fix the dweller surprise, but if 'n ye mess it up—" Here he drew a scarred forefinger across his own throat.

"Wouldn't you already be dead after you make the dweller surprise?" Rohoh asked.

Not if I can help it, Wick thought.

A few minutes later, after some of the feeling had returned to his hands, Wick stood on an empty ale keg in front of the kettle. The keg didn't sit terribly well on the uneven cave floor and he risked falling into the kettle every time he moved. Beneath the scorched iron bottom, flames licked out. Heat played over him. The goblinkin had even found a chef 's hat in the piles of clothing they used as bedding. Chief Zoobi had plunked it on Wick's head. Overall, Wick was not happy about his current situation.

"Careful, you little cannibal," the skink hissed.

"I'm not a cannibal," Wick whispered back angrily.

"Why? You *fix* dweller surprise but you don't *eat* it?"

"Don't talk to me."

Chief Zoobi glared at Wick. "Were ye a-talkin' to *me*, halfer?"

"Noooooo," Wick replied, smiling charitably. "I was talking to myself."

"Wouldn't make a habit of it if 'n I was ye."

On the verge of going into a goblinkin kettle for dweller surprise, I wouldn't think any habits would be forthcoming. But Wick kept that observation to himself. Instead, he cleared his throat. "I need the potatoes now."

While he'd been waiting for his hands to return to life, the goblinkin had been busy preparing vegetables at his direction. They handed over buckets of potatoes, some of them black with bruising. Wick didn't hesitate; he poured them into the bubbling kettle, then he stirred the pot with a ship's oar that was barely big enough for the job. The kettle was easily big enough for him to swim in.

"And some ale," Wick said.

"Ale?" Zoobi asked.

"Ale." Wick nodded. "It will help season the meat."

After a little grumbling, one of the ale kegs was broken open. Wick poured a bucket into the kettle. Then, as he'd hoped, the goblinkin fell to and quickly helped themselves to the rest of the ale. He stirred the kettle while they finished off the keg.

"Carrots," he called.

The goblinkin brought the carrots by the bucketful.

"More ale," Wick said.

"More ale?" the chief asked.

"If you want the true dweller surprise instead of a pale imitation," Wick said.

Another keg was opened. Another bucket was passed up to Wick, who poured it into the kettle and began stirring again.

While the goblinkin waited on their stew, they helped themselves to the open keg.

Wick started a song while he stirred, keeping an eye on the goblinkin.

Dweller surprise!
Dweller surprise!
Oh what a feast
For our hungry eyes!
Dweller surprise!
Dweller surprise!
It's warm and good,
I'll tell you no lies!

All of the goblinkin just looked at him.

"Onions," Wick called out. "And another bucket of ale."

They passed along the buckets of onions, then opened another keg of ale. He repeated the process with the salt and the pepper, asking for a bucket of ale after each. The kettle slopped over the sides from time to time. Steam boiled up as the liquid hit the flaming boards under the kettle. He stirred for a long time, hoping the ale the goblinkin had drunk would start to affect them, all the while singing his song over and over.

"Your singing really stinks," Rohoh muttered.

"They don't think so," Wick whispered back.

Several of the goblinkin started singing the "Dweller Surprise Song" in off-key voices. It sounded like several cats getting strangled at once. But they were singing.

"Firepears," Wick yelled, knowing it was the last ingredient before they plopped him in.

"Firepears!" the goblinkin yelled happily. This time when they formed a line to pass the firepears along, they weaved and swayed unsteadily. Several firepears spilled out of the buckets.

Wick led the song again, and this time the goblinkin readily joined in. After he poured the last of the firepears in, he called for more ale.

The ingredient caused a minor celebration. The goblinkin sang even louder. Wick gave them another song to sing.

Ale for me!
Ale for you!
Wouldn't you like to drink
Ale from a shoe?

Learning the song almost at once, the goblinkin joined in and their raucous voices filled the lair.

"You've gotten them drunk," Rohoh said.

"Yes," Wick agreed.

"Well that's stupid. Goblinkin are mean drunks."

"They're singing right now."

"If that's what you call it. This is still stupid."

"Want me to tell them that the last secret ingredient is skink?"

"No."

"Then be quiet and let me get us out of here." Wick stood atop the keg and turned to face the goblinkin. "Hey."

They looked up at him.

"Is it soup yet?" one of the goblinkin asked.

"Put the dweller in," another suggested.

"No," Wick said, holding his hands up. "It's got to simmer for a while. I need more wood for the fire and another bucket of ale."

The goblinkin lurched to fulfill his requests. Several of them shook his hand and thanked him for his time. A number of them told him the concoction bubbling merrily in the kettle was the finest thing they'd ever smelled. Then the latest keg of ale made the rounds.

Wick stirred some more, listening to the drunken versions of the songs he'd made up, and grew more hopeful about his plan. Then he turned to the goblinkin and put his hands together, clapping to a definite beat.

"It's time to dance!" Wick yelled out.

Crying out in excitement, the goblinkin raced around the lair. Three of them grabbed leather-covered drums and started laying down a fast-paced beat.

"Do ye know how to dance, halfer?" Chief Zoobi asked, grinning wildly.

"Yes," Wick replied.

"Then show us a dance step while we wait on the dweller surprise to cook."

Astounded, too surprised for a moment to even think straight, Wick listened to the rapid beat. Then he began a Swalian Grassroots Elven Clan dance that he'd choreographed in a recent book.

"What do you think you're doing?" Rohoh asked.

Wick waved his arms around. "Saving my life," he whispered to the skink.

"You've got an odd way of doing it."

Ignoring the comment, Wick tried to stay erect on his trembling knees. He'd mixed in all the ingredients. All that was left to finish off the dweller surprise was tossing in the dweller.

The goblinkin had trouble following the convoluted dance steps and gave up, complaining loudly. Upon reflection, Wick admitted that perhaps he'd selected the wrong dance. The Swalian Grassroots elves were given to complicated movements.

"You're losing them," Rohoh said. "They're going to want stew soon." The skink abandoned his position behind Wick's head and ran down his body to stand on the keg. He stood on his back legs and looked up at Wick. "Get off the keg. You don't have any rhythm."

Reluctantly, Wick abandoned his post. He jumped down and nearly lost the chef 's hat. He pushed it back to the top of his head. So far, that hat was the only thing that marked him as something other than a stew ingredient.

"All right now!" the skink bellowed in a voice that somehow filled the goblinkin lair. "It's time to party!"

The goblinkin just stared at Rohoh.

He, Wick thought, *is supposed to help me? When I get back to* One-Eyed Peggie, *Craugh and I are going to have a* serious *talk.*

"Is that a lizard?" one of the goblinkin asked. He struggled to keep his eyes open. The effects of the ale showed throughout the goblinkin ranks.

"Aye," another goblinkin said, "that's a lizard all right."

"Ye ever ate a lizard?"

"I have. Crunchy little thing, it was."

"But was it good?"

"It was good enough."

"Might be good in the stew is what I'm a-thinkin'."

"Get that lizard in the stewpot," Chief Zoobi ordered.

Three of the goblinkin staggered forward. For a moment, Wick felt sorry for the skink. Then he remembered all the hateful things it had said to him. Still, he was loath to see it thrown into the bubbling pot.

Wick glanced at the entrance to the lair and wondered if he could grab Rohoh and make a run for it. After all, the rude little creature might come in handy later. *The skink can run faster than me*, he realized.

Then he slid his right foot in the direction of the lair's entrance. None of the goblinkin even noticed. Emboldened, he slid his right foot out and took another step.

"Wait!" Rohoh cried out, lifting his tiny hands and arms.

The goblinkin halted, looking at each other in consternation.

"It's a-talkin'," one of the goblinkin said. "Anybody ever seen a *talkin'* skink?"

"Ye're not there to talk to it, Uluk. Just toss it in the kettle."

"I'm a magic skink," Rohoh shouted.

That stopped the goblinkin. Since he was talking and that wasn't a normal think for skinks to do, it was obvious that he was different.

"Magic, ye say?" Chief Zoobi forced his way to the front of the goblinkin.

"Yes," Rohoh said.

"What can ye do?" The goblinkin chief squinted at him.

"Well," Rohoh said, taking a moment to think, "I can talk . . . and I can dance."

"Let's see how he tastes," another goblinkin yelled out. "I get dibs on the head."

Rohoh stepped to the back of the teetering keg, waving his arms to keep his balance. Desperate, he yelled, "Also, I know the way to a fabulous treasure."

Wick groaned. *How often has* that *been used in the romances in Hralbomm's Wing? Talking fish. Talking snakes. At least if he was a talking bear he'd be big enough to defend himself*.

But the goblinkin hadn't read the romances in Hralbomm's Wing.

"A treasure, ye say?" Chief Zoobi asked.

Rohoh held his tiny arms as far apart as he could. "A *huge* treasure. Toss me in the pot and you lose your chance at the treasure."

"Well now," the goblinkin chief said, "I could do with some treasure. This bears a-thinkin' on."

"Great," the skink said, clapping his hands. "While you're thinking, let's dance." He turned to the drummers. "Give me a beat. Something with some feeling. Remember, you're going to get a treasure!"

Enthusiastic now in addition to being well in their cups, the drummers pounded their instruments. The skink started dancing, waving his arms and tossing his head to the beat.

Wick was so mesmerized by the sight that he forgot he was supposed to be escaping. Then he noticed that the skink's hand and head gestures grew more pronounced. So did that of the goblinkin.

Aggrieved, the lizard stopped dancing long enough to stomp his foot and point toward the lair's entrance. "Go!" he shouted.

Immediately, the goblinkin followed his lead, stomping their feet and pointing at the lair's entrance. They also shouted together, more or less, "Go!"

Understanding then, Wick turned and fled.

"Hey!" someone yelled. "The dweller's gettin' away!"

Okay, maybe it would have been better if I'd figured this out for myself! But it was too late now. Wick ran as fast as he could. As he turned the corner to head outside, he ran straight into a bear.

7

Dwarven City of Industry

Actually, Wick didn't run into a bear. He just thought it was a bear. But that was before he bounced back from the huge bulk, landed on his backside, and was able to get a better look at what he had collided with.

A dwarf in full armor peered fiercely down at Wick. Thick and burly, with fair hair and beard, he stared at Wick through solemn gray eyes. He wore his hair back in a long braid that draped over a massive shoulder and was tied up with silver chains.

The dwarf had his battle-axe lifted over his helmed head and was prepared to strike. Moonslight glinted from the sharp, double-bitted blade.

Wick covered his head with his hands, yanking the chef's hat down over his eyes. "Don't!" he yelped, certain that he was about to become—mostly—asymmetrical halves.

The axe didn't descend.

Unable to bear the suspense, Wick peered under the edge of the chef's cap and between his trembling fingers. *I'm not cut in half!* He touched his middle because he couldn't believe his eyes.

"A halfer," the dwarf growled.

Wick saw that the dwarf wasn't alone. Of course, it would have been foolish for him to attack a goblinkin stronghold all alone. Gazing beyond the first dwarven warrior, Wick saw that at least a dozen others followed the first up the narrow trail leading to the goblinkin lair.

"What's the halfer doin' here, Bulokk?" another dwarf asked.

"Looks like he was cookin' for the goblinkin," Bulokk replied.

"No," Wick protested. "There's been a mistake. I was just—"

The arrival of the staggering goblinkin interrupted his explanation. "Dwarves!" one of them yelled. "Dwarves is upon us!"

"Axes!" Bulokk roared. He took his battle-axe in hand and set himself. Two dwarves flared out to either side of him, a full step back to give him plenty of room to swing.

The goblinkin responded as swiftly as they could, but the ale they'd consumed made them slower than normal. They fumbled with their weapons. Roaring a deafening war cry that echoed from the hilltop, Bulokk swung his axe. Goblinkin went down like felled wheat under a harvester's scythe. Covered in a wave of green goblinkin ichors, Wick rolled over and tried desperately not to get trampled. Getting to his feet, he found himself pressed along with the action, trapped between the advancing lines of dwarves and the goblinkin.

"Anvils!" Bulokk yelled.

Immediately, the dwarves shifted until they faced the goblinkin two by two. Bringing their shields up, they pushed the goblinkin back into the cave.

"Axes!" Bulokk roared once they were inside the cave that served as the goblinkin's lair. Lit by the flames under the boiling kettle in the center of the cave and by torches that were shoved into the ground, the battle continued.

Goblinkin and pieces of goblinkin rained down on Wick. He dodged, using his dweller's quickness, barely staying ahead of the axes, clubs, and cudgels. Once he'd even managed to get clear of the action and grab onto the wall. He panted, breathing hard, hoping to let the battle pass him by so that he could make his escape.

Then the fierce-faced dwarf with the braid spotted him. "So there ye are, cook."

" 'Cook'?" Wick put a hand to his chest and shook his head. "I'm no cook. I'm a—" He managed to stop himself before he said *Librarian*. Then the poofy top of the chef 's hat, which had somehow—for *once*—managed to stay on his head, collapsed slowly down over his face. He pushed it aside. "They made me wear the hat."

The denial seemed a weak defense at best. Especially with the sound of steel meeting steel all around them. Shadows danced on the wall as the battle was waged. There was no doubt about the outcome. One of the dwarves grabbed a goblinkin and threw him into the boiling pot.

"Ye're a-comin' with me, halfer," the dwarf promised grimly. "I'm sure Master Blacksmith Taloston can think of a suitable punishment for him who'd cook up his mates an' serve 'em to the likes of these here goblinkin."

"But I didn't serve the goblinkin anything!" Wick said. "I swear! You've got to—"

"Shut yer cakehole, halfer, afore I shuts it fer ye!"

Wick shut. The chef 's hat collapsed down in front of his face again. Surely *One-Eyed Peggie* was on her way back by now.

Only a few goblinkin survived the dwarves' surprise attack. The rest were quickly routed and went screaming down the hillside to disappear into the trees. Their longer legs served them in good stead in that regard.

When it was over, Bulokk spent time taking care of the wounded. Three of his warriors had to be carried out on litters. Despite his small stature, Wick was assigned one of the corners of a litter.

"We should just cut his throat here," one of the dwarves grumbled to their leader.

"No," Bulokk replied, giving Wick a hard stare. "We'll leave his fate to Master Blacksmith Taloston. Mayhap he'll think of something evil enough for the likes of a dweller what would cook up his own kind for goblinkin stew."

"It wasn't stew," Wick said before he thought about what he was saying. "It was dweller surprise." He clapped a hand over his mouth.

In the Vault of All Known Knowledge, he'd gotten used to speaking his mind when someone got his or her facts wrong. It usually saved that Librarian a lot of time and effort. Although Wick's contributions weren't generally acknowledged or appreciated, he couldn't help making them. He was in the business of correcting facts, after all.

Bulokk scowled at him. "Ye're beginnin' to tires me, cook."

Wick shook his head. He opened his mouth to deny the charges.

Throwing a finger into Wick's face, the dwarf said, "Ye want to stay alive long enough to find out what Master Blacksmith Taloston has in store for ye, ye'll grab ahold of that litter an' get to movin'."

Since it took both hands to lift the corner of the litter, Wick didn't have a free hand to keep over his mouth to remind him to keep silent. He bit his lips instead.

Then they were on their way.

The trip down the hillside, encumbered as they were by the wounded, took a long time. Going without sleep after being frazzled and worried for days aboard *One-Eyed Peggie*, then being an unwilling guest of goblinkin who wanted only to eat him, hadn't agreed with Wick's nerves. He barely had the strength to make the trip. He didn't even argue when Rohoh caught up to the procession and climbed up his leg, undetected by the dwarves.

At the bottom of the long, crooked trail down the hillside, was another long hike to the caves where the dwarves lived. After being around the dwarves in Greydawn Moors, who lived mostly outside, it was always a small shock to find dwarven villages inside the earth.

Only a few fortifications existed aboveground. The caves were vent holes for the volcano at the bottom. As they approached their destination, Wick felt the heated air and sulfur stink coming from them.

The dwarven entrance was little more than a hundred paces from the coastline, which told Wick at once that they lived below sea level. That seemed awfully risky to him. Parts of the Vault of All Known Knowledge extended down into the bedrock of the Knucklebones Mountains. In places, bridges to the lower levels even crossed the underground river that flowed through the area. However, the Vault of All Known Knowledge seemed so . . . invulnerable Wick never worried about drowning inside it.

Beyond the dwarven fortifications, the Rusting Sea rolled out and upward, meeting the sky. The sun was just beginning to rise in the east, coming out from behind the hillside they'd left. The light caught the shimmering orange coloration of the sea.

At the end of a short pier, a ship sat at anchor. Wick studied the vessel, hoping it might be *One-Eyed Peggie*. Even if Craugh wasn't there to admit that he'd shoved Wick into a job far too difficult and dangerous for him and was there only to berate Wick for laying waste to whatever carefully constructed plan he'd wrought, the little Librarian figured he would at least be among friends.

Not dwarves who chose to believe he was a cook for goblinkin.

But it wasn't *One-Eyed Peggie* who lay at anchor in the natural harbor. It was a human ship that was there merely to trade. A line of carts moved onto the pier, loading up and taking away cargo. Boom nets swung over the ship's side to make the transfer easier.

Idly, Wick wondered what the dwarves manufacture to trade. Locked on the island as they were, it was easy to see that the Cinder Clouds dwarves would need several things. Then he noted the shabby quality of the clothing under the dwarves' fine armor. *Maybe they're used to living hand-to-mouth.*

Once the carts were emptied then full again, the drivers drove them back among the fortification. A great, hinged stone gate swung open and allowed entrance.

"Move along, halfer," Bulokk's rough voice said. "Ye've done just about enough gawkin'."

Taking a fresh hold on the litter he helped carry, Wick trudged forward once more. He was looking forward to sitting down, but he was afraid it might be the last thing he would ever do.

"Who goes there?" The challenge rang out strong and bold from the stone fort.

Wick stood at the large stone slab that served as the gate. He was tired and ached all over, and his eyes were fatigued and grainy.

" 'Who goes there?' " Rohoh repeated. "Like he doesn't have eyes in his head to see."

"Quiet," Wick told the skink. "You're going to get us both killed."

"Bulokk," the dwarf called back up. "Open up. Ye've got injured warriors a-waitin', an' all of 'em tired."

The dwarf manning the gate tower grinned down from above. "Did ye do for 'em then, Bulokk?"

"Aye," Bulokk called back up. "We did. Got rid of one nest, but there's more of 'em out there."

"There always will be," the other acknowledged. "Until we find a way to take these isles back to ourselves. At least them beasties won't be tryin' to get our fishin' crews for a while." He turned and shouted over his shoulder. "Open the gate!"

The cry was repeated. Then, a short time later, the mechanical clank of a windlass ratcheted to life. Chain links clinked as they wrapped the drum. Slowly, grating smoothly, the huge slab of rock raised along the cunningly wrought tongue-and-groove channels fashioned for it. When it rose to its full height some five feet above (plenty of room for a dwarf to walk through), other gatekeepers locked it into place with stone chocks.

"All clear," the dwarf above called down. "Come ahead."

Stumbling into motion again, Wick walked through the gate.

"That's a big rock," Rohoh said. "If it fell, we'd be smashed flat."

Not, Wick thought, *a pleasant thought*.

"Probably be relatively painless, though," the skink went on.

Wick chose to ignore his unwanted passenger. Some of the fatigue dropped away as Wick's interest flared anew. He'd been in dwarven fortifications before, by himself and with Craugh, and he was constantly amazed at the architecture. Each underground village or city took advantage of the lay of the land, which resulted in a unique experience each time.

Inside the fortification, three hills filled the center. All of them, Wick knew, led to different and separate sections of the dwarven village. One would lead to the forge area. Another would go to the living quarters. And the third was reserved for the storage area and wells that tapped into groundwater directly or used a filtration process involving a limestone-lined cistern.

The carts unloaded in front of one of them. Bulokk's warriors headed for another. Wick followed along. They handed off the wounded warriors to dwarven women, who picked up their men and carried them down into the passage.

Then Bulokk grabbed Wick by the shoulder and aimed him at the third aboveground entrance.

Upon entering the tunnel, hot air circulated around Wick, letting him know that this passageway probably led to the forge. Bulokk and some of the warriors took up torches to light the way. Several twists and turns later, all of them part of a corkscrew descent into the earth, they arrived in the main forge chamber.

Intense heat baked Wick to the core. He couldn't imagine remaining in the large cave for long. Only dwarves with their natural resistance to heat could hope to endure a lengthy stay. The stink of sulfur was almost unendurable. Metallic thuds and clanks of dwarven hammers striking superheated metal resounded throughout the cavern.

At the other end of the chamber, an open lava pit glowed yellow-orange against the wall and ceiling above it. Judging from the wall that separated the lava pit from the chamber, the design was intentional, providing the dwarven blacksmiths some respite from the roasting heat.

A score of anvils stood on sturdy tables made of stone. All of them shared a form, but Wick knew from his studies that each of them had been poured from molten ore and beaten into the proper shape and hardness by the blacksmith. When a dwarven blacksmith worked on an anvil, he had to know it as well as the back of his own hand. Every flaw and imperfection showed on his work, and a blacksmith had to know how to use those to his advantage.

The dwarves plunged long-handled tongs bearing the metal they were working with to a point just above the sluggish lava. In a short time, the metal would glow red-hot and they withdrew it. Back on the anvil, they held the piece with other tongs and picked up their hammers to beat the piece into the desired shape.

Most of them, Wick saw, worked on pedestrian items like bands for wheels or barrels. Others made frying pans and pots. Others worked on chains and collars. Farm implements, plows, and harness tack were also in evidence. A few of the younger dwarves, noticeable because of their lack of beards, made nails.

Wick couldn't believe that the Cinder Clouds dwarves, who had once made some of the best armor ever to be found, had been reduced to making items for sale from a peddler's cart. Looking at the work they were doing, he felt incredibly sad for them. In the Vault of All Known Knowledge, he'd read a few books that had praised Master Blacksmith Oskarr and the dwarves of his forge for their work.

Bulokk shoved Wick forward so hard that he nearly fell. Stumbling, he came to a stop in front of a dwarf whose hammer fell with a rhythmic clangor. They stood waiting till the dwarf finished with the piece for the time. When he stepped back, his massively thewed body glistening with sweat and glowing from heat and exertion, he nodded to another dwarf.

The other dwarf picked up the piece with a set of the long-handled tongs. In that instant, Wick saw that the piece was a nearly finished shield. At least, it was the backbone of a shield.

"Master Blacksmith Taloston," Bulokk called.

"Aye," the dwarf said, watching as the shield was carefully hung back over the lava pit. "Is that ye, Bulokk?"

"It is," Bulokk replied.

"Did ye put an end to that nest of goblinkin the scouts spied?"

"We did. But we come up on a surprise."

Still holding onto the huge hammer, Master Blacksmith Taloston turned to face Wick. The dwarf's face was broad and scarred by battle and fire. Sparks burned in his brown hair and beard. His arms showed scars from the ironwork.

"Don't like surprises," the master blacksmith said. His glance took a quick measure of Wick. "A halfer?"

"Aye," Bulokk said.

"What'd ye bring him back here for?"

"Didn't know what to do with him."

The master blacksmith grabbed a ladle from a water bucket and took a long drink. Then he poured another ladleful over his head. "Shoulda let him go. There's other halfers in these islands. Mayhap he can stay free an' catch a ship like some of them others have. Otherwise he can be a slave in the goblin mines again. Either way, it ain't our problem."

"He's a goblinkin cook," Bulokk accused. He held the crumpled chef's hat out as evidence. "When we come up on that goblinkin lair, this 'un was fixin' them goblinkin a meal an' leadin' the dancin'."

"Dancin'?" The master blacksmith's bushy eyebrows closed together.

"Aye."

"I wasn't leading the dancing," Wick said. "The skink was leading the dancing."

"Skink?"

Moving quickly, Wick plucked the skink from his hiding place on his shoulder. "This skink." He held Rohoh up by his tail, dangling him for all to see.

The lizard tried to get free, but he didn't open his mouth to complain.

"Ye have a dancin' skink?"

"Yes."

Before Wick could go on, Taloston looked at Bulokk. "Is this halfer infested with them things?"

Two dwarven warriors quickly searched Wick. They didn't find any additional lizards.

"No," one of them answered. "That appears to be the only one."

"Good," Taloston said. "I can't abide them lizards. Ate me fill of 'em, I have. Dwarves wasn't meant to feed on such creatures. Them goblinkin can have 'em all."

Rohoh stopped squirming to escape. For a moment Wick thought the skink was going to protest the comment. That would have been fine because it would have brought further proof to his claims.

"So he was cookin' fer the goblinkin, eh?" Taloston rubbed a hand through his smoldering beard.

"Aye."

The master blacksmith nodded, said, "Take him up top, cut his throat, an' throw him into the bay," and turned back to his work.

8

Banished

What!" The exclamation burst from Wick before he knew he was prepared to launch it. The sound of his incredulous voice pealed over the forge, bringing an end to all work. He almost dropped Rohoh to the cavern floor. "You're going to just order them to cut my throat and throw me into the bay?"

By that time, Bulokk had his hand on Wick's shoulder and was dragging him back from the master blacksmith.

"I'll be merciful," Bulokk said quietly.

"I don't want merciful," Wick bellowed.

"No?"

Realizing what he'd said, Wick held up his hands, one of which was still holding onto the skink. "What I mean is, I don't want to die."

"Should have thought of that before you started whipping up dweller surprise," Rohoh said only loud enough for Wick to hear.

"Ye shouldn't have been cookin' for the goblinkin," Taloston said.

"I'm not a cook." Wick felt entirely helpless.

Shoving his face into Wick's, making the little Librarian cringe, Taloston asked, "An' do ye know any recipes for cookin' dwarves?"

At last! Wick thought happily. *A question I can answer!* "I do! I do!" He put his free hand to his head and started imagining the pages of Prendergorf 's *A Short Course of Dwarven Dishes: Being a Horrifying Account of Famous Dwarves Eaten by Goblinkin*. "There's dwarf tort with spiced apples. Creamed dwarf. Jellied dwarf.

Dwarf-ka-bobs. Dwarf cake, though that's generally served for holidays and is made out of dried dwarf bits that have gotten particularly leathery with age and—" He was suddenly aware of every dwarven eye in the forge on him.

"An' how many dwarves have ye cooked up?" Taloston asked.

"None," Wick answered immediately. "I swear. The Old Ones strike me dead if I'm lying."

At that moment the lava pit bubbled violently, throwing up a huge gout of lava and causing a massive *boom!* that echoed through the forge. Thinking that the volcano below was about to erupt and throw burning lava everywhere, Wick dropped to his knees and covered his head with his arms. Cowering, he waited for the end.

The skink, which he'd dropped, ran up his arm and curled once more behind his head. "Get up," Rohoh said. "You're embarrassing me. If you're going to die, at least go out with some dignity."

Cautiously, Wick opened one eye. He looked around. Dwarves stared at him with derision and dislike. But that was okay. While he was on the mainland, that was how most beings looked at him.

"The lava pit didn't erupt?" he asked.

"No," Taloston said. "Get this cook outta me sight."

Strong hands gripped Wick. He tried to fight against them but it was no use.

"They were going to cook me and eat me!" Wick wailed.

"Oh, that's just softening them right up," Rohoh said.

Taloston turned and looked out at the lump of metal hanging over the lava pit. It was starting to glow cherry-red.

"I didn't escape from the goblinkin mines!" Wick shouted as he was dragged away. "A wizard sent me here in search of Master Blacksmith Oskarr's magic battle-axe!"

Bulokk stopped dragging immediately, calling to his men to halt. The dwarven warrior looked at Wick. "Are ye tellin' the truth, halfer? About comin' here fer Oskarr's magic axe?"

Terrified of answering, Wick just stared at the dwarf, wondering which response would let him live and which would get him instantly killed. Because he felt certain that was what it was coming down to.

"Yes," Wick squeaked, gazing into Bulokk's eyes. "It's true." He waited for the end.

After a moment more spent staring at him, Bulokk swung to face Taloston. "Did ye hear what the halfer claimed? That he came here fer Master Oskarr's axe?"

Slowly, Taloston faced Bulokk. "Aye," the master blacksmith said. "I heard him." He shook his head. "Doesn't mean it's true. Master Oskarr's axe has been lost fer a thousand years. Mayhap it was destroyed."

Wick thought Bulokk was going to argue, but the dwarf maintained his silence.

"Don't go gettin' yer hopes up, Bulokk," Taloston said.

"The axe . . . means a lot to me family," Bulokk said.

Sighing, Taloston picked up his hammer and walked over to Wick. "There's tales ever'where about Master Oskarr's enchanted battle-axe an' how it was lost when Lord Kharrion caused the volcanoes to erupt an' bury them islands in the sea while spewin' up new ones. Is that what ye're hopin', halfer? That some half-told story about Master Oskarr is gonna save yer neck?"

"You're in for it now," Rohoh whispered in his ear.

"It's true," Wick insisted. "I was sent here for the axe."

"Why?" Taloston demanded.

"The wizard, he thinks he can use it to find out what really happened at the Battle of Fell's Keep. He doesn't think that Master Oskarr betrayed the other warriors holding Painted Canyon while the south evacuated ahead of the goblinkin hordes." Wick met Taloston's accusing stare.

"What do ye know of all that?"

Slowly at first, but becoming immersed in the story just as he had back at Paunsel's tavern in Greydawn Moors, Wick told the dwarves the tale of the Battle of Fell's Keep.

Later, as Wick wrapped up with what he knew of the battles fought in the Cinder Clouds Islands—embellishing the telling with all the skills he'd learned as well as the sense of the dramatic he'd picked up from the romances he'd read in Hralbomm's Wing—the dwarves sat around him like dweller children during story time.

The clangor of the hammers falling on metal had silenced. Only the bubbling of the lava pit continued. Water buckets were passed around, and one had been made readily available to the little Librarian.

Finally, though, he was through and had once more sunk the Cinder Clouds Islands beneath the Rusting Sea. Looking out at the sad reaction of the dwarves, Wick felt a little sad for them himself—even though they'd been ready to cut his throat and heave him in the bay only a few hours ago. He knew at least that much time had passed because he was starving.

"Do ye know where Master Oskarr's axe is?" Bulokk asked.

"No," Wick answered truthfully.

Taloston scowled at him. "Then how were ye gonna find it?"

"I've seen—" Wick stopped himself from saying *map* because no one outside the Vault of All Known Knowledge had ever seen one. "I've *heard* a number of tales about how the islands were before Lord Kharrion sank them. I think, after I travel around on a few of them, that I'll be able to figure out where Master Oskarr's forge was."

"Likely it's at the bottom of the Rusting Sea," Taloston growled.

"There's tunnels," Bulokk pointed out. "All the minin' the goblinkin been doin', they've uncovered some of the vent tunnels that blew out of the volcanoes. Some of them dwellers we freed an' put on ships—"

Oh ho! Wick thought. *They've helped other dwellers who have escaped the clutches of the goblinkin! But not me!*

"—have said the goblinkin have dug up remnants of dwarven cities," Bulokk finished.

" 'Tis a forlorn hope ye're insistin' on," Taloston said.

"I would know that Master Oskarr was not the traitor the humans an' the elves believe him to be," Bulokk stated.

"What the humans an' the elves think of us or of Master Oskarr don't matter," Taloston said.

"It matters to me," Bulokk disagreed.

"An' me," another dwarf said.

"An' me," another echoed.

"It's the past," Taloston said. "Ain't no way of changin' the past."

" 'The past lays the bedrock for the future,' " Wick quoted. " 'If you want to change your future, find a way to change your perspective of the past in your present.' "

"What are you talking about?" Rohoh asked.

"What's yer meanin', halfer?" Taloston growled.

Bulokk looked at Wick with interest. "What he's a-sayin' is that if 'n we find Master Oskarr's lost battle-axe, there's a chance we can know what really happened at the Battle of Fell's Keep. An' if 'n we know, it'll change how we see ourselves today."

Taloston looked at Bulokk and shook his head. "Ye get a lot more from what that halfer's a-blatherin' about than I do."

"Mayhap," Bulokk said, "it's 'cause I'm willin' to listen."

Waving the comment away, Taloston stood. "We're a-wastin' time here now." He looked around at the other dwarves. "On yer feet. We got things to make. There'll be another ship along soon."

Bulokk pushed himself up, too. "What about the halfer's story?"

"It's a story, Bulokk," Taloston said. "Just like them tales the elders tell around the community firepits in the common rooms at night. It's just entertainment fer the young, that's all. Don't go a-gettin' all caught up in his story. It's hard beatin' disappointment out of a tender heart. Without a-losin' the heart it's attached to."

Silently, Bulokk studied his leader.

"What wizard in his right mind would send a halfer to do somethin' so important?" Taloston asked.

Bulokk kept his own counsel, setting his jaw stubbornly.

Something's going on, Wick thought. But he didn't know what it was. He didn't dare utter a word.

"Don't work that ore," Taloston said in a softer voice. "It's too hard for ye, an' when ye get it hot enough, ye're just gonna shatter it."

After a moment, Bulokk broke eye contact with the master blacksmith and nodded.

"Now take him on out of here," Taloston said. "Mayhap ye don't want to kill him, in case ye believe him, but make certain that halfer's off this island. Put him aboard one of the trade ships what's out in the harbor an' send him on his way, if ye like. But get him outta here. He's banished from our home."

"All right," Bulokk replied. He shoved Wick from behind and got him moving.

Long minutes later, Wick was once more above ground. The outside air was cooler, almost chill after he'd gotten acclimated to the forge chamber. Shivering a little, he pulled his light cloak more tightly around him. Rohoh scampered up under his hair to lie along his collar. Wick reached for the skink twice, but the creature avoided his efforts with ease, hiding inside his coat.

Bulokk and a dozen dwarves escorted Wick to the huge gate. Dusk had settled over the Rusting Sea, leaving black clouds hanging in a chartreuse sky. Land lay in that direction, Wick knew, because the sunset would have been practically colorless over the water. In order for the sky to have color, it had to pick up dust in the wind over land, not sea.

After they passed through the gate, during which time Wick once more had the uneasy feeling while walking under the immense stone, the wind held more of a chill, but he willingly admitted that the fear inside him may have caused that. On the other side, Bulokk steered him to follow the well-worn cart ruts that led down to the harbor.

Wick looked up at the moons and wondered if Craugh could see him. And, if the wizard could see him, if Craugh was unhappy with the way things had turned out.

Of course, there was always the possibility that Craugh had sent Wick on ahead simply to use as bait and was finding Oskarr's fabled axe himself even now. That seemed to be a favorite tactic.

"Halfer," Bulokk said.

"Yes." Wick was trying to work up the courage to ask for something to eat. He was certain he wouldn't get anything aboard a trading vessel if he weren't paying passage. And realizing that led to even further worries. Where would the trade ship put him ashore? He didn't have any gold as he usually did. It was possible they'd simply dump him over the side and have done with him.

"Do ye really think ye can find Master Oskarr's forge an' mayhap his axe?" Bulokk walked beside him but wouldn't look at him.

Wick measured his words carefully, well aware that they held the possibility to change his course. He tried to figure out if it would be safer to go on the cargo ship and hope to find another vessel that traveled to Greydawn Moors and try to take passage on it.

Still, the question was almost a challenge to his skills as a Librarian.

"Yes," Wick said. "I think I can."

"Why?"

"Because the Cinder Clouds Islands were made a certain way, in a half-moon shape that's distinctive." Wick looked out at the sea and saw the furled sails along the ship's 'yards riffling in the breeze. "I memorized some of the landmarks. There were lighthouses, cliffs, and reefs that I can use to figure out where I—where *we*—are in relation to where Master Oskarr's forge was. If we can find them." He gave the dwarf a sidelong glance. "Your familiarity with the islands would help us in that search."

They walked a while longer in silence.

"Do ye think it's still there?" Bulokk asked.

"Do I think what's still there?"

"The axe. Master Oskarr's axe."

Wick considered his answer, letting the strained silence gather weight and speculation. "I do. Magic weapons have a tendency to outlast all attempts to destroy them."

"An' through it ye could know what happened at the Battle of Fell's Keep, could discover what took place all them years ago?"

"The wizard who sent me here has such powers," Wick said. "If anyone could do it, he could."

Bulokk looked at him. "Do ye believe that in yer bones? 'Cause that's the bedrock of a man."

"I do," Wick said. Even though he wasn't absolutely sure of Craugh's powers, over the years he had seen the amazing things the wizard could do.

"All right then. Wait here." Bulokk turned back to his fellows.

Wick stood alone at the side of the cart trail and wished he were back home in the Vault of All Known Knowledge. Or at least safe back on *One-Eyed Peggie* where he could finish reading the romance about Taurak Bleiyz.

He stared at the lanterns along the rails of the human ship anchored out in the harbor. With the sun setting behind the vessel, the men all but lost in the shadows aboard her, the sight was beautiful. His hands itched to take out his journal and writing utensils and capture the memory in inks. More than that, he wanted to write up his latest adventures, all the things that he had seen and the people he'd met.

"Stop your wool-gathering," Rohoh admonished. "We need to find that forge."

"I don't even know if that's possible," Wick argued in a low voice. He looked out over the broken masses of islands scattered over the Rusting Sea.

"Craugh sent you here."

"As I recall, he sent you here as well. Why?"

"To help you."

"How?"

The skink was quiet for a moment. "I don't know. Craugh just said I was to keep you out of trouble."

"Well," Wick said, "that hasn't worked so far."

At that moment, the dwarven huddle broke up after a fierce, final debate. Bulokk returned to Wick.

"We're a-goin' with ye," the dwarven warrior declared.

Wick blinked at him. "Why?"

"Why? Why to find Master Oskarr's lost axe an' clear his good name is why!"

"Oh," Wick said.

"Yer quest, halfer, whether 'tis yer own or ye're a-workin' fer or with someone else what cares about Master Oskarr's relationship, 'tis a noble one."

"That's why you want to accompany me? To get glory?"

"No," Bulokk said more somberly. "I'm part of Master Oskarr's kith an' kin, halfer. 'Tis me own family we're a-talkin' about here, too." He sighed. "Master Taloston is a good 'un. He's a-runnin' this forge the best he knows how to, but we've gone a far piece down in the world."

The sadness in the dwarven warrior's words touched Wick's heart.

"Was a time," Bulokk said softly, "when armor made by the Cinder Clouds Forge with Master Oskarr's mark on it meant somethin'. It meant a warrior—be he a human, dwarf, or elf—could stand up in a battle an' know he was protected. But since them accusations after the Battle of Fell's Keep, no one wants to buy anything from us. Except a pittance of what we used to make." He pulled at his beard. "By the Old Ones! We're a-makin' nails an' horseshoes an' plows when we should be a-makin' armor an' weapons meant to be carried into battle by kings an' heroes!"

Several of the other dwarves came closer to Wick and Bulokk, as if finally making the last decision to throw in their lot with him. They murmured similar feelings.

"Ye're the first one what's ever come to these islands a-sayin' ye could find Master Oskarr's axe," Bulokk said. "So if 'n ye'll have us, we'd be right proud to journey with ye."

"If I'll have you?" Wick stood dumbfounded.

Rohoh moved so that he could whisper in the little Librarian's ear. "This is the part where you say, 'Yes, thank you.' And then you swear undying fealty to one another."

Bulokk looked uncomfortable. "We know we said some unkind things about ye—and *to* ye—be we're a-hopin' ye'll find room in that tiny little heart of yers to overlook that. At least fer a while. Ye see, it's a-mighty dangerous out there where ye'll be lookin'. Goblinkin roam unfettered over several of these islands. If ye're a-gonna be a-searchin' fer that axe, ye might want some help."

Gathering himself, Wick said, "Of course. Of course I'd like help."

The dwarven warrior shoved out his big hand. Unconsciously, Wick took it, finding his own hand engulfed in Bulokk's.

"But won't Master Taloston be upset?" Wick asked.

Bulokk turned him and started him toward the harbor again. "Aye, that he will, because he don't like no one a-questionin' his authority none. But it ain't his ancestor we're a-talkin' about. It's mine. An' come what may of our little hunt, I'm through a-makin' nails an' horseshoes. I'm wishful of a-doin' true dwarven armorer's work." He laid a heavy hand across Wick's shoulders, almost crushing the skink.

They walked down to the harbor but turned away from the ship. Several dwarves and humans called out to Bulokk, for he was known to a number of them.

They chose one of the single-masted longboats tied up at shore. From the lay of the boat, Wick guessed that it was used for ferrying goods among the islands, possibly to supply other dwarven outposts that weren't as large. Bulokk quickly assigned three of the dwarves to gather food and water to supply them on their excursion. After a short while, they returned with a cart loaded with several water skins and bags of food.

Wick crawled into the longboat with Bulokk and most of the other twelve dwarves. Four of them remained on shore to push the boat out into the retreating tide. The waves crashed against the longboat's side and the cold spray dappled Wick.

"Good job," Rohoh whispered in the little Librarian's ear. "Now just keep a civil tongue in your head, and maybe they won't cut it out."

9

Collision!

Once they had the craft shoved out into the ungentle caress of the sea, the four dwarves heaved themselves into the boat, aided by the others who grabbed their armor and pulled. They crowded together in the small boat, and Wick's stomach heaved, certain they would all sink under the combined weight. For a moment he sat petrified among the dwarven warriors, constricted between their massive shoulders.

After a while, a few of the dwarves assembled the single mast and raised the sail, which promptly filled with wind and drove them forward. The wind wasn't directly behind them, so they canted over to port. Bulokk sat in the stern and managed the tiller with a sure hand.

Then, with the tangy scent of pepper cheese in Wick's nostrils reminding him how hungry he was, his stomach growled. He immediately felt embarrassed.

That broke the tension on the boat and several of the dwarves laughed. Hunger was something they all understood and shared.

"Are ye hungry then, halfer?" one of the dwarves asked.

"Yes," Wick answered timidly, not knowing if his admitted weakness was merely going to be made sport of.

"Didn't get yer fill of goblin stew, I suppose?"

Wick didn't know what to say.

"Dweller surprise, I think it were, Hodnes," another dwarf said, chuckling. "I believe them ugly goblinkin was properly surprised, too!"

They all had a good laugh at that for a moment, and the sound combated the darkness of the night that pressed in all around them. Wick even laughed a little.

Then Hodnes opened one of the bags of food and carved up a cheese wheel, passing it out while another dwarf handed out biscuits.

"What's the landmarks ye was needin' to find?" Bulokk asked after they were well into the impromptu meal and the dwarven fort was fading in their wake.

"There was a lighthouse," Wick said. "It was built in the shape of a hammer." He crossed his arms to demonstrate. "During those days it was called Zubeck's Hammer, named after the dwarven god of the stars. It was supposed to be over a hundred feet tall. Red and green lanterns hung in either end to let ships' captains know whether they were on the sea side or the lee side of the island."

"I've never seen anything like that," Bulokk replied.

"Mayhap I have," a dwarf said.

"Where did ye see something like that, Drinnick?"

" 'Twas north of here." Drinnick glanced up at the sky, seemed to study the stars a minute, then pointed more or less in the direction they were traveling. "It ain't above water no more, but if'n ye know where to look, ye can find it."

"What's another landmark?" Bulokk asked.

"A domed amphitheater," Wick answered. "It was called Trader's Hall. Back before the Cataclysm, there were several such structures. Guildsmen and craftsmen met there twice a year, in the summer and in the winter, to show their wares and do business. The Trader's Hall in the Cinder Clouds Islands was unique. Besides being shaped like a dome, the builders had hammered blue foil all over it, making it very distinctive. According to what I've re—been *told*, the dome could be seen from miles away."

Apparently, none of the dwarven warriors had ever seen the amphitheater in their travels and battles with the goblinkin.

"Anything else?" Hodnes asked.

Quickly, Wick described Hullbreaker Reefs (two of them thought they knew where that might be), the Dragon's Aerie (so named because it once was home to a dragon), Delid's Circle (a semicircle of underwater mountains whose peaks appeared above the surface of the sea), and Jerrigan's Landing (a natural port that was too small to be used for commercial industry, but was renowned for a shelf of vertical granite that set it off from the rest of the island).

The dwarven warriors compared notes to what they had seen over their years of traveling through the Rusting Sea, describing in detail the things they'd observed and heard about. Wick continued eating till he was full, then grew sleepy. The skink's slight rustle as he burrowed through his clothes in search of the fresh crumbs didn't inspire the little Librarian to chase the creature down. He wanted his pipe and he wanted a bed instead of being jammed between the dwarves, but he went to sleep anyway.

Only a little while later—Wick was certain about that because he knew from the way he felt he hadn't slept long—dwarven cursing woke him.

“ ’Ware there!” someone said. “It’s a-comin’ straight fer us!”

Wick tried to dive for the bottom of the boat—not that there was any real room there, but it seemed safer there than sitting up if they were under attack. Being caught out in the open was one of the worst things to happen to anyone under attack. However, he was jammed too tightly among the dwarves to move.

“Show ’em the lantern,” Bulokk ordered.

One of the dwarves brought out a small pot of coals they’d kept out of sight. So far, Bulokk had wanted to remain unseen. When the dwarf removed the lid, the glow formed a translucent orange ball in the moonslit darkness.

Wick was curious about what had changed the dwarven leader’s mind about remaining hidden. Fatigued and a little frightened, he turned and gazed in the direction the dwarves seemed to be focused on. There, parting the great steam clouds that lay over the area from the volcanic activity, a ship designed solely for speed bore down on them. If it hit the small boat with its narrow prow, the ship would only leave splinters in its wake.

“Ship!” Wick squalled, managing to lever up an arm and point at the approaching craft. *“Ship!”*

“Ship!” Rohoh squealed in his tiny voice in Wick’s ear. The dwarves didn’t appear to have heard the skink’s cry of warning, but the shrill scream in Wick’s ear almost deafened him.

“Aye, we seen it already,” Bulokk said, holding the tiller hard so the boat cut back toward the land. But the smaller craft was coming around too slowly to avoid the oncoming ship.

Staring through the darkness, Wick realized the ship was sailing without running lights, like a smuggler might. *Like we’re doing*, he thought.

Her sails were black-gray, almost invisible against the sky and noticeable only because they were blank fields and held no lights. She was fully strung, even flying jib sails, not moving with any trepidation, obviously familiar with the waters.

The lantern wick caught flame from kindling lit by the coals. Handing the coal pot off, the dwarf replaced the hurricane glass on the lantern and turned the wick up. Bright, cheery light filled the lantern.

“ ’Ware!” the dwarf called as he stood and waved the lantern. “ ’Ware! There’s a boat out here!”

Figures shifted on the black boat, all of them lean shadows. Moonslight glinted on steel. Then, between a momentary gap of sails that allowed the moonslight through, Wick spied an archer bending his bow.

“Look out!” Wick called. “Archers!” even as he was wondering who would just fire at them without hailing.

Before his voice drifted away, an arrow crashed through the dwarf’s lantern, shattering the glass. Another arrow took the dwarf through the chest. Oil splattered the boat, then the wick fell through and the oil lit the dwarf holding the lantern and the boat on fire. Flames wrapped threatening tendrils around both.

The burning dwarf cried out in alarm and beat at the flames with his hands. He flung the remnants of the lantern into the sea.

Fear clawed through Wick and his instinct screamed at him to burrow as deeply into the press of dwarves as he could. Instead, he fought to get free, to try to reach the burning dwarf, but he couldn't.

"Adranis!" Bulokk barked. "Get him into the sea!"

Instantly, one of the dwarves pushed up, caught the burning dwarf in his arms, and threw them both from the boat into the sea.

Another arrow found a second dwarf. Two more arrows were embedded in the gunwales. Eight or nine shafts (things were confusing at this point) pierced the boat's sail. And a half dozen more arrows spiked the water around the boat as it pitched.

"Got me in me leg!" the wounded dwarf yelped. His big hands closed around his thigh. Flames from the spilled oil licked at his boots.

Wick gazed in disbelief as he drew his own feet up. *Where did they come from? Why did they attack?*

"To port!" Bulokk roared. "Turn the boat over! Save her if'n we can!"

The dwarves reacted to their leader's orders at once, standing on the port side and grabbing the gunwales. Three of them even took hold of the mast and boom and pulled those over to port as well.

Overbalanced, the boat turned on its side as the ship came abreast. Wick held onto the seat, not wishful of dropping into the deep, dark water. The ship collided with the boat, hammering it unmercifully. Then it was done. The boat capsized completely and he submerged. The dark water pulled at him but he held onto the bench.

Long, loud crashing filled the water around Wick. Holding onto the seat, Wick felt the longboat shudder and shake as the black ship ran up against it all along its side. More *thumps!* signaled the arrival of more arrows. One of them cut a furrow along the back of one of the little Librarian's hands. He grew instantly more worried because blood in the water would draw marine predators.

Once the boat stopped bucking and pitching in his grip, he took a fresh hold and pulled himself up into the dark of the upside-down boat. He felt at least three more arrows that had poked through the boat's hull.

Then he thought about the dwarves, wondering how many of them had learned to swim.

Taking a deep breath, Wick ducked under the side of the overturned boat, swam free of it, and popped up above the surface of the water. Shaking the wet hair from his eyes, he gazed around, glad of the full moon.

"What were you trying to do?" Rohoh squalled. "Drown me?"

"You're welcome to take your leave at any time," Wick invited. He wasn't sure where the skink had gotten to, but he was certain wherever it was couldn't be dry.

Adranis surfaced near Wick. The dwarven warrior was striving to keep his head above the water and was failing miserably due to the weight of his armor.

Wick pulled his knife from his water-filled boot and seized hold of Adranis's support straps. In the pale moonlight, the little Librarian saw the dwarven warrior's face.

Stay back from him, Wick told himself. *If he lays hold of you, he'll drown you as well as himself.*

As Wick started to saw at the support straps with the knife, Adranis figured out what he was doing.

A fierce, "No!" escaped from Adranis's mouth, emptying his lungs of air. Bubbles from his unheard bellow rushed through the water. But the deed was done quickly because Wick had learned to keep his knife sharp if he was going to keep it at all. The dwarf 's armor peeled away from his body and slid away into the sea.

Angry, Adranis closed his hand over Wick's arm, pulling the little Librarian underwater. Sinking, Wick fought to free himself but couldn't manage the feat by strength alone. Lungs burning, he gripped the knife in his free hand and tried not to let fear claim him entirely. Drowning was a horrible death.

But Adranis couldn't remain underwater any longer either. Releasing Wick, the dwarf kicked upward. Wick swam up as well, aiming for the other end of the overturned longboat.

Partially submerged in the sea, the longboat still maintained a little buoyancy. Wick grabbed hold of the stern and clung there, sucking in deep breaths. *No matter how many times I venture to the mainland, I'll never get used to the idea of death dogging my footsteps!*

Gazing around the longboat, listening to Adranis's curses, Wick saw that the mystery ship had continued on its way. Relief washed over Wick. The vessel could have stuck around to either finish killing them or take survivors as slaves.

"Ye stupid halfer!" Adranis growled. The dwarf thumped the longboat's hull with his fist. "That was me family armor ye just sent to the bottom!"

"You would have looked really good wearing it there," Rohoh snarled.

Before Wick could assure the dwarf that he hadn't said that, Adranis erupted in a torrent of foul curses that left the little Librarian in fear for his life. If he could have found the skink, he would have thrown him into the sea.

"Ain't no replacin' that armor!" Adranis worked his way around the lifeboat, obviously meaning Wick bodily injury. "I'll thump yer melon for ye, I will!"

For a moment, Wick continued around the boat in order to avoid the angry dwarf. Then he gripped the longboat's edge and flipped himself up onto the hull, which was riding a few inches out of the water. His weight (slight for a dweller!) didn't affect the overturned boat's buoyancy.

Adranis, unable to pull himself up out of the water, had to content himself with cursing Wick soundly.

A few feet away, Bulokk surfaced, spluttering and gasping for air. He, too, had sacrificed his armor. Still other dwarves came up as well.

When Bulokk asked for a quick count, they discovered that three of the dwarves had been lost. The warrior who'd held the lantern and gotten shot and set on fire had been sunk in the depths without recovering. Arrows had accounted for one more, dead with an arrow through his neck before the boat flipped. The third had evidently gone down too fast. Repeated diving turned up no results.

Setting his sights on continued survival, Bulokk gave the orders to those who could swim (and only about half of them could) to push the longboat to shore while the others held on.

Wick dove from the boat and joined the swimming effort. His mind raced, trying to remember everything he could about the black ship. Then he focused on swimming because, with the tide going out, getting to the beach was almost impossible.

Nearly an hour later, winded and worn, the dwarven party and Wick made a landing. The beach was inhospitable, craggy and rocky, but at least they wouldn't drown there. They pulled the boat up on shore. Bulokk and two other dwarves tore out the arrows and examined the extent of the damage.

Wick sat by himself, as far away from Adranis as he could manage. Even in the moonslight he could see the dislike the dwarves held for him.

They think this is my fault, he thought. *If I hadn't arrived and gotten Bulokk interested in finding Master Oskarr's lost axe, they wouldn't be here now*. He wanted to argue with them and point out the fact that he had nothing to do with the attack.

"The damage can be repaired," Bulokk told the group after he returned from the longboat. He put the lantern he carried on the rocky shoal. They'd found it floating to shore and miraculously intact. The light played out over the semicircle of glum faces. "With the tools we have at hand."

Wick knew the dwarves had packed for the eventuality they would have to work on the boat. Or, perhaps, another boat if they couldn't repair this one.

"The food an' fresh water remained on board, too," Bulokk said. It had been strapped under the benches in waterproof containers. "So we have a choice about what we do."

The impulse to tell the dwarves about *One-Eyed Peggie* thrummed inside Wick. When *One-Eyed Peggie* arrived, they would all be safe. But in the end he chose to tell them nothing about the Blood-Soaked Sea pirate ship. *In case Craugh keeps them away too long*.

"We can turn back," Bulokk said, "an' hope that our absence hasn't been noted."

"But if 'n we has been noticed missin' an' someone has told Taloston that the halfer wasn't on that ship, he won't be happy with us," Adranis said.

"I know." Bulokk scowled, striding across the rocky shoal where they'd landed.

"If Taloston grows vexed with us, we'll be out on goblinkin patrol permanentlike. Ain't gonna live any too long if 'n that's the case."

"I ain't afeared of Taloston's displeasure," Bulokk said, "but I set out to find Master Oskarr's axe." He glanced around at his men. "That still ain't been done, an' I mean to see it finished."

Slowly, then with increasing alacrity, the dwarven warriors echoed his sentiments.

"Then, in the mornin'," Bulokk said, "what we'll do is patch up the longboat as best as we can an' continue with what we're about."

Sullenly, the dwarves agreed. Their leader chose to ignore their lack of enthusiasm.

"Until then," Bulokk said, "get what sleep ye can. Ain't none of it gonna be easy."

"Wait," Wick said, not knowing he'd spoken out loud until all the dwarves were looking at him.

"What?" Adranis growled.

For a moment Wick thought about telling them to never mind. But he knew he'd never sleep that night if his curiosity didn't get assuaged. "Did anyone know that ship?" he asked. "The black ship that nearly ran us down?"

" 'Tweren't but one out there," Adranis said unkindly.

"Does it make a difference if 'n someone's seen it afore?" Bulokk countered.

Wick hesitated. "I don't know. But generally, according to Dreizelf Mochanarter, the more that is known about a problem, the better able the solver is to deal with it."

"So," Drinnick said, clawing fingers through his thick beard, "mayhap the knowin' will prove important?"

"Yes."

"I never seen the ship meself," Drinnick said, "but I heard she plied her trade in these waters."

"What trade?"

"She has an alliance with the goblinkin."

"What kind of alliance?"

"The ship's captain is interested in things that the goblinkin find in their mines."

"What things?" Bulokk stepped closer, taking over the questioning. "The ore?"

In that moment, Wick realized that the goblinkin were actually in competition with the Cinder Clouds dwarves, all of them ripping iron ore from the guts of the earth. He hadn't even considered that before, just assumed that the goblinkin were there in hope of finding gold or silver mines. But with the islands vomited up by the sea-based volcanoes, chances of finding those kinds of mines would be unlikely. The goblinkin were there supplying other forges, ones the goblinkin ran themselves with dwarven slaves or had trade agreements with.

"Not just the ore," Drinnick said. "I heard these humans—"

"They're human?" Wick asked, picturing the image of the lean archers along the ship's railing again in his mind. Those lean shapes could have been human or elven. They'd been too narrow and tall to be dwarves or dwellers.

Of course, the possibility existed that they were other kinds of creatures. Humans, dwarves, elves, dwellers, and goblinkin comprised most of the population of the world, but certainly not all of it.

"Aye," Drinnick said. "They're human."

"How do ye know?" Bulokk said.

"I spied on 'em a time or three whilst I was on patrol."

"Then surely others among you have seen it," Wick said.

No one answered.

Drinnick scratched at his beard. "I sometimes go a mite closer than these here warriors."

Bulokk took a deep breath, obviously not pleased about this revelation. "I told ye to stay away from the goblinkin."

Narrowing his eyes, Drinnick nodded. "I will. Just as soon as I get me four more Nathull Tribe heads. I told ye I'd claim ten of their heads for them a-killin' Broor the way they done. I swore me out an oath of vengeance. I means to live up to it."

Bulokk cursed and told Drinnick that he was being a fool, but Wick knew from the calm way Drinnick listened to his leader that the assessment was falling on deaf ears. A dwarven oath of vengeance was a fearful thing.

"Where did they do their trading?" Wick asked.

"West of us." Drinnick pointed in the general direction they'd been headed. "Not far from here."

Bulokk glanced at Wick. "Do ye think this is important?"

Wick pondered the question, and all the questions his fertile mind had already raised. "How often do you hear about humans traveling to trade with goblinkin?"

Shaking his shaggy head, Bulokk said, "Never. Leastways, *never* afore this. It's always them goblinkin what's a-tryin' to trade with humans. Ain't no dwarf or elf gonna work with 'em. But humans, now, they got short memories."

"Then it couldn't hurt to keep our eyes peeled for this ship while we're searching," Wick said.

With years of long practice behind them, the dwarves chose up guard shifts and made themselves as comfortable as could be on the hard rock. Wick took his own bed beside a tall stand of rock, telling himself that sleeping up next to a rock wall wasn't the same as sleeping out in the open. He didn't really fool himself, but he was so fatigued that he quickly went to sleep.

10

"D'Ye See Anythin', Halfer?"

Someone planted a toe in the middle of Wick's back, kicking the little Librarian hard enough to get his attention but not hard enough to injure him. Still, the unaccustomed violence—at least, it was unaccustomed in the Vault of All Known Knowledge—filled Wick with fear and he threw his free arm over his head to protect it. His other arm had gone numb from pillowing his face from the hard rock and now flopped rather uselessly.

"Wake up, halfer," a dwarf muttered. "Got no time fer beauty sleep. An' it ain't gonna help ye none anyway."

Dwarves, Wick grimaced, relaxing a little. Groggily, he pushed himself into a sitting position, not wanting to get kicked again because he suspected it would only get harder after the first effort. Dwarves weren't ones to lollygag around. They were always ready to do something.

To the east, the sun was barely peeking above the horizon. Gulls cried low in the sky overhead, evidently hoping for some left-behind morsel. Gesa the Fair looked like an empty silver ring in the western sky.

Bulokk gathered the dwarves quickly, breaking them into two groups. One was responsible for repairing the longboat and the other was supposed to fish for breakfast. Adranis and Wick were assigned to gather coal.

In short order, three of the dwarves waded out into the water with fishing lines and Bulokk led the five remaining ones to the longboat, which they immediately dragged completely onto shore and flipped over so they could start working on the holes made by the arrows the night before.

Adranis crossed over to Wick and kicked his feet. “C’mon then, halfer. That coal ain’t gonna find itself.”

Reluctantly, Wick got up and went.

Finding coal wasn’t a simple affair, Wick discovered. Although all the upheavals caused by volcanoes in the past had revealed much of the bedrock and mineral underpinnings of the land comprising the islands and the sea floor, coal wasn’t readily found. Cooling lava formed most of the islands, but here and there throughout most of them, chunks of the ocean floor had been shoved up as well.

Wick trudged in Adranis’s wake along through the hills and valleys of the island. He’d seen coal before, of course. A few communities outside Greydawn Moors used coal as a primary source of fuel. Most of them preferred to use wood logs, but if they couldn’t get that, they burned coal.

Only a little while later, Adranis called a halt and dropped down into a shallow crevasse.

Alert to the danger around them, Wick found himself interested nonetheless. More than anything, though, his fingers itched to be at his journal. There was so much he needed to record. For a while last night, he’d been able to sneak his journal out and make a few quick notes, just to make certain he didn’t forget anything when he had a proper chance to catch up with his thoughts and experiences.

Adranis ran his hand across the jagged faces of the crevasse. An uneven black stripe showed on both sides. When the dwarf picked at it, pieces of black rock tumbled down.

He looked up at Wick. “What are ye a-doin?”

“Watching you,” Wick answered.

“Hmmph. Ain’t ye ever seen coal mined afore?”

“I have. It’s still interesting.” Wick felt a little embarrassed about his curiosity, but not so much that he quit watching.

Adranis scowled. “Ain’t near as interesting as minin’ gems or iron ore. An’ minin’ ain’t what I’m for anyways. I’d rather be at me anvil, a-workin’ on armor.” He reached into the pack he carried and drew out a pickaxe. He kept his battleaxe close to hand. Drawing back, he swung the pick. The point dug into the black vein and broke chunks free. “Get on down here an’ make yerself useful.”

Wick slid over the side and scooted down.

Working like an automaton, Adranis dug into the crevasse side. Coal chunks flew and dropped at his feet. “Pick up them pieces an’ fill that bag.”

Kneeling, Wick did so. “Did you know that you’re digging into history?”

“What do ye mean?”

“Do you know where coal comes from?”

Adranis scowled at Wick as though he were a buffoon. “From the earth, of course. Can’t ye see me a-excavatin’ it?”

"Yes, but do you know how the coal got in the earth?"

"I never give it any thought." Adranis returned to his pick work.

Wick sorted through the coal chunks, picking up the smaller ones rather than the larger. The large pieces would have filled up the bag with too much wasted space, and a fire burned better with the smaller pieces close together.

"Finding coal here means that this land was above the sea once," Wick said.

"It is now."

"I know, but judging from all the metamorphic rock lying around, I think this section was once part of the ocean floor that got ripped up and pushed to the surface again."

"So?"

"Thousands of years ago, though some say it was millions, forests grew here," Wick said. "Trees grew to maturation and fell, covered over by more trees and organic growth. Eventually they rotted and were buried by more and more trees that kept growing on top of the old ones. Then, when enough time, heat, and pressure was applied to the organic rot, it became coal."

Adranis paused and looked at Wick. "So coal was once trees?"

"Yes," Wick replied. "Trees and plants. Everything that grew in the forest."

"An' this is true?"

Wick nodded.

"I have to admit, halfer, that's mighty interestin'. But it don't make no difference to me. Ain't gonna change the way I do things." Adranis shook his head. "Don't know how come ye to fill yer head with such useless knowledge. At least it ain't as bad as knowin' how to cook dwarves."

No, Wick agreed. *At least that bit of knowledge about coal is only wasteful, not offensive.*

Adranis put away his pick, then grabbed his battle-axe and laid the weapon across his broad shoulders. "I'm gonna warn ye about somethin' else, too, halfer."

A cold chill chased down Wick's spine. He dropped the coal chunk he'd been fumbling with and glanced up at the dwarf 's hard expression.

"Bulokk seems taken with ye," Adranis commented. "Even when we found ye with them goblinkin, was his hand what spared ye when ever' other warrior there would have spilled yer tripes for ye on general principle on account of bein' with them goblinkin."

Wick hoped that wasn't true because such an announcement was in nowise restful, but he suspected the statement was exactly what was on the dwarven warriors' minds.

"Bulokk's one to get to the truth of somethin'," Adranis said. "Me an' the others, we've mostly had hard lives an' are set to keep on livin' 'em."

"But Bulokk wants more," Wick said.

Narrowing his eyes, Adranis glared at Wick. "Ye seen that in him, did ye?" he demanded. "Plannin' on takin' advantage of it, are ye?"

"No. That's what he said last night before we left the fort. The part about being tired of smithing the things you've been making out here."

"It's work with a hammer an' anvil," Adranis said. "Good work for a dwarf.

I ain't ashamed of it. An' it's what the Old Ones has give us to do. Fer now." He took a deep breath. "What I'm a-doin' here, halfer, is a-givin' ye fair warnin'. I don't even owe ye that. But I'm a-doin' it to save Bulokk if 'n I can."

"Save him from what?"

"From gettin' his hopes up just to have ye bring 'em a-crashin' down, is what!" The dwarf's voice thundered in the stillness around them.

"How would I do that?"

"By a-leadin' him on a wild goose chase around these islands. Mayhap it ain't too late for us to go back to the fort. Taloston might be somewhat peeved, but he ain't gonna banish us. Not if 'n we go back soon enough."

Wick thought about the threat but didn't know what to say. Suddenly, everything he remembered about the area and about Master Blacksmith Oskarr seemed jumbled in his mind. Even if it hadn't been, the land where all those things had taken place was jumbled. By Lord Kharrion's evil magic, by volcanic eruptions, and by time.

It's not fair to hold me accountable for so much, Wick thought desperately. He met Adranis's hard gaze with difficulty. "I can't promise that we'll find Master Oskarr's axe. Or that we'll even find his forge. For all I know, it may still be underwater. You can't just—"

Snarling, Adranis lifted his battle-axe as if preparing to swing it.

Throwing up his arms to defend himself, Wick closed his eyes and ducked his head, certain he was about to be killed. *This is all Craugh's fault! He should be the one getting beheaded! Not me!*

He waited. Then he took another breath. And waited some more. Finally, he opened one eye and saw Adranis glaring at him.

"Ye do yer best then," Adranis said. "An' don't ye take too long to get it done."

Don't take too long? Don't *take too long*. Wick couldn't believe it. Since he'd arrived on the island, everybody had been willing to kill him. Then, when he was simply trying to accomplish the impossible task Cap'n Farok and Craugh had left him to do, dwarven warriors wanted to take over. But not be responsible for the task. *Oh no, never take on the responsibility. Just figure out whom to blame.*

And kill. That was a very important part to remember.

Adranis climbed to the top of the crevasse and glared down. "Are ye a-gonna fill that there bag or do ye expect them chunks to up an' jump in theirselves?"

"I'll fill it," Wick grumped.

"Then get 'er done."

Wick felt a slither over his right shoulder. "If I was you," the skink whispered to him, "I'd fill that coal bag. Adranis looks like he'd push you over the side of a cliff and tell Bulokk you slipped and fell."

Silently, Wick agreed. "You know," he said, "you might let the dwarves know you can talk."

"Why?"

"Because we could convince them I have magical powers. Maybe they wouldn't treat me so harshly then."

"Why do you have to have magical powers?" Rohoh asked. "Why couldn't I have magical powers?"

"Because," Wick said, thinking furiously.

"Because why?"

"I need to be the important one. It'll empower me."

The skink slithered out onto Wick's shoulder and sunned himself while the little Librarian worked. "You're already empowered."

"How?"

"They can't find Master Oskarr's forge without you."

That, Wick knew, was true. *However, I don't know if I can find Master Oskarr's forge.*

The skink slithered back into his coat and became still. Wick concentrated on gathering the loosened coal.

When the bag was full, Wick passed it up to the dwarf, then clambered up. At the top, Adranis handed Wick the bag again, claiming that he had to have his hands free to defend them in case of attack. Wick sighed and shouldered the bag, following the dwarven warrior back to the campsite.

"I says we let the halfer cook," one of the dwarves suggested. "After all, he was cookin' fer the goblinkin when we found him."

Wick sat and looked out to sea, deciding not even to deign notice of the slight the men threw at him. The dwarves quickly put the suggestion to a vote. The little Librarian wasn't at all surprised to find himself suddenly in charge of the makeshift kitchen.

As he built a proper fire there on the beach, he set up—with Adranis's assistance—a clever framework of metal rods that became a spit. The dwarves fishing the waters off the bank had experienced good luck and brought in several edible fish, and other dwarves had dug up clams in the mud.

In short order, with the addition of the cooking supplies, Wick had fish smoking over the fire on the spit and a large pot of clam chowder simmering on the coals. He also made pan bread in a large iron skillet that Drinnick proudly admitted he'd made. Wick made the bread partly because he had a hankering for it and partly because he wanted to prove to the dwarves that he could cook. If he could cook, there was at least some worth he could continue to bring to them once his days as guide were over.

If we don't get killed looking for the axe, he told himself.

The dwarves' disparaging comments quickly gave way to interest as the concerns of their empty stomachs outweighed the work of heckling Wick. The pan bread was new to them, and was something Wick had picked up in his travels. He'd even added the recipe to the book of favorite recipes he was in the process of writing.

The dwarves kept themselves busy with the repairs to the longboat and with guard duty. They rotated in and out at regular intervals. Lunch was ready before the boat was, but only just.

Once Wick announced everything fit to eat, the dwarves chose up and posted guards, then hunkered in and started eating.

While he was serving, Wick went ahead and cored a few apples, stuffed them with cinnamon, butter, and sugar and drenched them in firepear juice to heat up the flavor even more. During that, Rohoh kept slipping down his arms and snatching choice bits. Even though the dwarves protested that they couldn't eat another bite, Wick saw that the apples disappeared easily enough.

Afterward, Bulokk pronounced the longboat seaworthy again, then gathered his men and said a few words about the companions they'd lost. The sun was setting in the west, and the sky was bleeding orange shot through with purple veins.

Seeing the dwarves with their caps and scarves doffed and in hand touched Wick's tender heart as they listened to Bulokk's words. Wick had seen similar scenes aboard *One-Eyed Peggie* while on his excursions aboard the ship. Humans had a tendency to float among families, taking what they needed wherever they were at the time. Arrogance kept elves together, and avarice and fear generally kept dwellers together.

But love and a long sense of history bound dwarves. Their world was the earth, given to them by the power of the Old Ones during the Beginning Times when things were created.

"All right then," Bulokk said, clapping his hat back on his head. He gestured to the setting sun. "As ye can see plainly as the nose on yer faces, we ain't goin' nowhere tonight. We'll rest up once more, get us a fresh start in the mornin'."

The dwarves grumbled, not truly happy spending life out under the stars when they were used to being able to burrow up whenever they liked.

Wick wasn't happy about it either. Especially when he realized that he was going to have to cook another big meal. This time, though, Bulokk posted guards and assigned two dwarves to help the little Librarian.

"The meal ye fixed were helpful," Bulokk said in an aside to Wick. "Kept them men from feelin' hollow, it did. So I'm gonna see to it ye get help."

"Thank you," Wick said. "I won't let you down."

Bulokk looked at him and smiled a little. "I don't think ye will, halfer. Just get me to where I can find Master Oskarr's lost axe, I'll be thankful to ye the rest of me days."

Weakly, not at all certain he could deliver on the promise he was being asked to give, Wick nodded. Then, when his crew showed up, he put his plans into action to organize the evening meal.

Later, with fish chunks floating in a seaweed soup made a little more exotic with the firepear pulp he'd saved from juicing earlier, Wick wiped sweat from his brow with a forearm and wondered where Craugh and *One-Eyed Peggie*'s crew were. The bottom of the cook pot glowed cherry-red and the soup bubbled.

Several of the dwarves looked on with fond expectation. Bulokk had organized a guard rotation and taken one of the posts himself.

"Them stories ye were a-tellin' back at the burrow," Drinnick said. "The ones about Master Oskarr, them was true stories, wasn't they?"

"They was, er . . . were," Wick agreed.

Drinnick scratched the back of his neck with a big forefinger. "Would ye, uh, mind tellin' us a few more of 'em? We ain't ever heard the like. An' the way ye tell 'em, why folks would pay to hear ye a-tellin' 'em."

So as he cooked and fried (and tried frightfully hard not to think that his life might be on the line), Wick told the dwarves stories about the Cinder Clouds Islands dwarves. He included tales of Master Blacksmith Oskarr as well as that worthy's ancestors.

During the telling of Varshuk's Blockade, when a human pirate named himself king of the area and tried to enforce his laws, none of the dwarves said a word. Wick employed all the tricks he'd learned in Hralbomm's Wing to tell the tale properly. He continued the tale while he filled the dwarves' metal plates and tankards, then feigned distraction to the point that they washed the dishes in the sea so that he would be free to speak. It was a bit of chicanery he'd learned while making his way across the mainland hunting down lost books.

Later, when the coals had burned low and were deep orange, Bulokk put an end to the tale-telling. Several of the dwarves thanked Wick for the meal and for the stories. That night, the little Librarian slept without wondering if he was going to wake up with his throat slit.

But he kept wondering where *One-Eyed Peggie* and Craugh were, and why they had abandoned him.

"*Easy*. Go easy there, ye great-eared lummox," Bulokk growled from the longboat's stern. "We got this boat fixed up good as we could, but she ain't gonna take a fierce poundin'."

Despite the dwarves' best efforts, the longboat scraped the jutting teeth of the rocks they passed through. The hoarse sound carried over the water.

Wick swallowed hard, telling himself that the water probably wasn't that deep there if the rock was jutting above the sea surface. But he knew that might not be true. Slender spires of rock drove up from the sea bottom a hundred feet and more sometimes. The forces contained within the earth and unleashed through the open sores of the volcanoes festered with tremendous power.

All around them, the gray fog closed in swirling waves. The manifestation happened every time cool air came down from the north and hit the blast furnace that was the Cinder Clouds Islands.

Wick sat in the longboat's prow and peered out. The dwarves had since admitted that Wick had some of the best eyes among them. The fog glided over Wick's skin like damp silk and he resisted the impulse to claw it out of his face.

Although it was mid-morning, darkness covered the Rusting Sea and the sun couldn't be seen. Gull cries echoed across the water so much that Wick couldn't determine the true direction of the birds.

Stiff and sore from sleeping on the hard ground a second night in a row, Wick disliked acting as lookout now. There was too much moving around involved.

"D'ye see anythin', halfer?" Drinnick asked.

Wick sighed. He wanted to be angry, but he was afraid to be. Even though he'd told them stories last night, and cooked meals for them, he didn't trust the dwarves to be so thankful that they wouldn't throw him overboard while reacting to their own frustrations. Wick had already seen two saurian creatures gliding through the murky water.

However, *D'ye see anythin', halfer?* from the dwarves was becoming as irritatingly monotonous as, *Are you sure that brushstroke was made by the Dalothak Canopy Elves, Second Level Librarian?* from the Novice and Third Level Librarians. (And, truthfully, even a few Second Level and First Level Librarians still asked that! Wick thought that was shameful.)

The demand was repeated on the heels of Wick's sigh. "D'ye see anythin', halfer?"

"These dwarves," Rohoh whispered irritably, "are awfully short-sighted." Then the skink laughed at his attempt at humor.

Turning, controlling his ire only through excessive fear, Wick said (as politely as he could while trying to sound capable), "No. If I had seen something, I would have said that I had—"

Of course, at that point the longboat ran aground.

11

Landmarks

Loud grinding filled Wick's ears. From the deep-throated sound and the way the longboat continued to glide evenly over the surface of the hidden object, Wick believed they'd hit stone. Then his thoughts immediately flew to the holes that had been so recently repaired in the longboat's hull.

"Good job," Rohoh commented. "Maybe you should have been watching instead of getting all sensitive."

"Reverse!" Bulokk commanded, keeping his voice down because it carried across the water and he didn't want to alert anyone that might be in the area that they were there, too. *"Reverse!"*

Immediately, the dwarves churned their oars in the other direction, pulling back away from whatever they had hit. Their efforts yanked the longboat backward.

Caught unprepared, Wick nearly went ears over teakettle into the water. He flailed for a moment, certain he was going to land in the sea and be a mere gobbet for some passing monster. Then Adranis flicked out a lazy hand and caught him, keeping him in the boat.

"Ye think ye mighta seen *that*, halfer," Adranis griped.

Chagrined, Wick sat in the prow and concentrated on staying aboard and staying alive.

Adranis peered forward. "Don't see nothin'."

"We hit somethin'," Bulokk said.

"Aye. I know that. But I'll be jiggered if 'n I can find it."

Curious, though he felt certain he should just try to stay out of everyone's way, Wick turned and looked into the water. A small fish broke the surface only a few feet away. Reaching into the small bag at his feet, Wick palmed a handful of pan breadcrumbs and scattered them over the water's surface.

"What do ye think ye're a-doin'?" Drinnick growled. "Tryin' to bring us face-to-face with one of them beasties?"

"Face-to-face with ye, Drinnick?" another dwarf asked. "I'm a-thinkin' there ain't a monster in these waters what's brave enough fer that."

A few of the other dwarves chuckled at that.

"Quiet!" Bulokk ordered.

They all fell quiet.

As Wick watched, several small fish broke the surface and fed on the crumbs he'd spread. "There's something down there," he announced.

"Why?" Bulokk asked.

"That's a school of small fish. You won't find them out in the open because the bigger fishes eat them." Motivated by that same powerful pull of curiosity that had gotten him into so much trouble over the years, Wick grabbed the sides of the longboat and peered down into the water. He still couldn't see anything.

"Are we ashore, then?" Bulokk asked.

"Don't see no shoreline," Adranis replied.

"It's an underwater structure." Wick was certain he was right. He thought about how the longboat had glided across the submerged surface. "A big one."

"What makes ye say that?" Drinnick challenged.

"Because we moved across it evenly. If it were the shallows, it would have tapered up and probably stopped us in our tracks. And it has to have hollows or be porous in some way to hide the small fish." Wick searched the bottom of the boat and found the weighted line they used to test the depths.

"D'ye think it's Zubeck's Hammer?" Bulokk asked.

"That's what we were here searching for." Wick wasn't really thinking about the dwarves or their reaction to him. He was excited about possibly finding the dwarven lighthouse.

Standing in the prow of the longboat, Wick cast the line. But the rope was more tricky to manage than he'd thought. When he released it after spinning it around, the weight sailed backward.

Dwarves cursed and covered their heads.

"Give me that!" Adranis snarled. "Afore ye brain somebody!"

Meekly, Wick handed the line over and knelt in the prow again.

After a few casts, Adranis found the underwater surface about twenty feet forward and to port. The weight landed solidly on it.

"Slow," Bulokk said. "Slow an' easy as we go."

The dwarves barely moved the oars and eased the longboat through the water. A moment later, they bumped up against it again.

"All right," Bulokk said. "Drop anchor an' let's see what we found."

The water, though shallow, still came up to just under Wick's chin. Although he didn't want to, he had a tendency to bob on the tide and Bulokk had finally assigned

Adranis the task of keeping the little Librarian anchored. It wasn't a task Adranis was particularly fond of, and he occasionally waited until Wick was over the edge and had started to swim. Then the dwarf would yank Wick back like a wandering toddler. The skink clung to the back of the little Librarian's head, hidden by his hair.

Thankfully, the Rusting Sea was warm. On the negative side, though, there appeared to be plenty of depth for a sea monster to come by and try for a quick catch. Wick's attention was divided between the mystery of what they'd found and survival. In the end, though, the discovery devoured his attention.

Walking across the underwater surface, Wick found that it was thirty feet long and eight feet wide. Although Wick and two of the other dwarves had dived and followed the line of the submerged structure, they hadn't been able to go more than forty or fifty feet down.

Given the measurements, Wick was certain they'd found Zubeck's Hammer. The lighthouse was in surprisingly good shape. Nothing had appeared broken, though there were some pitted places on the surface.

Unfortunately, the ocean held too much sediment for Wick to see the lighthouse. The only way he'd ever see Zubeck's Hammer would be for some freak of chance to thrust the structure to the surface once more. Since the Hammer was reputed to be one hundred forty feet tall, he didn't see how that would happen.

And besides, he thought glumly, pacing across its submerged surface once more with his bare feet, *it was a miracle that the lighthouse wasn't destroyed when it sank.*

"Is this it then?" Bulokk asked.

"It has to be," Wick said.

"Then where should we head next?"

Wick sighed and ended up with a mouthful of salty, metallic-tasting seawater for his trouble. He also snorted some up his nose and it burned strong enough to bring tears to his eyes.

"Do you understand how important this is?" Wick asked. "We're standing on a piece of history."

Bulokk frowned. "There's lots of history. Everywhere you go, there's old things."

"But don't you realize how much those old things can tell us?"

"About what?"

"The past," Wick moaned. He gestured at the lighthouse, a feat that was incredibly hard to do because he had to wait between waves of the incoming tide and even then the water was up well past his armpits. "Can you even imagine what it would be like if we could get inside this place?"

"We'd drown," Adranis said. "This place is underwater." He shook his head. "Ye know, to be as smart as ye are, ye got some awfully dumb ways."

"He's speaking the truth there," Rohoh muttered in Wick's ear.

"Not while it's underwater," Wick argued. "If we could somehow raise it up and go inside."

"Everything inside is ruined," Bulokk said. "The only thing that survives the sea is gold. Even silver rots away."

"Some enchanted things survive, too," Wick said.

Bulokk frowned. "I don't hold much with magic. Can't see a need fer it."

"But you want Master Oskarr's battle-axe."

"Master Oskarr's axe ain't magicked up none," Bulokk replied. "It's just . . . Master Oskarr's axe. Something that touches all them before times."

Wick was thinking of all the books that might have survived. Some books were magical in nature and couldn't be easily destroyed by the vagaries of weather. But other books, especially ones that were kept around water or the constant threat of fire, tended to be kept in protective bindings. Just as his own journal was wrapped securely in oilskin beneath his clothing.

There have to be books in there, he thought desperately. *The Rusting Sea can't have claimed them all.*

"Which way?" Bulokk demanded.

Wick had difficulty wresting his thoughts from books and maps and journals that might still be lurking in Zubeck's Hammer. The lighthouse would have been a natural gathering place for seafarers, tale spinners, and those seeking their fortunes in legends and maps of old.

"Which way is the sun?" Wick asked.

Bulokk pointed.

Squinting up at the light that had grown somewhat brighter, Wick silently admitted that the sun probably did lie in that direction. He thought about it for a moment, then turned back to Bulokk. "Is it morning or afternoon?" He'd lost all track of time. It had been morning the last he'd looked.

"Afternoon," Bulokk answered.

"Then that way is west?" Wick pointed toward the sunniest part of the haze.

"Aye."

"We need to go still farther east, but in a northerly direction."

"Then let's be about it." Bulokk turned and walked toward the anchored longboat.

Wick couldn't make himself move. He was loath to leave the lighthouse and whatever treasures it might have inside.

"Perhaps we can get inside," he said, thinking about Luttell's *Guide to Undersea Vessels in Fact and Fiction: Their Design, Construction, and Uses*. Nearly all of those used magic in one form or another, though. Still, there had been a few workable designs, and dwarves were certainly most capable when it came to manufacturing things that—

"We're a-leavin'," Adranis declared. He yanked Wick and the little Librarian's feet left the lighthouse as he skimmed through the waves like a fat-bellied merchant's cog. Closing his eyes against the spray, Wick clapped a hand over his mouth and nose to protect himself from inhaling the ocean.

Hours later, Wick glumly sat in the prow of the longboat. In short order, proceeding on the information he remembered, they'd found Hullbreaker Reefs and managed to stay well clear of them, then Delid's Circle. Both of those landmarks had been above the ocean's surface.

Now, if everything was right, Wick felt they had to be closing in on—

"There!" Drinnick said, standing and pointing, which caused the longboat to tip precariously and take on a little water.

The rest of the dwarves set about cursing Drinnick's thoughtless action, but he protested and said he'd never claimed to be a sailor. The imprecations and defense didn't last long. The sight out in the middle of the ocean drew all of their attention.

For there, only a couple feet above the whitecaps rolling in from the sea toward the Cinder Clouds Islands, the very top of a blue dome could be seen. Wick's heart leaped. He knew from Brojor's *Physical Laws of the Natural World* that a dome often maintained air pressure in quite the same manner an empty tankard could be pushed to the bottom of a sink filled with water. In fact, that thought had been buzzing through Wick's mind because he was thinking that one of the devices he could use to get inside Zubeck's Hammer was similar in nature.

But the Trader's Hall had windows. Only the top half of the dome might have maintained an air pocket. Surely nothing had been up there.

But it might have floated, Wick thought optimistically. *Pots. Trunks. Kegs. Anything that might have an airtight seal.*

"No one knows this is here?" Wick asked, having trouble believing that.

"These ain't the primary trade routes," Bulokk said. "We're well away from them right now. Few comes through here, an' them not often." He looked at the blue dome. "Besides, what ye a-gonna do with somethin' like that a-stickin' up outta the water except make sure ye don't hit it?"

Wick had to concede that the dwarf had a point. As they got closer, though, the little Librarian's heart broke. Over the years, someone had broken through the dome, punching a big hole in the top. From his vantage point, he clearly saw the sea sloshing around inside.

He barely heard Bulokk asking him which way they were supposed to go. Despondent by the terrible realization that probably nothing inside Trader's Hall yet remained, Wick took a moment to get his bearings, then pointed north.

The dwarves immediately set out on the new tack, pulling all the harder as if they were racing the sunset to the west.

Twilight draped the Rusting Sea as they came within sight of the island chain. The water turned muddy black with it, and the white curlers held a glow like glimmerworms.

Wick had grown tired with the passing of the day. He wasn't used to having to spend whole days without something to distract his thoughts. He hated spending hours by himself with nothing but thinking to dwell on. Left to their own devices, his thoughts often chose to spin around and around like water gurgling through plumbing. Only he was unable to divest himself of those thoughts because he was afraid that he'd never rethink them. That was different when he had quill and paper at hand, because then he could jot down whatever was on his mind and trust that nothing would be forgotten.

It was terrible having a headful of thoughts with no proper place to put them.

His mind and fingers cried out for the luxury of putting quill to paper, of transferring all that thinking to a more forgiving and permanent medium, then sorting through it to make it make sense.

"Is that it, halfer?" Bulokk asked in a quiet, reverential voice.

Wick studied the coastline, looking for landmarks that he could recognize from the maps he'd seen of the Cinder Clouds Islands. Although most Librarians were able to remember prodigious amounts of information, he was more able than most of his fellow Librarians.

"Sail to the east," Wick said. "We need to travel up the eastern coast for a bit."

Bulokk gave the orders. "But is this the island where Master Oskarr's forge was?"

Wick shrugged. "I don't know. It could be. We need to be in closer."

The skink slithered on his shoulder. "This is it," Rohoh whispered. "And this is where this thing starts to really get dangerous."

"Hug the coastline," Bulokk ordered his warriors. "Keep a weather eye peeled."

Later, when the full dark of the night had descended upon the Rusting Sea and the island as well, Wick spied campfires nestled in a cove that looked like the scar from an old axe blow. Steep cliffs forty and fifty feet tall soared above the ruins of a city. Alabaster rock showed signs of expert quarry work. Since no one had truly built like that among the Cinder Clouds Islands in a thousand years, Wick assumed the village was at least that old.

Thin wisps of fog floated through the chill breeze that continued from the north. The campfires filled the ruins with orange light. There was no mistaking the creatures that maintained watch over the area.

"Goblinkin," Adranis whispered with real loathing. "Quite a mess of 'em, too."

Wick silently agreed. The goblinkin encampment was spread throughout the ruins. It was easy to see that they had been there for some time. A stone pier made up of broken rocks thrust a short distance out into the Rusting Sea. Two ships, both of them ragged and worn, jostled against each other on the tide.

Most interesting, though, was the ship lying at anchor next to the pier. Lanterns lit her deck and dark figures that might have been human moved around onboard. Her sails were furled and her rigging rang against the masts and 'yards in the breeze.

If that's not the black ship that tried to run us down, Wick thought, *then it's her sister*. He didn't think it was a coincidence.

"Slavers," Drinnick growled. "They got halfers there."

Shifting his attention from the buildings he could see, Wick spotted the slave pen tucked at the back of the canyon. Wire nets made up the enclosure. Skulls—most of them from dwellers but some from humans, dwarves, and elves—hung on the wire nets and picked up a warm cast-off glow from the campfires. Nearly a hundred slaves lay practically on top of each other on the stone floor. Goblinkin guards lounged around the slave pen.

"Are they a-sellin' 'em then?" another dwarf asked.

Wick surveyed the rest of the city. Then he spotted a narrow trail that had been cut into the cliff wall. The trail zigzagged up the wall. A torch burned at the entrance to a cave mouth.

"They're digging," Wick said.

"Fer what?" Adranis asked.

"I don't know." Farther up the cliff, Wick made out the block-and-tackle assembly that he assumed was used to lower excavated rock to the ore cars on the ground. A worn path led from the ore cars to the stone pier.

"Are they a-diggin' fer gems?" Bulokk asked. "Or fer gold?"

"Maybe it's iron ore," Wick said. "You mentioned that the goblinkin were mining iron ore and shipping it to the mainland."

"This ain't an iron mine," Bulokk said.

"No," Adranis agreed.

"How do you know?" Wick asked.

"Can't smell any iron," Bulokk said. He touched his nose.

Adranis and the other dwarves agreed.

"Was iron here once," Adranis said, sniffing again. "But it's been gone a long time."

"Mayhap even a thousand years or more," Bulokk conceded. "Master Oskarr an' his forge smiths had to import iron ore even durin' his day." He paused. "Either way, we have to find out what they're doin' there. An' this is the spot where ye said Master Oskarr's forge was."

Wick had been afraid the dwarves were going to come to that conclusion. Even though he was afraid, part of him was hypnotized by the possibilities the goblinkin presence presented. The goblinkin wouldn't be there if no reason existed.

Neither would the mysterious black ship.

"Time to get moving, halfer," Rohoh said. "This is what you've come all this way to find."

"How do you know that?" Wick whispered back, knowing the sound of the sea would carry his words away before they reached dwarven ears.

"Because," Rohoh said, "this is what Craugh sent me here to help you find. Now you just have to stay alive long enough to find it."

And what about after *I find it*? Wick wondered. *What then?* But he was afraid to ask.

12

A Daring Plan Is Made

"I think the halfer should stay here," Adranis said. "He'll just be underfoot."

"So do I," Wick piped up. "I think the halfer should stay here, too."

All of the dwarves shot the little Librarian a glance of annoyance.

"Or not," Wick whispered.

"You can't stay here," the skink told him. "Your place is down there. Either you can go with them, or you'll have to go alone."

Wick didn't want to go alone. "Of course," he added swiftly, "if you think I can help . . ."

Bulokk had given the order to set up camp on the other side of the island. A half mile of crooked rock and ridges separated their camp from the ruins of the city where the goblinkin had set up base. A hidden reef lay only a few feet below the ocean surface where they'd tied up. The longboat had negotiated the area with difficulty, so they knew the black ship couldn't close in on them without risking its hull.

The main focus of the mission, though, was not to get caught observing in the first place.

"He's goin' with us," Bulokk declared, "an' that's that."

"Why?" Adranis asked.

So I can be the slow one if we get caught, Wick was certain. *The sacrificial lamb. By the time the goblinkin get through tearing me to pieces, you'll all have made your escape.*

"Do ye know anyone else who might know his way around

them ruins?" Bulokk demanded. "We get down in them ruins a-runnin' fer our lives, might be a good idea to have a guide."

"Ummmm," Adranis said. "Hadn't thought about that."

Oh, Wick thought, and realized that he hadn't considered that either. Upon reflection, Bulokk's reasoning was without fault. Wick was of mixed emotions, though. He didn't like the idea of potentially ending up in slaver's chains (or dead!), but he knew that Bulokk and his men wouldn't recognize a book if they saw one.

If *any* of the books Master Oskarr used, or—and the hope left Wick giddy with anticipation—wrote himself, that knowledge would be worth every risk he took.

As long as I don't die, Wick told himself.

Wick's back and feet hurt by the time they reached the ruins. The dwarves acted like the rocky climbs and journey over the rugged terrain was something they did every day. Given that they lived on an island a lot like this one, though, Wick had to admit that they probably did.

They came to a stop on the side of the canyon across from the block-and-tackle. No goblinkin guarded the boom arm or the mine entrance. Since the coast was clear, they went to the other side and soon grouped under the block-and-tackle assembly.

Bulokk quickly divided the dwarves into two groups. One was assigned to stay by the boom arm to manage a retreat. The other was descending down into the goblinkin camp to assess the possibility of freeing the slaves.

Wick didn't even have to be told which group he was going with. Heart in his throat, he crept along behind Bulokk and the other dwarves as they sneaked down into the goblinkin camp.

The stone steps tracking up the cliff were so narrow Bulokk almost had to go down while turned sideways. Of course, carrying his battle-axe in both hands made the effort even more difficult. But he managed. The steps were uneven and sometimes poorly placed. Dwarves hadn't made those steps and Wick had the feeling that dweller or human slaves had.

But why? Despite the terror that never stopped vibrating through him, Wick couldn't let go of the question. If Bulokk and the others said there was no iron ore coming out of the mine, he believed them. *So why would the goblinkin be interested in a mine that didn't promise gold or gems or some other wealth? And what relationship did the ship have with the goblinkin?*

Finally, after what seemed like an eternity to Wick, he reached the ground level and stood in hiding with Bulokk. But that just meant that although he was no longer in fear of falling over the edge of the narrow steps, it was now a long way back up to safety. He would have felt better if there had been a few elven warders with longbows posted among the dwarves.

Craugh, he thought miserably. Surely the crew of the pirate ship could see where he was and how much trouble he was potentially in.

"It's here."

Wick clapped a hand over his mouth automatically. Glancing back over his broad shoulder, Bulokk glared at him.

It wasn't me, Wick thought desperately. Of course, at first he'd thought it had been him who had spoken. Then he'd realized that the voice was tiny, not a whisper or an inadvertent slip.

"Oskarr's axe is here," the tiny voice said.

The skink, Wick realized. Keeping one hand over his mouth to show Bulokk that he wasn't talking, Wick frantically searched for Rohoh with the other. Then he figured he probably looked like he was patting himself on the back.

"Should have slit his throat when we found him a-cookin' fer them goblinkin," Hodnes growled.

"It ain't too late to do it now," Drinnick whispered.

"If you two keep talking, maybe you'll wake the goblinkin and they'll come after us," Rohoh said. The skink crawled out from hiding and stood on Wick's shoulder waving an angry, curled-up claw at the dwarves.

"Ye got a talkin' lizard?" Drinnick asked.

Now he decides to talk. Anxious, Wick peered around the goblinkin camp amid the ruins. So far none of the goblinkin appeared to have heard them.

"It dances, too," Hodnes reminded. "We saw it dancing when we found the halfer a-cookin' fer the goblinkin." He smiled. "A dancin' lizard what knows how to talk. Now that could fetch a pretty price."

Rohoh crossed his forelegs and stood up on his hind legs. "You two are idiots."

" 'Course," Drinnick said, "he could have him a better disposition."

"Don't you think the important thing is figuring out why he chose *now* to speak?" Wick asked.

"Quiet!" Bulokk commanded.

All of them quieted.

"Lizard!" Bulokk pointed at the skink.

"Yes," Rohoh said.

"Why do ye talk?"

"Because I have something to say, you ninny."

"Enough to get all our throats slit?" Bulokk demanded.

"Look," the skink said, "I was sent here by a powerful wizard to make sure this numbskull—"

Numbskull! Wick thought indignantly.

"—managed to find Oskarr's battle-axe," Rohoh went on.

"Why?"

"Because the wizard wants to find out the truth of what happened at the Battle of Fell's Keep in the Painted Canyon."

"Why does he want to know that?" Bulokk demanded.

"It's time everyone knew what happened in those days," Rohoh stated.

Glowering, Bulokk leaned in close. "Does he think Master Oskarr betrayed them warriors?"

"I don't know. He doesn't talk to me about things like that."

Nor me, Wick thought glumly.

Bulokk ran his fingers through his beard thoughtfully. He clearly wasn't happy about the turn of events. "So why did this wizard—"

"Craugh," Rohoh said.

That does it, Wick thought, and prepared to run for his life. Craugh had a large reputation, but those who'd heard of him either liked him or hated him. The wizard tended to divide people into those two camps immediately. Generally the ones who didn't care for him had a relative who had been turned into a toad.

"Aye," Bulokk said. "I've heard of Craugh."

Wick's legs quivered. He thought if Bulokk chose to vent his anger on the skink he might gain a step on the certain pursuit. Of course, he'd be running straight into the arms of the goblinkin and the mysterious humans.

Of course, there existed the possibility that Bulokk would choose to take off Wick's head and cut the skink in twain in one fell swoop.

"Craugh's been around for a long time," Bulokk said. "There's some even say he was around for the Cataclysm and fought against Lord Kharrion."

Wick knew it was true. He'd read journals and books of the Cataclysm, and Craugh had been featured prominently in them.

"Why is Craugh interested in this?" Bulokk asked.

"He wants to know the truth," Rohoh said.

"Why?"

Wick couldn't keep quiet any longer. He stepped forward on trembling knees. "Bulokk."

The dwarf turned his harsh gaze on the little Librarian.

"I really think this is neither the time nor the place to discuss this at length," Wick said. "We've already been longer at it than we should have. What matters is that we're all here to recover Master Oskarr's axe."

Bulokk wanted to argue. That showed in every hard line of his body. Finally, he sighed. "Ye're right. But we're not even sure if the axe survived—"

"It did," Rohoh insisted. "In fact, we're not far from it."

"How do ye know that?"

"Because finding things is one of my skills," the skink answered. "That's why Craugh put me with this inept dweller."

Inept? Wick didn't know whether to be hurt or angry. He supposed he was both.

"Ye *find* things?" Bulokk asked. "How?"

"By magic," Rohoh said.

"Ye're a wizard?"

"No. I just have a talent for things like this. It's more like a—" The skink hesitated. "—a *knack*."

"Like a dwarf what can put his hand on a chunk of iron ore an' know he's gonna find something special in it," Adranis said. "A sword. An axe. A ring with a little extra good luck in it."

Rohoh nodded. "Exactly like that."

Immediate curiosity filled Wick. Although he'd heard of *knacks*, he'd never before seen anyone who possessed them. Magic was something that came two different ways: either as a discipline through years of tutelage, or as a more primitive means of tapping into the elemental forces that drove the power. Having a knack for finding magical things only made sense.

If you accepted the existence of knacks, Wick thought.

Bulokk didn't appear convinced.

"What this un's talkin' about," Adranis told the dwarven leader, "I've seen it fer meself. It's a true thing. Just seldom seen, is all." He turned and peered down at the skink standing on Wick's shoulder. "Ye're a-sayin' ye can sense Master Oskarr's axe?"

"I can."

"How did ye get the scent of it?"

Wick wanted to know the answer to that question as well.

"Craugh gave it to me," Rohoh answered. "He knew Master Oskarr and had touched the axe. It was enough to give me the scent."

"Even after a thousand years an' more?" Bulokk definitely had a hard time believing that. "Where's the axe?" Bulokk asked.

The skink pointed. "Somewhere inside the mountain. It's buried in there. But it's near."

Bulokk took a deep breath. "All right, then." His gaze raked the goblinkin and the mysterious ship. "First things first. We need to see what we're up against."

Wick decided he didn't like the sound of that. He liked it even less when Bulokk told him what he intended they do.

"An' ye," Bulokk threatened the skink, "no yappin'. Ye talk again before I tell ye it's okay to do so, an' we'll be a-takin' our chances on findin' Master Oskarr's axe ourselves."

The goblinkin guards stood their posts but didn't put any effort into it. There was more activity aboard the mysterious ship.

Of course, that was where Bulokk insisted they go. Even worse, he ordered Wick to follow him.

Cautiously, they crept down to the small harbor, easily avoiding the goblinkin guards, most of whom slept or stood in bored groups grumbling about their lot in life. The worst thing (if the constant fear of getting caught was discounted!) was the noxious smells coming from the great cauldrons that continued to simmer over fires in the center of the goblinkin camp.

Wick tried very hard not to think about what was cooked in those vast metal pots. That was hard to do when he saw the pile of bones—most of them from humans, dwellers, and dwarves with a few elven bones thrown in for good measure—that lay scattered at the water's edge on one side of the stone pier.

Lanterns glowed in the stern of the ship, stronger than the moonslight that peered again and again between clouds. Hidden in the shadows gathered at the base of the cliffs where they met the Rusting Sea, Wick hunkered down beside Bulokk and listened.

Up close, Wick saw the ship was crisp and clean, showing definite signs of immaculate care. The captain and his crew obviously cared about her the way a dwarven warrior cared about his axe. In the darkness, Wick couldn't make out her name, or even if she carried one. She rode light and easy on the tide, obviously carrying no cargo.

She carried something into the port, then, Wick thought, unable to keep from puzzling it out. *But what?* He gazed around the camp and knew at once. *She's a slaver.*

But that didn't sit right either. A ship that clean, that well cared for, Wick knew from experience that she shouldn't be a slaver. Ships used in that profession tended to be slovenly and piggish, cared for enough to keep afloat and keep turning a profit, but there was no pride in those ships. No matter what a captain and crew did, they could never wash the stink off such a vessel.

So who made you a slaver? Wick wondered. *And why did you agree?* All of the crew appeared to be human. *How did you come to deal with goblinkin if you're as successful as you look?*

After a few more minutes, Bulokk waved them back. Wick went willingly.

Once more at the foot of the stone steps, Bulokk conferred with Adranis. "We've got a two-fold problem," the dwarven leader said. "I want to find the axe, an' I'm not leavin' here without at least attemptin' to rescue them prisoners."

"An' I wouldn't let ye shirk on either of them duties," Adranis declared.

"The way I see it," Bulokk went on, "we've got to manage both of them things at the same time."

"Means splittin' our forces," Hodnes said.

"Not till we get the prisoners to the top of the cliff."

"We get them free," Adranis asked, "how are we gonna get them off the island?"

"Once we get them free an' up the cliff, we'll alert the goblinkin—"

"Assumin' they ain't already been alerted," Adranis said sourly.

Bulokk nodded. "Even so. As long as we get 'em clear, it should only take a few men to hold the cliffs against the goblinkin. All we need to do is hold the goblinkin fer a while, long enough for the prisoners to circle around the island. Then whoever holds the cliff top simply has to outrun the goblinkin to the longboat."

"Simply, he says," Drinnick grumped.

"At the longboat, them defenders will cast off. If 'n we get lucky, an' the Old Ones are known to favor the bold, them goblinkin will think their prisoners got away in other boats an' aren't circlin' around the island to take their ships."

"That's a daring plan," Wick said, because it was. "But even if the goblinkin fall for the trick, I don't think the crew of the black ship will leave their vessel unprotected. They'll be aboard her."

"That's a risk we'll have to take," Bulokk stated. "I don't see anything else we can do." He paused. "We ain't got all night, so let's be about it."

13

Walls of History

Crouched in the shadows, Wick watched in helpless terror as Bulokk and his handpicked warriors crept across the shadow-covered space. They moved in concert, as if they'd committed actions like this all their lives. Swiftly, each of them targeted a goblinkin guard and brought him down, finishing them all off quickly with their knives.

At that moment, the risk elevated to the point of no return. All it took was one goblinkin guard checking on another to throw them all into danger.

"Relax," Rohoh said, standing on Wick's shoulder. "Bulokk and his warriors know what they're about. They're good at this sort of thing."

"You've never seen them at work before," Wick whispered back.

"I saw them in front of the goblinkin you were preparing the banquet for."

"You were the entertainment."

"Under protest, though. And if you'd been able to save yourself, I wouldn't have had to bother."

Wick didn't say anything, caught up in the drama taking place in front of his eyes. In seconds, Bulokk had the attention of the prisoners, then had the locks picked. Adranis took the first one under his care and guided him through the shadows to the stone steps.

Several of the prisoners struggled to remain quiet as they made their way across the back of the campsite. They took advantage of the massive stone blocks that remained of the city, making Wick wish again that he could see the ruin in the light of day (which would have adversely affected the escape plan, though).

Only a few moments later, they began a staggered line back and forth up the stone steps cut into the cliff. Humans, dwarves, and dwellers aided one another in their bid to escape the goblinkin.

For the first time, Wick thought about how much the rescue attempt was like the Battle of Fell's Keep during the Cataclysm. He only hoped that this present effort didn't end so badly as that one had.

At Bulokk's direction, Wick joined in with the procession toward the end so they could split off once they reached the mine entrance. He went up and his legs ached with the effort. He couldn't remember sleeping last night, and now fatigue was hammering him. He truly wished he were back home, safely in bed at the Vault of All Known Knowledge, the only plunder on his mind one of the books from Hralbomm's Wing that Grandmagister Frollo frowned upon.

The escape proceeded at a snail's pace.

Long minutes later, the goblinkin noticed the escape attempt. It didn't happen the way Wick thought it would, which was pretty much through chance as a goblinkin went to relieve himself, or happened to glance up while a stray beam of moonslight penetrated the cloud cover and highlighted the fleeing prisoners.

Instead, what happened was that one of the escapees became too weak and lost his footing about thirty feet up the cliff face. Panicked, the man grabbed the man next to him and plucked him clean from the steps as well. Both of them screamed as they plummeted to the rocks.

Neither of them moved after they hit. Unconscious or dead, they weren't going to make their escape tonight. Wick felt badly for them. But only for a moment. Then panic exploded within him.

"What was that?" one of the goblinkin guards yelled.

"Something at the back," another called.

Hugging the cliff face because he'd suddenly grown aware of how far he had to fall, Wick glanced below, using his bare feet to search out the next step.

At first, three or four goblinkin started toward the back of the canyon. They took torches from supplies near the campfires.

"Hurry!" Adranis admonished from above.

But even though they were afraid of the goblinkin, the fleeing prisoners were suddenly afraid of the climb, too. Doubtless some had fallen while on their way to the mine from time to time.

The goblinkin guards called out. No answers came. Sensing that something was wrong, several other goblinkin roused from their beds and picked up torches as well. In practically no time at all, a horde of goblinkin had taken up the hunt.

"The prisoners have escaped!" a goblinkin yelled. "The slave pen is empty!"

"Over there!" someone shouted. "They're climbin' the wall to the mine!"

Immediately, the goblinkin started for the steps and the fight began in earnest. Thankfully none of them appeared to have bows. But Wick remembered that the human crew aboard the mystery ship did. And they knew very well how to use them. They didn't leave the vessel, though, presumably choosing to stay aboard and protect it.

Bulokk and two of his warriors protected the flank, using short-hafted axes and shields to alternately attack and defend. Their efforts slowed the goblinkin attack, but also distanced them from their comrades.

"Quickly!" Wick cried out. "Quickly as you can! More help is waiting at the top! Quickly!" As he moved, he helped the elderly human behind him, grabbing him once before he lost his balance and tumbled over the side.

Loose stone, Wick discovered, also made footing more problematic. But it also gave him an idea.

Adranis reached the mine entrance first.

Wick thought about passing the mine entrance by and continuing up the steps. It would have been safer to do so, but he wouldn't have gotten the opportunity to see if Rohoh was right about the axe. He stepped off the steps only with extreme reluctance.

A torch flared to life, causing Wick to jump a little.

"Well, halfer," Adranis said, "I see ye made it."

"I did," Wick agreed. But he didn't know how the dwarven warrior felt about that, or if he felt any way at all.

Hodnes and another dwarf stood inside the mineshaft with Adranis. The shaft was narrow and long, swallowed up in darkness beyond the reach of the torchlight. Scars from the iron wheels of mine carts scored the stone floor. Four carts lined the wall.

Wick ran to the carts and peered inside. "Here," he pointed to the first two. "Pour this one into that one."

"What?" Adranis demanded.

Grabbing hold of the cart, Wick barely managed to shift one of the wheels from the floor. "If you want to help Bulokk and the others, listen to me. *Empty this cart into the other one.*" Despite the fact that he'd been yelling loud enough that he heard his voice echo down the mineshaft, Wick didn't really think the dwarves would listen. In fact, he didn't know to whom he thought he was to give orders.

Surprisingly, Adranis and the others put the torches aside and helped him lift the cart. Outside the door, the last of the escaping prisoners filed by. The gap opened up between them and Bulokk's delaying action.

"To the entrance!" Wick yelled. "Hurry!" He pushed the cart and—unbelievably—got it moving. The wheels creaked.

With the dwarves' help, Wick got the cart outside to the steps but he made sure to leave room for Bulokk and the others to get by. They were below, in anvil formation, taking the blows of the goblinkin on their raised shields. A dwarven prisoner filled out the quad formation.

"Here!" Wick yelled. But he was so scared he felt like he was going to throw up. Despite Hallekk and Cobner's efforts to train him, he wasn't a warrior. He was a Librarian. Thankfully, as such, his mind was his greatest weapon. He leaned down and chocked the cart's wheels. "Come on now!"

"Axes!" Bulokk roared.

The dwarves shifted into attack mode and chopped at the goblinkin, temporarily driving them back. A few of them fell, but others fell in pieces. Bulokk and his warriors were merciless.

"Back!" Bulokk ordered.

The dwarves moved together, thundering up the steps. Bulokk was bleeding from three or four wounds, but none of them appeared serious. At the bottom of the landing, the goblinkin regrouped and charged up after the dwarves.

Wick shoved on the cart, rocking it against the chocks. "Turn it over!"

Adranis and the others helped Wick lift the cart. A cascade of small rocks tumbled free and skidded down the steps. The initial plunge knocked a few of the goblinkin down, but the loose rocks tripped others. They screamed as they fell.

"Great idea," Rohoh said, hanging onto Wick's shoulder tightly.

"Thanks," Wick said. He stood watching till the goblinkin got everything sorted and started back up the steps more slowly.

"You're not as useless as you look."

Wick frowned, but he didn't let Rohoh's unkind words rip the glow of victory from him.

"Maybe you should get into the mine," the skink suggested.

A goblinkin threw a club that smacked into the wall only a few feet from Wick's head.

"You're probably right," Wick said. He ducked back inside the mine entrance.

A quick glance up the steps revealed that the last of the fleeing prisoners was now disappearing over the crest of the ridge.

Inside the mineshaft, Bulokk picked up one of the lit torches and wiped blood from his face. He had his shield slung over his back along with his battle-axe, and carried a short-hafted double-bitted axe in his other hand.

"That was quick thinkin', halfer," Bulokk said.

Wick nodded. "It won't buy us much time."

Bulokk grinned. "Then we'd best make the most of it, shouldn't we?" He nodded toward the other dwarf. "This here's Rassun. He knows this mine an' has an idea about what the goblinkin is after an' who owns that ship down to the pier." He nodded toward the mineshaft. "We can talk on the way."

Wick struggled to keep up with the dwarves as they ran pell-mell through the mineshaft. The flames clinging to the torches fluttered and snapped as they ran. Within a short distance, the mineshaft split into three different shafts.

"Which way?" Bulokk asked.

Rohoh stood on Wick's shoulder. The lizard's tongue flicked into the air a few times. "To the right."

"Ye have a talkin' lizard?" Rassun asked. He was fairly emaciated from his long imprisonment and the harsh life afforded at the mine. Scars crisscrossed his face and hands, offering testimony to past battles and hardships. Gray streaked his long, ill-kept brown hair.

"Aye," Bulokk replied. "An' one that knows what we're seekin'."

Only a short distance ahead, the mineshaft split again, but this time the choices were up and down.

"Down," Rohoh said before anyone could ask.

Bulokk plunged ahead, holding his torch high. Shadows swirled and twirled around on the narrow walls of the shaft.

In several places, building blocks and archways—the bones of the old dwarven city that had existed aboveground before the island sank or was covered in lava—showed through. Before he knew it, Wick stopped at one of them and studied the inscriptions he found there.

There weren't many words, of course, because the author had been dwarven. Most of the dwarven languages that had existed before the Cataclysm forced everyone to learn a common tongue were abbreviated. Except when it came to forging and armament. In those areas, the dwarven language waxed eloquent.

The inscription was in the Cinder Clouds Islands dwarven tongue. It was also short and to the point.

Welcome
This is Master Blacksmith Oskarr's Forge
Metalwork Done Here
Intruders Will Be Killed

"Halfer!" Bulokk called. "What are ye a-waitin' on? Fer them goblinkin to catch up?"

"No." Wick struggled to take his eyes from the stone block. He pointed. "This was a warning to everyone who entered Master Oskarr's Forge. This stone was once placed at the entrance to the master blacksmith's inner circle." Drawn by other stones with engravings, he stepped slowly toward them to begin a deeper examination.

"How do ye know that?" Bulokk asked.

"Why, it's plain as the nose on your face," Wick said, not thinking. He was so used to having to explain to Novice Librarians that he didn't realize what he was doing. "That's written in the original Cinder Clouds Islands dwarven language." He wiped at the blocks in front of him.

"Hey!" Rohoh whispered in Wick's ear. "Ixnay onay ethay eadingray."

It took Wick a second to process the broken verbal language the skink used. In all his years, Wick hadn't heard it more than a handful of times. *Nix on the reading*. Only then did he realize what he'd said.

"Writ, is it?" Bulokk asked. Suddenly he was there in front of Wick, a grim look on his face. "Ye can read, can ye, halfer?"

Wick cringed back, but the wall was behind him. He held his hand up with only a small gap between his thumb and forefinger. "Maybe a *little*."

"A little, is it?"

Wick waited, heart beating frantically.

"Okay," Rohoh said, "so the halfer can read. A little. You can teach a monkey to wear clothes. Doesn't mean it suits him."

"Goblinkin kills them what can read," Drinnick said. He added his glare to Bulokk's. "They hate readin' an' writin'."

"It's not like the goblinkin aren't already after us to kill us," Rohoh said.

Wick glanced at the skink and wished he would shut up.

"Is that how ye come to know all them stories ye told us?" Adranis asked.

"Yes," Wick said. "The wizard that sent me has a few books. He taught me to read." Guilt stung him as he lied. Grandmagister Ludaan had given him the gift of reading, as the Grandmagister had done for hundreds of other dwellers who were brought into service to the Vault of All Known Knowledge. But he didn't want to reveal anything about the Library.

Adranis turned to the other dwarves. "Think about all them stories he's done went an' told us over the last few days. Stories *we* didn't know, or only halfway misremembered." His voice thickened. "He give us a gift is what he done. Without him, we wouldn't know where to even start lookin' for Master Oskarr's battle-axe."

"Master Oskarr's battle-axe?" Rassun echoed. "That's what the goblinkin are here lookin' for."

Bulokk wheeled on the onetime slave. "What?"

"The goblinkin," Rassun said. "They've been a-lookin' fer Master Oskarr's axe, too. That's why they've had us a-rootin' around in these caves."

"Maybe we could be moving while we're talking," Rohoh suggested sarcastically. "Or does standing around waiting for the goblinkin to catch up to us work for you?"

Wick raised his torch and studied the engravings made into the stones again.

"Do they tell ye anythin'?" Adranis asked. His voice was softer than normal.

Unconsciously, Wick raked dust and earth from the lines of the etchings. "These engravings," he said, "tell me that we're near Master Oskarr's forge. It also tells me some of the history that the town faced while they were here. This was part of the town's history wall, a place where travelers could visit and see much of what had taken place here."

Adranis pointed toward a block showing a goblinkin and ships out in the harbor. "Was this attack part of the Cataclysm?"

Wick rubbed the inscription across the top and translated the words with ease. "No. This was from hundreds of years before that. A goblinkin slaver raid that followed on the heels of a storm."

"An' did the goblinkin succeed?" Adranis asked.

Shaking his head, Wick grinned. Happiness filled him. "No. I recognize this story. This was Farrad's Stand."

"Farrad was Master Oskarr's da," Adranis said.

"He was," Wick agreed. "But he was also Master Blacksmith during his time. The goblinkin slavers came in greater numbers that year than ever before. There was some talk that the storm that ravaged the coastline was summoned by a wizard so the goblinkin would have an easier time of it."

The next block showed dwarven warriors standing on a bridge above two massive stone gates. Since Wick hadn't seen those gates when they'd sailed in, he assumed that they'd been lost during the Cataclysm.

"Master Farrad stood with his warriors above the gates to Hammer Cove."

Wick indicated an oval of islands and reefs that included the dwarven forge. "Hammer Cove was held together by the Treaty of Vovaln, which was made when the Master Blacksmiths all acknowledged Master Sarant—one of Master Oskarr's ancestors—as the greatest among them. In exchange, Master Sarant taught those blacksmiths and their sons all the secrets of his forge. That was when the Cinder Clouds Islands armor became prominent among warriors."

"I didn't know that," Adranis said.

"There's a lot you don't know," Rohoh said. "Like where Master Oskarr's axe is. Come on!" He marched to the end of Wick's shoulder and halfway down his biceps like it was a bridge.

Wick shifted his attention back to the previous stone. "Master Farrad and his warriors triumphed against the goblinkin slavers. In fact, the beating the goblinkin received was so vicious that no slavers ever again tried their luck in the Cinder Clouds Islands."

"Not until the Cataclysm," Adranis said in a low voice.

"The goblinkin didn't try to enslave dwarves then," Wick said. "They came only to finish the destruction of the forges."

"They've been enslavin' ever since. An' now they're here to steal Master Oskarr's axe."

"Running," Rohoh said. "Us. Going to go get that axe. Does that sound familiar?"

Ignoring the skink, Wick turned his attention to Rassun. "How long have the goblinkin been here looking for Master Oskarr's axe?"

"Three, mayhap four, years," Rassun answered. "I been here the last five months. Been right hard work we been doin'."

"Why are they looking for the axe?"

"Them thieves hired 'em to."

"What thieves?" Bulokk asked.

"Them in the black ship."

"They're thieves?" Wick asked.

"Aye. What did ye take 'em fer?"

"Slavers."

Rassun spat and shook his shaggy head. "They're thieves. Part of some guild down to Wharf Rat's Warren."

Wick had only heard rumors of Wharf Rat's Warren. Located far into the Deep Frozen North, the port city provided a haven for the murderers and cutthroats that profited from robbery and death. Filled with pirates, thieves, and assassins, Wharf Rat's Warren was a lawless place of superstition, avarice, and double-cross.

"Why would a thieves' guild be interested in Master Oskarr's battle-axe?" Wick asked.

Rohoh marched back up Wick's arm. "Because they want Craugh to keep from finding out the truth of what happened at the Battle of Fell's Keep!"

"What good would that do?" Wick asked.

"If Craugh can find out what truly happened during that battle," the skink replied, "he might be able to engineer a peace treaty along the mainland that can start to rebuild the Unity."

The Unity.

The words struck a chord deep within Wick. Was this what it was truly all about? This mission that Craugh had sent him on? If that was what the stakes had been, why hadn't Craugh told him?

Because you'd have gotten scared, Wick told himself. *Just the way you're doing now.*

He was a Librarian, not part of a diplomatic corps. He wasn't trained to deal in the fates of nations. Well, now that there weren't truly any nations left, he supposed he couldn't be afraid of that, but he couldn't be responsible for the fates of towns or even small villages. Give him a book and he could translate or copy it (provided it was written in one of the many languages he knew and read), or ask him to give reports about any number of subjects and he could do that.

"If 'n the goblinkin find Master Oskarr's axe," Bulokk asked, "what are they gonna do with it?"

"I don't know," Rassun said. "But I'm guessin' they're gonna destroy it. Get rid of it once an' fer all."

Goblinkin yells echoed within the mineshaft, some of them near and some of them far. It was so confusing it was hard to tell where they were.

"They'll have split up to look for us," Rassun said. "It'll make for smaller search parties, but once they find us they'll come a-runnin'. Ain't no way back out of the mineshaft 'cept through the entrance. Ye can wager they'll put guards over that."

"Escape is all about the timin'," Adranis said. "We'll worry 'bout that *after* we get Master Oskarr's battle-axe."

"That ain't gonna be easy," Rassun said. "The goblinkin got creatures what helps 'em with the diggin'."

"What creatures?" Bulokk demanded.

14

Master Oskarr's Forge

"They call them Burrowers," Rassun said as they ran. "They look like giant worms. If worms had mouths big enough to swallow boulders the size of cows."

"How do they help the goblinkin with the diggin'?" Bulokk asked.

Rassun waved at the mineshaft. "Burrowers dug this mineshaft."

Wick glanced around at the mineshaft, which was at least eight feet in diameter. For the first time he saw how smooth the walls were. They hadn't been made by pickaxes. There were no tool marks. He thought back to the bestiaries and ecologies he'd read while at the Vault of All Known Knowledge.

Since he'd begun his journeys along the mainland, Wick had increasingly read more about flora and fauna and animals he'd found and would probably find there. Several of them he hoped he'd never meet, but there were others he looked forward to seeing.

But a Burrower? He'd never heard of a Burrower. At least not as the name of a species.

"When the goblinkin were first set to this task," Rassun said, "the thieves were unhappy with the amount of progress they were makin'. They brought over the first Burrower, then they brought over three more."

"What do they do?" Bulokk asked.

"They eat through the rock," Rassun said. "Faster than a pickaxe. 'Course, ye gotta clean up after 'em. They digest what minerals they want outta them rocks, then the rest passes on through."

"Ye mean ye're a-shoveling worm—"

"Aye," Rassun said. "But it ain't as grim as ye'd believe. They break the big rocks into little rocks. Most of 'em ain't no bigger than yer fist when they pass through."

"Does it stink?" Drinnick asked.

Wick couldn't believe they were running for their lives and the dwarven warrior thought to ask such a question.

"No," Rassun answered. "Ain't no foulness to it." Torchlight played across his emaciated face and showed the grimace carved there. "Leastways, ain't no foulness to it when them Burrowers just eats rocks. They eat a dwarf or an elf, it's a whole different tale I have to tell ye."

"Burrowers eat people?" Wick asked. Now that, he believed, was an important question to ask.

"Aye," Rassun said. "Burrowers eats flesh an' blood people like they was gingersnaps. One gulp an' a body's gone afore he even knows he's been et."

With all the wonders of the world, Wick wondered again why so many of the large ones seemed intent merely to eat everything else out there.

"What passes through a Burrower, the leavin's of a man or a beast," Rassun said, "why there ain't enough to fill a hat, there ain't. Bone chips. There's something in a person or an animal that don't quite agree with them. An' once they get the taste of blood, why Burrowers becomes a danger to the goblinkin for days. They have to keep 'em penned up till they forget they ever had the taste of flesh an' blood. 'Course, Burrowers, they ain't exactly long on memory."

"Left," Rohoh announced when they came upon another choice of three tunnels.

Bulokk took the lead, thrusting his torch into the opening and following it down. Wick's attention was divided as he saw still more stones that had once been part of Master Oskarr's town. The little Librarian's heart ached to pass up all the treasures from the past without even taking time to make rubbings of the stones.

"Where did they get the Burrowers?" Wick asked.

"Ain't exactly sure," Rassun answered. "There's a rumor that some wizard magicked 'em up fer the thieves' guild."

So they might not even be natural creatures, Wick thought. He immediately felt better about his lack of knowledge about the Burrowers. He had friends among the elven warders on Greydawn Moors and often talked with them about their creatures and others they'd seen or heard of in their own craft.

"How much farther?" Bulokk asked.

Clinging to Wick's shoulder and hair, Rohoh said, "Not much. We're almost there."

The band kept running through the darkness.

All the while, Wick wondered if the other escapees had made it over the ridge and if the dwarves Bulokk had posted there were canny enough to hold what they had. Even then, they'd have to have a lot of luck to take one of the goblinkin ships without getting killed.

Wick fretted over how things would eventually turn out. Then he realized he might not even live long enough to find out.

Long minutes later, the mineshaft Rohoh directed them to opened up into a large chamber. Given that they'd been running steadily downhill for nearly the whole time, Wick knew they were well below sea level. He didn't like thinking about that.

But his fears quickly evaporated as Bulokk held his torch high and revealed the surroundings. The torchlight didn't reach far enough to reveal the rest of the chamber, but if it was anything like what Wick saw before him it would have been an impressive sight.

Elegantly made buildings, homes as well as shops, stood out from the cave walls. The dwarven structures had been carved from quarried rock that was bluish-white and no match at all for the reddish-alabaster of the native stone.

"They used different stone to make the city," Bulokk said in awe.

"They did," Wick agreed. "I'd forgotten." Holding his torch high, he walked to the nearest building and ran his hand along the smooth sides of the stone. "Back when Hammer Cove's homestone was laid—"

"Homestone?" Rassun asked.

Wick looked at the dwarf in disbelief. How could a dwarf not know his roots? Then the little Librarian realized how much had truly been lost in the Cataclysm.

"A homestone," Adranis said in a voice filled with quiet reverence, "was the first stone laid of the first building built in a true dwarven city. A lot of thinking went into it, into the making of it, because it carried the hopes and dreams of the dwarves who built it. They carved images of history, legend, and aspirations on all six sides of the homestone and imbued it with all their love."

Adranis's voice carried throughout the empty space, indicating just how large it was.

"Then," Bulokk said, "the homestone was laid as cornerstone of the first building an' the city began."

"That's correct," Wick said. "As I was saying, back when Hammer Cove's homestone was laid, the builders decided to choose a rock not overly natural to the area. They wanted stone that could be found wherever there were dwarves. So they chose this." He tapped the rock and it made a hollow sound. "Limestone. Wherever there is a dwarven city, there is generally limestone. Even here in the Cinder Clouds Islands."

"But ye don't find much of it here in the islands," Adranis said.

Wick nodded. "Still, they quarried some of it. For the rest, though, they took in donations. Together, they built a city for all dwarves who wanted to learn to forge in the heart of a volcano."

"Volcano?" Rohoh piped up. "I suppose that's why I feel so hot."

For the first time, Wick noticed the heat as well. He'd been too overcome with worry and fear to be aware of it earlier.

"We're sitting on top of a volcano, aren't we?" the skink demanded.

"Aye," Bulokk said. He raked a massive arm across his sweating brow. "It is gettin' a mite heated in here."

"It's the forge," Rassun said. "It's still operational."

"Master Oskarr's forge?" Bulokk whispered.

"Aye." Rassun smiled grimly. "I been a miner all me life. Wasn't one to ever be overly interested in the makin' of things. I prefer findin' them in the earth. Give me a rich vein of gold or a gem mine, an' I'm happy as can be. But I ain't no blacksmith. Nor did I ever wish to be."

Following Rohoh's directions, the group of dwarves and Wick walked through the center of Hammer Cove. The buildings were three and four stories tall, straight and square. Many of them showed signs of stress fractures that ran through the stone, but nearly all of them were whole. But there were obvious places where others had once stood.

Since there were no pieces of buildings in the main walkways or in the buildings, Wick assumed that the goblinkin had ordered the area cleaned. He hated thinking about all the things that had been thrown away. Much about the past could always be told through everyday utensils in addition to books and records.

"I helped clear some of this area," Rassun said. "When I was first brought here. The goblinkin had most of it done by that time. It took a long time. When the goblinkin found out there were buildings here, an' they was likely to be them what held Master Oskarr's forge, they didn't want anything damaged. They kept the Burrowers out then, 'cause the Burrowers woulda et everything in sight."

"This was all cleared by hand?" Wick asked.

"Way I heard it," Rassun said, "this area was kept pretty much like this. Like a big bubble formed over most of it an' kept it mostly from harm durin' the Cataclysm, an' fer a while when it was under the sea."

"A bubble?" Bulokk repeated.

"Aye," Rassun said.

"It could have been caused by the heat of the forge," Wick mused. "If the volcano that fed the forge didn't erupt, that might explain it."

"I was also told Master Oskarr's forge was protected by magic," Bulokk said. "I heard that a wizard put a protective glamour over the forge."

"I don't know about that," Wick said. "Dwarves, as a general rule, don't hold with magic."

"But we're inspired by luck at times," Bulokk said. "I could see a dwarf wantin' a bit of good luck for his forge, especially with his family's fortunes an' wellbeing tied to it."

Only a short distance farther on, with Rohoh growing more excited with every step, Wick and the dwarves found themselves standing in front of an arched doorway that stood ten feet tall, an impressive height to a dwarf, though not so much to a human.

Engravings and writing stood out on the beautiful stonework. The engravings showed images of war and weapons, of brave warriors locked in battles where they'd just cut down enemies and ferocious beasts while dressed in beautiful armor and carrying splendid weapons.

The writing over the doorway simply bore the legend: *Welcome to Master Oskarr's Forge. If you're a friend, you have nothing to fear. If you're an enemy, may you die on one of our finely crafted weapons.* Baldly stated, but there it was.

Inspired by their good fortune, the dwarves took fresh grips on their weapons and strode through the forge entrance. It was smaller than Wick thought it would be. From the descriptions of the forge, he'd believed it would be huge, a vast series of anvils, one after the other. It was said that Master Oskarr had an anvil for every piece of armor that he made. Of course, Wick had mistrusted that piece of information because dwarves learned how to make everything they ever wanted to primarily on one anvil.

Without the ringing of dwarven hammers against metal, the forge seemed surreal, unfinished. Cracks ran the length of the floor, testifying to the elemental forces that had ripped through the city as lava covered it. Despite the goblinkin's orders to clean the area, gray ash still collected on most surfaces.

At the far side of the room, a pit of molten lava burned red-gold behind a cracked stone wall. The heat rolled over Wick and covered him in sweat at once. The lava stirred restlessly, like a baker's bread dough, constantly folding into itself as the top cooled and the hotter liquid rock below bubbled up to take its place.

Anvils lay tumbled from the specially carved stone tables. Engravings decorated each of the tables, making each unique.

As if under some spell, the dwarves slowly made their way through the forge, touching each anvil and each stone table in awe. Mesmerized as well, Wick followed them. His quick hands darted over the engravings.

Unable to help himself, he took out his journal and began taking quick sketchings, but only of images that he didn't recognize or couldn't tie into one of the dwarven stories he'd been told. None of the dwarves even took an interest in him.

"We were sent here to get Master Oskarr's battle-axe," Rohoh said.

"I know," Wick said. "But—but—*this* is *history*." Journal in one hand and charcoal in the other, he gestured at the forge. "Can you even imagine the armor and weapons that came from this place? The blacksmiths that toiled here? Can you imagine what their lives were like? The hardships they had to endure?"

"Getting attacked by Lord Kharrion was probably pretty bad," the skink mused. "Probably even worse than if the goblinkin and those thieves catch the lot of us down here in this forge."

Wick craned his head around to face the skink. He focused on the lizard's face, then remembered again the danger they were in. There was, after all, only one way out of the forge.

"Where is Master Oskarr's axe?" Wick asked.

"There." Rohoh pointed toward the bubbling lava.

"Where?"

"In the forge."

Wick regarded the molten mass. "It can't be. If the axe were in there, it'd be melted to slag by now."

"It's not."

Although he didn't want to believe it, Wick put his journal and charcoal away. Slowly, he made his way through the overturned anvils and studied the lava pit.

"Where are ye a-goin', halfer?" Adranis growled.

"To find the axe," Wick replied, his mind searching desperately for a way the skink's words could be true. Even dwarven-forged iron couldn't stand the heat of lava. Especially not a thousand years and more of it.

Wick's announcement drew everyone's attention. They abandoned whatever had distracted them and fell in with him. Close up to the rolling lava, the torches were no longer necessary because the bright glow filled the immediate surroundings.

"Where's the axe?" Bulokk demanded.

"He says it's in the forge," Wick answered.

The expressions on the dwarven faces around him told him at once that they didn't believe him.

Wick took an involuntary step back from them and pointed to the skink. "He's the one saying it. Not me."

Bulokk cursed. "Only a fool would believe that. Ain't no way even Master Oskarr's axe would escape bein' burnt to a crisp."

"It's there," Rohoh insisted. He slithered to the end of Wick's arm, then sprang to the low lip of the retaining wall holding the molten lava back. "I *smell* it. And I'm never wrong."

"Nobody's ever never wrong," Adranis said.

"Well," the lizard mused, scratching his chin in thought, "there was that one time in the Wizard Ekkal's treasure room that I was . . . incorrect. But how was I supposed to know that the Cup of Weligan had been turned into a person? I mean, that just hadn't been done before. In the end, though, I was right and just didn't know it."

Together, Wick and all the dwarves peered closely into the lava pit. Wick got so close the heat nearly blistered his face. Tears filled his eyes and dropped into the lava. They hissed into steam before they even reached the molten rock.

Suddenly, Drinnick yelped. He danced away from the lava pit, flailing with his free hand at the flames in his beard from where he'd gotten too close. The smell of burning hair filled the air. By the time he'd reduced the flames to smoking patches, his once beautiful beard was a charred mess.

Angry, he raised his axe and strode toward Rohoh. "Ye vexin' little varmint! Why I oughtta pound ye into jelly, I should! An' mayhap I will at that!"

"Wick!" the lizard squeaked, scampering along the wide lip of the retaining wall.

"You're on your own," Wick told the skink.

With incredible athletic ability, the lizard leaped and caught hold of the smooth wall. His claws managed to find precarious holds and he scampered up toward the roof and stopped out of Drinnick's reach. He stuck his tongue out, cursed, and waved a threatening clawed fist.

Wick ignored them and turned his mind to solving the puzzle. If Rohoh was right, and there was no reason other than logic that dictated the skink was wrong, then Master Oskarr's axe lay somewhere in the lava pit.

"What are ye a-lookin' fer?" Bulokk asked.

"Aren't there tongs somewhere?" Wick asked. "Isn't the metal heated and softened by plunging it into the lava?"

"Aye," Bulokk said. "That's one of the secrets of a lava pit. Fire-hardenin' the metal is a lot easier." He started looking around as well. "An' they did use tongs. An' a sieve in case somethin' were dropped." He raised his voice and gave orders to his men to find those tools.

They scattered with their torches. Even Drinnick abandoned his pursuit of the skink to help.

15

Unwanted Truth

The tools, tongs, and the sieve—all equipped with long metal poles encased with wooden handgrips at the end—were quickly found. Bulokk and some of the others began sorting through the lava pit, but they had to frequently stop because even with the wooden grips to cut down on the heat transfer, the metal got too hot.

Hodnes was even able, through the use of padded gloves and iron will, to leave one set of tongs in so long that the metal turned liquid and dripped off at the end. The other dwarves cursed and slapped Hodnes for ruining one of their tools.

"It's no use, halfer," Bulokk said after a while. "If that axe is in there, it ain't comin' out." He spat. "This is a fool's errand, is what it is. I just hope them prisoners got away of a piece."

And I hope we can do the same, Wick thought. "The axe has got to be there."

"It can't be here," Rassun said, coming over to them. "I tell ye, them goblinkin's been all over this area. After them Burrowers uncovered this part of the city, especially when they found the forge, they went over every inch of it. If Master Oskarr's axe had been here, they'd have found it."

Wick's mind examined all the angles, looking for a lever. He lifted his torch and gazed at the anvils. "Where is Master Oskarr's anvil?"

"Over here." Bulokk led the way to one of the anvils.

Rather than the pristine thing he'd thought it would be, Wick saw a battered, much-used anvil sitting on the floor. The anvil arms were still straight, and every line looked as though it planed true. But stamped on the sides, the design still bravely cut, was Master Blacksmith Oskarr's forge mark. The design showed a hammer upright over an anvil, declaring the owner to be a full master of title and rank, with Oskarr's name and the Cinder Clouds Islands symbol below.

"Where's his table?" Wick asked when he found that the anvil was devoid of further illustration. Evidently Master Oskarr hadn't cared much for bragging.

A quick search ensued before Adranis found the table. "Here," he called.

The table lay on its side. A corner was chipped from it, but otherwise it was unharmed. Soot and ash covered much of its surface.

After tearing a sleeve from his shirt, Wick set to work cleaning all the images.

"Is there anythin' there about the Battle of Fell's Keep?" Bulokk demanded.

"No," Wick answered. And he couldn't help thinking how strange that was. Had Master Oskarr deliberately chosen not to reveal anything about that fight? Were the rumors true? The little Librarian sincerely hoped not.

Then, in small writing around the edge of the table, barely discernible in the torchlight, Wick found the newest entry, dated over a thousand years ago.

"What is it ye've found?" Bulokk knelt beside the little Librarian.

"This is the last entry on the table," Wick said. "It's written in an archaic dwarven tongue. The old language of the Ringing Iron Clan in the Iron Hammer Peaks."

"Master Oskarr's ma was from the Ringing Iron Clan," Bulokk said. "But I never heard of the Iron Hammer Peaks."

"They're called the Broken Forge Mountains now," Wick said idly. He translated the inscription with no little difficulty. The Ringing Iron Clan had always been small. "In addition to destroying Teldane's Bounty—which is now renamed the Shattered Coast—Lord Kharrion also made a deal with the dragon Shengharck to take over the Iron Hammer Peaks. The dragon lived there." He paused, remembering the dragon's treasure lair at the heart of the volcano where he and Cobner had fought for their lives. "Until very recently."

"The Ringing Iron Clan worked metal in volcanoes as well," Bulokk said.

"Yes." Wick nodded. "But they were never as successful as the Iron Hammer Peaks Clan. Many of the Ringing Iron Clan was apprenticed by the Iron Hammer Peaks Clan."

"That's how Master Oskarr's ma was born out here," Bulokk said. "But all I knew was that a few dwarven blacksmiths from near Teldane's Bounty ended up on the shores of the Cinder Clouds Islands. I don't remember anything being said about the Iron Hammer Peaks." He leaned in closer to Wick. "Can ye read it then, halfer?"

Satisfied with his translation, Wick started over at the beginning and read aloud in his best voice. " 'Let it be known that we are facing the end. Lord Kharrion has come calling for us, and we are all prepared to die this day. Let none say there were cowards among us, because we all stand prepared to shed our life's blood fighting the Goblin King. We are not merely blacksmiths, but we are warriors, too.' "

"Aye," Bulokk whispered, "they was. An' fierce ones, too."

" 'I fought Lord Kharrion's forces at the Battle of Fell's Keep.' " Wick's heart raced as the translation came faster and easier. " 'There we were betrayed.' "

"They *was* betrayed!" Bulokk said. "There's proof enough fer ye that it wasn't Master Oskarr who betrayed the Unity!"

Wick didn't agree with that assessment, but he wisely kept his thoughts to himself. He wasn't fleet of foot enough to scamper to the top of the room as Rohoh had been. He continued with the translation.

" 'My axe,' " Wick read, " 'that I forged myself under the watchful eye of my da, Master Blacksmith Farrad, was cursed during that battle.' "

"*Cursed*!" Bulokk exploded. He grabbed Wick roughly by the shoulder and shook him, feet dangling above the ground. "What do ye mean the axe was cursed?"

Out of self-defense, Wick grabbed onto the dwarf 's big hand. "I don't know. I'm just reading this part, too." He looked into Bulokk's eyes and saw the fear and hatred there, whipped into flames by the orange glow of the lava furnace. "Let me finish, Bulokk. This is what I do. For good or ill, this is what I can do."

"I don't want to hear Master Oskarr's good name sullied," Bulokk said harshly. His statement was a threat in Wick's ears.

"I know," Wick whispered. "I don't know what that inscription says, but I could lie to you." He paused. "If that's what you want." Hanging above the ground as he was, the little Librarian had to admit to himself that he'd have told the dwarven leader anything he wanted to hear at that moment.

Adranis stepped forward and put an arm around Bulokk. He looked at the younger dwarf and spoke calmly. "Is that what ye want, Bulokk? A lie? Even if it's a good one?"

Bulokk didn't take his eyes from Wick. "This was a mistake," the dwarf choked out. "We shouldn't ever have come here."

"Likely as not, there's a lot of freed slaves out there that don't feel all we done this night was for naught," Adranis said. "We done forged some good outta tonight. Freed them prisoners. Killed some goblinkin. No matter what else happens, we done that." He took a measured breath. "Now ye decide what ye want: the truth or the lie. An' try not to scare this little halfer so much that he ain't got him enough backbone to give ye the truth if it is bad."

Wick hung helplessly at the end of Bulokk's arm. *Where are Craugh and* One-Eyed Peggie*? It can't get any worse than this!*

Slowly, Bulokk uncurled his fingers and let Wick drop to the stone floor. The little Librarian's knees were shaking so bad that he fell on his rump.

"The truth then, halfer," Bulokk growled. "An' I'll know if 'n ye try to lie to me."

"The truth," Adranis said, reaching down to help Wick to his feet. "Bulokk's made of stern stuff. He can take it."

Trembling, Wick turned back to the inscription. He traced his finger along it, finding his place. " 'I didn't know about the curse till later,' " Wick read. " 'We were too busy escaping, running for our lives after the sickness took so many of us and rendered so many others unable to fight. Then, back on the Cinder Clouds Islands and once more in this forge, I began to have nightmares of Lord Kharrion.

He and others whom I can't name tried to talk to me. Every day their voices became more clear.' "

Bulokk growled.

Wick lifted his hands, covering his head and thinking that wouldn't truly help because then his head would be lopped off only with his hands holding onto it. He closed his eyes.

The blow didn't come.

"Continue," Adranis stated quietly, stepping up to place himself between Wick and Bulokk.

Wick didn't know if Adranis was there to reassure him, which it did, a little, or to stop Bulokk in case he couldn't control himself—which kind of wiped out all the reassurance. He turned back to the inscription, driven as much by curiosity as survival.

" 'Afraid of the nightmares, I tried to destroy the axe,' " Wick went on. " 'You will never know how hard this was to contemplate, let alone try to accomplish. The axe, *my* axe, would not break or bend on my anvil no matter how hard I tried. The magic that had infected it had become too much a part of it.' "

Silence hung over the dwarves. Wick was certain that none of them could imagine trying to destroy something they had worked so hard to make. That was a true horror for them, and the curse only made the story more horrific.

" 'In despair, I sank the axe into the lava furnace and hoped that Lord Kharrion's forces wouldn't find it there. The axe,' " Wick read, " 'was one of the main reasons the goblinkin invaded the Cinder Clouds Islands.' "

"They came fer the axe," Hodnes said.

"An' they're still here today a-lookin' fer it," Drinnick said.

The fact amazed them all.

There is so much Craugh didn't tell me about this task, Wick thought. But he focused on the words and continued his translation. " 'Years ago, my da, Master Blacksmith Farrad, made home of this forge to an elemental being named Merjul. He is a fire elemental, one of those few oddities that exist even after the Darkling Times that came before Lord Kharrion, when it was said the Old Ones warred and destroyed several of the worlds they had created.' "

"An elemental?" one of the dwarves whispered. "There's no tellin' what one of them things will do. Likely as not, it'll melt ye down in yer tracks as look at ye."

Wick sincerely hoped not because he knew Bulokk wouldn't be able to let the matter rest. " 'Unless Merjul has died in Lord Kharrion's attack, he will still remain there. If you are of my blood, if you know the names of your ancestors, then you may call upon Merjul and he will bring you the axe from the fiery depths. Have a care, though, for the axe is cursed. My only wish is that you find a way to free it because it is the most beautiful weapon I've ever hammered out upon my anvil.' " He looked up at Bulokk. "It's signed, 'Master Blacksmith Oskarr.' "

Without a word, Bulokk crossed to the lava furnace. "Merjul!" he spoke in a loud voice.

Drawn by curiosity but well basted in fear, Wick followed. He stood beside Bulokk, hoping that the dwarven leader wasn't drawing down the wrath of an elemental. Not many lived through such a thing.

"Merjul!" Bulokk called again, impatient this time.

At first, the surface of the lava pit merely continued to roil. Then, out in the center, something *moved*. Lava elongated in a bubble, then suddenly popped and a fearsome, hulking creature stood atop the lava.

Elementals, Wick knew, could take myriad shapes. All of those shapes were fluid, based more on power than on any kind of skeletal frame. That was only one of the things that made them so hard to destroy.

Merjul stood at least nine feet tall, fiery skin smooth as worn stone and the color of ochre. The facial features were ill-defined, consisting only of two eyes and a mouth like a slash. Reflections of shimmering heat twisted against his skin. He faced Bulokk.

"Who are you?" the elemental asked in a deep, sonorous voice.

"I am Bulokk, descendant of Master Blacksmith Oskarr, come to claim his axe," Bulokk declared.

Wick took a tentative step back. Being intrigued, he'd often found, was something akin to having a death wish.

The elemental appeared unimpressed. "The axe was left with me. That you know my name is one thing, but I was told a true descendant would know all Master Blacksmith Oskarr's lineage. He said that his descendant would know that."

"I do know the lineage," Bulokk declared.

"Then give it to me," the elemental challenged. "And know that if you fail, you will die."

"I am Bulokk, son of Farrad, son of Thumak, son of Azzmod, son of—"

"You're an imposter!" the elemental shouted. The fiery eyes narrowed and the slit of a mouth tightened in anger. "You don't know the lineage." Bending, he reached down into the lava and cupped a handful of molten rock. With the speed of a thought, the lava shot out in both directions and became a heavy war spear with a flared head. He poised to throw it, and there was no doubt that his target was Bulokk.

Bulokk raised his shield, which—in Wick's opinion—seemed like a pathetic thing to do. It was obvious that the elemental would strike the dwarf down.

The other dwarves scattered, except for Adranis, who chose to remain at Bulokk's side.

"Wait!" Wick yelled. Of course, he regretted speaking at once. It was evident that his mind responded much more quickly to solutions to puzzles than to self-preservation.

However, the elemental paused. "Who are you?" the creature demanded imperiously.

"Nobody, but I know why you believe Bulokk is an imposter. Which he isn't."

"He doesn't know the lineage," Merjul insisted.

"*You*," Wick said, "don't know the lineage."

"I was taught—"

"You were taught what the lineage was back in Master Oskarr's time," Wick interrupted, fearing that the elemental would choose to strike at any moment. "But a thousand years have passed since Master Oskarr met his fate in these islands."

Merjul seemed undecided for a moment. He kept the spear resting easily on his shoulder. "A thousand years," he mused. "Truthfully, I didn't count how long I've been here. Time holds no meaning to someone such as I. Even with the sun to mark its passage, I often don't pay attention. Oskarr's friendship, though it lasted years, seems like such a brief thing."

"This," Wick said, "is Master Oskarr's descendant. Blood of his blood. And if you gave your word to Master Oskarr, then you are honor-bound to Bulokk as well."

"Perhaps," Merjul agreed. He shifted his attention to Bulokk. "Tell me the lineage again."

Wick turned to Bulokk. "Again. Only this time begin with Master Oskarr."

Bulokk did. In spite of his fear, his voice rang out clear and strong as he worked back through the dwarven genealogy. At last he was finished, and everyone stood pensive, awaiting the elemental's judgment.

"You are as you claim," Merjul said. "You shall have your ancestor's battle-axe." The thin mouth curved into a frown. "I have to tell you, though, I will be glad to be rid of it. It's been a discomfort the whole time it's been here. The curse laid upon it is a powerful thing." He dropped the lava spear, which took back its original shape, and held forth his empty hand.

A tendril of lava plopped up, then grew like a vine. In its coils was a beautiful dwarven battle-axe. With careless strength, the elemental flung the weapon at Bulokk.

Wick ducked back, watching as Bulokk effortlessly caught the great axe. He fully expected to hear the dwarf yell out in anguish from the super-heated metal.

But Bulokk didn't. He acted as though the axe wasn't hot at all. Awe filled his face as he gazed upon the mirror brightness of the finish. Even after all those years in the lava pit, the wooden haft wasn't scorched. "By the Old Ones!" he gasped. "I have never seen such a blade!"

Merjul smiled. "Now I know for certain you are Master Oskarr's kith and kin. You share his love for the craft."

"With all me heart," Bulokk agreed.

Bowing, the fire elemental said, "Then I am glad I could keep my promise."

"Thank ye," Bulokk said, smiling. "I know me words ain't enough, but they're all I have. If 'n ye ever need anything that I can ever help ye with, let me know."

If we live, Wick thought, remembering the goblinkin even now searching the mineshafts for them.

"Use the battle-axe in good health," Merjul said. "My friend would have wanted that." His face darkened. "But beware the curse. Master Oskarr wanted to trust no one except his own family with the weapon because of that curse."

"Why have you never left here?" Wick asked, unable to curb his curiosity.

"My promise to Master Oskarr held me here," Merjul answered. "Now that I have fulfilled that obligation, I am free to go."

"How?" Wick asked. "You can't travel except through the fire routes."

The elemental smiled. "I can travel. When I wish to. I can walk through the lava rivers that reach under the sea to the mainland, or I can become a candle flame and travel in a lantern. For now, though, I'll explore what's to be had here in the islands. Many things have changed since Lord Kharrion brought his destruction here."

"Wait!" Wick cried. "I have other questions!" *How often do you get to talk to an elemental face-to-face?* Without *dying*?

"This isn't exactly time for a parlor room conversation," Rohoh said. The skink ran across the ceiling and dropped back to Wick's shoulder, curling a claw in his hair at once.

"Another time, perhaps," the elemental said. Then he dropped into the lava and disappeared. The molten rock dimmed at his passing and Wick knew he was gone.

"Well then," Bulokk said, "I suppose it's time we should be findin' out if 'n that escape attempt we planned for the prisoners is workin' out. Luck willing, they should be around the island by now." He slung his own battle-axe and shield, and took up his ancestor's, giving it an experimental swing. "By the Old Ones but this is a fine weapon." He smiled in pleased satisfaction, then took off at a trot.

Wick followed, falling into the middle of the group of dwarves, hoping that they all remained safe. That hope was quickly shattered, though. Only a few tunnels back, surely not even halfway back to the entrance, they were discovered by a goblinkin patrol.

"Halt!" a goblinkin ordered.

Turning, peering between the dwarves, Wick saw nearly twenty goblinkin in a pack just coming out of the mineshaft they needed to pass through in order to get out of the mine.

"There can't be more'n twenty of 'em," Adranis said. "I like the odds just fine."

Apparently so did the other six dwarves. They hefted their weapons. Then another goblinkin patrol closed on them from behind. Wick quickly verified that there were nearly twenty in that group as well.

"By the Old Ones," Adranis said, "most of the goblinkin must have been sent into the mine after us."

"This whole setup has been to secure the return of Master Oskarr's axe," Wick said. "It makes sense that they would safeguard that first."

"Well, it's to our rotten luck," Drinnick snarled. "Twenty goblinkin we could account for. Forty is pressin' the limit."

"In here," Bulokk said, dodging into the mineshaft to his right.

"No!" Rassun cried.

But it was too late. The dwarves, and Wick, had already plunged into the new mineshaft.

"This shaft holds the pens for the Burrowers!"

16

Burrowers!

"By the Old Ones!" Adranis shouted, coming to a stop in front of Wick.

Unable to stop so quickly, Wick ran into the dwarf's backside and fell backward, tripping Hodnes.

"Stupid halfer tanglefoot!" Hodnes yelped. "Walkin' ain't that hard to—"

From the way the dwarf stopped in mid-deprecation, Wick assumed Hodnes had gotten his first sight of the Burrowers, too. It did take the breath away.

The torches lit up the large chamber surprisingly well. Or maybe it only seemed like that because the Burrowers could be seen well enough to inspire instant nightmares.

They were at least thirty feet long and nine feet in diameter, and they lay in a writhing mess at the bottom of a twenty-foot pit. A narrow ledge ran around the pit, but it went in an irregular oval, leaving only the one entrance to the chamber.

Their pale pink and cream skins looked tough as leather but gave them a deceptively harmless appearance. They had no eyes or ears or nostrils, only a huge gaping maw that opened the full diameter of their bodies so they looked on the verge of turning themselves inside out. Rows of serrated teeth occupied the thick purple tongues that showed in the vast hollows of their mouths.

The tongues moved out again and again, like battering rams. Nets made of metal links covered the Burrowers' mouths/faces, though, and every time the tongues came in contact with the net, the tongues would withdraw at once. Chains attached to the nets were locked onto stakes driven deeply into the stone floor of the chamber.

"They can't chew through them metal nets," Rassun said. "An' the goblinkin put some kind of foul-tastin' brew on the net links to keep 'em from tryin'."

"How do they control them?" Wick asked.

"Got riders," Rassun said. "Humans with some kind of magical talisman what allows them to control the Burrowers. A little bit, anyways. If 'n nobody watches after these beasties all the time, why they'll get loose an' wander off on their own. It's hard bringin' 'em back under control."

Wick didn't doubt that. What he had trouble believing was that anyone could exercise any control at any time. He pressed against the wall so hard that the stone dug into his back.

"Ain't any way forward," Bulokk said, face grimy and grim in the torchlight. He nodded back toward the entrance. "Gotta go back through them goblinkin."

Evidently the goblinkin knew that, too. They stood in the doorway, grinning and waiting in anticipation.

"There's only one way we're getting out of here alive," Rohoh yelled into Wick's ear.

Wick had forgotten the skink was riding there. "What?"

"We've got to set a Burrower free," Rohoh said. "Let it chase the goblinkin back."

Wick peered over the side of the pit. "I'm not going down there."

"Why would ye go down there?" Adranis asked, not taking his eyes from the goblinkin.

"The lizard says we should free one of the Burrowers to chase the goblinkin," Wick said.

Peering over the side, Adranis shook his head. "It's just as likely to chase us as them." The other dwarves quickly agreed.

"I've seen what them things can do to flesh an' blood," Rassun said. "I ain't goin' down there."

"We don't have a lot of time to mess about," Rohoh said.

Without warning, white-hot pain flooded Wick's ear. It took him a second to realize that the skink had bitten him, managing to hit one of the few nerves in the ear. Screaming with pain, he tried to knock the skink loose, but it only chomped down harder and tore at his ear. Before Wick knew it, he stepped over the side and fell.

Noooooooooo! Then he hit something hard and leathery, spongy like a melon gone bad. Panicked, totally afraid that he knew exactly where he was, he rolled from his back to his stomach. His torch lay farther down on the ground, burning against the stone floor and driving the four Burrowers away from it. They didn't like heat. He filed that away for future reference even as he plastered his face up against the hide of the Burrower he was currently on.

Then light from other torches flooded the pit as the dwarves and the goblinkin peered down at him. Wick looked around, feeling the Burrower shifting beneath him. He didn't know if he was on top of the creature or clinging to its belly. Maybe it didn't even make those kinds of distinctions.

One thing he became certain of: The Burrower didn't like him on it.

"What are ye a-doin' down there, halfer?" Bulokk demanded. "Ye're gonna get yerself killed! Get back up here!"

For the first time Wick noticed that most of the pain in his ear was gone. The skink had stopped biting him, but it hadn't been lost in the fall. Rohoh clung tightly to his shoulder and hair again, digging his claws in deep.

"Come on, halfer!" the skink cried out. "Get up there and free this thing before the goblinkin kill those dwarves!"

Wick didn't think about freeing the Burrower or saving the dwarves. He only knew he wanted off the gigantic creature, and that the head was probably safer than anywhere else.

Grabbing fistfuls of the Burrower's leathery hide, the little Librarian pulled himself forward. If he reached the head, he was certain he could leap back to the ledge. Falling would no doubt mean instant death, crushed beneath the raw tonnage of the writhing creatures.

By the light of the torches held by the anxious dwarves, Wick reached the chain net that guarded the Burrower's maw. The creature felt him there then, and it gentled somewhat.

It thinks I'm its rider! Wick couldn't believe it, but he took advantage of his good fortune. He gripped the chain and prepared to leap to the ledge. Unfortunately, at that moment the Burrower chose to shift, maybe growing impatient. It shook its massive maw-end like a dog.

Wick tumbled down, scrabbling for a fresh hold, and caught the chain net again. Something clicked against his palm. When Wick looked up, he saw that he'd accidentally grabbed the locking mechanism. As he watched, the maw-net came loose.

"Move!" Rohoh yelled. "You're going to get us both eaten!"

Digging in with his bare toes, Wick climbed to the top of the Burrower again as the chain net fell away. The Burrower rose up immediately, twisting itself into a proud S shape and bugling like a moose—a very large, very angry moose. The sound filled the pit and the cavern.

Tensing like a bowstring, the Burrower lunged from the pit, sliding up the wall and over the ledge directly toward the doorway where the goblinkin were. Either it sensed the entrance or the goblinkin, or it remembered the direction. Wick had no clue. He clung on tightly, flattening himself against the Burrower's body, certain that he'd be scraped off on the entrance with every bone broken.

Instead, Wick sank down a little as the Burrower flattened its body and eased through the entrance. Goblinkin shouted in terror as the massive creature grabbed several of them with its maw and swallowed them whole. Immediately, the Burrower's teeth went to work, cutting and grinding, and its stomachs shivered into action.

Out in the main mineshaft, the Burrower took off in pursuit of the goblinkin fleeing down into the mine. Wick lost his hold and struggled to remain on top of the creature as it bounced and jarred beneath him. He finally gave up and wrapped an arm around his head and hoped he didn't have his brains bashed out or—Old Ones forbid!—end up *beneath* the Burrower.

Abruptly, Wick ran out of creature. He dropped off the posterior end and plopped to the floor. He landed in a pile of the foulest, gooiest mess he'd ever felt or smelled. As he tried to stand, his feet kept sliding out from under him.

The dwarves came out of the Burrowers' chamber with their axes and torches in hand.

"There he is!" Adranis shouted. "He's still alive!"

Wick finally got to his feet just as they arrived. Although they seemed happy enough to see that he was still alive, none of them wanted to touch him.

"That was a brave thing ye did, halfer," Bulokk said. "I don't think I coulda done that."

"Now you're a hero," Rohoh whispered into Wick's punctured ear.

Some hero, Wick thought sourly. *I'm battered and bruised, and have an ear that will probably never look right again, and I'm covered in—in—* He looked at the greenish paste that covered him from head to toe. Then he looked at Rassun.

"What is this?" Wick asked.

"Burrower leavin's," Rassun said solemnly.

Wick gazed back down at himself in disbelief.

"Goblinkin go right through 'em," Rassun said. "Told ye they digested fast. Goblinkin ain't no good for 'em nutritionally, but they do love to eat 'em. Like treats."

"Dung?" Wick cried. "I'm covered in goblinkin dung?" The foul stench nearly made him sick.

"It's not exactly goblinkin dung," Rassun said. "Though that's pretty foul, too. No, this here's Burrower dung. Usually it's rocks and suchlike. But this is, well, it's—"

"Right disgustin' is what it is," Adranis supplied.

Wick silently agreed. He wanted a hot bath with scented soap. He wanted a change of clothes. He wanted a book and a pipe, and to *never* be reminded that he'd once wallowed in Burrower poop made out of goblinkin.

The skink climbed down Wick, careful of where he trod. "If you don't mind," Rohoh said, "I'll manage on my own from here." The lizard was somehow miraculously clean of foulness.

"Come on," Bulokk said. "We've got an escape to attend." He trotted back up the mineshaft.

Wick took a moment and kicked as much of the dung from his feet as he could. He wished he had a stick to clean out between his toes, but he didn't. When he saw the dwarves leaving, he finally gave up and ran after them, avoiding the Burrower trail that had been left in the creature's wake.

Farther down the mineshaft, the goblinkin shrieked in terror, but the shrieks came less and less often.

They gained the front entrance without further incident, but there were ten goblinkin standing guard.

"Axes!" Bulokk yelled.

Immediately, Adranis, Hodnes, and Drinnick formed on Bulokk. The goblinkin tried to stand their ground, but they went down before the dwarven axes like wheat before a flail. The battle was short and vicious, with no mercy given to the goblinkin. Rassun and the other dwarf took on any that managed to escape the whirling death that was the dwarven axes. By the time they reached the entrance, all of them were covered in the blood of their foes.

Stumbling over the bodies of the fallen goblinkin, Wick peered outside. It took a moment for his eyes to adapt to the night.

"To the docks!" Bulokk roared, taking off at once. "They've made it around to the goblinkin ship!"

Glancing down, Wick saw that the escapees and the rest of Bulokk's warriors *had* made it around to the stone pier. A massive battle was taking place on the pier. Not all of the goblinkin had abandoned their posts to pursue the fleeing slaves.

Looking up, Wick saw that a number of dead goblinkin littered the stone steps leading up to the ridge. More of them had fallen to the hard-packed ground.

Wick followed the dwarves down the steps even though it meant running into the battle. He definitely didn't want to remain standing at the mine entrance by himself in case any goblinkin survived the Burrower's attack and decided to come out. Or if there were other groups that hadn't yet gone down before the Burrower.

Several of the loose rocks Wick had dumped down the steps remained and he had to be careful. Still, he slipped twice and ended up barely keeping himself from going over the edge, and he had new sets of bruises to show for his efforts.

When he reached the bottom of the steps, he was even with the dwarves. He was faster than they were, more sure-footed in spite of the falls he'd taken, and unburdened by armor.

Wick guessed that most of the prisoners had made good on their escape, because most of them appeared to be with Bulokk's warriors. They used weapons they'd taken along the way or picked up when they arrived at the harbor. Some of them threw rocks into the milled mass of goblinkin trying to keep the dwarves from reaching the anchored ships.

Within a few steps, the skink leaped onto Wick's leg and slithered up. At first Wick had started to beat the skink away, thinking that one of the dead goblinkin around him wasn't quite as dead as he'd looked. Then he recognized the lizard and relaxed a little.

"I guess maybe I don't stink so bad now," Wick said.

"I'm too short to wade through this makeshift battlefield," Rohoh replied. "I might get squished."

Maybe that wouldn't be a bad thing, Wick thought briefly, then chided himself for being so small-minded. Despite the skink's harsh nature, finding Master Oskarr's battle-axe would have been almost impossible without the creature given the logistics of the search.

Bulokk and his mineshaft team enjoyed a brief but telling advantage when they raced out of the darkness and slammed into the goblinkin warriors from behind without warning. The goblinkin went down in pieces, felled again and again by the dwarven battle-axes.

"Wick!" Bulokk roared, using his name for once instead of calling him *halfer*. "Get them women an' children to one of them ships! Adranis, you an' Drinnick give him a hand!" He was in the thick of the battle, standing ankle-deep in the incoming tide, scattering dead goblinkin in all directions. But still they came. The dwarf looked every inch the warrior, as at home on the battlefield as he would be at a blacksmith's anvil.

Wick looked around and spotted the women and children huddled in a mass on the other side of the stone pier. He ran to them. "Quickly!" he cried. "We've got to get you onto a ship! You have to hurry if you're going to have any chance at all!"

"It's a halfer!" a woman grumbled. "I'm not going to listen to a halfer!"

"Ye will!" Adranis thundered. "Elsewise we'll leave ye here fer them goblinkin to lock up again!" He bristled angrily. "Now ye get on up here an' do as he says!"

The woman climbed to the top of the stone pier. Yelling over the confusion, Wick organized a line that helped the weaker adults and smaller children to the stone pier where they were temporarily out of the way of the brunt of the battle.

Looking over his shoulder, Wick saw that the goblinkin had already reorganized, taking a step back to put both dwarven fronts ahead of them again. Now they were once more pressing their superior numbers. Worse than that, the human archers onboard the black ship had decided to weigh into the fight as well. Their shafts flew, but they seemed to be indiscriminate about whether they hit dwarves or goblinkin. Both were wounded and killed in the fusillades, and confusion swept across the combatants.

Once he had the women and children behind him, Wick led them to the goblinkin ship anchored on the other side of the pier from the battle. Arrows sped toward them as well, sometimes thunking into the stone pier and sometimes hitting the goblinkin ship on the battle side. Either way, the human archers from the black vessel were aware of the attempted escape by ship.

What are they waiting on? Wick wondered as he helped the escapees on board. "Do any of you have sailing experience?" he yelled.

"Aye," an elderly human man said. He was long in years as humans went, with gray hair flowing down past his shoulders. Arthritis or old injury had rendered him largely infirm, and Wick knew the old man had probably only been days away from death by overwork or by execution once the goblinkin deemed his work wasn't enough to justify whatever meager amount they were feeding him to keep him barely alive. "I've sailed afore."

"You're the captain," Wick said, addressing the man like he would a Novice or a Third Level Librarian back at the Vault of All Known Knowledge. "Until you're relieved of command."

"Aye," the man replied, and immediately straightened his shoulders with the acceptance of the responsibility.

"Get a crew together and get us squared away," Wick called out. "I want to be able to leave as soon as we're able."

"You probably know as much about sailing as he does," Rohoh said.

"Probably," Wick admitted. "But most humans, dwarves, and elves would rather take orders from a human or a dwarf before they would an elf or a dweller." *Especially one covered in Burrower dung that had once been goblinkin.*

"Aye," the human replied enthusiastically. Instantly, he started separating the escapees into groups, those with sailing experience and those without.

When the last of the women, children, and elderly had been loaded aboard the ship, Wick glanced back at the dwarven front. Bulokk and his warriors were starting to crumble now. Two more of them were in the water, unmoving. Another had three arrows jutting from his chest but somehow still found the strength and courage to continue fighting.

"Bulokk!" Wick yelled.

Some of the human archers had quit the ship now, coming ashore in a longboat pulled by steady stroke. A tall man with a moon-white face under his bloodred cowl stood in the stern. He held a staff beside him.

That, Wick decided, *doesn't look good*. He scampered to the end of the stone pier, calling Bulokk's name again and again. But the dwarves couldn't disengage without exposing their backs to the goblinkin. Wick knew they would never make the distance to the ship.

The longboat with the humans landed.

"Back!" the man in the bloodred cowl roared.

Most of the goblinkin pulled away at the command, but there were some that didn't.

The man in the bloodred cowl waved. Instantly, the humans lifted their bows, drew and fired in one smooth motion. The arrows cut through the goblinkin and dwarves alike. Seven goblinkin and two dwarves went down. Bulokk and two other dwarves remained standing, their bodies pierced by the arrows.

"Give me the axe," the man in the bloodred cowl ordered.

Bulokk drew a throwing knife from somewhere on his body and flicked it forward. The blade caught the moonslight as it whirled end over end.

The man in the bloodred cowl lifted a hand. The throwing knife stopped in midair less than an arm's length from the man. Casually, he flicked a hand and the knife shot back along the path it had come.

The blade took Bulokk high in the chest even as the dwarf strove to avoid the unexpected attack. Before he could recover, the man in the bloodred cowl gestured again, flinging his fingers wide as if flicking away a bothersome pest. In response, Bulokk went flying backward.

At another gesture, Master Oskarr's battle-axe suddenly flew upward. Bulokk tried to hang onto the weapon, blood streaming down him from his various wounds, but it was no use. Ultimately whatever magic the red-cowled man wielded was stronger than Bulokk's grip.

The battle-axe flew to the red-cowled man's hand. A grin split the moon-white face. Without a word, the wizard turned to go. The human archers closed ranks behind him and sent a few more shafts into the goblinkin and the dwarves.

Seeing that made Wick's heart sick as he took cover behind the stern of the goblinkin ship. But his keen vision also spied the identical tattoos under the right eyes of the archers: It was the black image of an unfolded straight razor overlaid with crimson lips.

No thieves' guild wears identifying marks, Wick thought. Then he remembered, from a book he'd borrowed from Hralbomm's Wing rather than a nonfiction source, that some thieves' guilds did mark their members. They were members of the elite, the special thieves that victims never saw and kings hired for clandestine missions or revenge.

But why would a thieves' guild be interested in Master Oskarr's battle-axe? How had they known where to find it? Questions tumbled through Wick's frantically jumping mind.

The goblinkin lay low while the thieves' guild members once more boarded their longboat and began rowing back to the black ship.

"C'mon, halfer," Adranis said at Wick's side. "We gotta go rescue them what's still alive."

Although he didn't want to, Wick went with Adranis and Drinnick. Hodnes brought up the rear. Wick couldn't sit idly by and watch the dwarves get killed even though he wanted to hide in fear for his own life.

They ran to the end of the stone pier and to the dwarves, humans, and elves that still stood and could wield weapons. Wick ran to Bulokk, who lay on his back with arrows and a knife sticking out of him. The little Librarian felt certain the dwarven leader would be dead.

Instead, Bulokk was in shock from his wounds and whatever mystical force had been used against him. His breath came in gasps as blood leaked out of him.

Even if we manage to get him out of here, Wick thought, *he's not going to live*. But Wick couldn't give up on Bulokk any more than the dwarf could quit laboring for his next breath.

Stepping behind the dwarf, Wick grabbed Bulokk's shirt and started trying to pull him toward the ship as arrows struck the ground around them. Having no other choice, Wick unhooked Bulokk's shield and stood guard over the fallen dwarf like any shieldmate would on a battlefield.

But Wick's thoughts were his own. *Please don't let me throw up*, he pleaded as his stomach swirled threateningly. *Heroes don't throw up on other heroes. I know I'm no hero, but I don't want to throw up on Bulokk. I'm already covered in Burrower dung—the* worst *kind of Burrower dung at that—and it just wouldn't be fair to be so inept.*

Slowly, inexorably, the goblinkin line advanced. Behind them, the black ship lifted its sails and raised anchor. It shifted, rolling on the tide, and got the wind behind it, heading into the fogbank that blew over the Rusting Sea.

Then, without warning, dwarven war horns trumpeted across the bay. The sound gave pause to the warriors battling on the beach.

Hunkered down behind Bulokk's shield, the wounded dwarf's breathing rasping in his ears, Wick gazed out to sea and saw the black ship slide right by *One-Eyed Peggie* as the pirate ship came into the harbor under full sail. The skull and crossbones fluttered under the topgallant.

"Pirates!" the goblinkin shouted.

Not just pirates, Wick thought with pride. *Those are pirates of the Blood-Soaked Sea. They don't come any more fierce!*

One-Eyed Peggie came about smartly, dropping anchor and sail less than fifty paces away, evidently taking her mark from the goblinkin ships floating at the pier. A longboat filled with dwarves smacked into the sea as a few of the pirates with bow skills feathered the goblinkin with a few shafts.

"Row!" Hallekk's lusty voice rolled across the sea. "Row, ye seadogs, or by the Old Ones I'll dangle yer corpses from the 'yards an' watch the gulls strip the flesh from yer bones!"

Wick knew that the harsh words were more for benefit of the onlookers than for the crew. Hallekk and the pirates wouldn't hesitate to give everything they had to rescue him.

Or maybe Master Oskarr's axe, Wick had to admit.

"Pirates?" Bulokk whispered weakly.

"Not pirates," Wick assured the dwarf. "You're among friends, Bulokk. Hallekk and his bunch, why, they'll set things to rights soon enough."

Bulokk's eyes closed, and for a moment Wick thought he'd lost the dwarf. Then Bulokk whispered, "That man took Master Oskarr's axe."

"I know," Wick said, watching as goblinkin dropped from bowshots and tried to get reorganized. "But we're not finished with that either, I'll wager." *Craugh won't let this go.*

In the next moment, the two longboats bearing Hallekk and the pirates arrived. The dwarven pirates jumped boat at once and ripped their axes free, wading into the goblinkin with a ferocity that sparked a second wind from those Bulokk had called in to battle.

Horrified but mesmerized at the same time, Wick watched Hallekk walk into the thick of it. The big dwarf whooped and hollered in a properly piratical fashion as his axe lashed out again and again. The crew of *One-Eyed Peggie* hated slavers, too.

In a short time, the goblinkin line broke. Survivors ran screaming for the stone steps. Hallekk and the pirates pursued them all the way to the ridge, managing to catch a few of their opponents, killing them outright or sending them plunging into broken heaps at the bottom of the cliff.

"Just stay with me," Wick told Bulokk. "Everything's going to be all right." He took the dwarf 's hand and held on tight, hoping for the best because his grip was stronger than Bulokk's. "Just stay with me."

epilogue

The Razor's Kiss

"Wick."

Certain that he had to be dreaming that voice and that no one would be trying to wake him, Wick rolled over and nearly fell out of his hammock. He caught himself just in time, his heart threatening to explode in his chest. Angry and embarrassed, he turned to whoever had called for him.

"What do you think you're doing?" he demanded. "Don't you realize that I've nearly been killed several times in the last few days and—" He stopped at once when he saw who the offender was.

Scowling, Craugh stood in the small crew's room and looked at Wick.

I'm going to be a toad, Wick thought morosely. Still, he couldn't go down without pleading for his life. "I'm sorry. I didn't know it was you."

"Of course you didn't," Craugh said. "You've barely had enough sleep to know anything."

Wick looked at the wizard, waiting for the jaws of the trap to snap closed on tender flesh. What would it feel like to be turned into a toad? "I haven't. I didn't mean to—"

"Get out of bed," Craugh said, waving impatiently. "We need to talk."

Wait, Wick thought heatedly. *Just because you haven't turned me into a toad doesn't mean . . . doesn't mean . . .* He sighed and threw the blanket off. *Doesn't mean you won't if I make you angry enough.*

"Slops has a meal prepared, I believe," Craugh said. "Get dressed and let's go eat."

Holding the blanket tight around him, Wick took out a fresh set of clothes from the sea chest under his hammock. He looked at Craugh. "Uh, would you mind waiting outside?"

"Why?"

"I'm going to change clothes."

Exasperated, Craugh rolled his eyes up. "Old Ones help me. In addition to being a bungler, he's also modest." He let himself out and closed the door.

"I'm not a bungler," Wick called to the wizard's departing back.

"We didn't get Master Oskarr's axe," Craugh growled. "I'd say that was fairly bungled."

"I found the axe, though." Wick dressed quickly. "That's what you sent me there for."

"I didn't send you to find it so you could let the enemy have it," Craugh responded.

True, Wick told himself. "I didn't even know there *was* an enemy. If I'd known, I might have handled things differently." *Although I don't know how that would have been possible.*

"There is. And they're still out there. That's one of the things we have to talk about."

Wick opened the door and joined the wizard. Together, they went topside and entered the galley. The smell of fresh, warm biscuits and firepear jelly, sweet butter, bacon, sausage, pepper gravy, and journeycakes made Wick's mouth water in anticipation.

Few people were in the galley so they took seats by themselves. Wick piled his plate high, but discovered that his engineering lacked by comparison with Craugh. They dug in and ate without talking for several long, satisfying minutes.

When they were finished with their second helping, resting up before they rallied for a third attempt, Wick asked, "How is Bulokk?"

"Still alive," Craugh said. "That one is very tough. He comes from good stock. He's very disappointed to have lost his ancestor's battle-axe."

Wick sipped his razalistynberry wine. After the battle, Hallekk and the pirates had secured the shoreline and gathered all the scattered mine slaves. Instead of trying to get them out on one of the goblinkin ships, Cap'n Farok had ordered everyone aboard *One-Eyed Peggie*. There had been no chance of catching the mysterious black ship. Knowing the slave ships could never be made anything more than what they were, Hallekk had ordered them burned to their waterlines and sunk in the harbor.

They'd remained at anchor for nearly a full day, tending to the wounded and giving the dead a proper burial. Bulokk had also requested that Master Oskarr's anvil be rescued if at all possible. Cap'n Farok had ordered that done, and Hallekk and a group of the ship's crew had gone down into the mine and brought the anvil back up.

There'd been a brief set-to with the Burrower, but Wick let Hallekk know that Burrowers didn't much care for fire and it had given them a wide berth after they'd doused it with oil and set it aflame. In the end, though, Craugh had gone after the Burrowers and dispatched them all. Leaving the creatures to eat their way through the islands wasn't possible. There had been no sign of the fire elemental, Merjul.

"I'm not a bungler," Wick said, when he could no longer stand the guilt the wizard had heaped upon him. "There was a lot I didn't know. Mostly things you didn't tell me. And you should have."

"I'm aware of that." Craugh reached into his robe and took out Wick's journal.

Only then did Wick realize that he hadn't switched the journal out of his other clothes back in his room. "Did you read that?"

"I did." Craugh nodded.

"That's not my best work," Wick said defensively. When he hadn't been helping with the wounded, Wick had climbed up to the crow's nest and worked on the journal. As a result, his work at recording the events that had taken place after he'd reached the Cinder Clouds Islands was hurried, more in the form of notes than in anything presentable.

"It isn't," Craugh agreed. "But I know it's an unpolished first draft. You'll get it right as you work on it. I just wanted to get an idea of what you'd been through."

Wick flipped through the pages, making certain everything was there. Every time he started a new journal, he always numbered the pages ahead of time, so he would know if anything had ever been removed.

"It's all there," Craugh grumbled. He tossed the protective oilskin pouch and writing supplies onto the table as well.

"Wizards have a habit of making things disappear," Wick returned. "They don't always put those things back where they belong."

"We have to get Master Oskarr's axe back," Craugh declared.

"How?" Wick asked. "We don't even know who took it."

Craugh snatched the journal from Wick's hands, then opened it to a page displaying the thieves' guild symbol of the straight razor and lips. "We do." He tapped the tattoo on the drawing Wick had made for reference. "The thieves were members of the Razor's Kiss, a thieves' guild that operates out of Wharf Rat's Warren."

Wick thought about that. He'd never been to Wharf Rat's Warren. Nor had he ever wanted to go. The port city was in the Deep Frozen North and was said to be one of the most lawless around. Only thieves and murderers lived there, safe from the vengeful arm of anyone who tried to make them pay for their crimes.

"You recognize the tattoo?" Wick asked.

"I do."

"How?"

"I've been there and seen it."

Wick resisted the impulse to ask what business had taken Craugh there. No doubt it wasn't good business. Craugh wasn't exactly a good person. The wizard tended to chase after his desires and seldom addressed the needs of others.

"That being the case," Craugh went on, "you'll have to go search for the thieves' guild." He sipped his wine.

At first, Wick couldn't believe he'd heard correctly. "No," he said, folding his arms across his chest. "I'm not going."

"Second Level Librarian Lamplighter," Craugh said in tones that sent a shiver through Wick just as surely as though they'd been uttered by Grandmagister Frollo, "you have a duty to protect the Vault of All Known Knowledge."

"I don't see how going into Wharf Rat's Warren is going to accomplish that."

"That's because you have limited scope of vision."

"My vision," Wick insisted, perhaps a bit emboldened by the razalistynberry wine, "is perfectly fine."

Craugh looked at him.

For a moment, Wick felt certain he was about to be threatened with toadification, and he wasn't certain how he was going to react to that. But for the moment he held onto his newfound belligerence.

"We still need to know what happened at the Battle of Fell's Keep," Craugh said.

"We know that Master Oskarr didn't betray anyone," Wick countered.

"Do we? Aren't some of those books in the Vault of All Known Knowledge sometimes in conflict with each other about events?"

Grudgingly, Wick had to admit that was true.

"Someone's lying then," Craugh said.

"Not necessarily," Wick replied. "It just depends on when the account took place."

"The victors always write the histories."

Sitting there looking at the wizard, Wick felt torn. He didn't know if it was better to argue with someone who didn't acknowledge books or the information in them, or with someone who was suitably educated. *And opinionated*, he added unkindly.

"Do you have Master Oskarr's stone table in which he writes he was betrayed?" Craugh asked.

"No. You know we don't." Wick hadn't even thought to bring it. "I have the rubbings I took of his statement, though. They're legible. And if we need to, we could go back for Master Oskarr's table."

"How many people can read that statement, Second Level Librarian Lamplighter?"

Wick drummed his fingers on the tabletop irritably. *Okay. Point taken*. He sighed. "No one who doesn't work at the Vault of All Known Knowledge. Even of those there, only a few can read it."

"I see. So can you prove your claim?"

"No."

Craugh nodded. "Then there's the red-cowled wizard who was with the black ship."

Wick looked at Craugh in surprise. "You knew him!"

"I know *of* him," Craugh corrected. "He's a very dangerous man. A wizard-for-hire to the highest bidder."

Unconsciously, Wick turned to the page where he'd drawn the red-cowled wizard's face. Wick had drawn the man four different times, using his memory of the wizard to remember how he'd looked and moved. Even rendered in charcoal, the man looked dangerous.

"His name is Hauk Kerbee," Craugh said.

Automatically, Wick asked for the spelling and inscribed it at the bottom of the page.

"He's an albino," Craugh said.

That explains the coloration I saw, Wick thought.

"As such, you don't find Ryman Bey often out in the daylight hours," Craugh went on.

"Is he part of the Razor's Kiss?"

"Not to my knowledge."

"Why would Ryman Bey be with them?"

"That's one of the questions we'd like answered, isn't it?"

Not we, Wick wanted to reply. But he couldn't. Not simply because he didn't want to anger Craugh, but because he was curious, too.

"The Razor's Kiss is for hire as well," Craugh said.

"You believe someone hired them to look for Boneslicer."

Craugh nodded. "I do."

"Why?"

"Because someone doesn't want the truth of what happened at the Battle of Fell's Keep to come out."

"Who?"

Craugh smiled. "If I knew the answer to that, we might not have to go to Wharf Rat's Warren."

Wick looked into Craugh's green eyes. "What if I choose not to go there?"

Craugh started to speak, then Cap'n Farok's rough voice blared through the galley.

"If 'n ye chooses not to go," the dwarven captain said from the doorway, "then ye'll not go."

"What if I want to go back to Greydawn Moors?" Wick asked.

"Then I'll take ye there, Librarian." Farok glared at Craugh. "I've had me fill of slave ships. I'll not abide bein' made part of one."

Craugh was silent for a moment, then gave a tight nod. "All right then, Second Level Librarian Lamplighter. The choice is yours." Without another word, the wizard got up from the table and stalked outside.

For some reason that he couldn't explain, Wick felt ashamed, like he'd somehow let the wizard down. *That's stupid*, he told himself. *You don't owe him anything. You've already risked your life several times for him*. But he couldn't shake the feeling.

"Are ye all right, Librarian?" Cap'n Farok asked.

"I am," Wick answered. *I will be*.

"Will ye be wantin' to go back to Greydawn Moors, then?"

"I'd be safer there," Wick said, hoping the old pirate captain would understand.

"Aye." Farok nodded. "Ye would be. An' it's a more fittin' place for ye than out here on the sea or on the mainland."

Somehow, though, even though Farok said that, Wick still felt guilty.

"I'm gonna see them we rescued to home first," Farok said. "They's closer an' we could use a few supplies afore we cross the Blood-Soaked Sea again. All these extra mouths we took on to feed ain't doin' our supplies any good." He clapped Wick on the shoulder. "Just let me know what ye've a mind to do."

"I will. Thank you."

Hours later, Wick sat up in the crow's nest with a fresh journal, the one he'd taken notes in, and his writing supplies. After the time he'd spent in the Cinder Clouds Islands, he enjoyed the simple and familiar task of rendering his notes into properly stated text.

He used one of the codes he'd invented to record his adventures and the events that had propelled him into them. Even as he reworked the argument in Paunsel's Tavern, beginning with how Paunsel had dragged him away from the adventure of Taurak Bleiyz, a vague wave of discontent filled Wick.

He hated unfinished things.

Since he'd been back on *One-Eyed Peggie*, he'd tried to focus on the book. He hadn't even been able to get the intrepid dweller hero across the spiderweb spanning the Rushing River high in the Death Thorn Forest. Swinging Toadthumper with Taurak just hadn't seemed . . . right.

So many things about the Battle of Fell's Keep remained undone.

It's not yours to do, Wick told himself. *You're a Librarian, not some larger-than-life dweller hero from a romance on the shelves of Hralbomm's Wing.* He watched the sun slowly sinking into the west, painting the sky fiery orange and red above the silvery water. *You don't even* want *to be a hero.*

Still, he knew that Taurak Bleiyz would have been able to slip unnoticed into Wharf Rat's Warren and spy on a thieves' guild.

And that was what Craugh was proposing. It was the only strategy that made sense.

It's also the strategy that could get you strung up from a net for the birds to eat, Wick reminded himself. *Or tossed to the sharks.*

He looked down at the page he'd been working on. It was an image of the Battle of Fell's Keep, pulled from the few pictures he'd seen drawn of it and from the descriptions he'd read. His picture centered on Master Oskarr standing atop a boulder in the heart of the Painted Canyon, swinging Boneslicer at goblinkin and the trolls that accompanied them.

Master Oskarr gave his life, Wick thought sadly, *maybe not then, but eventually all the same. And he was branded a traitor for that.* The realization didn't set easily with the little Librarian. He'd seen in Bulokk how those hurts from the past could still wound. *How long will they continue to do so?*

In the end, Wick knew he had no choice. What if he went back to Greydawn Moors, to the Vault of All Known Knowledge, and couldn't find peace to do his work or enjoy a good book?

It could happen. It was happening now. He could only imagine Grandmagister Frollo haranguing him for his absence, then for his inattention to the tasks before him. If he couldn't find it within himself to finish the Taurak Bleiyz adventure, how could he ever return home?

When it was almost dark, Wick packed the two journals away. He was too unsettled to work anymore, and it was even more unsettling realizing he knew what he had to do about it. He folded up his writing supplies and made his way down the rigging.

Critter and Rohoh were involved in some argument on one of the 'yards. It was evident from the ungainly way they were swinging upside down from their claws that they'd been raiding Slops's cooking brandy.

Once he reached the deck, Wick made his way to Craugh's room. Before he even knocked on the door, the wizard called, "Enter."

Sighing, Wick thought, *I hate when he does that.* Craugh had a habit of laying wards on the doors of rooms where he slept.

Inside the small room, Craugh sat cross-legged on the narrow bed.

"Why did you get a bed?" Wick asked, thinking of the hammock he'd been sleeping in. He'd never visited Craugh's room.

"Because I asked," Craugh answered. He closed the book he'd been reading and tried to hide it from sight.

Before he could stop himself, driven by curiosity, Wick grabbed the book. Craugh didn't let it go. Green sparks leapt from the wizard's baleful gaze. Wick saw the title anyway. He released the book.

Craugh tucked it into his traveler's pack. "Well?"

"That book was one I wrote," Wick said in surprise.

"You gave it to me."

"I know. As a gift." Wick shook his head. "I didn't think you'd still have it."

"I just found it in my pack," Craugh said. "Obviously I forgot to remove it."

Wick knew that wasn't true. The book had shown a lot of careful attention, but it also looked decidedly well read. Like a favorite book should. Wick had written it about his adventures with Craugh down in the Seltonian Bogs when they'd gone in search of Ralkir's hidden library.

"Was there something you wanted?" Craugh demanded.

Wick squinted up at him. "Some days, Craugh, you're a miserable excuse for a person."

Craugh glared at him.

"If it wasn't for the whole toad thing you do," Wick said, "I think more people would tell you that."

"Hmmmph," Craugh responded. "And more people would be toads."

"You know why I'm here, don't you?"

To his credit, Craugh didn't gloat.

"I can't leave this unfinished," Wick said, realizing the wizard was going to make him say it.

"I know," Craugh said.

"There are too many questions that need to be answered. And I've started taking some of them personally. During the last few days, I've gotten to know Bulokk. He's a good person. He shouldn't have to suffer under the weight of the accusation of Master Oskarr."

"I agree."

Wick regarded Craugh suspiciously. "But there's more to this, isn't there?"

"Yes."

Wick waited, then sighed as he gave up. "You're not going to tell me, are you?"

"No."

"Why?"

"Because I know too much to be neutral the way a good investigator should be. I have too many preformed suspicions."

"Do you know who hired the Razor's Kiss?"

"Perhaps."

"Then why should I go there?"

"Because we need proof before I start making accusations."

"I could get killed in Wharf Rat's Warren."

"I sincerely hope not. But it is a distinct possibility. I never said any of this was going to be easy."

At least that, Wick thought, *is the truth*.

A Note from Grandmagister Edgewick Lamplighter

I look back on this document after so many years have elapsed and it seems like only yesterday. The task that Craugh and Cap'n Farok set before me on that day was far more perilous than even they believed.

Well, I think that Craugh knew more than he was telling. He usually does.

As you can plainly see from this note, I lived through it all. But many didn't. And even now if all the truths come spilling out that we left hidden, more people will die.

"Secrets are such hard things to manage when you're not the only one who knows." Of course, as any Librarian worth his salt would recognize, that's a quote from Gart Makmornan's Cashing in on Secrets: A History of Blackmail in the Higher Elven Courts.

In all, there are three of these books, these journals of my travels during this time of trouble. I have divided them up to forestall any inadvertent discovery of them before their time. Timing is, as they say, everything. And it was never truer than now. The trouble I was witness to, the discovery of Lord Kharrion's Wrath so long after the Cataclysm, was not ended. I knew that when I walked out of the Forest of Fangs and Shadows.

But it was finished enough for the time. The danger was put aside.

The second book details what happened to me during my travails at Wharf Rat's Warren, of how I tracked down the Razor's Kiss, Ryman Bey, and the person who hired them to search for Master Blacksmith Oskarr's battle-axe, Boneslicer.

That journal, as with the third, will not be found with this one. Only one person knows where this journal may be found. And I will teach only one other Librarian—an apprentice I know whose heart and mind I can trust—the trick of the code I have used to record this narrative.

Only you, my apprentice, know the code to these books. And I will have taught you the way to find them. But know that the secrets they guard are dangerous things. I cannot impress that strongly enough upon you.

To find the second book, you must first find Ordal the Minstrel, who is as eternal as the wind. When you find him, ask him, "What rides in on four legs, stands on two legs, and stumbles away on three legs?"

Ordal doesn't know anything of the book that has been hidden, but his answer will give you a clue as to where you should look for the second book.

May your journey be successful, apprentice, and may your search be compelled out of curiosity rather than need.

Sincerely,
Edgewick Lamplighter
Grandmagister
Vault of All Known Knowledge
Greydawn Moors

Afterword

Worn and bleary-eyed from working by lantern light aboard *Moonsdreamer*, Juhg pushed up from the small table in the cabin Raisho had given him. He'd been sitting so long that his sea legs had evidently swum without him because he found the ship's deck seemed to be tilting beneath him.

Suddenly aware of the hunger that consumed him, Juhg lurched out into the corridor and made his way up onto the deck. He was surprised to find that it was night and that *Moonsdreamer* was rolling in the clutches of a storm.

He'd been so consumed by Grandmagister Lamplighter's narrative that he hadn't even noticed the storm's descent on the ship.

Fierce rain raked the deck, deep enough to slosh small tides back and forth as the ship rocked. Lightning blazed across the sky, burning through the dark masses of clouds swirling overhead. The hollow booms were so close and so loud they shivered through *Moonsdreamer*.

Looking back at the stern, Juhg found Raisho standing near the pilot. When a storm was on, there was nowhere else Raisho would be.

"When did this start?" Juhg asked his friend as he joined him.

Raisho stood dressed in a dark cloak, his face concealed in the shadows except for when the lightning struck. "Right before dusk. We're hours into it now." He squinted and turned his face up against the rain. "Thought it'd be played out by now, but it just keeps comin'." He shook his head and looked back at

Juhg. "Don't care none for this storm, I tell you. It's got a bad feel 'bout it. Like it ain't natural."

Juhg remembered the bog beasts they'd fought back in Shark's Maw Cove. Someone had sent those creatures. Could a storm have been sent as well?

A wave caught *Moonsdreamer* broadside and twisted her. The helmsman struggled to hold onto the large wheel. Crossing over to the man, Raisho threw his strength into the task as well.

Stumbling, Juhg managed to grab onto the railing and keep his feet. But only just.

"Been thinkin' maybe we should 'ead into port somewhere," Raisho shouted. "But didn't know which way we should make for."

"Calmpoint," Juhg said.

Raisho looked at him. "Ye finished translatin' that book?"

Juhg nodded. "I did."

"Does Craugh know?"

"I just came up," Juhg said. "I thought he'd be up here."

Shaking his head, Raisho said, "I haven't seen 'im since before the storm 'it."

Juhg didn't much care for the coincidence of the two events. "Make for Calmpoint."

"What are we gonna find there?"

"Not at Calmpoint," Juhg said. "We'll have to go up Steadfast River to Deldal's Mills."

"Why?"

"There are three books in all," Juhg said. "The book that Craugh brought me told me how to find the second."

"Where's the third?"

"I don't know. Perhaps the second book will tell us that."

Another wave slammed *Moonsdreamer*. Raisho fought with the wheel as a deluge of water slapped over him. The helmsman lost his footing and started to slip away. Moving with surprising quickness, Raisho managed to grab the younger sailor and haul him to safety with one hand.

Then Raisho lifted his voice and started calling out orders to bring the ship around on the correct bearing.

Feeling a little panicky but trusting his friend's instincts when it came to sailing, Juhg went belowdecks. He lurched through the companionway using his hands. The lanterns swung and batted against the walls, the flames flickering from the abuse.

At Craugh's door, Juhg knocked and waited. When there was no response, he knocked again, louder this time. "Craugh!"

No response.

Opening the door, Juhg stepped inside. Darkness filled the small room. A coppery scent was on the air, and it seemed disturbingly familiar.

Juhg stepped back into the companionway and took down one of the lanterns. He returned to the room.

Craugh wasn't there. But the coppery stink came from the pool of blood on the floor. Beside it, using the same blood, someone had written BEWARE.

Standing there in the room, feeling Craugh's absence, Juhg knew that even out on the Blood-Soaked Sea they weren't out of reach of the mysterious enemy who pursued them.

BOOK TWO

Seaspray

Foreword

Ordal the Minstrel

The rain followed *Moonsdreamer* into Calmpoint, further evidence that the storm wasn't a natural occurrence. The ship was at sea for six days before making port, all of them filled with anxiety.

No one knew why or how Craugh had disappeared. The wizard's blood—at least Juhg assumed it was the wizard's—still stained the cabin where he'd been lodged for the voyage. All of his effects were gone as well.

"This is a dangerous place, scribbler," Raisho declared as they stood on deck. In the rain cloak he wore, with his ebony skin dappled and inked with blue tattoos marking him as a sailing man, he looked every inch the warrior. Lantern light gleamed on the red fire opal headband. "I've been here before."

"So have I," Juhg replied. "Long before you were born." He smiled at his friend. Raisho, because of the disparity of their sizes, tended to sometimes treat Juhg as a child. Juhg didn't mind because there was a difference between being protective and being patronizing.

Raisho dropped a hand to the worn hilt of his cutlass. "True, scribbler, I keep forgettin' ye've been around a lot longer than me."

The coastline looked gentle. A solid harbor fronted the Gentlewind Sea to the south. To the west, the Forest of Hawks offered a barrier against any fierce weather that might wander in from the Gentlewind Sea. Although the local shipwrights lobbied every year to start logging the Forest of Hawks, the elven warders there denied them.

Shantytown occupied the area right behind the docks, but there were much nicer houses to the east behind the Customs House and Harbor Watch headquarters. To the far east stood the three tall buildings that housed the three shipwrights' guilds. The middle sector of the town was a mix of shops that provided services or sold goods either made in Calmpoint or imported from other places.

Juhg stood at the railing and remembered past times he'd been there. It had always been with Grandmagister Lamplighter.

Now Craugh was missing and Juhg felt he was putting Raisho at risk in the search for things that might have been better off forgotten.

Except the past will always return to haunt you, Juhg thought. Then he thought of the bloodstains on Craugh's cabin floor. *Or maybe it will kill you*. The possibility was sobering.

"Do ye think mayhap it might be best to put this behind ye for a time?"

Juhg clambered into the longboat over *Moonsdreamer*'s side and looked back at Raisho. For six days his friend had been trying to talk him out of what he was going to attempt.

"No," Juhg said.

"Whoever these people are that are tryin' to keep whatever happened at the Battle of Fell's Keep from becomin' public knowledge, they're serious about it."

"I know," Juhg said. He could recall the bog beasts with distinct clarity.

"An' they got Craugh," Raisho pointed out. "Right under our noses."

"It might not be the same people." Juhg sat in the longboat's stern. He disliked looking up at Raisho because the incessant rain kept hitting him in the face. "Craugh had—" He stopped, realizing the slip he'd unconsciously made. "Craugh *has* a lot of enemies. What happened aboard *Moonsdreamer* may be about another matter entirely."

Raisho gave a disgusted snort. "What are the odds of that?"

"I don't know. But I have to do this."

"Go seekin' Minstrel Ordal?"

"Yes."

Raisho waved an arm toward the city. "Calmpoint is a big place. That's a lot of lookin'."

"I won't find him here in Calmpoint," Juhg explained. "He'll be in Deldal's Mills."

Frowning, Raisho said, "I've 'eard of it."

"It's a lumber town farther up the Steadfast River," Juhg explained. "Lumberjacks float logs down river to Deldal's Mills rather than all the way to Calmpoint. They've had to go farther and farther upriver to claim them these days and don't want to risk the long ride when they can get just as much from Deldal's Mills."

"'Ow far away is this town?"

"A day. The Steadfast River is usually lazy, not too hard to paddle upstream. With this rain, that may change."

"Ordal the Minstrel will be there at that town?"

"Yes. Ordal, in one form or another, has been there for generations."

"Is 'e an elf?"

"No." Juhg smiled. Everyone always thought that. Dwarves weren't known for their singing voices even in a dwarven tavern, and elven minstrels were rare.

"A 'uman then?"

"Yes."

Placing his hands on the railing, Raisho shook his head. "Ye know I'm far too curious for me own good."

Juhg said nothing, but he smiled.

"An' I like even less settin' ye loose on yer own, scribbler, without someone to look over ye."

"Beggin' the cap'n's pardon," one of the young sailors in the longboat said, "but I resent that. Ye asked us yerself to care for the Librarian, an' we're gonna do that."

"No disrespect intended, Tellan, but I own up to a pertective nature when it comes to this particular scribbler."

"We can see him safe to this Deldal's Mills," Tellan said. He was tall and youthful, his hair the color of straw and eyes blue as the sky at twilight. Dressed in a cloak, he looked large and ready. A sword hilt stuck out above his left shoulder. The other men in the longboat were similarly equipped.

"Mayhap ye can an' mayhap ye can't," Raisho said. "But ye ain't gonna do it alone." He pointed at one of the men. "Outta the boat, Trotner. Ye're stayin' here."

Looking relieved, the older sailor climbed back out of the longboat.

"Raisho," Juhg said, "you shouldn't come."

"Because it's dangerous?" Raisho shook his head. "If it's dangerous, I shouldn't be lettin' ye go, now should I?"

"Not because it's dangerous," Juhg said. "Because you're captain of this ship. You've got obligations and duties here. This is my task to see through."

"Oh no ye don't, scribbler. There'll be no war of wits this time. 'Cause I win. Craugh done vanished offa me ship an' I don't know the reason—yet. I'll not 'ave ye disappearin', too."

"You've got a family," Juhg said, knowing it was his last point of attack.

"I told ye all them years ago, an' I'll tell ye again now, scribbler. Ye're me family. Just as much as me wife an' kids. Just as much as me ma an' da ye 'elped me find when we went looking fer *The Book of Time*." Raisho caught a kit that one of the other sailors tossed him, then dropped it into the longboat and followed it. "Until we find out what 'appened to Craugh, I ain't leavin' ye outta me sight. An' that's that."

Some of the tension Juhg felt melted away at Raisho's words. It felt good not to be alone in the world, and facing unknown adversaries and odds. He respected his good friend's wishes and didn't protest any further.

"Thank you," Juhg said.

Raisho picked up an oar and settled it into its lock. "What ye're a-doin', scribbler, I know it's fer the good of a lot of people." He grinned. "Just make sure ye give me proper credit when ye write up the story of this 'ere journey."

Juhg took up an oar, too, then waited for Raisho to call off the count. Together, then, the longboat crew rowed for the public dock.

Juhg paid for horses at the livery after negotiating a fair price for them. The seller threw the tack in for free because Juhg had paid in gold rather than offering something in trade.

"Ye know payin' in gold could cause some problems," Raisho said as they guided their new mounts out into the rain. "Word gets around town quick when ye're an outsider payin' in gold."

"I know," Juhg said. "If I didn't feel pressed for time we would have walked to Deldal's Mills."

At the mercantile, Juhg purchased a few supplies for a cold camp to enhance what they'd brought from the ship. Raisho made it a habit to keep some supplies on hand for times when they had to go ashore because of bad weather, to repair the ship, or to avoid pirates, but Juhg wanted to ease the trip if he could.

Once he had everything squared away to his satisfaction, Juhg pulled up his cloak and went back out into the rain.

Raisho and the other sailors divvied the supplies among them, placing them in bedrolls and saddlebags. Then they headed out.

They rode along the river, on the hard-packed trail that lined both sides of the Steadfast. Under Crossing Bridge, called that because it was the only bridge in Calmpoint that crossed the river, Juhg made certain they were on the Deldal's Mills commercial side rather than textiles.

The river's running high farther north, Juhg thought. *The storm front covers more than just the Gentlewind Sea.* He wondered if he should think any more about that, or worry anymore. Although, frankly, with Craugh inexplicably missing from *Moonsdreamer* while at sea, Juhg didn't know how he could worry any more. *Grandmagister Lamplighter, I do wish you were here right now. You've had far more experience with this kind of roving than I have.*

The wet saddle leather creaked. The horses' hooves thudded against the muddy ground. Gradually, Calmpoint fell behind them as they rode deeper inland. Instead of the forest that had once grown there after the land tried to heal, only scrub brush and farms could be seen.

To the right, within a cornfield that stood tall and green, a garish scarecrow kept watch. As he passed the straw man, Juhg got the uncomfortable feeling that it was staring after him with its charcoal-blackened eyes and stitched mouth.

It's your imagination, he chided himself. He turned his attention northward again, focusing on the narrative he'd translated about Grandmagister Lamplighter's adventures in the Cinder Clouds Islands. How had the Grandmagister fared in Wharf Rat's Warren while seeking the thieves' guild known as the Razor's Kiss?

Juhg knew his mentor had survived, but what must Grandmagister Lamplighter have seen there? And why had the Grandmagister never seen fit to tell Juhg about it? Of course, just from reading books in the Vault of All Known

Knowledge, Juhg knew that there were a great many things Grandmagister Lamplighter hadn't told him.

He sat the horse as best he could, though it was not a favorite mode of travel for him.

"Ye doin' okay, scribbler?" Raisho asked beside Juhg.

"I'm fine," Juhg replied.

"Ye appear to be doin' some deep thinkin' there."

Juhg hesitated a moment. "I am."

"We'll get Craugh back," Raisho said. "Ye got nothin' to worry about. The stories I 'eard about 'im, he can tree a bear with a switch."

"Perhaps," Juhg said, "but it wasn't a bear who took Craugh from a ship at sea." *It was something far worse.*

" 'E's 'ard to kill, scribbler. Ye just got to remember that."

"It would help if I knew who was after us."

"Ye said yerself that it wasn't Master Oskarr who betrayed the Unity at the Battle of Fell's Keep there in the Painted Canyon during the Cataclysm. According to the information Grandmagister Lamplighter uncovered, why, it was Master Oskarr was one of them betrayed."

"Then why didn't Grandmagister Lamplighter let people know when he found out?"

"Could be like Craugh pointed out to 'im all those years ago. 'E just didn't have proof."

"He had the rubbings he took from Master Oskarr's forge table."

"Ye're talkin' about a thousand years of 'ard feelin's. They don't just go away like sugar in tea."

Juhg sighed. "I know. But I have to wonder why anyone from all those years ago would even care now."

"Secrets are terrible things. They grow faster'n, bigger'n, an' stronger'n weeds. Somethin' ten years ago that might 'ave brought down one man, why now it might 'ave grown up big enough to bring down a whole town."

"You're a very wise man, Raisho."

Raisho grinned in the shadows of his cloak. "I 'ad me a very wise teacher." He reached out and clapped Juhg on the shoulder. "We're doin' this, scribbler. Whatever else comes from it, ye know ye're doin' all ye can. Take some solace in that an' 'ave a little faith."

With the rain beating down on him, Juhg tried to take his friend's advice. But he couldn't help feeling scared and doubtful.

They were moving forward, much more slowly than Juhg would have wanted, but still forward. And now something from a thousand years ago—*something tainted with the evil of Lord Kharrion!*—was trying to reach out for them again.

They camped just before nightfall. Thankfully they'd reached the outskirts of the Deldal's Mills forest. If it ever had another name, it had been forgotten.

Raisho waited until full dark had fallen before he would allow them to start a campfire. Then, after he'd spent a long time searching for the lights of other campfires and listening for other riders, he built the fire himself, just big enough to seat the small cauldron they used to make a shepherd's stew in. They used some of the meat they'd brought and added in some of the wild vegetables in the area.

Once the stew started to boil, Juhg sat by himself and took out his writing kit. He worked in the rough journal he carried, bringing the entries up to date and adding images of the Steadfast River, the campsite, and the men who journeyed with them.

When the stew was ready, all of them crept close and ate out of wooden bowls, thankful for the heat. The meat was decent and the vegetables added extra flavor.

After he'd finished eating, Juhg took the first watch, wanting to get it over and try to get a full night's sleep. He fed oats to the horses tied to a rope they'd put up between two trees.

Raisho relieved Juhg after a couple of hours. The rain continued unabated and the river gurgled by constantly.

Juhg made his bedroll as comfortable as possible, grateful to be out of the rain. For a while he lay there, unable to go to sleep. Then, mercifully, his thoughts gradually unlocked themselves and let him fall through them.

"Wake up, Grandmagister Juhg. Wake up."

At first Juhg believed the child's singsong voice was a memory that had threaded into the dark dreams he had of Grandmagister Lamplighter's visit to the Cinder Clouds Islands all those years ago, and of Craugh's bloody disappearance. It was something that didn't belong but didn't overly concern him.

Then something wet and stiff and prickly touched his nose.

That was real! Juhg thought. His eyes popped open and he was staring into the garish face of a monster.

"Wake up, Grandmagister Juhg," the thin, whispering voice taunted.

The coals of the campfire had burned low, casting a soft orange glow across the scarecrow's face. Juhg didn't know if it was the same one from the cornfield he'd seen earlier or if it was one that resembled the other.

It had the same moon-shaped face made out of burlap. The eyes were charcoal-colored triangles over a red button nose and a black-stitched mouth. A hat that would have been otherwise comical sat atop its head. A bright purple kerchief was tied around its neck. It wore patched and faded blouse and breeches, both tarred so they would stand up to the elements. The clothing was stuffed with thick straw.

It held a hand scythe at the end of its right arm.

Juhg sat up and started to cry out.

The scarecrow moved quickly, shoving the sharp scythe blade against Juhg's neck, pinning his head back against the tree where he'd laid his bedroll.

"Quiet, Grandmagister Juhg!" the scarecrow warned. It held its left arm to its stitched mouth, which never moved despite the fact that Juhg heard the words it spoke. It didn't have hands, just bunches of straw that stuck out the ends of the shirtsleeves. Yet somehow it held onto the small scythe. "I don't want to slit your throat if I don't have to."

Despite the fear that pounded through him, Juhg focused on the incredible creature holding him prisoner. He knew the scarecrow wasn't actually alive. It was a simulacrum for a wizard somewhere. Probably not far away. He'd seen things like the scarecrow before, but never so large. Usually they were paper dolls or stuffed toys. Animating a simulacrum was difficult work which became even more of a struggle the larger the host object was.

"What do you want?" Juhg felt his Adam's apple bob over the sharp blade. He thought he even felt a trickle of blood running down his neck.

The stitched mouth tightened up into a smile. "To give you a warning. If I believe you're taking my words to heart, I won't kill you."

"Who are you?"

"Not someone you know," the scarecrow assured him. "Not someone you wish to know."

"Did you take Craugh?"

"Craugh," the scarecrow grated, "has proven himself something of a nuisance."

Has. Not had. The word choice wasn't conclusive, but it was indicative.

Craugh escaped! The realization flooded through Juhg, but he immediately wondered where the wizard had gone and why he hadn't been in touch with them.

"Don't get your hopes up, halfer!" the scarecrow snarled. "The wizard hasn't gotten away for long. There are others tracking him down even now."

"What do you want?"

"I want to know what you're looking for."

"A book." Juhg hoped a book would be innocuous or so ominous that the wizard would abandon his efforts at threatening him. However, seeing as how a wizard animated the scarecrow, a wizard wouldn't be frightened of a book.

"What book?" the scarecrow asked.

Juhg silently wondered how much he could tell without giving away too much. Instead, he jerked his head to the side of the tree away from the scythe, went flat and brought up his knee. If the scarecrow had been a human, dwarf, or elf, Juhg would never have been able to dislodge it. But it wasn't. It was a scarecrow.

The enspelled creature went up and over.

"Raisho!" Juhg yelled as he rolled and got to his feet.

Only a few feet away, Raisho came up out of his bedroll at once. His hand closed over his dwarven-forged cutlass and the orange glow of the coals played over it. The young sea captain had always been a man of action.

"What is it?" Raisho demanded, looking around. His black hair was in wild disarray.

At that moment, the scarecrow pushed itself back up and came at Juhg, swinging the scythe in large pendulum arcs. Juhg dodged back, barely avoiding each swing.

Raisho cursed. By that time the rest of the camp was up, grabbing weapons.

The two guards turned and came from their posts at dead runs. That gave Juhg some heart. At least the scarecrow hadn't seen fit to kill either of them.

Moving and twisting, Juhg stayed out of harm's way. Then Raisho stepped in front of him, handling his cutlass with superb skill. The scythe rang against the cutlass as they met, and sparks flew.

"I'll kill you all!" the scarecrow threatened.

Juhg knew that Raisho was superstitious. Most sailors were. But his friend was worse than most. Many of the tattoos he wore were wards against evil and ill luck.

Raisho stood his ground, though, and turned aside every attempt the scarecrow made to slash Juhg. The ship's captain cut and thrust at the scarecrow time and time again to no avail. The heavy blade passed though the scarecrow's straw body without harming it, scattering only a handful of straw and slicing the tarred clothing to ribbons.

Dodging back, thinking quickly, Juhg grabbed a lantern from their equipment, opened the oil reservoir, and emptied the contents over the scarecrow's back. Raisho kicked the scarecrow's feet out from under it, causing it to fall flat on its hideous face. Before it could get up, Raisho took out one of the long knives he habitually carried in his boots and brought it down hard into the scarecrow's back.

The knife blade passed through the scarecrow and into the earth below. Raisho left the knife there, pinning the creature to the ground, then rolling back to avoid the scythe.

"Listen to me, Grandmagister Juhg!" the scarecrow screamed, kicking and flailing like an insect pinned to a display board. "If you continue poking around into this, you're going to get killed! Your friends will get killed, too."

"Mayhap," Raisho growled, "but it's gonna take better'n ye to make that 'appen."

Juhg plucked one of the larger coals from the campfire with two wet twigs he found. With a flick of his wrist, the coal landed on the scarecrow's back. It took a little while, but the lantern oil caught and a gentle flame spread across the scarecrow's body.

Abruptly, the scarecrow started screaming and flailing with renewed vigor. It beat its handless arms and footless legs at itself but only succeeded in setting its extremities on fire as well. That was the negative aspect of the spell. The wizard's life was at risk as long as he maintained control of the scarecrow.

After another moment, the scarecrow gave out a final scream and relaxed. No one moved until the fire had consumed the scarecrow, leaving only a husked-out mass of ashes and burned straw.

Raisho looked at Juhg. "What was that about?"

"You heard it," Juhg replied, kicking the scythe from the unmoving thing's arm. "It was a warning."

"Why didn't 'e just slit yer throat while ye was sleepin'?"

"Maybe it would have wasted the whole warning bit," Juhg answered.

"No reason to get snippy about it," Raisho said.

Juhg sighed. "I didn't mean to. I just . . . did *not* expect anything like that." Now that the violence was past, adrenaline flooded his system. He sat down weakly. "But Craugh's still alive, Raisho. You heard the scarecrow."

"I did. Doesn't mean 'e didn't lie to ye an' Craugh's lyin' somewheres done fer."

"Maybe we could be a little bit more positive."

Raisho kicked the remnants of the scarecrow's body. Charred straw scattered over the wet ground. "At least we ain't dead. That's about as positive as I care to be right now." He recovered his knife and replaced it in his boot. Then he caught the three pieces that remained of the scarecrow and hauled them over to the campfire.

Juhg joined his friend at the fire as the flames jumped up greedily to consume the straw. The renewed wave of heat washed over Juhg, taking away some of the chill that had soaked into him. He held out his hands and was surprised to see that they were shaking.

"Did ye know who it were?" Raisho asked.

Gazing around at the darkness, Juhg shook his head. "No."

Raisho stirred the burning straw with his cutlass. Embers leapt up into the night sky. "Well, that's not good," he grumped.

Juhg silently agreed. "I can stay up for watch duty. I don't think I'm going to be able to go back to sleep."

With a grim grin, Raisho looked around at the sailors. "I don't think none of us are. If 'n we don't, that'll be fine. But them that 'as watches will be up. Ever'-body else can get sleep if they want it." He spoke for the benefit of the men.

A couple of the more seasoned veterans went back to their bedrolls and covered up. Juhg didn't know if they were actually sleeping or only easing their bones after the long, unaccustomed ride.

Returning to the tree where he'd set up his bedroll, Juhg took out his writing supplies from his pack. He lit a single candle, drove a needle into the tree above him, then speared the candle onto the needle so it would burn levelly. Opening his journal, senses alive to the night and the raindrops sounding like footsteps all around him, he concentrated on his work, focusing hard enough that the fear could no longer touch him.

In the morning, they rose with the dawn and saddled the horses.

"I 'alf expected to find the 'orses with their throats cut," Raisho admitted as he finished saddling his mount. "With us all 'uddled up close to the fire, they'd 'ave been easy targets in the dark. An' walking to Deldal's Mills would be a lot 'arder than ridin'. Not to mention 'ow vulnerable it would leave us."

"You thought of this just now?" Juhg asked, irritated with himself for not thinking of it. He was cold and stiff in the morning, not rested at all from the brief sleep on the hard ground he'd managed or from the hours he'd labored on the journal. Toward dawn he'd finally managed a little more sleep, but it was interrupted by nightmares of what had happened to Craugh, and by the maniacal scarecrow's face shoved against his.

"I thought of it last night." Raisho swung effortlessly up into the saddle. He raised the hood of his cloak over his head.

"And you chose to do nothing?"

"Didn't want to spread out our forces too thin."

Juhg leaped up against the horse, managed to snare the saddle horn, then pulled himself up high enough to get a foot in the stirrup. Horses weren't made for dwellers and dwarves.

The horse whickered, stamped its feet and blew.

As Juhg looked at Raisho, he realized how much his friend had grown and learned in the past eight years. The Raisho of old would have been more concerned about missing a night's sleep or trying to figure out if there was any way to find gold through the scarecrow.

Sometimes Juhg missed the Raisho of old, and it saddened him to think that one day he would miss him altogether.

Your thoughts are too dark, he told himself. So he forced a smile and said, "I'm ready when you are."

"Oh," Raisho said, "I've a feelin' ain't neither of us ready for what Craugh 'as involved us with."

Shortly after midday, though the rain never relented and Juhg never felt the passage of time through a forest that constantly dripped from unending rainfall, they reached Deldal's Mills.

"Looks quiet enough," Raisho commented as they followed the well-worn trail toward the town.

Juhg didn't comment.

" 'Course, a quiet place is where bandits and assassins works best out of." Raisho eased his cutlass in the sheath he wore down his back.

Out on the Steadfast, the ferry between the two banks of the town bumped over the rolling water. Mule teams drew the ferry either way across the river, taking passengers as well as cargo. At noon it made a delivery every working day to the mill workers, supplying lunches that the mill owners paid for then charged the workers for.

"Where are we goin' once we reach town?" Raisho asked.

"The Wayside Inn." Juhg adjusted his hood to keep the light rain out of his face.

"This Minstrel Ordal will be there?"

"In all likelihood. If not, we can send word or meet him somewhere." Juhg's body ached with the constant motion of the horse. He looked forward to sitting by a roaring fireplace.

"Minstrel Ordal?" The tavern owner looked over Juhg's head. Juhg had to tiptoe slightly to look over the counter in the Wayside Inn. "I haven't seen her today, but she should be along with the evening crowd."

" 'She'?" Raisho repeated.

The tavern keeper was a portly man with a beard and a wandering eye. He'd introduced himself as Fhiel, but most of the other patrons seemed to call him

Jolly. Juhg assumed it was because the tavern keeper laughed at all the jokes he was told, no matter how old those jokes happened to be.

Fhiel nodded and looked a little confused. "She. That's right. Haven't you met Minstrel Ordal?" Suspicion hardened his features.

"No," Raisho said.

"I have," Juhg replied. "But it has been a few years. The last Minstrel Ordal I saw was a man."

A broad smile split Fhiel's face. "Ah, well then, kind sir, you're in for a treat, you are. No one quite plays the harp the way this Minstrel Ordal does."

Juhg paid for ales for Raisho and his men, then got a tankard of hot mulled cider for himself. "We'll wait for Minstrel Ordal. If you'll just let her know we're here." He put coins on the countertop.

With a practiced move, Fhiel scooped the coins away. "Perhaps you'd like something to eat while you're waiting."

"No, thank you," Juhg answered. "We'll eat when we buy supper for Minstrel Ordal."

"Good, good." Fhiel rubbed his hands together in anticipation. "I'll make sure the bread's baked fresh by then, and that we have plenty." He ran his good eye over the group of sailors with renewed appreciation. "You look like a hungry bunch. Nothing like cold rain to bring up an appetite."

Juhg took his mulled cider to one of the tables near the large fireplace. Logs blazed in the hearth as he shed his cloak and hung it from a coat tree in the corner. Sinking into one of the big, stuffed chairs, he sipped the cider and let out a contented sigh. Once more among civilization, in front of a fire and with a warm drink in his hand, the fight with the scarecrow seemed far in the past.

Raisho sat across from him. "I thought ye said Minstrel Ordal was a man?"

"I did," Juhg agreed. "In my experience, he always has been in the past. But I guess things change."

"How did Minstrel Ordal change from a 'he' to a 'she'?"

"Minstrel Ordal is an hereditary title," Juhg explained. "Usually it's passed on from father to son. I guess this time there was no son to carry on." He sat staring into the fire for a time, then got out his journal and started working.

It didn't take long before his actions drew the attention of the inn's guests.

"Halfer," a thick, bull-necked man bellowed across the room. "What do you think you're doing?"

"Writing," Juhg answered. *It feels so good to be able to say that!* But some of the old fear stirred within him.

"Writing?" The bull-necked man stood. He looked like a logger, his arms and back big and strong, and his hands marked with scars from knives and axes. "Is that a book?" He said it like an accusation.

"Yes." Juhg looked up. "It is a book." He took pride in that fact.

"Are you stupid?" the man bellowed. "Are you trying to bring the goblinkin down on us? If they find we've got a book here, they'll likely burn the town down around our ears." He started across the room. "I don't know where you got that, but you need to toss it into the fire. Toss it into the fire right *now*!"

"No," Juhg replied.

"Then I'll do it for you." The man came at Juhg.

Casually, stretching smooth and quick as a great cat, Raisho shot out a foot and tripped the man. By the time the man hit the floor, the sea captain had his cutlass out and the point resting against the big man's throat.

The big man froze at once.

Three of his companions shifted in their seats and started to get up.

Immediately, Raisho's men loosened their blades in their scabbards.

Tense silence filled the tavern.

"I wouldn't," Raisho said in a carefully measured voice, "was I you. We've come a far piece under 'ard times, an' we didn't come 'ere to be 'andled like rough trade."

The men stood for a moment, obviously trapped by their pride. They didn't like being bearded in their own tavern.

"This 'ere's me friend," Raisho declared. "A learned friend who knows more'n any of ye will ever learn if 'n ye devote the rest of yer lives to it. I'm not in the 'abit of lettin' me friends go unaided, an' I won't see 'is position disrespected. 'E's a Librarian. The Grandmagister of the Vault of All Known Knowledge. An' if 'n ye 'aven't 'eard of 'im yet, ye will."

One of the men looked at the others. "What's a Librarian?"

Both his companions shook their heads. Still, confronted by the hard-eyed sailors from *Moonsdreamer*, they resumed their seats.

"Books ain't nothin' to fear no more." Raisho took the cutlass from the logger's throat. "They're good things. Things worth respectin'. And I won't stand fer it to be any other way." He glared back at the man on the floor. "Do we 'ave us an understandin' then?"

The man shot silent resentment at Raisho for a moment. Then he grudgingly nodded. "Yes."

"Ye can get up, then." Raisho caught Fhiel's eye at the bar. "We didn't come 'ere for no trouble, but we've 'ad some what give it to us on the trail 'ere." He nodded to the loggers' table. "Set 'em up with a round on me." Reaching into his coin purse, he took out a silver coin and flipped it to the barkeep. "Let 'em drink that up."

Looking somewhat relieved, Fhiel pulled ale from the cask behind the bar. "Yes sir."

The logger on the floor got up but didn't look at Raisho or Juhg. He returned to his table and the free ale. The men talked in low voices. Juhg overheard "Grandmagister" three times. He was aware of being the object of covert scrutiny.

"Do you think that was wise?" Juhg asked in a voice that carried only to Raisho.

"No, 'twasn't wise at all." Raisho grinned. "We're 'ard-lookin' men, scribbler. 'E should 'ave 'ad 'imself at least twenty more men afore 'e come over 'ere a-threatenin' the way 'e did. They're loggers, not trained warriors."

Juhg sighed. "That's not what I meant. I was talking about making an announcement about me being the Grandmagister and about the Vault of All Known Knowledge."

Raisho laughed. "I thought ye were in Shark's Maw Cove to convince all them people they should be a-buildin' schools."

"I was."

"An' ye were talkin' about the Library."

Frowning, Juhg said, "You know I was."

Grinning under the shadow of his hood, Raisho looked around at the inn's patrons. All of them quickly looked away rather than risk accidentally meeting the sea captain's fierce gaze.

"Don't ye think they'll be talkin' about ye after ye're gone from 'ere?"

Juhg's cheeks burned.

Raisho laughed at his discomfort in good-natured humor. "They'll be talkin' about ye."

"I'd rather they didn't equate violence with an education."

"Really?" Raisho shifted, obviously enjoying himself. When they'd lain fallow onboard *Windchaser*, Raisho had often instigated arguments just to draw conversation from Juhg. The fact that he possessed a canny mind and a quick facility for learning had always made him a worthy opponent. "Wasn't it Baomet Sunkar that attributed much of education to invadin' armies what brought new learnin' back to both countries?"

In disbelief, Juhg looked at his friend. "You *have* been reading."

Shrugging, Raisho said, "It's a way of easin' long voyages."

Smiling in deeper appreciation of his friend, Juhg returned his attention to his journal. The cheery fire warmed him.

"Grandmagister Juhg."

Startled, Juhg looked up from his journal. A young woman with long red hair and her father's honest brown eyes regarded him. Her smile was open and friendly. She wore a yellow blouse with alabaster fringe and tan breeches. A feathered red cap sat on her head at a jaunty angle. She carried a pack over one shoulder and a small harp in one hand.

Gladness touched Juhg's heart and momentarily lifted the grave doubts and fears that his work on the journal barely kept at bay. He closed the journal, capped his inkwell, and put them both into his pack. He stuck the quill he'd been using behind his ear.

"Yurial!" Juhg exclaimed as he got to his feet and opened his arms. The young woman came to him eagerly, but he was surprised again at how tall she was. She had to kneel to take him into her embrace.

"I'll be Yurial to you," she said, "but to everyone else, I'm the Minstrel Ordal."

"Of course, of course." Releasing her, Juhg stepped back and looked her up and down. "You've grown."

Yurial laughed in delight. "I have. There was no alternative, I'm afraid."

"You were just a girl when I last saw you." Juhg waved her to one of the overstuffed chairs.

"That was twenty years ago, Grandmagister."

Juhg thought about it. Keeping timelines of outside things—dynasties, science, and other fields of study—was simple, but his personal timelines often blurred. One year seemed to leap headlong into the next.

"Twenty years brings about a lot of changes," Yurial said.

"It does. And don't call me Grandmagister. You're my friend."

"You have that title of office," Yurial said. "I wouldn't take it from you through casual address."

"Forgive me oafish friend," Raisho said, stepping forward to introduce himself. "I'm sure that sooner or later 'e would've remembered I were 'ere." He doffed his cloak to bare his head and smiled. "I am Captain Raisho, Master of *Moonsdreamer*, currently in port—"

"—at Calmpoint," Yurial said. "It's a pleasure to meet you, Captain Raisho."

"Ye seem to find out things pretty quickly," Raisho observed.

Yurial smiled. "Generally, if it happens in Calmpoint, Deldal's Mills, or a dozen other towns around here, I know about it." She sat in the chair Juhg had waved her to.

"We came straight from Calmpoint," Raisho said.

In that moment, Juhg realized why Raisho was being so inquisitive. "Raisho, Yurial didn't have anything to do with what happened to us last night."

"Then 'ow did she know *Moonsdreamer* was in Calmpoint?"

Yurial raised an amused and inquisitive eyebrow. "For one, Captain, you can't very well sail a deep sea ship up the Steadfast River. For another, a group of miller's men were returning to Deldal's Mills when you arrived, and they carried the news of your arrival. Then there are the horses outside that carry Ganik the blacksmith's mark. Another indication that you hadn't brought your ship upriver." She smiled again. "Unless you've some magic that allows you to fold your ship up and put it into your pocket."

"No," Raisho growled.

Juhg knew from experience that the young sea captain was embarrassed.

"I meant no disrespect," Raisho said, directing his gaze to Yurial as well as Juhg. "I just don't want nothin' to 'appen to the scribbler 'ere."

"So I judged," Yurial said, "from the reports of the near altercation in here earlier." She sat back calmly, her fingers plucking quiet notes subconsciously from the harp in her lap.

"Where's your da?" Juhg asked, hoping to steer the conversation away from the last few minutes.

"He's dead." Sadness touched Yurial's brown eyes.

"I'm sorry for your loss," Juhg said.

"As am I," Yurial said. "He was taken by Torlik's Fever three years past. One of the logging camps deep in the forest came down with it. Da went there because he couldn't bear the thought of those women and children dying without the all too brief happiness of stories and songs to tell them good-bye. So he went." She paused. "Da had been around Torlik's Fever on three other occasions. Survived it himself once. He thought he would be safe. He wasn't. We had to burn his body there with the others. But I placed a headstone for him in the graveyard. It gives me a place to go talk to him."

"You still have his songs," Juhg told her. "All those he taught you, as well as the ones he wrote."

A smile lightened her features then. "I know."

"I didn't know he was gone," Juhg apologized. "Otherwise I would have visited."

Yurial plucked sweet, sad notes, but she smiled. "I know you would have. You and Grandmagister Lamplighter. And since Wick's not here, am I to assume that something has happened to—"

"No," Juhg said. "Grandmagister Lamplighter abdicated his position to go off on a most remarkable journey." He didn't know how else to describe his mentor's disappearance with *The Book of Time*.

"Hopefully, Wick will return soon to us with marvelous tales of where he's been and what he's seen," Yurial said. "There's never been a talespinner like him."

"Never," Juhg agreed. "I wish he were here now to advance the idea of starting schools to teach reading and for the building of Libraries."

"From what I hear," Yurial said, "you've been doing well."

"Changing opinions is hard and slow."

"You're combating a thousand years of fear. That won't be an easy task."

"But if people could only understand what the Libraries have to offer," Juhg said, "they would take to the idea more quickly."

"All they know right now is that books may draw the goblinkin to them. The goblinkin still sack towns. Especially in the south near Hanged Elf 's Point."

Juhg knew that. One of his Librarians was assigned to assessing the growing threat of that situation. Several of the leaders he'd talked to were afraid another goblinkin war was brewing. He couldn't discount that possibility.

"But enough of that," Yurial said. "What has brought you here when you have so many other important things to do?"

Juhg waved the innkeeper over to bring fresh drinks all around, then he proceeded to tell the tale.

"Craugh wants to ferret out the betrayal that happened at the Battle of Fell's Keep?" Yurial sat back in her chair and delicately strummed the harp. The music was hauntingly familiar. Juhg was certain he'd heard it before, probably played by her father, but Yurial had made it her own.

"Yes."

"Why?"

"Because, as he insists, the world—or at least the mainland—is getting smaller. The goblinkin activity in the south has bunched up the northern empires, kingdoms, and port cities. The populations there have increased, so trade and travel have become more important. It's hard enough to work out those things without the mystery of who betrayed who at the Battle of Fell's Keep standing in the way."

Yurial nodded. "I agree with that."

"As do I," Juhg said.

"But what brings you here to Deldal's Mills?"

"Grandmagister Lamplighter left a book at the Vault of All Known Knowledge detailing his search for the traitor. I finished translating the code only a few days ago. At the end of that book, he left a clue to the location of the second book."

"There are two books?"

"There are three in all," Juhg said.

"Is the third with the second?"

"I don't know."

Yurial thought for a moment. Her quick mind instantly provided an answer to the question she hadn't even asked. "You came here to see me because you think I know the location of the second book."

"Because Grandmagister Lamplighter said Minstrel Ordal did."

Yurial shook her head. "He never gave me a book. Or my da. We helped Wick find a couple."

"Actually," Juhg said, "the Grandmagister said asking Minstrel Ordal a question would unveil the location of the second book."

"What's the question?"

A wave of nervousness passed through Juhg. The Grandmagister had been referring to Yurial's da, a man who had dealings with Edgewick Lamplighter on a personal level, swapping stories and humor and songs. Even though one Minstrel Ordal passed on all his knowledge to his apprentice, that didn't mean everything was handed down.

"The question is, 'What rides in on four legs, stands on two legs, and stumbles away on three legs'? I thought at first it might refer to the ages of a man. Crawling on four legs as a babe, walking as a man, then with the aid of a staff when he's bent with age."

Yurial smiled. "That's a good guess. Except it doesn't explain the bit about riding. Babes don't necessarily ride on four legs."

"Do you know the answer?"

"Of course I do. It's an easy question to answer if you knew Wick and my da."

"It escaped me."

Yurial stood and slung her pack and harp once more. "Come with me and you'll get your answer. Let's take care of Ganik's horses first. They look sad standing tethered outside."

"We don't need them?" Raisho asked.

"Not unless you intend to leave tonight."

Thinking about the scarecrow they'd encountered in the forest, Juhg shook his head. "We'll take rooms here tonight."

"You're welcome to stay at my home." Yurial looked at the sailors, who were also getting to their feet. "Of course, it will be crowded."

"We'll be fine here." Despite her status as Minstrel Ordal and the respect she had in the community as such, she had only a small house and was of modest means.

Together, after reassuring Fhiel they would return for supper, they departed.

Later, after the horses had been safely moved to the livery, Yurial led them through Deldal's Mills, through the shops and trade stores. Farther back, following a winding path between some of the older buildings in the town, they reached a small building that Juhg remembered.

It was three stories tall and narrow, a seeming clapboard building that was part shop and part residence. Though old, it had stood the test of time and looked solid enough to stand for several more years. Lights burned in the first floor.

An empty pottery jug painted with a sunburst (even though in the darkness that had fallen over Deldal's Mills Juhg couldn't see it) hung from the chain over the front door. It was the only advertisement, and it was all that was needed.

Evarch's Winery and Spirits was a legend along the Shattered Coast.

"I should have remembered Evarch's," Juhg said.

"You had a lot on your mind," Yurial told him as they walked up the tall wooden steps to the vintner's. She knocked on the door.

"Who is it?" an irritable voice demanded from within.

"Minstrel Ordal," Yurial answered, "Grandmagister Juhg, and friends."

"Go away. It's late."

"I know it's late, Evarch. I wouldn't be here if it weren't important. Come on. Open up."

"Tomorrow."

"Grandmagister Juhg is here."

"I heard you the first time. He can—" Evarch caught himself. "Did you say Grandmagister *Juhg*?"

"I did."

A moment passed as a shadow appeared on the curtained window. Locks ratcheted. Then the door opened. Evarch stuck his head out. Moonslight gleamed on his gray hair and beard. His leathery face was seamed with wrinkles.

"What happened to Wick?" Evarch demanded. "You didn't go and let something bad happen to him, did you?"

"No," Juhg answered. "Grandmagister Lamplighter is off on an adventure."

"Another one, huh?" Evarch shook his shaggy head. "I swear, Wick has never acted like any halfer I've ever known." He narrowed his eyes at Juhg. "You neither."

Juhg didn't know how to respond to that so he didn't.

"I suppose you're to blame for the interruption to my evening," Evarch accused.

"I am," Juhg admitted. "Grandmagister Lamplighter told me to come see you."

"He did, did he?" Interest flickered in the old man's eyes then. "Before he left?"

"The Grandmagister left the Library eight years ago. I was working on a book he'd written. There was a passage in there that sent me to Minstrel Ordal."

"Then to me?"

"Yes."

Evarch scratched his chin. "How did you come to me?"

"The Grandmagister sent me."

"Yes, I understand that. But how did you get the message? Did he just tell you to come see me? And you waited eight years to get around to it?"

"No."

"Because I can see that happening with you halfers. Dwarves and elves, too. You act like you have all the time in the world. But there are those of us who count days more dearly."

"It was in the passage in the book," Juhg said.

"What book?"

"One of Grandmagister Lamplighter's journals about the Battle of Fell's Keep."

"When he went seeking Master Blacksmith Oskarr's battle-axe Boneslicer in the Cinder Clouds Islands?"

Juhg nodded.

"What did this passage say?" Evarch asked.

"I was to find Minstrel Ordal and ask him—"

"Not a *him* this time around," Evarch said.

"—and ask *her* the answer to the following question, 'What rides in on four legs, stands on two legs, and stumbles away on three legs?' "

"You should have known the answer to that," Evarch said. "Without Minstrel Ordal's help. Then again, you never had the same interest in razalistynberry wine that your teacher did."

"No."

"Still not as interested?"

Juhg shook his head. "Sorry." He'd never developed a taste for wine or pipe-weed.

"Oh spare me from the uncultured palate. At least Minstrel Ordal was able to guide you to my door. The answer to your teacher's question is obvious. A thirsty man rides up on his horse's four legs to Evarch's Wine and Spirits, stands on his own two legs while he drinks his fill, then stumbles back using every lamppost along the way as his third leg."

It made sense to Juhg, but he knew he wouldn't have gotten the answer without Yurial's help. *Well, I might have even if Yurial hadn't been here*, he told himself. *Knowing the answer was in Deldal's Mills might have been enough. Once I'd started thinking clearly*.

"If that riddle led you here," Evarch said, "then you've come about the book."

"The second book of the trilogy?" Juhg asked.

"I don't know anything about that." Evarch stepped back and waved them into his house. "Years ago, Wick delivered a book to me for safekeeping and told me that one day his apprentice would show up for it. He claimed that only his apprentice would be able to read it."

Juhg followed Yurial through the door into the house. Nothing about Evarch's house smacked of business. It was a home first, and as such the first room was large and spacious, filled with decanters, tankards, and glasses from everywhere in the Shattered Coast.

Evarch waved them to comfortable furniture. There was room for all of them with space left over. Evarch sometimes entertained large numbers of guests, which belied the curmudgeonly persona he displayed.

"Juhg, light a few of the lanterns," Evarch directed. "We'll need illumination."

Juhg used the flames in the fireplace to light the lanterns. Soon, the room was cheery and bright. The flames reflected off the glass, stone, and metal containers arranged on the shelves around the room. The windows held stained glass images of grape fields and decanters, a concoction as audacious as the man who lived there.

Evarch returned in a few minutes with a large book in his hand. The blue cover caught Juhg's eye immediately. It was a reptile hide of some kind, and it immediately made him remember Rohoh.

"Before I give this book to you," Evarch said, "even though I know you, I want to abide by Wick's wishes in this matter."

"Of course," Juhg answered.

"He said whoever came for this book would know how to read it. He said that not even every Librarian he knew would be able to do that."

"Because he invented a code to write it in," Juhg said.

"Yes." Still a little hesitant, Evarch handed over the book. "I will know if you can read this."

Juhg opened the cover of the book with the reverence Edgewick Lamplighter had taught him to have for books. The code in this book was the same that had been used in the last. After days of translating the other book, Juhg could read the code with a little speed.

" 'Read this passage to Evarch the Vintner to prove that you know how to read the code.' Signed, 'Second Level Librarian Lamplighter.' " Juhg took a breath and deciphered the next section. " 'Evarch, obviously the situation I pursued regarding the Battle of Fell's Keep and Lord Kharrion's Wrath has become worse than I had imagined. Some old secrets never go away, and fear remains just as sharp for those that have done wrong. Please rest assured you have carried out to the best of your abilities the favor I have charged you with. Drink that bottle we set aside to seal this agreement in good health.' "

"Then he is truly gone." Tears showed in Evarch's eyes. "I'm going to miss that little halfer. I have known few friends like Wick."

The old man's emotion touched Juhg and made him more aware of his own loss. "I don't know that he is gone for good, Master Evarch. Only that he has been gone these eight years."

Evarch sat in one of the overstuffed chairs. "Eight years. I'd feared something had happened to him. In the whole time that I've known him, I've never known more than two or three years to pass before I saw him again. I knew too many years had slipped by this time, but I continued to hope that I would see him once more."

"You may still yet," Juhg said, but he knew he was hoping that more than he believed it. The power wielded by *The Book of Time* was incredible, and Juhg could only guess at the number of worlds it had opened up to Grandmagister Lamplighter.

"The book will help you?" Evarch asked.

"I think so," Juhg said. "There's still a lot to learn." He flipped through the pages, glancing at the pictures Grandmagister Lamplighter had drawn all those years ago when he was a Second Level Librarian. "While Grandmagister Lamplighter was in the Cinder Clouds Islands, he crossed the path of a thieves' guild called the Razor's Kiss."

"They operate out of Wharf Rat's Warren," Evarch said. "I've heard of them."

"So have I," Yurial said. "They're very dangerous."

Thoughts of the scarecrow that had attacked them the night before and of the bloodstains that were all that remained of Craugh aboard *Moonsdreamer* collided within Juhg's head, worrying at him. He wanted to get up and get moving, get back to Calmpoint and return to the ship. But Grandmagister Lamplighter's words—even across the years—seized his attention once more and pulled him into those events that had happened so long ago.

1

Wharf Rat's Warren

Act like a thief, he says, Second Level Librarian Edgewick Lamplighter thought crossly as he trod the icy streets of the city of thieves, murderers, assassins, brigands, thieves, cutthroats, cutpurses, thieves, burglars, thieves and—*I'm repeating myself. That can't be good.* He snorted in disgust. *Act like a thief, indeed. As if I know anything about being a thief. Why Craugh should—*

A howling wind from the Great Frozen North ripped through Whisper Street and distracted him. Out in the harbor, where a handful of ships sat sheltered in the Whipcrack Sea, so named because the sea had a tendency to freeze over with the sound of a whip cracking and crush ships mastered by unwary captains, rigging popped and rang against masts.

Wick pulled his black cloak more tightly around him and tried to remember the last time he'd felt his feet. They were frozen blocks at the ends of his legs that might as well have belonged to someone else.

As a dweller, he didn't really have a need for footwear. Generally his feet were tough enough for any task he had ahead of him. Today, however, he wished for a pair of boots just his size. Still, his discomfort was only an errant thought. The ruse he had yet to play consumed his thoughts.

He'd never before had to play the part of an assassin. Or was it a thief? For a moment, near frozen from his trek over the Ice Daggers, the small mountain range south of the city, and famished from not eating for what seemed like hours, Wick truly couldn't remember what part he was supposed to play.

He was supposed to be a thief or an assassin. He was pretty sure about that. The whole thing was Craugh's idea, which Wick had thought to be dumb from the beginning but hadn't had a better idea (or wanted to risk being turned into a toad by saying that), so he'd agreed to subterfuge. That had been onboard *One-Eyed Peggie*, though, and there'd been a meal waiting.

And he'd actually thought Craugh or Cap'n Farok would have become inspired and come up with something much better by the time they actually reached Wharf Rat's Warren.

He'd expected a hot breakfast that morning, too. Instead Craugh had roused him from his hammock, ordered him into his clothes, and marched him out to the little village where they'd dumped him.

Walking through the screaming wind, feeling the icy teeth of winter gnawing him all the way to the bone, Wick nearly tripped on his trousers again. The legs were several inches too long. Craugh had chosen to overlook that and told Wick he could simply keep them rolled up. Rolling them up hadn't lasted long. As soon as they'd gotten wet in the snow, they'd promptly unrolled and been a nuisance ever since.

He pulled the pants legs up again and felt the cold material slapping against his legs. The numbness seemed to be spreading. He had to pinch his ankles to discover that he *could* feel them even though he hadn't expected to.

To make matters worse, the donkey he was using as a combination mount and pack animal was becoming increasingly rebellious. Wick had to lean into his effort to bring the donkey along, and every now and then his efforts caused him to trip on a slippery spot and end up face-first in the snow. He didn't have a stitch of clothing that wasn't gunked up with mud.

When he fell again, Wick spat the dirty snow from his mouth and wiped it from his face. He was so cold that the snow actually felt warm against his skin, which was another bad sign.

I'm going to get frostbitten all over, he told himself. *If I somehow make it back out of here alive, Craugh and Hallekk are going to carve my toes, fingers, nose, ears, and other pieces off me.*

He turned to the donkey and stared the animal in the eyes. It was refusing to move again and strained at the end of the reins. Of course, since it outweighed him nearly ten times, the donkey didn't have to strain hard.

"Come on with me, you great lummox," Wick ordered. "You've got the easy part. At least all you have to do is act like a donkey."

The donkey swiveled its ears toward Wick as if it were listening intently. When he tugged again, it pinned its ears back, pulled its lips back in a big grin, and brayed donkey laughter. Then it sat on its haunches.

"I've got a mind to sell you to a renderer to be made into glue," Wick threatened. He set his feet and pulled with all his might.

Suddenly, laughter punctuated the howling wind.

Startled, Wick stepped back into the donkey's larger bulk for protection. He wasn't ready to start pretending to be a master assassin yet. Or thief. Whichever it was.

"Havin' trouble with your donkey, halfer?" one of the three men in front of the Tavern of Schemes asked. He was a tall human with a florid face and a big nose.

"No," Wick said, straightening to his full three and a half feet minus in height.

"You looked like you were having problems with him," the man continued.

Glaring, hoping the effect was both chilling and an expression of warning, Wick patted the donkey's neck. "No. Not any problems. This is where I wanted him to sit."

"In the middle of the street like that?" The man looked at Wick doubtfully. "Someone will steal him."

Let them, Wick thought. *If they can get him to move when they want him to, they can have him*. After all, the donkey wasn't part of his assassin's disguise. Or thief 's. He could gladly spare the stubborn beast.

"I'm toughening him up," Wick replied. "Having him sit in near-frozen mud puddles increases his endurance and strength. It's part of a training process."

The donkey yawned, smacked its lips, and stood, looking anything but trainable. Unbidden, it tramped toward the livery next door to the Tavern of Schemes, obviously smelling the hay and grain inside. The animal's sudden movement yanked Wick into motion and he stumbled along after it. Maybe he looked ridiculous, but at least he hadn't fallen on his face again. Still, looking in command of himself while being dragged by the donkey was impossible.

"And now I'm done punishing him," Wick said with feigned authority and confidence, falling into step with the donkey because he found the length of rope he'd tied around his wrist wasn't going to loosen up. "He knows who's boss."

The men laughed again at him, shaking their heads and going on with their business.

The donkey headed straight into the livery and Wick went with the animal, grateful to be out of the wind.

"How long are you going to be in town?" the dirty-faced young boy asked as he took the donkey's lead rope from Wick's wrist.

"I haven't decided yet." Wick gazed around the livery, surprised at how clean it was. Wharf Rat's Warren wasn't known for its cleanliness.

"The charges are daily or by the ten-day," the boy said.

"By the day," Wick said. "For now." Craugh hadn't been overly generous about funding his present mission despite Wick's protests. The wizard had insisted that Wick couldn't very well play the part of a thief looking for work if he was flush with gold. The little Librarian didn't want to spend what meager amount he had on caring for the cantankerous donkey when it might mean he'd have to skip meals himself.

The boy lifted his thin shoulders and dropped them. "Whatever. If you're late on a day's pay, though, my da will sell the donkey for whatever he can get."

"All right." *This could work out all the way around*, Wick thought. He wasn't looking forward to dragging the donkey back over the Ice Daggers.

Several horses stood in the paddocks, munching hay and oats, and snorting and stamping. A few coaches and carts occupied the far end of the livery. Wick didn't think the wheeled vehicles were often used. The streets in Wharf Rat's Warren were filled with potholes and covered only in oyster shells and loose shale.

Ryman Bey and the Razor's Kiss thieves' guild have Master Oskarr's battle-axe, though, and I can't allow that to continue. Especially since Wick blamed himself for losing the weapon while on the Cinder Clouds Islands. (Actually Craugh blamed him for it, and there was no arguing with the wizard once he became convinced of something.)

Bulokk was still recovering from his wounds during the battle against the Razor's Kiss. Upon discovering that Wick was about to leave *One-Eyed Peggie*, Bulokk had asked the little Librarian to promise him that he would do everything in his power to recover Boneslicer.

Wick, even though he hadn't wanted to promise such a thing, hadn't been able to say no. Of course, he'd envisioned he'd have someone at his back to do all the heavy lifting and sword-swinging that accompanied such promises. Bulokk would have been better off asking one of his warriors. Then again, maybe he'd asked everyone.

The other dwarves had volunteered to accompany Wick, but Craugh had forbidden that. Craugh insisted that Wharf Rat's Warren was primarily a human dwelling, albeit a lawless one, and that having a party of dwarves in their midst would alert the Razor's Kiss. There were dwarven bandits and thieves, of course, but they didn't live in Wharf Rat's Warren.

Reluctantly, Wick had admitted the wisdom of that. So, with the Cinder Clouds Islands dwarves and *One-Eyed Peggie*'s dwarven crew removed from the board, there had remained only two possibilities for the position of spy.

Craugh had quickly pointed out that no one would ever see him as anything less than a wizard. Wick had guilelessly (the threat of being turned into a toad always persisted when talking to the wizard) presented the opportunity for Craugh to pass himself off as a *thieving and selfish* wizard, and suggested that the role might require Craugh to do a lot of acting, but it wasn't beyond the realm of the imaginable.

Craugh had only given Wick one of *those* looks, and the little Librarian knew how things would go. Two days later he'd found himself at the small village of Bent Anchor and equipped with an ill-tempered and stubborn donkey.

Outside in the wind, Wick debated his choices. Twilight was coming on and snow was starting to fall again in thin white flakes.

He shivered, wishful of a warm fire, a good book, and a pipe. Maybe a pint of razalistynberry wine. That was the only way to properly enjoy weather like this.

Grimly, knowing that time counted and he'd lost days while traveling across the Ice Daggers, Wick headed for the Tavern of Schemes.

Like all of the other buildings in the city of thieves, murderers, assassins, thieves, etc., the Tavern of Schemes was heavily weathered by exposure and neglect. Windows were boarded over, the glass panes unreplaced, but space had been left for crossbowmen to take aim. Wick knew the place only because it was next to the livery.

The Tavern of Schemes was one of the most used buildings in the city. It was there that devious plans were hatched, daring robberies planned, and assassinations bought and paid for all along the Shattered Coast. The Tavern of Schemes wasn't the only such place to sell those services, but it was the only one in Wharf Rat's Warren.

Wick tried the door.

It was locked.

So what is an assassin—or a thief—supposed to do in this instance? Is this a test?

Wick gave the dilemma some thought. Finally, he reached into the small bag he carried and took out his thief's lockpicks. He'd just opened the kit up and set to work when he heard someone clear his throat behind him.

"I wouldn't do that if I were you," someone said.

2

Quarrel

Looking up and back, Wick saw a slim young man standing behind him. The young man wore heavy outer clothing and a thick fur cap. The hilt of a rapier jutted over his shoulder. A long knife was scabbarded at his right hip. His eyes were pale blue and the brows sharply arched. A scarf masked his lower face but his breath still blew a fog in the cold.

"Hello," Wick said, not certain what he was supposed to do.

"Hello," the young man replied.

Looking at the innocent-seeming blue eyes, Wick couldn't help wondering what the young man did as a vocation. Most of the other men the little Librarian had encountered while trudging through Wharf Rat's Warren had hard, selfish eyes.

These eyes seemed genuinely amused. And maybe a little suspicious.

"What are you doing?" the young man asked in a soft voice.

"Picking the lock," Wick said, gesturing with his pick. *There's no sense lying about it. Besides, this is the city of thieves, murderers, assassins, thieves, etc. It's not like they're going to call the watch to lock me up. Such behavior is expected here.*

"Why are you picking the lock?"

"Because the door's locked."

"Of course it's locked," the young man said. "This is the Tavern of Schemes. They don't just let anyone in. Saves them from getting surprised by any Watch members who come here looking for revenge or justice."

Wick could understand how the criminals of Wharf Rat's

Warren would see that as a defense. Several of the residents there had prices on their heads all along the Shattered Coast.

"But if you pick the lock," the young man went on, "you'll probably get a crossbow bolt between your eyes for your trouble. Utald rarely misses when he sets his sights."

Wick thought about that for a moment, then put his lockpicks away. "Well, that's not something I look forward to." He faced the door and spoke more loudly so that anyone who might be listening behind the door could hear him. "Sorry. Picking locks is a force of habit. I'm a thief." *Or an assassin.* He shrugged as nonchalantly as he could with the promise of a crossbow bolt between his eyes staring him in the face. "I find a locked door, I just naturally reach for my lockpicks." He forced a chuckle to break the tension, then looked at the young man again. "You know how it is."

"No," the young man said, "I don't." His eyes narrowed in irritation. "I'm not a thief."

"Oh." *That obviously leaves murderer or assassin.* Wick wasn't sure if either of those left him more comfortable than the other.

The door remained closed.

Feeling foolish, Wick jerked a thumb at the door. "Are you certain someone's on the other side of that door?"

A frown lowered the young man's arched brows. "Is this your first time here?" he asked.

"Yes." Wick stuck out a hand. "Righty Lightfingers at your service." *Should I have said that in a gruffer voice?* he wondered. *The thieves in Drelor Deodarb's tales always seem to be a scrofulous lot.* He made his voice deeper and added a hint of bravado. "I mean, the name's Righty. Righty Lightfingers."

"I see. But weren't you picking the lock left-handed?"

"A ruse," Wick said, thinking fast. *Why do I always get the ones with falcon's eyes?* It was enough to make him think being clever was not intended for him. Being intelligent, he'd found on several life-or-death situations, was decidedly different than being clever. Intelligence just didn't turn away axe blows and arrows with the same sort of success craftiness did. Intelligence involved learning, and sometimes learning was a direct application of the trouble he got into. "If I used my right hand, I'd give myself away."

"Most people," the young man stated, "are right-handed."

"Oh." In his hurry to cover his gaff, Wick had forgotten that. Being intelligent also wasn't a great defense when the other person was intelligent, too. Suddenly he felt like he was being taken to task just as he was by Grandmagister Frollo at the Vault of All Known Knowledge.

"Don't you know the secret knock?" the young man asked.

Wick blinked. *Secret knock?* "What secret knock?"

"The one that gets the guard to open the door."

"No."

The young man let out a breath of disgust that fogged the cold air for a moment.

Wick held his head up even though he wanted to drop it and turn invisible. "I did say this was my first time here," he reminded.

"So you did." The young man regarded him even more intently.

"I came here looking for work. Lots of thieves come to Wharf Rat's Warren looking for work."

The young man just looked at him.

"What's wrong?" Wick asked.

"You're the strangest thief I've ever met," the young man admitted.

"Maybe you haven't met many thieves," Wick suggested defensively.

"This is the place for meeting thieves," the young man pointed out. "I've met any number of thieves. After all, this is the city of thieves, murderers, assassins—"

"And thieves." Wick sighed.

The young man frowned. "I was going to say liars. There are a *lot* of liars here."

He said that as if Wick should take note that he knew all about liars.

"Of course," the young man went on, "lying doesn't pay as well as any of the other work. And *everybody* comes to hate you because once you start lying it's a hard habit to break. Once you start, you just sort of tend to forget you're doing it." The young man paused. "But it will get you just as dead. You might want to keep that in mind."

Wick gulped, but kept that reaction hidden. He hoped.

"Are you sure you want to go in?" the young man asked.

Actually, Wick was certain he did *not* want to enter the premises. One of the rumors he'd heard about Wharf Rat's Warren was that the Tavern of Schemes had a pit beneath it that allowed the disposal of bodies by way of an underground chute that led to the coastline only sixty yards away. Liars, cheats, and spies left the tavern with their throats cut and were given an impromptu burial at sea.

"Yes," he answered, and hoped that the young man didn't hear the momentary quaver in his voice.

The young man stepped to the door and banged on it with heavy-handed authority. The rapid syncopation of blows was answered from inside. Wick memorized both rhythms at once, in case he managed to emerge alive and ever had to go back to the Tavern of Schemes.

Then bolts slid and crossbars were lifted. The door opened and a huge troll shoved his blocky head through the space. He peered out with eyes large as a horse's and with sickly yellow irises. Nearly eight feet tall, the troll stood half that across, looking surely too broad to fit through the door. His skin, visible on his face and massively-thewed forearms, was the color of butter fat, pale and putrid with a hint of an ochre undertone. His hairless head was as square as a tree stump slapped into place atop his short neck. Pig's ears twitched atop his head, and the resemblance was carried out in his thick snout as well. Tusks in his lower jaw reached up past the outside corners of his eyes. He wore clothes fashioned from gray sealskin.

"Who is it?" the troll demanded in a voice even louder and deeper than a dwarf's.

"Quarrel," the young man announced. "You know me, Krok."

Quarrel fits you, Wick thought, surveying the young human. *Straight and sleek, no room for nonsense.*

The troll leaned down over the young human and blew out his breath in a great gray fog that enveloped Wick.

Wick almost threw up. Trolls smelled bad anyway, but whatever this one had been eating had been truly noxious. The little Librarian clapped his hand over his mouth and used his thumb and forefinger to pinch his nostrils shut.

Quarrel remained standing, arms folded over his chest.

He's got to be holding his breath, Wick thought desperately. *There's no way he can stand that stench.*

"I know you," Krok admitted. "You can come inside." He moved sideways and Quarrel slipped through easily. Then the troll turned his attention to Wick and blocked the way again, halting Wick in his tracks. "And *you*. Who are you?" He thrust his face forward.

With the troll's features only inches from his own, Wick removed his hand from his mouth, but he forgot to let go of his nose. His reply, "Righty Lightfingers," came out sounding high-pitched and nasal.

"*Righty* Lightfingers, huh?" Krok glared at Wick.

Realizing that he was gripping his nose with the wrong hand, Wick changed hands. He was pinching his nose again, still sounding nasal, when he answered, "That's right. I'm Right, er, Righty." He removed his hand and tried not to breathe.

"So what do you do, Righty Lightfingers?" Krok asked.

"I'm a thief," Wick said. "And a master assassin." He added the last quickly.

The troll regarded him with fascination. "Is that so?"

Still not breathing, Wick nodded.

"A halfer who's a thief and an assassin." Krok smiled. "This should be fun." He shot out a big, three-fingered hand, grabbed Wick's cloak, and yanked him inside.

Wick had time for one strangled, "Eeeep!" before he was yanked into the dark interior of the Tavern of Schemes.

"Lookit what I found at the door!" Krok roared as he held Wick up and carried him through the tavern in one big fist.

"A halfer," a man with an eye patch exclaimed in delight.

"Entertainment," a man with badly fitting wooden teeth added. "Didn't know there was going to be a sideshow tonight." His teeth clacked as he spoke.

Another man rubbed his hand and hook together enthusiastically. "It's been long enough since we had a halfer for sport. How many pieces do you want to cut him up in?" He leered in anticipation.

With the fear flooding him, thoughts of the cold water out in the harbor awaiting his body, Wick didn't mind the troll's stench so much. Actually, it wasn't that he didn't mind the stink, because he did, but it suddenly seemed like the sour odor was the least of his problems. He fought against the troll's grip but couldn't manage to get away.

"Don't get caught," Craugh had admonished Wick before they'd dumped him

out of *One-Eyed Peggie*. *"Don't do anything to raise suspicions. Do your best not to get noticed in any way. Slink. Skulk. Sneak. Act like a thief."*

Well, that wasn't working out. And, at the moment, Wick would have preferred getting turned into a toad to ending up in chunks for the monsters out in the harbor. Toads still got to eat and had warm beds.

Krok thumped Wick onto the scarred bar at the back of the tavern. Gazing around the room, the little Librarian got the feeling he'd stepped right into the pages of one of Drelor Deodarb's crime romances. Only Wick didn't feel like one of the tough mercenaries or thieves or assassins Deodarb wrote about.

At least twenty men were in the room. All of them sat in shadows at tiny tables scrunched in between high-backed booths. Single candles barely illuminated the harsh features of the men seated there. All of their faces carried lines formed of misery and cruelty. Scars and missing limbs were in abundance. The reek of desperation swirled through the room.

Wharf Rat's Warren divided the residents there quickly into winners and losers, with a subdivision of losers who died and those who survived with scars to show how close they had come. There were two other trolls and four goblinkin. With the darkness lurking in the room, the tavern seemed small. The low ceiling maintained that image.

"What you got there, Krok?" one of the trolls asked.

"Going to find out," Krok answered.

Not knowing what else to do, Wick sat on the counter. He blinked and tried to think of something to say. If he'd been one of Deodarb's antiheroes, he'd have pulled out hidden stilettos and pinned both Krok's hands to the counter for him. Or a hidden short sword and lopped off one of the henchmen's heads.

Even if he'd had stilettos, Wick couldn't have found it in him to pin Krok's hands to the counter. He didn't care for violence at all. Despite that, sometimes violence seemed to follow him around. Most of the time, it chased him, waving a weapon or baring fangs, and threatening the most awful things.

"Says his name is Righty Lightfingers," Krok said. "He's supposed to be a thief and an assassin. Anybody heard of someone by that name?"

A chorus of "nos" ran around the room.

Looking back at Wick, Krok growled, "Nobody's heard of you, halfer."

"A thief and master assassin isn't supposed to have a reputation," Wick said in a small voice. "Except by those looking to hire him." Thankfully he managed to say that without quavering. He tried to look fearless, but doubted he pulled that off sitting contritely like he was in Grandmagister Frollo's study to accept a verbal drubbing. "Does anyone here want to hire a thief or an assassin?"

The tavern patrons broke out in laughter. It was undecided whether "A halfer thief!" or "A halfer assassin!" got the greatest response.

"Maybe he offers *low* prices!" someone else chortled.

"Or he specializes in *little* jobs!" another cried.

"In those hard-to-get-to places!"

Wick's hopes of survival dwindled.

"Do you know how many people would want to hurt me if they suspected I was a thief or an assassin?" Wick asked, trying to find some way to excuse his anonymity. "I can't just go around letting everyone know who stole the king's crown or who poisoned an important merchant."

Krok scratched his head thoughtfully. "That's true."

"And people I've stolen from don't want to admit it. Who wants to admit they've had a fortune stolen by a dweller?" Wick went on.

"That's true, too."

"Or had someone they were supposed to be guarding assassinated under their very noses by me?"

"Of course it was under their noses. He's a halfer."

"You've done that?"

Wick started to say a dozen times, then thought the tavern crowd might not believe that and considered lowering the number, then figured he really needed to impress and—hopefully—throw a little fear in them. "Nearly one hundred times," he declared, thinking that surely that was a respectable number of victims.

3

The Assassin's Résumé

Laughter filled the tavern immediately.

"No way," a grizzled mercenary said. "A little pipsqueak like you couldn't have killed nearly a hundred people."

"I didn't do it with a blade," Wick said. "They had to look like accidents. That's what I specialize in. Trip wires on stairs. Snakes in beds. Death by horse—"

"Death by horse?" a man asked. "You hire the horse?"

"No," Wick said, finding himself curiously drawn to his stories, which were lifted from various compendiums on assassinations he'd read. Grandmagister Frollo hadn't exactly been thrilled about finding those on Wick's personal reading list, either. Grandmagister Frollo wasn't of the opinion that all knowledge should be saved. "You can put a burr under a horse's saddle. Or poison it so it temporarily goes mad. Then you can just talk them into killing their riders."

"Talk to horses?"

Too late, Wick realized that he'd selected a means that didn't come readily to anyone other than elven warders. "I was taught the trick by an elven assassin."

"An elven assassin?" The doubt was evident in the sailor's voice. "Elves don't take easily to that trade."

"Not easily," Wick agreed. "But sometimes the best solution to a problem is one corpse taken quietly so that ten others don't need to be taken." He paused. "Of course, the best tool of the trade is poison. I know how to make hundreds of poisons."

"Poisons," Krok repeated.

"Yes." Wick tried to act nonchalant. "I once walked into a

banquet room with an incense shaker and spread invisible poisonous dust over the meals of eight men whose deaths I'd been paid for. The first one was dying as I walked out of the room." He shook his head. "Still, it was a near thing. The poison had acted much more quickly than I'd wagered."

Silence filled the tavern, and most of the patrons pushed their unfinished plates away.

"Is this true?" Krok asked.

"Of course it's true," Wick replied, warming to the hope that he could emerge with a whole skin. He tried to act calm and detached.

In the corner, a quiet smile flirted with Quarrel's lips. It appeared that the young man didn't quite believe Wick's tales. Thankfully, it seemed he was the only one who didn't.

"Mayhap the halfer's telling the truth," someone suggested.

"We'd have heard of him here," one of the men said. "We get to know everyone in that line of trade who come through here."

"This is my first time here," Wick said. "I didn't want to be known to so many." He paused. "I wasn't exactly given a choice here today."

"How did you keep us from hearing about you?"

Wick thought quickly and snatched at the first idea he thought was believable. "I'm really good at, uh, thievery and assassinations."

Silence hung in the tavern for a moment, then the thieves, murderers, assassins, thieves, etc. started laughing. They slapped their legs and thumped on the table.

"*Nobody* is *that* good," a slim man in black and purple clothing stated. He stood and touched his chest, filled with pompous pride. "I'm Dawarn the Nimble. Perhaps you've heard of me."

"You're a burglar," Wick replied instantly. "There's a price on your head up in Kelloch's Harbor, a job waiting for you in Hanged Elf 's Point if you decide you want it, and merchants in Drakemoor, Talloch, and Cardin's Deep want you dead. Well, maybe not Merchant Olligar in Cardin's Deep because he doesn't think the warehouse fire was truly your fault, and it worked out for him. Oh, and the captain of *Wavecutter* still wants you to pay off on the percentage he was supposed to get for helping you in Bardek's Cove."

An instant hubbub of conversations started around the room.

Then, "You never paid off on that percentage to Cap'n Huljar?" someone demanded.

Dawarn instantly lost some of his pompousness, throwing up his hands to the crowd that suddenly bristled against him. "Hey! Hey! Stop snarling and snapping like a pack of wolves! I was going to pay him! I still am!" He frowned. "Things in Bardek's Cove just got . . . *complicated*."

"So complicated you stiffed Huljar?" someone said. "You don't stiff Huljar. You're lucky you're still walking around breathing through your nose instead of your neck."

"I'm not the one under suspicion here," Dawarn pointed out, taking his seat again, no longer wanting attention. "It's him!" He threw a finger toward Wick.

"Okay," Krok snarled, turning back to Wick, "so you know Dawarn, and you even know some of the work he's done. Including stiffing friends." He threw a sidelong glare at the offending burglar. "That doesn't mean you're who you say you are."

Wick gave the accusation consideration but didn't see an immediate answer.

"Test him," someone said.

Heads turned, all of them focusing on Quarrel. The young man sat at a table by himself. He'd unwrapped his face, revealing smooth-shaven, youthful features.

"He came in with you, Quarrel," Krok said.

"No," Quarrel replied. "He's not with me." He paused. "*You* let him in, Krok. If you want to make anyone responsible for his presence here, you have to take it. You could easily have left him outside."

Krok scowled. "Anybody else here want to get identified?"

No one volunteered.

"Just because he knows faces and names," Quarrel said, "doesn't mean that he's a clever thief or an assassin." He regarded Wick. "You should test him."

I hope you're caught in whatever your next endeavor is, Wick thought. Anxiety thrummed through him.

"All right then," Krok said. "A test. What kind of test?"

Wick thought he saw a way clear. He crossed his arms and looked as defiantly as he could out at the crowd. He was glad he was in baggy pants and not standing, because he didn't know if he'd be able to stand on his shaking knees.

"Pick someone for me to poison," Wick said, feeling certain that no one would be brought forth. Even if someone was, he could concoct something that would put a victim into a coma for several days. Provided the victim wasn't buried or thrown out into the harbor, he would recover. By then, with luck, Wick would be long gone from Wharf Rat's Warren.

"He doesn't just claim to be an assassin," Quarrel reminded. "He also says he's a thief. Let's see if he's as good a thief as he claims to be an assassin."

I really don't care for you, Wick thought.

"That's right! See if he's truly a thief," a man with a peg leg suggested. "Have him pick Utald's safe."

"A safe!" Wick cried, feeling instant relief. At the Vault of All Known Knowledge he was in the habit of tripping mousetraps so none of them would get hurt. He also kept the cats fed when no one was looking. "That's easy enough!" After all, he'd read several books on the manufacture of safes and lock-picking, which went surprisingly hand in hand in a lot of areas. *Surely they can't come up with anything I'm not familiar with.*

His enthusiasm, however, seemed ill placed. Evidently no one had expected quite that reaction. Everyone stared at him with increased suspicion.

Wick quickly realized that none of Deodarb's characters would have reacted in quite the same manner. He deepened his voice. "I mean, bring it on, you muttonheads." *There. That's tough enough, isn't it?*

" 'Muttonheads,' is it?" Krok slapped his big hands on the counter on either side of Wick, emphasizing the fact that he could crush him if he wanted to.

"I was talking to the muttonheads," Wick said weakly. *Was that too tough? It had to have been too tough.* "Not to you. You're not a muttonhead. I wouldn't ever call you a muttonhead." *Maybe a cold-blooded killer. Maybe stinky, but never to your face. Maybe—*

"Utald," Krok roared. "The safe." He fisted Wick's cloak and blouse in his big hand again and lifted him from the counter.

The barkeep, who until this point had been a silent spectator to the action, walked to the wall of bottles behind the counter and slapped a big hand on the wall. Tall and overweight with sloping shoulders and long gray hair, the barkeep looked like a mercenary who'd gone to seed.

At the end of the series of slaps, a section of the wall popped open. The barkeep grabbed the hidden door and swung it wide.

"My safe," the barkeep said. "Nobody gets into *my* safe."

It was impressive looking, Wick thought. The safe was a contraption of hammered metal plates, springs, gears, wheels, and levers. None of the safes Wick had ever seen had looked quite the equal of this one. When it came to safes, this one was a dreadnaught.

"There she is." Utald slapped the safe's side with obvious affection. "I call her Lusylle. She's the best of the best."

"No one's ever beaten Lusylle," Krok said. "There's a lot of thieves who have tried."

"They all call her 'heartbreaker,' " Utald said.

"Well," Wick said grimly. "We'll see about that." (He said that with much more confidence than he felt.) "If you'll put me down."

Krok looked at Wick dangling from the end of his arm. "Oh. Okay." He opened his fingers.

Unceremoniously, Wick plopped to the ground and landed on his posterior. After all the slips and falls with the donkey, that region was already overly sensitive. He pushed himself back up. His lock-pick kit fell to the floor and scattered.

"Say," one of the men said, peering over the counter, "isn't that a Gladarn's Lock-picking Kit Number Six?"

"It's a Number Nine," Wick said. "It's acid-proof."

An appreciative *ooooohh* came from the thieves in the audience. At least, the ones that were above the regular cut-and-slash or thump-and-run caliber.

"Acid-proof," one old man said. "Now I could have used some of those when I went up against Thomobor's Forbidden Chest. Took me three days to get inside his fortress and two shakes of a lamb's tail for me to lose my lock-picks." He shook his head. "I never got that close again."

Wick set himself before the lock. As he considered the problem before him, all his fear seemed to drain away. The only thing that seemed to exist in his world was the conundrum of the safe.

"Little halfer's got his work cut out for him," someone murmured.

"Where did Utald get that safe?"

"Don't know. He's always had it here."

"Ever seen it open?"

"Nope."

Spinning the dials, Wick worked the springs and plates, pushing and shoving as he tried to find the rhythm of the safe. The safe was like a living, breathing organism, and everything had to be in perfect balance.

Snikk!

"That was the first lock," a man whispered.

"Has anyone ever popped the first lock?"

"Langres," Krok said. "But that's been two years or more."

"Four years."

"I said 'or more,' didn't I?" Krok asked irritably. "Four's more than two."

Ignoring them, captivated by the challenge of the safe, Wick kept searching for hidden pins to the second lock. After reading the books on lock-picking, he'd practiced on locks around the Vault of All Known Knowledge, until he'd locked himself into a closet and couldn't get to the lock. He hadn't noticed that fact until he was standing in the dark. Grandmagister Frollo had found him still standing in the dark a few hours later, looking for a monograph Wick was supposed to complete on sail design of the Silver Sea merchant ships. After that, Grandmagister Frollo had taken away Wick's lock-picks and forbidden him to lock himself in anything again.

Claaa-aaack!

The second lock popped.

"He's got a *second* lock!"

"How many more to go?"

"Three, I think. Hey, Utald, how many more locks?"

Wick glanced up at the barkeep, who continued to stand there impassively, arms crossed over his chest.

Utald shook his head. "Let the halfer find out."

The third lock wouldn't surrender its secrets. Wick used thin silver wire to snake out the confines of the mechanism, but had trouble picturing the device in his mind. Every time he almost had the pins in place, they dropped back into locking position.

Finally, he concentrated on feeling his way through the lock, easing each of the five pins into place. They fell again.

"Arrrgggggghhhhhh!" the crowd gasped.

"What is it? What happened?" the mercenaries, murderers, and assassins asked.

"He can't get past the third lock. Keeps dropping the pins," the thieves answered.

I got past the first two locks, Wick thought plaintively. *No one has done that before. Surely you can believe I'm a thief now.*

But he knew they wouldn't. He wasn't that lucky.

"Ready to give up, halfer?" Krok grinned.

"No." Wick rubbed his hands together to warm them. Working on the cold metal of the safe for so long had left them chilled and leaden. *If I give up, I might as well just jump into that chute out to the harbor.* Besides, the problem of the lock had intrigued him.

He leaned into the safe again. This time he worked on each pin as it came free. On the third pin, he found a hole that shouldn't have been there. Going back to the first and second pins, knowing what to look for now, he found holes in them as well.

Wick smiled. *Clever. Clever, indeed.*

"He's smiling! The little halfer's smiling!"

I am, Wick thought, *because I know the secret of this one.* Using the wire, working by touch because he couldn't see into the lock, he searched for a hole on the front of the lock. When he didn't find one there, he searched from the back. After he found it, he ran the wire through the lock, threading the pins each in turn.

This time all the pins stayed in place when he pushed them back. He grabbed the lock lever, pushed a lever, and stretched two of the springs.

Kha-chunk!

4

Inside the Safe

"The third lock! He's got the third lock!"

Resting his cramping hands, Wick looked up to find an umbrella of faces peering down at him. The animosity was gone from them. It felt like they were all on the same team, all sharing the same expectations.

Unless I fail, Wick thought. *Then it's the chute for sure.*

"Hey, halfer," the man with the eye patch said, "let me buy you a drink. You can't keep working at that so hard without a drink. Utald, it's on me." He flipped a coin into the air.

Utald unlimbered an arm and snatched the coin from the air as effortlessly as a falcon taking a dove. He tested the coin between his teeth, then shoved it into a coin purse.

"What'll you have, halfer?" the barkeep asked.

"Razalistynberry wine," Wick said, grateful to have the drink.

"That's a sissy drink," one of the big mercenaries grumbled. "You should get you a shot of busthead. That'll settle your nerves just fine."

"Just the wine, please," Wick said. Then he thought about the response he should have made. He frowned and glared up at the mercenary. "Who are you calling a sissy? I'm not just a thief. I'm an assassin, too. Maybe you want to remember that before you go to sleep tonight and don't wake up in the morning."

The tavern's patrons broke out laughing, and slammed their fists against the counter.

"He's got you there, Jolker!"

Quick as lightning, though, Jolker pulled his sword and had it tucked under Wick's chin.

"You might have a care there, halfer," the mercenary growled. He jabbed Wick hard enough with the sword to make him step back. "Won't be any trouble to snuff you out with the candle before I got to bed tonight."

Wick froze, leaning uncomfortably back.

"Jolker," a calm voice said.

Heads turned toward the voice.

In the lantern light, Quarrel stood there with a bow drawn. The arrowhead nocked on the bow gleamed.

"Sheath that sword," Quarrel said.

"And if I don't?" Jolker asked.

A thin smile curved Quarrel's mouth. "At this distance, this arrowhead will split your head like a melon." He paused. "I won't miss."

But people on either side of the big mercenary drew back. Just in case.

"You're taking a part in this?" Jolker asked. "Normally you don't involve yourself in anything that goes on here outside of a job."

"One," Quarrel counted evenly. "Two." The arrowhead never wavered.

Cursing, Jolker took his sword back. He grabbed up his tankard and abandoned the counter.

"You just made a big mistake, Quarrel," Jolker snarled. "A *big* mistake!" He left the tavern.

Trembling, Wick accepted the mug of razalistynberry wine from Utald. He tried to drink without spilling it all over himself, and for the most part managed that. As he put the mug on the bar, the little Librarian wondered what Quarrel thought he was doing, and why the young man had taken part in the argument. But Wick was already starting to not think so badly of Quarrel.

"Go on then, halfer, let's see if you can defeat Lusylle," Utald challenged.

Taking a deep breath, Wick turned back to the safe. In seconds, he'd worked through the fourth and fifth locks. Neither had been anything special, and there had been no further tricks.

Click!

Ratchet!

Covered in sweat despite the chill that pervaded the room, Wick gripped the final lever and shifted the last spring.

"He's done it!"

"The halfer's done it!"

"Utald, whatever you've got hidden in that safe will never be safe again!"

A look of unease pulled at the barkeep's face. He took a step forward just as Wick gripped the doorframe and set himself to pull.

"Wait!" Utald commanded.

"Wait?" Wick echoed.

"Wait!" Utald repeated, stepping back.

That's not a good sign, Wick thought, stepping back himself.

"Why wait?" Krok asked.

Utald was silent for a moment. "Because the safe may be booby-trapped."

" 'May be?' You don't know?"

Scratching self-consciously at the back of his neck, Utald shook his head. "No."

"Why don't you know?"

"I don't know what's in there. It's not my safe. I stole it."

Wick looked at the big man in disbelief. "What?"

Utald shrugged. "I wasn't always a barkeep. I used to be with a group of bandits. We attacked a caravan and took everything they had." He nodded toward the safe. "That was one of the things they had."

"When was this?" Krok asked.

"Twenty-seven years ago. More or less." Utald looked at the safe. "I just kept it around, you know, in case I ever found someone that could open it."

"But you put it in the bar."

Utald nodded. "It made a good conversation piece, didn't it? Besides, I figured that sooner or later I would learn its secret."

"Do you know who the safe belonged to?"

"Could have been the caravan master's."

"I never heard of no caravan master carrying a safe like this," someone said.

"Or it could have been a wizard's," Utald said.

The tavern crowd drew back. "There could be anything in there," someone said. "Maybe even something the wizard wanted to get shut of. Maybe a monster. Or some undead thing that kept following him around."

Tense, the crowd took another step back.

Wick was suddenly aware that he was standing there alone. He slid his fingers around the doorframe, no longer prepared to swing it wide, but rather to slam it shut.

"Open it," Krok commanded.

"It is open," Wick insisted.

Krok drew a heavy two-handed sword. He gestured toward the safe. "Pull the door open."

Wick leaned on the door, hoping that if anything was inside it was dead or didn't know it had been released. He shook his head.

"Do it, halfer," Krok commanded.

"I'm a thief," Wick said. "Not a warrior."

"You're an assassin," the troll said. "If something bad comes out of there, assassinate it."

"Assassination, a good assassination," Wick insisted, "takes time. Something done in the heat of the moment, that's murder. I'm not a murderer. Any unskilled person can do that."

Utald scrambled over the bar, distancing himself from the safe.

"You've been curious about this for twenty-seven years," Wick said, feeling somewhat angry that the barkeep wasn't doing the door chores himself. "Haven't you wanted to see what you stole all those years ago?"

"Sure," the barkeep said, drawing a pair of long knives from somewhere on his person. "Open it up and let's have a look."

Wick fidgeted, trying to think of a way to escape opening the safe.

"Do it now, halfer," Krok said. "We're growing old waiting."

Closing his eyes, terrified of what he was going to find, Wick swung the door wide. He let the iron door carry him with it, hoping to use it for cover, and closed his eyes tightly.

"Bless me," Utald whispered in the stillness that followed, "for I am a rich man."

Since he hadn't been struck dead (by lightning, fire, or a death bolt) or mauled to death (by a gargoyle, a dragon, or a banshee), Wick grew curious. Across the bar, the patrons stepped forward again and looked inside the safe in amazement.

"I've never seen one of those made out of gold," one of them said.

"It looks comfortable," another said.

"Do you really think it's worth a fortune?"

"You melt that gold down, if it's pure enough, and it'll keep Utald living easy for the rest of his life."

"I don't know about that. You know how Utald is when he gets deep in his cups and gets around women. It's like closing your fist in a pool of water."

"Or slow horses. Utald stays an inch away from the poor house because he has an eye for slow horses."

Krok grinned. "Maybe you should pay to let people use it before you melt it down, Utald. Won't hurt the gold. I'll be your first customer."

"No!" Utald leaped the counter with the vigor of a much younger man. "Nobody's sitting on that! Or doing anything else either! It's mine! I've dragged it around for twenty-seven years, and put it up here at the Tavern of Schemes!"

So curious he could no longer stand it, Wick looked around the door and into the safe. At first he thought the safe held a chair. Then, since it was made out of solid gold and encrusted with a few gems, he guessed that it was a throne. Hypnotized by the deep yellow luster of the gold, he peered more closely.

On deeper examination, he discovered that the chair had no seat. Well, actually, it only had part of a seat.

"It's a privy," Wick said.

"Not *just* a privy," Utald corrected. "It's a solid *gold* privy. *My* solid gold privy."

Most of the people in the Tavern of Schemes broke out into laughter at Utald's good fortune, twenty-seven years in the making, and others cursed him for it. The barkeep didn't care. Overjoyed, Utald bought the whole tavern a round.

Later, mostly accepted into the fraternity of thieves, murderers, assassins, thieves, etc. that frequented the Tavern of Schemes, Wick drank razalistynberry wine and speculated on how the golden privy had gotten into the safe, and whom it had been intended for. No one knew for sure, and too many years had passed for Utald to remember whom it had been stolen from.

After they'd flushed the subject of the privy from their minds, the tavern's patrons told tales about past jobs and past employers. Wick listened to the stories the men told. Of course, being the storyteller he was, Wick was soon telling them of his own adventures as a thief and assassin.

He told them about the time he'd stolen King Iakha's magic mirror that kept him from aging (a story borrowed from Hralbomm's Wing), and the way he'd tricked Northern Giants into letting him know where their lair was (from an unfinished story he'd started working on with Taurak Bleiyz as the main character), and how he'd assassinated a dragon by destroying its magical heart.

By the time Wick had walked the tavern crowd through the lava-filled antechamber of Shengharck's lair (Wick actually renamed the dragon and his own purposeful destruction of it, as well as working in a vengeful king who'd hired him to do the deed—not mentioning, of course, that the deed had been accomplished through sheer accident and not design), many of the men were sleeping at their tables or in their chairs.

Wick walked along the countertop much as he had back in Paunsel's in Greydawn Moors when he'd first gotten involved in the search for what had truly happened at the Battle of Fell's Keep back during the Cataclysm. He was slightly tipsy from the wine, for it was a good vintage, but not so much off his game that he wasn't already wondering where he should spend the night. Particularly since he wanted to wake up in the morning.

Then the door opened and four hard-eyed men walked into the tavern. All four of the men wore the open razor tattoo on their cheeks that marked them as members of the thieves' guild Wick had come to Wharf Rat's Warren to scout.

Quietly, the little Librarian walked to one end of the counter and made himself as invisible as he could. He didn't look at the thieves, but he kept track of

them through his peripheral vision. He also noticed that Quarrel was keeping watch over them as well.

The Razor's Kiss guild members bellied up to the counter and ordered. "Hey, Utald. Where'd you get the privy?"

"Oh, this old thing?" Utald asked, jerking his hand back toward the privy in the safe. "I've had it for a long time."

"I've never seen one before," the tallest of the men said.

"They're rare and unique things, Vostin," Utald agreed.

A sleek shadow slunk along the counter bottom beneath Wick's feet. The cat was huge, with tortoiseshell coloration and startling gray eyes. Just past Wick's feet, the animal sat on its haunches and gazed up at him in the way that only cats could.

Then, with a lithe leap, the cat jumped up to the counter next to him.

"Hello, kitty," Wick said. He reached to pet the cat.

The animal turned to him and hissed a warning. One paw lifted and filled with sharp claws.

Hastily, Wick drew his hand back. He didn't want to risk injury to his fingers because that would affect his ability to write. In the past, he'd hurt his hands and fingers, and the time he'd been unable to write had been almost unbearable.

"Not the friendly sort, are you?" Wick turned his attention back to the four Razor's Kiss thieves as they made small talk.

"What are you doing in here?" Utald asked.

"Meeting a man," Vostin said.

"Business?"

"Yes." Vostin tossed back his drink and looked hard at the barkeep. "None of it yours."

Wick's ears pricked up. Craugh was of the impression that someone had hired the Razor's Kiss guild to steal Boneslicer. As far as Craugh and his contacts in the city could ascertain, Boneslicer hadn't left the hands of the Razor's Kiss.

Sipping his drink, Wick wished his head would clear.

Nearly an hour later, after a dozen men came and went through the tavern, a new visitor walked through the door. He hadn't known the secret knock, which had marked him instantly as someone from someplace else, but he'd produced a marker of some sort that got him past Krok.

Wick watched with interest. Beside him, the cat yawned, pink tongue rolling out for a moment before curling back in.

The new arrival was a man of indeterminate years. He wore dark clothing against the cold, and carried a longsword at his hip. After an almost casual glance around, the man settled on the four Razor's Kiss thieves. He tapped his cheek.

Vostin nodded and hooked a chair from another table with his foot. The man came over to sit.

After a brief conversation with the new arrival, the thieves got up from the table and headed out the door. The mood inside the tavern lightened almost immediately.

"I suppose they're not exactly popular around here," Wick observed to the man next to him.

"Razor's Kiss," the big mercenary muttered. He was deep in his cups and his gaze was a little slack. "Think they're something special here in the Warren." He took another sip. "They're not. Just thieves." He shrugged. "Thieves that will slit your throat as soon as look at you, though. Better to stay away from 'em."

"I will," Wick said, and wondered if he'd be able to. He had no intentions of—

"Follow them," a woman's voice ordered.

Wick looked down at his feet. He thought that was where the voice had come from. It was hard to imagine, though, because he hadn't seen any women in the tavern.

Only the cat lay there.

"Did you say something?" the mercenary asked.

"Not me," Wick said.

"Coulda sworn I heard a woman." Looking around, the mercenary pulled at his beard. "But I don't see any in here."

Okay, Wick thought, *we're imagining the same thing*. He was just thinking how strange and improbable that was when—

"Follow them."

The tone was more insistent this time. It also wasn't finished.

"Get up off your duff, halfer, and get moving."

Now there was no mistaking *who* the voice was talking to.

5

"Is That *Your* Talking Cat?"

Wick was distracted by Quarrel as the young man got up and departed the Tavern of Schemes. Movement erupted at his side. When he turned back to the counter, he found the cat sitting there staring at him with those large gray eyes. At the moment, those eyes looked particularly intelligent.

And angry.

"Get up," the cat said, baring her fangs. (Wick was suddenly certain the cat was a she.) "Get up and get moving. This is what you're supposed to do. If you'd made it to the meeting, you'd have known that."

Meeting? Wick thought rapidly. Now that he considered everything that Craugh had told him, he did seem to recall some mention of a meeting. But he'd thought that wouldn't take place until he found Boneslicer.

The mercenary leaned in from the other side. "Is that your cat?"

"Nooooooo," Wick answered cautiously. He was fairly certain that talking animals would not be well received in Wharf Rat's Warren. With all the paranoia prevalent throughout the outlaw town, the animal would doubtless be hung as a spy. Or drawn and quartered. Or simply thrust into a bag with a brick and tossed out into the harbor.

The chances were also good that anyone with the cat would receive the same treatment. At his size, Wick thought it was possible he would fit in the same bag as the cat.

"Move it," the cat yowled. She struck at Wick with extended claws.

Wick barely got his hand out of the way. The claws sliced neatly through the sleeve of his cloak.

"Did you hear that?" the mercenary asked.

Looking innocent, Wick said, "I didn't hear anything."

"You didn't hear that cat talking?"

"No." Wick shook his head.

"You did," the cat insisted. She stood and stretched, arching her back and moving closer. The threat was evident. "Now get up."

The mercenary raised his glass and peered into it. "Utald must be forgetting to water his drinks. They don't usually have this much kick."

The cat swiped at Wick's arms again, chasing them from the counter. "Let's go. You need to find out where they're going."

Wick stood.

Moving with ease and grace, the cat dropped to the floor. Her tail flicked imperiously. She stopped and waited, clearly not happy about Wick's reluctance.

Jerking a thumb toward the door, Wick said, "I'm going to let the cat out."

"You'd better," the mercenary said. "She sounds really upset with you." He drained his drink and banged the empty glass against the counter, signaling for another.

Wick went. Now that the tavern's patrons were pretty drunk, none of them seemed to care that he was leaving. Seated near the door, Krok looked up at Wick.

"The cat," Wick said, pointing.

The cat waited impatiently at the door.

Krok nodded. "Who let it in?"

"I don't know."

"Filthy beasts," Krok growled. "Always carrying in vermin."

"Look who's talking," the cat hissed. "Is that your head? Or did your neck throw up?"

"What?" Krok roared, pushing up unsteadily.

"I didn't hear anything," Wick said.

"Get the door, halfer. You're losing ground."

"Is that *your* talking cat?" Krok demanded.

"No." Wick shook his head. "Definitely not."

"Then why are you taking it outside?"

"Because . . ." Wick thought furiously, "I'm tired of listening to it. I can't get it to shut up." That was the truth. "But it's not mine."

"You're going to be polite to a troll," the cat accused, "but you can't listen to me?"

"See?" Wick said, smiling as inoffensively as he could.

"Get it out of here."

Wick opened the door and followed the cat out. He thought just for a moment of staying inside the tavern. But he'd been fortunate enough the first time to survive the encounter. Besides, now that the cat had mentioned it, he did remember that Craugh had given instructions about some meeting with someone named—

"Alysta," Wick said, looking down at the cat.

Regal and confident, the cat sat on her haunches and gazed up at him with gray-eyed command. "I am. You are the Librarian."

Wick glanced around to make certain no one had overheard the cat. Full dark filled Wharf Rat's Warren's streets, leaving thick shadows everywhere.

"I am," Wick admitted. "Second Level Librarian Edgewick Lamplighter."

"*Second* Level Librarian?" The cat, Alysta, looked displeased. "Craugh couldn't have arranged for a more *experienced* Librarian?"

Wick drew himself up to his full height. He was certainly taller than a cat, had opposable thumbs, and didn't cough up hairballs. How much experience could a cat have at spying?

"I'm the most experienced available," Wick said. "None of the other Librarians have ever been to the mainland."

"So you're out on an island, are you?" The cat smiled.

No more information, Wick thought. Evidently the cat didn't know as much as he'd thought. And now it had one more piece of information about the Vault of All Known Knowledge.

"I'd thought the Librarians were based deep in the interior."

Wick refused to answer.

"And what does Craugh think?" Alysta demanded. "Just because you can read and write doesn't mean you're suited to find the lost sword."

"Reading and writing," Wick said, "are the two most important—" He stopped, suddenly realizing what the cat had said. "What sword?"

"Seaspray."

Wick racked his brain. For a moment, he couldn't place the weapon. Then it came to him in a rush. "Seaspray? Captain Dulaun's Seaspray?"

The sword was one of legend, just as Boneslicer was. Captain Dulaun of the Silver Sea trade empires had fought at the Battle of Fell's Keep a thousand years ago with Master Oskarr. In his own right, before the Cataclysm, Captain Dulaun had helped defend the Silver Sea holdings against the encroachment of goblinkin and anyone else that dared raise sails against them.

"It wasn't always Captain Dulaun's," the cat said.

"How do you know this?"

"You're not the only one that can read and write."

Wick was amazed. "You can read and write?"

"It's not that difficult," Alysta said. "I taught my daughter to read and write."

The image of a mother cat teaching her kitten to read filled his mind and seemed very strange. Wick was so captivated by that image that he didn't realize the cat was speaking to him again.

"What?" he said.

The cat hissed angrily. "You're wasting time. When we finish this, I'm going to tell Craugh exactly what I think of him for pairing me up with you."

You're not the only one, Wick thought.

"Now come on." The cat took off.

Reluctantly, Wick fell into step. "Where are we going?"

"To follow the Razor's Kiss thieves, of course." The cat leaped over a wide hole filled with freezing water, broken ice, and mud.

Wick saw the hole too late and nearly fell in. "Why are we following them?"

"Because they know where the sword is."

"You don't?"

The cat shot him a reproachful look but kept moving. "If I knew where the sword was, we would go there. Now be quiet. If those men find out we're following them, they might choose to kill you."

Then following them at all is a bad idea, Wick wanted to say.

The four Razor's Kiss thieves added six more to their number when they reached the livery.

Trailing after the cat, Wick circled around behind the livery to the back door. It wasn't locked. Alysta squeezed through the gap and disappeared inside. Wick sipped a breath of cold air that bit into his lungs. The odors from inside the livery hit him, too. After a moment, he eased through the door.

"Quiet," the cat admonished, like she was talking to a child. "And get down so you can't be seen."

Wick hunkered down behind the stalls. In the romances from Hralbomm's Wing, Deodalb's antiheroes and Decarthian spies managed to escape certain death all the time and never once doubted their skills. He was terrified to the point of being fumble-fingered. The happy buzz he'd enjoyed in the Tavern of Schemes was now a thing of the past.

Horses snorted and stirred in the paddocks. The sharp scents of oats, barley, and hay tickled Wick's nose. He caught himself right before he sneezed.

"Don't you dare," the cat hissed.

Wick held a finger under his nose. He needed to sneeze so badly that his eyes watered. Only the threat of painful death kept him from succumbing. Gradually, the pressure in his head went away. He let out a tentative breath.

Easing forward again, he joined Alysta and crouched at the end of the paddock. Peering around the corner, he spotted the Razor's Kiss thieves saddling horses while the livery boy looked on.

"You can't just take my father's horses," the boy whined.

One of the thieves turned and slapped the boy down. After he hit the ground, the boy stayed there. Tears streamed from his eyes as he looked at the thieves.

"Be glad it's just the horses we want," one of the thieves said. "Another word from you, and your father will come here in the morning and find he has to bury you."

The man who had hired them stood nearby. He wasn't saddling a mount. "How long will this take?"

The thief who had slapped the boy down turned to their employer. "As long as it takes, Captain Gujhar. Not one moment sooner."

In a crowd, the thief would have faded from view almost at once were it not for the distinctive tattoo on his cheek and the burn scarring over his right eye that pulled at that side of his face. In the cold, the scarred flesh was almost white as paper against his dark skin.

"That's not an acceptable answer, Flann," Captain Gujhar replied. He stood with military erectness.

Looking at the man, Wick now recognized the bearing and self-discipline. He was a man of authority, used to being obeyed.

So why is Captain Gujhar in Wharf Rat's Warren dealing with thieves? Wick wondered.

At the corner, the cat watched with supreme concentration, like she'd spotted prey. Her tail coiled and uncoiled behind her with methodical slowness. She looked ready to pounce.

Flann led his mount toward the livery's door. "I'm here to achieve results," the thief said. "If you think you can do it any sooner, then I suggest you be about it." He paused, waiting.

Captain Gujhar stood silent and still for a moment. His hand toyed with the hilt of the longsword at his hip.

Even with the odds ten against, he's thinking about fighting them. Wick was amazed. The man was either foolhardy or very good. Wick was curious as to which it was, chiefly because it was likely they were going to be enemies, or—at the very least—competitors for Boneslicer.

"No," Captain Gujhar replied.

"Then let me be about my business," Flann suggested. "That way we can both keep your employer happy. We handled that situation on the Cinder Clouds Islands the way you wanted us to and it very nearly cost us when that other ship appeared."

"I don't know how the dwarves found out about Boneslicer," Captain Gujhar replied.

"Or how they happened to have a fighting ship at their beck and call that night," Flann said. He grinned. "Seems there's a lot you don't know. You'd be better off letting us do what your master paid us to do."

The captain said nothing.

The cold wind howled through the open door and sucked what little warmth there was out of the livery. The horses whinnied and stamped in displeasure.

"Going to wish us luck then?" Flann smiled.

"Good luck," the captain said.

Flann pulled himself into the saddle as the horse reared and bucked, evidently in no hurry to get out into the freezing weather. Leaning forward, the thief seized the horse's ear and bit it, hanging on till it stopped fighting.

The other thieves quickly mounted as well, then they thundered down the street, heading back into the Flowing Mountains at the other end of Wharf Rat's Warren.

Captain Gujhar watched for a moment, then left without a word. The door slammed loosely behind him.

Still crying a little, the livery boy got up and closed the door. He cursed for a while and promised death to the thieves if he ever saw them again.

Wick started to move.

The cat pressed herself back against him. "Wait," Alysta said.

Before Wick could ask why, movement in the rafters caused him to sink back against the paddock wall. Then Quarrel dropped from the rafters into the area between the paddocks by the front door, startling a scream out of the livery boy.

"It's all right," Quarrel assured the boy. "I've come for my horse." He fished a coin from a small leather purse.

Always alert for details, Wick spotted a curious symbol stamped onto the leather purse. It was small and artfully done, a rose clasped in the thorny embrace of a vine.

The livery boy caught the coin in the air and made a fist around it.

Moving quickly, Quarrel saddled his horse, negotiated the price of a bag of apples for the horse, and led the animal outside. With his cloak wrapped around him, Quarrel galloped out after the thieves.

"All right," the cat said.

"All right what?" Wick asked.

"Now we follow them." Alysta walked out into the walkway between the paddocks.

Wick had been afraid the cat was going to suggest that. "Shouldn't we stay here? Until Craugh and the ship arrive?"

"Why should they come? You haven't found anything of importance yet."

"We're following those thieves."

"Yes, and that trail may lead us nowhere. We don't know yet."

"Doesn't Craugh know what we're here looking for?"

"That man," the cat replied. "Captain Gujhar."

"Why?"

"Because he's from *Wraith*."

"*Wraith?*"

"The ship that took Boneslicer from the Cinder Clouds Islands."

"Is Boneslicer still on the ship?"

"I don't know."

"Shouldn't we try to get the battle-axe back?" Wick still clung to the hope that he'd end up in a warm bed for the night.

The cat turned around and looked up at Wick. "All right."

Wick halted and looked back at the cat. "All right?"

"As in, 'All right, we'll steal the battle-axe back from a ship of armed guards before we follow that pack of thieves and see what they're up to.' "

Wick almost sneezed again. He lifted his fingers to his nose. "Armeb guarbs, huh?"

The cat gave a solemn nod.

Removing his hand from his nose, Wick said, "Maybe we could follow the thieves. At least for a little while."

"Splendid idea," the cat said.

"Sarcasm really isn't an endearing trait," Wick stated.

"Are you talking to that cat?" the livery boy asked. He stood in the walkway, a rag shoved up against his nose.

"No," Wick said.

"Yes," Alysta said. "We've come for the donkey."

The boy looked at Alysta. "I've never seen a talking cat before."

"I wouldn't say a word," the cat said, "if I thought the halfer could handle this on his own. Let's have the donkey. Come on. Quick now."

Dazed and befuddled, Wick joined Alysta at the paddock that held the donkey. Inside the paddock, a feedbag covered the donkey's lower face. He munched contentedly, but without any real interest.

Before Wick knew what was about to happen, the cat pounced on him, landing on his shoulder, then springing to the paddock.

"Well," the cat asked, "what have you got to say for yourself?"

Initially, Wick thought Alysta was talking to him. Then he noticed that her attention was on the donkey.

"The fact that we're behind schedule is partly your fault," the cat went on.

The donkey locked eyes with the cat. "It's not my fault," the donkey said. "Have you seen how dense the halfer is?"

Wick couldn't believe it. He leaned heavily against the paddock door. The livery boy gawped beside him.

"You can talk, too?" Wick whispered.

The donkey rolled his eyes, looking even more comical because the feedbag made him look like he was wearing a veil. "Do you see what I have had to put up with? He's not exactly the brightest candle in the bunch."

"You knew where the rendezvous was supposed to be," Alysta said. "You could have gotten him there."

"It was cold," the donkey said. He shivered and flicked his tail. "It's still cold."

"Doesn't matter," the cat told him. "We've got a job to do."

"We can wait till morning," the donkey suggested. "It'll be warmer in the morning."

That sounded good to Wick, too. He deserved at least one night in a warm bed.

"No," the cat said. "We're leaving. *Now*." She flattened her ears against her skull and eyed the donkey with dark-eyed threat. "Or perhaps you'd care to be a toad again instead of a donkey."

The donkey sighed. "All right, all right." He shifted his attention to the livery boy, who was staring in wide-mouthed astonishment. "Give me a refill on the feedbag. I'm taking it with me. Put it on the halfer's tab."

Minutes later, equipped with a replenished feedbag for the donkey and enough supplies for a few days, Wick mounted up. The cat leaped onto the donkey's haunches, who complained that they could—and should—both walk.

Outside the livery stable, Wick took up the chase of the Razor's Kiss at a sedate pace. He wrapped himself tightly in the cloak. At least this time he was riding instead of nearly dragging the donkey. Overall, he had to admit that it was an improvement. Except for the fact that it was so cold, so dark, and that he was probably headed straight into trouble.

6

Caught

Falling snow blew through the air. The howling north wind picked up more dry, white powder from the ground and mixed it with the new flakes. Wick felt them touch his face, brief moments of icy cold, then a stinging numbness that lasted just a short time.

After hours of riding, Wharf Rat's Warren was a collection of lights in the distance amid the foothills of the mountains. Wick had also begun to doubt the luxury of riding the donkey. In the beginning, he'd rather liked the idea of controlling the animal. Or at least having the illusion of controlling the animal. The donkey claimed to be an expert tracker, one of the many talents he professed to owning, and didn't have any problems cutting the sign of the Razor's Kiss horses.

Wick knew about tracking, too, and was confident that the donkey was on the right track. He was so cold he was miserable, even under the heavy folds of his traveling cloak. If he could have just closed his eyes for an instant, he felt certain he'd have fallen asleep.

Do that, he thought again, *and you'll be abandoned by the cat and donkey. They'll leave you lying, and since there's no true spring thaw up in the Great Frozen North, no one will ever find your body.*

Dropping the protective wrap of the cloak from his face, Wick peered forward. With all the snow blowing, it was hard to see, but the road was clearly defined between the trees. Going any other way was out of the question because the deep snowdrifts covered treacherous terrain. Traveling that way in the dark would have meant a broken leg for a horse. As it was, even with the road fairly well traveled, the donkey had a hard time pushing through.

"How much longer?" Wick asked.

"Oh, please shut up," the donkey snapped. "I'm the one doing all the work here."

Wick had to admit that was true. But it also sharpened the question of *why* the donkey and the cat were helping the wizard seek out Boneslicer. And now Seaspray. The cat, if she knew and Wick thought she did, wasn't talking. Even for a talking cat, she acted strangely preoccupied.

He turned his attention once again to the histories of the dwarven and human weapons, and to what he recollected about the Battle of Fell's Keep. Nothing new came to mind. Craugh claimed that his only goal was to settle the old injustice against Master Blacksmith Oskarr and prove that he wasn't a traitor to the brave warriors of the Battle of Fell's Keep, but Wick no longer believed that. Craugh had some ulterior motive in mind. Wick just didn't know what it was.

Scanning the skyline again, Wick tried to remember what was up in the mountains. He'd read about the area, but he would have liked to have read more. Primarily he remembered what had been written about the port city and the thieves, murderers, assassins, etc. who lived there. There were even a few outlying towns and villages that did a little business with Wharf Rat's Warren, bartering food and wood for trade goods such as cloth and farming equipment the pirates brought in from cargo ships they took.

Wick hadn't read anything about what lay beyond. Whatever it was, though, he felt certain they were headed there.

Sometime later, a pale glow took shape in the darkness ahead. It grew larger as they got closer.

"Stop here," Alysta ordered.

The donkey stopped and swung his head around. "This isn't the best place to spend the night."

"That's a campfire up ahead," the cat said. She uncoiled from Wick's back and stretched, arching her back and working one leg at a time. "We're not going any closer."

Wick gazed around wildly, not believing what the cat was intending. "We're going to spend the night here? *Here?*"

"Yes." With a lithe vault, the cat sprang from the donkey's backside and grabbed hold of a low-hanging limb on a massive spruce tree. Snow fell thick as fog for a moment from the branch, then thinned out.

"But we'll freeze," Wick protested.

"No you won't." The cat sat in the crook of the tree. Her head turned to watch the silent flight of a passing owl.

The donkey turned and lumbered into the open space beneath the spruce. He pressed up against a pile of boulders and rock that had been shoved there by the road builders all those years ago. Earth had washed down the mountain and formed a berm that splashed up over the boulders.

"Get off me," the donkey ordered.

Without a word, Wick slid off. *I should be the one giving orders*, he thought. *Craugh sent me to do this*. But that only made him think that the wizard should have been trekking up the side of the snow-covered mountain, not him.

Sheltered by the boulders from the wind, Wick rummaged through his supply pack. He took out a bundle of kindling.

"What are you doing?" the cat asked.

"I'm going to start a fire," Wick explained.

"No."

Grudgingly, Wick looked up at the cat. "If I don't have a fire, I'll freeze."

"Sit close to the donkey."

"He stinks," Wick said.

"Hey," the donkey replied, "you're not exactly an apple blossom yourself."

Wick realized that was probably true. He'd been on the road for several days, and there had been no way he was going to bathe in a freezing stream or pond. Still, he was certain he smelled better than the donkey.

Wick was determined not to sit next to the great, smelly donkey. He took an additional blanket from his pack and pulled it over himself as he sat in a spot he hollowed out in the snow. Despite his best intentions, though, he slid over close to the donkey, acting like he was falling asleep. Then, after a moment, he started feeling warmer and he went to sleep.

"Hey."

The voice woke Wick. He clawed through the blanket for a moment to peer out.

Quarrel sat hunkered down in front of him. The young man held his bow and a nocked arrow in his hands. In the moonslight reflected from the snow, he was smiling.

"What are you doing out here?" Quarrel asked.

The donkey came awake beside Wick and swung his big head around to survey the situation. Instead of being concerned, the donkey only yawned and smacked his lips.

Glaring up into the tree, Wick saw Alysta sitting there on the branch. Evidently the cat had gotten caught sleeping as well. She stared down with baleful eyes.

"I got a job," Wick explained.

"Awfully fast work," Quarrel commented. "When I left the tavern, you were still telling stories."

"That's how it goes sometimes. Unemployed, then you're employed."

"By who?"

Wick remembered a line from the Spymasters of Darcathia romance. "If I told you that, you'd have to kill me."

Quarrel looked at him as though he were odd. "You *are* the strangest thief and assassin I have ever met."

"I meant," Wick said, realizing that he'd gotten it wrong, "that *I'd* have to kill *you*."

Grinning again, Quarrel nodded. "I thought that's what you meant. It's just as well. Knowing that you would do me harm if you had to makes what I'm about to do even easier."

What you're about to do? Wick sat up a little straighter. "Maybe we could talk about what you're about to do."

"I'm going to let the thieves find you," Quarrel said.

"Thieves?" Wick swallowed, peering over Quarrel's shoulder at the forest. Shadows seemed to slip among the trees.

"I got too close to the camp," Quarrel explained. "My mistake. I was overzealous, I suppose. But it's nothing I can't fix now that I found you."

Wick heard the snow chuffing under footsteps then. Someone was closing in on his campsite. He tried to stand up but got tangled in the blanket and his cloak and couldn't get up.

"I do hope they don't kill you," Quarrel said. "Good luck with it." Then he sprang over Wick's head and ran with sure-footed grace up the pile of boulders. He was out of sight before Wick realized that he should be running, too. He made another attempt to get up and succeeded.

The chuffing sounded closer.

"Some watchdog you were," Wick growled at the cat as he staggered through the snow. He grabbed the donkey's harness and tried to urge the animal to his feet.

"I'm not a watchdog," Alysta protested. "I was sleeping up here." She craned her head around and kept her voice soft. "Too late, halfer."

Abandoning his efforts to move the donkey, Wick turned and tried to run through the chest-high—on him—snow. His feet twisted and slipped beneath him. Before he got three steps, an attacker came up behind him and hit him at the base of the skull. He remembered seeing the snow-covered ground coming up to meet him, but blackness swallowed him before he hit.

Captured, he thought morosely, his thoughts swimming in pain. *I hate being captured.*

"Anybody recognize him?"

Someone grabbed Wick by the hair and flopped his head around. He tried to resist, but he was still too groggy. The headache exploding inside his skull seemed to be doing just fine, though.

"I think I saw him," someone else said. "Back at the Tavern of Schemes."

"Are you sure?"

"How many halfers do you think there are in Wharf Rat's Warren?"

"Not many," the other voice admitted.

"And even fewer of them with red hair like this one."

Forcing his eyes open, Wick found himself bound hand and foot and lying on his right shoulder.

"He's awake," someone said.

Instantly, a sword swooped down and rested heavily against Wick's throat.

"Have a care there, halfer. I'll split you open as soon as look at you."

Wick believed the speaker. The Razor's Kiss had gotten their name first from the method they'd employed to rob their victims: slitting open the fat purses of merchants and letting the contents drop into another bag. But the thieves' guild had slit a fair number of throats, too. He lay still.

"He's not dead, is he?" One of the thieves leaned in for a closer look. "You hit him a pretty solid knock on the noggin, Flann."

"He's not dead." The grizzled veteran holding the sword squatted down beside Wick. "I've hit plenty more a lot harder. Besides, everybody knows halfers has got thick skulls. Takes a lot to get through one of 'em. Or to break one."

Pain rushed through Wick's thoughts, so violent and fierce that he thought he was going to throw up. Then, horrified, he realized he was going to. "I'm going to be sick," he croaked. He made gagging noises.

Reluctantly, Flann took back his sword.

Wick turned over and threw up. He felt immediately embarrassed, which was exceedingly strange because he should have been frightened for his very life. Then he realized he was still scared as well. He felt very confused.

After a while, his stomach was empty of the wine. Worn out, chilled to the bone, he slowly rolled over to look at the Razor's Kiss members.

"Who are you?" Flann asked.

"Nobody," Wick said hoarsely. The taste in his throat threatened to set off another wave of sickness.

Flann prodded him with the end of the sword. "I'll have your name, halfer, or I'll bury you here without one." He raised an arched eyebrow. "Which is it going to be?"

"Tevil," Wick croaked. "My name is Tevil Bottleblower."

"Bottleblower?" one of the thieves repeated. "That's a strange name."

"I'm a glass blower by trade," Wick said. "I make . . . well, bottles."

"Bottles of what?"

Wick blinked at that.

"Bottles of what?" the thief asked again. "Ale? Pickles? Spices?"

"Just . . . bottles," Wick replied. "I don't put anything into them. I make them so that other people can put things into them."

"And you can sell an empty bottle?" The thieves marveled at that idea.

"Yes," Wick said. "Some bottles are worth hundreds of gold pieces."

"Really?"

Wick clung to that. If they thought he could make bottles worth hundreds of gold pieces maybe they wouldn't kill him out of hand. "Yes."

"How do you make a bottle?" one of the thieves asked. "I've always been curious. I thought maybe you might chip them out of glass, but I don't see how you can do that without breaking them."

"You don't chip them out," Wick said. "You cook glass, make it out of sand and other things, and heat it till it's molten. When you get it right, you scoop some of it up on a pipe and you . . . blow it."

"Ah," another thief said. "That's why you sometimes see bubbles in the glass. I always wondered about that."

"Enough about bottles," Flann growled irritably. "I want to know what you're doing following us, halfer."

Wick thought for a moment. "This, uh, is the *only* road out of town."

"He's right there," one of the thieves said.

"I wasn't following you," Wick insisted. "We just happened to be headed in the same direction."

"In the middle of the night?" Flann narrowed his eyes in suspicion.

"I had to get out of town," Wick said, thinking quickly.

"Why?"

"I picked the wrong pockets back in the Tavern of Schemes."

"That's him!" one of the thieves exclaimed, pointing at Wick.

For a moment, the little Librarian feared that the man was going to say, *That's him!* As in, *That's him! The halfer from the Cinder Clouds Islands!* But he didn't.

Instead, the man said, "That's the halfer who picked Utald's safe."

"So you're a thief, are you?" Flann asked.

Wick shrank back from the sharp edge of the naked blade. "Yes."

"Were you planning on thieving from us? Is that what you were doing in our camp?"

"I wasn't in your camp," Wick said. "I was here. Asleep."

"You weren't asleep when we got here."

"I was. I swear. Right before you got here."

"You heard us coming?"

Wick nodded. The back of his head squeaked against the snow.

"You didn't hear us coming," Flann said. "Hearing you even suggest that makes me want to gut you right now."

Being gutted wasn't a pleasant prospect. Several medical and history books in the Vault of All Known Knowledge had pictures of such barbaric procedures. Wick swallowed and gagged on the vile taste at the back of his throat again.

"So how did you really know we were coming?" Flann asked.

"Quarrel told me," Wick answered.

"Quarrel's your partner?"

"No," Wick said, wanting to be as truthful as he knew how. "The cat is my partner." He pointed up into the tree. "Or I'm her partner. I'm not sure exactly how that works. But I really think she's supposed to be my aide. She just takes far too many liberties to be a proper aide, though."

Alysta spat at him from the tree branch and flattened her ears in annoyance.

"The cat?" Flann repeated.

Wick nodded.

"You have a cat for a partner?"

"It wasn't my idea," Wick said honestly.

"The cat's name is Quarrel?"

"No. The cat's name is Alysta."

"Then who's Quarrel? Another partner?"

"No. Quarrel's a mercenary I met at the Tavern of Schemes. He's not my partner. You can't trust him." Wick had trouble reconciling the young man's actions in the tavern to save him and his recent betrayal.

"He was out here?"

"Yes."

Flann waved four of his men into motion. They quickly drew their swords and eased through the brush.

"Do you have any other partners I should know about?" the thief leader asked.

From the tone in the man's voice, Wick knew he had to be as completely honest as he dared. "I think maybe the donkey can be considered a partner. He talks, too. Not as much as the cat, but he's stubborn."

"Talk, do they?" Skepticism wrinkled tight lines through Flann's face.

Wick nodded.

Flann sighed in disgust. "I'm through talking to you, halfer. You lie every time you open your mouth. Make your peace."

Wick blinked. "You're going to kill me?"

Nodding, Flann said, "Don't worry. I'll make it quick and painless. We aren't enemies, after all. You were probably just following along, intending to rob us—which isn't the smartest thing you could have done. But I can respect that."

"Why are you going to kill me?"

"I can't very well have you following us around, now can I?"

"I could promise not to."

"I wouldn't believe you."

"Well, that's hardly fair. You don't really know me enough to make that judgment."

"Fair's only good in checkers," Flann said. "And that's only if you keep both eyes on the board." He waved a gloved hand. "Now hurry up with it. I can still get a few hours' sleep."

You can just kill me and go back to bed? Wick couldn't believe it.

"Flann," another thief spoke up, "don't kill him yet."

Anger showing on his face, Flann looked at the speaker. "Why not?"

"You weren't in the Cinder Clouds Islands," the other man said. He was young and intense. "I was."

"So?"

"While I was there, some of the goblinkin talked about a halfer they'd caught. A little red-haired halfer. Talked a lot, they said. Like this one. He was supposed to cook for them."

I'll never, Wick moaned to himself, *live that down. Even if I live through this. It will pursue me forever.*

"The dwarves rescued him," the younger thief went on. "Later, he was at the buried foundry. He was with the dwarves that found the axe we were sent for."

You were sent for the axe? That interested Wick intensely. Was it just happenstance that the subject of the Battle of Fell's Keep had arisen that night in Paunsel's Tavern, or was there something more diabolical afoot? His native curiosity weighed in heavily against his fear.

Flann regarded Wick. "Were you there, halfer?"

For a moment, Wick was torn, not knowing which way was the safest to answer. *Saying* no *in this instance*, he believed, while looking at the sword in Flann's hand, *is probably a . . . dead end. Or a life-altering one at best.* He took a deep breath and let it out. No brilliant ideas came to him and he was decidedly disappointed.

"I don't have all night," Flann said. "Tell me the truth, and I'll know it when I hear it—"

Wick had serious reservations about that statement since the thief leader didn't believe him about the talking cat and donkey.

"—or you'll never wear a hat again," Flann finished.

"I was there," Wick answered. Then he set himself to be as coy as he could. *They won't get any more answers out of me! I'll die before I tell them anything that will make them think they can kill me immediately.*

Without a word, Flann lifted his sword and slammed the hilt against Wick's forehead with a dull *thunk.* Blinding pain consumed the little Librarian and he dropped once more back into darkness.

7

Krepner the Goblinkin

The whole world moved as Wick swam up through the cottony darkness. *I'm alive!*

Of course, that discovery wasn't as inviting as it might have been if he'd been certain he was out of the hands of the thieves' guild and had woken up instead in his bed at the Vault of All Known Knowledge. At first, he didn't move—he was sure of it—but the sensation of moving stayed with him. Nausea wormed through his stomach.

Then he felt rough wood against his hands instead of snow. He also realized that he was no longer wearing his travel cloak. That woke him at once. His writing kit was secreted away in the cloak's hidden lining.

His journal was missing!

Cracking open an eye, Wick discovered that he was in a ship's brig. The heavy iron door rested awkwardly in its frame, and rust patches showed inattention. The interior of the brig stank of excrement and vomit. Not at all the kind of place Wick would ever hope to be. Although it had been exciting to "borrow" those places for a time in his reading.

Lantern light glowed on the other side of the iron door.

"Haw, haw, haw!" a deep voice boomed. "I beat ye again, Dolstos!"

"I swears, Krepner, ye're a-cheatin'! I know ye are!" The second voice was falsetto and angry.

"Ye can't prove I'm a-cheatin'," Krepner said.

"It's like ye're a-seein' me thoughts," Dolstos protested.

"Just pay up an' cease yer whinin'."

"Let's go again," Dolstos said. "Double or nothin'."

"Ye'll just end up owin' me double," Krepner warned. "Can't say I didn't warn ye."

"Ye can't be lucky forever, an' if 'n ye're a-cheatin' I'm a-gonna catch ye."

Curious, Wick pulled himself up the iron door and looked around. He was on a ship. The gentle sway of the vessel resting at anchor told him that. The iron door revealed to him that he was down in the ship's brig. And the stench that even overpowered the stink of the brig, well, that told him he was being held by goblinkin.

Peering out into the brightness of the lantern light, lifting one hand to partially block the rays that seemed to pierce his head, Wick saw a lone goblinkin sitting at an uneven table. He wondered where the second voice had come from.

The goblinkin shook his right hand, stuck out two fingers, roared, "Even!" then chortled with laughter. "Haw, haw, haw! I beat you again! I'm a-tellin' ye, Dolstos, ye can't beat me!"

"Cheater!" the falsetto voice screamed. "Dirty, rotten cheater!"

The big goblinkin rocked back and forth as he guffawed. "I tell ye, Dolstos, doin' guard duty without ye to play with would be mighty borin'. Mighty borin' indeed."

"Nobody else will play with ye because ye cheat all the time," Dolstos accused.

Then Wick saw where the second voice was coming from. At least, he saw where the second voice was supposed to be coming from. He couldn't believe it. A shiver of fear rattled along his spine.

The goblinkin used his right hand to play the odds and evens game, but he played it against himself. His left hand was dressed up in miniature clothing like another guard and a face had been drawn on it in charcoal. A worn piece of sheep's wool created a patch of hair on the back of the hand.

When the goblinkin, Krepner, wanted the other player to talk, he flexed the thumb like a lower lip and raised his own voice, then spoke out of the corner of his mouth. As Wick watched, the goblinkin played himself again, and beat the hand puppet once more. Krepner howled with glee and slapped the table with his good hand while his other hand thumped in agony.

"Cheater!" the falsetto voice shrilled. The high-pitched voice filled the brig. "I'm gonna kill you!"

Moving quickly, Krepner drew the long knife at his side and held it against the hand puppet's wrist, just under the fake lower lip created by his thumb. Where a goblinkin's neck would be if the hand puppet were another being. "Don't ye be a-threatenin' me, Dolstos!" he roared. "Ye knows I can't stands it!"

The puppet struggled against the knife. Krepner pinned his left hand against the top of the table. A thin line of blood trailed the knife blade.

A new wave of nausea rattled through Wick. He was certain the goblinkin was about to amputate his own hand for talking back to him.

"Don't."

The voice surprised Wick. It was even more surprising when he discovered it had come from him. He knew that when the goblinkin's head swung around and locked on him.

"So," Krepner said, "ye're awake. I thought for sure they'd kilt ye." He kept his knife at the hand puppet's throat.

"Yes," Wick said nervously.

"Ye saw him!" The hand puppet squirmed against the knife, trying to get out from under the blade. "Ye saw him a-cheatin'! Tell him ye saw him!"

Krepner glowered at Wick. "Are ye goin' to accuse me, too?"

"No," Wick answered. "I didn't see you cheating." *And I also don't see how you couldn't be.*

"He was a-cheatin'!" Dolstos yelled.

Losing interest in the shouting match, Krepner leaned back in his chair. He left the hand puppet lying on the table. "I'm here to watch ye, halfer. Don't give me no trouble an' ye'll live until they kills ye."

Oh, and that's so comforting, Wick thought, not relaxed at all. "Okay."

The goblinkin stared at Wick for a long time. Wick stood his ground on the other side of the iron door and looked at everything but Krepner.

"Want to play odds an' evens?" Krepner asked.

"No."

"What?" Krepner asked belligerently.

"No. Thank you," Wick added.

"An' why not? Do you think I cheat?"

Wick pulled back from the door. "I didn't say that."

"Well, ye'd best never—"

"You're a cheater," a woman's voice declared. "You're cheating Dolstos out of everything."

"*What!*" Krepner thundered. He vaulted from his chair and stood with his knife in his hand. The stacks of copper coins on the table behind him (most of them on Krepner's side and not Dolstos's) scattered in a tinkling rain.

Wick jerked backward and bumped into the back wall of the brig. "Nothing!" he said anxiously. "I didn't say anything!"

"I heard ye, halfer." Krepner strode to the brig. He thrust his knife through the iron bars of the door. "Ye best watch yer unkind tongue, or I'll have it from yer head, I will."

"You're a cheat. I'll say it again in case you didn't hear me with those pig-ugly ears."

Shaking his head, Wick said, "Not me. I didn't say that."

The cat lay curled up in the back corner of the brig. Her tail flicked lazily. "I said it," she announced.

"Ye better tell yer cat to shut her lyin' mouth, halfer." Krepner glowered at Wick.

"I can't," Wick pleaded. "She doesn't listen to me."

"Don't make me come in there."

"Why?" the cat demanded. "Do you think we're afraid of you?"

"Ye should be!"

"Because you cheat Dolstos?" The cat pushed herself up on her forepaws and wrapped her tail around herself. Her eyes glinted mockery. "Dolstos doesn't even have any arms to defend himself."

"What are you doing?" Wick demanded of the cat.

"Do you really want to die a slow death in the belly of this rat-infested ship?" Alysta asked.

"All right, halfer, I've had me about enough of ye an' yer blasted cat!" Krepner fumbled for the keys hanging from his hip.

Alysta turned to Wick. "Get ready," she said.

"Get ready?" Wick stared at the goblinkin, who was easily three times his size.

The cat got on all fours. "Keep your head, Librarian. It's only one goblinkin. Surely you can handle one goblinkin."

"No," Wick said, pretty certain that he couldn't. "I'm not a fighter. I'm a Librarian."

The cat spat in disgust. "We're all fighters when we have to be."

Not me, Wick thought.

"Just stay away from him," the cat said. "You've seen for yourself that he's not overly bright."

He talks to his hand, Wick thought desperately. *That's a sure sign that there's no mind lingering in that thick skull. How can you reason with a mad goblinkin?*

By then, amid curses and threats of bodily harm, Krepner opened and swung wide the heavy iron door. It clanged against the wall.

"I'll have the tongue from yer head!" the goblinkin roared.

"An' the tail of the cat as well!" Dolstos shouted in his falsetto voice.

Together, goblinkin and hand-goblinkin charged into the brig.

Krepner reached for Wick with his free hand, intending to grab his hair. Instead, the little Librarian ducked and rolled between the goblinkin's legs too fast to be caught.

By that time, the cat was in motion, springing from her haunches and launching herself up the goblinkin in a series of lightning-fast jumps that took her up the body of their foe. Then she sat atop his head and started clawing and scratching and biting Krepner's ears and nose.

Wick watched in stunned fascination.

"The keys!" the cat yelled. "Grab the keys!"

Krepner flailed at the cat, barely missing her as she sprinted over his head and shoulders. Her claws dug into fabric and flesh. Off balance, screaming in terror and anger, the goblinkin collided with the rear wall of the brig and the bars.

"Get the *keys*!"

Galvanized into action, Wick darted forth, swallowing his heart, which was pumping frantically in the back of his throat. His hand closed on the heavy key ring and yanked.

It didn't come off.

"Get the keys!" the cat yelled. The goblinkin's efforts to seize her got closer and closer.

In another moment Wick felt certain her foe would have her. Redoubling his efforts, Wick seized the key ring again and yanked with all his strength.

Cloth tore. The keys came away in Wick's hand, but the goblinkin turned on him at once.

"Ye done made a *bad* mistake, halfer!" the goblinkin growled. He stepped toward Wick, who shrank back at once. The little Librarian was certain that his life was at an end. He raised his hand before him, hoping to ward off any blows, but knowing that the knife would probably nail his hands to his skull.

Then the goblinkin's pants, torn loose by Wick's efforts to claim the keys, fell and tangled around his ankles. He tried to take another step, but he tripped. "I'm gonna—gonna—ullllllppppp!" He crashed to the floor.

"Go!" the cat commanded. "While he's *ullllpppping!*" Lithely, she jumped over the fallen goblinkin.

Krepner flailed with his knife and reached for his pants at the same time. He yelled and screamed and cursed.

"Out!" the cat shouted, throwing herself at Wick.

Standing, Wick rushed out the door and threw it closed behind him. He fumbled with the key as Krepner got to his feet and leaped toward the door. The lock engaged with dull, grating clicks.

Krepner reached through the bars with the knife, slashing at Wick. "C'mere, ye terrible little beast! I'll rip ye to pieces an' gnaw on yer bones!"

All the more reason to stay away, Wick thought. He was glad he remembered to yank the keys from the lock.

Krepner continued to roar and rage. "Stupid, stupid halfer!"

"Who are ye callin' stupid?" Dolstos demanded. "Ye were the one that let him out!"

"I didn't let him out! *Ye* let him out!"

"He took the keys from *ye*!"

"It was ye supposed to be watchin' me back!" Krepner slashed at his other hand, but missed. The hand dressed up as Dolstos slapped the knife from Krepner's hand. Then it lifted and drove at Krepner and started strangling the goblinkin. Overwhelmed, Krepner went backward, tripping over his dropped trousers again.

That goblinkin is not *right in his head*, Wick told himself. He watched, hypnotized by the action as Krepner rolled across the floor of the brig fighting his own hand.

"Have you taken root?"

Yanked back into the danger that immediately surrounded him, knowing that he was in more danger outside the brig than in it because the goblinkin that discovered him free aboard the ship might decide to kill him at once and ask questions later, Wick glanced around the room.

"Let's go," Alysta said. She bounded toward the door that led to the hallway.

Instead, Wick turned his attention to searching the room. He ran quickly, fearing that at any moment a goblinkin might wander down from the upper deck.

"What are you doing?" the cat asked.

"Looking for my cloak." Wick sorted through the pile of outwear in the corner. Evidently a lot of the goblinkin crew dropped their cloaks and coats there.

Or maybe there were a lot of victims that had ended up in stewpots and no longer needed them. It was a sobering and chilling thought.

Exasperated, the cat said, "Grab any cloak. Better an ill-fitting cloak than fitting back inside that cage again."

"You don't understand." Wick kept turning cloaks.

"I'm not going to help you out of here again. It was hard enough sneaking onto the ship after you this time. I nearly ended up in a stewpot."

"It's not just my cloak," Wick said. "My book is in there."

That caught the cat's attention. "You brought a book from the Library?"

"Not a book. A journal."

"What's a journal?"

Wick didn't bother to explain. Two coats later, he found his cloak. Frantic, he felt through it and discovered that his journal and writing kit were missing. "No!"

"Let's go," the cat said. "That's your cloak."

Worried about the journal's absence, Wick pulled the cloak on. He'd written the journal in a special code that he'd devised, so reading it wouldn't be easy. But it could still be done. As a Librarian, he'd learned all codes were eventually broken.

Having no choice, Wick followed the cat. Perhaps the journal had fallen out when he'd been taken prisoner. Thinking of the journal, made with his own two hands, languishing out in the snow pained him. His journal surely deserved a better fate.

Also, the journal had been carefully and craftily hidden within his cloak. It couldn't have easily fallen out. By the time they reached the ladder leading up to the waist, he was convinced that someone had to have removed it.

But who?

"Carefully here," the cat whispered when they walked through the ship's waist.

Wick nodded and followed slowly. The waist of the ship was low on a human or an elf, and would have caused any from either of those two races to have to bend over to proceed. Waist decks were sandwiched below the upper deck and above the cargo area. On the particular ship Wick found himself on, space was at a premium.

Throughout the whole vessel, the stench of goblinkin pervaded. Wick stopped breathing through his nose and breathed through his mouth. It helped a little.

Together, one after the other, he and the cat made their way through the waist, tiptoeing quietly past rooms where goblinkin slept in swaying hammocks. No one had roused to hear Krepner's shouts and curses. Then again, walking through the waist now Wick couldn't hear them. Of course, it was possible that Krepner had managed to strangle himself, though Wick hadn't ever heard of that being done.

The next ladder took them to the upper deck. At the top of the ladder, Wick slowly opened the hatch, surprised to see gray daylight instead of night awaiting him. But it made sense. He'd been brought in at night.

"I'll scout ahead," Alysta said.

"All right," Wick replied, opening the hatch wide enough to allow the cat through, then closing it back down once she was on the deck. He watched her through the slit he'd left.

Alysta walked back and forth, very much like a real cat would. Wick started wondering if she'd always been a cat.

She turned and looked at him with those big eyes. "Come on, then. Be quick about it."

Hating the fact that he had to put so much trust in the cat's talents, but knowing at least she wouldn't be noticed as much as a dweller hanging around on the main deck, Wick slid through the opening and closed the hatch behind him. He stood for a moment in the shadow of the main mast.

Wharf Rat's Warren lie spread out to port. Snowflakes swirled through the air, large and fat, but with plenty of space between. It would gradually accumulate, but it would take time.

Wick couldn't believe what he was seeing. He'd spent all that time, and he was farther away from his goal than he'd been.

"Let's go," the cat said.

Wick started forward.

The cat went ahead, bounding for the stern. Gazing up at the stern castle, Wick saw three goblinkin lazing around a bucket of coals on the deck. The smell of cooking meat lingered in the air. Wick didn't want to think about what was cooking.

Just then, the door to the captain's quarters swung open. Wick took advantage of the brief respite he had to clamber into one of the two longboats the ship had on the port side. He slithered up under the tarp while the cat kept watch.

8

Escape

The man who had come to the Tavern of Schemes the night before walked out onto the deck. As he passed by Wick's hiding spot, the little Librarian saw that the man consulted a book.

Wick's heart leapt for a moment as he believed the book to be his own journal. Then he saw that it was bound differently, and in another color. Still, it was a book and that was exciting enough. Before he knew it, Wick started wondering about other books that might be in the man's quarters.

That one, Wick felt strongly, *and any others he might have, belong in the Vault of All Known Knowledge so they can be preserved and protected.*

The man walked to the stairwell leading down to the galley.

The cat called for Wick.

Reluctantly, feeling overly exposed in the pale gray daylight, Wick climbed out from under the tarp and out of the longboat. He crossed to the port railing and looked out at the dock. Ice chunks floated in the water. The span was too far to jump, and the water was near freezing, assuring him of a quick, relatively painless death. He hunkered by the longboat, using it to shield him from sight of the goblinkin in the stern.

"Har," one of the goblinkin said. "I wonder if Krepner is still down in the brig cheatin' hisself at odds an' evens."

The other goblinkin laughed.

"One of these days," another goblinkin said, "he's gonna get tired of cheatin' hisself at odds an' evens an' kill hisself over it."

They all had a good laugh about that as they warmed their hands over the kettle of coals.

"Go," the cat said.

"Where?" Wick asked. Surely the cat couldn't be suggesting that he dive into the water. That would be the end of him. Even if he made it to shore, which Wick doubted, his clothes would be sodden and heavy. He'd never get away.

"The ship is tied up to the dock," Alysta said. "If we reach the stern, we can climb along the mooring rope."

"I'll be seen," Wick said.

The cat twitched an ear in irritation. "I'll provide a distraction. These goblinkin would love nothing more than to put me in a stewpot."

Except maybe a dweller for the stewpot, Wick thought but didn't say. He didn't want to get into an argument over who would provide a finer goblinkin repast.

"Now get ready. On my word." The cat bounded away, moving so quickly that she appeared weightless. She leaped and landed on the railing of the stairwell leading up to the stern castle. Quickly, she ran along the railing until she stood at the railing's center.

Then she meowed, loud and long, like a hungry cat standing outside the door and wanting in. It was, Wick had to admit, one of the most annoying sounds ever.

The sound caught the attention of the goblinkin immediately. The biggest one of them slapped the two others and shushed them. Like a pack of predators, which Wick knew they were, they stared at the cat with anticipatory gleams in their eyes.

Deliberately, the cat squatted on the railing and wrapped her tail around her paws. She meowed again, acting innocent and vulnerable.

Wick was really starting to wonder where the cat had been before she had appeared to help him. She was too arrogant—well, perhaps not. Cats, by their nature, tended toward arrogance and filled everyone's life whose path they crossed with demands.

"A cat," one of the goblinkin said, reaching for the knife sheathed on his hip.

"Stew meat," another goblinkin hissed. "Get him, Rido."

Rido slipped his knife free and drew it back to throw. Alysta meowed again, as if totally unaware of the danger.

Fearing for the cat, certain he was about to see her pierced by the knife and dead soon after, Wick watched helplessly. He slid a hand over his face to hide his eyes. But he found himself transfixed, unable to cease looking on.

With some skill (goblinkin were more accustomed to bashing and slashing and even gnashing things with their fangs rather than true ability), Rido flung the knife. It came with greater speed than Wick would have imagined, glittering through the intervening space.

Looking almost bored, the cat flicked out a paw as she dodged to the right and batted the knife away. The blade flew over the stern railing and clattered to the deck.

"Did ye see that?" one of the goblinkin asked. "That cat knocked the knife away!"

Alysta flicked her ears and meowed, sitting comfortably once more on the railing.

"Why, it's laughin' at ye, Rido," one of the goblinkin said.

Growling curses, Rido picked up a stone war hammer leaning against the back stern railing. "I can't promise ye stew meat after this," he stated as he hefted the huge weapon, "but ye'll at least get broth an' a few bones to suck the marrow from." He took up the hammer in both hands and moved slowly toward the railing.

Alysta continued sitting there and meowed again.

"Nice kitty, kitty," Rido rumbled soothingly. "Nice kitty. Just ye keep a-sittin' there. This'll be over in a bit." He kept slide-stepping forward, raising the hammer over his head. "Nice kitty, kitty."

The other goblinkin watched expectantly.

Wick almost couldn't bear to watch.

Then Rido swung the hammer with all his prodigious might. Alysta uncoiled from her haunches and leaped to the left, catching hold of one of the lines and clinging by her claws. Rido's hammer crunched through the stern railing and the sound of splitting wood filled the air.

"Oh, that's bad," one of the goblinkin said. "Cap'n Gujhar's gonna be pretty vexed at ye."

"Me? It was me ye sent after that blasted cat!" Rido drew the hammer back from the wreckage of the railing.

Alysta yowled, and the sound was almost laughter.

"Get that cat!" Rido roared.

The other goblinkin sprang to pursue the cat, drawing weapons. Alysta ran through the rigging, drawing them on down the starboard stairwell away from the stern castle. The whole time, she remained tantalizingly close to the goblinkin, as if she didn't have her wits about her and was running in fear and only just managing to avoid sudden death. That perceived luck only drew the goblinkin into a greater frenzy.

Taking advantage of the moment, Wick sprinted from hiding and ran for the other stairwell on the port side of the stern castle. The goblinkin were so intent on their prey that they never noticed him. But new goblinkin arrived from below, coming out of the stairwell amidships to see what was going on. They saw the cat, too, and immediately gave chase.

Afraid he was going to be seen, Wick ducked into hiding beside the stairwell instead of going up it. He sunk back and tried to become another layer of the wood as the goblinkin chased the cat through the rigging. The goblinkin threw knives, axes, and belaying pins at the cat, setting up all kinds of noise.

Even the man, Captain Gujhar, came up from belowdecks to see what the matter was. The man held a finger in the pages of his book to mark his place.

That reminded Wick of his own missing journal. He wanted it back. Then he noticed that he stood next to the captain's quarters. He eyed the door latch. Before he knew what he was doing, his hand dropped to the latch and flipped it.

The latch opened.

In the next instant, Wick was inside.

The captain's quarters were cramped, much as they were aboard *One-Eyed Peggie*. Shelves and boxes and chests took up all the space that wasn't occupied by the bed. Light poured in through the stern windows. A small leather bag sat on one of the shelves. A quick inspection revealed that it held a handful of gold and silver coins.

But Wick's eyes were immediately drawn to the small desk built into the wall. Three books lay on top of the desk. One of them was his journal.

Before he knew it, Wick stood at the desk, his hands sliding over the books. He immediately tucked his journal into the cloak again, once more in its hiding place. Then he opened the larger of the two remaining books.

The volume was written in a human tongue, one of the old ones before the Cataclysm. He recognized it and the words came to him swiftly.

THE LOG OF THE WRAITH

Drawn by curiosity that overrode the fear clamoring at him, Wick turned the pages. The man who had penned the ship's log had an inelegant hand. It wasn't the language as much as the writing that inhibited Wick's almost instant translation.

Wraith had taken leave of her port home in Illastra deep within the Forest of Fangs and Shadows eighty-seven days ago. She'd been fully stocked with provisions and trade goods, and had a crew of thirty-two goblinkin that—

Someone banged on the door. "Who's in there?" a voice roared. "I saw you go in there! Come out at once!"

A crew of goblinkin that are even now banging on the door, Wick thought fearfully. He closed the book and ripped a pillowcase from the bed, fashioning a makeshift knapsack for the books. Thinking of the water he had to go over in the harbor, he wished he had better protection for the books.

But that couldn't be helped.

Knocking slammed the door in its frame again. "Is that you, dweller?" the man demanded.

First you have to save yourself, Wick told himself. He tossed the bag of gold and silver coins into his makeshift bag as well. Working quickly, he knotted the pillowcase, then tied the ends together to make a sling that he pulled over his head and one shoulder. Sliding the knapsack onto his back and out of the way, the little Librarian ran to the stern windows.

The beating resumed on the door. Captain Gujhar called to his goblinkin crew. "Stop chasing that cat! Get over here and break down this door!"

Wick opened the stern windows. If he'd been a normal-sized elf, dwarf, or human, he wouldn't have had room enough to escape. He stuck his head out. The stern window was almost twenty feet above the freezing harbor water. Wind plucked at his clothing and hair. The dock was thirty feet away, way beyond his reach.

Panic thundered through Wick in time with the pounding on the door.

"What are you waiting on?"

Hearing the cat's voice above him, Wick looked up and found her hanging headfirst on the anchor rope. "I'm trapped," Wick said.

"Use the mooring rope." The cat crept along the rope herself, placing one paw neatly before the other with effortless grace.

For the first time, Wick noticed the rope that angled down from *Wraith* to the dock. The hawser rope was thicker than a dwarf 's wrist. It would surely support his weight, but he wasn't as fleet as the cat, who he was certain could run along it if need be.

But he had an idea from one of the romances in Hralbomm's Wing. Turning, he opened the sea chest beside the bed and took out a leather razor strop. The wide leather band looked suitable for his purpose.

Wood split behind him. The door shoved inward a little. It wouldn't take much more abuse before it gave way.

Returning to the stern window, he slipped outside again. Standing on the narrow ledge of the window, he tiptoed in an effort to reach the hawser. His fingers were several inches short of his prize.

The door shuddered inward, falling in pieces inside the cabin. Goblinkin poured into the room.

"They're going to catch you!" The cat paused, already halfway to the dock.

Desperate, barely maintaining his balance on the gently bobbing ship, Wick held the leather strop in one hand and flipped it over the hawser. Jumping up, he caught the other end, gambling that he could catch it and not drop into the harbor.

His hand closed around the strop and he held on tight. Immediately, the smooth leather slid across the hawser, gaining speed. He shot toward the cat.

"Look out!" Wick yelled.

Voices rang out above him. Twisting uncontrollably at the ends of the razor strop, Wick saw that goblinkin lined *Wraith*'s stern, too. Several of them threw knives, hand axes, and belaying pins at him. Luckily, all of them fell short.

The leather zipped along the hawser and he was on the cat. Alysta cursed him soundly as she gathered herself. Wick feared that she would be knocked from her precarious perch by the strop.

Instead, at the last moment possible, the cat leaped up from the rope and the strop passed harmlessly underneath. He expected to see her land again on the hawser, managing a child's trick of jumping rope. She came at his head, though, her paws flailing and her claws extended.

Wick couldn't help it. Instinct forced him to duck. The cat missed him with three of her paws but managed to hook him with her left foreleg. Her claws dug into his hair and his scalp.

Yelping in pain, Wick was distracted from the sudden stop waiting at the end of the hawser. The cat clung to him, digging all of her claws in deeply enough to draw blood. From the corner of his eye, Wick saw the piling ahead just before he slammed into it.

For a moment, he thought he'd knocked himself out. He'd knocked the wind out of his lungs and his senses spun dizzily inside his battered skull. Ice and water lapped at the piling below his feet. From where he hung, he had a clear view of *Wraith*'s prow. The ship's figurehead had been carved into the shape of a monstrous looking thing rising from the ocean. Wraiths took many shapes, Wick knew, but there was no doubting what that one was.

"Are you going to hang there all day?" the cat demanded.

No, Wick thought. *I'm going to hang here and listen to my heart stop.* He felt certain that was going to happen. Then he managed to take a breath as his lungs finally started working again. Unfortunately, that started an onslaught of pain.

The cat leaped from the top of Wick's head to the dock. At her urging, he managed to heave himself up and lay gasping on the dock.

Onboard *Wraith*, Captain Gujhar called out to the goblinkin. Some of them grabbed bows. Arrows thudded into the dock as Wick climbed with renewed enthusiasm. Keeping his head covered with his hands, he ran down the dock amid cargo handlers who dove for cover.

"Avast there, ye blasted goblinkin!" a tall human yelled. Then he reached for his own bow and nocked an arrow. A heartbeat later, he seated the shaft in the chest of a goblinkin who squalled in mortal agony.

"This way," the cat called.

Wick ran blindly, trusting the feline even though he didn't want to. He turned to the right at the end of the dock, scattering a gathering of seagulls that took flight from the fish heads and entrails left by the morning fishermen. By that time, a proper fight had started between the goblinkin and the human sailors along the dock. In the next minute he was gone, lost among the twisting alley of Wharf Rat's Warren.

9

Seaspray

Heart pounding and lungs burning, Wick couldn't go on anymore. He halted in the last alley they'd come to and leaned against the wall.

"Come on," Alysta said. She stood ahead of him, looking as cool and composed as if she'd just wakened from a nap.

Wick shook his head. "I can't go on any farther." He sucked in air, believing he was about to die.

"All right then," the cat said reluctantly, "rest. I'll go make certain we're not being followed." She ran to the front of the alley and peered out. Her tail twitched behind her, keeping perfect time.

Still trembling from the close call, not willing to believe that he was actually going to make good his escape, Wick held his arms up for a moment to let his lungs fill more easily. Then, before he knew it, he took the ship's log from the knotted pillowcase. His eyes moved restlessly across the pages, scanning information. As always, he got lost in the words almost at once.

"What are you doing?"

Wick ignored the cat and kept reading. "Getting information."

"What information?"

"About the people on that ship. *Wraith*."

"They want to kill us."

"Yes."

"There's not a whole lot more to know."

"Actually," Wick said, licking his thumb and turning the page, "there is. The man who hired the Razor's Kiss thieves here isn't just after Boneslicer and Seaspray. He's also after—"

"Deathwhisper."

Wick frowned. "You knew."

The cat turned over a paw, then sat and wrapped her tail around her feet. "Honestly, I can't believe you know so little."

"Craugh didn't tell me anything other than to come here. And that someone would be here to help me."

"Didn't you study the stories of the Battle of Fell's Keep?"

"I did," Wick said.

"Then you should have known what the people we're up against were after."

Wick suddenly realized what those prizes were. "Boneslicer, Seaspray, and Deathwhisper."

"Magical weapons are a rarity in this world," the cat confirmed. "Nothing like them has been made since the Cataclysm."

"I know," Wick said.

"And they were all present during the retreat from Teldane's Bounty. That was one of the reasons the defenders were able to hold out as long as they were." Sadness touched the cat's gray eyes. "If they hadn't been betrayed, maybe more of them would have escaped being overrun."

"How do you know about the Battle of Fell's Keep?"

The cat stood. "We need to be moving. You've got your breath back."

"Where are we going?"

"To find Seaspray." The cat started off.

"No," Wick said.

"No?" Alysta turned, and despite the fact that she was a cat, irritation showed in every line of her body.

"We can't go on alone. It's too dangerous."

"We're already nearly a day behind, thanks to your capture."

"I didn't get captured on purpose. But we should stay here. Craugh, Cap'n Farok, and Hallekk will be here soon."

"Do you think it's wise for *One-Eyed Peggie* to drop anchor in the harbor at Wharf Rat's Warren?"

Actually, now that he thought about it (in other terms than simply of his rescue), Wick thought maybe *One-Eyed Peggie* putting in to port at the city wasn't a good idea. She'd be set upon at once by several of the pirates who traveled to the city of thieves, murderers, assassins, thieves, etc.

"No," he sighed.

"Good, because I don't think Craugh would believe it was safe, either. You might wait there for a long time." Alysta got underway again. "Our time would be better spent finding Seaspray."

Reluctantly, Wick put the ship's log away and fell in behind the cat.

"You *sold* my donkey?" Wick stared at the livery boy in disbelief. Alysta had told him his captors had used the donkey to bring him back to town. They'd left it at the livery.

Cautiously, the livery boy stepped back. Bruises showed on his face where the Razor's Kiss thieves had hit him the previous night. It looked like he had a few new additions, so maybe his father hadn't necessarily believed his story about the stolen horses. "I told you when you left it here yesterday that if my da came in an' it wasn't paid for, he'd sell it. Those men didn't pay for it. So, he did."

"To whom?" the cat asked.

The livery boy hesitated. "To the . . . renderer."

"You knew he wasn't a normal donkey," Alysta protested.

Sullen, the boy said, "Let the donkey tell the renderer that, then. I tried to tell my da it could talk." He touched a painful looking bruise on his forehead. "I got clouted extra hard for that one, let me tell you."

"When did the renderer pick up the donkey?" Wick asked. He couldn't help thinking about the dreadful fate that awaited the donkey. In a few days, what was left of him could be made into pretty decent glue. *People need glue*, Wick thought. *It has to come from somewhere.*

"This morning," the boy answered. "He always picks up unclaimed livestock in the mornings."

"How quickly does he . . . does he . . . ?" Wick couldn't go on thinking about it.

"Is he already dead?" Alysta asked.

Pensive, obviously a little afraid of Wick even though the little Librarian was smaller than he was, the boy lifted his shoulders and dropped them. "I don't know."

"Where can I find the renderer's place?" Wick asked.

The livery boy gave him directions and Wick left quickly.

Outside, Wick hurried after the cat. The goblinkin searched through the city even now. If the boy knew that, if he went to the goblinkin, they would have time to intercept them.

"He won't tell," Alysta said.

Wick kept pace. "What makes you so certain?"

"He's afraid of the goblinkin, and of his father," the cat said. "He was even afraid of us."

Wick tried to believe that. He just hoped that the donkey wasn't sitting in little pots of glue already.

The renderer kept a small shop outside of town, not far from the trail that led up into the mountains. The little stone shack leaned against a hill of snow and ice, looking like it might blow over at any moment. Only a short distance away, a ramshackle barn bracketed by trees looked bowed under the weight of the snow on the slanted roof. A few horses and two donkeys stood listless in the corral out front. Gray breath plumed from their nostrils.

Seeing the animals there, knowing the fate that awaited them, Wick felt a pang of sorrow for them. *Concentrate on what you need to do*, he told himself. *It's the same as one of the chickens that end up in a pot, or a fattening pig.*

He trudged through the snow on his bare feet, which he—by some miracle—could still feel. The cat rode his shoulders, no longer able to break through the high drifts. Wick glanced hopefully at the steady stream of smoke pouring from the chimney against the slate-gray sky. Surely it would be warm inside.

A trail existed between the corral and the shop, and to the well out back, but there was no other. Wick made his way to the uneven porch and pulled himself up. Drifts covered the porch and the two rocking chairs that sat there.

Gathering his courage, Wick knocked on the door.

"Who is it then?" a voice called from inside.

"Wick of . . . of Meek's Crossing," the little Librarian said. Meek's Crossing was a small town outside Wharf Rat's Warren.

"What do you want?" the voice demanded.

"There's been a mistake," Wick said. "A terrible mistake." The stink from the corral hit him then, thick and cloying in the cold wintry air.

The cat leapt from Wick's shoulders to a window sill. She peered inside and her breath frosted the glass.

"I ain't made no mistakes. And I'll club the man that says I made one. When I make glue or paste, it's good. It'll hold anything you're of a mind to put together. That's my guarantee."

"There's no mistake about your work, sir," Wick said. "The livery boy made a mistake. He wasn't supposed to—"

The door opened suddenly and a shaggy old man stood there in patched-over clothing. His gray beard hung to his waist and looked wild and unkempt. Under an ill-made fur cap, he was bald. His pale, runny eyes didn't look in the same direction.

"You've come about the donkey, then," the man said. He extended his hand.

Almost overcome by the strong chemical smell coming from inside the shop, Wick didn't know what to do. He shook the man's hand. Heavily callused and covered in patches of glue that held horse's hair and other disagreeable things, the man's hand spoke of cruel strength.

"I, uh," Wick said, trying to figure out what was happening, "uh, I have. About the donkey."

The man grinned and the effort looked slapped on and forced. "Well then, it's good to see you. He said you might be coming by for him."

"He did?" Wick was astonished. "He told you that?"

The man nodded. "He did. I'm Rankle. Come on in."

Trepidation stirred within Wick. He didn't trust the renderer.

"Wick," the donkey called from inside. "It's all right. Come on inside."

Hesitantly, Wick followed the man inside the home. Shelves lined the walls and tables took over the open space in the center. Pots and bottles filled the tables and shelves. The chemical stink was even stronger inside the room, but it was warm.

The donkey sat on his haunches near the fireplace. He looked comfortable and rested, not like the other poor beasts out in the corral.

Alysta walked into the room with Wick.

"Is that your cat?" Rankle asked.

Wick waited for Alysta to answer, but she didn't. Obviously she didn't care to let the renderer know she spoke.

"Yes," Wick said.

Rankle scratched his beard and looked at Alysta longingly. "Are you particularly attached to it? Out here, with winter on us so fierce, it's just another mouth to feed. I could make you a good deal on it. Can always use cat guts for strings and such. And there ain't nothing quite as delicate as cat glue."

"Uh," Wick stuttered, at a loss.

Alysta hissed at him and flicked her tail disdainfully.

"The cat is mine," the donkey said, looking back over his shoulder.

"Yours, is it?" Rankle asked. He smiled and turned back to the donkey. "Well, Prince Dawdal, I wouldn't harm a hair on your cat's head."

"Prince?" Wick looked at the donkey.

The donkey nodded. He flattened his lips and grinned. "Yes. *Prince*."

Wick hadn't even known the creature had a name. He couldn't be a prince. Could he?

Rankle waved to a chair in front of the fire. "Sit. Be comfortable. Would you like something to drink? To eat?"

Still dazed, Wick said, "Yes. Very much." Rankle pushed him into motion and the little Librarian walked to the chair and sat.

The donkey had a deep bucket of some kind of oat mash in front of him. Bits of apples and carrots showed in the mixture.

"Want some?" the donkey, Dawdal—maybe even Prince Dawdal—asked.

"No," Wick said. "Thank you." Even as hungry as he was, the bucket's contents didn't look appetizing.

"I've got oatmeal," Rankle said.

Minutes later, Wick sat with a bowl of warm oatmeal as the heat in the fireplace burned away the wintry chill he'd carried in with him.

"Prince Dawdal told me the whole story," Rankle said.

"He did?" Wick asked, anxious to hear the tale himself.

"Of course, at the beginning I didn't know he was a prince," the renderer said. "I got him this morning and was going to slit his throat out in the barn. Then he started talking." He shook his head. "In all my days, I never heard an animal talk." He lowered his voice. "You ask me, it's kind of unnerving the first time."

Wick silently agreed.

"Anyway, he told me about the curse," Rankle continued.

"About the curse?" Wick asked. He spooned up oatmeal, grateful for the simple meal. Rankle had also put out a loaf of bread and chokeberry jelly. The bread tasted fresh and the jelly had a sugary tang.

"The curse Wizard Hardak put on him," Rankle said.

"The one that turned me into a donkey," Dawdal said. "I told Rankle about how my father, the king, had put you in charge of finding me."

"On account of no one would suspect a halfer," Rankle said. He leveled a forefinger at Wick and grinned. "Clever plan, that one."

"Right," Wick said. "Clever." But he was wondering where the donkey got his imagination. During the days they'd shared together earlier, the creature had shown no sign of intelligence.

"I also told him about the treasure," the donkey said.

"You told him about the treasure?" Wick asked.

The donkey nodded solemnly. "I told him we were trying to find it because it had a cure for the curse that keeps me a donkey. I also promised Rankle a portion of it for sparing my life." He paused and looked at the renderer with sorrowful eyes. "It was the least I could do for his generosity."

"Yes," Wick agreed. "It was."

Only a short time later, once more fortified with supplies, Wick set out with the donkey and the cat. Rankle stood on his uneven porch, waved at them, and wished them well.

"Remember your promise, Prince Dawdal," Rankle called after them.

"I will," the donkey replied. Then he swiveled to face forward again and muttered, "When pigs fly."

Given what he'd seen the last two days with talking animals, Wick wasn't so certain that he wouldn't see that before his journeys were over.

"You're not really a prince, are you?" Wick asked.

The donkey looked at him. "What do you think?"

Wick gave the question serious thought. At the moment he wasn't getting to ride the donkey and was being forced to lead him. Perhaps appealing to the donkey's ego would get him up out of the snow.

"I think you are," Wick answered.

"Idiot," the cat snarled.

The donkey brayed with laughter. "You're not riding me. Those days are over."

As he trudged through the snow, Wick missed those days. Why couldn't Craugh have arranged for someone who would actually *help* him? Only the thought of tracking down Boneslicer for Bulokk drove him on. That and the certain knowledge that toads couldn't turn pages in a book or write with a quill and ink without a great deal of difficulty.

They headed into the mountains, once more taking up the trail.

Near nightfall, they reached one of the small outlying villages on the way down the mountains to Wharf Rat's Warren. No more than a dozen small structures jammed together with fifty or so houses scattered behind them, the village framed the road as it twisted to the east.

Candlelight burned soft yellow against a few windows. Only a few people were about on the street. They gazed curiously at the small group that wandered into their town.

Wick felt uncomfortable under the weight of the stares. During the last few hours of breaking through the new-fallen snow and staring through the flakes that continued to fall, he'd thought of nothing but the three magical weapons that had been at the Battle of Fell's Keep. He couldn't help wondering why Captain Gujhar was looking for them. Of course, the captain was working for someone else, but he'd purposefully not mentioned his employer.

What was it about the three weapons, though? Wick wondered. *Why were they so important after a thousand years?*

Nothing in anything he'd read offered a hint of that. In fact, he didn't know why Craugh had come to Greydawn Moors and been so interested. Though looking back on the situation, neither Craugh nor Cap'n Farok was the type to just go searching for the truth of a battle that took place during the Cataclysm on a whim.

So what weren't they telling him? The thought rolled uncertainly in Wick's mind. He didn't like thinking like that, but the truth of it stared him in the face. But even as he felt anger over being used, he knew that Cap'n Farok—and probably Craugh—wouldn't have gambled his life without good reason.

That could only mean that the danger he was walking into was even greater than he feared. Wick almost felt sick with anxiety, but curiosity drove him as well.

He stumbled tiredly down the street, knowing he had to have someplace to rest. Thankfully, there'd been no sign of pursuit from either the goblinkin or the Razor's Kiss.

A man with a sword stood on a porch in front of a tavern. "Greetings, stranger."

"Greetings," Wick said, bringing the donkey to a stop. Alysta popped her head out of the pack of supplies she'd been riding in. Wick hadn't seen her for hours and guessed that she'd been sleeping.

"What brings you to our village?"

Wick wondered if the place even had a name. Some of them were so small they didn't.

"I'm just passing through," Wick answered. "But I'd like a night's lodging if I could."

The man shook his head. "We don't have lodging here. Even this tavern's just for drinking and eating. Most that travel this road never stop here." He looked around. "There's a few who take in lodgers." Stepping out into the snow-covered street, he pointed out the houses. "Give 'em a try. Tell 'em Enil sent you."

"I will," Wick replied. "Thank you." He moved through the street, leaning into the harsh wind and the swirling snow.

The first two houses didn't even answer his knocks. The third offered lodging, but apologized, saying there was no room for the animals.

Back out in the street, Wick spotted another building that held a leather harness and an apron, advertising the shopkeeper was a leatherworker. Without a written language, shops did the best that they could to advertise what they were.

The detail on the apron, made large enough to nearly cover the expanse of leather, caught his eye. It was a rose caught in the thorny embrace of a vine. He remembered exactly where he had seen such a design: on the leather bag Quarrel had carried.

The leatherworker's shop had been one of the places the man at the tavern had pointed out.

Drawn by his curiosity, Wick went to the shop and rapped on the door. He felt encouraged because a lot of light came from inside.

A man in his middle years opened the door. "Yes?" He was lean and composed, dressed in a leather apron and a dark shirt and trousers. His face was hollow and tired.

"Enil said you might have a bed for the night," Wick said. "I can pay."

The man looked at the donkey and at the cat, who had her head poked up through the supply bag. "For the animals as well?"

"Please."

The leatherworker suggested a price that was fair and Wick agreed. The man said, "There's a small shed in the back. The donkey can stay there. The cat can come inside."

"Thank you," Wick said.

"I'll show you." The man pulled on a heavy coat. "I'm Karbor, by the way."

Wick introduced himself, again claiming to be a glassblower. Together, they took the donkey around back to the small shed and saw to his needs, then returned to the house next to the modest shop.

10

The Leather-Maker's Tale

Inside the house, Wick helped Karbor in the kitchen, setting out dishes for a small but scrumptious repast.

"I apologize for the meagerness of the meal," Karbor said. "I've not had company for a while, and I've been somewhat distracted of late."

"The meal looks good," Wick replied. "It's been days since I've eaten this well." He hadn't gotten to eat in the Tavern of Schemes, and there'd been no decent meal since he'd left *One-Eyed Peggie*. The renderer's oatmeal had been just enough to keep his stomach from meeting his backbone.

Dishes held venison, sweet potatoes, fresh-baked sourdough bread, and a canned vegetable medley with a pepper seasoning particular to the south.

"One of my affordable vices," Karbor grinned as he poured the glass jar of vegetables into a small kettle to heat in the fireplace. "I do like exotic flavors. Up here, usually it's potatoes or other root crops, things that the farmers can get this cold earth to give up in ready numbers. I have to warn you, though, if you're not used to peppers, they can burn."

"I love peppers," Wick assured him. The fragrance of the peppers opened his nose and made his stomach rumble.

"Then you've been beyond Wharf Rat's Warren." Karbor put out a dish of honey butter.

"Several times," Wick agreed.

In minutes, everything had been heated and they set to at the small table. Wick ate with more than his usual appetite, devouring sourdough bread, cheese, venison, vegetables (which were even hotter than he expected), and sweet potatoes.

"You eat bigger than you look," Karbor observed. He dangled a piece of venison out for Alysta, who took it with proper disdain.

Embarrassed, Wick apologized. "I'll pay extra. I hadn't meant to. But, as I said, it's been a long time since I sat down to a meal like this."

Karbor waved the offer away. "It was just conversation. These are the winter months up here, and I'm not used to having company. During this time, I generally do a few commissioned pieces and put back others for sale in the spring when the traders start their regular trips back and forth across the mountain."

Curious as always, Wick talked to Karbor about the goings-on of the community. It was hard acting like he was knowledgeable about the area while at the same time trying to get an idea of what might have drawn the Razor's Kiss up into the mountains.

To cover his inadequacies, and because he didn't like silence at the dinner table without a book in his hand, Wick summoned up some of the old legends he knew about the northlands and spun them out in great detail. Most of them were about cursed pirates, shipwrecks bearing lost fortunes, and monsters that tore men to pieces high in the mountains. And a dragon or two. Dragons always made for some of the best stories.

"Are you sure you're a glassblower?" Karbor asked during a break while they retired to the fireplace to smoke their pipes.

"What do you mean?" Wick asked, at once worried that he'd somehow given himself away.

"You could be a storyteller." Karbor puffed on his pipe and stared into the flames. "You have a knack for weaving a tale."

"Thank you," Wick said. "You're too kind."

"No," Karbor said. "I know a good taleweaver when I hear one, and you're better than any I've ever heard." He puffed for a moment. "I only wish that my daughter were here to hear you. She always loved a good story."

"You have a daughter?"

"*Had*," Karbor said quietly. "I lost her."

"I'm sorry for your loss."

"It was only a few months ago. She wasn't my daughter by blood, but I raised her from the time she was eleven years old. She's seventeen now. Her name was Rose." Karbor took down a piece of leather from over the fireplace. "She was gifted in leatherwork, though it wasn't her calling. She crafted the design I've been using for the last few years." He tapped the rose wreathed in the thorny vine. Smiling at the memory, he traced the imprint. "She did this as a lark. I chose to use it to mark our work. Not many do that, you know. Because the goblinkin see such a mark as writing."

"I know," Wick said.

"She was a precious child," Karbor said as he put the leather piece back on the mantle. "But sad. I never could get her past the melancholy that plagued her as a child."

"Why was she sad?" Wick asked, before he realized that he might be prying. He couldn't bear to leave a tale untold.

Karbor packed his pipe and got it going again. "Her parents, my good friends in younger and more profitable years, were killed by goblinkin. Rose barely got away. When I found out what had happened, I went down the Shattered Coast to see to her. She had no other family, so I brought her back here to live with me."

"The goblinkin overran her village?" Wick asked. That wasn't an unusual tale. Goblinkin ferocity had been building across the mainland as the tribes turned outward to work out their aggressions instead of fighting with each other as they had in the past.

"No." Karbor's voice was soft. "As it turned out, the goblinkin were searching for her family."

"Why?"

"Because they are the present descendants of Captain Dulaun, the hero of—"

"The Battle of Fell's Keep during the Cataclysm," Wick said. Although the large meal had made him sleepy, he was once more awake.

Karbor glanced at him with concern.

"I collect tales," Wick said. "The Battle of Fell's Keep is one that remains on everyone's mind."

"It does." Karbor nodded. "Many people—humans and elves—distrust the dwarves due to Master Blacksmith Oskarr's betrayal of those brave defenders."

Master Oskarr didn't betray anyone! Wick curbed his response with difficulty. "Your daughter was Captain Dulaun's descendant?"

Karbor nodded. "She was. On her mother's side. I didn't know it at the time. Rose told me that later. Her ancestor wielded the sword Seaspray in a thousand battles, and he lost his life there at the Battle of Fell's Keep."

"And the sword fell into goblinkin hands," Wick said, remembering.

"Yes, and during the last thousand years, it was lost in time. No one knew where it was. But there was someone who believed he knew." Karbor puffed on his pipe. "In fact, he felt certain Seaspray was somewhere in this area."

Wick's heart quickened. "In Wharf Rat's Warren?"

"No, but somewhere nearby." Karbor waved to the north. "A dozen empires and kingdoms have risen and fallen in the mountains. One of them, I don't know which, was supposed to have found Seaspray."

"Was the sword found?"

Karbor shrugged. "I don't know." He sounded tired and old.

Wick felt sorry for the man then. Karbor was in the winter of his years, alone and without family. No one should have to die like that, he thought. Then Wick realized that he had a chance of doing exactly that while on the task Craugh had set for him.

Unless, of course, he was able to learn enough to save himself.

"They came here to find my daughter," Karbor said.

"Who came here?" Wick asked, fighting the fatigue that filled him.

"The goblinkin. Under the direction of a despicable man named Gujhar."

Karbor scowled. "I was next door. In the shop where the hides are cured. I heard the sounds of a fight and ran outside. By that time the goblinkin already had Rose." Tears showed in his eyes and his hand trembled as he held his pipe. "She fought them. With tooth and nail, she fought them. I swear, you've never seen a girl who could fight so well. Her mother was a warrior, trained in swordcraft and hand-to-hand arts. A child was chosen in each generation to train so."

"Why?"

"In the event that Seaspray was recovered."

"Who trained your daughter?"

"Her mother, for a time. But even here she felt the need for more training. There's man in the village, a blind man who was once part of a king's bodyguard, that trained Rose in hand-to-hand techniques. And not far from here, I know another man who was once a sellsword. I bartered for lessons for her because she wanted so badly to learn."

"You don't know what happened to her?"

Karbor shook his head. "I went down to Wharf Rat's Warren and tried to spy on the goblinkin ship. I nearly got killed for my trouble." His voice broke. "But I learned enough to know not to hold out any hope for Rose."

"While I was in Wharf Rat's Warren," Wick said, "I saw a man who carried a small bag with the rose emblem on it."

"A bag?" Interest flickered in Karbor's wet eyes.

"Yes." Wick looked around the room. "You make a lot of leather goods—gloves, blacksmith's aprons, and harness—but I don't see any bags or backpacks."

"I don't make them," Karbor said. "The communities I sell to are all working people. They don't have enough wealth for excesses. A leather bag when a cloth one would do is excessive."

"So you didn't make that one? I saw the emblem with my own eyes."

"I made one," Karbor said. "But only one. For Rose." His voice thickened. "Tell me the man's name. I'd like very much to talk to him if I'm ever given the chance."

"Quarrel," Wick answered.

"Was he human?"

Wick nodded.

"Part of Gujhar's group, no doubt."

"I don't think so," Wick said. "Why would Gujhar want your daughter?"

"Because Seaspray is ensorcelled," Karbor replied. "The magic inside the sword can't be wakened without one of the true heirs holding it. Only Dulaun's family can evoke that."

"Why would the goblinkin want her or the sword?"

"I don't know. According to the legend Rose told me, all three of the weapons—Master Oskarr's battle-axe Boneslicer, Captain Dulaun's sword Seaspray, and the elven warder Sokadir's mighty bow, Deathwhisper—were used to strengthen the wards protecting the defenders there at the Battle of Fell's Keep."

"How?"

"By tapping into the magic within them."

That was the first time Wick had heard such a story. He sat up a little straighter. "Rose told you this?"

Karbor nodded. "She did. Her mother told her the story, though her mother never mentioned it to me. Only a handful of the defenders at that battle knew about that."

After a time, Karbor excused himself and went off to bed. He made up a pallet in front of the fireplace for Wick.

Despite a full stomach and not much rest, Wick found his mind was too busy to allow him to drift off to sleep. His thoughts kept chasing themselves inside his head. Instead, he'd taken out his journal and his writing tools and set about putting down the events of the day. The work went quickly by the firelight, even though he knew he would have to revisit it at a later date.

Still restless, he turned to the books he'd taken from *Wraith*. The journal detailed Captain Gujhar's progress in his search for Boneslicer and Seaspray, and even mentioned that Deathwhisper was rumored lost somewhere deep within what had been Silverleaves Glen. There was even a series of maps detailing the elven city of Cloud Heights and the environs as they had been and as they currently stood.

One of Captain Gujhar's notes said: *I have been told* (Wick noted that never once did *Wraith*'s shipsmaster acknowledge who might have told him) *that anyone with two of the weapons in hand will be guided to the third. With the successful location of Boneslicer, all I need is Seaspray to find Deathwhisper. The men among the Razor's Kiss that I've been dealing with swear they know where Dulaun's sword is. We will see.*

"You should get to sleep," Alysta said softly.

Blinking, Wick looked over at the cat. She hadn't spoken while Karbor was around, which was understandable, but she'd seemed aloof and lost in her own thoughts even after the man had gone to bed. He wondered if he'd done something to upset her and was afraid to ask.

"I will," Wick said. "I usually stay up far later than this at the Vault of All Known Knowledge."

"Not," the cat insisted, "after you escaped goblinkin earlier in the day, and after spending the night trying to stay warm in a snowdrift."

Wick studied the cat. "Are you worried about me?"

The cat glanced away. "No. But I'm not going to be blamed for your failure to escape early in the morning in case the goblinkin come here looking for you."

Wick didn't truly think that was likely, but that didn't mean it wouldn't happen. The cat's demeanor intrigued him. "You're worried about something."

Without another word, she rolled over and faced the other way, soaking up the heat of the fireplace.

For a while, Wick read but didn't learn much. Words escaped him and twisted inside his normally agile mind. After a bit, he put away his journal and writing kit, then hid the books as well. He made himself as comfortable as he could on the pallet, turned so that his back was turned to the flames. After a moment, he was warm and toasty, and he dropped right off to sleep.

In the morning, Wick set off again into the teeth of the blustering winds. Karbor added to his provisions, and he thanked Wick for his generous payment.

"There is one favor I would ask of you as you travel this road," Karbor said.

"If I can," Wick answered.

"If you hear any news of my daughter, if you hear any news of Rose, I ask only that you trouble yourself enough to let me know what you find out."

Wick nodded. "I will."

Then he set off, once more leading the donkey because Dawdal wouldn't allow him to ride.

Three miles up into the mountains, the trail Wick followed split out into a Y. He stood there for a time, not knowing which way to go. The cold pinched his face and his feet longed for a fire to be propped next to.

There was no clue as to which direction the Razor's Kiss thieves had gone.

Alysta roused herself, obviously put on notice by the halt of the donkey. "What's the matter?" she asked.

"I don't know which way to go," Wick replied. He walked back and forth in front of the two roads, trying in vain to find evidence on which to base an answer.

"That's why I came," Alysta said. She put her dainty nose into the wind. "To the left."

Wick looked to the left. That fork led more deeply into the mountains. On the face of things, there wasn't a better place to hide a magical sword than more deeply into the mountains. Still, the right fork might take them to an area where hiding such a thing was even easier.

That's assuming Seaspray is still in existence, he told himself. But he didn't have any doubts about that.

"How do you know it's to the left?" Wick asked.

The cat looked at him with her cool agate eyes. "I don't. I'm guessing."

"Guessing?"

"Yes. Guessing is much better than walking back and forth till you wear a trench in the ground."

Wick looked back the way he'd been pacing. It was true, he supposed, that he had been rather heavy-footed in his indecision.

He sighed. "I'd have much preferred a scientific basis for reaching that decision."

"How about a mathematical one?" the cat asked. "It's a fifty-fifty chance."

Unwilling to argue such a point with the cat, Wick started forward, taking the left fork. They would find out the truth of the matter soon enough.

At sundown, Wick stopped to make camp. He was cold and tired and scared. In his exhaustion, he was beginning to sense shadows flitting around him and imagining them as ravening beasts waiting to take him down and feast on his bones.

He went off the road for thirty yards or so, thinking to hide himself and his camp better than last time. The snow flew thicker now, gathering intensity again as if in the night it found a new strength.

The forest was thick around him, and it was alive with nocturnal creatures. He cut the trail of a fox and heard an owl pass overhead with a heavy *whoosh* of its wings before ducking down and spotting it only a heartbeat later. Thankfully he found no bears or wolves, which could have provided uneasy slumber at best.

He had a cold dinner of jerked meat and journeycakes and longed for the warm meals he'd enjoyed at Karbor's home. He thought again of the leather worker, how his daughter had been taken by the goblinkin and poor Karbor didn't know what had happened to her.

He sat under thick blankets with his back to the donkey, who munched contentedly on a feedbag of oats purchased from Karbor. The cold was kept at bay by thick woolen blankets. Alysta slept near the donkey, more vulnerable to the cold because of her small size.

Wick hated the darkness. It was too dark to travel any farther, but his mind wasn't yet tired enough to sleep despite his physical exhaustion. He needed a book. Not even a pipe or a glass of razalistynberry wine. Just something to occupy his mind. Unfortunately, it was also too dark to read, although the moon occasionally broke through the cloud cover for long silvery moments.

In the silence of the night, amid the calls of the nocturnal hunters and the wind, Wick heard the sound of a trickling stream. He'd crossed the stream once and been aware of its presence most of the day. It came down the mountain, clear and pure.

Grudgingly, he took the water bag from the pack the donkey had carried and went in search of the stream. He stumbled another twenty yards through the forest, pushing at the pines and getting the scent of them all over him in the process before he found the stream.

The stream meandered through the forest, running between the trees and boulders. It wasn't any wider than six feet across and was only inches deep.

Making his way through the snowdrifts, Wick tripped and fell. As he pushed himself back up, irritated now because he had snow all over him and would probably be wet soon when the flakes melted back at the camp, the clouds passed for a moment and moonslight touched what he'd tripped over.

It was a body.

11

The Fortress

Pale, anguished features peered up from the snowdrift where Wick had inadvertently uncovered it. In life, the victim had been a young man, a human of few years, a man by their standards, though not long so.

Wick automatically thought of him as a victim because his throat had been slit. Getting to his feet, the little Librarian discovered that he was in the cold camp of the dead. Hypnotized, recognizing the lumps around him for what they were, Wick brushed away the snow and found six more people.

They'd all been humans, traders by the look of their rough clothes and some of the supplies that had been left in their packs. All of them had died by violence, not far from the cold, dead ashes of their campfire.

Wick knew they'd been killed only a short time ago. The scavengers hadn't been at them yet. He stood in numb horror, gazing down on the faces.

"There's nothing you can do for them." Alysta stood near a tree outside the camp.

Wick said nothing, but the howling wind made him feel near-frozen inside.

"Did you hear me?" the cat asked.

"I heard you," Wick mumbled.

"There's nothing you can do for them," Alysta repeated.

"A burial," Wick suggested.

"You have neither the tools nor the energy." The cat gazed solemnly at the scene. "And the earth is frozen solid." Her voice was quiet. "Better to leave them as you found them and hope that someone else finds them to give them a proper burial."

Stunned, Wick recognized the truth of the cat's words. He nodded.

"At least we know we're on the right track," Alysta said.

"What do you mean?"

"The Razor's Kiss thieves came this way."

Tearing his gaze from the dead men, Wick looked at the cat. "How do you know that?"

"The wounds," Alysta said. "Most of them were made by razors, not swords. These men, the majority of them, were murdered in their sleep. The razor is the chosen weapon of the men we're pursuing."

Wick knew that. "It could be another group of thieves."

"I doubt it. Thieves don't often come up into the mountains."

"That doesn't mean there *wasn't* another group of thieves."

"No, but common sense would dictate that we're following the men we trailed from Wharf Rat's Warren." The cat looked through the forest and slunk back as a great owl passed by. The predator's shadow almost found her in the darkness. "Fill the waterskins and come back to camp before you lose your way."

Wick stood frozen, peering down at the bodies and fearing that he might end up just like them. It was a wonder that he wasn't dead already. *I'm a Librarian*, he thought desperately. *Not an adventurer. Not a sellsword. Not one of those heroes like Taurak Bleiyz from Hralbomm's Wing.* He took a small, deep breath and tried to steady his spinning senses. *I'm a dweller, and I'm a long way from home in a land that will kill me if the men I'm chasing after don't.*

In the dark deep of the night, Wick wished only that he could go home. Someone else could solve the riddle of the Battle of Fell's Keep and who had really betrayed whom out there. It had happened a thousand years ago. Those events should have no bearing on what was taking place now.

But they did. The arguments that took place in Paunsel's Tavern back in Greydawn Moors. The loss Bulokk still felt over his ancestor's battle-axe and Master Oskarr's good name. The kidnapping of the girl, Rose, who was supposed to be the descendant of Captain Dulaun. All of those things had happened because of the Battle of Fell's Keep. There were many who needed to know what had happened.

"Second Level Librarian Lamplighter," the cat called with more intensity. "Do you hear me?"

Wick pushed away his fear. Fear clouded a person's thoughts and killed him faster than an opponent's weapon. "I hear you."

"Fill the waterskins or return to camp," the cat said gently. "You can't spend the night looking at those men you can't help."

I know. With an effort, Wick got himself started. He went to the stream and filled the waterskins, made himself drink until he could hold no more, and headed back to camp after the cat.

They had chosen the right direction at the fork in the road. That had to mean something. But he was afraid that it only meant he was walking to his death.

The fortress came into view by late morning.

Wick rode the donkey instead of walking now. Rags wrapped his feet to stave off most of the chill. Dawdal wasn't happy about being ridden and having to suffer Wick's slight weight, but Alysta had given the donkey no choice. When Dawdal had pressed her for a reason for the change, the cat had declined to answer. She rode in front of Wick and he shielded her with his cloak.

The donkey saw the fortress first and had stopped. New-fallen snow, showing no signs of interruption, covered the narrow trail up into the mountains. When Alysta had demanded to know why they had stopped, the donkey had pointed his blunt nose at the fortress and told them where to look.

The building sat atop the mountain amid a thick copse of pine and spruce trees. The overcast sky didn't allow much sunlight to illuminate it.

The main structure was a tumbled-down wreck, and several buildings ringed it. Humans didn't build with the same care that elves and dwarves did. Their lives were fleet and filled with more violence than those of elves and dwarves, and even goblinkin. They had a tendency to build and abandon, seeking something new or different, or simply exhausting what the land had to give them in certain areas.

They also reproduced much more frequently than any race except the goblinkin. Elves planned each birth as a special event, and dwarves bore strong sons to help their fathers. The Old Ones had given the seas to the humans because the seas covered more space than the earth, which was given to the dwarves. The elves claimed the magic of the air, of the high and lofty places. And goblinkin had been birthed in fire.

As a result of the humans' proclivity for reproducing and moving around, the Shattered Coast and the islands were littered with abandoned homes and settlements. Few human cities lasted more than a few hundred years.

Upon viewing the fortress, Wick felt certain that it had been vacant much longer than it had been occupied. Fire had claimed the fortress at some point, burning away the wood and cracking the mortar. Piles of stone poured out into the snow, and most of those piles were covered by snow as well.

When it had been a place where people had lived, the fortress had four towers at the corners of the structure, flanked on both sides by guard towers. Now two of those towers had fallen, spilling across the fortress and the broken land that led up to it. Spruce and pine trees and brush had started to claim the area inside the broken fortress walls as well.

It was a place, Wick felt certain, that had been looted over and over again. Nothing could lay in that tangle of stone that hadn't been found. It wasn't possible.

We're on a fool's errand. Sickness twisted Wick's stomach and soured the back of his throat. *If Captain Dulaun's sword was ever here, it's surely gone by now.*

Smoke from three separate campfires curled into the leaden sky, mute testimony that someone was still there.

"The sword is still at the fortress," the cat said, as if guessing his thoughts.

"Do you know that for certain?"

“Why else would the Razor’s Kiss thieves be here?” the cat asked. “Why else would we be here?”

Because we’re idiots, Wick thought, but he refrained from saying that.

Turning away from the trail, hoping their arrival had gone unnoticed in the thick flurry of snow that continued to fall, Wick and his companions forged more deeply into the forest. Once they found a grade they could climb, Alysta and Wick left the donkey in a thick copse of trees that kept him out of the weather for the most part, and tied his feedbag on for him. He was munching away, probably the only happy one of the group, when they headed up into the mountain.

The way was hard and made harder by the snowdrifts that came as high as Wick’s chest as he carried Alysta. But after a while, he broke through the last of them and made his way around to the cave Alysta had spotted on the western wall of the mountain.

The cave was small and shallow, more like a divot in the mountainside. It also smelled strongly of animal musk, indicating that it was sometimes a home for wild things. Thankfully, none of those were about at the moment.

Wick wanted a fire, but he knew the smoke would give away his presence. If the Razor’s Kiss thieves hadn’t already spotted him.

Instead, he tried to enjoy the relative comfort of the cave and tell himself that not having the wind blowing against him was good enough. For a while, he watched over the fortress.

The thieves kept a watch over the area, but it was too big for them to maintain properly. Also, they stayed busy poking about in the ruins.

There was no sign of Quarrel. Thinking about the young man, Wick wondered if he had been one of the victims he’d found last night. He regretted now not looking then, but then he hadn’t wanted any more of those dead faces permanently painted in his memory.

“What are they looking for?” Wick whispered to the cat.

She sat beside him, her eyes busily watching the thieves as well. “Clams.”

The reply jarred him. “Clams?”

The cat glanced at him with preening disdain. “What else do you think they’d be looking for?”

Wick grimaced. *You left yourself open for that.*

“Why don’t you act like a Librarian?” the cat suggested.

“What do you mean?”

“You have Captain Gujhar’s ship’s log. Maybe you could *read* it and find out why the Razor’s Kiss thieves are here.”

Actually, Wick had been itching to read the books but hadn’t thought Alysta would appreciate the effort. Rather than react to the sarcastic tone the cat had adopted, he reached into his pack and pulled out the book. Last night at Karbor’s, Wick had labored through the man’s crabbed handwriting (oh, for a raconteur who had been trained as a Librarian and could write neatly!) but hadn’t been able to read too much in the weak light of the fireplace.

He'd started with the latest entries and worked his way backward. Most of those entries, though, had concentrated on Gujhar's search in and around Wharf Rat's Warren, mundane things. Before that, there had been the excavation by the goblinkin in the Cinder Clouds Islands.

In all, Wick decided that the captain kept rather good notes. But then, that was probably because whomever he represented demanded them that way.

He kept turning pages, leafing through narrative and illustrations. Alysta had come to peek over his shoulder as he sat on the cold stone floor on several occasions, but she'd walked away in obvious ignorance. Perhaps the cat had taught her daughter to read (a claim Wick still doubted somewhat), but she couldn't read the captain's hand or his language.

After a bit, he opened their provisions and ate jerked meat, feeding tidbits to Alysta without being asked. The cat didn't refuse the offerings.

Hours later, toward midafternoon, Wick found the answer they sought.

"After the Battle of Fell's Keep," Wick said, summing up what he had translated from the ship's log, "the goblinkin kept Seaspray for almost four hundred years. Then they lost the sword."

"To whom?" Alysta peered intently with her cat's eyes.

Wick shook his head. "Captain Gujhar's narrative doesn't say. They only thing they were certain of was that Seaspray was taken by a man of Captain Dulaun's bloodline."

"But not his direct bloodline," Alysta said. "It was a descendant through another ancestor."

Wick looked at her. "You know more about this than you're telling."

"Keep reading," the cat said. "I would know more."

Closing the book, Wick returned the cat's measured gaze. Outside, the sky was starting to darken with twilight. "Tell me what you know."

"When I'm ready."

"No," Wick said, drawing on reserves of courage he hadn't known he'd had, "*now*." And those stores of courage evaporated even as he gave utterance to the word.

"What?" Alysta's ears flattened. Her furred face grew taut. She launched herself unexpectedly, catching Wick in the chest and knocking him backward. She remained atop him and unsheathed the claws on one paw. "Don't trifle with me, halfer! I would kill you for that!"

Wick lay stunned. He didn't know what to say, and he feared to make a move.

Alysta trembled. With a flick, her claws disappeared. "I'm sorry. I shouldn't have done that." Her tone carried contrite apology.

"No," Wick agreed. *You almost scared me to death.*

The cat walked off him, then sat and peered out the cave mouth. "I have been searching for that sword for a long time," she said in a voice barely above a whisper.

Cautiously, Wick sat up and picked up the book.

"I gave up more than you know, more than you could possibly comprehend, in the search for that sword," the cat went on.

"Why did you search for the sword?"

"Because finding that sword became entrusted to me. I'm of Captain Dulaun's bloodline, and my family is charged with returning that sword to his rightful heir. There is only one out there now who can carry that sword and wield the magic in it. My granddaughter." Alysta's head rose proudly. "My time for it has past, but not my granddaughter's. She must carry the sword for us all."

Silent and eager, Wick listened and marveled at what was being revealed. Now that he knew this, he could guess at so much more.

"I swore upon my father's bedside that I would find that sword or die trying." Alysta shook her head. "Instead, it has come to this. I'm a cat."

"But you weren't always a cat."

"No. Once I was human. Once I was young and beautiful. But now . . . now I've grown old. And I'm no longer human. I gave up being a mother and a grandmother to pursue that sword."

"You taught your daughter to read," Wick said. "You told me that."

"I did," Alysta agreed. "But I never stayed to see if she taught her daughter to read. Then . . . then it was too late for all of us." She looked at Wick. "That's why the sword is so important. That's why I allowed myself a second life as a cat. So I could finish what I started. Or die trying. There's no other way for me to accept what I've done."

Wick thought about that, and he began to see the cat in a whole new light. "The man who stole the sword from the goblinkin—"

"Thango," the cat said.

"You're welcome," Wick said, thinking she was acknowledging his decision to reveal what he knew. "That man—"

"No," Alysta told him, "the man's name was Thango Enlark." She spelled it.

Wick took out his journal and wrote as he spoke, jotting down the gist of the information he'd distilled and guessed at. "Thango took the sword from the goblinkin down in the south, at a place called Pinanez Narrows."

"Where the Steadfast River flows out of the Forest of Fangs and Shadows," Alysta said. "I've been there. I'd even heard that Thango took back the sword there, but I couldn't confirm it."

"According to Captain Gujhar's notes, he did. The battle was bitter and bloody, and it took place over four days, a series of skirmishes that went up and down the Steadfast River." Wick drew illustrations of the river. He'd been to the Pinanez Narrows. The terrain came easily to hand, and so did the small figures engaged in battle. His craft with illustration was as good as his handwriting. "Finally, though, Thango took possession of the sword."

"He always denied it," Alysta said bitterly. "My ancestors, the true ones to whom the sword belonged, didn't believe him. But they couldn't prove elsewise. So they searched for him, and they searched for the sword. Given our destiny, our lives were always at risk."

The little Wick had read about the search for the sword bore out the truth of that statement.

"Soon there were more funerals than births," the cat went on, "till our line came down to just my father. He sired me and an older brother, then they were killed by goblinkin. I held my brother in my arms as he died, and on that day I gave up hunting for the sword for years. I met a man I could love, settled down, and had a daughter. I struggled not to feel that I was betraying my heritage, and I didn't tell my daughter or my husband who I truly was."

Wick turned the page and sketched the cat, drawn by the melancholy that clung to her. Her large eyes were pitiful.

"But then a rumor reached me," Alysta said quietly. "A whisper. Nothing more. But someone said the Razor's Kiss in Wharf Rat's Warren was searching for Seaspray, and that they knew where Boneslicer and Deathwhisper were as well. If all three weapons were being searched for, I knew something terrible was about to happen."

The wind stirred the snow outside the cave and chased it inside.

"I was old by that time. Truly too old to do what I did. I'd buried my husband five years before that. Maybe if he'd been alive I would have stayed. You'd think that a daughter and a granddaughter would be enough to keep me."

"But it wasn't," Wick whispered. He made no accusation; just stated fact.

"But it wasn't," Alysta agreed. "My blood is drawn to that sword. I told my daughter and my granddaughter who we were, and what our legacy was." Pride glinted in the cat's eyes. "My daughter was afraid. She didn't want me to go. She said that a thousand years lost was forever. But my granddaughter—" Pride and pain thickened her voice.

Listening to her speak, knowing that Alysta was once more in those days in her mind, Wick felt tears in his eyes.

"My granddaughter was only a child, but she promised me that if I didn't find the sword, she would. If I had fallen, my granddaughter would have taken up the hunt. She never got the chance." The cat's voice broke. "The goblinkin killed her mother and father just a few years ago. She was lost. *My* granddaughter was lost." The pain echoed in her words. "And I'm here with you, hoping that you can lead me to Seaspray, that I can at least redeem myself that way."

"If there's no one in your bloodline left," Wick said, "what good will it—"

"Perhaps another bloodline can carry the sword now that my bloodline has ended," Alysta said. "I think that might be true. By the Old Ones, I *hope* that is true."

Silence filled the cave for a time, and kept even the wind and the cold at bay.

Finally, Wick could no longer control his curiosity. "How did you become a cat?"

"I got into a battle with a band of goblinkin near Hanged Elf 's Point. I'd gone there to get information about the Razor's Kiss guild because I'd heard they made port there. I'm old, and my body at that time had seen nearly all of its years after all the hardship I'd put it through."

After only begetting two generations? The thought struck Wick as odd until he remembered Alysta had been human. They were the only race that didn't live to see many generations of offspring.

"The goblinkin took me down and mortally wounded me," Alysta said. "I was near death when they closed in on me. I lay there helpless and dying, with nothing I could do to defend myself. They would have cooked and eaten me, except Craugh arrived."

"Craugh?"

Alysta nodded, and the response looked strange coming from a cat. "That was when I first met him." She paused. "I'd heard of him, of course. His name is spoken in all the dark places throughout the Shattered Coast, and there are many who fear him."

Not without reason, Wick thought.

"To my surprise, he knew who I was," Alysta said, "and he knew what I searched for. He slew most of the goblinkin, and those he didn't slay he drove away. He is fierce in battle, and he will neither give nor ask quarter."

Wick had seen the wizard in battle a few times. Alysta's assessment of Craugh was fair.

"Afterwards," Alysta said calmly, "he told me I was dying. Of course, I already knew that. He asked me what I was doing. I told him I was searching for the sword, for Seaspray. He told me that was a worthwhile cause, something that he had an interest in as well. When he offered to put me into the body of this cat, which was all he could do, I accepted."

"The cat died in your place?" Wick wasn't entirely happy with that possibility.

"No." Alysta hesitated. "Craugh made this body with his magic. Scooped up some earth and shaped it into what you see before you. I'm not flesh and blood, Librarian. I'm something else."

"And Dawdal?" Wick asked.

"I don't know what Dawdal is. Perhaps he's only a talking donkey. But once, he told me when he'd been eating fermented berries, he'd been a toad for a few years because he'd angered Craugh."

Wick absently drew a toad with incredibly long ears and a toothy grin. He thought it favored Dawdal well.

"Since that time I've hunted Seaspray." The cat stared out at the fortress. "I've never been closer to finding it."

Quietly, Wick said, "Seaspray is here."

"You're sure?"

"I am." Wick gazed out at the ruins of the fortress. "When Thango Enlark fled, he came here and built a small keep."

"Why?"

Wick tapped the book. "If Captain Gujhar knew, he didn't write why."

"That is Thango's keep?"

"No. Thango's keep is buried beneath those ruins. At least, his keep is beneath one of those ruins somewhere in these mountains. Since the Razor's Kiss has concentrated their efforts on that one, I would guess those ruins would be where Thango held the sword."

"Is Seaspray still there?"

"Captain Gujhar and the Razor's Kiss believe so. According to what I've read, Thango concealed the sword within a maze of hidden walls and secret passages."

"That explains the need for the thieves."

"Yes," Wick said, thinking of the tricks and deadly traps that probably lay in wait.

"Then we must go there," Alysta said.

A sinking sensation dawned in Wick's stomach. He knew the cat was going to say that. But he had to admit to some concerns himself. According to a few of the notes in *Wraith*'s ship's log, Thango had assembled a small library of books about arms and armament. He desperately wanted to find those and get them back to the Vault of All Known Knowledge.

"Tonight," the cat said, watching the thieves prowling through the ruins.

Glancing at the sun, Wick saw that the time was only a few hours off. He made himself eat, not knowing if he would find an appetite. But he did.

12

At Sword's Point

"If they catch us there, they'll kill us." Wick hadn't said that once for all the hours he'd thought it, but he couldn't let it go unsaid any longer.

"Then," Alysta said calmly, "it would be in our better interests not to get caught."

Wick refrained from further comment as they made their way down the mountainside. Thankfully the trees stayed thick, but creeping through the snow was difficult, especially when it reached to Wick's chest. Even worse, when he looked back he saw that the trail he left was clearly marked.

The Razor's Kiss thieves kept guards stationed around the perimeters of the fortress ruins, but none of them ventured much past. Campfires lit the interior of the ruins and created long shadows that danced against the stone structures and piles.

The men talked in low voices.

Alysta leaped through the snow and occasionally fell through, but never for long. Dawdal had remained at their camp.

They stayed with the trees and went past the fortress, then hooked back around, following along the broken coastline till it met the outer perimeter wall. The stones hadn't been set flush, and the mortar had cracked and fallen away. There were plenty of hand- and footholds.

Swallowing the sour taste of his fear, steadying himself and hoping the night kept him in its shelter, Wick followed the cat up the wall. They climbed twenty feet up till they reached the top.

Wick hung by his fingertips, cautiously peering over the edge in case a guard had been stationed there. The way was clear.

"Come on," the cat hissed, barely audible over the wind that rushed in from the seaside. They had made their way back around to the coastline farther south where the keep had been.

Throwing a leg over, Wick pulled himself up and onto the top, then hunkered down in the shadows. During the climb, his hands had gotten cold. His bare feet had proven up to the task and to the chill touch of the stones, but he was always protective of his hands. The thought of losing his hands, even a finger, terrified him. There would be so many things he couldn't do.

He shoved his hands under his armpits to warm them, then crept around the wall till he could look down into the Razor's Kiss camp.

"Someone's coming," Alysta said.

From his vantage point, Wick saw a line of riders coming up the trail he and his companions had taken earlier. *Something important brought them out at this time of night*, he thought. He hid behind the low crenellation atop the wall and watched.

Two of the eight riders carried torches. The flames stood out hard and bright against the darkness. The men in the camp greeted the new arrivals and brought them into their camp.

Wick studied the men and discovered Captain Gujhar was among them. He also recognized another of the Razor's Kiss members. There was no mistaking Ryman Bey, the leader of the thieves' guild.

Ryman Bey was a lean man of medium height, with nondescript features save for the ruined right eye he hid under a crimson leather patch embroidered with a straight razor. His long hair brushed his shoulders, and he wore expensive black clothing.

All it would take, Wick realized, was a change of clothing and the distinctive eye patch, and Ryman Bey would disappear in a crowd.

Bey and Gujhar talked to the men in the camp only for a short time, then disappeared into an entrance in one of the tumble-down buildings.

"What place is that?" Alysta whispered.

Wick pictured the sketches he'd seen in the ship's log. Gujhar had maps of Thango's keep as well as the later structures. "It was the main house. It was located almost directly over Thango's keep."

"There are piles of earth around that building," Alysta said. "Some of it is fresh-turned."

Wick noted the dark earth staining the new-fallen snow then. The cat's eyes were better than his. Several wheelbarrows stood nearby.

"They've been excavating," the cat said. "We need to get in there."

"The entrance is too well guarded."

"There has to be a way. We have to get in. They didn't bring Ryman Bey and Gujhar out here for no reason."

Fearfully, Wick followed the cat as she padded through the snow piled atop the wall. At least there were no footprints in the snow, no sign that anyone else had come this way. Hopefully that meant they wouldn't encounter a guard.

Several long minutes later, the cat found a set of broken steps leading down to the ground level. After a brief pause, Alysta headed down the snow-covered steps. Wick's breath blew out gray but the wind quickly tore it away. The snow made the steps slippery, but he took care.

On the ground, they remained behind broken piles of stone and went soundlessly. The Razor's Kiss thieves remained hovering around the hissing campfires under the thin shelter of oilskin tarps that kept most of the falling snowflakes from the flames.

Despite his observation of the thieves around their campfires, Wick got the distinct impression he was being watched. He halted in the inky shadow of a broken wall and listened. In the humid winter air, sound carried farther.

"I'll be glad when they finally find that sword," one of the thieves grumbled. "I thought they'd have by now for sure."

"I'm in no hurry to see it," another thief said. "The way I hear it, there's a curse on that sword. Anybody who touches it is doomed to die soon after."

"I'm not touching it," a third thief said.

"What are you going to do if Ryman Bey orders you to carry it back to Wharf Rat's Warren?" the first asked.

The man cursed. "I'll take my chances with the curse. Not with Ryman Bey. He carries more blades on him than the number of years he's lived."

The other two men agreed. One of them threw another piece of wood on the fire, starting a brief stream of sparks that leaped into the air.

"I just hope this new place they found doesn't have the sword, either," the first man said.

"That man Gujhar thinks it does, though."

Wick leaned against the wall at his back and kept his breathing slow. If the Razor's Kiss found Seaspray, they would take the magical weapon and go. He wouldn't be able to catch them or take the sword away.

He gazed around the snow-covered inner courtyard and saw three other entrances. He suspected there were more. But all of the ones he saw now looked like they hadn't been entered in weeks.

Except for two of them.

Wick's eyes narrowed as he studied the trail leading into those entrances. Had the thieves gone that way of late? Snow nearly covered the footprints. Before morning, they would be completely disguised again.

At that moment, a shadow stepped into view at the end of the wall. The man held a sword naked in his fist. When he saw Wick, he grinned.

Fear washed through Wick, leaving him more frozen than the weather for a moment. He'd been discovered.

"Well, well, halfer," the man taunted. "I cut your trail back there while I was headed to the privy. I knew somebody was out here. Wouldn't have thought it was you. Figured you'd be too smart to come here again."

Desperately, Wick looked around for an escape path. None presented itself. As soon as he ran, even if he proved more fleet than the thief in the snow, the others would run him down.

"Heard from one of our new arrivals that you'd escaped Gujhar." The thief took another step closer. "He wouldn't admit to it, but there was plenty who saw you. Too bad you didn't have enough sense to stay away from us." He gestured with the sword. "Get over now, or I'll kill you where you cower."

I, Wick thought, *am having no luck at all when it comes to staying concealed.*

Beside him, Alysta cursed and spat. She padded around him and headed for the thief. "Get ready to run," the cat said.

Wick slowly stood.

"You've got a talking cat?" the thief asked.

"A m-m-magical cat," Wick stuttered. "She knows spells."

"Then why is she a cat?" the thief asked.

Alysta chose that instant to spring for the man's throat, claws silvered by the moonslight. The thief swiped at her with his sword but missed. He staggered back under her attack, throwing up his free hand to protect his face as she scratched again and again. The thief screamed in fear and pain, crying out for assistance.

"Run!" Alysta shouted.

For a moment, Wick didn't know which direction to run. The wall seemed too far away, and hiding behind the broken structures of the inner courtyard would only delay the inevitable. He took two steps one way, then two steps in the other, and noticed that he was running in the direction of the thieves, who had left their campfires and were coming on the double.

"The wall!" Alysta shouted as she climbed on top of the flailing thief 's head and kept slashing.

Wick yelled in terror before he realized he was wasting his breath and stopped. He devoted his energies to running. Glancing back over his shoulder, he saw two of the thieves drawing back knives to throw.

"Get down!" a voice ordered.

A foot darted out in front of Wick and tripped him, sending him sprawling through the snow. The throwing knives shot by overhead. He rolled and tried to get to his feet at once.

"Stay down if you want to live." Quarrel nocked an arrow to string while he stood behind a tall column, then turned and took aim at the rushing thieves. The young man had three other arrows fisted in his left hand holding the bow. As smoothly as Tongarian spidersilk, Quarrel released the first arrow, flipped the next around to the string, drew the fletchings back to his ear, and released again. In the space of a man's exhaled breath, the young archer had three arrows in the air.

All of the arrows hit their targets with meaty thunks. In quick succession, three of the Razor's Kiss thieves tumbled to the ground, hit dead center in their chests.

Wick was impressed. He'd seldom seen archery so swift and certain outside of elven warders.

The surviving Razor's Kiss thieves scattered, taking cover behind broken buildings, scattered piles of stone, and a few of the larger trees that had taken root inside the inner courtyard.

Thinking quickly, Wick felt confident that three of the thieves were either dead or dying. Originally, ten of the Razor's Kiss thieves had ridden out to the ruins. They'd been joined by seven more, including Ryman Bey. Gujhar made eighteen. That number was down to fifteen.

Even as he thought that, though, Quarrel put another arrow into the chest of the man fighting to get Alysta from his head. The man was dead before he hit the ground, and Alysta jumped free of the body as it fell. Immediately, arrows followed the cat but hit the ground well short of her.

Then an arrow fired by one of the thieves thudded into the snow-covered ground only inches from Wick's head. *Not good*, he thought.

"Get over here," Quarrel ordered. He knelt and whirled around the stone column, drawing and firing again effortlessly. His arrow just missed the man who'd fired at Wick.

Scrabbling through the snow, in truth staying under it most of the way, Wick joined Quarrel and hunkered down. Arrows from the thieves shattered against the column or whistled by.

"We can't stay here," Quarrel said.

Wick agreed, but he looked around. "Where did the cat go?"

"The cat?" Quarrel shrugged and peered around the column, then ducked back as an arrow glanced off, narrowly missing him.

"I had a cat with me," Wick said.

"Whatever for?"

"Because she wanted to come."

"Why couldn't you have picked a bear?" Quarrel asked. "A bear would be more of a deterrent than a cat."

"I didn't exactly have a choice in the matter."

Muffled voices reached their ears.

"They're going to surround us." Quarrel looked around, rolling to his right and drawing the fletchings back to his ear. He released and Wick saw one of the thieves drop to the ground.

More cursing suddenly filled the air. Shouts of promised revenge followed the dying man's last cries.

"We'll never reach the wall," Wick said. "Even if we did, they'd pursue us."

"I've no intention of leaving here till I get what I came for."

"Seaspray?"

Quarrel looked at Wick. The young man's eyes narrowed. He looked even younger with his smooth face. A beard or a mustache would have added more maturity.

"What do you know about Seaspray?" Quarrel demanded.

"Practically nothing," Wick lied.

Quarrel shook his head. "I knew I should have let the thieves kill you."

"Actually," Wick said, changing his mind when he thought it wouldn't be any trouble for Quarrel to boot him out into the open and use him for a distraction while he made his own escape, "I know a lot."

"What do you know?" Quarrel's gaze was filled with challenge.

"I have a map of the keep that was here before this fortress."

"Where?"

Wick took out the ship's log and tapped the cover. "Here."

"Give it to me."

Taking a step back, Wick hid the book once more in his cloak. "No. You'll leave me out here."

Quarrel showed him a thin-lipped smile. "Perhaps."

"Are the two of you going to stand here and natter all day?" The cat sat atop a heap of stones only a few feet away. She looked no worse for wear despite her fight. "Or do you think possibly you could avoid getting killed or captured?"

"A talking cat?" Quarrel asked.

"It's not as amazing as it sounds," Wick said. "And not nearly worth the trouble, I tell you."

"They're coming," Alysta said.

"Follow me." Quarrel turned and ran, staying low and within the shadows.

Wick trailed after the young man. They ran a zigzag trail through the tumbled buildings of the inner courtyard. Some of the statues of people and creatures startled Wick. He hadn't seen those in his earlier observations.

Quarrel cut across other trails, confusing their own tracks with those of others. He obviously had a destination in mind, but he took a circuitous route to it. Finally he headed into one of the doorways that opened a throat down into the earth.

With the dank moldering smell all around him, Wick couldn't help feeling he was descending into an open grave. Broken rock lay strewn about. Snow had blown in through the entrance and sat in heaps.

Inside the chamber, the thieves' voices reached Wick's ears more readily. They'd gotten confused and anxious, becoming more certain their quarry had somehow managed to escape.

"Did they get over the wall, then?" someone asked.

"If they'd gone over the wall, we'd have seen them," another answered.

"They're still here," another voice, more commanding in tone, announced. "They're hiding. Spread out and find them. I want to know who they are and what they're doing here."

"Ryman Bey," Quarrel whispered in the quiet of the chamber.

Wick had assumed that. "What are we going to do?"

Quarrel frowned at him. "I should have let them kill you."

"Perhaps they wouldn't have killed us," Alysta replied.

Quarrel snorted derisively. "They'd have killed you."

"Then you were a fool to interfere," the cat accused.

Ignoring the comment, Quarrel slid his bow over his shoulder and drew his sword. He stared at Wick. "Let's have another look at that book."

Wick hesitated.

Quick as a wink, Quarrel placed his blade tip at the little Librarian's throat. "Now would not be a time to vex me, halfer." Even though his voice was soft, there was no lack of menace in it.

13

To the Dungeon

Swallowing hard, feeling the keen edge pressed up against his neck, Wick weighed his chances. Everything in him that was a Librarian (which was *everything* in him) screamed out not to surrender the book. It held clues to the person who had sent Captain Gujhar in search of the three magic weapons that had been at the Battle of Fell's Keep. The pages offered hints at where Seaspray was located.

And it might even tell what was at stake, why the weapons were being gathered after Lord Kharrion had fallen and a thousand years had gone by.

"Your word," Wick bargained in a croaking voice.

Quarrel stared at him in surprise over the length of sword steel between them. "What?"

"Your word," Wick repeated. "Before I give you the book, I want your word."

"On what? That I won't kill you?" Quarrel nodded. "Done."

Wick knew that was no trade. Quarrel had already risked his life to save his. He didn't think the young man would just as quickly take it. Even if he did have a sword at his throat.

"Your word that you will give the book back to me," Wick said.

Quarrel cursed. "You bargain too far, halfer. I could just as easily pluck the book off your dead body."

"And I could just as easily start yowling and draw the Razor's Kiss thieves down on you," Alysta said.

Silence stretched between them for an instant.

"Perfidious cat," Quarrel snarled.

Alysta sat on her haunches a safe distance away, her tail curled around her paws. "That's just one of my more endearing qualities," she replied. Her large eyes winked in amusement.

"Do we have a bargain?" Wick asked.

Quarrel didn't answer.

Alysta purred, on the verge of a yowl. "Don't mind me," she said. "I'm just tuning up my voice."

Heaving a great sigh, Quarrel dropped the sword from Wick's neck. "Old Ones preserve me, the two of you don't know what you're in for or what I've had to do to get this far." He gestured with his free hand. "Very well, you've got my word. Now let's have a look at that book."

Relaxing a little, Wick took the ship's log from his cloak and handed it over.

Quarrel sheathed the sword and took the book in both hands. "Where did you get this?"

"From *Wraith*."

"How?"

Wick related the story of the escape from the goblinkin ship (perhaps playing up the nearness of the escape and his amount of derring-do a little, but he felt entitled since it *was* his story) and his subsequent journey to the ruins. The cat hissed at several of the more fragrant points, but offered no comment. As he talked, Quarrel walked more deeply into the chamber.

Wick was grimly aware that the thieves could enter the tunnel at any time. He wondered how far back the tunnel went. As narrow and barren as it was, there didn't appear to be many places to hide. Defending their position was out of the question; all the thieves had to do was starve them out.

Two turns later, Quarrel stopped in a work area that Wick could barely discern in the low light. Quarrel, with only his human's eyesight, had to trail a hand along the tunnel's side to find his way. In the work area, a lantern hung on the wall. Using a tinderbox on a shelf near the lantern, the young man lit the lantern.

The soft yellow glow filled the work area.

Quarrel opened the book and leafed through the pages. "I can't read it," he admitted.

"You can read?" Wick asked, surprised when he thought he wasn't going to be any further surprised.

"Yes." Quarrel frowned at the pages as he continued turning them. "But not this."

"The halfer can read it," Alysta said.

Quarrel looked at Wick. "Is that true?"

Blabbermouth, Wick thought at the cat. He sighed. "Yes."

"How?"

"With my eyes," Wick said. He didn't mention that he could also read with his fingers, by scent, by sound, and even by taste. After all, he was in training to be a First Level Librarian.

"That's not what I meant." Quarrel looked exasperated.

"Oh."

"Who taught you to read?"

"Someone," Wick answered.

Quarrel shook his head. "Fine. Keep those secrets. But not this one. Can you read this?"

"Yes."

"What does it say?"

"I haven't read all of it. There wasn't time." Wick glared at the cat, indicating that lack was purely her fault. Alysta just winked at him in disdain and wrinkled her nose. If Quarrel caught the look, he gave no indication.

"But it talks about Seaspray?" Quarrel asked.

Wick nodded. "The text refers to Seaspray and Boneslicer and Deathwhisper."

Quarrel frowned. "All of the weapons that were at the Battle of Fell's Keep."

"Yes." Wick was quietly surprised that the young man knew so much about the weapons. He wanted to ask how Quarrel had come about that knowledge, but he didn't dare.

"Why?"

"I don't know. The captain of *Wraith*, a man named Gujhar, was sent to retrieve them." Wick almost added that he'd been on hand when Boneslicer was taken.

"For what reason?"

"I don't know. Yet."

"Who sent him?"

Shaking his head, Wick said, "I don't know that, either."

"Perhaps the ship's log will reveal that."

"That's what we're hoping."

" 'We?' "

Wick pointed to Alysta. "The cat and I."

"How did you become partners?"

Alysta interrupted. "Do you think we really have time to talk about this now? The thieves outside aren't going to give up looking for us."

"She's right," Wick said.

Quarrel held the book closer to the light. Wick had to hold his tongue. In the Vault of All Known Knowledge, flames weren't used. Illumination was provided by lummin juice from glimmerworms. Several dwellers, Wick's father among them, raised glimmerworms.

The young man flipped the ship's log till he found the maps of the ruins. He studied them.

"The thieves gave up on this site," Quarrel said, "but I felt that something more was hidden here." He placed a finger against the map. "What's this?"

Wick peered at the page. The small picture at the edge of the old keep Thango had built was of a ship with full-bellied sails.

"It's a ship," Wick said.

"Here in the mountains?"

"Perhaps there's a cave at the bottom of the mountain that leads to the sea," Wick said.

"I've been there," Quarrel said. "I didn't see a passage to a cave."

"Maybe you didn't know what you were looking for," Alysta suggested. "In any event, staying here only makes us increasingly vulnerable. It's better if we put some distance between us and our foes."

Wick was antsy, too, eager to be moving.

"I'll take you to this spot," Quarrel stated. He handed the ship's log back to Wick. "Let's go."

Carrying the lantern, his sword naked in his fist, Quarrel led the way down into the ruins. Looking around at the layers of earth that had piled on top of the past structures, Wick was reminded of the caves in the Cinder Clouds Islands. How much history had been lost in the world even before the Cataclysm? At one time, writing hadn't existed. It troubled him to think of how many people's stories would never be told.

Down and down they went, following Quarrel and the swinging lantern. Soon, though, he halted at an opening.

"We'll have to go easily from this point on." Quarrel shined the lantern into the next section. "This leads to Thango's main house. To the dungeon area. There are a number of passages. They are in relatively good shape."

"Hold on." Wick opened the book, knowing from memory where the map of the pre-existing keep was. He studied the drawing for a moment, looking at the scale at the bottom of the page.

"The opening to the dungeon is ahead." Quarrel held the lantern closer.

Instinctively, Wick pulled the book back from the lantern's heat. "The dungeon wasn't filled in?"

"I don't think anyone even knew it was here before Gujhar and the thieves found it."

"You've been there?"

"I have."

"Did you see a ship?" Alysta asked.

"No."

"Was there a passage down to a cave at the bottom of the mountain?"

"There still is," Quarrel replied.

"Could that be the ship on the map?" the cat asked. "A reference to a hidden port?"

Wick thought about that. Several cities and keeps had smugglers' paths. Contraband existed everywhere, though it was generally goods that the sellers and buyers didn't want to pay heavy taxes on. He trailed a finger down the map, tracing the passageway marked on the paper.

If the passageway led to a secret port, why wasn't the ship drawn at the bottom of the passage rather than the top? That troubled him.

"There's nothing there," Quarrel said.

Wick read through the script under the picture. "According to these notes, Gujhar—or whoever he works for—is convinced that this room holds a secret of some sort."

"What secret?"

"It doesn't say."

"What's in that room?" Alysta asked.

"Nothing." Quarrel looked disgusted. "If Seaspray was ever in that room, it's long gone. That was probably the secret."

"Then why hasn't the sword ever been found since Thango brought it here?" Alysta asked.

"Perhaps Seaspray has been destroyed." Quarrel sighed.

The cat looked at him. "Do you believe that?"

Hesitation showed on Quarrel's smooth face. "I hope it's not true."

"Why?"

Quarrel's eyes narrowed. "Because I want that sword."

Alysta hissed in displeasure. "You can't always have what you want, boy."

"Let's go have a look at this room," Wick suggested, hoping to remind the others why they were there. "Provided we get out of here alive, I'll wager we don't get many chances to come back this way."

"Agreed," Quarrel replied.

The cat sniffed.

Quarrel turned back to the open area. "This excavation gives us a way to reach the dungeon entrance. After we enter that, the way becomes much more dangerous. Not all of the traps have been sprung."

Traps? Wick thought. *There are traps?* Then he sighed. Of course there were traps. There *had* to be traps. He wondered if Craugh and the crew of *One-Eyed Peggie* were near. He hoped that they were because the situation at the moment didn't look good.

The entrance to the dungeon was a hole in the floor set next to an excavation wall. Obviously the excavation had been done some time in the past because the wood was rotting. New braces had been set into place over the old ones, but nothing about it looked safe.

"Will it hold?" Wick asked nervously.

"There are no guarantees," Quarrel replied. He ducked down and climbed down into the dungeon.

When the light left with the young mercenary, Wick realized he was about to be left standing in the dark. He stepped into the entrance and followed Quarrel down.

Steps cut into the wall led down at least twenty feet. Wick judged that by the fact that the steps were each about eight inches high and there were thirty-two steps in all. The actual height was twenty-one feet and four inches, but he didn't quibble. It made for a solid shelf of rock overhead, even with the generous headroom.

"Carefully through here." Quarrel shined the lantern around, revealing the iron-barred cages set in the wall to the right.

Rats ran among the bones of the deceased. No flesh remained on the ivory underpinnings, but there were several insects that lived in the detritus left by those who had tramped through the dungeon looking for Dulaun's lost magical sword. They protested the invasion of the light with high-pitched squeaks.

It was obvious that those who had opposed Thango had met bad endings once they'd fallen in his hands.

Past the four prison cells, the torture room offered a glimpse into past horrors. Two iron baskets held skeletons. Other skeletons hung from chains set into the wall.

"I take it Thango wasn't the forgiving type," Wick commented.

"No," Alysta said. "By all accounts, he was a vindictive man even before his frustration with Seaspray."

"What do you know about the sword?" Quarrel asked.

"More than you do."

Quarrel grimaced, but thought better of saying anything. He turned and followed the lantern again. He stopped against a wall on the other side of the torture chamber.

"I found a secret passage here." Quarrel hung the lantern on a nearby hook, then put his hands on the wall and pushed on two separate stones. "The thieves had found it before me. They'd found more than a few of them, but they left some of them untripped and set to catch anyone who happened upon the way and wasn't wary."

Wick surveyed the map and saw that a passage did go on past the area on the drawing that he now knew to be the torture chamber. At that same moment, a section of the wall turned to a ninety-degree angle, swinging on concealed hinges. Grinding filled the room and echoed down the hallway ahead.

"It leads to the room with the secret passageway to the sea." Moving cautiously, Quarrel entered the passageway. He kept his sword at hand and moved with cautious speed.

Only a short distance ahead, a skeleton in tattered clothing stood pinned against a wall, pierced by a long metal shaft. A callous later visitor had used one of the skeleton's eye sockets as a candle sconce. Melted wax filled the empty space and wept waxy tears down the cheekbone into the soundless scream of the mouth.

"Evidently Thango wasn't simply protecting his wine cellar," Alysta said.

The next trap was a yawning pit with sharpened metal stakes at the bottom. It was ten feet across, built so that an unwary man couldn't just stretch out and save himself as he fell. It also held a dead man at the bottom amid the other bones of past victims. The dead man had evidently been in that condition for months.

"Did you know him?" Wick asked.

"No. As I said, there have been a lot of luckless that came this way in the past."

"Oh." Wick tore his eyes away from the sight with effort.

Quarrel looped the lantern to his hip with a piece of rope, then made his way across by way of the pegs sticking out from the wall. He made the crossing look effortless.

Wick tucked the ship's log into his cloak and reached down for the cat. Alysta flattened her ears, raised a paw in warning, and hissed.

"Do you think you can navigate that climb unassisted?" Wick asked reasonably.

Grudgingly, the cat hissed again and lowered her paw. Instead of letting Wick lift her, though, she ran up his arm and spread herself across his shoulders.

"All right," she said.

14

Hiding Place

Wick stepped onto the first peg at his feet and reached for the ones well above his head. He was barely able to reach, and felt certain if the climb had been a long one he wouldn't have had the strength or endurance to manage it. The cat's weight across his shoulders further increased the difficulty.

Quarrel waited on the other side of the chasm, holding the lantern to better light the way.

Making the journey without incident, Wick stepped down onto the next ledge. Without a word, Quarrel turned and they went on.

Ahead, bones lay in scattered disarray beneath four axe blades that had swung out from both walls, the floor, and the ceiling. All of them had been set off by a weight-activated stone. Now the axe blades were heavily rusted and falling to pieces.

"Some of the traps sprung themselves over the years," Quarrel said, indicating a crumbled section of wall. He directed the light inside to reveal the rusty shards that had once been steel spikes. "The traps that relied on venomous snakes hold only dead things now, but there are some venomous spiders that have propagated down here and done well."

Suddenly aware of the cobwebs that lay against the back of his neck, Wick flailed at the webs and shivered.

"Also, the traps armed with acid and poison might have diluted over the centuries, but they can still poison you or make you sick." Quarrel went on.

Down and down they went, sometimes on inclined hallways

and sometimes by way of corkscrew stairs. Evidently the dungeon had a few levels.

"I'm taking us to that room," Quarrel explained. "The one on the map. By the safest route possible. It's not necessarily the shortest."

Wick's legs ached from the effort of walking. With all the floor changes, he was reminded of the Vault of All Known Knowledge. A much gloomier version of the Great Library, to be sure, but just as serpentine.

Along the way, they passed several other victims of the traps left scattered throughout the dungeon levels. Many of them were scattered literally instead of merely figuratively.

Thango's trap designers were very thorough, Wick noted grimly.

Only a little while later, they reached the room that was supposed to have held Thango's greatest secret.

"Stay here," Quarrel said. "This room, more than all the others, continues to be dangerous." He held up the lantern. "Each time a person leaves this room, the traps reset themselves. More than that, they move around, shifting where they are and what they do."

"Wizardry?" Wick asked. In the romances in Hralbomm's Wing there had been any number of stories about moveable traps. All of them had been fueled by magic.

"I don't know. It has to be." Quarrel walked into the room slowly and began lighting other lanterns hanging on the wall. When he touched one of them, a section of the opposite wall popped open and a crossbow fell into position. It fired automatically and the bolt leaped across the space.

Quarrel dodged out of the way. The sharp blade, not blemished at all by rust, smacked into the wall right where the young man had been standing.

"Forgot about that one," Quarrel admitted. He went through the room and turned off five other traps. "That's not all of them, but it will allow you to enter and look at the passageway down to the sea."

With the lanterns lit, the room stood revealed. Instead of a simple stone floor, this one held a patchwork of blue and black tiles measuring two feet square. It looked like a giant chessboard. When Wick counted the tiles, he found they were arranged eight by eight, exactly like a chessboard. A bloodred border ran around the room.

Friezes decorated the walls, depicting human heroes in battles on the land on snow-covered mountains as well as in rich woodlands, and on the sea. Ships under full sail were frozen in battle against others while sea monsters roared up from the depths.

Cautiously, and curiously, Wick peered into the room. "Maybe I could just stay out here," he suggested. "Like you said, if there was something here to find, you would have already found it."

"Then why did we come down here?" Quarrel sounded angry. "I've already been down here. I could be looking in other places."

"No," Alysta said, easing into the room. "What we seek is here. Somewhere."

"The sword?" Quarrel walked toward the cat.

Despite his trepidation, Wick's curiosity about the friezes drew him into the large room. He stayed to the outside walls as well, circling the chessboard floor. "Is the floor booby-trapped?"

"Yes," Quarrel answered. His attention remained on the cat. "What makes you certain the sword is still here?"

The cat padded silently to the wall with the image of the sea battles. "I can *feel* it."

"You can't do that." Quarrel approached the frieze as well.

Alysta stretched up and touched the frieze. "I can."

Wick studied the frieze. There was something familiar about it. In seconds, his fear was forgotten. The frieze wasn't merely carved into the stone wall. Shaped colored stones were set into the hollows, bringing more immediate color to the images.

Looking around the room, Wick saw that none of the other friezes were like that. He wondered why this one was different. He took one of the lanterns from the wall and walked closer, studying the images.

Then it came to him.

"This is the Battle of the Dancing Waves," Wick whispered.

"What?" Quarrel demanded.

"The Battle of the Dancing Waves." Wick touched the frieze. "Of course, it wasn't called that at the time. It was just a skirmish between Captain Dulaun's ship, *Tolamae*, and a pirate ship called *Death's Grin*." He pointed at the flag on the second vessel, almost lost in gray fog.

"I've never heard of the battle or those ships," Quarrel said.

"I have," Alysta said. "It's an old story. Handed down to me by my father, and his father before him. This was the battle where Dulaun harnessed the power of the waves with Seaspray for the first time."

"That's right." Wick scanned *Tolamae* and saw Dulaun standing on her foredeck with his sword pointing straight into the air. The ship's captain was spare and lean, a man long hardened by the sun and the sea. His brown hair had streaks in it. He wore rolled-top black boots, tight black breeches, and a blue and red striped shirt. "That's Captain Dulaun."

Quarrel peered at the man's image made up of specially selected stones. "He's not as tall as I'd thought he would be."

"No," Wick said, remembering the pictures he'd seen of the human. "Dulaun wasn't heroic in stature, but in his heart. He never once gave up."

"Dulaun was killed in the Battle of Fell's Keep," Quarrel said. "When the dwarven blacksmith Oskarr betrayed the Unity defenders who stayed to protect the evacuation of the southern Teldane's Bounty."

"Master Oskarr didn't betray them," Wick said.

"That's the way I've always heard it told," Quarrel said.

"So have I," Alysta said.

"I only recently learned that story was false," Wick said, remembering the time he'd spent in Master Oskarr's forge. Neither of his listeners appeared interested in his opinion.

"This could be the ship the map referred to," Alysta said.

"I'd already thought of that," Quarrel said. "But what would that have to do with the sword?"

"It was during this battle that Captain Dulaun harnessed the power of the sea for the first time," Wick repeated. "The Old Ones gave the power of the water to humans, and those powers were invested in a few weapons made by humans. Seaspray was one of those enchanted creations. While locked in this battle, coming to the aid of a stricken merchant, *Tolamae* and her crew were vastly outnumbered by pirates from the Cage Islands. For a time, it looked like the end."

"But Dulaun used the sword, right?" Quarrel asked.

"They say Dulaun had always been blessed by the Old Ones," Wick said. "That from the day of his birth he was destined to be a hero. He'd studied the ways of the sea, and when he forged the sword himself, he asked the Old Ones to infuse it with power. The way most scholars interpret it, Dulaun asked only that the sword not break during a battle. Instead, given the way he led his life and tried to champion those not able to stand up for themselves, he was given much more."

"He commanded the seas that day," Alysta said. "When he thought all was lost, he stood upon that deck and hoped that the sea would rise up and swallow his enemies. It did."

As he listened to the cat speaking, Wick felt a curious warmth dawn in the frieze. The chamber itself was near freezing and only his traveling cloak managed to keep him warm. He ran his fingers over the stones.

There's a puzzle here, he realized.

"What?" Alysta asked.

"Steganography."

"What's that?" Interested, Quarrel stepped forward.

"It's a craft, very deceitful and very sly," Wick said, "of hiding a message within a picture."

"What message?" Quarrel demanded.

"That," Wick replied, "remains to be seen." Picking at one of the stones with a fingertip, he was surprised to find that it easily popped out. He quickly searched out others. When his hands filled, he laid the stones down on the floor.

"Why did you pick those?" Quarrel asked.

"They're of fish." Wick scanned the images of fish jumping in the water. Not all of the pieces were the same shape, which was what he had expected. The message wasn't in the fish; they were only the link.

"There are plenty more of fish," Quarrel said.

"Yes, but not all of the others are depicted cresting the ocean with their tails tilted to the left." Wick worked to fit the pieces together.

"The fish shouldn't be in the picture," Alysta said.

"Very good," Wick said, smiling at the cat. "Why not?"

"Because whenever a large predator is in the water, all the small fish leave the area."

"Right," Wick said. "A sea creature's first instinct is survival, as are many others'.

In the sea, if you're small, you're prey. Food for someone else. By the same token, small fish often avoid dead things in open water because they attract larger predators."

"But the fish are in the frieze," Alysta said.

"Yes." Wick reached for another piece, testing it. As he'd quickly discovered, not all the frieze pieces were loose. Most were mortared into place. Gazing at the pieces, Wick saw that they created a pattern. He wasn't tall enough to get all the pieces he thought he needed. Quarrel had to get a few of the higher ones for him.

"They were put there to draw attention," Quarrel said.

"I believe so." Wick's fear of his situation had all but vanished, its bones taken away as his curiosity filled him.

"To what purpose?" Alysta asked.

" 'Throughout the course of his life, a man's hand often slips from the tiller,' " Wick said softly.

"What's that?" Quarrel asked.

"A quote," Alysta said. "That's one of Captain Dulaun's most prized sayings."

"Dulaun was referring to the fact that most men tend to wander through life without purpose or aim," Wick said. "They go wherever the sea dictates." He surveyed the fish tiles in front of him. There were seventeen of them. "I'm certain that these pieces were put in that picture to provide direction for those who came looking for the sword."

"You believe Thango left clues?" Alysta asked.

"This frieze," Wick said with grim certainty, "is far older than Thango's time." He continued moving the fish pieces around, fitting them together so they were almost seamless. The design was flawless.

The cat crept in closer, sitting nearby and curling her tail around her paws. "I've never heard of this frieze."

"Neither have I," Wick said absently. "But I've heard of the artist."

"What artist?"

Wick pointed at the signature in the lower right corner. It was an icon of a gleaming star. "Lazzarot Piknees," the little Librarian answered. "He was one of the finest artists the Silver Sea Trade Empire ever saw." He turned his attention back to the tiles. "He was a contemporary of Captain Dulaun."

"They knew each other?" Quarrel asked.

"I didn't say that. It's possible, of course. And Piknees did make this mural."

"A signature at the bottom doesn't necessarily mean that Piknees made this mural," Alysta challenged.

"I," Wick said forcefully, "am familiar with Piknees's work."

The cat blinked at him, obviously ready to fight further, but she chose not to.

"What are you doing?" Quarrel asked, kneeling beside Wick. He eased his bow from his shoulder and laid it close to hand.

"These pieces form a puzzle," Wick said. "I'm trying to figure out what their secret is." As he worked, another piece slid to a neat fit.

"This one," Quarrel said, "goes here." Using his forefinger, he pushed one of the pieces against two others. When the sides touched, all three fused with an audible *clank* and triggered a brief spark of blue light that rivaled the lanterns' glow.

Wick leaned back, thinking that the pieces were going to catch fire. When nothing happened, he asked, "What did you do?"

"I just fit the stones together. I didn't cause that." Quarrel had his sword in one hand and a long knife in the other.

Wick had never seen the young man draw either weapon. The little Librarian tried to slide the piece Quarrel had touched from the others.

It wouldn't move. Somehow, the pieces had fused.

Returning his attention to one of the pieces he'd placed, Wick found he could easily slide it away. He lifted his hand from it and pointed at it. "Do this one."

Hesitant, Quarrel laid his blades aside and nudged the new piece into contact with another. The *clank* sounded again just before the blue light flashed.

"You're causing this," Wick whispered.

"It's not me," Quarrel said.

Wick thought again of the leather-maker's symbol on the bag that Quarrel carried. He tested the two new pieces and found they were fused as well.

"This is magic," Quarrel said. "I don't know magic."

"Apparently," Wick said, "the magic knows you."

"But how?"

"This makes no sense," the cat spat.

"Perhaps you'd care to piece the puzzle together," Wick offered.

Haughtily, the cat stepped forward and pushed pieces together with her paw. The pieces fit but there was no other reaction.

"It doesn't mean anything," Alysta said. "Maybe it's just because he's been down in this room before. Whatever magic is here could have an affinity for him."

"Perhaps," Wick said noncommittally. At his direction, Quarrel continued fitting the pieces together. Each time the pieces touched, they fused with a *clank* and the bright explosion of blue light.

The cat sniffed at each one, but her efforts grew less certain.

In a short time, the seventeen pieces had become a rough oval with flukes on one end.

"A fish," Quarrel whispered.

In truth, the assembled piece did look very much like a fish. Wick lifted it from the floor, amazed at the way it held together, as if it had always been of a piece. He turned it over, switching the side of the tiles that showed fish cresting the waves with their tails turned for the blank one on the other side.

Only now the other side wasn't blank. Words were written there. The language was the high trader tongue from the Silver Sea. He translated, amazed that the words rhymed even in the common tongue.

Fair blows the wind,
Driving iron men and wooden ships.
A hero far from home,
Unafraid to die alone.

Say his name, friend,
And ride the fierce Silver Sea as she dips!

"What does it mean?" Quarrel asked.

"Captain Dulaun," Wick said.

Nothing happened.

The little Librarian looked at the young mercenary. "Say his name."

Quarrel hesitated.

"Say his name," Wick repeated.

"Captain Dulaun," Quarrel whispered.

Immediately, the inscription on back of the fish lit up in roping, bright blue veins. Wick felt the piece vibrate in his hands. "Again. Louder. Put your hand over the inscription."

Dropping his hand over the inscription, nervousness showing bright in his eyes, Quarrel licked his lips. And he spoke the name of the hero of the Silver Sea once more. "Captain Dulaun!"

Abruptly, the fish piece flew from Wick's hand, sliding out from under Quarrel's. In an eyeblink, the fish elongated into a boarding plank. One end of the plank dropped against the floor and the other fell against the frieze.

Wick tried desperately to catch the plank, certain that it was going to destroy the image wrought from hundreds of stone pieces. He missed. The end of the plank fell *into* the frieze, coming to a shuddering rest on the edge of the artwork like it was a window ledge.

Fog spewed from the image.

Suddenly, the noise of crashing waves filled the underground chamber, followed immediately by the salty smell of the sea. Heat swept some of the chill away, warming Wick as he gazed up at the fog-covered frieze. He could no longer see the images there.

"Come aboard!" a deep voice rang out.

15

Captain Dulaun

uarrel slid his bow over one shoulder, then took up his blades. He started forward.

"Where are you going?" the cat asked.

Placing a foot on the boarding plank, not even looking back at Alysta, Quarrel said, "To see where this takes me." He walked forward, leaning into the incline. The fog reached for him, softening his image as it took him into its embrace.

Alysta hesitated only a moment, then followed, quietly padding up the board.

Unwilling to remain behind, though drawn more by curiosity than by a fear of being left behind on his own, Wick reached down and took up the nearest lantern. He stepped onto the board and followed it up.

The fog swirled into him until he couldn't see. The rhythmic sound of waves crashed against the prow of a ship. Seven steps later, he felt the familiar up and down sway of a vessel at sea.

Then he was through the fog and could see the blue sky open around him. He stood on the ship's deck and knew that he was nowhere near Wharf Rat's Warren.

Quarrel and Alysta stood in front of the ship's captain. There was no mistaking him.

Captain Dulaun was an unassuming man. Sun-streaked brown hair that blew in the gentle wind and a warm brown-eyed gaze looked average, not heroic. He wore a mustache that curled on the ends, and he smiled as if he'd never seen a sad day in his life. His clothing was plain, black boots and breeches, a red shirt with belled sleeves.

"Welcome, my friends," Dulaun said.

"This can't be," Quarrel whispered, dazed. "You're dead. You died a thousand years ago."

Dulaun smiled again. "Of course I'm dead. Otherwise you wouldn't be here now seeking Seaspray." He laid an affectionate hand on his sword hilt.

"How did you arrange this?" Alysta asked.

"Magic, of course. Borrowed from Seaspray and linked to me through my family." Dulaun clasped his hands behind him. "You are my family. At least one of you. Otherwise you would never have figured out the secret of the frieze and would not have been able to activate the spell that allows you to come here."

Family? Wick thought. Then he realized another of the truths that had been staring him in the face. He gazed around at Dulaun's crew. The captain's men all looked battle-hardened and ready.

Beyond them, the Silver Sea shimmered under the midday sun. An albatross glided through the cloudless blue sky. The white canvas sails trapped and held the wind, mastering it as the ship continued to crash through the waves.

Dulaun walked to the ship's prow. "Come. Come. I'll tell you how you came to be here. But first I would show you my world. Hopefully it's still your world."

As if hypnotized, Alysta and Quarrel trailed after Dulaun.

"Due to the construction of the spell and certain constraints that are part of the nature of time," Dulaun said as he gazed out to sea, "I can answer your questions here and now, but I won't remember them."

"Who made this spell?" Alysta asked.

"A wizard named Rivalak." Dulaun sounded pleased.

"Rivalak," Wick said, "was one of Dulaun's contemporaries."

"More than a contemporary," Dulaun insisted. "He was a friend." He gazed at Wick. "And who might you be? I know you're no relative because you're a dweller. Not unless something went truly and drastically wrong with my lineage."

"No, I'm not family," Wick answered. "I came here with these two. As an advisor."

"Splendid." Dulaun smiled again.

Wick had to wonder what the man had been doing before they arrived. Dulaun was too pat, too sure of himself. Even before the Battle of Fell's Keep, Dulaun's self-confidence had caused fights that had sorely tested him upon occasion.

"Why are you here?" Wick asked.

"Because of this." Dulaun whisked the sword from his hip, slashing the blade through the air. "You know my blade?"

"Seaspray," Wick answered. "It has the power to call on the magic of the waves."

Seaspray was a gleaming length of steel three and a half feet long. Double-edged and inscribed with runes that blazed blue even in the bright light, the sword commanded instant respect. The guard above the hilt was shaped like two dolphins swimming around the blade. They had sapphire eyes and lines of carved gold filigree. It was beautiful.

"Aye." With a flourish, Dulaun returned the blade to its sheath. "There are many who want this sword. But no one can have it but one of my descendants. That's why this place was made."

"Where are we?" Alysta asked.

Surprised, Dulaun knelt and reached for the cat. "A talking cat?"

Alysta drew back, flattening her ears and hissing a warning.

"She's not exactly a cat," Wick said. "Her name is Alysta. She's one of your descendants."

Surprised and dismayed, Dulaun stood. "That's impossible."

"It's the truth," Alysta said.

Dulaun shook his head. "But a cat can't wield my sword." He looked at Wick. "I have no issue to give my sword to?"

"You do," Quarrel said.

"You do," Wick said. "It was her touch that activated the spell in the frieze."

" 'Her'?" Alysta looked at the young "man."

"This," Wick said, "is your granddaughter. Rose." He knew it could be no other.

"You?" Alysta padded around to better survey Quarrel. "*You* are Rose? I left you and your mother when you were so young."

Quarrel looked at Wick then, and her eyes were soft. "You knew?"

"Not until you put the puzzle together," Wick said. "I talked to Karbor the leathermaker. He told me that he adopted the daughter of friends who were related to Captain Dulaun."

"My granddaughter," Alysta whispered. She padded up to Quarrel. "You are Rose?"

The young woman smiled, but there was sadness in her eyes. "I am. But that was the name Karbor gave me when he found me and kept me hidden. I am Quarrel now, and I will be Quarrel until the day my parents' murderers are brought to justice."

"I'm your grandmother."

Quarrel's eyes widened. "Alysta?"

"Yes."

"We thought you were dead."

"I very nearly was." The cat touched her chest in a very human gesture. "After this happened, I couldn't return. Then I heard your parents were dead. When I returned then, I found no trace of you. I believed you dead as well. Until that night Karbor talked of rescuing you—only to lose you again."

"Captain Gujhar's men came for me," Quarrel said, "but I escaped."

"Your mother," Alysta said pridefully, "trained you well."

Quarrel smiled. "She always said she had a good teacher."

"*You* are my descendant?" Dulaun asked. "A girl?"

Quarrel looked at him and lifted her chin in reproach. "I'm a woman."

Dulaun laughed and shook his head. "You're a slip of a thing. If you're sixteen I'll eat my boots."

"I'm seventeen," Quarrel said, "and I won't be made sport of. Not even by you. My mother gave her life to save me so that our line would be complete to take up your sword once more."

The captain shook his head. "You won't get my sword, girl. You would only take it from this place and lose it."

"How dare you!" Alysta hissed angrily.

Quarrel moved before Wick knew she was in motion. In an instant, she doffed her cloak in the warm breeze that propelled *Tolamae* through the Silver Sea. Her long blond tresses were tied back and hung below her shoulders. She was all suppleness and grace—and her sword leaped into her hand like a live thing. Her body fell into perfect line behind the point, which hovered only inches from Dulaun's right eye.

The crew drew their weapons and started forward at once.

Captain Dulaun held up his hand and stopped the sailors in their tracks. His lips twitched into a smile. "All right, child. You've got fire in your belly. I'll admit that. But you're not good enough to challenge me."

Without a word, without warning of any kind, Quarrel followed her blade and nicked Dulaun's right ear. Bright crimson blood dripped from his lobe.

"Don't disrespect me," Quarrel said. "I'll kill you. My mother gave her life to live out your legacy. You died at the Battle of Fell's Keep, and you lost your sword."

"I . . . *died*?" Dulaun pronounced his sentence in grave dismay.

"Yes. At the hands of Lord Kharrion's goblinkin."

"No!" Wick shouted. "Don't tell him anything of the future! If you change the past, none of us might be here! If Captain Dulaun isn't at the Battle of Fell's Keep, the evacuation of the south won't take place! Or more might be lost! You could change the course of the war! Lord Kharrion could win!"

Too late, Quarrel realized what she might have done.

Dulaun held up a hand. "There's no reason to worry about that. This place, this moment, it's all stolen. Rivalak engineered this spell so that this crew and I will never remember these visits."

" 'Visits'?" Wick repeated.

Touching his bleeding ear, Dulaun nodded. "When the sword is lost from my descendants, it can be returned here for safekeeping till one of them comes to claim it. The magic of this spell won't open until the riddle is solved, and only my descendants can trigger it." He wiped his crimson-stained fingers on his shirt. "Now, where were we?"

The captain's question was deceptive by design. Even if Quarrel wasn't going to reply, she at least thought about it. That was enough time for Dulaun to rip Seaspray from its sheath and take a step back. His blade crashed against Quarrel's.

Without a word, the battle was joined. Steel met steel, and the ringing clangor filled the air, beating back the noise of the creaking canvas and rigging.

Then the cheering began. The sailors rallied around their commander, calling on him to give greater and greater effort.

Quarrel fought well past her years. Her reflexes were honed and certain, unflinching in spite of Dulaun's attack. The captain smiled, arrogant and filled with confidence. He knew his skill in a thousand battles and more, and was in the prime of his life. The Battle of Fell's Keep lay months or years in his future.

Despite her youth and speed, Quarrel gave ground more often than Dulaun did. They fought in a tight circle, and Wick knew from his research and reading of swordplay that it was Dulaun's skill and expertise that drove the fight. Neither combatant seemed willing to be the first to call enough. Sweat streamed down both of them.

Then Dulaun flicked his blade, stepping up the pace and tempo. He slammed Quarrel's sword aside with more power and authority. In another blinding pass that was too fast to follow, the Silver Sea captain suddenly had his blade at Quarrel's throat.

Quarrel froze, looking up at Dulaun fearlessly. "If you're going to do it, get it over with," she stated.

Laughter burst from Dulaun's lips. He reversed his sword and handed it to her, hilt first. "You're blood of my blood," he acknowledged, "and fit enough to carry the sword of your ancestors."

Slowly, Quarrel took the proffered blade. Holding it in front of her, the blade pointing at the sky, she admired the sword.

"It's beautiful," she whispered.

"It is," Dulaun agreed. "And now—it's yours. Take it and use it in good health against your foes."

Lowering the sword to hold at her side, Quarrel looked at the sea captain. "What about you?"

Dulaun smiled at her. "I'll go on to whatever fate has in store for me. There's no other way."

"But you're going to die."

"Everyone dies, girl," the captain said softly, but this time there was no disrespect offered in his words. He smiled. "Even if this spell were not crafted in the way it was, and I could remember meeting you after you are gone, I can't change who I am. Wherever I die, however death comes for me, I trust that I chose to be there because of the man I am. I couldn't turn away from that."

"It's worse than death," Quarrel said. "At the Battle of Fell's Keep, you're betrayed. By one of those that you assume is your ally."

Some of the lightness vanished from Dulaun's smile. "Then I hope that my descendants stand truer for me than some of my friends."

"You shouldn't go there."

Dulaun shook his head. "There's no other way for me, Quarrel. I chart my life by the same stars I always have. If I were to remove those stars from the heaven, what would be the reason for living?" He took a breath. "I'd rather die than surrender. But tell me one thing."

Quarrel tried to speak and couldn't. Tears glimmered in her eyes and trailed down her cheeks.

Wick felt the heat of tears on his own face as well. Their presence surprised him. He looked at the young captain and his crew. He knew from his reading that Captain Dulaun and his men had always acquitted themselves bravely against pirates, enemy crews, goblinkin, and sea monsters. But they would soon be sailing to their deaths. Would it truly have been the same if they had known that? Looking at the man, Wick believed that it would have been.

"What?" Quarrel asked in a voice tight with pain. Wick knew the young woman wasn't just facing Dulaun's loss, but those of her parents as well.

"My death," Dulaun said. "Did I die well? Was it for something I would have been proud to die for? And did my death make a difference, or was it all a waste?"

"You helped save a great many people," Alysta said. "Lord Kharrion's goblinkin forces would have slain them all if they'd been able. Your sacrifice, and that of your companions, it made a difference."

"Good." Dulaun smiled again, nearly as cocky as he'd been when they'd arrived. "That's all I've ever asked." He looked at Quarrel. "Be true to the spirit of the sword and it will never let you down."

"I will," Quarrel said.

"Now go, and may the Old Ones watch over you." Dulaun placed his hand on the hilt of Seaspray sheathed at his side. Quarrel still held her own version of the sword. For the moment, with the power of the spell, the sword—past and present—existed in the same time and space.

The gray fog rose suddenly around Wick, Alysta, and Quarrel, obscuring the Silver Sea and the blue sky. The fog seeped into the little Librarian's lungs, bringing with it the biting cold of the buried keep.

He blinked, and they were once more standing in front of the frieze. Only Seaspray hanging at the end of Quarrel's arm testified that the incident had happened. The walkway had disappeared and the pieces containing images of the fish had returned to the frieze.

"We're back." Quarrel examined the sword, which gleamed like it was newly minted in the lantern light. Blue fire ran along the edges and the runes.

"But not any safer than we were," Alysta said.

Quarrel sheathed the sword and took up her bow. She looked at the cat. "It's true? You're my grandmother?"

Alysta padded over to Quarrel and placed a paw against the young woman's boot. "I am. But when I knew you, your name wasn't Quarrel."

"No," Quarrel agreed, kneeling down and touching the cat's head and scratching. "I was Nyssa."

"Yes."

"I chose my name after my parents were killed." Sadness touched her pale blue wolf 's eyes. "My father nicknamed me 'Quarrel' because he thought I was argumentative. He always insisted that I came by my nature honestly, that I got it from my grandmother."

Alysta preened. "That's true. You did."

"He thought my querulousness was a bad thing."

"Well," the cat said warmly, her breath gray in the cold, still air of the chamber, "your father was a good man. You'll never hear me say anything else but that. However, he was a man after all, and not always capable of the best judgment when it came to the nature of young women." Her eyes blinked at Quarrel. "Frankly, I like the way you are."

"Perhaps we could save the family reunion for later," Wick said. "We're still trapped on this mountain with Captain Gujhar, Ryman Bey, and the Razor's Kiss thieves."

Quickly, they gathered their things and prepared to leave.

"We could use the passage to the sea." Quarrel pointed to the opening beside the frieze.

"You've been that way?" Alysta asked.

"Yes."

"Is there a boat?"

"No."

"Dawdal's still back at camp," Wick reminded them.

The cat sighed. "He could probably make his way back to Wharf Rat's Warren on his own. Then again, Dawdal doesn't have a true sense of direction. He could get lost out here. Or goblinkin or a bear could eat him." She shook her head. "We'll have to go back for him."

Quarrel took the lead once more.

16

Pursued

Long minutes later, after all the surviving traps had once more been navigated, Wick and his two companions stood at the entrance to the excavation site. The snowfall had increased, filling the air with thick flakes that obscured vision.

The snowfall helped, Wick knew, but they would still stand out against it if someone saw them. Staying there till the dawn was out of the question and would be tantamount to suicide. They had to press on.

The thieves' camp was still in turmoil. Gujhar and Ryman Bey were convinced that the interlopers hadn't escaped over the wall. The thieves were searching the campsite and the inner courtyard, brandishing torches to drive back the darkness and cursing their luck.

"Quietly," Quarrel whispered, "and stay close to me." She went, hunkering low to the ground. She carried her sheathed sword in her left hand, her right hand resting on Seaspray's hilt to draw it quickly.

Fear hammered inside Wick. Even though he'd been through several horrific struggles over the last few years, he didn't believe he would ever get over the fear of dying suddenly in some violent manner.

They slipped through the night without incident and crouched in the shadows at the base of the wall. After a moment, when it seemed none of the torches carried by the thieves was near, they scaled the narrow steps leading up the wall.

At the top, the clouds parted and silver moonslight streamed down, raking the wall with incandescence, blunted somewhat by the swirling snow. Wick was reaching for the crenellation on the other side when Alysta hissed, *"Look out!"*

Ducking instinctively, Wick put both hands over his head and hoped nothing bad would happen to him. Something with leathery wings skated just above him and raked claws through his hair. An eerie, ululating, screaming whistle ripped through the still of the night.

"Up on the wall!" someone shouted down in the inner courtyard. "There they are!"

"Get up, Wick," Quarrel called. "We've been spotted."

Wick lifted his head, holding his arms up to protect himself. He got warily to his feet and looked up into the night. The ululating whistle continued, circling low overhead. Scrabbling for the crenellation, he spotted the winged zarnk diving at him again.

The creature was a flying scavenger with a five-foot wingspread. Three horns, two over its fierce eyes and one at the end of its cruelly curved beak, made the zarnk's face look like a knotted fist. Copper-colored scales covered the elongated body, leading down to a darker shade along the whiplike tail with the barbed end. Opening its razor beaked jaws, it screamed again.

Three others joined it.

Terror raced through Wick. Although he'd never seen the creatures outside of an ecology book, he knew what they were. According to the information he'd read, a dozen zarnks could strip a cow down to a mass of bones in minutes. He didn't want to find out if that was true.

Alysta moved, bunching then unbunching, hurling herself at the attacking zarnk and landing on its back. Knocked aside by the cat's weight and fury, the zarnk screech-whistled again as it tumbled to the top of the wall in a flurry of wings. The feline struck with clean, white teeth. Even though the zarnk was bigger than Alysta was, she weighed easily three times as much. The zarnk flailed helplessly as it tried to get up.

Another zarnk veered toward the cat, reaching for her with razor claws. Wick reacted almost immediately, unable to face the thought of Alysta ripped to shreds in front of him. He threw himself at the predator, and that was what saved him from the third's attack as it glided in at him.

Wick grabbed the zarnk's wing and neck, riding it to the ground. *Don't let it bite me! Please don't let it bite one of my fingers off or permanently damage one of them!* Nightmare images of the creature doing exactly that plagued him as he held on. He was surprised at how light the zarnk was, but it also possessed a wiry strength.

"Break its neck," Quarrel said.

Wick tried to find leverage but couldn't. In truth, he didn't know if he could actually kill the zarnk. He didn't like killing. He wasn't a warrior; he just didn't want to watch Alysta get hurt. The zarnk flailed and dug its claws into the wall, crawling up despite Wick's efforts. Lying on his back, suddenly trying to keep the zarnk from his throat, Wick saw Quarrel smoothly nock an arrow and track one of the other two flying zarnks.

The bowstring thrummed. The arrow pierced the heart of its target. Like a broken kite, the zarnk tumbled from the night sky and disappeared over the edge of the wall. Then Quarrel nocked another arrow, drew, and fired. The shot didn't hit the second flying creature's body, but it shattered a wing and dropped it into the inner courtyard.

Wick fought to keep the zarnk's curved beak from his eyes, yanking his fingers back each time he turned his attacker's efforts. Without hesitation, Quarrel flicked out her foot and slammed the zarnk's head up against the wall. Bone crumpled. The zarnk suddenly became dead weight in Wick's arms. He shoved the dead thing from him and scrambled to his feet.

Only a short distance away, Alysta jumped away from the dead zarnk she'd fought. Her muzzle was bloody. The winged predator lay curled up in a ball, its throat torn out.

"Is that all of them?" the cat asked more calmly than Wick felt she had any right to.

"For the moment," Quarrel answered just as calmly.

Then the first arrow from the thieves splintered against the wall. Sparks leaped from the razor-sharp iron blade.

Below, the thieves raced toward the wall. Two of them stopped long enough to nock arrows and draw back. They released too early, though, and both deadly missiles went wide of the mark. By an uncomfortable few feet.

"Go!" Quarrel ordered, drawing back another arrow. She centered herself, calmly and dispassionately despite the crossbow bolt that skidded from the stone only inches below her boots.

For a moment, Wick watched her, drawn by the sight of the elegance of intent that the young woman evidenced. She reminded him of an elven archer, every line of her centered exactly so behind the bow. Her fingers opened like the petals of a flower, releasing the shaft. The missile sped true, catching a man just above the breastbone where a chain mail shirt would have ended, then pierced him and knocked him back.

By then Wick was scrambling over the crenellation, realizing too late that the side they'd gone over on faced the sea. He was also more than twenty feet above the ground.

"Hurry!" Alysta growled as she leaped to the top of the crenellation.

"It's too far," Wick protested. "I could break my leg. Or my neck."

"You say that like staying here is an option."

Wick turned to face the cat, figuring to appeal to Alysta's good sense. *If we're not killed outright, and we shouldn't be—maybe—Craugh and Cap'n Farok will be after us soon enough.* Only before he could say anything, the cat launched herself at him, striking him heavily in the chest.

Off balance, Wick went over the wall backward. Alysta hooked her claws into his traveling cloak. He yelled in surprise and fear as he fell. The cat yowled. For a moment, her furry face was nose to nose with his. He flung his arms around her and held on.

When he hit the ground, the snow cushioned his fall. The impact still drove the breath from his lungs, but nothing felt broken. He plunged down into a drift that was taller than he was, disappearing at once inside the snow.

"Get up!" Alysta commanded, detaching herself from Wick and squirming from his panicked grip. "They'll be on top of us in seconds."

Wick nodded, still struggling to suck air into his deflated lungs. Grabbing fistfuls of snow, he heaved himself from the drift till he stood on his feet. He caught half a breath, then another, and finally—*thank the Old Ones*!—he could breathe again.

Then Quarrel plummeted into the snowbank beside the little Librarian. She came up out of the snow like a dervish, throwing snow in all directions. It suddenly looked like it was snowing *up* as much as it was down.

"Run!" Quarrel ordered.

"Which way?" Wick asked frantically.

Neither the cat nor the young warrior answered him. Both of them ran straight for the tree line nearly forty yards away.

"Dawdal isn't that way," Wick cried after them. He had to struggle through the snow because it was up to his chest in most places.

Alysta scampered across the snow and Quarrel ran in quick strides that seemed to defy gravity.

Wick took another breath, ready to protest the direction again, then an arrow hissed into the snow ahead of him, probably only missing him by inches. He reconsidered the value of protesting the direction and decided that *any* escape would be a good thing at the moment. He spared a fleeting glimpse at the thieves and saw a half dozen men scrambling over the keep wall and dropping to the snow. When he turned back around, he stubbed his toe and pitched headlong into the snow.

Quarrel stopped and came back for Wick, grabbing him by an arm and jerking him to his feet. Together, with the cat urging them on, they ran for the trees while arrows rained down around them.

Later, Wick was never able to completely remember the struggle they had as they dodged through the forest. Several times they tripped over fallen trees or had to fight their way through drifts and brush. Pines and firs tore at their faces and eyes. Snow dropped down on them from the limbs by the bushel.

The land remained roughly level for a time, then quickly fell away toward the sea. In a short distance, they were falling down the treacherous landscape at nearly the same speed they were running.

Wick bounced and thudded against the mountainside. The wild cries of the thieves, excited now because their prey was almost at hand, filled the little Librarian's ears. Terror raked at him.

Before he knew it, they were all out of running room. They burst free of the forest unexpectedly and found themselves out on a pointed shard of rock covered in snow that hung above the sea a hundred feet below.

"No!" Wick gasped. It wasn't fair. They'd risked everything to claim Seaspray, solved the puzzle of the boat room when the Razor's Kiss thieves hadn't been able to do that. They couldn't end up without a place to run.

Quarrel turned, bow in her hand and an arrow already nocked. Her breath exploded out of her in ragged gasps that stranded gray clouds in the cold air. Even Alysta seemed winded.

Wick gazed around, spotting an incline that went down the side of the mountain that offered him a fleeting hope. With luck, it went all the way to the bottom of the mountain. And with greater luck they would never lose their footing on the narrow trail.

"This way," Wick said.

"Too late," Quarrel said in a low voice.

Turning, Wick spotted the predatory shadows gathering in the tree line. Moonslight glittered on swords and knives. Involuntarily, he took a step back and nearly stepped over the ledge. Quarrel reached for him without taking her eyes from their enemies and steadied him.

"Careful," she said.

Wick almost tittered at the idea of being careful. *We're one word away from being dead. Careful doesn't even figure into this.* Or maybe they were two words. If Gujhar decided to say, "Kill them," instead of, "Kill."

"Who are you?" a man's voice rang out.

"Someone who will kill you if you give me half a chance," Quarrel replied.

"Then I shouldn't give you a chance." The voice mocked her.

"Are you a coward then?" she demanded.

"Actually," Wick whispered, "now wouldn't exactly be the time to antagonize him. Orlag Sonder, in a very excellent work called *A Sharp-Tongued Diplomat Stays Only One Step Ahead of Impending Retribution*, suggests that when overpowered and outnumbered, remaining pacifistic is the best way—"

"I am Ryman Bey," the man declared as he stepped from the tree line. His eye patch caught the moonslight, marking him instantly. "I lead the men that will kill you if you don't surrender what you took from the keep."

Showing no apparent strain, Quarrel kept her bow bent. "I could kill you where you stand. And I will if you don't call off your dogs."

Ryman Bey laughed, confident in his ability. "Even if you succeeded, these men would cut you to doll rags."

Quarrel smiled, but Wick could see that the effort was forced. "You won't live to see that happen."

"Oh, but I might," Ryman Bey taunted. "I just might. You'd be surprised to know what I've lived through."

Wick talked from the corner of his mouth. "We don't have to do this. Not yet."

"They're going to kill us," Alysta said. "They don't want to try to take us alive."

"They do at the moment," Wick said quietly.

"That's because they're afraid Quarrel will fall into the sea with the sword after they've killed her." The cat's voice was quiet and didn't go far.

"C'mon, girl," Ryman Bey said. "Make it easy on yourself."

With no indication of what she was about to do, Quarrel released the arrow. Wick's senses were spinning so rapidly he heard the shaft passing on the polished wood, then the deep, basso *thwang* of the string. He started to demand why Quarrel had fired the arrow when they were at the mercy of their enemies, then realized that her arm must have been growing tired holding the powerful bow ready. Knowing she'd never have the chance to draw back again, she'd obviously chosen to loose.

The arrow flew straight and true for the center of Ryman Bey's face. Incredibly, the thief leader whirled to one side and took a step back. The arrow sliced through his hair and several strands were sheared.

"No!" Ryman Bey shouted, throwing his hand up to still his men. "I don't want to lose that sword!"

By that time, Quarrel had thrown the bow down and slid Seaspray free of the sheath. The blue-etched blade caught and reflected the slight moonslight. Snowflakes whirled around her.

"Before I allow you to take this sword," Quarrel promised, "I'll throw it into the sea."

"Throw it!" Ryman Bey showed his teeth in a wolf 's grin. "If I can't stop you, I'll recover the sword from the sea. I'd rather not if we could come to an arrangement."

Wick stood frozen, not knowing what to do. It was plain to see that Quarrel felt the same way. The little Librarian looked out to sea, hoping against hope that *One-Eyed Peggie*'s sails were visible. Only a pale, ghostly fog drifted in atop the waves crashing against the jagged rocks below.

"The only arrangement we can come to," Quarrel said, "doesn't involve me giving up this sword."

"Perhaps I could take you with us," Ryman Bey said. "We only need the sword for a short time, so I'm told."

For what? Wick wondered, curious again at Gujhar's purpose and who had sent the man on his mission.

"No," Quarrel replied. "I don't trust you. I'll never trust you."

A voice from the ranks of the thieves spoke in a cant known only to them. Wick was familiar with the language from his studies, though he wasn't as fluent as he would have wished to be.

"I'm ready," the voice said.

Ryman Bey responded in the same tongue, never taking his eyes from Quarrel. "Do it."

Wick turned to Quarrel. "Look out. They're planning—"

Before he could finish speaking, an arrow sped from the darkness pooled at the tree line. A thin cord trailed after the missile.

Quarrel saw the speeding arrow, or perhaps guessed from the sound of the bowstring that she had been fired on, and tried to spin away. Wick believed that the hidden archer had aimed at Quarrel's chest, but the young woman managed to avoid the arrow for the most part. Instead, it transfixed her left shoulder with a *thunk*.

Staggered by the blow, Quarrel barely remained standing. She looked down at the arrow in disbelief. She thought fast, though, recognizing the cord attached to the arrow and what it represented. Bringing the sword up, she tried to cut the cord, but whoever had hold of the other end pulled on it and yanked her from her feet.

17

Escape

Screaming in pain as the arrow twisted in her flesh, Quarrel tried to fight, but she was dragged through the snow like a sled, plowing a furrow. Ryman Bey waited with his drawn sword.

Turning over on her back, Quarrel threw Seaspray toward the cliff.

"No!" Ryman Bey shouted as he watched the enchanted weapon spin through the air.

But Quarrel wasn't able to get enough strength behind her effort. Seaspray fell short of the ledge and lay on the snow, naked and vulnerable.

"Wick!" Quarrel yelled, drawing a knife from her boot and grabbing the cord in her free hand. "Throw the sword over!"

Alysta lunged across the snow and nuzzled the sword, trying to move it with her head. Unfortunately, she wasn't strong enough. She turned to Wick and yowled, *"Hurry!"*

Ryman Bey raced forward, grabbing Quarrel's knife hand in one of his and staying her blade. He plucked her easily from the snow and grinned at her. She tried to fight him, but he was too strong and too quick with his hands and feet, and she was wounded. He grabbed the arrow with his other hand and twisted it savagely.

Quarrel screamed and almost passed out, dropping down to her knees for a moment. When she rose again, she had the thief leader's knife at her throat.

"Don't vex me, girl," Ryman Bey said. "At the moment you yet live."

Wick sprinted toward the sword, but one of the Razor's Kiss thieves got there before he did. The man grabbed the hilt and lifted the blade, grinning in triumph.

"Keep coming, halfer," the thief taunted, waving Wick on with his free hand. "We'll see how you like the taste of cold steel. And maybe we'll see if this sword lives up to the legend that surrounds it."

Having no choice, Wick stopped.

Alysta threw herself at the man, but he was prepared and fast enough to slap her away. She hit the snow-covered ground and flopped miserably, mewling in pain.

"Take them to the edge," Ryman Bey ordered.

At sword point, the thief guided Wick to the ledge. He couldn't help looking down at the waves thundering against the rocks. The cliff wall was almost sheer, but there were ledges scattered along the way. None of them were close enough to safely drop down onto.

Ryman Bey brought Quarrel to the edge and stood her there in the wind. Several of the thieves kicked Alysta and drove her away, and the cat had no choice but to go.

Wick's mind worked desperately. *They're going to kill us. Ryman Bey just wants to gloat first.*

"Who are you?" Ryman Bey demanded of Quarrel.

"He's a mercenary," one of the thieves responded. "I've seen him around the Tavern of Schemes."

"This is no man." Ryman Bey pushed back Quarrel's hood and revealed her hair and soft features. "I will weary of asking you, girl. If you would live, you'll answer my questions."

Quarrel only returned the thief chieftain's gaze full measure.

Ryman Bey grinned. "You've meddled in something that you've no business being part of." He held out his hand and the thief holding Seaspray handed the sword over.

"I have every right," Quarrel replied.

Gujhar stepped forward then. "Get me a torch."

One of the thieves pulled a torch from his equipment pack and lit it.

Taking the torch, the mercenary captain held the flame up and toward Quarrel. The wind whipped the flames, seeking to extinguish them. "I know you," he said. "I recognize your face." He reached inside his cloak and took out a book, flipping it open to a familiar section.

"A *book*!" one of the thieves gasped.

Most of them stepped back in consternation.

"If the goblinkin discover you have that," another thief said, "they'll be down on you in a second with naked steel and clubs. They hate books."

"I'm certainly not going to tell them," Gujhar replied. "And even a goblinkin would think twice about taking a wizard's book of spells."

A wizard? Wick didn't believe for a moment that Gujhar was a wizard. He was like none of the wizards Wick had ever seen. Wizards were proud and haughty men. (And sometimes women, though he'd only encountered one of those.)

But the book was magical in nature. Gujhar spoke a couple of words and the blank pages that Wick could see suddenly filled with images. One of them was of Captain Dulaun and his wife. Quarrel favored both of them.

"You are one of Captain Dulaun's descendants," Gujhar said excitedly. "That's how you were able to find Seaspray when we weren't. I knew it had been hidden, but I had no idea where."

Quarrel said nothing, but she couldn't hide the truth either. "You're not fit to carry that sword."

"Oh, I won't be carrying it," Ryman Bey said. "I'm ransoming it to Gujhar's employer." He eyed the blade appreciatively. "As pretty as this sword is, it's worth a lot of gold." He smiled. "Consider me crass if you will, but I'd rather have the gold. Besides, I could never unleash the power it wields."

"Neither can Gujhar's employer," Quarrel said.

"Gujhar's employer has other intentions for the sword than using it as it was created," Ryman Bey said.

"Careful," Gujhar cautioned irritably. "You're speaking out of turn."

Ryman Bey smiled. "A few minutes from now, it won't matter."

Wick swallowed hard. For the first time he noticed that the other end of the rope attached to the arrow in Quarrel's arm was looped around one of the bigger thieves' waist. A desperate—and risky!—plan formed in Wick's brain.

You've clearly been reading far too many romances from Hralbomm's Wing, he told himself. But it was doable. Neither he nor Quarrel weighed half of what the thief weighed.

All they needed was a moment. And a lot of luck. By the Old Ones, they would have to be *awfully* lucky to survive what he had in mind.

"That sword," Quarrel said, "is meant for our family."

"Not anymore." Ryman Bey held the sword level before him. "Gujhar's employer plans on stripping the magic from this blade and using it for something else." The thief chieftain looked at Gujhar, who stood in silent fury.

"That can't be done," Quarrel argued.

Ryman Bey smiled. "I'm told it can be. The betrayal at the Battle of Fell's Keep ran deep. Deals were struck and the people involved trusted each other far too much. Lord Kharrion placed his agent within the ranks of the defenders and planned well."

The news shocked Wick. It was the first confirmation of a traitor among the defenders that he'd ever heard of outside of rumor and the elemental in Master Blacksmith Oskarr's forge. The story was becoming more tangled, and more relevant to things that were going on in the world now.

Just as Craugh and Cap'n Farok had told him. It even lent to the belief that it was something of a legacy Lord Kharrion had left.

"When Gujhar's employer is done with this sword," Ryman Bey taunted, "it won't be anything but a trinket."

During the thief chieftain's exchange, Gujhar had been gazing with deep interest in Wick's direction. "You were in the Cinder Clouds Islands."

The accusation hung in the cold despite the harsh wind coming in from the sea.

"No I wasn't," Wick squeaked. He cleared his throat, hoping he sounded more firm. "I've never been to the Cinder Clouds Islands."

Then one of the thieves spoke up. "There was a halfer there."

"There were a lot of halfers there," another thief snarled. "The goblinkin had slaves working those mines."

The first thief shook his head. "You don't often see red hair on a halfer. This one has red hair. So did the one in the Cinder Clouds Islands."

"I think you're right," a third said. "I saw him, too."

Gujhar approached and stood in front of Wick. "You *were* there. Searching for Master Oskarr's axe."

"It was someone else," Wick insisted, but his voice cracked and he knew he sounded like he was lying. "Some other dweller. Not me." He hated the way his voice came out. Just as guilty sounding as it did when Grandmagister Frollo wanted to know who'd smeared jam on the pages of a book or who had (accidentally!) forgotten to return a much-used reference book to its proper place. He hated sounding guilty. Terrible things always followed.

"It was you," Gujhar said. "What were you doing there?"

"I escaped," Wick said. "I was one of the mining slaves."

"You," Gujhar stated clearly, "were with the dwarves searching for the axe. They found it when no one else could."

"Not me," Wick said weakly.

"And now," Gujhar mused, "you helped this girl find Dulaun's sword in a place we had searched repeatedly." His eyes narrowed. "What do you know about this, halfer? What do you know about Deathwhisper?"

Deathwhisper. So Gujhar was looking for the third weapon from the Battle of Fell's Keep. Just as the journal had indicated. But why? The question tumbled endlessly through Wick's mind. Why was Gujhar's master planning to strip the action from the weapons? How had they been bound together a thousand years ago? Had that been why they'd been lost all that time?

He didn't know. The fact that he didn't have a clue made him so curious he couldn't stand it.

"Do you know where Deathwhisper is?" Gujhar asked.

Wick didn't say anything. Dread filled him. He knew what was going to happen next, and knowing that gave him strength to think about the wild scheme that had occurred to him.

"You should tell me," Gujhar said casually, as if he were talking about the price of apples or whether the ale at the top of a tankard was more flavorful than the ale at the bottom. "It will save you a lot of painful torture."

Actually, Wick was for anything that saved him painful torture. If he'd known where Deathwhisper was, he'd have told. Immediately. However, he also knew that he'd probably be tortured anyway because Gujhar wouldn't choose to believe him till he'd been tortured for a while. Of course, if he told the truth immediately, there was also the possibility that Gujhar would torture a *lie* out of him. It would be a clever ploy.

But that meant putting up with the torture, and Wick wasn't looking forward to that. Even when he ascribed to the fantasy that *One-Eyed Peggie* would arrive with Craugh, Cap'n Farok, Hallekk, and the crew, Wick didn't care for even a *little* torture.

Without taking his cruel eyes from Wick, Gujhar asked, "I trust you have someone who's good at torture?"

"I do." Ryman Bey cleaned his nails on his cloak. "I usually attend to it myself. I'm the best we have."

"Good." Gujhar smiled. "I wouldn't want anyone but the best available to handle the chores on this."

"We'll have to discuss the price, of course. Helping you recover these things is fine, but you didn't mention anything about torture when we made our bargain."

Frowning, Gujhar turned to glare at the thief leader. "Do you really want to spend more time looking for the elven bow? When you have someone right here who knows where it is?"

"*Might* know," Ryman Bey countered. "I find I believe the halfer. I don't think he's lying."

"He lied about being at the Cinder Clouds Islands."

Ryman Bey grinned coldly. "Yes, but we all knew he was lying about that, didn't we? He's not a very good liar. Doesn't come by it natural enough."

Idly, Wick wondered if he should feel insulted. Then he decided there really wasn't any room for considering an insult with all the fear running rampant in his mind. Maybe he was quiet on the outside, but he knew he was running around screaming inside his thoughts.

"We had a deal," Gujhar protested. "I can't have you just assigning new costs to every little thing."

Shrugging, the thief leader said, "You can always take care of the torturing yourself." He paused. "If you don't have any tools for it—spikes to drive up under his fingernails, crimpers to shred his ears, knives to split his fingertips—"

Wick shuddered and sour nausea bubbled at the back of his throat.

"I don't have any of those things," Gujhar said.

With a smile, Ryman Bey said, "I'll be happy to rent you a set."

Wick knew that he'd never have a better chance of escape. He steeled himself for the course of action he'd chosen, then hoped that he didn't get Quarrel or himself (or *both* of them!) killed.

He sprinted forward, quicker than the thief watching him had expected. Wick felt the man's fingers brush against the back of one shoulder, but he was free, running straight for Quarrel.

"The rope!" Wick yelled. "Grab the rope!"

A startled look flashed across Quarrel's face as she realized Wick was coming too fast to stop short of the ledge. Instinctively, she braced against his charge. If she'd been a full-grown man or a dwarf, perhaps even an elf, Wick knew he would have never been able to knock her from her feet. But she was slight, and she was weak from her injury. He just hoped she wasn't too weak to help save herself. She thought quickly on her feet. He knew that and he was counting on that skill.

"Stop him!" Ryman Bey yelled.

"Stupid halfer!" one of the thieves said.

"No," Quarrel said, trying to move out of the way.

Then Wick was on her, hitting her at her waist, below the arm she threw out to stop him. He reached up and caught the rope with his right hand, flipping his arm to catch a loop behind his right elbow.

For an instant they hovered on the brink of the cliff, teetering as Quarrel fought back and tried to stop the impending fall. "Grabtherope!" Wick yelled. *"Grabtherope!"*

They fell, spinning over the empty space above the sea and the jagged rock. Wick slammed against the cliffside and felt the breath leave his lungs. He got his left hand around the arrow in Quarrel's shoulder and snapped it off so that it wouldn't be savagely jerked from her flesh. She screamed in pain, or it might have been she was already screaming in fright, he wasn't sure. But she grabbed the rope with both hands.

Wick hoped that his arm wasn't torn out of its socket when they ran out of slack. He was still screaming—*something*, he wasn't sure what—when that happened.

They hit the end of the rope still seventy feet from the sea, slamming into mountainside as the thief above (evidently figuring out what was going to happen and fearing the worst) tried to dig in. Whatever the thief did, Wick knew, was potentially doomed to failure. That was quickly proven true when he and Quarrel began falling again. Only this time they were close enough to the mountainside to slide down to one of the ledges.

Wick hit the ledge with bone-jarring force and skittered along, flailing helplessly as he shot over the edge. He managed to grab hold of the ledge and chinned himself, mewling with fear. Quarrel had landed on the ledge and was in no danger of falling off. She lay silent and still, and he feared she was dead. Blood covered her wounded shoulder.

Motion above Wick caught his attention. He looked up and saw the thief falling from the ledge, arms and legs flailing. His scream echoed, growing closer. Then Wick realized that the rope was still around his arm. He whipped his arm from the coils as the thief fell within inches of him, screaming, "Letgooftherope! *Letgooftherope!*" to Quarrel.

Weakly, she shifted and shook free of the rope as well. Wick got the rope off his arm last, noticing from the stiffness in his fingers and palms that he'd suffered burns and abrasions from struggling to hang onto the rope. The cold wind threatened to tear him from the ledge and he didn't think he had the strength to climb up.

The thief turned end over end and smashed against the rocks below. His body lay there for just a moment, then the waves crashed in and carried it away. Somewhere in the foggy darkness, the dead man disappeared without a trace.

Wick tried to pull himself up, digging his toes into the mountainside and heaving with all his strength. Above him, he heard the shouts of the thieves. Two arrows splintered against the stone as archers tried to pick him off. Quarrel lay sheltered under an overhang, but she leaned out with her good arm and caught hold of Wick's cloak. Leaning back, she helped him clamber up while another arrow whizzed by. He huddled under the overhang.

"That was idiocy," Quarrel accused.

Nodding, Wick said, "It was. But if we'd stayed up there, they would have killed us."

"That shouldn't have worked."

"You only think that because you haven't read Daslanik's *Practical Applications of Dual Penduluming Bodies*. It's a fascinating book. Daslanik did a lot studies regarding penduluming weights with no fixed points."

Quarrel shifted and got to a sitting position.

"You shouldn't be moving," Wick said. Blood smeared the stone surface where the young woman had lain.

"Staying here for them to climb down and slit our throats isn't a good idea. Neither is staying here to freeze to death."

Wick nodded, realizing that it was a lot colder on the mountainside. He helped her to her feet. They crouched under the overhang, then peered upward.

Gujhar looked down at them over the side. "You got lucky, halfer."

Wick didn't bother to argue or point out the mathematics of his actions.

"If you know what's good for you," Gujhar went on, "you'll make certain we never cross paths again."

"I'll have my sword back," Quarrel promised.

Gujhar smiled at her. The light from the torch he held exposed the cruel lines of his face. "You're welcome to try, girl. I don't like leaving loose ends."

The thieves had spread out along the cliff, but none of them had yet found a way down to the ledge where Wick and Quarrel were. But their efforts to find one were reason enough to go.

"Can you walk?" Wick asked.

"If I can fall down a mountain and live," Quarrel said, "I can walk."

Wick took the lead, marking their path with a trained eye. He hadn't navigated the steep and twisting staircases of the Vault of All Known Knowledge's subterranean recesses without learning a few things. They went slowly, but they went, switching back and forth as they needed to. Occasionally, till they reached the rocky shore seventy or so feet below, arrows still skittered down the mountainside or splashed into the sea.

At the water's edge, they walked east along the coast, thinking that the more distance they put between themselves and Thango's keep the better. Wick felt certain Gujhar would return to *Wraith* and set sail as soon as he could.

After all, the elven bow Deathwhisper yet remained to be found.

Quarrel stumbled and almost fell. Wick took her good arm across his shoulder and supported her as well as he could. He kept them moving through the snowstorm. A few minutes later, he heard footsteps behind them. His heart stopped inside his chest, then he turned around and saw the cat had joined them.

"Is she going to be all right?" Alysta asked.

"Yes," Wick answered, though he wasn't sure. The wound looked horrible, and the rough trip down the mountain (the climb as well as the fall) hadn't been good on her. "She just needs some rest. We need to find shelter." He turned and continued on.

The cat fell into step beside them, trudging through the snow with a definite limp.

"Ryman Bey and the Razor's Kiss thieves are leaving the keep," Alysta said. "They have what they came for."

"And they think we're as good as dead," Wick said grimly.

"If we live through the night and manage to return to Wharf Rat's Warren, they'll be waiting."

Wick went on, forcing himself to move through the physical pains and exhaustion that plagued him. The pain was dulled somewhat by the questions that revolved endlessly inside his head.

epilogue

Safe Harbor

"Over here!" someone cried. "They're over here!"

"Thank the Old Ones!" a familiar voice growled. "Are they still alive?"

Wick struggled against the lethargy that filled him. He tried to move but wasn't able to. Even fear seemed walled off by the cold that filled him. He sat hunkered in the folds of his cloak where he, Quarrel, and Alysta had decided to take shelter beneath a stand of spruce trees when they could go no farther.

They'd walked for an hour or more and found no sign of habitation. That part of the coast appeared completely desolate. The bright spot was that they hadn't crossed paths with the Razor's Kiss thieves, either.

Unless they've come calling now, Wick thought grimly. He kept still, trusting the snow that had fallen to keep them covered. The snow now felt several inches thick. He wondered how they'd been found. With the snow around them and falling fast, he'd believed they'd safely dug in and disappeared.

Then hands dug at the snow and uncovered them. Torchlight burned bright and hot against his eyes.

Hallekk peered at Wick. "Are ye truly alive, then?" Snow clung to his beard, and his breath had formed ice crystals in his mustache.

"I am," Wick whispered. Heartened by the sight of his friend, the little Librarian tried to stand. Past Hallekk, *One-Eyed Peggie* sat at anchor well away from the rocky shoals. A longboat sat beached on the shore. Craugh stood nearby, his staff blistering the frigid air with a trail of green sparks. "It's good to see you. I hoped you would come soon—soon enough." He tried to take a step and almost fell.

"Go easy there with ye," Hallekk cautioned, throwing his big arms around Wick and lifting him as he would a child. "I got ye. Don't ye fret none. I got ye."

"What about Quarrel and the cat?" Wick whispered.

Hallekk peered into the cloak nest. "They're alive. We'll take care of 'em."

"Please," Wick asked. Then the fatigue that filled him claimed him and took him into the yawning blackness.

When Wick woke again, he was on *One-Eyed Peggie*, sleeping in a bed this time instead of a hammock. For a while he simply lay there, luxuriating in the warmth he'd thought he'd never again feel while he'd huddled in the thin protection of his cloak. The ship was in motion, riding the ocean waves, rising and falling regular enough to let him know they were making good time—wherever they were headed.

Thoughts of Quarrel and how the young woman was faring drove Wick reluctantly from the bed. He still wore the clothes he'd gone roving in while at Wharf Rat's Warren. A bath, he knew, was in order at his earliest convenience.

He found his cloak on a chair beside the door. He pulled the garment on, then went out into the waist. In the hallway, two dwarven pirates carried supplies up from the cargo hold to the galley, replenishing Cook's supplies. After a brief conversation, Wick found out that Quarrel was resting and that Craugh and Cap'n Farok were topside making plans to pursue *Wraith*. While the idea of the two making further plans didn't make Wick's heart leap for joy, he was still glad that Gujhar and Ryman Bey hadn't escaped undetected. Although he was afraid of crossing paths with the two again—and the mysterious master Gujhar worked for—the little Librarian didn't like leaving any mystery unsolved.

And this one looked like the biggest he'd ever seen.

On the main deck, Wick found the wizard and the ship's captain on the stern castle, heads together as they consulted a map. Wick hailed them.

"So," Craugh said, "you've risen." He didn't look particularly relieved or glad to see Wick. Doubtless, he was thinking that Wick had managed to let yet another of the weapons escape their grasp.

Wick gazed at the sun and judged it was only a couple of hours past sunrise. "I have. And you're lucky that I did after all that I've been through. You found us early this morning. I've only gotten a few hours of sleep. I'm surprised I'm even up."

"You've gotten more than a few hours' sleep," Craugh said. "You slept through one whole day."

The news shocked Wick. He never slept that long. His ability to sleep so little had helped him keep up with the work Frollo assigned him at the Vault of All Known Knowledge.

"A day?" Wick repeated.

"Aye," Cap'n Farok said. He ran a withered hand through his gray beard and smiled a little. "Me, I never seen a halfer go so long without a meal. Unless he was chained up somewheres an' food couldn't be had, of course."

"Of course," Wick said, dazed. *A day? I slept a whole day away?* He looked at Craugh. "We've lost time."

"We have," Craugh agreed. "But we've learned more."

"What?"

"We've learned that the three owners of those mystic weapons had hidden them," Alysta said. "They didn't just disappear over the years."

Wick turned toward her voice only to see her leap gracefully to the table where the map was. The cat sat on her haunches and wrapped her tail around her feet. "So?" he asked.

"That means someone was looking for them a thousand years ago," Alysta said. "Otherwise there would have been no reason to hide them."

"Who's looking for them?"

"That's just one of the questions we need answers for," Cap'n Farok said. "There's somethin' more than meets the eye to this."

"The monster's eye?" Wick asked, thinking of the great eye kept in the jug under the captain's bed.

Cap'n Farok frowned and waved a hand. "No. This doesn't have anythin' to do with that there eye. I meant the eye." He pointed to one of his eyes. "Me eye. Yer eye. Just . . . just . . . the *eye*. It were a figure of speech."

"Oh," Wick said, realizing he was thinking too literally. Then he thought of something else. "How is Quarrel?"

"Mendin'," Cap'n Farok said. "Hallekk took the arrow out of her shoulder. He says it missed everythin' important. Gonna be painful comin' back from it, but she'll get it done all right. She's young yet. Got a lot of healin' left to her."

"She's a very strong young woman," Alysta added. "I look forward to getting to know her."

"I'm glad," Wick said.

"Although I'm not too happy with you." The cat focused her unblinking gaze on the little Librarian. "When you threw both of you over the cliff, I thought you'd committed suicide and taken her with you."

" 'Threw yerself over the cliff '?" Cap'n Farok looked totally shocked.

"It had to be done," Wick insisted. "It was the only way."

In a disapproving tone, Alysta quickly related the events.

"Ye hadn't mentioned that when we talked," Cap'n Farok said when the cat finished her tale.

"We had other things to discuss," Alysta said.

Cap'n Farok dropped a trembling hand on Wick's shoulder and grinned, pleased and proud. "Jumpin' offa cliffs, is it? Wait'll I tell Hallekk. Or Cobner! By the Old Ones, that crusty warrior'll have hisself a laugh now, won't he? An' claim all the credit fer yer courage an' skill. 'Course, he'll probably leave ye yer trickery an' such fer thinkin' of such a thing."

In spite of the situation, Wick grinned. Cobner, who still claimed that Wick had saved his life that night in Hanged Elf 's Point, would rejoice in the telling of the story. No doubt Cobner would further embellish it when he told it in taverns.

By the time Cobner was finished with it, Wick was likely to be nine feet tall and to have taken at least fifty Razor's Kiss thieves with him. It would be something to hear, that was certain. He looked forward to it and felt a pang of wistfulness to see his friend again.

"I swear," Cap'n Farok said, still grinning, "since ye started a-hangin' out with proper pirates, Librarian Lamplighter, ye sure have picked up some almighty un-Librarian ways."

"I suppose," Wick replied, but he felt proud of his accomplishments. He felt proudest of the fact that he'd lived through everything. Looking at Craugh took some of the celebration out of the moment, though.

Craugh gazed out to sea, his brows knit in consternation.

Wick hadn't often seen the wizard worried. "Do you know where *Wraith* is bound for?"

"Perhaps," Craugh said.

"Where?"

Craugh glanced at Wick in a way that let the little Librarian know he'd rather not answer that question. But Cap'n Farok and Alysta were waiting on a reply as well.

"There can be only one place," Craugh said. "The Forest of Fangs and Shadows."

A chill passed through Wick. He'd spent a little time in the area, but never enough to get completely comfortable with it. The Forest of Fangs and Shadows was a dangerous place, filled with monstrous spiders, elves that had chosen solitary lives apart from the rest of the world and didn't welcome intrusion, and frightful beasts left over from the Cataclysm.

"Why there?" Wick asked.

"Because Sokadir lives there," the wizard answered. "Somewhere."

"Sokadir is still alive?" Wick asked. Sokadir was the elven warder hero who had taken up arms with Deathwhisper, the enchanted bow, at the Battle of Fell's Keep more than a thousand years ago.

Craugh nodded and took out his pipe. He tamped it full, then muttered an incantation to light it. "He is an elf, you know. They live for a long, long time. Unless they're killed, of course."

"You never mentioned Sokadir was still alive," Wick said.

"No."

Wick couldn't believe it. "That's something worth knowing."

"Now you know it."

"I could have known it days ago, before we left Greydawn Moors."

"Knowing Sokadir was alive wouldn't have helped us find Boneslicer or Seaspray," Craugh replied testily.

"If we truly want to know what happened at the Battle of Fell's Keep," Wick pointed out, "all we have to do is ask Sokadir."

"Except that Sokadir doesn't want to be found," Craugh said. "I went looking for him before I went looking for you."

Wick thought about that. It was the first admission Craugh had made that his arrival in Greydawn Moors hadn't been exactly fortuitous happenstance.

"I couldn't find Sokadir," Craugh said. "But I encountered others who were looking for him as well." He paused. "These were very dangerous beings."

Beings. The description slammed into Wick. *Beings. Not people. Not creatures. Beings.*

"It was their interest," Craugh said, "that made me most curious about why they would be looking for him after all these years."

Wick cleared his throat. "What . . . *kind* of beings?"

A small, mirthless smile pulled at Craugh's mouth. "The very dangerous, murderous sort, of course."

Of course. Wick sighed. "Gujhar believes that with Boneslicer and Seaspray in his possession he'll be able to track down Deathwhisper because of the magic spell that bound them at the Battle of Fell's Keep."

"That's probably true. Magic ties all things together, after a fashion. Those three weapons shared a binding."

"Then we need to catch *Wraith.*" Wick looked at the ocean, but there was no ship in sight.

"I'm keeping watch over *Wraith,*" Craugh said. "I can do that for a time. I've managed to place a compatriot on board that ship while it was at Wharf Rat's Warren." He puffed on his pipe. "More than that, though, I can also track Sokadir and Deathwhisper. When the time is right."

"How?"

"Through Master Oskarr and Captain Dulaun's descendants."

"Why couldn't you have done that before?" Wick asked. "Bulokk is with us, and you sent Alysta to me. You had their descendants before I ever entered Wharf Rat's Warren."

Craugh regarded the cat. "Alysta is not . . . quite who she used to be. When she lost her old body, she lost that tie to Captain Dulaun."

Wick looked at the cat, feeling a little sad for her and all that she had given up. After all, how could a person live as a cat after years of having hands?

"Now we have my granddaughter," Alysta said, "and we have the scent of our enemies. I will have my ancestor's sword back where it belongs."

"We'll have them all back," Cap'n Farok promised. "Afore this affair gets any more outta hand." Then he shifted his gaze to Wick. "There's breakfast a-waitin' belowdecks, Librarian. Best get at it while it's hot."

At the thought of breakfast, Wick's stomach rumbled. He was too hungry after a day's sleep to feel nervous over where *One-Eyed Peggie* was headed. He took his leave and headed belowdecks. Whatever trouble was brewing, it would come soon enough. He chose to be fortified for it.

In the galley, Bulokk and the Cinder Clouds Islands dwarves were regaling each other with tales while stuffing themselves with breakfast. *One-Eyed Peggie* never stinted on feeding her hands and passengers.

As soon as Wick arrived, some of the pirate crew greeted him and called him to their table, which sparked an immediate good-natured battle between them and the Cinder Clouds Islands clan as they entreated Wick to sit with them. In the end, they made way for Wick in the middle of both groups and he gave in to their demands for his stories in Wharf Rat's Warren.

With a full plate ahead of him and plenty more to hand, Wick sat among the pirates and warriors and spun his tales. He couldn't help thinking how out of place Grandmagister Frollo would have thought him among them. But surely there was no finer place for a storyteller than in front of a willing audience.

A Note from Grandmagister Edgewick Lamplighter

After my recovery, which was thankfully short in returning, I spent time at my journals. I have written this one and placed it with a friend of mine in Deldal's Mills. Since you have that book, my apprentice, doubtless you know that my friend was none other than Evarch. Hopefully the Ordal that helped you solve the riddle to find this journal was known to me. He was a good friend.

Better yet, you should never be given this book, for it will mean that an Old Evil has once more risen. And, quite possibly, that an end has come to me. If that is true, try to find time to come to my grave and read to me every now and again.

I'm reminded of Alysta, the cat, in this instance. At least she had paws to turn the pages of a book with if she had a mind. I shudder to think of an eternity spent without books. I have hopes that every book that was ever lost is somewhere waiting for me when my life here finally ends.

There is yet a third book, of course. One that will complete this trilogy you've come seeking. You'll find it deep within the Forest of Shadows and Fangs. Look for that journal in the Crocodile's Throat at Jaramak's Aerie just off Never-Know Road.

Due to circumstances beyond my control, I couldn't take that book from that place. Even that book is somewhat unfinished, though. I fear you're going to have to write the end to that one.

Just don't let it be the end of you. You're facing horrible foes who don't know the meaning of mercy. If the Old Ones are willing, Craugh will be with you. He was the one who helped us escape from the madness of the Darkling Swamp when the time came. But even he couldn't destroy Lord Kharrion's foul legacy.

That's all I can say for now. To say any more would reveal too much at the wrong time. A story has to unfold at a natural pace, and—sometimes—so does life.

If you've come this far, and you're the one I taught my secrets to, then I must have cared for you. Hopefully you cared about me. Even more so, I hope that my life mattered and that I did good works. But mostly I hope that I got to read every good book there was.

Go forth then, my apprentice. Step lightly and with care. Everywhere you go now, there will be only danger. I wish that I could save you from this undertaking, but obviously I can't. So I wish you good luck from afar.

Sincerely,
Edgewick Lamplighter
Grandmagister
Vault of All Known Knowledge
Greydawn Moors

Afterword

Tears wet Juhg's cheeks as he finished reading the last words in his mentor's second journal. The fire still blazed brightly in Evarch's fireplace, so someone must have kept it fed while he was reading, though he'd been swept away by Grandmagister Lamplighter's words and hadn't noticed.

He wiped his face with a hand and looked to his companions.

"Are you all right?" Yurial asked. Concern showed on her youthful face.

After a moment, when he found his voice, Juhg nodded. "I am."

"It must be hard," she said.

"What? The translation?" Juhg shook his head. "Grandmagister Lamplighter taught me his codes. Most of them are almost second nature now."

"I meant it must be hard reading his last words."

"These aren't his last words." The declaration came out more defensively than Juhg had intended.

"Wick isn't here," Yurial said quietly. "If this is as important as you say it is, as important as Craugh has led you to believe, I know that Wick would be here." She smiled a little. "Despite his protestations contrariwise, he was never one to miss out on an adventure." Her eyes searched his. "You don't know if you're ever going to see him again."

Juhg returned her gaze and found he couldn't lie to her. Or to himself. "Wick is gone," he whispered, "off on an adventure like none have ever before taken." He shook his head. "I don't know if he will ever return. Or if he will even be permitted."

"That's why this journey is hard," Yurial said. "You're being offered one last chance to walk in your mentor's footsteps. I felt the same way when I found songs in my father's things that I'd never heard him sing." She smiled a little. "Wick taught my father the secret of writing."

"Grandmagister Lamplighter did that?" Juhg was surprised. Grandmagister Lamplighter had always taken pains to keep his abilities secret, and had believed that none on the mainland knew how to read except wizards.

"He did," Yurial said. "Learning to write didn't come easily to my father. If it hadn't been for Evarch's wines and spirits, I don't think either of them would have made it through that education."

"Do you know how to read?"

She nodded. "I do. It was hard not to learn with them railing at each other. My father made me practice the lute every day for hours. While I played the lute, he worked with ink and paper till he finally grasped what Wick was teaching him." She smiled at the memory. "I think I learned more than my father did, but he learned enough to capture songs on paper. While he was busy at that, I taught Wick to play the lute. He'd played the lute before, of course, and I never found anything he couldn't play, but he didn't quite have the fingering down. I helped him with that."

Juhg felt the weight of the book on his leg. Fatigue leeched the strength from him and he could barely keep his eyes open.

"When I first started playing my father's songs," Yurial said, "I felt only sadness and despair. Gradually, I came to love my father's songs. Someday you'll be able to feel better about these journals you're after."

"There's only one more," Juhg said. "After that—" He couldn't go on.

"There are others," Raisho said, leaning forward with his hands on his knees. He looked tired as well. "Just in readin' that book, ye've learned that there are other books the Grandmagister wrote what ye 'aven't read yet."

"I know," Juhg said. *But do they still survive?* There were days, sometimes, when he didn't think of the trap he'd unwittingly brought to the Vault of All Known Knowledge that had destroyed so many books. Even with the addition of the second Library he'd discovered while looking for *The Book of Time*, several of those books hadn't been replaced.

They were gone. Forever.

"It's only the end when ye give up on it," Raisho said. "Ye used to tell me that when I'd get to feelin' dispirited. I'd 'ate to think ye were just a-tellin' me that."

"It's just that I don't know if I'm up to this task," Juhg said. "We were nearly killed last night—" He stopped himself, then corrected his statement. Gray dawn was already touching the windows of Evarch's distillery. "—*two* nights ago. Someone is looking for us." Tired as he was, he dreaded sleep, knowing the scarecrow thing would be waiting for him in his dreams.

"You can do this," Evarch said. "Elsewise Wick wouldn't have put you on the track like he did."

"He didn't put me on the track," Juhg said. "Craugh did. And now he's missing." He could still see BEWARE written in blood in the wizard's cabin aboard

Moonsdreamer. What had happened to Craugh, and who had taken the wizard unawares on board a ship full of Raisho's best pirates?

"That's where you're wrong," Evarch stated evenly. "Wick put you onto this trail." He pointed his pipe at the journal Juhg held. "He's even talking to you through those pages, asking you to finish what he started."

"It wasn't just what he started," Juhg said. "It was what he *couldn't* finish."

"Have you ever read Krumwirth?" Evarch asked.

"Yes." Juhg frowned. "Don't tell me that you read as well?"

"No, no. I knew Wick did, but I never had an interest."

"There's a lot you could learn about wine and spirits," Juhg said. "At the Vault of All Known Knowledge, there are thousands of books about fermenting and distilling."

Evarch waved the idea of the books away. "You can keep them. I know all I need to. I can't keep up with the orders I get now." He puffed on his pipe. "Anyway, what I was getting to was a quote Wick gave me at one time that stuck with me. Of course, he was talking about wines and such at the time, but I've found the quote fits a great deal of occasions. It fits this one now." He cleared his throat. " 'For every vine there is a season, for every rhyme there is a reason, to do less than all you can is treason.' "

"I remember the quote," Juhg said.

"Good. Then you'll know Wick put a lot of store by that thought." Evarch grew more serious. "All those years ago when Wick passed through here, I knew what he was dealing with was dangerous. I saw him go up the Steadfast River, and I saw him come back down it. He looked better going up it. When he came back, he didn't talk about all that he'd lost, or all the warriors that he'd gone with who didn't come back. I didn't ask. I've seen men who've gone through war before, and I knew that was what Wick had been through."

For a moment, silence filled the room except for the crackle of the wood burning on the fire.

"Juhg," Yurial said.

Juhg looked at her.

"Could you really turn around now? After you've come so far?"

Taking a deep breath, Juhg shook his head. But he couldn't help wondering if all the schools he was trying to get started would still be built and organized if something happened to him. Could he better protect the future he was trying to build by continuing to build, or by tracking down whatever villainy lay in the past?

Then he knew there was no choice. Old villainy had a habit of popping up when least expected. Just as it had now.

"No," he said. Then he looked at his three companions. "But if we're going up the Steadfast River to combat whatever Grandmagister Lamplighter was unable to defeat, we're going to need help."

BOOK THREE

deathwhisper

Foreword

The Bowman

Startled shouts drew Juhg's attention from the journal he worked on down in the ship's galley. He glanced up, only then aware that the vessel had subtly shifted her course. Somewhere on *Moonsdreamer*'s top deck sailors yelled in panic.

"Over here!" someone screamed. "There's more of 'em over here!"

"Get it off me! Get it off me!"

"It's bit me! Help!"

Capping his inkwell, Juhg placed blotting paper on the freshly inked pages and hoped that they didn't smear. He'd been working down in the ship's galley, picking at a plate of breakfast Cook had fixed for him even though it was after hours in the mess.

He hurried up the stairwell, pausing only to open a cunningly concealed hiding place and stash the book inside. *Moonsdreamer* was a pirate vessel that hailed out of Greydawn Moors. As such, she had a number of hiding places and voids that were located from stem to stern.

At the top step, Juhg reached down for the knife he wore in his boot. The blade was good Teholian steel, eight inches long, and sharp as a razor.

"There's another one over there!" a pirate yelled.

"Kill it!" a second squalled.

"They're everywhere!" The third voice held fearful dread.

"Stop yer caterwaulin' an' get to stompin'!" Bulokk shouted.

The sounds of boots thudding against the deck exploded and rolled over the deck.

“Stand yer ground, blast ye!” Raisho’s deep voice rang out. “Show me ye got guts fer fightin’, or I’ll get me own look at ’em when we’re done ’ere!” His tone was just as fierce as his words. “Get them fishin’ nets up ’ere! Stretch ’em across the riggin’ an’ make a shield!”

Several of the pirates sprang to do their captain’s bidding.

Peering out from the stairwell, Juhg saw dozens of plate-sized spiders dropping from the dark green leafy canopy. The Forest of Fangs and Shadows earned its name, stockpiled with things that hunted and fed on the weak and unwary.

Covered in dark green chitin that provided limited armor, the fat-bodied spiders dropped to the sails, the deck, and the men. The spiders died easily enough, but they came down as if powered by a sudden cloudburst. Some of them died from the fall, but others scuttled across the deck in search of prey or clung to the rigging to drop again.

Gathering his courage, Juhg stepped out onto the deck. “They’re trance spiders,” he called out to them. “Their bites won’t kill you. Just make you sick.”

“Make ye sick enough ye’ll wish ye was dead,” a black sailor with gray hair said, ripping one of the arachnids from his neck and clubbing it with an armored fist. “I seen ’em afore. Nasty creatures. But it ain’t the little ones what ye should be afeared of.”

Glancing up, Juhg saw that *Moonsdreamer*’s masts sometimes raked against the tall trees. Branches rattled and sometimes splintered against the masts. The crew carrying the nets crawled quickly through the rigging, avoiding most of the spiders because the creatures had dropped to the ship below.

The vibrations through the branches had drawn the trance spiders. Webbing hung everywhere above, looking like dirty gray mausoleum sheets scattered among the branches.

The crew kept smashing and hacking the spiders to pieces. Yellow ichors stained *Moonsdreamer*’s scarred deck. Four of Raisho’s sailors had dropped to their knees and were heaving up the contents of their stomachs. One of Bulokk’s dwarves was down as well.

Juhg joined the fight on the deck, stomping on the spiders where he found them.

Spiders died by the dozen, but for every one that perished two others seemed to plop down to take its place. They crawled and cowered, and some even leaped two feet or more, eliciting startled yells from the crew and the dwarves.

Finally, though, the sailors navigating through the yards had strung the huge fishing net over the pirate ship. Used for deep ocean fishing to bring up cod and other edible fish, the net was big enough to cover two vessels *Moonsdreamer*’s size.

Spiders continued to drop onto the net. In moments, they clustered over the strands so thick that it was hard to see the trees for the spiders.

“We should stop,” a pirate complained. “They might make their way through that net, an’ then where would we be?”

“We ain’t stoppin’.” Raisho gazed down at his crew from the stern castle. His dark face held grim resolve.

The scuttling noise made by the spiders crawling across the net sounded loud.

Somewhere in the rigging a loose sail luffed in the slight breeze afforded upriver and would have to be tightened.

"If 'n we don't stop, them spiders is likely to cover us over," a sailor said.

As if to underscore this possibility, a few more meaty plops sounded against the net.

"An' likely as not, they'll find a way to come a-creepin' under that net," the sailor went on.

"If they do, we'll kill 'em," Raisho growled. He raked his men with a hard gaze. "Ye were all conscripted to 'elp take care of the Vault of All Known Knowledge. Some of ye've been at it longer'n I 'ave. Ye draw yer pay whether ye're fightin' goblinkin what's tryin' to get to Greydawn Moors an' the Library there, or whether ye're tradin' up an' down the Shattered Coast in the 'opes of linin' yer own pockets with profits."

The pirates didn't say anything. They knew it was true.

"Now, no less than the Grandmagister 'isself 'as come callin' on ye to 'elp 'im out," Raisho thundered. "By the Old Ones, ye'll stand up an' be counted like fine sailin' men an' proper pirates—ever' one of ye—or I'll 'eave the lot of ye overboard an' conscript the first bunch of farm boys a-wantin' to get out of town that I see." He glared down hotly, arms crossed over his broad chest.

"Farm boys?" one old sailor cried indignantly. "Would ye be after havin' our fine ship an' home turned over to the grubby hands of *farm boys*?"

"No," a few of the crew muttered.

"Well then," the old sailor said, looking displeased, "if that's all the spirit ye've got in ye, the Grandmagister sure picked himself a sorry crew to get him through this. I might as well jump overboard an' save Cap'n Raisho the trouble of heavin' me." He pointed up. "Or open that net an' let them spiders have at ye."

"No!" the crew roared.

"Then let's make sure we keep me ship clear of them spiders," Raisho ordered. "We've come too far into 'em to turn around, an' I don't fancy travelin' overland to the Crocodile's Throat meself. I'm a sailin' man."

The crew hooted and hollered with more vigor—except for the six crew and two dwarves down with the trance spider venom—and set about their chores. They kept vigilant watch, though Juhg knew they all feared spider invasion.

Juhg walked to the ship's prow and stared out at the turgid water. This far upriver, the Steadfast rolled along slowly, wide and deep instead of the faster waters around Deldal's Mills and Calmpoint. Getting permission to come through the gates at Calmpoint had required heavy bribery. Luckily Raisho never sailed anywhere without enough gold to ransom his way out of trouble he couldn't fight his way through.

He'd spent two days bargaining with the city official before *Moonsdreamer* had been allowed upriver toward Darbrit's Landing. Before the Cataclysm, Darbrit's Landing had been a strong port city, a place where traders and caravan captains met to agree to terms, a place where artisans and guildsmen came to sell their wares, or to buy.

Juhg had never been through Darbrit's Landing, but he'd heard of it. These days it was supposed to be a place of dead things, of ghosts. But the lure of treasure drew fortune hunters in time and again, and the gruesome stories continued about what went on there.

"What are ye thinkin' about so hard, scribbler?"

Glancing up, Juhg found Raisho standing beside him. "Actually, I'm wondering if I'm leading us into a trap," he admitted.

Raisho frowned. "Not so loud. Some of 'em's got keen ears, an' we're 'avin' problems enough without spookin' 'em further."

Silently, Juhg nodded. He peered through the gloomy murk that was present despite the fact that it was shortly before the noon hour. Spiders continued to plop onto the net. Several of the arachnids scuttled over the net in front of Juhg's face.

"Ye know we're a-goin' in the right direction," Raisho said. "Don't ye?"

"I do." Juhg took a deep breath.

"Well then, ye just need to remember that it's the time an' toil of the travel that takes a toll on the traveler, not the frettin'."

Looking at his best friend, Juhg smiled. "You almost got it right."

"I knew frettin' wasn't right," Raisho said. "I read that poem a lot. It's one of me favorites."

"You read it?" Juhg was surprised.

"I do."

"How?"

"I bribed one of the Novices to make me a copy of that book of poems ye wrote," Raisho answered.

"*Bribed?*" *Librarians don't take bribes.* At least Juhg didn't think they did. "He charged you? For a book? That *I'd* written?" He'd heard of such things, of course, back before the Cataclysm. However, he planned to give books away for free. If a person or town would lodge and feed a Librarian. And provide the paper and ink, of course.

Raisho shrugged. "Only a little. Cost me a 'am an' a couple snozzgrape pies."

"Pies?" *My writing, my poetry, is worth* pies?

"Two." Raisho held up two fingers defensively. "An' the 'am weren't a cheap one. 'E wanted a fair price for 'is time, 'e did."

"Two pies and a ham."

"A good 'am."

Juhg couldn't believe it.

Raisho looked at Juhg in concern. "Are ye sure one of them trance spiders didn't bite ye? Normally ye're much better at conversations."

Juhg was flummoxed. He cleared his throat. "That volume of poetry wasn't meant for public consumption."

"Ye read it to me."

"You're my friend."

"Would ye 'ave made me a copy if I'd asked?"

Juhg hesitated. "Yes." But he also knew he would have found ways of putting that task off. Reading the poems to Raisho had been impulse. Before, when the muse had taken him, he'd always had Grandmagister Lamplighter to read to.

"Well then, I just saved ye the trouble of 'avin' to do it yerself. Ye should be thankin' me."

Juhg didn't know what to say about that.

"An' who would have thought it?" Raisho asked. "That ye, who prides yerself on makin' libraries an' books fer people, would try keepin' one out of people's 'ands."

Standing there, Juhg listened to the spiders plopping against the net overhead. He realized then that Raisho had only mentioned the poem as a distraction. He let out a tense breath.

"Maybe I should get back to work," Juhg said.

Raisho gazed up at the spider-laden net. "Ye should. We're gettin' closer to Darbrit's Landing. Ain't gonna be much more time that ye can work in a safe place."

Juhg turned and went back across the deck strewn with dead spiders. But the sound of the spiders scuttling overhead echoed in his head and reminded him that all their lives might be forfeit.

"Is this a ship or a pigpen?" Raisho roared.

"It's a ship, cap'n," came the immediate reply from a dozen throats.

Juhg smiled at that. Raisho had turned into quite the ship's captain.

"Then why ain't there no buckets an' mops out 'ere clearin' this mess away?"

Feeling a little more lighthearted, Juhg returned to the galley with book in hand and set to work. His spirits were further buoyed when he discovered the ink hadn't run or smeared when he'd had to put it away.

"You're going to ruin your eyes working by lantern light."

Juhg hung in the rigging over *Moondreamer*'s prow. It was his customary position when he was aboardship. He cradled his journal on his knees and worked in charcoal. He looked up at the young woman's voice.

Minstrel Ordal's long red hair brushed her shoulders and warmth reflected in her brown eyes. She carried her lute in one hand and a bowl in the other. As usual, she wore the Minstrel Ordal trademark yellow blouse with alabaster fringe and tan breeches, though these were cut for a woman. The feather in her red cap fluttered as the chill night wind plucked at it.

"I'm used to working by lantern light," Juhg said.

"At the Library?"

"Yes."

Yurial frowned. "Then it's a wonder you're not blind as a bat."

Juhg smiled at her. "I'm a dweller. Our eyesight is a little better and a little more indestructible than a human's."

"I'll take your word for it." She looked at the rigging beside Juhg. "Do you mind company?"

"Not at all." Juhg put his charcoal into a bag and closed the journal.

"I brought you something to eat." Yurial offered the plate.

"I've already eaten."

"Not nearly enough, according to Raisho."

"How would he know? He's been looking out for the ship all day."

Yurial settled in beside Juhg. "Because he has spies *everywhere*," she replied mysteriously. She said it in a half whisper and in such a conspiratorial manner that Juhg was chuckling in spite of the danger that surrounded them.

"I truly wish you hadn't come," he told her.

Sniffing with feigned disdain, Yurial said, "I have to admit, I've had far better reactions to the offer of my company."

"It's not your company I'm worried about," Juhg said. "It's your safety."

Yurial leaned back against the rigging and wrapped her arms around her knees. "I can look out for myself, Grandmagister."

Juhg frowned. He remembered Yurial as a child, and that had only seemed like yesterday. He was never going to get used to how quickly human children grew. "I meant no insult."

"Then don't treat me as if I were a child," Yurial stated flatly, but without anger. "I am, for better or worse, the Minstrel Ordal now. I will carry on my father's office to the best of my ability." She took a deep breath and relaxed a little. "That also means not trying to get myself killed, thank you very much."

"I apologize," Juhg said.

"You should. It's hard enough being the first female Minstrel Ordal in five generations without everyone making a fuss about it."

"Everyone?"

She shrugged. "Perhaps not everyone," she grudgingly admitted, "but enough so that it is a sore point. The thing is, no one knows more about the Steadfast River than Minstrel Ordal. Even me." She looked at him. "Why else do you think Wick sent you to the Minstrel Ordal to answer a question that you should have known yourself?"

Juhg had to admit that was true. If he hadn't been so tired from the long trip and paranoid about being attacked in his sleep as he had been on the way to Deldal's Mills where he'd encountered Minstrel Ordal, he would have known the answer to the puzzle Grandmagister Lamplighter had left in his first journal from the Cinder Clouds Islands.

Yurial gazed out into the darkness. "I know this river and these lands. If not from my time on it and through it, then from the stories I've had from the previous Minstrel Ordals. I had to memorize a good bit of history and lore, I'll have you know."

"Yes," Juhg agreed. "I know that you have." He gazed at the plate's contents. "What are these?"

"Cookies."

"I'd guessed that from the round shape," Juhg said dryly.

"I baked them myself," Yurial said. "My mother created the recipe. Wick liked them a lot as I recall."

Not wanting to chance offending his friend any further, Juhg picked up a cookie and took a bite. It was surprisingly sweet and still warm from the oven. "Delicious," he said.

“Have another.”

Juhg helped himself to another but said, “You didn’t come out here to feed me cookies.”

“No.”

“You don’t know any more about the Crocodile’s Throat than I do, do you?”

“Unfortunately, no.” Yurial sighed. “I came out here to tell you to trust yourself, Juhg.”

“Me?” Juhg was surprised.

“Yes.”

“I do trust myself.”

Yurial looked at him knowingly. “Not yet you don’t. You have doubts about your ability to handle whatever lies ahead of us.”

Juhg started to object automatically, then thought better of it. “Do you think that you can handle whatever is ahead of us?”

“I don’t know. That isn’t what I’ve decided to concentrate on.”

“Then what?”

“I’ve decided,” Yurial said, “that I will meet whatever lies ahead of us to the best of my ability. That’s the promise I made to my father as he lay dying.”

Juhg remained silent.

“And at some point, since Wick took his leave of you by choice and knew that potentially what we’re here to do now would come back to haunt you, I think he elicited the same promise from you.”

After a moment, Juhg said, “He didn’t ask in so many words.”

“But you knew what he wanted.”

“Yes.” Juhg nodded. “He told me he knew he was leaving the Libraries in the best hands available. He also knew that I would be more able to send the books back out of the Libraries and into the hands of the people than he would ever have been able to do.”

“Wick did love to protect those books.” Yurial smiled.

“Did you know—” Juhg’s voice failed him for a moment. “Did you know that *I* was the one responsible for almost destroying the Vault of All Known Knowledge?”

“I did. My father told me. He learned it from Craugh.”

“Craugh.”

“Craugh said you were not to blame,” Yurial went on. “He was very clear about that. He explained that the book you carried was a trap, one so clever that not even he nor Wick had puzzled it out. Until it had already snapped closed.”

Juhg remembered the roaring fires and the bloody violence that had erupted within the Vault of All Known Knowledge. Those images would never leave him as long as he lived.

“You’re fallible, Juhg,” the young woman said. “Just as Wick was during the years that I knew him. He didn’t always know what was best. But he always tried to do his best.”

“I know.”

“You can’t let the fear you’re feeling stop you.”

“But what if I make a mistake?” Juhg asked quietly so that none would hear.

"Evidently Craugh has already made a mistake, or else he would be here now and there wouldn't have been blood all over his cabin."

"Exactly what happened to Craugh remains to be seen," Yurial said. "I've seen that old wizard walk through situations that left everyone around him dead."

Juhg looked at her.

Yurial sighed and shrugged. "Okay, that's probably not what I should have said."

"No."

"But what I'm getting at is that Craugh is a survivor. He's always told me not to count him out till I see his smoldering corpse."

Juhg knew that was true.

"What I'm saying," Yurial told him, "is that Wick sent *you* to see this through to its completion. Not Craugh."

"Why?"

"I don't know. I suppose when we find the answers to the other questions we have, we'll know the answer to that one as well."

If we live, Juhg thought morosely. *Old Ones willing, if I'm to be taken, don't let it be in failure.*

"Your redemption for what happened to the Vault of All Known Knowledge," Yurial said, "doesn't lie in dying for the right reasons. You're supposed to *live* for them."

"I know," Juhg said. "I know."

Darbrit's Landing stood cloaked in shadows, vines, and the low branches of tall trees. Remnants of stone buildings and of the ten-foot stone wall that had surrounded the city lay mired in the thick black mud. All of them tilted at crazed angles. Creatures moved within the tall brush on either side of the Steadfast River. A bridge, somehow miraculously whole, curved in an arch above the water and blocked *Moonsdreamer*'s progress. Bird calls, cat screams, and lizards bellowing filled the thick silence.

"Drop the anchor," Raisho ordered. "Archers, stand alert."

"Aye, cap'n," the crew responded.

Raisho joined Juhg at the prow. Together, with Yurial, they stood staring out over the dead city.

Gently, her sails furled so that she no longer felt the weak push of the wind that had brought her to Darbrit's Landing, *Moonsdreamer* floated back to the length of the anchor chain and rode the rise and fall of the slow current.

"Is this it then?" Raisho asked.

"This is Darbrit's Landing," Yurial answered. "What's left of it, anyway."

"Ye ever been 'ere?" Raisho asked.

"No."

"'Ow 'bout ye, scribbler?"

"No," Juhg replied.

"Well," Raisho mused, "Grandmagister Lamplighter musta been. Otherwise 'e'd never have sent ye up this far." The young captain glanced around. "All this black mud, though, makes me think of them bog beasts we ended up fightin' in Shark's Maw Cove."

Silently, Juhg agreed.

"Guess there's no 'elpin' it," Raisho commented.

"What?" Juhg asked.

"If 'n nobody's come out 'ere to meet us, looks like we'll be goin' over there to meet them."

Nearly two hours later, Raisho was finally satisfied the warriors going ashore were fully provisioned. Juhg knew his friend hated splitting his crew, but there'd been no helping that. Fortunately, Raisho had been carrying an extra complement of warriors from Greydawn Moors because he'd been providing protection for Juhg out in the Blood-Soaked Sea.

Juhg clambered down the fishing net hung over the ship's side and into the waiting longboat. Yurial joined him next. He knew better than to protest her choice to accompany him. He'd only have been wasting time, and she did know more about the area than he did.

He sat in the stern and watched monkeys capering through the branches, chattering with anxious fear. Thankfully they hadn't encountered any more spiders. But the temperature was greater than Juhg would have thought. Where Calmpoint had been cool because of the Gentlewind Sea, and even Deldal's Mills was only slightly warmer, Darbrit's Landing was almost sweltering.

Raisho climbed down into the longboat to join them.

"Shouldn't you stay aboard the ship?" Juhg asked.

The young captain seated his cutlass over his shoulder and shook his shaggy head. "Not with ye out an' about by yerself." He rolled his shoulders. "Besides, I'd rather be runnin' from trouble than sittin' in that ship a-waitin' fer it to find me." He grimaced. "From the looks of this place, that won't take any time at all."

The boat crew rowed for shore at Raisho's direction. Their oars made little noise in the water. Above, monkeys raced along the trees, squealing threats and tossing down branches.

"What are we lookin' for again?" Raisho asked.

"Jaramak's Aerie," Juhg answered, remembering the passage from Grandmagister Lamplighter's last journal.

"Do ye know what it is?"

"No. But it stands to reason that it would be above ground. Something like that, I think we'll notice." Of course, that wasn't necessarily true. Many woodlands elves had gotten good at hiding their homes and cities in the branches of trees. Even the rope bridges connecting them were often unnoticeable.

The boat crew rowed to the nearest pier. All of the piers were made of stone and jutted out into the wide river at certain points. If there were any docks that had been made of wood, nothing of them remained.

"Weapons drawn," Raisho said. Then he nodded to the young sailor standing in the boat's prow. "Toss that line an' pull us alongside."

The sailor flipped the end of the line expertly over one of the stone pillars sunk into the mud holding up that end of the stone dock. Hand over hand, he pulled the boat up next to the dock.

At Raisho's instruction, swordsmen took the lead, flanked swiftly by archers.

Thankfully someone in the past had crafted a flight of stairs leading up to the dock. If they hadn't, Juhg would have been hard-pressed to climb up. Peering down into the murky water, he got the sense that the stair extended down into the depths for a ways, proof that the whole city had at one time sat higher on the river. Or perhaps the river had risen.

The chatter of the monkeys continued, growing in cadence and volume, till the noise seemed all-consuming.

Raisho cursed the tiny primates. "They're relentless," he grumbled. "Ain't no way we're gonna sneak up on anybody with them there." He took the lead, though, walking down the runway leading to the massive city wall gates.

Juhg walked beside Yurial. Only a short distance farther on, they walked through the open doorway. The massive gates were marked by roaring lions, not alligators.

"Lions?" Juhg asked the minstrel.

"Art only," Yurial said. "No one has ever spotted any lions in the Forest of Fangs and Shadows. But there are occasional tigers."

Juhg pressed on, pushing his fear to the back of his mind. He kept wondering if Grandmagister Lamplighter's adventures while investigating the Battle of Fell's Keep had ended here or somewhere else. There was no way of knowing.

"Where are we 'eaded?" Raisho asked as they walked through the entrance. The gates were all but destroyed. Creeper and vines were deeply rooted in the mortar between the stones.

Juhg looked at one of the few remaining tall buildings. "High ground. There."

Turning, Raisho strode through the buckled streets, avoiding jagged ruptures of the cobblestone streets where tree roots and vegetation had torn through. Juhg followed his friend. Their footsteps sounded loud and out of place.

"Wait," one of the sailors on the right said.

They froze. Juhg waited anxiously.

"What is it?" Raisho demanded.

"I thought I heard something."

"So did I," Yurial said. She reached into her tall boots and withdrew two short sticks not quite two feet in length that were capped in iron at both ends. She cocked her head to one side and listened intently. "There."

Juhg listened as well and thought he heard furtive footsteps. He didn't think the sounds were made by a beast; they were too weighted, too careful. The cadence was all wrong for a truly wild thing.

Raisho waved his men into action, dividing two small three-man groups from their fifteen, nearly halving their strength. Moving quickly, the two groups surged forward and surrounded the portion of a wall they judged the noise to be issuing from.

As they closed in, the noise suddenly erupted into a crescendo of sounds. An elven boy leaped to the top of the wall with acrobatic grace. Slender and graceful, he wore only a modest loincloth, a knife at his belt, and a bow slung over one shoulder. His hair was the color of summer wheat and his skin deeply tan. Bright aquamarine eyes peered at them.

The archers raised their bows.

" 'Old yer fire!" Raisho bellowed, throwing up a hand.

The bowmen held their arrows nocked.

From the shadows near the young elf, a pirate darted forward and tried to grab his feet. With a lithe leap, the young elf threw himself into the air and caught a tree branch. With the speed and skill of a monkey, he darted through the branches and was twenty feet up and hidden by the tree trunk.

"What are you doing here?" the boy called down.

Raisho glanced at Juhg, letting him make the choice.

"We don't mean you any harm," Juhg said, stepping forward and showing his hands.

"Is that why you tried to capture me?" he challenged.

"We've come a long way," Juhg said, "and we know that we're among enemies."

"I'm not your enemy," the young elf replied. "Not yet, anyway. But I can be. The Forest of Fangs and Shadows is my home. You've not been given permission to come here."

"Juhg," Yurial whispered. "May I?"

"Of course," Juhg said.

Yurial stepped forward. "Do you know me, elf?"

High above them, the young elf peered around the tree trunk, allowing only a small part of his body to show. "You look like the Minstrel Ordal."

"I *am* the Minstrel Ordal," Yurial shot back.

"No," the young elf insisted, "you're not. I've met the Minstrel Ordal."

"That was my father."

The young elf peered more closely. "Minstrel Ordal did have a little girl with him when he visited our sprawl."

"I was that little girl," Yurial said.

Suspicion deepened in the young elf 's voice as he looked around. "Where's your father?"

"He . . . died."

"Oh." The young elf seemed uncomfortable.

Death made a lot of elves uneasy, Juhg knew. If they were properly insulated from the rest of the world and there was no violence in the community, death was a seldom-seen and alien thing except in the animal world. They had the longest lives of all the races.

"I'm sorry for your loss," the young elf said. "He sang very well."

"Thank you."

"What are you doing here?"

"We've come seeking the Crocodile's Throat."

Even at the distance, Juhg saw the perplexed look on the young, beautiful face.

"Why?" the young elf asked.

"We were sent there by a friend."

"What friend?"

"Edgewick Lamplighter."

"Wick the taleteller?"

"Yes."

The young elf looked harder at Juhg, then out at *Moonsdreamer* anchored in the river. "Is Wick aboard the ship?"

"No," Yurial answered. "He's not with us this time. Do you know Wick?"

"I do. He's been to our sprawl before. Is this one a taleteller, too?"

Juhg cleared his throat. "I know stories."

"Good ones?" The young elf 's voice sounded eager.

"I think so."

"I've never met anyone who knew as many stories as Wick. Or as good." The young elf glanced at Yurial. "Except, perhaps, the Minstrel Ordal."

"Thank you for that," Yurial said. "But I've never met anyone who could tell as many stories as Wick." She smiled a little. "Minstrel Ordal doesn't just tell stories, though. Minstrel Ordal carries news to all the people along the Steadfast River and the Never-Know Road."

The elf looked at Juhg. "Who are you?"

"Juhg."

"You know Wick?"

"He's my teacher," Juhg answered.

"The Crocodile's Throat is a dangerous place."

"That's why we brought so many men."

"Will you harm me?"

"No," Juhg answered. "But there are men who seek to harm us. It might prove dangerous to you to come among us."

The young elf smiled. "No one can catch me in this forest if I choose not to be caught." He took two steps out along the tree branch, then vaulted from limb to limb in a dazzling display of acrobatics.

It seemed he barely touched any branch before he was gone again, flipping and twisting and arcing through the air. Then, with a flourish, he vaulted once more and plummeted twenty feet to land effortlessly in front of Juhg.

"I'm Kimaru," the young elf announced. "I can take you to the Crocodile's Throat. It isn't far from here, but the way is dangerous."

"Mayhap ye should just give us directions an' let us find our own way there," Raisho suggested.

"You wouldn't find it," Kimaru told him. "The way is known only to elves." He smiled. "And to Wick, once." He turned abruptly on his heel and brushed through Raisho's pirates. All of them looked twice as big as the young elf, but there was something about Kimaru that spoke of nobility and hinted at danger.

" 'E's too young to be so arrogant," Raisho commented quietly.

"Kimaru is probably three or four times older than you," Juhg replied. He fell in behind the young elf.

"Still," Raisho grumbled, "such an attitude doesn't wear well."

By the time it started getting dark, Juhg wondered if Kimaru knew anything at all about distances. They'd trekked for hours, walking deep into the Forest of Fangs and Shadows and leaving *Moonsdreamer* and the rest of the crew far behind. They also left behind the thought of safety offered by the ship's greater size.

Juhg felt the increasing anxiety among his companions as the woods turned darker and more inhospitable. They seldom spoke, all of them intent on listening to the myriad noises around them. Movement filled the forest as well. Monkeys chattered and threatened in their wake, and flying squirrels sailed through the treetops, mixing with brightly colored birds.

Near dusk, Kimaru stopped. "We'll camp here."

Raisho looked around the tightly packed forest. "There's no place for a camp."

"Not on the ground." Kimaru pointed up. "We'll stay in the trees. There's an old sprawl in these trees."

"In the trees, is it?" Raisho didn't look happy.

Juhg had stayed with elves before and the idea of hanging suspended high above the ground didn't bother him. "It's not much different than sleeping in a hammock aboard *Moonsdreamer*," he told Raisho.

"Only about thirty or forty feet," Raisho growled.

"I've never been on a ship," Kimaru said. "I can't imagine getting a night's sleep above that much water. Here, the fall might kill you, but at least you won't drown along the way."

He has a point, Juhg thought.

"Gather firewood," the young elf told them.

"Ye're gonna start a fire in the treetops?" Raisho asked.

"A fire will help stave off the night's chill," Kimaru said as patiently as though he were speaking to a child.

Raisho scowled. "I know that. But what I'm gettin' at is, won't ye set them trees ablaze?"

"Not if we're careful. I intend to be careful. Don't you?"

Raisho gave the order to his men. Juhg helped, gathering small limbs and branches, breaking them so they were no more than a foot and a half in length. When he had a sizeable group of them, he used a leather strap from his backpack to tie them together. Then he looped them over one shoulder.

Similarly burdened by firewood, Kimaru leaped up into the trees, going through them as easily as one of the pirates might scamper aloft rigging. Thankfully, that same training with the ropes allowed the pirates to climb more readily and they followed.

The abandoned sprawl hung scattered in the trees, most of the components no longer connected by rope ladders. Two of the trees supporting structures were dead, withered and gray. That was a sure sign there was no elven habitation. Elves would never allow a tree to die if it was in their power to save it, or continue to live in a dead tree if it couldn't be saved.

They gathered in one of the large houses in the center of the sprawl. Kimaru reached the front porch and kicked down a rope ladder that unrolled as it came. Raisho caught the ladder and tied it to the tree trunk, but it still spun and shifted as the pirates climbed along it.

Standing on the plank floor of the house, Juhg was reminded of standing on a ship's deck. Just as the ship rolled and shifted subtly underfoot at all times, the tree house rolled and shifted on the breeze. A hint of the fragrances from the mineral oils used to keep the wood walls supple and replenish the health of the tree tickled his nose. All elven homes smelled of flowers and herbs. Many of them created unique fragrances.

A porcelain bowl occupied the center of the living chamber. Black and gray-white ash from previous fires occupied the bottom of the container. A flue above it ran through the two-story house and out the roof. All the furniture had been taken by the previous occupants when they departed.

Kimaru tended the fire and got a cheery blaze going in short order. By that time full dark had descended and the Forest of Fangs and Shadows had begun its nocturnal life. Screams of hunter and prey sounded in the distance.

"Why are you seeking the Crocodile's Throat?" Kimaru asked.

Raisho and the pirates brought out their food bags and passed out bread and dried meat. The wineskins made the rounds, too.

"I'm looking for something Grandmagister Lamplighter left behind," Juhg answered.

"What?"

Juhg hesitated for a moment. "A book."

"He was always very careful about his books," Kimaru said. "I don't think he would leave one behind by accident."

"It wasn't by accident. It was by design."

"What book is it?"

"A narrative of his travels. He came to the Forest of Fangs and Shadows seeking Sokadir and Deathwhisper."

Kimaru frowned, then bit into a chunk of fresh bread. "Why would he do that?"

"Have you heard of the Battle of Fell's Keep?"

The young elf nodded.

"Sokadir was one of those who survived and still yet lives."

"There is another," Kimaru said.

"Who?"

"Larrosh, Prince of the Laceleaves sprawl."

"I don't know of him."

Kimaru pointed. "He lives to the north, near the Darkling Swamp. He is Sokadir's cousin."

"Have you seen Sokadir?"

Shaking his head, Kimaru said, "Very few people have seen him since Lord Kharrion's defeat by the Unity, and he never talks to anyone. He went off to himself and remains hidden."

"Why?"

"His two sons were at the Battle of Fell's Keep. Qardak and Palagan. They were twins." Kimaru said that with a tone of reverence. "After they were lost to him, when the dwarf Oskarr betrayed the defenders at the Battle of Fell's Keep, it's said that Sokadir was never the same. He never made peace with his loss. He had lost his wife in battle only a year before that."

No one wrote that up, Juhg realized, and wondered how much history of the Cataclysm had been lost during the confusion of the time and immediately following.

"A thousand years of grief?" Raisho asked. "That's a long time."

"Sokadir loved his family," Kimaru said. "With them gone, he was . . . hollow. Rootless."

Juhg understood that. Elves, partially because of their long lives, developed deep relationships. But Sokadir must have been hurting badly to walk away from his community. Especially since they would have supported him during his pain till he accepted his losses.

"Sokadir isn't entirely rootless," Juhg pointed out, "if he's still in the area. He'd have been gone from here."

"An elf is often tied to the land that birthed him," Kimaru said. "Sokadir couldn't stay away from this forest for the rest of his life." He crunched into a firepear that he'd taken from one of the trees below. Juice ran down his chin and gleamed in the firelight.

"If he's still here," Juhg asked, "do you think you can find him?"

"Not if he doesn't want to be found," Kimaru replied. "And I wouldn't intrude on his solitude." His aqua eyes rested on Juhg. "Likely, he'll kill anyone who does."

One of the guards Raisho had posted alerted them shortly before the goblinkin attacked. They came early, after the moons were gone and the sun was just beginning to swell in the eastern sky.

Raisho shook Juhg awake, holding a hand over his mouth. Over the years of their relationship, Rashio had waked him like that before. Juhg opened his eyes.

Putting a finger to his lips, Raisho removed his hand from Juhg's face. "Goblinkin," he mouthed, so quiet the word barely stirred the air.

Juhg nodded, then got quietly to his feet and woke Yurial in a similar manner. In the space of a breath, they were all awake in the elven tree house.

"Out the back," Kimaru whispered. "We'll have to go quickly. Stay close to the trunk. Perhaps they won't see us."

Juhg knew the chances of that were slim. His heart thudded inside his chest.

"Archers," Raisho said to the four crewmen who had bows, "ye'll stay up 'ere till the last. After them goblinkin attack, feather 'em. We'll split their attention as best we can."

The men nodded tensely but stood their ground next to the windows.

"Juhg," Kimaru whispered at the door, "stay with Minstrel Ordal. She knows this forest better than anyone."

"Where are you going to be?" Juhg asked.

The young elf grinned. "Wherever I can do the most good." He curled a finger over the arrow nocked to his bowstring. "I've killed a few goblinkin before. They don't normally come this far into the forest." He nodded to the door. "Now go."

Yurial went first, sliding down the rope ladder effortlessly while staying in the shadows of the trunk. She drew fire from the goblinkin archers at once.

Raisho ordered the pirate archers to loose their shafts. Their arrows flew into the pack of goblinkin and struck targets readily.

Juhg grabbed the rope next and began his descent. He plunged down, scraping against the rough bark and taking hide from his hands and his jaw. He ignored the stinging pain and dropped to the ground beside Yurial. She already had her batons in her hands.

Three more ropes spilled from the tree house. Raisho and his men slid down the ropes like they were bailing after furling the sails during a savage storm. They hit the ground in ungainly heaps and quickly sprang to their feet. Goblinkin arrows struck among them.

Juhg took cover behind a nearby tree, following Yurial.

A strange, savage cry ululated from the upper tiers of the trees. Drawn by the sound, Juhg spotted Kimaru leaping from branch to branch. The young elven warrior had an arrow nocked to his bowstring every time he came to a stop on a branch. He drew and released smoothly, and every arrow hit a target with unerring accuracy. Raisho's archers accounted for others, but all they did was succeed in dispersing the group. Then he yelled again, and the sound was even more attention-getting.

Most of the goblinkin advanced in a wave, running toward the pirates now grouped around the tree. A few goblinkin archers lit fire arrows and launched them in high arcs. Several of the flaming shafts landed on the tree house's thatched roof. A blaze sprang up immediately.

As dry as the untended tree house was, fire quickly engulfed the structure, grabbing purchase like a great snarling beast. In seconds, the tree house was a roaring bonfire that greedily lashed up into the tree, setting it ablaze as well.

"Archers!" Raisho roared.

The archers sprang into position, dropping to one knee to fire into the advancing ranks of the goblinkin.

"Release!"

Arrows flew from bows. Several of the lead goblinkin tumbled to the ground. Those following closely behind tripped over them and went sprawling. Kimaru rained down more death from above, piercing the misshapen triangular heads of the goblinkin.

The brutes were close enough now that Juhg could see them clearly by the light of the tree house inferno. Black woolly hair clung to the inverted triangles that were their heads. The chin was the narrowest point, but the eyes were close-set around a piggy nose. Their skin (by daylight) was a sickly gray-green color that looked mottled by the hand of Death. Huge ears stuck out from their heads, many of them wrinkled and folded and flapping as they ran. Yellow fangs glinted in their cruel mouths. They wore the bones of enemies—humans, elves, and dwarves—in their clothing, hair, and puny beards. They wore little in the way of clothing, sometimes breeches and a shirt, and sometimes merely a twisted loincloth or animal skin.

When Lord Kharrion had gone among the goblinkin, he'd had to fight his way through the hordes to make them listen to him. Legend had it that he'd killed several of them so that the others would fear him. And they did fear him, but they also came to love him because he guided them to undreamed victories over the hated humans, elves, and dwarves.

Even since Lord Kharrion's death, the goblinkin had changed. Juhg had seen that when he'd gone among them. They had started creating a culture of their own, and they hadn't returned to preying on each other as quickly as they had before. They had developed a racial consciousness that they'd never before exhibited. Even in defeat, they'd learned, and they continued repopulating their ranks at an alarming rate.

"Back!" Raisho bellowed. "Back, lads! We're gonna take the 'igh ground!"

Trust Raisho to know where the high ground is, Juhg thought, feeling proud of his friend. Raisho had proven himself every inch the warrior time and time again.

"On me, lads!" Raisho called. "Just stay focused on me!"

Kimaru continued loosing shafts into the goblinkin as he sprang again and again through the trees. Every couple heartbeats (even the rapid, frantic ones that hammered Juhg's ears) a goblinkin dropped stone dead in his tracks. The foul creatures left a trail of their dead behind them. But they continued coming.

Juhg ran, keeping up with the pirates and Yurial only because he was fast enough to take two and three strides to every one of theirs. He dodged trees and slid through brush. He tripped several times on the treacherous terrain but managed to push himself back to his feet each time.

Then he saw the hill, the high ground that Raisho intended for them. They ran up it, only a few feet ahead of the goblinkin.

" 'Ere!" Raisho yelled. "We 'old 'ere!" He turned, a dark, fierce shape in the pale dawn, and met the closest goblinkin head-on. Raisho blocked the goblinkin's sword blow by batting his opponent's arm aside. He brought his cutlass down in a blistering arc, aiming for the goblinkin's head. But the goblinkin blocked the cutlass with a metal bracer.

The goblinkin grinned and growled, leaning forward to snap at Raisho's neck with his curved yellow fangs. Raisho twisted and turned in a cunning move that cause the larger goblinkin to sail over his head and land hard on the ground, the wind knocked from his lungs. Before the goblinkin could recover, Raisho slit his throat with the cutlass. Taking a hand-and-a-half hold on the cutlass, Raisho whirled to engage the next foe.

Beside Juhg, Yurial fought with her twin batons. She used them together to block an overhead hammer strike by a goblinkin, then swiveled and diverted her opponent's size and strength, hurling him to one side. He tried to raise the hammer in both hands, but before he could she broke his wrist with one of the weighted batons and crushed his jaw with the other. Unconscious or dead, the goblinkin fell back among his fellows.

Fierce roaring filled the hilltop. Juhg lost sight of his companions as a goblinkin bore down on him with a spear. Moving quickly, Juhg dodged away but grabbed the spear hilt and yanked it toward the ground. The spear broke nearly in half, leaving a piece a little over three feet in length imbedded in the ground.

The goblinkin roared ferociously, throwing the broken spear away and reaching for the hatchet at his side. As he ripped the weapon free, Juhg seized the broken spear from the ground and gripped it like a staff. He'd studied staff work for a time, learning the skill from a book so that he could train one of the young dwarves that guarded the Vault of All Known Knowledge.

When the goblinkin lunged at him with the hatchet, Juhg held the staff, right hand over and left hand under, then blocked the hatchet away and quickly flipped the staff 's other end around to slam against the goblinkin's face. Surprised, the great brute yelled in pain and took a step back. Juhg gave him no quarter, though, flipping the staff once more and driving the end into his throat. The goblinkin stumbled away, getting in the way of the one behind him.

Juhg fought the next, holding the goblinkin back with a dazzling display of staff strikes. In the end, though, he knew their efforts weren't going to be enough to save them. There were too many goblinkin. Two crewmen were already down and the rest were beleaguered.

A great shadow suddenly appeared, swooping out of the forest. Juhg heard the crack as its wings spread and caught the air. He recognized the large bird as an owl just before it clawed out the goblinkin's eyes with its sharp talons.

His face a ruin, the goblinkin squalled out in fear and pain and stumbled away. Blood seeped between his hands.

The owl took to the air again, never making a sound. Its huge yellow eyes locked on Juhg for just a moment. For an instant, Juhg felt like it recognized him.

Then another ululating wail, this one different than Kimaru's, echoed over the battle, freezing the approaching combatants. The ones engaged kept to their tasks.

From the corner of his eye, Juhg saw another elf leaping effortlessly through the trees, flitting and changing direction like a dragonfly, as if gravity held no laws for him. Then he was suddenly fifty feet away, kneeling on a branch as he drew back a great golden bow with the face of a snarling mountain lion embossed on it.

The elf was slender, of indeterminate years as were all of their kind in their middle years. A supple chain mail shirt of black rings covered his upper body over a green and brown shirt that faded him into the trees behind him. Breeches of the same material covered his legs and were tucked into thin snakeskin boots. He wore his silver hair tied up in a topknot and it looked long and hacked off rather than properly cared for. Light purple eyes gleamed like a cat's. A smile of anticipation split his lips.

Juhg knew in an instant who he must be. Kimaru confirmed it. "Sokadir," the young elf breathed.

The goblinkin knew the new arrival, too. His name ran through their ranks. "Sokadir," they called. "It's Sokadir."

The elven warrior released his bowstring. A gleaming ruby shaft leaped from the golden bow and seemed to disappear before Juhg's eyes as it took full flight.

An instant later, a goblinkin warrior *exploded*, seemingly from within. Before the various pieces of his body descended, a blaze erupted and consumed them. Ash rained down from the sky.

In quick succession, two other goblinkin were summarily dispatched in the same fashion. Their ashes whirled on the breeze as well.

Then a great brown bear lumbered from the forest under Sokadir's feet. When it rose to its hind legs, the bear stood almost fourteen feet tall. It snuffled mightily, then roared and dropped back to all fours. In motion at once, the bear streaked for the goblinkin.

Raisho and the pirates stood to one side. Then the great bear was among the goblinkin, ripping and shredding with its great claws and biting. The goblinkin line broke, shattered into knots that quickly retreated. The bear flung the ones it had caught into the air so they crashed down several feet away. Most of them weren't moving, but the ones that did were quickly put to death by Raisho and the pirates.

Sokadir's magic bow, Deathwhisper, churned out burning death. As the elf drew back the string, another arrow formed out of thin air, summoned by the spell beaten into the bow.

In less than a minute, the goblinkin were in full rout. They headed back to the north, and only then did Juhg realize that they hadn't come upon them from behind. With any luck, *Moonsdreamer* still awaited them at the port in the ruined city.

Slowly, Sokadir stood on the tree branch where he'd taken up position. The owl returned to him, alighting on a specially constructed leather stand the elven warrior wore upon his left shoulder. Snuffling with displeasure, the bear padded toward Juhg and sniffed him. When the large creature was satisfied with his inspection, he turned and lumbered back to the elf.

"Greetings, champion," Kimaru said in the woodlands elf tongue.

Sokadir balanced his bow on the toe of one of his snakeskin boots and leaned slightly on his crossed arms. "You bring trouble on yourself, little brother," the elven warrior said.

"These people seek you," Kimaru said.

"I know. I don't want to be found. If not for you, I wouldn't be here now."

"I thank you for your help, honored one."

"I did it so that you can help others," Sokadir replied. "Use my gift wisely. These days I don't give out many."

"I will."

"Sokadir," Juhg called.

The elven warrior looked at him. "I don't know you."

"I wish to talk to you."

"Why?"

"I want to know what happened at the Battle of Fell's Keep."

Sokadir regarded Juhg in silence for a moment. "Careful what you seek. What you ask could get you killed."

"I'm not hunting you or Deathwhisper," Juhg said. "I only want the truth."

"The truth is a dangerous thing," Sokadir replied. "And it will kill innocent and guilty alike."

"I don't understand." All the weariness and fear and curiosity he'd felt since Craugh had come for him in Shark's Maw Cove came apart inside Juhg. "I *need* to understand."

"I would not kill you if I didn't have to," Sokadir said. "But I will if I must. You need to go from these woods. I won't make the mistake of helping you again."

Unconsciously, Raisho stepped in front of Juhg.

Without another word, Sokadir turned and leaped, vanishing into the forest with hardly a rippling leaf in his wake. The owl glided beside the elven warrior while the bear lumbered along beneath.

"I don't understand," Kimaru said in a child's voice. "Sokadir has never harmed an innocent."

" 'E saved us this night," Raisho said. "Doesn't make sense, 'im threatin' us like that."

"Didn't you feel the pain in him?" Yurial asked.

"I did," Juhg said. "A thousand years of it." But was it pain from what had happened, or guilt over what he'd done?

A day later, on a foggy morning that held a cloud layer close to the land, Kimaru brought Juhg and his companions to the Crocodile's Throat. They stood high on the hillside of a low valley and stared at the water coming through a cave mouth and spilling down into one of the tributaries to the Steadfast River.

"There." Kimaru pointed at the cave mouth on the cliff face. "That's the Crocodile's Throat."

Rushing white water poured through the tunnel and dropped to the wide bowl of the river below. The water look cool and deep, then narrowed again as it found its way to the Steadfast River. Crocodiles lay in the mud along the riverbank.

As Juhg watched, a gull dipped down to the river's surface for a fish and became prey instead as an alligator opened its jaws wide, surfaced and snapped the bird from the air in a flurry of feathers.

From the hill where he stood, Juhg could just see the Never-Know Road going over another hill in the distance. "Where is Jaramak's Aerie?" he asked.

"Not far from here," Kimaru answered. Over the past day and a half, the young elf had been quiet and kept mostly to himself. Sokadir's reaction to them that night had weighed on him heavily. Juhg guessed that only Kimaru's curiosity and need to see what it was that Sokadir feared had brought him this far.

Jaramak's Aerie was a small tree house less than a hundred yards from the Crocodile's Throat. Age had weathered the wood, but greenery still wrapped it. If Kimaru hadn't pointed it out for them, Juhg doubted they would have found it.

"Does anyone live here?" Juhg asked.

"Not in a long time," Kimaru answered. "Jaramak was a lookout for the Laceleaves sprawl."

"What 'appened to 'im?" Raisho asked.

"He died," Kimaru said, as if that were strange. "I knew him for a time. It's strange to think that he's no longer there."

"Does anyone come 'ere?"

"It's a place of the dead," Kimaru answered. "Jaramak died in that place. No one will go there."

The dead were anathema to elves. With their long lives, they didn't like to be reminded of what awaited them in the end. When elves died, they were given back to the air, placed in baskets and tied high in trees so their bodies could waste away out of sight.

"I've been told," Kimaru said in a quiet voice, "that people can still hear Jaramak speaking inside that house."

For a moment, Juhg looked up at the house, then he walked to the tree.

"What are you doing?" Kimaru asked.

"I'm going inside."

"Why?"

"Because I was told to go to the Crocodile's Mouth inside Jaramak's Aerie."

"The Crocodile's Mouth is back the way we came. You saw it for yourself."

"I know. But I have to see. There was a reason the message was worded like that."

Kimaru took a step back. "You could be cursed."

"I don't think I will be," Juhg replied. He couldn't argue with the years that had taught the elves to fear death. He found handholds and footholds, and climbed forty feet till he reached the dwelling. Yurial followed at his heels, trailed by Raisho.

Juhg paused at the door, touched the handle, and found it wasn't locked. He opened the door, walked in and looked at the shadowed recesses.

The tree house consisted only of four rooms in a two-story stack. The living room and the kitchen were on the bottom, and two bedchambers were on top. All of the furniture remained, presumably the way it had been since the day Jaramak passed away.

The elven warder had lived simply. Everything was neat and orderly, although covered with dust. Empty bird nests occupied shelves that contained tiny carvings. Evidently Jaramak had enjoyed whittling, judging from the tiny wooden figurines.

One of those figurines was a miniature crocodile. On impulse, Juhg picked the crocodile up and turned to the window to allow light into its mouth. A bird, nesting in the curtain above the window, suddenly exploded into motion, flew around the room, and out the window.

Juhg ducked back and his heart trip-hammered. He took a deep breath and forced himself to relax. Beside him, Raisho had his cutlass half drawn.

"Mayhap we're all a little nervous," Raisho growled in embarrassment.

"This," Yurial said grimly, "is an appropriate time to be nervous."

It wasn't just the thought of being in a dead elf 's house, Juhg knew. It was the expectation of finding . . . something. But he was going to have to look elsewhere, for there was nothing inside the crocodile figurine. He reported his findings to the others and put the figurine back on the shelf.

In Jaramak's Aerie, he mused, remembering what Grandmagister Lamplighter had written.

"Juhg," Yurial called from the circular staircase leading to the second floor.

He went, climbing the steps, and followed her to one of the bedrooms. Vines moved inside the bedroom, shimmying and shaking under their own power for there was no wind.

A slight keening reached Juhg's ears, something he could almost understand but that stayed just beyond his reach. The almost-voice was intoxicating. Then he realized what he had overlooked.

"Jaramak's Aerie," he told the others. "It isn't just the tree house. Not with the symbiotic relationship the house and the elf that lives inside it has with the tree. Jaramak's Aerie includes the whole tree."

Quickly, Juhg descended the ladder and called Kimaru to him. "I need to talk to the tree," Juhg said.

A fearful look filled the young elf 's face. He shook his head. "It is a dead place. It knows death."

"It may know the secret I'm looking for," Juhg replied. "Please. Help me."

"It is a dead place."

"The tree isn't dead," Juhg implored. Then he reached deeper, remembering how the young elf had looked on Sokadir with hero worship. "Sokadir is a prince, yet he hasn't been among his people in a thousand years. Would you have him stay away forever? Until it's too late? Do you want him to die rootless?"

"No." Kimaru's faced tightened.

"Then help me. Can you talk to the tree?"

"I can try." Reluctantly, Kimaru approached the tree and laid his hands upon it. He sang in a soft voice, then his eyes opened in surprise. He looked at Juhg. "Come here. It wants to talk to you."

Juhg joined the young elf, taking the proffered hand. Feeling the buzzing thrill of contact almost at once, Juhg had to suppress his urge to immediately disconnect. He had a feeling of great age and a timelessness that was similar to the feeling he'd gotten when he'd handled *The Book of Time*. This was magic, Juhg knew, in its most elemental form.

"Librarian," a deep voice said inside Juhg's mind.

"Yes," Juhg responded.

"You . . . are . . . not . . . the . . . other," it announced ponderously.

"No. I'm Juhg. You knew Grandmagister Edgewick Lamplighter."

"Yesssssss." Above, the branches clacked and rustled restlessly. "He wassss . . . known . . . to . . . me. He . . . said . . . one day . . . another . . . would . . . come. He . . . left . . . a gift."

Juhg waited, the breath locked in his throat.

"There . . . isssss . . . a tessssst. A quesssssstion . . . you . . . mussssst . . . anssssswer."

"Ask."

"Name . . . the . . . three."

The three? Juhg was confused. The three what? Three was a magical number, one that was used over and over again in stories, in magic spells, and in coincidence and jokes. Then his mind cleared and he knew there could only be three names that Grandmagister Lamplighter would give to the tree. The three names of the weapons that had held at the Battle of Fell's Keep and were now in jeopardy.

"Boneslicer," Juhg said. "Seaspray. Deathwhisper." As the last name left his lips, he felt the connection with the tree grow stronger.

"Yessssss," it exclaimed. "Look . . . up."

Juhg looked up just to see a section of the tree bark split open. A rectangular shape wrapped with a cloth tie tumbled free. He knew instantly what it was. He caught the book easily, feeling the solid weight of it.

"I . . . bore . . . the fruit . . . of your . . . mastssster," the tree said. "Live . . . long. Live . . . well."

Juhg studied the book. He could tell from the look of it that it had been made in the Vault of All Known Knowledge. He'd made several reams of the paper himself while he'd been a Novice. When he opened the cover and peered at the first page, he recognized Grandmagister Lamplighter's elegant handwriting at once.

Like the other two books, this one was also written in code. Hypnotized by the words, he thanked the tree for its help, then he ascended the tree house once more, telling Raisho that they would camp there while he worked through the book.

"Returnin' to *Moonsdreamer* would be safer," Raisho said.

"The ship is three days away," Juhg called back. "And there may be goblinkin along the way." From the doorway, he peered back down at his friend. "I need to translate this as quickly as possible, Raisho. Once you learn something, once you know something, no one can take it away from you. That was one of the first lessons Grandmagister Lamplighter taught me. If we lose this book before I translate it, we may never know what we need to."

Raisho growled a curse, but agreed with obvious reluctance.

Juhg settled in at the small work table in the tree house living room. He took out the blank book he'd brought to record the translation in, and set to work, dipping his quill as his mind manipulated the coded entries. In the space of a drawn breath, he was no longer in the tree house in the Forest of Fangs and Shadows, but was once more upon the Blood-Soaked Sea with Grandmagister Lamplighter.

1

Battleground

Edgewick Lamplighter, Second Level Librarian at the Vault of All Known Knowledge, sat at the table in *One-Eyed Peggie*'s galley and wished he were somewhere else. He didn't like magic. Especially when it was a powerful spell being done right in front of him.

At the moment, the pirate ship fought the strong winds of a building storm front. She rocked back and forth between the waves, slowly cresting one, then falling headlong down another. The lanterns lighting the galley swayed and thumped the walls.

Craugh sat at the table.

The wizard's long gray-white hair fell past his shoulders and his beard rested at the bottom of his chest. His nose was a savage blade set between two green eyes that held lambent fires. A slouch hat shadowed his seamed face as he murmured the Words of Power that activated the spell he wove.

No one spoke. The waves crashing against the pirate ship's hull sounded loud.

Cap'n Farok sat at a nearby table.

Craugh focused on the two people seated at the table. Bulokk and Quarrel sat quietly, awaiting his command

"Give me your hands," Craugh bade them.

The three—dwarf, human, and wizard—held hands at the center of the table around a candle with a dancing flame.

Although he didn't like magic, Wick watched with interest.

As Craugh's droning voice died away, the candle flame turned green and sputtered. In response, a cloud of green-tinted smoke floated up and hung in the air between the three. Green embers darted inside the smoke sphere.

"Yes," Craugh said, and Wick thought the wizard sounded a little surprised at his own success.

Craugh had hoped that he could track the third weapon through the ties the descendants had to the weapons through their blood. Actually, Craugh had claimed he could do such a thing, but Wick felt certain it was only a hope.

Now, however, it was reality.

Wick sat to one side, a journal open in one hand and a stick of charcoal in the other. He'd been blocking out images of the gathering, putting them into the journal he kept for stray and random thoughts. Later it would be transferred to the journal he kept that recorded his adventures. He'd almost finished the second, and planned on dropping it with Evarch in Deldal's Mills.

Images swirled within the smoke sphere. Warriors—human, elven, and dwarven—fought with goblinkin. Swords, spears and battle-axes chopped down foes as war chariots thundered through the battlefield. Dead lay strewn in all directions.

"This is the Battle of Fell's Keep," Craugh said, with a slight frown.

"I thought you were using this spell to discover the location of Deathwhisper," Quarrel said. As always, she was frank and forward.

At her elbow, the tortoiseshell-colored cat flicked her tail lazily.

"I was," Craugh admitted. "This is . . . unexpected."

The images continued coming.

Wick turned the page and worked on a blank sheet, quickly blocking out the relative positions and capturing some of the armor details he could see. He recognized some of the standards and emblems of the great warrior houses that still existed along the Shattered Coast, but there were several others he didn't know.

"There's still a lot of emotion that's tied to those days," Cap'n Farok spoke up in his gravelly voice. "Perhaps it's that what draws ye there."

"Perhaps," Craugh replied. But he kept his eyes fixed on the smoke images.

Wick knew it was true.

"There's Captain Dulaun," Alysta said, sitting up straight now and wrapping her tail around her feet.

Automatically, Wick moved to a new page, staring into the smoke and locating the human hero at once. Wearing silver armor with a blue standard tied around his arm, Dulaun cut an impressive figure. He stood at the forefront of a ragged line of dwarves and humans with two groups of elven archers flanking them.

"It's you," Alysta whispered to Quarrel. "You're bringing this vision."

Wick sketched the figures locked in battle, then added Quarrel and the cat. He knew from experience how determined the young woman was to find her ancestor's sword. She'd posed as a mercenary in Wharf Rat's Warren.

"I don't mean to," Quarrel whispered.

One-Eyed Peggie rolled suddenly, causing everyone in the galley to grab hold of something in order to keep from being pitched about. Except for Craugh, Quarrel, and Bulokk. They stayed in place as if they'd been mounted there.

Farok glanced about uneasily. *One-Eyed Peggie* had been in the grip of the storm for hours now. When they'd seen it forming, they'd tried to outrun it, but it hadn't proven possible.

In the smoke sphere, the goblinkin warriors met Captain Dulaun and the smaller team that tried to stand their ground. Several of the humans and dwarves stumbled and seemed unsure of their footing.

"They're sick," Wick said in disbelief.

"This is the morning of the last battle," Craugh said. "After they were betrayed."

Sadness leeched onto Wick. That had been part of the story of the Battle of Fell's Keep: that someone among the defenders had deliberately made the warriors too sick to fight any longer. Some of them had actually died during the night from whatever they'd been given.

The goblinkin had rolled over most of the ones that had been left.

In the smoke, the goblinkin did that anew. Several of them dropped, victims of the unrelenting elven archery, but in the end there were too many goblinkin. Captain Dulaun went down with a pike through his chest, driven by a troll that stood head and shoulders above the goblinkin. Crimson smeared across the battered silver armor.

Wick wanted to look away but found he couldn't. He'd met Captain Dulaun, after a fashion, in the mystic frieze where his sword had been hidden and stored. He'd been young for a human, too young to die in such a manner.

But he did. The troll bore down hard on the pike and kept Dulaun pinned to the barren earth. A second troll joined the first and raised his double-bitted axe.

"No!" Quarrel cried out, taking her hands from Craugh and Bulokk's.

The smoke sphere ruptured and poured up toward the galley ceiling, dispersing entirely.

"I'm sorry," Quarrel said, tears in her eyes. "I could bear no more."

Craugh looked a little irritated. "The spell isn't working as I'd thought it would, but we mustn't give up on it. This may be the only way we have of finding out where Sokadir and Deathwhisper are."

With obvious reluctance, Quarrel extended her hands once more to the wizard and the dwarf. Craugh spoke Words again, and the candle flame once more turned green and released a steady stream of smoke that formed a sphere.

This time the image formed and showed a dwarf in thick armor. He swung a mighty battle-axe, cleaving through his foes and leaving a trail of bodies in his wake.

"Master Oskarr," Bulokk whispered.

Wick didn't think the dwarf could be anyone else.

Oskarr moved through the canyon battle, shoving through the goblinkin line to reach comrades-in-arms who were in trouble. Several times he rescued people in confrontations that looked like they would take his own life in forfeit.

Then he saw Dulaun lying at the mercy of the trolls. Though there was no sound with the sight, Wick saw Oskarr flip his blood-smeared helm mask up and shout, *Nooooooo!*

But there was no undoing what had been done that day. Dulaun was stretched dead upon the ground, and the trolls took away his sword, Seaspray.

"That was when Seaspray was lost," Alysta said. The cat somehow managed to look sad.

The sheer numbers of the goblinkin drove Oskarr back, flowing over Dulaun's corpse and concealing it from view. Then the goblinkin were in Oskarr's face, pulling down dwarves at a high cost, but pulling them down all the same.

A moment later, Oskarr grabbed the nearest standard-bearer and called for the retreat. The standard-bearer blew the horn. Reluctantly, the dwarven line collapsed and fell back.

"He ran," one of the dwarven pirates muttered.

Angrily, Bulokk looked over his shoulder for the offender. "He didn't run," the dwarf growled, "an' I'll break the head of anyone that says he did."

"Not on me ship," Cap'n Farok said. "I'll decide any head-breakin' that needs to be done." He glared around the packed galley. "Anyone tries something like that, I'll toss him in the brig, an' think about puttin' him out at the next desert island we come across."

"The world," Craugh said, "could always use a few more toads." He added his glare to the captain's.

"What ye're lookin' at there," Cap'n Farok said, "is war. Most of ye've been blooded somewhere, whether at sea fightin' true pirates or goblinkin, or in a tavern brawl." He nodded toward the images trapped in the smoke sphere. "But that there's war. No rules. No give an' take. Only survivors an' them that died. Ain't none of ye got any rights judgin' a single man there for what he done—unless ye were there, too."

The crew looked shame-faced and offered apologies.

"Master Oskarr done only what he could," Cap'n Farok said. "Comes a time when a warrior has done all he can for the cause an' his country, an' it's time to pack it in so he can fight again another day." He ran his trembling hand through his beard. "Master Oskarr did himself proud, he did. After the Battle of Fell's Keep, he returned to the Cinder Clouds Islands an' made the best armor a warrior could hope for."

"Until Lord Kharrion tracked him down there an' killed him there," Zeddar, *One-Eyed Peggie*'s principal lookout, said.

The battle continued, and even though he knew he was seeing something that no one alive today—save one!—had seen, Wick wished that it would end.

This time it was Craugh who took his hands away. He frowned. "Something's wrong. I can use the spell to tie our vision to the Battle of Fell's Keep, but I can't locate Deathwhisper."

"Perhaps it's because you don't have one of Sokadir's descendants," Alysta said.

Craugh appeared to consider that. Then he looked at Wick. "Join us," the wizard said.

"Me?" Wick didn't like the idea of being that close to a magical spell. Although he'd never seen one of Craugh's spells backfire, he knew that spells sometimes did go awry.

"Of all of us," Craugh said, "you are the most curious to know the end of the story, and what has happened to Sokadir and Deathwhisper. And you've touched Boneslicer and Seaspray."

Wick looked around desperately. "Not me." He shrugged it off. *Haven't I already gotten involved enough in this?* He really didn't want to be drawn into the center any further. He was quite content working from the outside from here on out and watching events unfold, thank you. "I'm not curious. Not at all."

Craugh frowned. "Get over here."

"No thank you." Wick smiled to show that he meant no offense. Being rude was never a good idea. Being rude to a wizard was just foolish.

"As a dweller or as a toad," Craugh threatened, "with warts or without, you'll serve for this spell."

"In that case," Wick said. With a true feeling of dread, he closed his journal and put away his inks, charcoal, and quills.

"Would you hurry up?" Craugh snapped.

Wick jumped and quickly finished.

"Holding this much power open this long is taxing." Craugh gestured to the table.

Wishing he'd stayed in his room and chiding himself for his curiosity, Wick sat on the bench bolted to the floor. He kept his hands in his lap.

"Your hands," Craugh said in exasperation.

Fearfully, Wick brought up his hands. They were his most prized possessions. Without them, his whole life would change. Reading books wouldn't be the same (he could use his nose to turn pages, he supposed, except on days when he had a cold). Writing would be a lot harder (though he'd read that some authors and artists who'd suffered physical disabilities had learned how to use their feet). And the privy—well, he honestly couldn't see how that could be done at all!

"Wick."

Recognizing the level of frustration in Craugh's voice as dangerous, Wick met the wizard's glare. "Yes?"

"Are you quite through wool-gathering?"

"Actually," Wick said, "I was just thinking. Maybe you can't do this even with my help—"

"I can," Craugh interrupted.

"—and since doing this spell is taxing and everything—"

"Give me your hands."

"—maybe we could just try doing this another time. I mean, maybe the storm, the atmospheric conditions, aren't good for—"

"*Give me your hands! Now!*"

Shaken to his core, remembering how Craugh had once vaporized a whole building just to get someone's attention, Wick handed his hands over. Craugh put him between Quarrel and Bulokk. Then the process was repeated, this time with more favorable results.

2

Monster!

A tingling sensation spread through Wick as the candle flame sputtered again. Smoke formed into a sphere that filled with an image. This time the focus was on an elven warder who fought with a mystic golden bow that fired ruby arrows that formed in his fingers every time he drew back the string. The loosed shafts plunged among the goblinkin, blasting holes through their ranks.

Tears slid down the elf 's face. He stood above the bodies of two other elven men. Both of them favored him in their looks. Wick knew that many would have thought that just because they were elven, but the little Librarian had drawn enough faces that he easily distinguished one elf from another.

"Sokadir," someone behind Wick whispered.

Another elf, this one who also favored the elven champion, though not nearly so much, caught Sokadir by the shoulder and pulled at him. Sokadir turned on the other for a moment, pointing one of the ruby arrows at him. Then he whirled again and fired the arrow into the heart of a lumbering jallackdross, one of the huge war beasts Lord Kharrion had brought to the battle.

The war beast disappeared in a blaze of fire. In the next moment, Sokadir gave the two elves on the ground a last look, then fled before the goblinkin army. The defenders were now in full rout.

"That was then," Craugh said. "We need to know where Sokadir is now."

Wick stared after the retreating elf. Curiosity rose high and strong inside Wick. *Who were the two men at Sokadir's feet?* So many died that day, that final day of the Battle of Fell's Keep, that it didn't make any sense. And Sokadir was a trained warrior; he knew that losses on a battlefield were inevitable.

"Think about Sokadir," Craugh commanded. "Where is he now?"

Wick considered the question. Oskarr had returned to the Cinder Clouds Islands and had begun smithing armor despite the rumors that persisted that he had been the one to betray the Unity defenders. Dulaun had died there on the battlefield, his sword lost and his body never seen again.

But Sokadir—

Wick thought about the elven warder. Sokadir had been from Laceleaves Glen. He'd been a prince there. Had he returned there after Lord Kharrion's defeat? Had he even made it back from the Painted Canyon? Wick didn't know. He wished he'd been at the Vault of All Known Knowledge. There might have been some mention of him in the journals and memoirs that had come out of the Cataclysm.

He knew where at least three histories on Sokadir were, and six books on Laceleaves Glen.

Would he have returned home? Sokadir was an elf. Nowhere else made sense. Most of them died within only a few short miles of where they were birthed. Wick thought of Sokadir going home to get healthy again. It was the only logical thing for the elven warrior to do.

Abruptly, the smoky sphere grew agitated. The clouds of smoke oozed and flowed into each other, then just as quickly, an image formed. An elf hunkered on the branch of a tree. He was lean and handsome, and his profile striking. A large brown bear lumbered under the tree branch, and an owl glided soundlessly to the branch over the elven warrior's head. The forest around him was tall and straight, a shipbuilder's dream.

"Sokadir," Wick breathed.

"Where is he?" Craugh asked.

Wick studied the forest. In the corner, he caught a blue flash of a stream or river. A moment more and he thought he had it. He focused on the mountain range in the distance, recognizing the Broken Forge Mountains from the time he'd gone there the first time he'd been shanghaied. The area shown him wasn't far from where they'd encountered Shengharck the dragon. "This has to be Laceleaves Glen."

"In the Forest of Fangs and Shadows?"

"Yes. As I recall, Sokadir was from Laceleaves Glen." There were other elven communities in the Forest of Fangs and Shadows, of course, but Sokadir was from the Laceleaves sprawl, so it was reasonable to assume he was there. "He was a prince there or something. He took several warriors from there with him when he traveled to the Battle of Fell's Keep."

"He was a prince," Craugh agreed. "Upon his return from the Battle of Fell's Keep, he withdrew from the fight and stepped down as prince of his people."

"Why?"

"He lost two sons in the Painted Canyon when the goblinkin overran the defenders. Most assume it was because he was grieving. As I understand it, he's stayed aloof from his people ever since."

"Rootless," Wick said, and the word sounded harsh and cruel in his ears. *And I'm not even an elf.* He watched the elven warrior for a moment as he stood in repose. Without warning, Sokadir turned to Wick, lifting the bow into the air and taking aim.

"Who are you?" the elven warder demanded, gazing at him with his purple eyes.

Watching him, Wick saw Sokadir's lips move, but he also heard the man, speaking like he was in the galley next to him.

"What are you doing spying on me?" Sokadir demanded.

"I'm not spying," Wick answered. With all the accusations he faced from Frollo, he'd learned to first deny all wrongdoing.

Rage mottled the porcelain skin and tightened the purple eyes. Quick as a striking snake, Sokadir released the string without firing the arrow and reached for Wick through the smoke sphere.

Wick was hypnotized by the action (he still couldn't believe the elven warder could somehow see him) and tried to dodge away too late. Sokadir's hand extended past the smoke sphere and caught the front of Wick's shirt.

Yelping in surprise, Wick found himself dragged from his seat. He caught Sokadir's wrist and tried to pull the elf 's hand from his clothing. But it was to no avail. The elven warder had a death grip on him. Wick was lifted bodily from his seat and hauled toward the smoke sphere.

Craugh barked a single word. The sphere lost its shape and floated up to the ceiling. Sokadir vanished and Wick dropped back into his seat.

"What happened?" Bulokk asked.

"Didn't you see that?" Wick asked, adjusting his shirt.

"What?" Quarrel gazed at him intently. "All we saw was you rising from your seat and sliding into the smoke."

Wick looked at Craugh.

"I didn't see anything," the wizard said.

"It was Sokadir," Wick exclaimed. "He saw me. He *grabbed* me!"

"Impossible." Craugh frowned.

"I didn't yank myself off that bench."

"No," the wizard admitted, "you didn't." He rubbed his long nose with his forefinger. "It only means that Sokadir has his magical defenses in place." He nodded to himself. "And he's stronger in his powers than I'd believed."

"He doesn't want anyone to bother him," Wick said. "I understood that well enough."

"Unfortunately, Sokadir doesn't have a choice in that matter. If we don't get to him first, Ryman Bey and Gujhar will."

"We also need to get our ancestors' weapons back from them," Bulokk added.

That was another part of the puzzle. They still didn't know why Gujhar's employer wanted the three mystic weapons the champions had used at the Battle of Fell's Keep.

One-Eyed Peggie staggered sideways without warning, heeling over hard to starboard. The candle tipped over and would have gone sliding across the table, but Wick's quick reflexes snatched it from the air. Pots and pans hanging from the galley hooks and in cupboards set off a ferocious racket.

"By the Old Ones," Cap'n Farok exploded, shoving himself to his feet with the aid of his crutch, "what was *that*?"

No one had an answer.

A moment later, the pirate ship heeled over again, this time to port. Timbers cracked somewhere below. *One-Eyed Peggie* righted herself with difficulty, knocked off balance by the blows and now struggling between the troughs of the storm-tossed waters.

A burst of crimson, blue, green, and yellow feathers burst into the room. Critter flew into the room screaming at the top of his voice, *"Cap'n Farok! Cap'n Farok!"*

"I'm here, blast ye," Cap'n Farok replied. "Right here in front of yer eye, I am."

Dropping to a table, Critter stood with his wings spread out around him for balance. "Oh," the rhowdor said. "There ye are. By my lights, ye can be hard to find when ye're not in yer cabin."

Another impact struck *One-Eyed Peggie* and heeled her hard over to port. Critter slid across the table, unable to dig his claws into the wood, and flapped his wings in an effort to recover, beating Quarrel and Bulokk till they covered up. He squawked fearfully.

"What is happenin' to me ship?" Cap'n Farok bellowed.

"We're under attack, Cap'n," Critter said.

"By who?"

"The monster, Cap'n. It's found us again."

Although the Blood-Soaked Sea was filled with monsters, only one of them actively hunted *One-Eyed Peggie*.

At Cap'n Farok's orders, the crew ran up the stairwell, then he hobbled up himself. Wick trailed after, aiding the old sea captain when he could, which wasn't something Cap'n Farok would often allow anyone to do. But he had a soft spot for Wick.

Another impact shook *One-Eyed Peggie*, battering them up against the walls. Cap'n Farok lost his footing and would have gone down except for the aid Wick gave him. The old captain took a moment to gather himself, then once more pressed onward.

"Gettin' old an' feeble isn't good, Librarian Lamplighter," Cap'n Farok said. "No one should have to endure such a hardship."

"It's the price we pay for wisdom," Wick replied, holding onto the old dwarf's elbow. Personally, Wick looked forward to his elderly years as a Librarian. A *First* Level Librarian, of course, so much more of his time was his to command.

Water slopped onto the main deck when Wick stepped outside with Cap'n Farok. The storm had made the night darker, though that was alleviated from time to time by the whip-crack of lightning. Thunder exploded overhead, sounding as if it were right on top of them. The ship rode awkwardly in the sea, tipping restively as she was caught in crosswinds and waddled through the troughs. Canvas cracked overhead, and Wick knew the sheets strained at the rigging.

"Where away, Zeddar?" Hallekk cried from the stern castle near the ship's wheel.

"Off to port now. Two points." Zeddar was aloft in the crow's nest. He hung on for dear life, swinging wildly from side to side as the ship plunged over another tall wave.

Wick stared through the darkness, searching for the monster. He'd seen it before, but it was always incredible to witness. From *One-Eyed Peggie*'s present descent down the other side of the wave, it looked like they were sailing straight to the bottom, that the incoming wave would swamp them and send them to the depths below.

The crew played lanterns over the black sea, searching for the creature.

Bulokk and the Cinder Clouds dwarves came on deck, but Hallekk bawled orders at them to stay out of the way. With only a little show of resentment at being ordered about, Bulokk and his warriors lined the stern cabin, holding their ground as best as they could.

Quarrel stood only a few feet away from Wick and held Alysta in her arms. The cat had her head flattened and kept twitching her ears against the rain.

Then Wick saw the monster as it swam through the sea and came at them at amazing speed. Although *One-Eyed Peggie* was a large ship, capable of carrying tons of cargo, the monster dwarfed her, being more than twice her size in length. The creature resembled a whale at first glance, but it possessed a horny carapace on its head and back that protected it from attacks from above. Six twenty-foot tentaclelike legs equipped it for grappling with prey. On a few occasions, the creature had managed to grab hold of longboats with hapless pirates and take most or all of them to the bottom of the sea.

"Brace yerselves!" Zeddar cried in warning. "It's comin' in again!"

Cap'n Farok grabbed hold of the nearest railing. Wick did the same. He watched in fear-filled fascination as the creature cut through the sea so fast it sprayed a steady stream of water into the air, as if it were slicing through a layer of the ocean and peeling it back.

The huge head was visible for just a moment above the waterline. The jaws were large enough to open wide enough to swallow half a twenty-foot longboat in a single gulp. The hard ridges of bone had proven a number of times that they could crunch through wood. Oval in shape, the creature's head had whiskery projections that stuck out in all directions. In daylight they were deeply purple, fitting well the wart-covered wattles of purple and black skin that sheathed the onyx-colored head when it withdrew it to safety. The empty eye socket remained a mass of pestilence and had never healed. Wick could only imagine the pain that must have blazed through the creature with its constant immersion in salt water.

Then the creature was once more upon the pirate ship, slamming into it at full speed.

3

"A Lie Will Get You Killed"

The creature struck *One-Eyed Peggie* with a resounding boom that temporarily deafened Wick as he hung onto the railing. Cap'n Farok shuddered and went down, landing asprawl and hanging onto the railing with one arm while the other held tight to his crutch.

Despite his tight hold, Wick lost his grip and started to slide away. A massive wave of water, created by the creature's attack, rained down on the deck. For a moment Wick thought he was going to drown, then he realized he was sliding across the deck, heading for the starboard side. Caught at the crest of a wave, *One-Eyed Peggie* twisted violently so that only swirling black water was on the starboard side.

Wick knew that if he slid through the railing on that side he'd be lost for good. Then something hard looped just under his chin and caught him by the throat. Instinctively, he reached up and caught hold of it, recognizing by touch that it was Cap'n Farok's crutch.

"Hold tight there, lad!" Cap'n Farok commanded. "I ain't a-gonna lose ye!"

Scrambling, digging his feet against the deck in an effort to find purchase, Wick looked up in disbelief and saw that the old dwarven captain was holding onto the railing with one hand and managing to keep them both safe. *That's not strength*, the little Librarian realized grimly. *That's stubbornness!*

A moment later, the pirate ship righted herself. Water swirled across her deck and washed over the side.

Wick pushed himself up and crossed over to Cap'n Farok.

He helped the old dwarf to his feet. "Thank you," Wick said. "I would have been washed over the side."

"I couldn't let ye go," Cap'n Farok said with a grin. "We ain't written me memoirs yet. I still have a lot of stories to tell ye." He gave Wick a wink.

"Harpooners!" Hallekk bellowed from the stern castle. "Stand ready!"

Two dozen pirates grabbed long harpoons from the hold and got ready on deck. As he helped Cap'n Farok up onto the stern castle deck, Wick still felt immensely frightened. The day would come, he knew, when the creature or *One-Eyed Peggie* would destroy one or the other. When that day came, he didn't know which would lose, but he was afraid the ship was more fragile than the creature's rock-hard carapace.

Wind whipped across the deck, making the salt spray smack into them more vigorously. Wick squinted against it and stood beside Cap'n Farok and Hallekk.

The ship's crew stood ranked with their harpoons.

"Give it a taste of sharp steel," Hallekk growled. "See if it likes it any more than last time it found us."

Green lightning gathered at *One-Eyed Peggie*'s prow. Staring through the spray and the rigging, Wick saw Craugh standing there. Green embers whirled dizzyingly around the wizard. In his hand, his gnarled staff glowed lambent emerald.

"Where's the beastie, Zeddar?" Hallekk demanded.

"Ahead!" Zeddar yelled back down from the crow's nest. "Dead ahead!"

Staring forward, Wick spotted the creature once more cutting through the water on a collision course with the pirate ship.

"Hard to port!" Hallekk ordered. "Hard to port!"

Behind them, the helmsman fought the big ship's wheel, cutting *One-Eyed Peggie*'s direction to port. Rigging creaked as the sails caught full hold of the wind and yanked at the masts. The crew shifted over to starboard to confront the creature as it shot past.

But the creature altered course as well, resuming its bearing on the ship.

"Brace yerselves!" Zeddar called from above.

Curses ran the length of the ship.

This time the creature came up out of the water. Four of its tentacles reached for *One-Eyed Peggie*'s prow. Craugh struck in that moment, unleashing a wall of lightning that hammered the creature. The stench of ozone filled the air and Wick went deaf with the sound of the *boom*!

Incredibly, the creature lifted from the water, almost totally emerging. *One-Eyed Peggie* sailed within mere feet of it but was never touched as the tentacles wildly waved. Most of the dwarven pirates were too stunned to react, entranced by what they had just witnessed, but a few launched their harpoons. Even fewer struck the creature.

"Is it dead?" Cap'n Farok asked, whipping his head around as they passed the creature.

Drawn by the need to see what had happened, Wick abandoned his position at the railing even though the ship's deck still jerked and shifted as the helmsman fought to find a proper course for her. At the stern railing, he peered out at the sea. The creature floated limply on the water, but it still moved its tentacles.

"It's alive!" Zeddar yelled from aloft. "It's still alive!"

But at least it's not giving chase anymore. Wick watched as the creature slowly sank beneath the waves. Before it disappeared, though, the pirate ship crested a wave and started down the other side, losing sight of the creature.

Cap'n Farok took control of the ship, issuing orders that calmed the crew while Hallekk went below to assess the damage. Wick went forward to join Craugh, who was staring out to sea. For a time, the little Librarian looked out at the rolling waves, but couldn't see anything that would interest the wizard so intently.

"What's wrong?" Wick asked.

At first the wizard didn't seem inclined to answer. Then he took a deep breath and let it out just as Wick was prepared to walk away. "That creature found us," Craugh said.

"It constantly searches for this ship," Wick replied. "That's always been true."

Craugh adjusted his slouch hat. His skin held pallor to it that Wick had seldom seen. Then he remembered that the wizard had been weaving spells for hours. Now there'd been a huge expenditure while he'd worked to save the ship. Wick knew from experience with Craugh that the wizard had a large physical debt to repay from using his power.

"It found us through magic," Craugh said. "Not magic of its own."

That thought chilled Wick. "You're saying someone sent it? After us?"

Craugh nodded, but held up a hand to quiet Wick. "The others don't need to know this. And perhaps I'm wrong."

Wick doubted that. Craugh was rarely wrong when it came to magical problems.

"Who would send it?" Wick asked. "Who would even know to send it?" Not even the people of Greydawn Moors knew about the monster and the eye. It was a story the crew of *One-Eyed Peggie* kept quiet because getting dwarven pirates was difficult enough without adding the fact they'd be permanently cursed by a vengeful monster after they signed on.

"I don't know. But I felt the magic that lured the creature here."

Wick considered that. "We still don't know who Gujhar is working for."

"No, we don't. That would help. But there's a simpler reason for this."

"What?"

Craugh looked at Wick. Fatigue ate into the wizard's features. His green-eyed gaze didn't blaze quite so forcefully. "The creature is an animal. It's not inconceivable that an elven warder charmed it and told it where to go. The magic that was used was simple, but very powerful. Primeval. Like that used by elven warders."

The thought took Wick's breath away. "That's not possible."

"It's not?" Craugh grinned mirthlessly. "Not all elven warders use their lore to work with natural animals of the lands, the skies, or the waters. Some of them use their gifts to build relationships with monsters."

Wick knew that was true. Selmanick Thostos had written several books on the subject of elven warders who learned to tame monsters to further their own goals.

"Who do you think sent the creature?" Wick asked.

"An elven warder," Craugh answered. "A very powerful elven warder."

Wick understood then. "You think Sokadir sent the creature after us."

"Possibly." Craugh grinned coldly again. "You must admit, after your confrontation with him, that Sokadir isn't predisposed to someone poking around after him."

Self-consciously, Wick touched his shirt collar. "No." He swallowed, finding himself a little dry-throated as he looked out at the sea. "But that doesn't have to be the answer."

"Then find me another," Craugh snapped. "Right now I'm second-guessing myself enough without having someone do it for me."

"I can try," Wick said, marshaling his courage. For the last few days, since they'd quit Wharf Rat's Warren and sailed south, he'd had his present predicament on his mind. "But to do that, we need to return to the Vault of All Known Knowledge."

"Out of the question," Craugh responded immediately, shaking his head. "We've lost too much time as it is. All we know is that our enemies are headed south and that they're after Sokadir."

Craugh had also managed to put a spell on Gujhar's ship, *Wraith*, and was presently able to track them.

"Sokadir is in the Forest of Fangs and Shadows," Wick pointed out. "He's not going to be easy to find. He's an elf on his home territory, and he's powerful." He thought for a moment and used Craugh's own thinking against him. "If he's powerful enough to send that creature after us within minutes—"

"He was just lucky it was in the area," Craugh snarled. "With the creature's interest in this ship already, sending it here was no problem."

"Within *minutes*?" Wick let his doubt sound in his voice.

"As I said, it was merely good fortune on Sokadir's part."

The wind blew around them for a few moments. Wick got the distinct impression that Craugh didn't try to walk back to belowdecks because he didn't want anyone to see him fall on his face.

Hallekk came up during that time and informed Cap'n Farok that there were a couple leaks down in the cargo hold, but that they weren't immediately dangerous. He had crews working to patch them.

"When you turned up in Greydawn Moors those weeks ago," Wick said, trying to pick his words carefully, "you didn't show up by accident."

Craugh didn't say anything.

"You planned to be there," Wick said, "and you planned to get me to go looking for the three magical weapons that were at the Battle of Fell's Keep. A dweller wouldn't be noticed the way a wizard would. Maybe—" He took a deep breath, remembering how worn and haggard Craugh had looked. "—maybe you'd already been found out searching for them."

Craugh kept his silence, but his frown was deeper.

Wick went on even though he knew he would have been far better off being paralyzed with fear. "You said that you were concerned because what happened at that battle—that who betrayed whom—was part of what is keeping humans, elves, and dwarves from uniting once more against the growing goblinkin hordes. I believed you."

Craugh regarded Wick with a glare of green-eyed steel. "Don't presume to lecture me overmuch, Librarian."

"You lied to me," Wick said, but he kept the anger out of his voice.

Although he maintained his silence, Craugh's staff suddenly became a beehive of buzzing green embers that circled it.

"Lying appears to be one of your greatest natural talents, Craugh," Wick said quietly. "I've never noticed that in you quite so much before." He took a deep breath, surprised that he hadn't already been consigned to an existence as a toad. Or thrown overboard. "You lie to others about anything you wish to, at any given time you choose to."

"You're daring far, far too much," Craugh whispered in a cold, deadly voice.

Shut up! Shut up! Wick screamed at himself inside his head. *Stop now and maybe he won't do anything to you that will leave scars!*

But he couldn't shut up and he knew it. What he had to say was too important. He'd seen how hard Bulokk and Quarrel had tried to get back their ancestors' weapons, how much they'd been willing to risk. The Old Ones knew he was no hero, he was just a dweller, a Second Level Librarian with grand designs on one day becoming a First Level Librarian.

"You can lie to anybody you want to, Craugh," Wick said in a quavering voice.

"I could strike you down where you stand," Craugh threatened. The glowing green embers whirled around him now like fireflies.

The power he was giving off made Wick's hair stand on end.

"I could *blind* you," Craugh went on. "You would never be able to read again, never be able to write."

There are books for the blind, Wick told himself, shoring up his courage. *You already know how to read them.* He made himself go on.

"You can lie to anyone you want to," Wick said again. "I don't think you can help yourself. It's not forgivable, but it's understandable. Knowing you."

Craugh gestured.

Helplessly, Wick floated up from the ship's deck. Several of the pirates noticed what was going on. One of them was sent to get Hallekk and Cap'n Farok. The others drew back. Whatever the wizard chose to do, there was no stopping him.

"But don't lie to yourself, Craugh," Wick made himself finish. "Don't you dare lie to yourself or even presume that you can. That would be the most dangerous thing of all. Not just for you, but for all of us. A lie will get you killed. It will get *us* killed. We need to know more about what happened at the Battle of Fell's Keep before we go any further. You know that's true."

Green embers suddenly blazed from Craugh's eyes.

Wick closed his eyes involuntarily, feeling certain that he'd never open them again.

"Craugh." The voice belonged to Cap'n Farok.

Wick was suspended a moment longer, then he dropped to the deck. He let himself go limp (or maybe it was that he was so close to passing out that he couldn't physically move!) and remained lying on the deck as it rose and fell. *I'm alive! And I'm still me!*

"Is there a problem here?" Cap'n Farok asked.

Craugh gazed down at Wick. Slowly, the embers stopped blazing from his eyes and they were just eyes again. "No," the wizard replied. "No problem."

Wick wondered if he had the physical ability to cringe. He thought cringing might be a good move under the circumstances. Actually, maybe it was a little late for cringing.

"Well then," Cap'n Farok said, and cleared his throat.

"There's a course change," Craugh said in a curious, detached tone.

"Aye," the dwarven captain replied.

Wick continued lying on the deck. None of the crew, not even Hallekk, came to help him to his feet.

"Make for Greydawn Moors," Craugh said. He turned to go, leaning heavily on his staff. "I'll be in my cabin. Make certain I'm not disturbed."

"Aye."

Wick thought that was unnecessary. After what they'd just seen, no one on the ship would dare bother the wizard. He lay there for a while longer, till he could no longer hear Craugh's staff thumping against the deck, or feel the vibrations.

4

Innocence

"Are ye fit then, Librarian Lamplighter?"

Wick held up a hand against the light that invaded the darkness of his cabin. He recognized Cap'n Farok's voice. "I'm fine," he replied, wishing that he hadn't been bothered. The last few hours had been very confusing. After the confrontation with Craugh, he'd returned to his cabin and threw up several times. The room was still rank with the stench.

"I expected to catch ye readin', or maybe writin' in them journals ye keep." Cap'n Farok lumbered into the cabin and hung the lantern on the wall. He adjusted the wick, making the light brighter till it filled the room. He grimaced and his nose twitched. "Ye need to air this room out some."

"I got sick," Wick apologized.

"Understandable. Very understandable, given what ye risked. Ain't no shame in that."

"I'm tired," Wick said, hoping the captain would take the hint and leave.

Instead, Farok limped over to the bed and sat himself. "Well, I won't keep ye long, then, but I feel there's some things that need sayin'. After what went on between you an' Craugh."

"I made a mistake," Wick said. *You mean I could have gotten us all killed or turned to toads. I know that.* "It won't happen again." Pain swelled at the back of his throat.

"Eh? An' what mistake was that?" Cap'n Farok put both hands on his crutch and waited patiently.

Feeling strange lying down when the dwarven captain was sitting, Wick levered himself up. "I told Craugh he was wrong."

"Ye did, did ye?"

"Yes." Wick sighed. "That has to be one of the stupidest things I've ever done."

"But was he wrong?"

Wick looked at Cap'n Farok suspiciously. *Is this some kind of trick? Did Craugh send you down here to terrify me further? Because I know he's not going to just drop this. He'll drop me first. Probably over the side.*

"We need more information if we're to pursue Sokadir," Wick said, deciding not to make it an issue of right and wrong. "I told him we needed to go back to the Vault of All Known Knowledge and find out what we could."

Cap'n Farok scratched his chin. "Aye, I think that's a good plan."

"Well, don't mention how you feel to Craugh. You'll probably end up turned into a toad."

The dwarven captain laughed at that. "Wouldn't that be somethin'? Me a toad? An' Hallekk an' them other brutes a-snappin' to whenever I croaked the orders?"

The image the possibility summoned *was* funny. Before he knew it, even though he truly didn't want to, Wick was laughing at the thought. Cap'n Farok joined in, and both of them were belly-laughing like a couple of fools.

"Them sails is a-luffin'!" Cap'n Farok said. Then added, "*Cro-oak!* Batten them hatches! *Cro-oak!*"

"Furl them sails or I'll have the hides from yer backs, I will!" Wick said in his best Cap'n Farok imitation, which he'd been told by several of the crew members was actually pretty good. *"Cro-oak!"*

"Wait just a minute now," Cap'n Farok said, suddenly serious. "That ain't what I sound like, now is it?"

Wick stopped laughing, suddenly realizing he might have offended yet someone else he considered a friend.

Then Cap'n Farok's face wrinkled, no longer able to stay straight. *"Cro-oak!"* he laughed, and slapped his knee.

Wick wiped the tears from his eyes. It felt good to laugh, but he knew it hadn't changed the fact that he'd angered Craugh. Gradually, both of them calmed.

"I know ye think ye're in trouble with Craugh," Cap'n Farok said.

"I'd like to keep it in its proper perspective," Wick said. "Basically, life as I know it is potentially at an end."

"I got to tell ye something, lad," Cap'n Farok said. "I'm mighty proud of ye."

Wick sat in stunned silence.

"I don't know another being alive that would confront Craugh as ye did," Cap'n Farok said.

Meaning all the ones in the past are dead? Wick wondered. *Or bouncing around on their new, plump behinds?* "Never argue with a wizard." He sighed. "I know. I've read all the books."

"Arguin' with a wizard ain't the smartest course ye could plot."

"I didn't exactly plot it."

"But we was in a storm, an' ye made the decision ye knew to be right."

"I was right?"

"Weren't ye?" Cap'n Farok searched his face. "Don't we need to know more?"

"Yes," Wick sighed. "We do. What we've discovered is confusing. And trying to beard Sokadir in his homeland is—is—"

"About as sensical as beardin' a wizard who's tired an' scared—"

" 'Scared'?" That choice of description interested Wick at once. "Craugh wasn't scared."

"Sure he is. He's been scared since we started this thing. He was scared when he went a-huntin' ye in Greydawn Moors."

Wick shook his head. "He doesn't seem scared to me." *Scary, though. Awfully, awfully scary.*

"That's 'cause ye don't know what ye're lookin' for when it comes to a man like Craugh." Cap'n Farok sighed and clawed his beard in momentary indecision. Then he stared at Wick with his rheumy eyes. "I'm gonna tell ye somethin', Librarian, that I expect never to hear again. Do ye understand me?"

Wick nodded.

"I'll have yer oath on this, I will."

"Aye," Wick said automatically. "I swear that I'll keep your confidence."

"Good." Cap'n Farok grinned, but the effort was forced. "Mayhap that way we'll both keep our skins." He paused a moment to gather his thoughts and choose his words. "Craugh's been alive an awfully long time. A thousand years. That we know of. Could be more."

Wick accepted that.

"A person don't live without makin' mistakes," Cap'n Farok went on. "*I've* made me share of 'em, too, Old Ones know. But with a thousand years to live, a thousand years to make mistakes, can ye even fathom the mistakes Craugh mighta made along the way?"

Wick couldn't, but he recognized the propensity was there. In the years that he'd known him, Wick knew that the wizard was pursued by a restlessness that he couldn't shed himself of.

"There's a pain in Craugh," Cap'n Farok went on. "Some hurt I can't ken."

"I don't see it," Wick muttered.

"Just because ye don't see it don't mean it ain't there." Cap'n Farok sighed. "Do ye remember when ye climbed up on that mast when the Embyr came?"

Wick did remember. It was something he knew he could never forget. The Embyr had been the most wondrous and wicked thing he'd ever seen.

"Where all we saw was a monster," Cap'n Farok said softly, "ye saw a little girl. One what was lost and alone. Ye climbed up that mast an' touched a part of her that saved us."

And I hurt her horribly in the process, Wick thought. He felt even worse in that moment, but he wasn't as fearful of Craugh.

"I'm tellin' ye now," Cap'n Farok said, "ye touch something in Craugh, too. Somethin' he didn't expect mayhap even existed."

"I don't know." Wick shook his head. He didn't believe it for a moment. Craugh had been on the verge of killing him or throwing him overboard only a few hours ago.

"Well then, when ye get to me years, mayhap ye'll know more an' be able to see more."

"Craugh used me. He came to Greydawn Moors to use me to try to recover those lost weapons."

"I know."

"If he'd have asked, I wouldn't have come."

"I know that, too. Ye forget, Librarian, I'm as much responsible for yer kidnappin' as he is."

Wick had forgotten. He blamed everything on Craugh.

"The wizard *did* go to Greydawn Moors lookin' for ye," Cap'n Farok said. "I went with him. He told me wasn't nobody else would do in this instance."

"I'm not a warrior. I'm not the person who needs to be doing this."

"An' yet, was it ye that recognized we need to get back to Greydawn Moors an' try to ferret out more information?"

Wick made no reply.

"Ye're the exact man for this job, Librarian Lamplighter. Wouldn't nobody else do it proper. Craugh knew that. That's why, when he figured on goin' to the Cinder Clouds Islands to recover Boneslicer, he wanted ye. Wouldn't nobody else do. Not the way he saw it. It's yer mind he wanted. Yer mind an' yer heart an' that little bit of innocence ye've managed to hang onto in spite of the worst things ye've gone through. Ye've got a child's eyes, Librarian Lamplighter. An' I 'spect ye always will."

Listening to the old dwarven captain's words, Wick didn't know if he was being complimented or not.

"It's that innocence, I think," Cap'n Farok said after a while, "that touches Craugh most. I fear he, like most of us who have grown up an' gone where we've gone in the darkest parts of our lives, has lost all his own innocence. So he borrows yers when he feels he needs strong counselin'."

"Craugh doesn't listen to me."

"He did today, didn't he? We're headed back to Greydawn Moors, ain't we?"

Wick couldn't argue with that.

"Craugh comes to ye," Cap'n Farok said, "he seeks ye out, when he seeks out the company of no one else. Ye need to remember that."

"He sought you out first," Wick objected. "You and Hallekk and the others brought Craugh to Greydawn Moors."

"Craugh wasn't seekin' us out. He wanted *One-Eyed Peggie*. He needed a ship." Cap'n Farok shrugged. "I take me some pride in the fact that Craugh trusts me an' me ship more'n he trusts any other that comes out of the Yondering Docks in Greydawn Moors."

Wick took a deep breath. "I thought he was going to kill me."

"But that's just it, lad. Craugh can't kill ye. He can't harm ye in any way. 'Cept mayhap yer feelin's now an' again." Cap'n Farok scratched his chin. "I think that's why he wants ye along, too. Ye can't help tellin' him when he's in the wrong, an' he'll listen to ye whether he wants to or not on account of who ye are."

For a long time only silence, permeated by the slap of waves against the hull, the creak of the 'yards and the rigging, and the banging Hallekk's repair crew was making below, stretched between them.

"Do you think that's really true?" Wick asked.

"Aye," Cap'n Farok responded, smiling and patting Wick's knee. "I do."

"Then maybe I can make him tell us the rest of it. Because I know he's not telling us everything he knows."

Cap'n Farok frowned a little at that. "Well now, Librarian Lamplighter, I wouldn't go pressin' yer luck now."

During the next six days while *One-Eyed Peggie* made for Greydawn Moors, Wick contented himself with his journals, transferring his notes and drawings to the coded copy he intended to leave with Evarch in Deldal's Mills.

He also added work to another journal that he kept on the ship and her crew. Occasionally, after bribing Critter to keep a weather eye (as if the one-eyed rhowdor had any choice in the matter!) peeled for Craugh, Wick worked among the crew, repairing rigging, scraping barnacles, and swabbing the decks. That was, he'd discovered, the best way to pick up stories about where they'd been and what they'd done and whom they'd met.

On several of those occasions, Quarrel, Alysta, Bulokk, and the Cloud Cinder-Islands dwarves joined Wick in the galley and talked late into the night. All of them told tales, and Wick kept notes. In exchange, he—with Cap'n Farok's guidance—told them about the Vault of All Known Knowledge and Greydawn Moors. Given everything that they had been through, none of them was truly surprised by the existence of the Library.

Craugh never put in an appearance. The wizard stayed in his room and took his meals by himself.

Despite the near-death experience (near-blinding, near-toadifying experience), Wick felt a little sorry for Craugh. He thought about going to the wizard's door and trying to talk to him. Once, Wick had almost gone to the wizard's door, but two crewmen who "happened" to be standing by Craugh's door engaged him in conversation, begging stories and songs from him. Gladdened to see that his company was desired—after fearing the reception he would get from Craugh—Wick went with them to the galley only too willingly.

On the morning of the seventh day, they reached Greydawn Moors.

Eagerness filled Wick as he stood in *One-Eyed Peggie*'s prow and strained his eyes to see through the layers of pale gray fog that continually surrounded Greydawn Moors and gave the island its name. He found he could almost see through it, maybe even enough to cry out a warning if he saw a ship in time for the pirate ship to take evasive action (which was actually Zeddar's job at the moment). Some days were better than others. This was one of the good ones. There was no rain.

One-Eyed Peggie's warning bell clanged out her presence and the sound pealed out over the Blood-Soaked Sea. There had been no further sign of the creature that hunted the pirate ship, but they had seen other monsters, none of which—thankfully—seemed interested in them.

Wick secretly hoped they were stuffed to the gills on the goblinkin pirates that sometimes plied the seas looking for merchant ships that might not be properly armed. When Cap'n Farok and his crew weren't spreading the rumors of the Blood-Soaked Sea being filled with monsters, they sank the goblinkin ships to the bottom.

Gradually, Greydawn Moors came into sight. Homesickness twisted in Wick's stomach, especially since he knew this was only to be a brief visit and he would have to set sail again, possibly never to return. That was always a sobering thought every time he shipped aboard *One-Eyed Peggie* to track down a myth or a rumor or a scrap of history that he'd turned up in his studies.

Under Cap'n Farok's guidance, they put in to one of the piers of the Yondering Docks. A few other ships sat at anchorage, most of them pirate ships unloading goods that the populace of Greydawn Moors wanted.

"Even when people have everything they need or think they want, often they want what their neighbor has. The sheer act of the neighbor wanting that thing sets up a desire in others that simply can't be explained." That was from Ardelph's *Laws of Supply and Demand: Beyond Necessity*.

It also summed up the populace of Greydawn Moors. When the Builders had magically lifted the island from the sea floor, they'd planned for everything. There was nothing the denizens of Greydawn Moors lacked. The limestone construction of the island provided for several natural wells that filtered out the sea salt, and cisterns and lakes that held fresh water. The forests in back of Greydawn Moors proper and before the Knucklebones Mountains teemed with wild game that elven warders tended to. Farmers raised still more and reaped plenty of grain for bread and livestock from the fields.

The island was, Wick had come to know, a veritable paradise. He closed his eyes and could almost smell the paper and ink of the books sitting on the shelves of the Vault of All Known Knowledge.

Several families came running to meet the ship. *One-Eyed Peggie* had been identified by the small cargo vessels ferrying goods in from the big ships that sat out from the docks. Wives, children, and friends all came to greet the pirates.

No one came to greet Wick. *Because no one knew I was gone*, Wick told himself. But he was a little surprised at his feelings of being left out as he watched the pirates climb the ladder and go among their families. Still, he knew Cap'n Farok and Hallekk wouldn't be going ashore either to be with families. Cap'n Farok had outlived his wife and two children (both of whom had died in battle against the goblinkin even before Wick had met him), and Hallekk had been orphaned as a child. Cap'n Farok was the closest thing to a father Hallekk had ever known.

"Are you going to get moving?" a cold voice asked. "Or are you going to just stand there and moon?"

Trembling a little, and feeling suddenly sick to his stomach, Wick turned and found Craugh standing there.

The wizard looked rested again, perfectly able to toadify someone, or blind someone, or blast someone to little bitty—

Craugh growled.

"I'm going," Wick responded, grabbing hold of the ladder and hauling himself up. He just hoped his weak knees didn't give way beneath him and cause him to fall on Craugh. He didn't think that would be well received. At the top of the pier, he tripped and almost fell.

Craugh looked at him oddly. "Are you all right?"

At the moment, I appear to be. Wick tried to speak, found he couldn't, and settled for nodding.

"Then we need to get going."

We? Wick blinked.

Quarrel and Bulokk both climbed to the pier behind the wizard. Bulokk's dwarven warriors stood to one side and closely watched Craugh. Wick had the distinct feeling that if Craugh had tried to harm him they would have interfered. *Or maybe that's just wishful thinking*, he told himself. *It's not like they could actually stop Craugh.*

"The Library," Craugh said. He scowled. "Don't tell me you've forgotten about it."

"N-n-nooooo," Wick said, sliding a foot out and taking a step away in case this was some kind of weird, cruel trick.

"Then let's be about it." Craugh strode past Wick toward the nearest livery that had rental wagons and horses.

Bulokk and his dwarven warriors followed. All of them gawked at the city, especially at the signs that adorned every building in Greydawn Moors. All the dweller shop owners and craftsmen advertised, and signs got bigger when two shops were in direct competition with each other. Of course, the advertising was wasted on the dwarves because they couldn't read.

Quarrel could, though. As could the cat. They went forward, too, following in Craugh's wake, which was wide because no one in Greydawn Moors who knew him wanted anything to do with him.

Alysta paused and looked back over her shoulder. Her tail twitched in irritation. "Aren't you coming?"

"Yes." Wick answered before he really thought about it. He considered what was about to take place: Craugh in the Library. When Grandmagister Ludaan had been in charge of the Vault of All Known Knowledge, Craugh's presence there had almost been a regular thing.

But not since Frollo had become Grandmagister. The two of them couldn't tolerate the sight of each other. When Craugh wanted to meet with Wick, he usually sent word to the Vault of All Known Knowledge.

Perhaps this wasn't such a good idea, Wick thought as he trudged after them.

"Are you nervous?" Quarrel asked when he'd caught up to her.

"About what?" Wick asked.

She looked at him, her blue eyes filled with bewilderment. " 'About what?' Craugh, for one. Sokadir for another. There's any number of things to be nervous about."

Wick sighed. "I know. I am."

"Well, take heart, Librarian Lamplighter."

Unbelievably, Wick's spirits soared just a little. It was the first time Quarrel had addressed him by his title.

"Cap'n Farok told us all that if there was anyone who could get to the bottom of this mess, it was you. He said that's why Craugh sent for you instead of coming himself or sending another." Quarrel looked at him. "The captain said you have a knack for puzzles, whether they're in words, mazes in lost treasure rooms, or . . . people." She clapped him on the shoulder. "After all, you found Seaspray when no one else could."

But I've been wrong about things before, too. Wick tried not to think about that. Besides, curiosity was thrumming through him. The answers had to be there somewhere.

5

Vidrenium

Wick rode in the back of the wagon as they went up the long, twisting trail to the Vault of All Known Knowledge. The Great Library's dark gray towers only stood out against the dark gray Knucklebones Mountains when a trained eye knew where to look. Nestled just above the Ogre's Fingers (it was still whispered that the Builders had made the mountains from two gigantic beings locked in combat, and that their feet anchored the island to the sea floor, though no one had ever discovered the truth of that), the structure was protected by a high wall of the same dark gray stone. Only the Ogre's Fingers held any color, and they were threaded with rust-red iron veins.

"This is so . . . beautiful." Quarrel gazed around in open astonishment. "I've never seen anything like this."

That was because she'd grown up around Wharf Rat's Warren, in the cold northlands off the Frozen Sea. Precious little had grown there that flowered or bore fruit.

"It is," Wick agreed. "I never really knew it till I left."

"If I lived here, I don't think I would ever leave."

"Not even to get your ancestor's sword?"

Some of the joy left her face, and Wick felt badly about that.

"I have to," she replied. "That sword is important to my family."

"I know," Wick said, hoping that he could truly help her find Seaspray and help Bulokk once more take possession of Boneslicer.

And find the name of the true traitor that day at the Battle of

Fell's Keep. Wick took a deep breath that made him push all of the various pressures away. Grandmagister Ludaan had taught him to whittle down a problem, to divide it into its separate components, and conquer each area of contention.

At the moment, he couldn't even consider the problem. He needed more background information. He'd been running willy-nilly across the countryside trying to follow Craugh's plans. If recovering the weapons had merely been a battle, the wizard's judgment probably would have carried the day.

But this wasn't a military strategist's problem. It was a Librarian's.

Even as he'd calmed himself during the final leg of the journey up to the Vault of All Known Knowledge, Wick discovered he faced yet another problem.

As always, dwarven guards stood post in front of the main entrance to the Library's inner courtyard. Wick recognized Varrowyn Forgeborn, their leader, instantly.

The dwarf was one of the most loyal and experienced warriors Wick had ever had the pleasure of meeting. His armor was polished and he held his battle-axe in one big hand.

"Greetings," Varrowyn said in his booming voice.

"Greetings," Craugh replied.

Varrowyn walked around the wagon filled with dwarves and Quarrel and Alysta. "Brung visitors, did ye, Second Level Librarian Lamplighter?" Strolling casually, he walked around the wagon.

"I did," Wick answered, standing. "They're all friends."

"That's good." Varrowyn smiled, showing his teeth, but even that could be construed as threatening. "We're a friendly lot here. Craugh, it's good to see that the wolves ain't pulled ye down while ye were out amongst 'em."

"Thank you, Varrowyn." Craugh sat quietly. He'd always gotten on well with the dwarves.

"I take it the Grandmagister ain't expectin' ye." Varrowyn stepped in front of the wagon again and raised his battle-axe to signal his men. Immediately they started raising the iron-bound gate, which clanked and banged against the runners as it rose.

"No," Wick replied.

"We're here on a private matter," Craugh said.

"A research project," Wick added.

"Hmmmm." Varrowyn eyed Wick speculatively. "The Grandmagister's been looking for ye."

A sick pit opened up in Wick's stomach. *All I need is the Grandmagister upset with me.* He spent a large part of some of his days trying to escape Grandmagister Frollo's attentions. Frollo tended to be uncomplimentary and demanding, and he never forgot when someone made a mistake. In those respects, he wasn't much like Grandmagister Ludaan.

"Apparently he didn't know ye was with Craugh," Varrowyn went on.

"I didn't know I was going to be with Craugh," Wick replied.

"I thought as much." Varrowyn nodded. "I tracked ye to Paunsel's Tavern the last time anybody seen ye. Was told ye was in the company of Craugh and Hallekk. Figured it likely ye went with *One-Eyed Peggie* when she filled her sails that night. Told the Grandmagister that as well, but he was about ready to order out the guard to search for ye. He muttered somethin' about postin' Librarians to keep watch over Hralbomm's Wing, that ye'd be along soon enough to get another one of them books."

"I see."

"Want me to send a runner to fetch the Grandmagister an' let him know ye've returned?" Varrowyn offered.

"No," Wick said weakly. "That won't be necessary. Thank you." He slumped back into the wagon bed and resumed his seat on the bag of potatoes that he'd used as a chair. *I'm doomed. If Craugh doesn't toadify me, the Grandmagister will have me scrubbing kitchens and bathrooms. Or copying books of dwarven love songs.*

Wick guided everyone into the main building through the back door, stopping off at the kitchens long enough to raid the pantry. He took supplies to make bacon and tomato sandwiches, then loaded up Bulokk's warriors with strawberry, firepear, and pecan pies. No one in the Library went hungry. He also added some cakes and two jars of chozelak jelly, and loaves of wheat, pumpkin, and corn bread. Four jugs of razalistynberry wine finished off the provender.

Then he guided his party to one of the little-used side rooms off Hralbomm's Wing. Few Librarians visited Hralbomm's Wing because most didn't share Wick's love of the romances; and the ones who did, feared Grandmagister Frollo's scalding tongue.

While Quarrel, Alysta, and the dwarves agreed to stay in the room, Craugh insisted on accompanying Wick. That made the little Librarian nervous as he hurried through the hallways and rooms of the Vault of All Known Knowledge. Added to that, he knew he stuck out in his clothing of breeches and shirt instead of his robe. He didn't look like a proper Librarian.

Still, the Librarians recognized him.

"Hello, Second Level Librarian Lamplighter," a Novice said. He was burdened with a dozen thick books that he barely managed.

"Hello, Grental," Wick responded. As he passed the Novice, he reached out and adjusted the top book, making them all more secure. "You should really carry those books in two trips."

"I thought one would—"

"Save time?" Wick asked hurriedly. "Not if you trip and drop them and rip the binding loose. Repairing a binding—"

At that moment, Grental did misstep. The sound of torn bindings echoed in the hallway.

Sighing, not breaking stride, Wick shook his head and forced himself not to look back to see how bad the damage was. *Thank the Old Ones those were reference volumes we have several copies of.* "I heard that, Novice. I read the titles of all those books. I expect them to be repaired. I'll be checking."

"Yes, Second Level Librarian Lamplighter," the Novice replied in a dispirited voice. "Did you know that the Grandmagister was looking for you?"

"Yes, I did." Wick hurried on.

Lanterns filled with lummin juice blazed blue-white in the hallways and in the rooms. The Vault of All Known Knowledge was a hodge-podge, and most would have sworn it held no rhyme or reason in its design. Four stories existed aboveground, and others were carved into the strata beneath the Library, making a honeycomb of a large section of the Knucklebones Mountains. A river separated two halves of the underground floors. Sometimes a lower floor had to be gotten to by ascending two flights of stairs only to descend three others.

There were proper maps made of the various floors and rooms, but only the more experienced Novices were allowed to carry them around. Managing a map meant not having hands free to carry as many books as a Librarian could.

The hallways of the underground were carved through the rock but held the same arch shape as the blocks that had been laid above had created. It was darker in the lower recesses with the absence of light, and it was a lot cooler. Dressed only in a shirt and breeches, Wick found himself growing cold.

As he walked, Wick listened to Craugh's measured stride behind him. No matter that he was moving nearly at full speed, Craugh paced him easily.

"Do you know where you're going?" Craugh finally demanded.

"Yes," Wick answered.

"It doesn't seem so."

Risking a look back over his shoulder, Wick saw a trace of concern showing on the wizard's face. *Is he worried that we'll get lost down here?* It had happened in the past. Sometimes only for hours, but sometimes for days. The Library was immense. That was why new Novices were never allowed to wander on their own, and why those somewhat skilled packed their pockets with food and a small waterskin while they walked.

"I know where I'm going," Wick said.

Craugh frowned but said nothing.

Two rooms farther ahead, Wick darted through the doorway. He walked among the shelves, trailing a hand across the spines of the books.

"What is this place?" Craugh asked.

"Military biographies of the Silverleaves Glen elves," Wick answered. "Some of them were from the Laceleaves Glen area and some of the smaller sprawls located in that area." He took down a book. "This is the journal of Captain Beetalmir, who was second-in-command at the War of the Twisted Snake." He held up the tome he'd kept for himself. "This is General Koffar's journal. He commanded the opposing army from the Dewy Rose sprawl."

"Why do you want to know about these two men?"

"Not these men," Wick explained. "The war. The War of the Twisted Snake. Sokadir and Deathwhisper played a major part in the outcome of that confrontation. Beetalmir and Koffar were two of the most literate writers of the time. Ones who had an eye for detail. They'll tell us things we need to know about Sokadir."

"There have to be biographies here on Sokadir."

"There are. But you can't always trust a biography. No matter who the person, no matter who the writer, I've found nearly every biography I've read to be slanted either for or against the subject." Wick paused, organizing his thoughts. "We need to isolate facts and check them."

"Why?"

Overcome by his own curiosity, Wick forgot his fear and discomfort with Craugh. "Think about it. We contacted Sokadir—by accident, to be sure, but contacted nonetheless—and he came at me. I have to ask myself why."

"He doesn't want to be bothered."

"He knew someone was looking for him."

"*I* was looking for him. Before I gave up and came to Greydawn Moors."

Wick remembered the haunted look in the elven hero's eyes. "There's something more here. Something we don't know about." He opened the book and began reading.

Craugh stood in frozen silence for a moment, then Wick dismissed the wizard from his mind. He had a mystery to solve.

Hours later, through a hundred books and a half dozen rooms, Wick got a glimmer of what they were ultimately after.

"The weapons," he said.

Craugh looked up from the book he was currently perusing. "What about them?"

"Do you know who made them?"

"According to legend, Master Blacksmith Oskarr made his. The others I don't know about."

Wick crossed to the wizard to show him the picture he'd found. "Look."

In the picture, a dwarf was being handed a glowing rock by a merman. The dwarf stood hip-deep in the water. The merman remained in the water, but his tail was flipped up to show above the waterline.

"What's this?" Craugh asked.

"It's where the metal came from," Wick answered. "The merpeople found a glowing rock at the bottom of the sea and offered it in trade to a dwarven blacksmith in the Clanging Reefs."

" 'The Clanging Reefs'?"

"It's the merpeople's name for the Cinder Clouds Islands." Wick turned the page and showed Craugh a series of maps. "I don't have a book with me, but if I did you could see that the coastline correlates to—"

"The Rusting Sea," Craugh mused, interested now. "I see that. But what does it mean? Is this Master Oskarr?" He glanced at the script on the opposite page. "I can't read this."

"I can. It doesn't say who the dwarf is, though. But look here." Wick pointed at a symbol inscribed on the dwarven blacksmith's chest plate. The symbol showed a dwarven hammer striking an anvil and flames shooting off the blow. "Do you recognize this symbol?"

"Yes. That belongs to the Cinder Clouds Islands dwarves."

"More than that," Wick said. "It belongs to Master Oskarr's family."

Craugh peered more closely at the dwarf in the picture. "Is this Master Oskarr?"

"No. The time period is wrong. This was illustrated hundreds of years before Master Oskarr was born. There's a possibility the tale was old even before it was written down."

"Who's the dwarf in the illustration?"

Wick shook his head. "I don't know." He shifted books to one of those he'd brought from an earlier room. "Here's an entry by Naggal, one of Master Oskarr's apprentices."

"It says the book is by Master Oskarr."

"It wasn't. A lot of masters passed their writing off onto junior apprentices. They didn't have time to do the work themselves but it needed to be done. So they assigned it to someone."

"And later claimed the work as their own?"

"Technically, the work was theirs," Wick said. "The writing wasn't, of course, but they claimed the writing of manuals based on their work as well."

"Even so, what does this tell us?"

"Well, where the metal came from, for one." Wick held up the second book. "But this tells us that all three weapons—Boneslicer, Seaspray, and Deathwhisper—all came from the same source. That glowing rock you saw in the other picture. And from the same master hand as the others." He flipped through the pages and showed Master Oskarr working at his forge. " 'From the remains of the fallen star—' "

" 'Fallen star'?" Craugh repeated.

"It's a rough approximation from the mer tongue."

"All right."

" 'From the remains of the fallen star my ancestor traded the merpeople for, I made three items,' " Wick read. " 'For the first time, I didn't plan out those weapons ahead of time. The ore called to me in a way I had never known. Of course, I fashioned an axe first. I'm a dwarf, after all, and my own nature will override anything else I'm confronted with.' "

"Vidrenium," Craugh whispered.

6

"I'm Grandmagister Of This Library, And I—*Ulp*!"

ick blinked. It took a moment for the reference to vidrenium to come to him.

"It wasn't a fallen star," Craugh said, taking out his pipe. He started to strike his thumb. "It was vidrenium. Had to be." A wisp of smoke curled up from his thumb.

"No," Wick warned, knowing a fire inside the Library would be a bad thing.

"Of course it was," Craugh declared imperiously, thinking that Wick was arguing with him. As soon as the wizard's thumb caught fire, a magical rain cloud formed over his head and drenched him. He cursed.

"I tried to stop you," Wick said.

Pipe clenched between his teeth, Craugh glared up at the miniature rain cloud. As if in open defiance, the rain cloud released a half dozen tiny bolts of lightning and rumbled with quiet but energetic thunder.

"The magic wards that protect the Vault of All Known Knowledge," Wick reminded.

Almost immediately, the stone floor sucked the water from the floor with a loud gurgling and returned the floor to its dry state. Craugh, however, was left drenched, but every drop that dripped off him was blotted up by the floor.

The wizard put away his pipe, then muttered a single word. Wick felt the heat of the spell sear into him and turned his head to avoid it. When he looked back at Craugh, the wizard was dry once more.

"You mentioned vidrenium," Wick reminded him.

"I did," Craugh agreed, pursing his lips in contemplation. "You're familiar with it?"

"I know the legend," Wick said. "It was a metal created by the best magical metallurgists of the time in Dream. The purest metals and the most powerful spells."

"Yes," Craugh said.

"I thought the metal, culled from white gold and invested with enchantments and magic, was just a myth."

Craugh studied the glowing chunk of rock the dwarf and the elf exchanged in the illustration. "I'd heard they'd finally done it, though. All of them that worked on it, Dadorr, Hosfeth, Klial, and Tormak all died in the Cataclysm. Whatever they discovered will probably remain hidden for some time. They gave most of their lives to creating that metal." He paused. "I remember when Dream died, after Lord Kharrion went into the city and unleashed the goblinkin hordes to run rampant. He caused explosions throughout Dream. There was a forge, a combination of dwarven manufacture and wizard spells, where they were working with vidrenium. I was told the magic spells safeguarding it were disrupted and caused even further destruction in the city."

"It's possible during the explosions that chunks of vidrenium were thrown into the Gentlewind Sea," Wick pointed out. Then he sighed. "So much of this is guesswork. And now, with Dream involved, there is even more research to be done."

"Guesswork or not," Craugh said, "I think you're on to something."

Wick took heart in that.

"But your efforts alone aren't enough," Craugh stated.

"I'm doing the best that I can," Wick protested before he realized those very words were about to doom him.

"I know." Craugh's voice was unmistakably soft and understanding. "You must become an army, Second Level Librarian Lamplighter, and there is only one way you can do that." The wizard's robes swirled as he turned and left the room. "Come."

In disbelief, Wick watched Craugh stride through the door. Then, hands and arms filled with books, the little Librarian hurried after the wizard. Wick didn't make a sound, but inside his own mind he was screaming in terror. *Grandmagister Frollo is going to find out about this! And he's not going to care for it! I'm going to be scrubbing kitchen floors for years! I'll never be allowed to touch paper again!*

Craugh strode through the halls and passages of the Vault of All Known Knowledge. Every Librarian, from Novice to First Level, the wizard ordered them all to drop whatever they were doing and fall in behind him. He didn't say "or else." That was inferred. The Librarians did as he bade reluctantly and with no little resentment (though none of it displayed to anyone except Wick because they thought Craugh's ire was all *his* fault—which, after a fashion, Wick had to agree that it was).

By the time they reached the main chamber (Craugh did have to stop three times and ask directions of Wick, but the little Librarian was surprised that the wizard knew as much of the inner workings of the Vault of All Known Knowledge as he did), an army of Librarians marched at the wizard's heels.

"This is all your fault, Lamplighter," First Level Librarian Cottle sneered. He was a rotund dweller with bulging eyes and a sweet tooth that was legendary, which was the cause of his immense fatness. "You brought the wizard here. You know Grandmagister Frollo doesn't want him here."

"But I didn't—" Wick started to protest.

"The Grandmagister is going to be properly vexed at you," First Level Librarian Amatard grouched.

"I couldn't stop—" Wick tried to add in his own defense.

"You're going to gain intimate knowledge of the kitchen floors after this," First Level Librarian Natter promised. "If Grandmagister Frollo doesn't make you scrub, I will!"

"He's a wizard—" Wick pointed out. But he stopped because he knew it was no use. *I didn't have a* choice! His arms felt as though they were about to fall off from carrying the books the whole way. No one offered to help him with his burden.

Finally, though, they were in the main chamber. Tables and chairs and bookshelves filled the room. More Librarians were there, all of them huddled over the various projects they worked at. They looked up at once as Craugh entered the room with his army of captive Librarians.

"Your attention, Librarians," Craugh said in a booming voice.

Wick quailed and felt as though he were going to faint. *I'm not going to be relegated to permanent kitchen duty, I'm going to be exiled from the Library!*

"On your feet!" Craugh's voice bristled with command. "I've got a project worthy of the finest Librarians at the Vault of All Known Knowledge!"

Grudgingly, the Librarians came to their feet.

"This project requires a lot of research on a multitude of levels," Craugh went on. "All the necessary information will be gathered and brought back to this room."

Knowing he was the center of a lot of malicious attention (surely the most that had ever been unleashed in the Library), Wick took a quiet step back. Then another. *Eleven more*, he told himself, *and you can reach the door.*

Without looking, Craugh reached back with his staff and hooked Wick behind the neck, drawing him up in a graceless, stumbling trot.

"You all know Second Level Librarian Lamplighter, I presume," Craugh demanded.

"Yes," a few Librarians answered.

Wick knew they all knew who he was. At one time or another, nearly all of them had come to him to take advantage of his knowledge, ask where a book was, or ask how to prepare something for Grandmagister Frollo. Even the First Level Librarians, although most reluctantly, acknowledged his acumen and familiarity with the Vault of All Known Knowledge.

"I said, you all know Second Level Librarian Lamplighter!" Craugh's voice thundered through the hall, sounding louder even than Grandmagister Frollo on his most surly day.

"Yes!" The reply this time was equally thunderous.

“Good,” Craugh replied. “He will be in charge of the research efforts. You will listen to him and do as he says and we’ll all get along just fine.”

Listen to me? Wick blinked in astonishment. A whole new wave of terror blasted through him. Surely he was going to be blamed for everything that happened from this point on.

“Craugh!”

Wick recognized the voice as Grandmagister Frollo’s at once. His knees fell out from under him. Swiftly, Craugh reached out for him, caught him by his shirt collar in one hand, and somehow kept him upright as they turned to face the Grandmagister.

Frollo strode imperiously through the Library’s main hall and all the Librarians gathered there. Dressed in the charcoal gray robes of Grandmagister, he didn’t look like an imposing figure. He was a blade-thin human, tall, and stoop-shouldered from all the long years working over books. A long gray beard trailed down to his narrow chest, partially masking his pinched, severe features. There was never a day in his acquaintance with the man, even before Grandmagister Ludaan passed away peacefully while reading and Frollo took over as the new Grandmagister, that Wick had seen Frollo happy.

Quarrel, Alysta, Bulokk, and his dwarven warriors trailed behind the Grandmagister.

“What is the meaning of this?” Frollo demanded. His hazel eyes flashed angrily. “You can’t just come into this Library and disrupt everything.”

“I’ve come,” Craugh said, straightening himself to his full height and towering over the Grandmagister—especially with the peaked slouch hat, “on a matter of grave importance.”

“Your problems are no problems of mine,” Frollo snapped, frothing at the mouth. “Or of this Library.”

“I need these Librarians to do research.”

“These Librarians already have tasks. *Important* tasks. They’re not here at your beck and call. You can’t just rush in here and interrupt schedules and procedures simply because you can’t figure something out on your own.”

Craugh’s face purpled in fury.

Wick pushed against the staff, hoping he might be able to take a step or five back from the impending collision of wills. Regrettably, Craugh kept his hold on the staff—and therefore Wick—quite firm.

“I came here tonight and discovered these interlopers,” Frollo said, throwing back a hand to include Quarrel, Alysta, Bulokk, and his warriors. “Here! *Without* my approval. You know we protect many important books and records here, Craugh. You, of all people, should know that.”

“I do,” Craugh said. “Those books and records are the very reasons I chose to come here.”

You *chose to come here?* Wick thought indignantly. He almost objected aloud, then realized that Craugh was not only taking the credit for their presence there, but he was also taking the blame. At least that part was good. Wick decided he could sacrifice one for getting out of the other.

"Faugh!" Frollo sneered. He turned his attention to Wick. "And you, you malingering excuse for a proper Librarian, are you the cause of all this?"

Unable to speak in his terror (unable to stand if it hadn't been for Craugh's staff propping him up), Wick could only shake his head.

"Don't lie to me!" Frollo commanded. "Craugh wouldn't have come here by choice. And you've been missing for days. Did you go off with one of those pitiful excuses for books from Hralbomm's Wing?"

Wick gave that consideration. That was tricky. That night in Paunsel's Tavern, he *had* taken an adventure about Taurak Bleiyz (which he still hadn't finished!), and there was the possibility that the Grandmagister was already aware of that. But the romance wasn't the reason he'd been gone from the Library for so long. He started to open his mouth and explain himself.

"And don't you dare tell me you were shanghaied again!" Grandmagister Frollo bellowed. "I'll have none of that this time!"

Stymied, afraid for his very life, Wick closed his mouth.

"Answer me!" Grandmagister Frollo shrilled.

Wick wished that somewhere along the way he had learned how to turn himself invisible. But since invisibility wasn't forthcoming, he took a deep breath, screwed up his courage, and—

"This is not his fault," Craugh roared. "He is trying to help solve the problem I'm dealing with."

"Again, Craugh," Frollo shouted back, turning to stare directly into the wizard's face, "your problem is not my problem."

Green embers circulated around Craugh's staff. His eyes glowed bright green.

"Uh-oh," someone said. "Now you've done it."

To Wick's horror, he discovered the speaker was none other than himself.

"I want you out of here!" Frollo pointed imperiously in the direction of the main door. "This instant! I'm Grandmagister of this Library, and I—*ulp*!"

Actually, the *ulp* came after Craugh moved, but the wizard moved *so quickly* that the *ulp* came out almost immediately. Taking one step in toward the Grandmagister, Craugh caught Frollo's head in one spidery hand that could have palmed a dinner plate. Green sparks scattered in all directions from Craugh's staff and eyes, spinning round inside the great chamber.

Then Craugh spoke a Word, just a single Word, but it boomed so loud that Wick was never certain what it was. Frollo seemed to collapse into the charcoal-gray Grandmagister's robes.

By the time Wick blinked, Grandmagister Frollo had disappeared. His robe lay on the floor.

"He's killed the Grandmagister!" someone shouted.

Again, Wick discovered that it was himself. And it was no wonder that he didn't recognize his voice because it certainly didn't sound like him. He'd never spoken so high-pitched.

"The wizard's killed the Grandmagister!"

Now that, Wick thought as he held his hand over his mouth, *was not me!*

"Craugh vaporized Grandmagister Frollo!"

"Someone get the dwarves!"

Two of the Novice Librarians and one First Level Librarian standing nearby fainted dead away and lay sprawled on the floor. Other Librarians moved back from them as if they feared Craugh had slain them as well, and that death might be catching.

Metal clanked as dwarves ran into the room and drew their weapons. They held pikes and battle-axes and stood at the ready. None of them appeared ready to jump Craugh. The green embers continued circling the wizard's head and tall hat.

"Wait for Varrowyn," one of the dwarves whispered, and it was so quiet in the main chamber that it sounded like a shout.

Several of the Librarians started edging away.

Craugh threw a hand out. Green lightning jetted from his hand and arced over the heads of the Librarians. The Librarians, from Novice to First Level Librarian, dropped to the floor. (And it was a good thing the Vault of All Known Knowledge was enchanted with the water absorbency spell, because more than a few robes were suddenly drenched.)

"No one leaves!" the wizard ordered.

"Aren't you dwarves going to get him?" one of the Librarians demanded.

"Uh," the sergeant-at-arms among the dwarves said. "Mayhap we should await Varrowyn's decision on this."

"He *vaporized* the Grandmagister!" someone cried. "You're supposed to protect the Grandmagister and the Library!"

"Well," the dwarf said, peering at the pile of robes, "it's a little late to protect the Grandmagister. An' the Library don't appear to be in no immediate threat of harm."

"Cowards!" another Librarian shouted.

The dwarf frowned and turned to the warrior next to him. "Did ye see which one of them quill-pushers said that?"

Before the man could reply, Varrowyn ran through the door. Wick was impressed. For Varrowyn to be there all the way from the front gate in such short time was impressive with all the armor he wore.

"What's goin' on?" Varrowyn held his battle-axe at the ready before him. "Where's the Grandmagister?"

All the Librarians pointed at the charcoal-gray robe piled on the floor.

Varrowyn's eyes widened in shocked surprise. "What happened to him?"

All the pointing fingers shifted to Craugh.

Varrowyn stood there for a moment, and Wick knew the dwarf had to be really undecided about what to do.

7

Solutions

Then the Grandmagister's robe squeaked. Everyone looked at the material as it jerked and shifted. All breaths were held (except for Craugh's) as a lump foraged its way through the clothing and emerged from the robe's hem. A moment later an ugly pink and tan toad covered in black warts followed its blunt snout into the open.

"Craugh, you're going to pay for this!" Frollo squeaked in his new toad voice. He stood on his hind legs and shook his tiny little foot at the wizard. "Mark you well my words! You're going to regret the day that you ever—"

Quarrel had been holding Alysta in her arms, possibly so the cat wouldn't get stomped on in all the confusion. But Alysta (possibly giving in to her cat instincts and recognizing the toad as possible prey), erupted from her granddaughter's arms and leaped for the irritated toad.

"Cat!" Frollo shrieked. "No! Don't let it get me!" He turned and fled, but even with the alacrity of a quick-legged toad at his disposal, Wick knew Frollo would never escape Alysta's quick fangs.

Craugh took his hat from his head and flung it. Just as Alysta pounced toward the toad, the hat descended upon her and trapped her. Green sparks sizzled and it locked down onto the floor.

Alysta hissed and meowed in feline displeasure. But despite her best efforts, she couldn't budge Craugh's peaked hat.

Shrieking and squeaking, Grandmagister Frollo hopped from the room as fast as his tiny legs would carry him.

"Was that—" Varrowyn frowned.

"The Grandmagister?" Craugh asked. "Yes. It was."

"Hmmmm," Varrowyn said, squinting at the wizard, and showing how he'd risen to command with the blessing of all the other dwarves by demonstrating both sense and sensibility, "then the Grandmagister truly hasn't been harmed."

The dwarves flanking Varrowyn sighed in unison and looked truly relieved.

"No. He's not been harmed a bit. I give you my word on that."

"You can't just let Craugh turn the Grandmagister into a toad!" one of the Librarians shouted.

Craugh pointed at the speaker—First Level Librarian Cottle, Wick was glad to see—and immediately the Toad Librarian population of the Vault of All Known Knowledge doubled.

"Oh no!" Cottle shrieked. Then he too sped off, waddling from side to side because he made a very fat toad.

"Well then," Varrowyn said, "since nothin's truly amiss"—he pointed toward the door—"we'll just go on back outside an' take care of guardin' the Library. Wouldn't want anythin' untoward to happen now, would we?"

"No," Craugh said, "we wouldn't."

Varrowyn ushered his command outside the Library. The main doors closed with a loud bang.

"Now," Craugh said, turning to the Librarians, "on your feet."

The Librarians moved incredibly quickly.

"I have a project that I need researched," Craugh said. He dropped a hand to Wick's shoulder. "Second Level Librarian Lamplighter will be my emissary in this. Obey him as you would me. Address the tasks he gives you with all due haste, or by the Old Ones, your rumps will thump!"

The Librarians stood fearfully.

"Get your assignments from Second Level Librarian Lamplighter," Craugh ordered. "Are you Librarians? Or are you *toads*?"

As it turned out, they all chose to be Librarians. Wick found himself in the middle of a panicked chaos.

The research took three days. Later, when he realized it had really been three days, Wick couldn't believe it. The time had seemed like hours, and Craugh had demanded updates on what he was finding out every few minutes. Once he knew how long it had actually been, he didn't feel quite so angry at Craugh for asking so much, but at the time it hadn't sat well with Wick.

When he was finished, he was exhausted. It wasn't that he was unused to hard work. The truth was that he worked hard every day. But he'd never had to think for so *many*, and all at one time, too. In the end, he'd finally had to make a much larger outline to map what he needed and from where he needed it.

He worked nonstop, feeding on the excitement of what he was learning. As quickly as he could, he compiled all the information into one journal, trying to figure out a timeline of when everything happened. And who had done it.

Finally, the reports started to trickle down. Soon no more information was coming from the military libraries or the biographical section or the shelves containing tomes on magic and spells and enchantments.

Wick became a bottomless pit of knowledge. He hadn't ever before known how much raw information he could hold at one time. He had to start the journal over twice, then finally gave up and worked the pages in loose fashion, sewing them up later only when he was finished with them.

The whole time, Craugh stood guard over him. At first Wick had thought it was only to make certain Wick kept his nose to the grindstone and didn't get distracted. Then he realized that the wizard was facilitating the handling of the books, the organization of the presentation of the material, and the meals. Wick never had to ask for sustenance; it was there when he was ready for it.

At times he'd had to take leave of the chair to go to the privy, of course, but there was a lot of pacing involved as well. Pacing helped Wick think, and there was a lot of thinking to do.

But finally, he had all of it: the history of the three weapons that went into human, elven, and dwarven hands.

And he understood why Lord Kharrion had been interested in Dream at the start of the Cataclysm.

"What did you find out?" Quarrel asked.

Wick tried to find a comfortable spot in the back of the wagon. Craugh sat in the driver's seat and handled the team. The wizard knew most of the story, having patched it together himself as Wick had uncovered bits and pieces of the events that had tied Dream and the heroes' weapons together.

"Almost all of it," Wick said.

"Who betrayed the defenders at the Battle of Fell's Keep?" Bulokk asked.

"That," Wick acknowledged, "I didn't find out. Let me begin with the vidrenium that was used to create the weapons."

The wagon creaked as it headed through the big gate past Varrowyn and the dwarves. Craugh had assured them that Grandmagister Frollo and Cottle would no longer be toads by the next morning, though it was the wizard's frank opinion that they could have used a life as toads for a while longer yet.

"Wizards and blacksmiths for centuries have labored to create armor that will withstand a dragon's fiery breath and sharp claws," Wick said. "So far, there's only one thing that will do that without fail."

"Dragon skin," Quarrel put in.

"Exactly. However, getting dragon skin to make armor with presents two problems."

"Ye hafta kill the dragon," Bulokk said.

Wick nodded. "Also, cutting the dragon skin is almost impossible. If it's magicked in any way to be made more supple and easier to deal with, it also loses its ability to withstand the attacks you're trying to design it for. So these wizards and blacksmiths of Dream came up with vidrenium. That's what they called the hybrid metal they created."

"What's Dream?" Bulokk asked.

"Dream was a city," Wick answered, "like no other. Built by elves, humans, and dwarves, it was constructed so that all the races could live there in peace and bring out only the best of each other."

"It sounds too good to be true," Quarrel said.

"Maybe it was," Wick said. "The goblinkin hated it. Dream signified the eventual fate that awaited the goblinkin. If all people could come together in the manner that Dream did, it wouldn't be long before those races living there decided to effect a more permanent solution to having goblinkin living around them."

"I could live with that," Adranis said, smiling mirthlessly. "No goblinkin sounds awfully good."

"Dream was the first city to fall during the Cataclysm," Wick went on. "Lord Kharrion struck there first, knowing that if he could take the city he would strike a major blow against the morale of those who would oppose him."

"Because each race would follow suit as they always did, and blame each other for the loss of Dream," Craugh said.

"But I think Lord Kharrion struck there first because of the vidrenium. It posed too big a threat."

"How did he find out about the vidrenium?" Quarrel asked.

"Lord Kharrion worked among the wizards and blacksmiths," Wick said.

"And they knew it?" Alysta asked.

"No," Craugh called back from the driver's seat. The horses' hooves slammed against the ground as they hurried along. "Lord Kharrion was there under another name."

"What name?" Bulokk asked.

"Wazzeln Phalto," Wick answered.

"No one knew that was Lord Kharrion?" Alysta asked.

"Not until later. The people who died there that day, I'm pretty sure they never knew."

"Lord Kharrion worked on the invention of the vidrenium?" Bulokk asked.

"Yes."

"Why?"

"Because during the Cataclysm, he enlisted the aid of dragons. Shengharck and others like him. If the humans, dwarves, and elves suddenly came up with armor that might stave off most dragon attacks, he'd have to rethink his plans of conquest."

"He went there to sabotage the creation of the vidrenium," Alysta said.

"I think so." Wick rubbed his tired and aching eyes. "It has to be what happened. It's the only thing that makes sense." *But you're so tired after three days of no sleep that everything or nothing makes sense to you.* He smothered a yawn. "After the forge where the vidrenium was being made—had *been* made, actually, according to papers from Master Blacksmith Kalikard that survived the explosion, the invasion, and the subsequent shipping to the Vault of All Known Knowledge—exploded, the goblinkin attacked Dream and sacked the city. By that time, the vidrenium was gone."

"Where?" Quarrel asked.

"It had to have been blown out into the Gentlewind Sea where the merpeople found it," Wick said. "Or perhaps it was carried aboard a ship fleeing the city that was later sunk and the merpeople found it then."

"How much later?"

"I don't know. It took Lord Kharrion nine years to secure his hold on Dream and the outlying country. The wars, the Cataclysm, was not an easily won thing. For either side."

"Either way," Bulokk growled, "this chunk of vidrenium found its way into the hands of the merpeople, then into the hands of my ancestor."

Wick drank from the wineskin Adranis passed him. He was thirsty but he didn't want it to make him lightheaded. "Yes," he replied. "It did."

Of course, once they reached the Yondering Docks, climbed aboard *One-Eyed Peggie*, and got underway, Wick had to tell the story all over again for Cap'n Farok and Hallekk.

"Why did the merpeople take the ore to Master Bulokk?" Cap'n Farok asked.

They sat down in the ship's galley. The rest of the crew that weren't on watch sat on the long benches and listened. Wick knew the story would get repeated several times when he'd finished with it. Everyone would know.

"Maybe it was only chance they took it there," the little Librarian said. "After all, who would have been interested in a chunk of ore? Even ore that looked different than any ore anyone had seen before?"

"Or because it were so different," Hallekk put in.

"True." Wick rubbed his face in an effort to stay awake. "The merpeople might have figured that difference made the ore even more valuable. At any rate, Master Blacksmith Oskarr took the ore back to his forge in the Cinder Clouds Islands and began working with it. He made Boneslicer, Seaspray, and the metal reinforcement parts of Deathwhisper." Remembering the elven bow from the vision Craugh had summoned up, he was certain it had possessed metal reinforcement arms.

"Why three weapons?" Cap'n Farok asked. "An' why not all three of 'em dwarven weapons?"

"At this point," Wick said, "I have to start guessing. But these are educated guesses. From the notes we discovered that were left by the wizards and blacksmiths, the originators of the vidrenium intended to make three enchanted weapons, one for a warrior from each of the races. They worked the magic of their designs into the metal as they constructed it."

"A battle-axe fer the dwarves, of course," Bulokk said. "Master Oskarr kept that himself."

"A sword for the humans," Quarrel said. "That went to Dulaun."

"Wait," Cap'n Farok said. "I thought ye said the three of them didn't know each other before the Battle of Fell's Keep."

"I didn't think they did," Wick admitted. "But when we researched ships' logs of vessels that traded on a regular basis with the Cinder Clouds Islands, we discovered that Dulaun shipped aboard *Wavecutter* as a boy and worked his way up in command. He was first mate when Master Oskarr gave him the sword."

"Why would Oskarr give such a blade to a young human?" Cap'n Farok asked.

"I don't know."

"In the stories about Dulaun," Alysta put in, "it's said that the sword was given to him by a dwarven blacksmith for an act of bravery. But the stories don't name the blacksmith or say what that act was."

"In the legends of the Cinder Clouds Islands dwarves, it's said that Master Oskarr gave the finest sword he ever made to a human who rescued his son from a sea monster," Bulokk said.

"When he was just a young man, before he made captain, Dulaun is supposed to have slain a sea monster that very nearly killed him," Quarrel said. "I only now remembered that story. There are so many."

"Aye," Bulokk said. "I know what you mean. All the way back from the Library down that windin' mountain trail, I had somethin' at the back of me head. Just couldn't pry it loose. Till now."

"So those two weapons are explained," Cap'n Farok said. "But why weren't the stories intertwined before now?"

"Because of what happened at the Battle of Fell's Keep," Craugh answered. "The defenders there were betrayed and overrun by the goblinkin. Master Oskarr was blamed for it."

"Because Dulaun died there, and lost Seaspray," Quarrel said bitterly.

"Why not blame Sokadir?" Cap'n Farok asked.

"Because," Wick said, flipping open the journal he'd made of all the research he'd done on the vidrenium and the weapons, "Sokadir lost his two sons there." He showed Cap'n Farok and the rest the illustration he'd made of the brave elven warder and his two sons.

"So Master Oskarr was the only one who didn't lose anything?" Cap'n Farok asked.

"If you don't count his warriors," Wick said.

"An' his honor an' his good name," Bulokk said in a quiet voice.

They all sat quiet and sober for a time. Despite the fact that he wanted to be abed more than anything, Wick reached for another of the sugar biscuits Cook had made and slathered it with apricot jelly. It tasted just as good as the first one. A full stomach also made him want to sleep. During the last three days of frenzied research, he knew he'd eaten, but it had only been when he'd gotten sick from not eating. He hardly remembered anything he'd had.

"What about Sokadir?" Cap'n Farok asked. "How did he come by Deathwhisper?"

"I don't know."

Cap'n Farok's brow wrinkled. "What do ye mean ye don't know?"

Wick hesitated for a moment. This was the part of the story that he most hated.

"The metal bow reinforcements were stolen from the Cinder Clouds Islands," Craugh said.

Leave it to you to put a bald face on it, Wick thought sourly. In truth, though, he knew there was no other way to state what had happened.

"Stolen?" Cap'n Farok asked. "By who?"

"We don't know," Craugh said.

Cap'n Farok pulled at his beard irritably. "Ye don't mean to suggest that it was Sokadir?"

"He did end up with the bow," Bulokk said.

"Mightn't it be another bow?"

"Wick got me ancestor's books out of the forge." Bulokk nodded at Wick. "There was a drawin' of the bow reinforcements."

"Blueprints," Wick said automatically. "I didn't catch it the first time through. It doesn't look like a bow. But the powers in the bow, what it's supposed to do, fit what Deathwhisper does."

"Didn' Master Oskarr recognize the bow at the Battle of Fell's Keep?" Cap'n Farok asked.

"I don't," Wick said quietly, "see how he could not have."

Silence hung heavily in the room when he finished the story.

"Well then," Cap'n Farok said, "I suppose we'll just have to ask Sokadir how he came by that bow when we find him."

When he finally got to sleep a short time later, Wick slept nearly a day and a half. He could translate the word *exhaustion* in dozens of languages, write it in almost as many, but he didn't think he'd ever truly comprehended what it was to be exhausted until after the marathon at the Vault of All Known Knowledge. He couldn't believe how tired he was.

After the first day, he tried to get up but only succeeded in staying up long enough to use the privy and get a drink of water. Then he was once more abed and nothing woke him.

Through it all, *One-Eyed Peggie* sailed relentlessly, canvas spread high and wide to catch as much of the wind as she dared, spending half a day fighting a storm that seemed to follow them as surely as a predator that had their scent. Hallekk later told Wick that the ship had foundered a couple of times and her deck had been awash with the Blood-Soaked Sea. Wick was only too glad to have slept through that.

When he finally got up, he found that his time was off and it was the middle of the night, not morning. Starving now, he retreated to the galley and whipped up a batch of cinnamon-flavored oatmeal and a rasher of bacon, then took servings to the two dwarves standing at the helm.

They thanked him and started spooning the oatmeal up before the cold wind whipping across the sea cooled it.

"What's our course?" Wick asked.

Telafin, the helmsman, answered. "Craugh says Boneslicer an' Seaspray are still in Torgarlk Town. We're headin' there."

That was curious. Since Gujhar and Ryman Bey had reached Torgarlk Town, they hadn't left. Or maybe they'd left but the weapons were there for safekeeping.

Of course, there was always the possibility that the weapons were in town as bait in a trap.

8

Torgarlk Town

Wick watched Craugh in disbelief.

The wizard slung a bedroll over his shoulder, then crossed it with a waterskin. He put on his hat last, then took a fresh grip on his staff.

"*You're* going to go?" Wick asked when he could hold the question no longer.

Craugh just looked at him. Then he walked toward the gangplank that connected *One-Eyed Peggie* to the pier.

"Good luck, Craugh," Cap'n Farok called down from the stern castle.

"Thank you, Captain Farok," Craugh responded, glancing up for just a moment, then setting his sights on Torgarlk Town again.

Wick turned to Cap'n Farok. "You're going to just *let* him go? Alone?"

"It's not like I have any choice, Librarian Lamplighter," Cap'n Farok said. "Craugh has made his wishes known."

Staring at Craugh, who had already reached the pier, Wick couldn't understand all the confusion that was racing through him. For the last two days that he'd been conscious, he'd worked in his journals and tried not to think about the fact that Craugh was going to send him into the middle of the outlaw town.

After all, Torgarlk Town wasn't as bad as Wharf Rat's Warren, but the citizens there condoned slavery (primarily of dwellers) and traded with goblinkin (which was generally only done for slaves—dwellers—and spices to season the bounty in their stewpots—dwellers who could no longer swing a pickaxe in a mine).

Trade caravans from Never-Know Road stopped by there to do their illicit business (contraband goods that were smuggled in without benefit of paying the local king's tax, and slaves), then continue on to other coastal towns farther north.

Nightmares had plagued Wick's last two nights when he'd contemplated being kicked out into the middle of Torgarlk Town.

He'd never once considered staying behind when Craugh went off alone. *I should be relieved*, he thought. Unfortunately, he wasn't. He looked at the bedroll he'd assembled for himself. *And what if Craugh gets captured or killed? Will I ever know the end of the story if that happens*? He knew he wouldn't. If a wizard (especially one of Craugh's caliber!) couldn't walk into Torgarlk Town and take what he came for, then no one aboard *One-Eyed Peggie* had a chance.

So he wouldn't know. Could he live with that?

As he mulled over the question, watching Craugh stride purposefully between the cargo handlers, passengers, and merchants scattered over the dock, Wick knew that living with the question wasn't the only problem.

Despite his faults and his mean-spirited nature, Wick had a friendship with Craugh. None of the acquaintainceships he had back at the Vault of All Known Knowledge or in Greydawn Moors even came close to what he shared with Craugh. Nor did his friendships with the captain and crew of *One-Eyed Peggie* or with Brandt and Cobner and the others.

Craugh was all Wick had left of Grandmagister Ludaan. Despite the fact that there would be no living with Grandmagister Frollo upon Wick's return to the Vault of All Known Knowledge, Wick didn't want anything to happen to the wizard.

Wick looked up at Cap'n Farok.

The old sea captain smiled at him, nodded, then raised his hand in farewell. "May the Old Ones keep watch over both of you."

"Thank you," Wick said, and bolted for his gear. He had it in his hands and was bounding down the gangplank. From the corner of his eye, he saw Quarrel and Bulokk start to follow.

"No," Cap'n Farok said sternly. "The last thing Craugh needs is the two of ye flounderin' around out there an' givin' away there's strangers hangin' about. Ye'll stay aboard *Peggie* an' wait—like the rest of us."

Wick knew Quarrel and Bulokk wouldn't take the order kindly, but they'd meet Cap'n Farok's demands. He didn't break his stride, didn't glance over his shoulder. At the bottom of the gangplank, he stepped into the crowd and started making his way through them.

People didn't give way to a dweller the same way they did for Craugh. Thankfully, with the peaked slouch hat atop his tall frame, the wizard was simple to follow.

Wick trotted through the street and kept Craugh in sight. He wasn't sure if the wizard knew he was there or not, but Wick didn't believe it was that easy to follow him without him knowing.

They ascended the cut steps along the ledges. Most of the structures there were two-storied combinations with shops on the bottom and personal dwellings on the second floor.

Wick tried to follow close enough to Craugh that anyone looking at him would believe he was the wizard's personal servant, but not so close that Craugh could hear him. If the wizard didn't already know he was there. He also made sure that he didn't make eye contact with anyone. On the mainland, those who lived in rough towns weren't used to having dwellers look them in the eye. It was simple subterfuge, but an effective one.

However, it didn't always work.

"Halfer," a fat man with a broadsword on his hip called out. He was as impressively tall as he was fat, and had a hard look about his piggy eyes.

Wick tried to ignore the man and keep going. That worked for about two steps, which was when the fat man inserted himself directly into Wick's path.

"Halfer," the man said in a vexed tone, "I'm talking to you."

Having no choice with the fat man blocking the way, Wick stopped. He stared at his toes. To distract himself, he wiggled them in the dirt, making sure he wouldn't glance up.

"What are you doing here?" the fat man growled.

"Following my master," Wick answered.

The fat man looked at Craugh. "I don't see any masters here. At least, I don't see your master."

Wick didn't say anything, hoping the big man would just let him pass.

Moving with speed and grace, the big man grabbed the front of Wick's shirt and yanked him from his feet. "I didn't say you could go, now did I?"

"Please." Wick continued staring at his feet. "I have to keep up with my master."

"The old man with the pointy hat? Hah! He appears to barely have the wherewithal to be master of himself." The fat man started laughing, bending down close to Wick so that all the little Librarian could see was his corpulent mass. Then there was the sound of an impact and the fat man's face screwed up tight in pain.

Wick saw the staff up between the man's legs where it had struck. Realizing the man was falling forward, Wick quickly stepped back. The human fell like a massive oak out in the forest, taking his time with it. He dropped to his knees first and tried to catch hold of Wick with his hands. Then he fell forward on his face and got sick.

The nearby pedestrians spread out from Wick and the fat man, who moaned in pain but still reached for his sword. Craugh stepped up and rammed the bottom of his staff into the fat man's chins.

"Don't," Craugh said softly, but his voice was like silk-covered steel. "It wouldn't hurt my feelings to leave your body here for whatever carrion-feeder comes along that isn't particularly finicky about what it eats."

The fat man's hand dropped away from the sword.

"That," Craugh said, "was for being disrespectful in talking about me. I've got keen ears, and not much mercy left in me these days." He flicked his eyes to Wick. "Come."

Wick shouldered his bedroll again and skirted the fat man to stand at Craugh's side.

"Don't let me catch sight of you again." Craugh gave the staff a final shove that started a coughing fit. Then he turned and strode along the cobblestoned street.

Wick followed. He kept waiting for Craugh to yell at him, but the wizard ignored him and headed for the nearest tavern. Three horses, all of them road weary and covered in dust, stood tethered at the railing. A carved statue of a bear on its hind legs stood beside the door.

Craugh entered the tavern and stood for a moment. The wizard stopped so suddenly that Wick almost ran into him. The little Librarian slid back a step or two and peered around Craugh's russet-colored robes.

"Welcome to The Big Ol' Bear's Tavern," an old man behind the scarred bar greeted.

Craugh nodded. "A table, if you please."

The tavernkeeper guided them to a table in the back and drew two ales at Craugh's direction, then departed quickly after the wizard paid him. Craugh reached into his pipe pouch, took out his pipe and filled it, then smoked a wreath around his head. He never once looked at Wick.

Wick sat across from him at the table. The chair wasn't made for a dweller. As a result, his legs dangled off the floor several inches and made him feel like a child. *I should have stayed on* One-Eyed Peggie, he told himself morosely. *Better still, I should have stayed at the Vault of All Known Knowledge*. Only that would have been no good as well. With Grandmagister Frollo only lately turned back from toad to human, things wouldn't have gone well there, either.

"Why?" Craugh asked finally.

Wick blinked at him. Why was such an open question. He'd learned to hate it while teaching Novices about the cataloguing of books. The answer to their *whys* most of the time was simply because that was the way the Grandmagisters wanted things done.

"Why what?" Wick asked.

Craugh frowned at him. "Why did you choose to accompany me when you could have remained on the ship?"

"I made a mistake," Wick said, thinking that was what the wizard wanted to hear.

"Then you can correct that mistake. Go back to *Peggie*."

For a moment, Wick considered getting up from the table and doing exactly that. Then he thought about the weapons they were searching for and the opposition they could be up against. He remembered most clearly Sokadir's rage at his appearance in his thoughts.

"I can't," Wick said.

"You can," Craugh said crossly. He waved his pipe toward the door. "I just gave you permission to take your leave."

Wick steeled his spine (though it still felt awfully brittle) and sat up a little straighter. "That isn't what I wish to do."

"What is it you wish, Librarian Lamplighter?"

Wick thought about that, sensing that he had to choose his words carefully. Craugh was not an easy man to know, though Grandmagister Ludaan had seemed to know him well.

"I wish to see the end of this," Wick said finally. "Bulokk stepped away from everything he's ever known in an effort to rectify his ancestor's honor—"

"And his own, to a degree," Craugh pointed out.

"Yes. Quarrel and Alysta have given their lives so far—Alysta even sacrificed her body—trying to get their ancestor's sword back."

"They also want to continue a legacy," Craugh said.

"I know."

"They have personal motivations to risk their lives. What is it that brings you to the brink of death?"

Wick blinked.

"For I can assure you that's what we're talking about here."

Taking a deep breath, Wick tried to calm the fear that clamored inside him. One thing he knew for certain when many other things seemed confused was that he wanted to live. He still hadn't finished that Taurak Bleiyz romance. "You talked about how important it was to find out what happened at the Battle of Fell's Keep. Do you truly believe that, or were those just pretty words you dropped in front of me to make me more amenable to what you wanted me to do?"

Craugh said nothing.

"Cap'n Farok believes in what you said," Wick went on, unable to bear the silence. "So does Hallekk. The crew of *One-Eyed Peggie* has laid their lives on the line to find out the truth." He paused and took another breath. "Even if you were just lying for your own ends, what you said was true. The goblinkin are rising in numbers and intent. One day they may try to rise up in the south again and pour north along the Shattered Coast. If they do, the land will once more run red with blood. I don't want to see that happen."

"You can't stop the coming war. The goblinkin have seen they can have more than they've ever had before. They won't be satisfied with what they have now."

Wick was acutely conscious of the fact that a number of goblinkin sat around other tables in the tavern. A few of them even appeared to be giving them undue attention.

"What those three weapons can do," Wick said, "what the truth can do, is help the humans, elves, and dwarves once more join forces. Knowing what happened at the Battle of Fell's Keep can remove a lot of hostile feelings."

"But the defenders in that place were betrayed," Craugh said.

"If Lord Kharrion was after the weapons, if he knew they were hammered from the vidrenium, maybe he did something to betray them."

"How?"

"I don't know."

"There's also the fact that the bow reinforcements were stolen from Master Oskarr's forge," Craugh reminded.

"Yes."

"Also, Sokadir also didn't like knowing you were spying on him."

"An honest reaction," Wick said. "Anyone, especially an elf who values his privacy, would feel the same way."

"Would they?" Craugh puffed on his pipe and the smoke formed an owl with wide, sweeping wings that flew around his pointed hat. "His reaction seemed a little . . . extreme."

"He's an elf."

"An elf with a guilty conscience, I wonder?" Craugh mused.

Wick shook his head. "His two sons, Qardak and Palagan, died there in that canyon, Craugh. What manner of person would sacrifice his sons to further his own ends?"

"A truly evil one." Craugh's green eyes held sparks that eddied within their depths. "A man with no conscience."

He talks like he knows what he's talking about, Wick realized. *How much does he know that I don't?*

"Have you ever known such a man, Librarian Lamplighter?" Craugh asked.

"I've seen them."

Craugh smiled, but the effort held no warmth and no gentleness. "You've seen them in your travels, and you've read about them in your books, but you haven't really *known* them." He took another puff and the owl figure was overtaken and slashed to pieces by a smoke dragon. "They're out there, and doubtless we're going to be up against one."

We're. Wick took heart in that. *We* didn't mean a wizard and an ungainly toad. So he didn't have to worry about that. However, *we* also meant that any danger that came Craugh's way would doubtless come Wick's as well. The choice between the two fates wasn't pleasant.

"You still have a chance to get clear of this thing," Craugh said.

Do you want me to leave? Wick wanted to ask. But he couldn't. He feared the answer. Craugh might tell him to leave, then they would both be stuck with what the wizard claimed were his wishes. *If you wanted me to leave, you would have sent me back to the ship.*

But even then, Wick had to wonder if he was being manipulated. Craugh was that good, he knew. Good enough to make him convince himself that what he was doing was totally of his own volition.

I should go, Wick told himself, and he thought he was going to say exactly that when he heard himself saying, "No. I'm going to stay."

Craugh appeared to be both relaxed and perturbed at the same time. He leaned back in his chair and sighed.

Thinking that Craugh might suddenly usurp control over his presence there, Wick said, "I'm a member of *One-Eyed Peggie*'s crew."

"So?"

"So Cap'n Farok can keep watch over us through the monster's eye," Wick said. "If we get into trouble, he can send Hallekk and the crew to help."

Craugh puffed on his pipe for a moment. "If we get into trouble, Second Level Librarian Lamplighter, it may well be beyond the scope of *One-Eyed Peggie* and her crew's ability to help us. That I can promise you."

Wick felt the anger seething beneath Craugh, but he didn't know if the wizard was angry at him or something else.

At that moment, a group of goblinkin who'd been talking among themselves and sometimes looking in Craugh and Wick's direction scooted back their chairs and approached.

This, Wick told himself, *can't be good*.

9

Trouble at the Big Ol' Bear's Tavern

Hey, graybeard," the biggest goblin said, placing his fists on his belt. "We notice ye have a halfer there."

Craugh smiled, and there seemed to be a flicker of interest and honest amusement there. "I do."

"Thought maybe we'd take him off yer hands," the goblinkin said.

"And why would you want to do that?" Craugh asked.

The goblinkin grinned as if the answer to that were the easiest thing in the world. "Why, to fill me stewpot, that's why."

The other four goblinkin with him laughed and elbowed each other in the ribs at their friend's joke.

"Fascinating," Craugh said.

Wick felt sick at his stomach. Though he hadn't wanted to leave Craugh on his own, staying aboard *One-Eyed Peggie* was looking better all the time.

"We'd be willin' to pay ye," the goblinkin said. "A fair price, of course."

Green embers circled Craugh's staff and occasionally issued from his eyes. "Of course. I'm sure that you would."

Cautiously, afraid he knew what was coming, Wick stretched his legs down and put his toes on the hardwood floor. He gripped the edge of the table, prepared to throw himself under it.

"Unfortunately," Craugh went on, "this particular halfer isn't for sale. I'm not done with him yet."

The goblinkin frowned. He reeled a little unsteadily, mute

testimony to how much ale and spirits he'd consumed. "We come over here to get us a halfer. Come to take him to supper, we did."

The other goblinkin cracked up at the old joke.

"We ain't leavin' without what we come fer," the goblinkin said harshly. "Won't be any problem to fold ye up into that stewpot as well, graybeard."

Craugh laughed, and it was a full-throated roar that Wick had seldom heard. Generally that reaction only came from two different sources: either something had truly tickled the wizard's funny bone, or else he was about to wreak a vicious smiting on some hapless enemy.

Wick knew which it was to be this time.

"Mayhap you'd like to try to take him," Craugh invited in a soft voice.

The lead goblinkin drew his sword, followed quickly by the others unlimbering their weapons.

"You amuse me," Craugh said. "Truly you do. But it's an amusement that will grow old quickly." He lifted his staff and slammed it down against the floor.

Green lightning speared from the staff and wrapped around the goblinkin swords and battle-axes. Immediately, the goblinkin started dancing, juttering and screaming as they bounced to and fro. Whenever they banged into each other, great showers of sparks erupted and lit up the whole interior of the Big Ol' Bear's Tavern.

Craugh continued laughing in great delight, but Wick sank beneath the table.

"Stupid goblinkin," a dwarf at a nearby table muttered to his mates. "Ought to know better than to pick a fight with a wizard."

Banging his staff against the hardwood floor again, Craugh stopped the lightning. The goblinkin spilled to the floor, unconscious or dead.

Peering under the table, Craugh said, "You can come out now."

With as much dignity as he could muster, Wick clambered from beneath the table. All eyes were on Craugh, who was bending down and going through the goblinkin's clothing. He stopped when he found a coin. "As I suspected."

Wick tried to peer at the coin in the wizard's hand, but Craugh closed his fingers over it too quickly.

Finished with his search, Craugh straightened and looked at the tavernkeeper. "I don't hold you accountable for this."

"Good," the old man declared, "for I had nothin' to do with it."

Craugh flipped his hand out. A gold coin flashed through the air. The tavernkeeper caught the coin effortlessly. "Find someone to dispose of the trash I've left. I'll not trouble you any further than that."

"Thank ye."

Turning, Craugh led the way through the door, ignoring the stares of the rest of the tavern's patrons. Other goblinkin sat at tables, too, but none of them seemed inclined to avenge their kin. As Wick pushed through the door, one of them even offered to rid the tavern of the bodies—for a tankard of ale.

The price of life in Torgarlk Town, Wick thought unhappily.

Out on the street, Craugh took a deep breath and looked to the east. The Forest of Fangs and Shadows lay in that direction, miles down Never-Know Road.

"That went well," the wizard observed.

"It did?" Wick couldn't mask his astonishment or his disapproval. "You may have killed them, Craugh."

"Would you rather have bathed in their stewpot?" Craugh looked at him.

"No."

"You didn't have to kill them."

"Perhaps they're not dead. In fact, now that I think on it, I think one of them was actually playing possum and another was twitching his foot." Craugh smiled and looked back at the Big Ol' Bear's Tavern. "Mayhap they'll rejoin us in a few moments."

"We could keep moving," Wick suggested.

Craugh got underway. "If you're going to accompany me, we're going to do things my way."

Wick knew he was expected to respond. "Fine," he said. *But I don't have to like it or even take part.* Not that he could take part in flinging lightning bolts and fireballs around.

"Those goblinkin got exactly what they had coming to them," Craugh said.

Although he didn't like goblinkin, Wick preferred putting distance between them as opposed to putting the goblinkin to death.

"After all," Craugh went on, "they were sent there to kill us."

That surprised Wick. He stumbled over a loose cobblestone and nearly landed on his face in a pile of steaming horse dung. Craugh's announcement, as well as the acrid scent that filled his nostrils, brought his senses to instant attention.

"How do you know they were sent there to kill us?" Wick asked.

Craugh flipped the coin he'd removed from the goblinkin's clothing into the air.

Instinctively, Wick caught the coin. It was solid and heavy. When he opened his hand, he found it was a disk, not a coin. It was embossed with a straight razor. *The Razor's Kiss thieves' guild*, Wick thought, recognizing the emblem.

"Actually," Craugh said, "they were sent there to kill *you*. After all, you've been identified by Ryman Bey and Gujhar."

"Oh," Wick said. Then he realized that maybe Craugh had been leaving him behind for just that reason: because he could be identified. Now he'd marked Craugh as a target as well.

"There's nothing to be done for it now," Craugh said. "We'll just be more careful."

Wick followed for a while as Craugh wandered seemingly aimlessly through Torgarlk Town. Finally, he could contain his curiosity no longer. "Where are we going?"

"To find Boneslicer and Seaspray."

"That's good." *But don't we need an army for that?* Instead Wick asked, "Do you know where they are?"

"More or less." Craugh took an emerald from inside his robe. Two silver dots, looking like faraway stars, gleamed in the green depths. "I'm tracking them."

"How?"

"Through the ties Quarrel and Bulokk have with them. Now that each of them has touched those weapons, and I'm able to use both of them and not just one, the ties are very strong."

Wick stared into the emerald for a moment and saw that the silver stars were getting bigger and glowing more brightly. "We're getting closer to them."

"Yes." Craugh pocketed the gem. He gazed down the Tiers and nodded at a large house that sat by itself not far from the port. "Unless I miss my guess, that's where the weapons are."

The house was huge, made of solid stone. A high wall ran around the estate, encompassing a forest of fruit trees and flower gardens. Stone gargoyles sat atop the wall and the house. Armed guards also held positions along the wall and at the main gate. Out in the water, anchored at a private pier with two other ships, Wick recognized *Wraith*, the ship Captain Gujhar commanded. One of the other two ships looked like the sleek black vessel Wick had encountered with Bulokk and his warriors in the Cinder Clouds Islands.

"That ship probably belongs to the Razor's Kiss guild," Wick said.

Craugh nodded. "It does."

Wick hesitated. He hated pointing out the shortcomings of Craugh's plans. On the other hand, he would truly hate to get caught by their enemies because of them.

"Do you really think the two of us—you and I—are going to be able to break into that house and steal Boneslicer and Seaspray?" Wick asked. "I mean, there's just the two of us. Even if we're very clever, and I know that we're clever because *you're* clever, and I would *never* intimate otherwise no matter how dumb an idea you concocted—"

"No matter how *dumb*?" Craugh asked archly.

Wick thought quickly. Dumb was a, well, *dumb* word choice. He was a Librarian, after all. A Second Level Librarian, no less. He knew words. Lots of words. Surely there was another word that wouldn't be quite so acrimonious as *dumb*. (Or as potentially toadifying!) But he quickly rejected *stupid*, *asinine*, *thoughtless*, and forty others in half as many languages.

"Did I say dumb?" Wick asked. "I didn't mean dumb. Dumb must have slipped out. I'm tired. We just had a close encounter of the goblinkin kind in the Big Ol' Bear's Tavern. I'm sure I'm not thinking straight. I'm sure I didn't mean dumb. *Dumb* would be a totally inaccurate assessement of our current situation and your ability to—"

"Quiet," Craugh growled. "Don't make me regret relenting and letting you come along."

Wick mimed locking his lips with a key and throwing the key away.

"Of course I don't expect the two of us to manage that feat," Craugh said.

Wick sighed with relief.

"That's why I've recruited help."

It took another hour to reach the top of the Tiers where the poor lived and cheap lodging was available. Staying silent that long, not knowing where they were going or who Craugh had "recruited" to aid them in the proposed break-in made the little Librarian intensely curious and anxious.

At the top of the Tiers, the housing was hardscrabble and dilapidated. Almost as many houses stood empty—roofs falling in, walls broken, windows empty—as held residents. The residents were living piled one on another. The economy of Torgarlk Town quickly broke into those who had (fierce and uncaring and bloodthirsty) and those who had not (who were willing or forced to live on the scraps offered or left by those who had).

Wick's heart went out to the wan and hungry faces of the children he saw playing in the alleys or helping their fathers with work, mending nets or smoking fish, or sorting through trash that had been brought up from the houses and shops farther down the Tiers. The poor or economically disadvantaged were never seen in Greydawn Moors because they didn't exist.

Once he had his bearings, Craugh turned and walked to the public well, standing a short distance off to one side while citizens hauled up buckets to meet their needs. Chickens gathered around the houses looking for food, and every now and again one of the stealthier children managed to grab one. That would trigger a celebration of sorts every time, because the quick-handed hunter would run back down an alley squealing for his mother while a parade of gamins followed.

"What are we doing here?" Wick asked. He judged it safe to ask since they appeared to be doing nothing and no one showed any interest in them.

"Waiting," Craugh said.

"Oh." Wick waited quietly for a moment but soon grew bored. "Waiting for what?"

"For me," a quiet voice said.

Wick turned and his heart sped up. He recognized the voice immediately. "Sonne!"

She stood just behind him, not quite two feet taller and still as slender as she'd been when he'd met her a few years ago in Hanged Elf 's Point. She wore a dark blue cloak with the hood pulled up because females didn't often walk around by themselves in Torgarlk Town that Wick had seen. Under the hood of her cloak, her short-cropped blond hair hung only to her jaw. Freckles scattered over her upturned nose. Her pale green eyes crinkled as she smiled to see him.

In addition to the cloak, she wore rather plain brown clothes and scarred knee-high boots. She was no longer the teenager she'd been when Wick had first made her acquaintaince but the years had been kind to her. She also carried more throwing knives on her person than anyone Wick had ever met.

"Greetings, dear Wick," she said, smiling with real affection. She grabbed him and hugged him, then glanced at Craugh and back at him. "I didn't know you were coming along on this trip. At least, not this part of it."

Sonne was one of Brandt's Band of Thieves, a ragtag group devoted to stealing from the wicked and evil to build a war chest to make a bid to get Brandt's kingdom back from the man who murdered his parents.

"Craugh never mentioned that you were to be part of this either," Wick said.

Sonne grinned broadly. "According to Craugh, there's quite a fortune waiting to be claimed for any who's careful, quick, and greedy." She cocked her head to one side. "That fits us in every way."

"How long have you been here?"

"For days. Ever since Craugh sent a message by way of a Dread Rider."

Wick looked at Craugh. "You didn't think to tell me this?"

"You've been busy working on this problem with your own special talents," Craugh said. "I saw no reason to distract you from what you were doing. Nor was your knowledge necessary."

"With Craugh planning to rob the house of a wizard," Sonne pointed out, "who else would he call on?"

That was true. Wick sighed. He should have known Craugh wouldn't have walked into Torgarlk Town on his own.

"Did you track the goblinkin that attacked us at the Big Ol' Bear's Tavern?" Craugh asked.

Sonne nodded. "After the two that lived recovered, they went straightaway to Kulik Broghan's house."

"Kulik Broghan?" Wick put in.

"The wizard who currently holds Boneslicer and Seaspray," Sonne said. She grinned impishly. "Of course, *that* won't last much longer."

"Brandt has a plan?" Craugh asked.

"Brandt," Sonne said, "*always* has a plan. I think you'll like this one. Cobner even likes it. A little." She clapped Wick on the shoulder. "Having Wick will not only be like old times, but it will make our task easier."

"Easier?" Wick repeated. *Easier* generally meant things were more dangerous for him. *Easier* generally meant risking his neck first before all the others risked theirs. *Easier* generally wasn't *easier* at all. "Maybe we should rethink the situation if having me here is going to make things *easier*. Maybe we should just go along with the plan the way it was originally conceived." *Back when I wasn't here to make things easier.*

Sonne laughed. "Come on." She linked her arm through Wick's. "The others will be glad you're here. Cobner especially. He always enjoys your visits."

Wick had mixed feelings about seeing Cobner again. Back in Hanged Elf 's Point, in the Serene Haven Cemetery where the Keldian mosaic puzzle had led them, Wick had saved Cobner's life. Maybe. That was the way Cobner told it, and in every telling Wick got braver and braver. Instead of merely taking an arrow in the posterior, Wick usually defeated six or eight warriors in single combat, then somehow managed to leap out and catch the arrow in his teeth to save Cobner's life. The romance writers on the shelves of Hralbomm's Wing had nothing on Cobner's tall tale-telling.

But looking at Sonne's winning smile, Wick knew he couldn't refuse.

"All right," he said, and walked with her, hoping that the short walk didn't lead him to his doom.

10

"Cake! That's What This Will Be!"

Brandt and the Band of Thieves took one whole floor of the building where they were renting rooms. Since there were only four rooms on the floor, that wasn't as impressive as it sounded.

The human who rented the rooms to the thieves knew something was in the wind, but he was an old hand at criminal activities and his price had been met. In addition, Sonne had said, Cobner had offered to slit his throat if he ratted them out.

Inside the building, Sonne led them up two staircases to the third floor. She paused at the closed door and held Wick and Craugh at bay with a raised hand. Cautiously, her left side turned to the door, she used the thin handle of a throwing knife to rap on the door.

The cadence was one Wick knew the thieves used when they were on operations. He recognized the answering signal when he heard it, then Sonne pushed the door open and went inside.

Hamual, tall and lanky, his light brown hair hanging down into his gray eyes, wore a mustache these days, but still looked younger than his years. He had the soul of a poet and Wick had taught him how to play a lute. Today he wore a warrior's light leather armor under his long cloak. Before Brandt rescued him and brought him into his little family of thieves, Hamual had been a slave. Cuffs covered the scars on his wrists.

"Look who I brought," Sonne said, gesturing to Wick.

"Wick!" Hamual exclaimed in delight, then knelt on one knee and hugged him.

Touched, and a little hurt to see how much the boy had become a man in his absence, Wick returned the hug. "Hamual, you're looking fine."

Breaking the embrace, Hamual pulled a flute from his cloak. "I've been practicing." He fingered the instrument and fit it to his lips. Instantly, a happy tune piped through the hallway.

"Yes," Wick agreed. "You have been. You'll have to show me what you've learned."

"A few things, though probably nothing you've never heard. The Minstrel Ordal teaches me songs now and again when we happen to meet him in his travels."

"He's a good teacher," Wick agreed. "He'll instruct you more than I ever could."

"Perhaps," Hamual said. "But it was you that taught me to love making music."

Face reddening with the praise, Wick said, "The music was always within you. I merely pointed out to you what it was."

Karick, an older, heavier human stood guard on the door with Hamual. His hair was dark brown but was shot through with gray these days. He was usually taciturn and quiet, a man given to deep thoughts, but he nodded and smiled and greeted Wick.

At the far end of the hallway, Tyrnen and Zelnar, twin dwarven pickpockets, kept watch through a window overlooking Kulik Broghan's house and the harbor.

"See?" Zelnar, or maybe it was Tyrnen, asked, slapping the other twin. They were young and usually in one trouble or another. "I told you I thought Wick was with Craugh."

Tyrnen, or maybe it was Zelnar, rubbed his shoulder and frowned. "I didn't say he wasn't."

Wick exchanged greetings with both of them, got their names sorted out, and was pulled into the nearest room by Sonne.

"Wick!" Cobner bawled as soon as he saw him. The dwarf thundered across the floor and grabbed Wick up in a bone-breaking embrace.

"*Can't breathe*," Wick said with what little breath remained to him.

"It's good to see you, too, little warrior," Cobner said. He was a little shorter than Hallekk but broader across the shoulders. Scars creased his broad face, running into his sandy-gray beard.

"*Can't breathe*," Wick repeated, growing desperate and slapping Cobner on the back in an effort to get him to loosen his grip.

Cobner slapped Wick on the back as well, mistaking the effort. "You're a sight for sore eyes, you are."

Just before he was about to pass out from not breathing, Wick was released and stood on unsteady legs. Black spots danced in his vision.

"You feel like you're getting stronger," Cobner said, pinching Wick's bicep. "Have you been working out? Doing the exercises I told you to do?"

Wick thought about all the running he'd been doing for the last month or so. "Yes."

"Well, it's been working wonders on you," Cobner said. He was bound and determined to turn Wick into the fiercest dweller warrior who ever lived. "Whatever you're doing, keep it up."

Spotting a chair, Wick stumbled over to it and sat. He gazed around the room and spotted Brandt sitting behind the big desk littered with small wooden models. At the same instant he saw they were models, Wick figured out what they were models of.

Kulik Broghan's house was reproduced there, down to the gargoyles on the high retaining walls.

"Greetings, little artist," Brandt greeted. He sat at ease in the chair on the other side of the desk. Dressed all in black, even down to kidskin gloves, he cut an imposing figure at a glance. But only when he wanted to. When he wished to disappear in a crowd or even alone in a street at night, it only took him a heartbeat to do so.

When he was playing a role for some con or scheme or theft he'd dreamed up, Brandt oftened passed himself off as nobility. He came by the title honestly. His father had been a baron in the Sweetgrass Valley before being murdered by the current self-styled king. Brandt's black hair was carefully coiffed and bangs hung down over his close-set black eyes and thin nose. His black eyebrows turned his eyes into hollows of black fire. His black goatee jutted arrogantly.

Little artist was the nickname Brandt had first given Wick when he'd met him back in the slave pens of Hanged Elf 's Point. Brandt had been there casing a possible job and had happened to catch Wick working on the homemade journal he'd fashioned while aboard *One-Eyed Peggie* after being shanghaied in Greydawn Moors. The master thief had flipped through Wick's journal and thought him an artist at first, but had reasoned that there was more. At the time, Brandt had needed someone who knew art, and he'd purchased Wick and set off the adventures that had led them to the Broken Forge Mountains and the deadly encounter with Shengharck.

"Greetings, Brandt," Wick replied, leaning in with interest and studying the model. "Kulik Broghan's home?"

"It is," Brandt said, smiling. "A close approximation, at least." He regarded Wick with keen interest. "And how is it you're here in Torgarlk Town? I wasn't informed that you were going to be coming." He glanced up at Craugh.

Brandt was the one person Wick knew that was almost as innately curious as he was. "It was a last-minute decision." Wick pushed himself up from his seat. Now that he was puzzled, his shortness of breath and dizziness were of secondary importance. "So Kulik Broghan is the target?"

Smiling lazily, Brant flipped over a hand and said, "The man does appear to have what we're after. And we're determined to change that."

"How?"

"Cake!" Brandt said enthusiastically. "That's what this will be!"

Wick brightened a little at that, but he'd been around Brandt and the Band of Thieves long enough to know that even the best of plans didn't always turn out well.

"Speaking of cake," Cobner said, rubbing his big hands together briskly, "Lago said something about the food being almost ready. Let's have a look. See if Wick can still come close to eating me under the table."

"We've been here for six days," Brandt said. "As soon as we could get here after getting the offer from Craugh."

"Offer?" Wick sat in the dining room they'd arranged in one of the rented rooms. The thieves had brought in two long tables and they now stood laden with food that Lago had prepared.

Lago stood nearby, a smile beaming on his ancient, seamed face. He wiped his big hands on an apron. As long as Wick had known Brandt, Lago had cooked and baked for them, always preparing meals wherever they ended up. Age had bent his body and robbed it of strength, but he still knew his way around a kitchen. Part of their leasing arrangement had included use of the kitchen, which—Lago had informed Wick—was nothing to be proud of. But he'd turned out a fine meal. Wick had seen the old dwarf do the same thing with nothing more than a camp cookfire.

"An offer," Brandt affirmed. He shrugged a little, enjoying the telling of the tale. "Knowing that his adversaries partially consisted of the Razor's Kiss, Craugh knew he would have to eventually have thieves."

"It did," Craugh added, "seem prudent."

"And it was. Since Craugh knew that Boneslicer was probably in the Cinder Clouds Islands, and that Sokadir still held Deathwhisper somewhere in the Forest of Fangs and Shadows, he had us on hand in Calmpoint."

Wick chewed a delightful raspberry-nut cake covered with hickory-honey and sweetened peppers that burned just enough to tantalize the palate before the cake extinguished the flames.

Calmpoint made sense. It was at the other end of the Steadfast River. The Never-Know Road crossed the river twice early on and ran parallel at other times. A fast, determined rider could make the distance between Torgarlk Town and Calmpoint in less than three days, but a trade caravan would take weeks to negotiate the rough terrain.

"Once Craugh discovered the weapons had been brought here," Brandt said, "he asked us to come. And here we are."

"The weapons are there?" Wick asked.

"They are."

"You've seen them?"

"I have."

"How?"

Brandt smiled. "Why, I was invited, of course. After all, I'm Baron Lorthord, a collector of fine and unusual weapons."

"Baron Lorthord?" Wick repeated.

Brandt sipped his wine and picked at a piece of turkey breast. "Yes. A very rich and influential man. From the Spoonhorn Pass."

"A good choice," Wick said. "Spoonhorn Pass is on the other side of the Broken Forge Mountains and is supposed to be a gathering place for the rich and indolent. I knew you'd gone there because you told me tales of the city. But who is Baron Lorthord?"

A wide smile split Brandt's face. "Why, *me* of course. I am Baron Lorthord. After we looted what we could of Shengharck's treasure and retreated from the Broken Forge Mountains, we went to Spoonhorn Pass and lived extremely well for a few months. With all the gold at my disposal, becoming Baron Lorthord was an easy task. A lot of people who live there were someone else before they arrived. Most of the gold they bring to the city wasn't originally there. In fact, while we were there—as I have doubtless told you—we saw two blackhearts get their just desserts. One was overtaken by a group of men he'd robbed, and the other was robbed by good-hearted thieves who stole back the money he'd taken that had left a poor town behind."

"I take it you charged a commission?"

Brandt laughed. "Of course. No one does that kind of business for free. Not even good-hearted thieves. Trust me, those poor people were grateful to see their treasures returned to them. Even after subtracting the commission."

"So you entered the premises as Baron Lorthord," Wick went on.

"You should have seen it, Wick," Sonne gushed. "It was one of Brandt's most masterful performances. He played every inch the fop and had Kulik Broghan eating out of his hand."

"Tell me about Kulik Broghan," Wick requested. Giving up after finishing his second big piece of cake, he leaned back in his chair and took out his writing utensils. As he talked and listened, he drew the faces of his friends and some of the details they brought out regarding Kulik Broghan's estate.

"Kulik Broghan is a collector at heart," Brandt said. "A greedy man by nature. He fancies himself something of a wizard as well, I suppose, because one of the things he collects are spellbooks from dead wizards."

"A very dangerous preoccupation," Craugh said, frowning.

"Perhaps," Brandt agreed. "But every safeguard can be beaten. Provided the proper motivation and the right tools." He cocked an eye at Craugh. "Even yours."

Craugh sniffed in disdain. "We'll see."

"When that day comes," Brandt said, "*you* won't be here to see. If there's anything too dangerous to be left lying about, any spells or secrets, you'd be better served taking them to the grave with you."

"Duly noted," Craugh said.

"Why is Broghan interested in the weapons?" Wick asked.

"Primarily," Brandt said, "I think it's because they are a set. A trilogy of known death-dealers, if you will. They were all carried by fallen heroes."

"Sokadir hasn't fallen," Wick pointed out.

"So you say," Brandt replied. "I only know that no one has seen him in years."

"I saw him only days ago."

Brandt looked at him with keen interest. "Where?"

Wick took a moment to explain about the visions Craugh had tried to summon, and the fact that the elven warder didn't want to be found.

"His son was the one who bound the weapons at the Battle of Fell's Keep," Brandt informed them. "Did you know that?"

Craugh tugged at his beard in sudden speculation. "No, I didn't."

Wick shook his head.

"Evidently Qardak, the eldest, was something of a wizard," Brandt said.

"Unusual," Craugh said. "Elves go for a more natural magic, something that comes from Nature and enhances Nature. With the magical creation of the vidrenium, it should have been anathema to elvenkind."

"Deathwhisper was created for the elves," Brandt reminded.

"True," Craugh agreed, "but that is a spell that's friendly to the user. A binding spell like the one you're talking about should have been beyond his ability."

"There are some elves who tinker in the more chaotic magicks," Wick said. "Hallinbek's *Compendium of Mislaid Spells and Wardings* lists no fewer than fourteen elven practioners. Those are only fourteen that he knew of."

"I've known them, too," Craugh said. "They're usually not very successful at them. Elves have an innate sympathy with Nature. They hate to see anything violated. Even those who have gone rogue or outlaw are limited in their abilities to warp the essence of something. Shape-shifting. Tracking. Charming. Those are all areas where elven expertise is the order of the day." He put his pipe in his mouth and snapped his fingers, lighting the bowl. "But at the level you're suggesting? That's very rare."

"But not impossible."

"I would bet against it. Every time."

"Why did Qardak bind the weapons?" Wick asked.

"To strengthen—" Brandt began.

"There would be—" Craugh started at the same time.

Smiling, Brandt gestured to Craugh. "I bow to your area of expertise."

"I can think of only one reason to do such a thing," Craugh said. "To shore up whatever magical defensive wards he had in place around the defenders." He puffed on the pipe thoughtfully. "While the weapons were bound, their special powers couldn't be called into play."

"No one's ever mentioned this before," Wick said.

"Kulik Broghan mentioned it," Brandt said. "To me."

"How does he know what we don't?"

Brandt wiggled his eyebrows. "It's all rather interesting, isn't it?"

"What does he plan to do with the weapons?" Craugh asked.

"He told me he was actively seeking Deathwhisper, that he knew the bow was somewhere in the Forest of Fangs and Shadows."

"Sokadir has it," Wick said.

"He didn't," Brandt said, "tell me that."

Craugh puffed on his pipe. "I trust you offered to buy Boneslicer and Seaspray from him?"

"I did. I offered more gold than I've ever seen. If he'd accepted, if we truly meant to pay his price, we'd have had to dig out the top of the Broken Forge Mountain and find Shengharck's treasure trove again." Brandt sighed—more, Wick thought—upon reflection of how much gold they'd lost when the volcano had exploded and filled the interior of the dragon's chamber. "But he refused. Although I swear I saw temptation in his eyes."

"Did he mention Lord Kharrion's Wrath?" Craugh asked.

Wick held his quill still, pausing in the middle of drawing a profile view of

Sonne. He hadn't ever heard of Lord Kharrion's Wrath. In all the time he'd been searching for the three mystic weapons with Craugh, the wizard had never mentioned it.

"No," Brandt answered. "Should he have?"

"It would be better," Craugh said, "if he didn't. But I'm afraid that may be what this is all about."

"What's Lord Kharrion's Wrath?" Wick asked.

Craugh sat forward on his chair. Everyone drew in close to hear him. "No one knows for certain," the wizard answered. "Even midway through the Cataclysm, Lord Kharrion knew he was hard-pressed to seize victory from the jaws of defeat. In the beginning, his successes came easily and cheaply. He had thousands of goblinkin to call on, and he'd studied his targets."

Wick changed pages and took notes, drawing small goblinkin in the margins.

"The Goblin Lord brought his forces up from the south," Craugh went on. "He knew the goblinkin would be less than enthusiastic about venturing into the north to fight in the snow-covered mountains."

"He was right about that," Lago said. "They still tell stories about how the goblinkin cried tears of ice and ate their own frozen feet."

Wick blinked at that. "If they ate their own feet, how did they march?"

Lago scowled. "I don't know. Mayhap they hurried about on their stumps afterward. It's just a story. But a good one."

"The fact was, after Teldane's Bounty was destroyed and the coast shattered," Craugh went on, "Lord Kharrion had a harder time earning each conquest. In the early years of the Cataclysm, the humans, elves, and dwarves didn't get along and seldom worked together on anything."

"Except in Dream," Wick said.

Craugh nodded. "Except in Dream. But Lord Kharrion's pursuit of them, his destruction of all their books and ways of life, bonded them in ways; they had never before had to rely on each other. If they were going to survive the goblinkin onslaught, they had to join forces. They did, and the tide of battle began to turn. But those days were dark and filled with loss."

Wick remembered. The journals he'd read from that time—tired and unkempt things barely held together with second-hand glue, thread, and ties for the most part—had all carried a note of inevitable sorrow and pain.

"Lord Kharrion knew he needed more in his arsenal," Craugh said. "In Silverleaves Glen, he used dark, arcane powers and perverted the elven princesses, turning them into fierce and vicious Embyrs that fought the Unity warriors till the end when Lord Kharrion's hold over them ended. On other battlefields, he raised dead goblinkin, twisting them and shaping them into Boneblights. Then there came the second uprising at Dream."

"The first battle," Cobner said soberly, "killed most of them who lived there and scattered the rest to the wind."

Craugh nodded. "After Lord Kharrion moved on north, the Unity leaders decided to try establishing a beachhead at Dream and raising an army of the survivors there. The effort was premature. They hadn't counted on the Goblin Lord's ability to raise the goblinkin dead and have them fight again as Boneblights. This time when Lord Kharrion took Dream, he shattered the city and tore it down to rubble."

Wick still recalled the fountain he'd seen in Hanged Elf 's Point that had let him know what the city overrun by goblinkin had been before it had been destroyed. He remembered how hopeless he'd felt standing there in a slaver's chains.

But that changed, he reminded himself. *Just as this can change.*

"No one knew why Lord Kharrion didn't raze the city the first time they passed through," Craugh said. "Many suspected it was because he wanted more, faster victories to keep his goblinkin hungry and not surround them with the losses they'd suffered. Perhaps that was true, but he also may have had another reason."

"The vidrenium," Wick said, knowing immediately what the cause for the decision had been.

"We didn't know what he was doing there," Craugh said, "but now that we've learned what we have, it stands to reason."

"What are you talking about?" Brandt asked.

Craugh nodded to Wick, acknowledging the little Librarian's skills as better to summarize the story. Quickly, Wick sketched out the events as they'd been able to put them together.

"Lord Kharrion went there to retrieve the weapons?" Sonne asked when Wick had finished.

"That's what it looks like," Wick said.

"You said Lord Kharrion was there in disguise," Hamual said. He'd traded places with one of the dwarves to come in and eat.

"He was, as best as we can reconstruct the events that happened then."

"What if he wasn't after the weapons?" Hamual asked.

"What do you mean?" Craugh said.

Hamual shrugged. "Just that when we steal a unique and well-known piece of jewelry, one or more with original settings, we have to break them apart to resell them. Otherwise they'll be recognized."

Brandt leaned forward and put his chin on his forefingers, resting his elbows on the table. "Ah, Hamual, you are starting to think like a true thief."

Hamual blushed and smiled. "What if Lord Kharrion wasn't after the weapons? Remember, they weren't made until later by Master Oskarr."

"Then what else would he be after?" Lago asked.

"The vidrenium," Wick said, seizing on the idea at once. "In its purest form. He intended to make a weapon from it himself."

"Or else he already had," Craugh said, "and wanted only the magic bound into the metal to fuel his latest creation."

"Lord Kharrion's Wrath," Wick said, looking at the wizard. "Do you have any idea what it is?"

"No," Craugh answered.

"Then someone, somewhere, must," Brandt said. "Otherwise there would not be so much interest in collecting these three weapons." He leaned back in his chair. "All we have to do to stop them is to steal the weapons." He grinned. "And that's one of the things we're best at."

11

The Magic Sword

You are a master thief. You're traveling with master thieves. You won't get caught. You are the wind. No one will know you're there until you're gone. You're as quiet as a tear sliding down a cat's whisker and—

"What's wrong, little warrior?" Cobner whispered behind Wick.

The sound of the dwarf 's voice nearly caused Wick to jump out of his skin. He started and hit his head on the top of the drainpipe he, Cobner, and Sonne crawled through.

"Nothing," Wick said, rubbing the top of his head. "I was just waiting till my eyes adjusted to the darkness."

"Well? Are they adjusted?" Sonne asked with a trace of irritation.

Except for the stars I'm presently seeing, Wick thought. "Yes."

"Then get a move on. We don't have all night."

"Stay off the little warrior," Cobner said. "He knows what he's doing. He's a seasoned veteran."

"Your voice carries in the tunnel, you know," Brandt whispered from the opening they'd entered on the other side of the Chop River.

Reluctantly, Wick went forward, trailing his fingers along the side of the drainage tunnel. Brandt and his thieves had found the drain tunnel early on and explored it as much as they dared. Of course, it didn't lead where they wanted it to, but it got them closer to their ultimate goal. If everything worked right, it brought them close enough.

Kulik Broghan's fortress had been built long before the

wizard had taken up residence. During that time, the fortress had been added to and remodeled on a number of occasions. It would have been too much to hope that the tunnel would have led directly into the treasure room where the wizard kept the captured weapons. However, Brandt had used his time as "Baron Lorthord" well.

Claiming to want to repay Kulik Broghan for his hospitality, and to seal a bargain they'd both agreed on to exchange lesser items, Brandt had given the wizard a mobile of a miniature elven city made up of glistening trees overlooking a large lake that was actually a mirror. The mobile was magical in nature, and Brandt had shown the wizard how—with a phrase—the mobile would come to life, progressing through the seasons in a matter of moments. Tiny, multicolored leaves would fall from the trees into the lake, rise again as snowflakes and become buds and leaves to repeat the whole season. Over and over.

Since it was magical in nature, and the spells had been laid closely together, only a truly trained wizard could see the additional spell that had been hidden that allowed someone to access the mirror through another made with the same spell.

"Here," Cobner said. "Just ahead there."

Wick spotted the mark on the wall. Most people would never have seen it, but he'd been told what to look for. He stopped by the mark.

Quickly, Cobner took his leather pack off and unpacked the mirror inside. He laid it on the uneven ground.

"We already tried to get in this way," Cobner said. "Even sent Sonne, but she wouldn't fit neither. She's too big."

"Too tall," Sonne muttered. "I was too tall."

In truth, Wick knew that the young woman was larger proportioned than he was.

"Craugh could probably explain to you why it's so," Cobner said, "but the farther the two mirrors are from each other, the smaller the opening between them."

"Kowt's *Magical Theories of Transportation Reduction and Mass Shifting*," Wick said automatically. Reading about magic wasn't one of his favorite pastimes, but he'd gotten familiar with some of the things written. "Magic isn't without limitations, and when you confine a spell to a thing that's not inherently magical, those limitations increase exponentially."

Cobner just looked at him. "I'll take your word for it, little warrior. If it was me, I'd try a magic potion that would allow me to walk through the walls."

"Even if you could get through the walls with a discorporal potion," Wick pointed out, "you'd still cross Kulik Broghan's magical wards and set off alarms. With the mirrors, you can cross that space and it's like you were never there."

"I'll take your word for it. You know more about it than I do. Shuck your gear and step lively. There are still some patrols around the wall now and again."

Trembling a little, Wick dropped his gear and stood only in shirt and breeches.

"Here." Sonne held out a knife.

"I hope I don't need it," Wick said.

She smiled at him. "Me too. But you never know."

Nodding, he took the knife, then walked over and put a foot on the mirror. He closed his eyes, knowing he was about to get sucked into the treasure room like a boiled egg into a bottle with a fire at the bottom.

"Uh, Wick?"

Oh no! They know me! It was a trap! Then he opened one eye and saw Cobner and Sonne facing him. "Am I back already?" Maybe this wasn't so bad.

"The Word," Cobner said. "You've got to say the Word."

"Right." Wick took a deep breath and said the Word. Instantly the mirror's surface took on a rippled look, like a pond blown by the wind. He dipped a toe in and found it was cold, but not uncomfortably so. "Hey, this isn't too—"

The spell yanked him into the mirror with a loud *SPLOOSH!*

Instinctively, Wick held his breath as he was pulled under what felt like liquid. Cold blackness pressed in against him. For a moment he felt like he was coming apart. Then just as quickly he felt compressed and knew he was coming up to the moment of no return. His breath exploded from him as the spell sucked him through the opening.

No! he thought. *I'm too big! I'm not going to make it!* He felt as though a mule were sitting on his chest, as if a pair of mules were sitting on his chest. He screamed, and he felt the last of the air leave his lungs in a rush. This was where Sonne had said she'd been caught, and she had thought she was going to drown before the spell gave up and tossed her back out.

He flew through the air in a rush, landing in a pile on the hard stone floor. He coughed and sucked in a breath. "I'm sorry," he said when he had his breath back. "I'm too big. I didn't fit, either." He looked up for Cobner and Sonne—

—and discovered he wasn't in the drainage tunnel anymore. Soft lamps glowed in the corners of the room, throwing golden light over the chests of gold and gems sitting on the floor.

The sight took Wick's breath away. Stunned, he sat up. *I made it! I'm in Kulik Broghan's treasure room!*

Heart beating rapidly, he pushed himself to his feet and looked around. He'd arrived only a few feet from the elven mobile that had magically transported him into the room. The mobile was a thing of beauty, elegant and fragile looking. It sat next to an elven helm cut into the features of a snarling wolf on a stone head.

Wick couldn't believe he was alone. He had half expected to find Kulik Broghan there. Or a small army of armed guards. Either one of those wouldn't have been too big a surprise. Luck wasn't something that came easily to him.

The treasure room was small but contained fortunes. Besides the gold coins and ingots and gems, there were a number of weapons. Swords, spears, bows, knives, and axes all occupied weapons racks.

Get moving! Wick told himself. *They'll be worried about you!* On his way over, though, he couldn't help stuffing the bag Cobner had given him, advising him to do as much "shopping" as he could while he hunted the weapons. Before he reached the weapons racks, the bag was filled to overflowing with gold coins and gems, surely a small fortune that would pay whatever Brandt was charging for helping them recover the two weapons.

Tying the bag back to his belt, he approached the weapons racks, spotting Boneslicer immediately. Grasping the battle-axe, he eased it free of the rack.

At that moment, the jewel-encrusted broadsword next to the battle-axe opened its eye. The eye was elongated like a cat's but it looked vaguely reptilian. It blinked and focused on him.

Wick stood hypnotized. He'd read about animated weapons before, but he'd never seen one. Cautiously, slowly as he could, he leaned to the left.

The eye followed him.

Thinking maybe that was just a trick of the light, Wick took two steps to the right.

Effortlessly, the eye followed him again, looking right at him.

Metallic lips formed on the blade. "Greetings."

Greetings? Wick thought rapidly, trying to come up with a ploy. All he came up with was, "Greetings."

"What are you doing?"

"Nothing."

"Yes you are."

"No I'm not." Wick suddenly felt like he was trapped in one of those endless conversations he had with Grandmagister Frollo. Of course, when he got back there was going to be a new wrinkle in those conversations. *Second Level Librarian, you're the reason I was a toad!*

"You took that axe."

Wick looked down at Boneslicer as if he were surprised to see it. "This axe?"

"Yes. That axe." The voice sounded petulant as a child.

"Oh. *This* axe. I thought you meant the other axe."

"Which axe?"

"The one I'm not supposed to shine."

"You're going to shine that axe?" the magic sword asked.

"Yes. I'm the new treasure polisher." Wick pulled out the tail of his shirt and started scrubbing on the battle-axe's haft. "Kulik Broghan told me I had to shine this axe."

"You're a treasure polisher?"

"Yes."

"We've never had a treasure polisher before."

"Well," Wick said with a hint of the conspirator in his voice, "if you ask me, that shows. Nobody should let their treasure get this dusty." He shined Boneslicer some more, spitting on it and polishing again, humming a happy tune as he did so. He also took a step backward.

The sword frowned, the eye half closing and the metallic lips pursing in frustration. "Why does that axe get all the special attention?"

"Does it get special attention?"

"You know it does."

"No," Wick said. "This is my first night."

"I didn't think I'd seen you before." The sword looked in the direction of the big door. "In fact, I don't remember hearing the door open."

"You must have been asleep."

"Maybe. It gets boring in here. When my master had me, we were always fighting dragons, rescuing princesses, and cutting the ribbons at market dedications."

"Really?"

"I'm a very famous sword. Maybe you've heard of me."

"Maybe I have. What's your name?"

"Frostfire."

"Really?" Wick asked, excited and interested in spite of the fact that he was meeting a magic sword for the very first time while in the treasure room of a wizard who had already hired people to try to kill him. "I *have* heard of you!"

"See?" the sword said smugly. "I told you."

"You slew the giant Konnard! And the banshee hordes of Bluesdale!"

"That was me." The sword seemed somehow to stand a little straighter in the weapons rack. "So I'm telling you that if anyone deserves polishing around here, it's me."

Then Wick remembered something very distressing. It was true that Frostfire had been the human hero Murral's sword, but when it had disappeared, it had been subjected to a spell by an evil wizard that had altered its nature. No longer content with aiding its hero, Frostfire had turned on him and given his position away again and again until the ice trolls had finally killed him.

"You're right," Wick said, suddenly feeling in danger again. "You do need polishing. Let me put this axe away."

"I'll be right here."

Trying not to panic, Wick walked over to the elven mirror, said the magic Word again, and dumped the axe in. Boneslicer slid through like it was sinking into a small rippling sea.

"Hey," Frostfire said.

"Yes?" Wick replied.

"Did you just shove that axe into that mirror?" The eye bulged on the sword as if trying to peer over the other weapons.

"No," Wick said, trying to keep his voice from trembling. "I laid it down over here by the wall."

"I can't see it."

"Do you want to see it?"

"Yes," the sword replied. "I'm supposed to guard everything in here."

"All right," Wick said, "but if I'm going to pick it up again, I might as well shine it."

"Never mind," the sword said. "I guess I need to get my eye checked. I haven't been out of this treasure room in a long time. Maybe I'm just seeing things."

Wick returned to the weapons rack, looked down at the sword, then picked up Seaspray.

"Hey," Frostfire called. "Over here." The sword jostled in place. "You grabbed the wrong sword. I'm the one with the eye. See?" He blinked rapidly.

"I know," Wick said. "I was just told to shine this sword, too." He carried Seaspray over to the elven mirror and saw the spell was still in effect because the surface was still rippling.

"I thought you were going to shine me."

"I am. I just don't want to forget these weapons. Kulik Broghan will be very cross with me if I don't remember to shine these two."

"Why are they his favorites all of a sudden?" Frostfire asked in a petulant voice.

"He doesn't tell me things like that."

"He hasn't told me, either," the sword said, "and I get tired of it, I tell you. I mean, how many other sentient swords does Kulik Broghan have?"

None, I hope, Wick thought. He dropped Seaspray into the mirror pool. It went in with hardly a ripple and only a slight *sploosh*.

"Hey," Frostfire protested. "You did it again!"

"Did what?"

"You put that sword in the mirror like you did the axe!"

"I'm sure it only looks that way from there."

"Actually, it looks that way from here, too."

Noticing the change in the sound of the voice, Wick peered over his shoulder and found Frostfire floating there, gently bobbing as if riding out an invisible ocean.

"I was watching you that time," the sword accused. "You dropped that sword into the mirror."

"Uh—" Wick thought furiously. "No I didn't."

"I saw you."

"I didn't drop it," Wick said. "It slipped."

"Slipped?" Frostfire blinked at him, as if considering the truth of what he was saying.

"Sure. I have polish on my hands. It gets slippery."

"You dropped the sword?"

"Yep." Wick showed the magic sword his best innocent smile. Maybe it didn't work on Grandmagister Frollo anymore, but surely it would work on the sword. After all, Frostfire hadn't been all that bright to begin with, and the evil spell had dulled its wits.

"Swords don't fall through mirrors," Frostfire said.

"I'm not responsible for the mirrors," Wick said, drawing himself up. "I'm just here to polish weapons."

Unfortunately, a rather large ruby chose that moment to spill out of the pouch he'd crammed so full of loot. The gem skittered across the floor and bounced against the wall.

Tilting forward, Frostfire examined the bag at Wick's hip. "That bag is full of gold coins and gems."

"I've got to polish those as well," Wick said, thinking it was at least worth a try.

Frostfire's eye narrowed in suspicion. "You know, suddenly I don't believe you. You know what? I don't think you're a treasure polisher at all. I think you're a—" The sword's voice rose by several decibels. "—*THIEF!* Help! Thief! Thief in the treasure room! Help!"

Immediately, the sound of running feet pounded in the room outside the door. Kulik Broghan obviously kept guards posted nearby.

"Thief in the treasure room!" the sword continued to yell. It spun around, bringing its blade up to engage Wick.

Moving quickly, Wick grabbed the snarling wolf-face elven helm from the stone head and used it to block the sword blow. Just as quickly, he reached out and poked the sword in the eye with a forefinger.

"Arrrrrrrgggggghhhhhh!" the sword screamed. "He poked my eye! He poked my eye! I'm blind! Help!"

The door rattled as it started to swing inside.

Unwilling to wait around any longer, Wick dove into the mirror, grabbing the loot bag and shoving it ahead of him because he didn't want to get hung up on it. There was a moment of the intense black cold again, then he shot through the other mirror and back into the drainage tunnel.

"Little warrior," Cobner called, starting forward. He held Boneslicer in both hands. His own battle-axe was slung over his back.

Sonne stood nearby with Seaspray.

Wick landed painfully on his head and immediately scrabbled to get to his feet. "Get back!" he called. "We've been found out!" He twisted toward the mirror and grabbed it in both hands while Sonne reached down for the loot bag. Only a few gold coins and jewels had spilled from it.

"What are you doing?" Cobner asked.

Not wanting to take time to explain, Wick lifted the mirror and swung it toward the wall. Just before the mirror made contact with the wall, Frostfire flew free and spun through the air. Then the mirror hit the wall and shattered into a thousand gleaming pieces in a rainbow spray of color that filled the drainage ditch.

"There you are!" the sword shrilled. It spun across the intervening space.

"Duck!" Cobner ordered.

Wick ducked, grabbing his head in both hands, knowing he was about to have it shorn from his shoulders. Metal shrieked. Daring to look up even though he didn't want to, Wick saw Boneslicer intercept Frostfire.

"Thief!" the sword yelled, withdrawing and hanging in the air.

"A magic sword?" Cobner asked.

"Nobody mentioned there'd be a magic sword," Wick complained.

"We didn't know," Cobner said. Frostfire feinted and drove in, screaming curses. Amazingly the dwarf blocked every attack and the tunnel filled with the clangor of ringing metal.

"I'm gonna get you!" the sword screamed. "I'm gonna get you!"

"By the Old Ones," Cobner said, "I hate talking weapons. Never know when to shut up."

"Help!" Frostfire screamed. "Helllllllppppppp! Guards! Thieves! Thieves!"

Sonne handed Wick the loot back, then grabbed his shirt and yanked him into motion. "Run," she ordered.

Wick ran, heading for the other end of the tunnel as fast as he could go. He didn't doubt that the alarm would be spreading inside the fortress. Kulik Broghan's guards would converge on them in seconds. The ringing duel followed him, coming quickly.

Outside, Wick ran down the short, steep incline toward the reeds where Craugh, Brandt, and the others waited in a small riverboat. For the moment, they'd decided to leave *One-Eyed Peggie* out in the harbor and try to keep from setting sail with a dozen ships nipping at their heels.

Besides, Sokadir and Deathwhisper were upriver in the Forest of Fangs and Shadows. That was where they needed to go. Provided they escaped.

Wick ran for all he was worth, but his steps got ahead of him and he tripped, spilling down the incline to the river's edge. He held on to the loot bag tightly, losing less than a handful of coins. Rolling to a stop on his back, he looked up at Craugh.

"What's going on?" the wizard asked.

"Magic sword," Wick said. "Nobody said anything about a magic sword."

"Well," Brandt said, lifting the loot bag from Wick's grasp and handing it back to Hamual, "no one mentioned there was a magic sword in the treasure room when I talked with Kulik Broghan."

Sonne ran from the tunnel, followed by Cobner, who was still battling the magic sword.

Wick tried to get up, then discovered he'd slipped and fallen in mud, thoroughly soaking his clothes. He groaned, then hoped that he lived long enough that wet clothing was the worst of his worries.

An arrow materialized between his feet. He stared at it, then realized it had been fired from above. Swiveling his head back, he looked up at the fortress wall. At least a half dozen archers lined the high wall, letting fly as quickly as they could.

"Shields!" Zelnar, or maybe it was Tyrnen, yelled in warning. He and his twin, joined by the four other dwarves—Baldarn, Volsk, Rithilin, and Charnir—lifted shields to protect everyone.

Arrows thunked into the shields.

Lago reached out of the boat and grabbed Wick by the shirt. "Get in here before you get feathered!" The old dwarf yanked him into the riverboat.

Wick yelped when he hit, collecting several bruises in the process. Getting his life saved wasn't always a gentle process.

"Bah," Craugh growled, "this is insufferable." Green embers darted from his eyes as he drew his hand back. A ball of swirling flames formed in his hand. A moment later, he threw the fireball, which swelled in size as it flew at the cluttered archers.

The archers suddenly decided they had other places to be and abandoned their positions. The fireball struck the wall and threw green flames in all directions. The stones blistered and cracked, exploding in a sudden chain.

Sonne reached the hillside then and dove in among the dwarves. Baldarn shifted his shield and caught her in one strong arm, delivering her gently to the bottom of the boat.

"Cobner!" Brandt called.

"I'm busy," Cobner yelled back, still fighting briskly with the magic sword.

"Lousy, flea-bitten slaves!" Frostfire yelled. "I'm going to get you!"

"Magic sword," Brandt observed.

"I see that," Craugh replied. "Nuisance is what it is. I hate magic weapons with personalities. It's the same reason I don't keep a familiar." He pointed in Cobner's direction. A green beam jetted from his forefinger and slammed against the sword, sending it spinning out of the air to slam into the fortress wall.

"Come on," Brandt urged.

Cobner turned and ran, skidding and falling down the incline. By that time, Hamual, Sonne, and Karick had bows ready and were firing back at the guards. A man tumbled over the side and hit the ground.

Brandt ran back to the tiller and settled in. Charnir joined him, raising his shield to defend them both. An arrow struck the shield and bounced off.

"Grab hold!" Brandt yelled.

Everyone hunkered down. Wick slid close to the side and took a good hold on the railing.

"Ready, Craugh," Brandt said.

Immediately, Craugh turned from throwing a second fireball into the midst of a group of guards that had just rounded the corner of the fortress. Several of them were on fire now, screaming and yelling and smoldering as they ran to the river's edge and jumped in.

Craugh threw an open hand toward the riverboat's single sail, which was fluttering a little in the slight breeze. The canvas glowed a pale green, then the sail filled as if it had just grabbed hold of a hurricane. The riverboat took out from the bank like an arrow launched from a bow.

Glancing back, Wick saw some of the surviving guards try to give chase, but they were quickly outdistanced by the magically powered boat. A few last arrows fell short, dropping into the river and thudding into the bank.

Sighing with relief, Wick tried to relax. They'd escaped. Now all they had to do was find Sokadir.

12

Never-Know Road

They traveled by riverboat and magically summoned wind all night, but toward the end, even Craugh's power was at last beginning to fail him.

"We need to rest," the wizard said. "I dare not use up all my reserves. We're going to be traveling in hostile territory for a while."

"Rest," Brandt said. "You've done more than enough for now." He glanced back over his shoulder at the dark river behind them. "We haven't seen any signs of pursuit thus far."

Gradually, the glow faded from the sail and it finally fluttered and died altogether. The thieves grabbed oars and put them into the locks, then started rowing, spelling each other off and on. The rowing was hard because the Chop River was named after the turbulent rush that spilled down it. Wick was convinced that a man walking along the riverbank would make better time than they were.

Only a few hours before dawn, Brandt called an end to it. They put the riverboat into the bank, then crawled out and hauled the craft up into the thick brush that filled the Forest of Fangs and Shadows.

Wick hurt all over and ached for sleep. He could attribute the pain to the falls he'd taken during the night, but he believed that traveling by magic had also done something to his body. He didn't know if he would ever be the same again.

They made a cold camp deep in the forest. Brandt posted four guards and set up a rotation schedule, placing himself and Cobner on alternating shifts. With luck, they would get two hours' sleep before morning. Wick intended to get all four hours and figured that he'd earned it.

Lago outdid himself by revealing the large picnic baskets he'd packed aboard the riverboat. They contained cold chicken, sweet potatoes, and fresh-baked bread. He'd even packed honey butter and a selection of three preserves, all made fresh while they'd been holed up awaiting Craugh's arrival.

"There isn't anything like snatching your fate from the grinning jaws of death to give a warrior an appetite," the old dwarf said.

Wick ate a little, but kept falling asleep. Finally giving in to exhaustion, he rolled up in his traveling cloak, laid his head on his arm, and closed his eyes. He was asleep before he took a full breath.

"Wick, wake up."

Still half asleep, Wick flailed at the arm that shook him.

"C'mon, little warrior. You don't want to be napping here when Kulik Broghan's men come upriver looking for whoever stole those weapons from his treasure room," Cobner said.

Wick sighed and reluctantly let go of sleep. It fragmented in his grasp, dissolving like spun sugar. When he blinked his eyes open, he saw that fog had settled in over the forest. Gray vapor pushed between the trees, blunting the distant morning sunlight so that it almost appeared to be twilight.

This, he thought, *is why they call it the Forest of Fangs and Shadows.*

No one knew why the forest attracted as much fog as it did. Some claimed it was because the Broken Forge Mountains housed a live volcano and because the Gentlewind Sea was so cold. The constantly churning masses of warm air and cold air contributed to the foggy conditions that often held sway over the area.

Lago had three campfires going and was happily moving between the various pots and pans, stirring and turning and mixing. Everything smelled good, but Wick was surprised he was already hungry again after last night's repast.

Brandt and Cobner weren't overly talkative. Each kept their own counsel as they studied the forest with watchful eyes. Their weapons were close to hand.

"Good morning, little artist," Brandt greeted. "Sleep well?"

"Well enough," Wick said, "but not nearly long enough." He helped himself to frying pan biscuits, bacon, and onions and potatoes. Sitting back on his haunches, he turned his attention to his meal.

"Eat all you can," Craugh advised. "We've got a long walk ahead of us to join the Never-Know Road."

"Won't Kulik Broghan look for us there?" Wick asked.

"If he or his men are there, we'll wait until the roads are clear." The wizard ate slowly. This morning he looked worn and haggard. "By now Hallekk will have seen that we were successful and will be bringing Quarrel, Alysta, Bulokk, and his warriors to meet us."

The plan was for Hallekk and the others to meet them along the Never-Know Road while Craugh and Wick headed on into the Laceleaves Glen territory where

Sokadir was. When they rendezvoused, they would have a stronger force to stand against Kulik Broghan and the Razor's Kiss thieves' guild.

At least, that was the plan.

Craugh still hadn't mentioned how he was going to pull Sokadir out of hiding.

It took them all day to march through the Forest of Fangs and Shadows to reach the Never-Know Road. The fog finally cleared at midday, but even then the weather never turned warm, but it did lose some of its coolness.

Wick's mind worked constantly as he walked through the forest. He tried not to remember how many vicious beasts and predators roamed the area, but he kept coming back to thinking about bears, wolves, harpies, goblinkin, trolls, spiders, snakes, wild pigs, and dragons. They weren't happy thoughts.

Thankfully, Hamual played his flute from time to time, and the dwarves swapped stories and sang. During the breaks from walking, Wick used the time to work in his journal. Craugh, he noted, kept to himself. If he didn't know how arrogant the wizard was, Wick would have thought Craugh was showing some of the stress they were all under.

Of course, that was ridiculous.

Still, the possibility that Craugh believed they were about to engage something he couldn't completely control left Wick feeling a little queasy.

Toward dusk, Hamual—who was scouting at the moment—called back to let them know they had to veer to the east instead of continuing north because of a spider colony that had left hammock webs everywhere in the forest. No one argued.

Walking along a ridgeline a fair distance away, Wick spotted the giant spiders crawling through the trees. Their legs spanned eight feet and their bodies were bigger than dwarves, almost as tall as a man.

A short distance ahead, they walked under abandoned nests. Dessicated bodies hung in the silken folds. They were so shriveled and missing so many pieces—really no more than clothing, hair, and bones—that Wick couldn't tell if they were human, elf, dwarf, or dweller.

A few of them were goblinkin. There was no mistaking the death stench that clung to some of the newer ones. Goblinkin smelled even worse dead than alive.

But by nightfall, they reached the Never-Know Road and only had to walk three more miles to reach a waystop.

The waystop was little more than a wide place in the well-traveled road. Over the years, the Never-Know Road had been beaten and ground down to bedrock. Ruts still marred the surface, but they couldn't go as deep anymore because hooves and boots and bare feet had trod the earth into the consistency of stone.

A lantern hung from a tree to one side of the road. The wide open space and ashes of old campfires showed that a number of people had camped there over the years. The brush and young trees had also been hacked down to ankle height so that nothing could come creeping out of the forest without being seen. Scavengers and predators had learned to lie in wait along the Never-Know Road, always open to whatever chance brought them.

The group built campfires. Wick sat close to the one he shared with Hamual, Sonne, and Cobner. The warmth pressed against him and he was grateful for it. Tonight promised even lower temperatures than the night before. Lago provided yet another feast, and the grumbling some of them had voiced earlier in the day at having to carry the packs he'd prepared were thrown back in the faces of those who had complained.

None of them talked overlong after they had their bellies full. With so little sleep the night before and all day spent tramping through the woods, they all went to sleep early.

Wick woke only once, to take a turn at guard as he'd volunteered. For a time, he worked by the moonslight in his journal, his ears alert to the slightest sound. He also looked up frequently, aware that the lives of his friends depended on his vigilance.

His shift passed without incident and he had no trouble returning to sleep. But this time his dreams were plagued with memories of the fighting he'd glimpsed of the Battle of Fell's Keep in the vision Craugh's spell had wrought.

By midday the next day, they caught up to a caravan heading east to meet up with the Steadfast River. There the caravan master would haggle for a couple days with the merchants and traders who'd come upriver to trade goods and buy others they would resell down in Deldal's Mills and farther downriver to Calmpoint. All those goods came by way of the farmlands passed along the way and at the trade fairs established by other traders that carried goods over the Broken Forge Mountains.

Craugh and Brandt negotiated joining up with the caravan for safety's sake, and it was agreed to. They fell in after the last wagon and spent hours walking in the dust before it started to rain that evening and finally the dust was knocked from the air.

When the caravan rested that evening, they sat apart from the rest of the wagons and traders, making their own camp but staying within the safety presented in numbers. Lago took advantage of the availability of trade for food and bargained for more supplies, spending the gold Wick had liberated from Kulik Broghan's treasure room.

Wick thought about joining Craugh and talking to him, but the wizard seemed preoccupied, so he kept with Hamual and Cobner, swapping stories and enjoying one another's company. Wick still missed being at the Vault of All Known Knowledge, but he'd come to enjoy the time spent with his friends—at least, those times he didn't spend running for his life.

"What do you think Craugh's thinking about so hard?" Cobner asked during a lull in the conversation.

Studying the wizard's profile, Wick shook his head. "I don't know."

"Whatever it is," Hamual said, fingering his lute, "you know if it's got Craugh thinking about it overmuch, it has to be bad."

Wick silently agreed.

Late the next day, they were delayed half a day by a broken wheel on one of the wagons. Since Brandt and Craugh had decided to stay with the caravan for safety and for the disguise it offered, they stopped with it.

With the impromptu break taking place, Wick lounged in the shade offered by the trees. His hands craved his journal and charcoal to capture the scenes of the people talking in groups, trading among themselves, and the caravan master impatiently trying to help the wagon driver replace the wheel.

Finally, unable to handle just sitting any longer, Wick excused himself from Hamual and Cobner's company and approached Craugh. The wizard looked up at him in idle speculation.

"What?" Craugh snapped.

"I thought we'd talk," Wick said.

"I don't know if that's such a good idea." Craugh shifted his staff restlessly. "With the mood and condition I'm in, I don't look forward to having my authority undermined at this point and in this place."

Wick stood on trembling legs, as afraid then as he'd been afraid two nights ago when Frostfire, the magic sword, had unexpectedly come to life in Kulik Broghan's treasure room. "I'm not here to question your authority or judgment, Craugh. I simply wanted to make certain you're all right."

Craugh continued looking at him suspiciously. "I'm fine."

"I'm glad." Wick hesitated, not truly knowing what to say, but feeling that he had to say something. "I didn't mean to undermine your authority on *One-Eyed Peggie*."

Craugh sighed.

For a moment Wick thought he was going to be turned into a toad just for apologizing.

Heaving himself up from beside the tree where he'd been sitting, Craugh turned toward the forest. "Walk with me."

"Uh, are you sure you wouldn't rather be alone?" Wick didn't want to take the chance that the wizard was going to take him out into the forest, toadify him, and leave him for the wolves and spiders.

"I want to talk to you." Craugh waited, looking more impatient by the moment. "There are things I must say."

Feeling like he was going to throw up, mostly certain he was walking to his doom, Wick joined the wizard. They walked into the forest. At least Cobner, Hamual, and Sonne had noticed that Craugh was walking with him. If he got changed into a toad, maybe they would come catch him and plead with Craugh to change him back. Or at least gather him up so he'd be safe and not get eaten. Wick truly didn't want to be alone in the forest, especially not as a toad.

"I've yelled at you, I've risked your life on several occasions during this little adventure, and I've lied to you whenever I felt the need. About things that you couldn't even imagine." Craugh shook his head. "And yet, you come to me this morning and ask after my health. Truly you are like no one I've ever known before."

Wick took a slow step back, certain he'd done something wrong, but not knowing in any way what that might be. *Maybe if I apologize really fast! Maybe if I told him I've got a fever and I didn't know what I—*

"Your care for me touches me," Craugh said, "in a way I haven't experienced in a long, long time."

That caught Wick totally by surprise.

"No matter what I've asked you to do," Craugh went on, "you've done it. You stood up to me on *One-Eyed Peggie* and made me do the thing that I should have known to do without being told. Or should have listened to immediately." The wizard took a deep breath. "When we went back to Greydawn Moors, when you were once more safely within the walls of the Vault of All Known Knowledge, you could have insisted on staying there. Where you'd be safe."

Not after you turned Grandmagister Frollo into a toad and yelled at him, Wick thought, but didn't say. *I wouldn't have been safe there. I might not be safe there when I go back.*

"I had a good friendship with Grandmagister Ludaan," Craugh went on. "Together, he and I managed to right a number of wrongs."

"He was a good Librarian," Wick acknowledged. "An even better teacher."

"I'm a better man for having known him. I know that's true." Craugh's green eyes locked on Wick's. "Just as I'm a better man for having known you."

A lump formed in Wick's throat. The silence between them seemed like a bottomless void. "I . . . I . . . I don't know what to say," he whispered.

"Nothing," Craugh said. "You don't have to say anything. This is my time to speak, and I've said things here today that I never expected to say again the rest of my life." He stood a little straighter. "There. I've said what I intended to say. I want to thank you for your care and concern, Second Level Librarian Lamplighter. I only hope you feel as though you've made a wise investment in your friendship."

Wick stood there. His senses reeled. *This didn't happen. I imagined all of this.*

"I'd rather you kept quiet about this conversation when we get back to the others," Craugh said.

No one would believe me anyway. Wick nodded, not trusting himself to speak, not daring to say one word that might change the whole tone of the conversation.

Craugh frowned, but only a little. "Close your mouth. You're going to attract flies."

Wick nodded and closed his mouth. He bit his tongue but didn't yelp in pain, didn't even flinch.

Peering back at the road, Craugh said, "I think we can return. It looks as though they finally replaced that wheel." He looked at Wick again. "Where we're headed, what we're going to find, I don't truly know. I want you to know you can speak freely with your counsel." He paused. "I can't guarantee that it will be well received at all times, but I will listen."

Nodding again, Wick refrained from speaking.

Craugh started to walk away.

Wick couldn't let it pass. As soon as the urge to speak hit him and he knew he couldn't hold it back, he was terrified. The wizard's name was past his lips before he could stop it. "Craugh."

The wizard turned toward him and gazed at him expectantly. "Yes?" For just a moment, there appeared a flash of vulnerability Wick had never before seen in the wizard. Then it was gone, and Wick thought perhaps he might have been mistaken.

"I've never known anyone like you," Wick whispered. "I've never had a . . . *friend* like you."

"You have lots of friends." Craugh nodded toward the Band of Thieves. "Them. The crew of *One-Eyed Peggie*. I know Captain Farok puts a lot of store by you. You seem to make friends wherever you go."

"That's because people aren't afraid of me," Wick said, then wondered if he'd been too honest. "I mean, the thought that I might turn them into toads never crosses their minds."

Craugh frowned. "No, I suppose it wouldn't."

"The thing I'm trying to say is, I don't fit any better in this world than you do," Wick went on. "We're, both of us, trying to make our own way, and that way isn't very clear. I'm a dweller Librarian who, for whatever reason, can't seem to simply want to stay at the Vault of All Known Knowledge and take care of books. And you—" He stopped. "Well, you're a wizard. But you can't simply be a wizard and tend to your own selfish interests, conquer towns, and terrorize people the way other wizards do. Just as with this investigation into what truly happened at the Battle of Fell's Keep. Both of us have contrary natures."

"Well," Craugh said, "I've been more selfish than you could even know." He took a deep breath. "Maybe one of these days I'll tell you all about it."

"I'd be glad to listen."

"Don't be too sure. There is much you still don't know." Craugh hesitated, then reached out and placed a hand on Wick's shoulder. "You're a good friend, Wick. There is innocence in you that I will never let anyone take from you as long as I live."

"Thank you," Wick whispered, not knowing what else to say. Craugh left him standing there, heading back to rejoin the caravan, already grumbling because it had taken so long. But for a long time, Wick could still feel the unbelieveable gentleness of the wizard's hand as it had rested on his shoulder.

13

Laceleaves Glen

Hallekk and the group from *One-Eyed Peggie* caught up with them that evening. Again, they'd taken a camp by themselves.

"Cap'n Farok expects us to continue on with ye," Hallekk told Craugh. "Told me I wasn't to come back without ye." He cut his glance toward Wick. "Nor without Wick."

"I'll have to thank Captain Farok upon our return," Craugh replied.

Wick marveled at the wizard's confidence. Here they were, in one of the worst stretches of wilderness there was, and Craugh acted like they were out for a lark. At that moment, an owl flew by low overhead. Several of the caravan drivers and guards warded themselves, spat and cursed, taking the arrival of the bird as an ill omen.

Breathless with anticipation, Bulokk and Quarrel received their ancestors' weapons. Both of them had held them before, but Wick knew what it meant to them to hold them again now, even if they were surrounded on all sides by the threat of the Forest of Fangs and Shadows. They both thanked Wick and hugged him fiercely, embarrassing him near to death. For hours afterward, stories were told about the weapons and the heroes that had carried them. Laughter and tears followed the stories. And Wick knew that Bulokk and Quarrel were nervous about their new duties. Living up to legends was hard.

Lago was hard pressed even with his resources to feed the big group, but he negotiated a few more purchases (at what he complained were a brigand's prices!) and soon had pots and pans bubbling. Several of the other caravan groups looked on in envy.

"Tomorrow," Craugh said, "we'll separate from the caravan. We'll strike out for Laceleaves Glen along the elven trade trail."

"If we do that," Brandt said, "the elves will know we're coming."

"When ye're a-dealin' with elves," Hallekk said, "especially if you're on their home ground, it's better that they know ye're a-comin'. Try a-sneakin' up on them, ye'll end up with more feathers than a winter turkey by the time they open up on ye with their bows."

Wick sat to one side of the group and listened to the stories, catching up on the adventures Hallekk and the others had had (there'd been a squabble with goblinkin along the way that had slowed them a little, but ended up with a lot of goblinkin left out for the carrion eaters), and listening to Cobner and Sonne relate their own adventures while in town waiting for Craugh's arrival or for the weapons to be removed from Kulik Broghan.

"There's quite a stir in town, too," Hallekk said. "Word's gotten out that some of Kulik Broghan's pretties has up an' got theirselves stolen. He's pitchin' a proper fit about it. Turnin' the town over lookin' for 'em."

"Good," Brandt said, "then he's not looking for them in this direction."

"Somethin's goin' on, though," Hallekk said.

"Why?" Cobner asked.

"Because for all the noise Kulik Broghan is makin' lookin' for them missin' weapons, I didn't see enough of his men doin' it."

"What do you mean?" Brandt asked.

"Way I heard it in Torgarlk Town," Hallekk said, "Kulik Broghan's had him a standin' army garrisoned there for some time. Lots of bad things have happened there when them men got bored."

"That's true," Sonne said. "We counted several warriors that Kulik Broghan had on his payroll."

"So then," Brandt mused, black eyes filled with fire, "where are the rest of his men?"

No one had an answer, and no one slept any better that night even with the extra guards posted.

Just before midday, Brandt went forward to talk to the caravan master and tell him they were taking their leave. Shortly after that, they were on the barely worn footpath that Craugh said led to Laceleaves Glen, where Sokadir had once ruled as prince.

"Why ain't there a better path?" Bulokk grumbled as he fought through the brush. "Seems like if elves used this trail to trade along, they'd take better care of it."

"Woodlands elves don't walk on the ground unless they have to," Wick said. He pointed up at the interlocking branches of the tall trees. "They prefer traveling through the trees."

"I see horses' hooves here." Bulokk pointed.

"Probably from traders going to the elven sprawl," Wick said. "When you're in the forest, you won't often find elves on the ground. The Old Ones gave them the air, the high places in the tall trees, just as they gave the dwarves the earth and the humans the seas."

"I never met no elves while I was on the Cinder Clouds Islands."

"Elves are," Wick said, "very much their own people with their own way of doing things."

For two days, they traveled through the forest. Although they ran short of fresh meat, Brandt and Hallekk didn't allow the men to take game. They were on elven lands now.

Several of the dwarven pirates started to get nervous, including Hallekk, because none of them were used to being far from the sea. But Craugh insisted they were getting closer to Laceleaves Glen, which no one else had been to.

According to the spell he had on Boneslicer and Seaspray, they were also getting closer to Deathwhisper. They reached Laceleaves Glen first. Actually, elven warriors from Laceleaves Glen reached them first.

The afternoon of the third day, Hamual stopped in his position of scout and held both hands up. Slowly, he turned around and said, "We're not alone. Stand still."

Knowing what he was looking for, Wick peered through the wisps of fog that still clung to the forest that day and looked up into the trees. He didn't know how many elves were up there, but there were a lot of them.

"How did they get up there so quiet like?" Bulokk asked. He fingered the haft of the battle-axe and unconsciously shifted his feet into a ready position.

"They were waiting on us," Wick answered. "They spotted us coming and knew we'd cross under them."

"Don't make any sudden moves," Hallekk advised. "We're trespassin' on their lands."

"This is a trade route," Bulokk countered.

"Aye," Hallekk agreed, "but they know we ain't no traders. Comin' up here empty-handed an' armed to the teeth like we done. They figure we're the next thing to an invasion force."

"Against an elven sprawl?" Alysta spat and hissed.

"They also might have sensed the magic in those weapons you carry," Craugh said. "Their power is naked. My own is masked from elven senses."

Wick knew that elves recognized magic much more quickly than any other race, second only to trained wizards.

Slowly, Craugh lifted his hands and walked apart from the group. He spoke loudly. "I'm Craugh. I've come among your people before."

"Perhaps you have, graybeard," an elf called down, "but that doesn't tell me why you're here now."

"I've come seeking Sokadir."

“Sokadir is rootless,” the elf replied. “You were told that before, Craugh.”

“I can find him this time.”

Several of the elves hanging in the trees clucked their tongues. “When an elf doesn’t want to be found, no one may find him.”

“Then there will be no harm in my looking, will there?”

After a brief discussion in an elven tongue that Wick recognized (most of it inflammatory and derogatory and directed at Craugh, and some of it good-natured cajoling toward the elven captain to let the group pass and look for Sokadir because none of them were elven and couldn’t possibly find Sokadir), one of them dropped from the treetops.

The elf plummeted like a shot sparrow for a moment, then caught hold of four or five branches on the way down (it all happened too fast for Wick to see), and finally came to a stop on a branch only a few feet from Craugh and a little higher.

Handsome and arrogant, the elf lounged on the branch on bent knees and regarded the wizard. “I am Alomas,” he declared, “captain of Prince Larrosh’s Royal Guard.” He was a little over five feet in height, smooth-faced and slender. His pointed ears stood out against his blue-black hair. Eyes as dark green as holly leaves held a hint of mischief. He wore a chain mail shirt, short breeches tapered so they wouldn’t catch on brush or branches as he passed through the forest, and carried a bow slung over his shoulder as well as a short sword in a reverse sheath on his back so it hung upside down. Leaf-bladed throwing knives hung in a brace over his chest.

“Greetings, Alomas,” Craugh said.

“Greetings, graybeard. You’ve come a long way for nothing.”

“Perhaps.” Green sparks whirled from Craugh’s staff. “But that remains to be seen.”

“I have seen you before.”

“As I told you.”

“You’ve looked for Sokadir before.”

“I have,” Craugh admitted.

The elf smiled. “You’ve never found Sokadir before.”

“This time,” Craugh said with grim conviction, “shall be different.”

“We’ll see, graybeard.” Alomas held his hand aloft.

A falcon dropped from a branch high overhead and came to rest on the leather bracer the elf wore on his right wrist.

“A message, Goodheart,” Alomas said. “Quickly.”

The bird dipped its head quickly, then leaped into the air, flapped its wings and arrowed unerringly through the forest.

“Now,” Alomas said, “we wait. Make yourselves comfortable.”

Wick sat beside a tree trunk and hid his journal from view as he worked on it. He used charcoal and broad strokes to lay out the scene, capturing the elves resting easily in the trees as if they were avian. Their animal companions—falcons, songbirds, squirrels, wolves, and other woodland creatures, including two brown bears—occupied themselves nearby.

It was the first time Wick had seen so many elves in one group outside of Greydawn Moors. There the elves lived in sprawls as well, beautiful tree houses that had been lived in for generations (which was a long time considering the elven life spans), but this was different. In Mossglisten Forest, Wick didn't ever once think that maybe the elves would kill him.

Here, he knew, there was every chance. It was unsettling, which made him more nervous, and the only way he could ease that was by working, which required a certain amount of clandestine behavior on his part. Thankfully, he was a dweller amidst nearly forty armed humans and dwarves who showed scars from blood they'd shed during violent encounters.

Craugh kept to himself, actually chatting amiably with Alomas as they waited for word. It wasn't long in coming. After a few more minutes, Goodheart came flying back and cried out for the elven captain's attention.

Alomas lifted his arm and Goodheart landed there. They talked for a moment, then the elven captain turned to Craugh. He smiled. "You're in good fortune. Prince Larrosh must be feeling generous these days."

They reached the sprawl at the onset of twilight, coming up over a ridge that kept the whole valley below hidden until the last moment. The sight took Wick's breath away. Even all the books he'd read on elves hadn't prepared him for what lay before him.

Laceleaves Glen was large for an elven community, which were normally small. More than a hundred tree houses occupied the tall, straight trees at the bottom of the canyon. Rope ladders connected several of them and knitted a hub of suspension bridges that provided communal walkways nearly a hundred feet in the air. A small stream cut through the heart of the sprawl, providing fresh water.

The elves knew they had visitors coming. Several males stood in combat armor and occupied defensive towers on the outskirts of the sprawl as well as key positions within it. Limbs and branches wound around the tree houses and blended them into the trees, but all of them had blue-white lanterns hung to stave off the night.

Lummin juice, Wick realized, knowing the elves had to raise glimmerworms to provide the fire-free lighting. The gentle, blue-white glow made the little Librarian homesick. The Vault of All Known Knowledge and all of Greydawn Moors used lummin juice to light their homes. Mettarin Lamplighter, Wick's father, replenished the street lamps so the town and Yondering Docks were lit at night, too. There was nothing like that familiar light.

Alomas led the way down the ridge, following a rarely used trail that zigzagged along the uneven contours. The rest of the captain's elven guards ran through the trees, sounding like a large flock of birds moving through the leaves and branches.

Wick felt the unease that swept through the elves. Once they had defined the area of their homes and lands, they hated anything new or different that entered those areas. If they wanted to see something foreign, they wanted to travel away from their homes to see it. A low buzz of conversation followed the group as they walked to the center of the sprawl.

Above, the elven palace sat, stretching from a center tree to seven outlying trees to make a massive structure. Unable to disguise the presence of the palace, the elves instead chose to emphasize it. The wood glowed a beautiful deep, rich red, as if it had just been polished. Intricate elven art decorated the sides. Beautiful lanterns created from shells, flowers, and rocks hung around it.

A beautiful elven male with silver hair put up with jeweled combs that glinted in the lamplight looked down at the arrivals. His gold link armor looked like it held inner fires. The crimson insignia of a bear's silhouette decorated the armor's chest plate.

"Craugh," the elf called down, "you're back among us one more time."

"Prince Larrosh," Craugh greeted.

"I see you haven't given up your quest to find my brother."

"Not yet. I find I've gotten stubborn in my later years."

Larrosh laughed. " 'Later years?' You're well past anything a human should live without some kind of pact with evil."

Wick thought that perhaps only he saw the pang of hurt that flashed through Craugh's green eyes.

"Maybe I've been blessed by the Old Ones," Craugh replied.

"Or cursed," the elven prince agreed. "I have to wonder at the sins you've committed in your long life, Craugh."

This time, Craugh's smile was forced. "And I thought this was going to be a pleasant visit."

"It will be. I just love to antagonize you. As I remember from our war years together, you never had much of a sense of humor. I guess some things never change."

"Have you seen your brother?" Craugh asked.

"Not in years. Certainly not since the last time I saw you." Larrosh paused a moment. "And the seasons haven't even changed since that last parting."

"No."

Interest showed on the elven prince's face then. "Have you learned anything new?"

"Perhaps. I think I know a way to find Sokadir."

"How?"

Craugh walked to Quarrel. "This is Quarrel, descendant of Captain Dulaun, fallen hero of the Battle of Fell's Keep." He tapped her sword, which instantly lit up in a cool azure color. "And this is Seaspray."

Surprise tightened Larrosh's eyes. "You found Dulaun's sword."

Quarrel wrapped her hand around the grip. "It's my sword now," she stated evenly.

Larrosh smiled. "I see."

"This," Craugh said, walking to Bulokk, "is Bulokk, of the Cinder Clouds Islands dwarves, decendant of Master Blacksmith Oskarr." The wizard touched the battle-axe in the dwarf 's hands, causing it to glow with a soft golden radiance.

"Boneslicer," Larrosh breathed, but it was so quiet in the sprawl that his voice carried to Wick's ears, and probably everyone else's in the party. "All you need is Deathwhisper to have all the weapons that were bound at the Battle of Fell's Keep."

"I think," Craugh said in a slow, steady voice, "that I can find Sokadir. What do you think?" Although he kept his voice quiet and even, there was no masking the challenge in his words.

For a moment, Wick got the impression—though he didn't know from where—that Larrosh might order the elves to descend on them in vengeful fury. Then the elven prince smiled. "You have my permission to cross Laceleaves Glen to search for my brother. When you find him, let him know that he doesn't have to be rootless. I—and his people—are here should he choose to return to us."

They camped outside the elven sprawl. Lago had enough supplies to fix a good meal, but the warriors threw lots for hunting parties in the morning. Larrosh had also afforded them hunting privileges, provided they didn't waste anything.

Wick sat at the campfire and worked in his journal. Although full night had descended and he could no longer see the elven dwellings, he still saw some of the light, and he remembered clearly what he had seen. He worked in quill and ink, tightening up the drawings he'd made earlier. He sat apart from the others, watching them as they talked.

Without warning, a soft voice sounded in his ear. "So you're a wizard, halfer?"

Snapping the journal closed, though putting blotting paper in so he wouldn't smear the lines, Wick looked around and rose to his feet. "Who's there?"

Cobner jumped to his feet and drew his battle-axe. "Who's where, little warrior? What do you see?"

Wick backed away. The hair on the back of his neck stood at attention. *Something* was there. He wasn't imagining things.

The voice laughed, again from behind him.

When he turned this time, Wick thought he saw a blur of movement. Instinctively, he reached for it, to make sure it was really there. His fingers brushed through smooth silk.

"You're very fast, dweller," the voice whispered again. "But I've never met a halfer wizard before."

"I'm no wizard," Wick said, circling, trying to track the voice.

"Then what are you?"

"I hear a voice," Cobner growled. "Someone's there." He hefted the battle-axe. Most of the others were on their feet now, all of them baring weapons.

"Prince Larrosh," Craugh called, "I'll ask you to reveal yourself now."

Incredibly, the elven prince's head appeared in midair, as if it had been struck off his shoulders and somehow suspended there. He smiled. "A little trick. I meant no harm. Just a lesson in how dangerous these woods can be."

We already knew that, Wick thought irritably.

Larrosh pulled at the cloak he wore. The garment was invisible, but Wick knew from the way he gradually came into view that it was a cloak. He turned the cloak inside out, revealing the dark blue inner lining.

"A gift," he said, "from someone I knew a long time ago."

Up close, Wick saw that the elven prince's eyes were different colors. One was light purple and the other dark brown. Since the elves preferred perfection, it was a wonder that he was prince. Then Wick remembered that Larrosh was only holding that position for his brother, till Sokadir returned or had another child to carry on the bloodline.

"I haven't seen one of Harrag's cloaks of invisibility in a long time," Craugh commented. "It must be quite the collector's item." Only then did Wick notice the flurry of green embers swirling around the end of the wizard's staff. Wick took a step back from the elven prince.

"I got it from a collector," Larrosh said, "in a trade." He cut his gaze back to Wick. "I'm something of a wizard myself."

"Really?" Wick asked.

"Not as good as Qardak, my nephew," Larrosh admitted, "but I learned a lot."

"Qardak was the one who bound the weapons at the Battle of Fell's Keep," Wick said.

"Yes."

"You were there, weren't you?"

"At the end," Larrosh agreed. Sadness tightened his mouth. "I arrived with reinforcements, but by then it was too little and far too late. The rout had begun." He flicked his glance over to Quarrel. "I saw your ancestor die. It was a very sad thing, a very beautiful thing."

"And you did nothing?" Quarrel asked, her face pale in the mixture of firelight and moonslight.

"There was nothing," Larrosh said softly, "to be done. You could not imagine the chaos that the battlefield turned into. The Unity defenders fell sick and the goblinkin overran their positions like they were made of paper." He paused. "Those men fell, weak as they were, but they sold their lives ever so dearly. They were, and *are*, heroes."

"What about my ancestor?" Bulokk asked. "Did you see him?"

"I did. When I saw him, he was headed away from the battle."

"Liar!" Bulokk shoved himself to his feet and lifted Boneslicer from the ground.

Instantly, Hallekk and Cobner stepped in front of the Cinder Clouds Islands dwarf and blocked him.

Larrosh seemed amused, not at all threatened.

"Bulokk," Craugh commanded, "sit down. Now. We are guests in this place."

Bulokk glared at the elven prince. After a moment, he broke eye contact and stalked away.

"Touchy," Larrosh said. "Even after a thousand years."

Cobner turned to face the elven prince. His scarred face was devoid of emotion. "Master Oskarr wasn't the only one to quit that battlefield without losing his life."

Larrosh smiled but took no offense. "It was, at the time, the only thing to be done."

"The thing Bulokk disagrees with," Hallekk said, "is his ancestor bein' responsible for betrayin' those men in that place."

"If you ask me," Larrosh said, "whoever set that sickness loose that night did everyone a favor. If that line hadn't buckled, every one of those men would have stayed there and died. Would that truly have been any better?"

"In the eyes of some," Cobner said, "yes."

"Not in my eyes." Larrosh looked out into the darkness. "It was everything we could do to get my brother to quit the battlefield. We finally had to render him unconscious before we could get him away."

"He left two sons there," Wick said.

Larrosh regarded him, then nodded. "He did." He shifted his attention back to Craugh. "I thought perhaps to while away some time here tonight, to trade a magic trick or two, but I'm afraid the atmosphere isn't ripe for that." He shook his head. "Even after a thousand years, what happened at that battle lives on in us. It's a shame." He smiled wanly. "So I'll bid you good luck on the morrow and take my leave."

Wick watched the elven prince leave, draping his magic cloak back over him and disappearing into the night. *What*, the little Librarian wondered, *had that been about?*

14

Sokadir

"Do you know where he is?" Wick asked as he gazed at the gem in Craugh's hand.

"I do," the wizard answered. "We're very close now." He put the gem back inside his clothing and resettled his peaked hat on his head to shade his eyes from the sun.

Standing on yet another one of the foothills that ran along the Broken Forge Mountains, Wick gazed around at the Forest of Fangs and Shadows. It was near midday, so the shadows were in somewhat of a retreat, but the fangs still prowled the brush, ready to attack.

"By the Old Ones," Cobner groused, emerging from the brush ahead of them, "there are some things a body needs to do in peace, and all manner of monsters and creatures just needs to leave him be." The dwarf was fastening his trousers and wearing spider silk across his head and shoulders.

Despite the tension that ran deeply in the group, most of the dwarves laughed and added insult to injury by teasing Cobner unmercifully.

"Mayhap them spiders object to bein' fumigated," Hallekk roared, slapping his knee. "After all, it's their home ye're a-takin' a—"

"How much do you remember from your reading about Qardak?" Craugh asked Wick.

The little Librarian assembled his thoughts and checked his notes in his journal. "Qardak was Sokadir's eldest child. There were only the two boys, born relatively close together, which is an event in elven families."

Craugh took out his pipe, packed it with pipeweed, and smoked. "Two sons, yes. And only the one learned wizardry?"

"I found nothing to suggest that the other did," Wick agreed.

"Sokadir didn't much care for wizardry. So where did Qardak learn his skills?"

"I don't know."

Craugh scratched at his beard as they walked. "Then there is the matter of the bow parts that went missing from Master Oskarr's forge. How do you suppose that happened?"

Wick thought about that and came up with the only two solutions it could be. "Either someone in Master Oskarr's forge took them, or someone from outside took them."

"Oskarr's notes don't mention any of his forge help disappearing at that time?"

"No. By process of elimination, someone went there to steal it."

Craugh sucked on his pipe and smiled. "Meaning whoever it was knew the parts were there."

"There's another possibility," Wick said as it struck him.

"Oh?"

"Someone went there looking for the vidrenium."

"Why would they do that?"

"Because Dulaun went back to the Silver Seas and began fighting Lord Kharrion and the goblinkin. His sword—was like no other. It might have been recognized by Lord Kharrion."

"But it wasn't given to Lord Kharrion," Craugh pointed out. "Instead, those reinforcement parts ended up with Sokadir."

"The parts were intended for an elven weapon," Wick said. "Maybe the magic was only meant for elves."

"Then, following our chain of logic, whoever stole those parts from Master Oskarr's forge—"

"Was an elf," Wick said softly.

"Not only was an elf," Craugh said, "but an elf who knew what vidrenium was. Interesting conundrum, isn't it?"

Wick worked that through his mind for a time. "It would be good," he said at last, "to know where Qardak learned his wizardry."

For two more days, they walked through the forest, changing directions as Craugh bade them, and he changed those directions only because the markings on his enchanted gem changed.

Finally, on the evening of the third day as they sat to dinner and tried not to think about how far they were from everything they knew, Craugh looked up into the trees and called out, "Sokadir."

Startled, Wick looked up from his journal and stared into the trees behind them. There, just barely against Jhurjan the Swift and Bold, he saw the barest hint of a silhouette against the branches.

Craugh stood but held his hands out to his sides. "You know me, Sokadir."

For a long moment, only the night sounded. Everyone in camp held their breath.

"You know I don't mean you any harm, Sokadir," Craugh said.

"I know you're a fool, wizard, to come looking for me so far from home." The voice was low and melodic. There was no sound of threat, surprise, or fear in the words.

"Yet, here I am." Craugh grinned up at the night. "It's been a thousand years. Don't you think we should settle this thing now?"

In the distance, a bear snuffled. Overhead, an owl rode the wind.

"I don't wish to speak to you," Sokadir said. "I'm more of a mind to put a shaft in your eye."

Cobner and Hallek reached for their weapons. Sonne's hands were filled with throwing knives. Quarrel already had an arrow to her bowstring.

"For over two days," Sokadir continued, "you've dogged my trail, my every move, through some wizard's trick that you've learned since last time you came here looking for me. I've told you before that I don't like wizardry. I've good reason to hate it."

Holding up a hand, Craugh motioned for them to relax. "I just want to talk."

"So talk."

"A thousand years ago, you fought in the Battle of Fell's Keep," Craugh said.

"Ancient history. Nothing of importance happened there."

"How dare you!" Quarrel exploded. "My ancestor gave his life there to protect the people that fled Teldane's Bounty before Lord Kharrion and the goblinkin."

"Who are you?"

"I am called Quarrel, and I am the descendant of Captain Dulaun."

"By the Old Ones, is that his sword? Is that Seaspray?"

"It is," she declared proudly. "We found it and recovered it. Just as Boneslicer was found."

"Boneslicer is here, too?" Awe and something else was in the elf 's voice. Wick's ears pricked up sharply.

Bulokk held up the great battle-axe. It glowed golden. Above, Sokadir was illuminated as Deathwhisper gleamed silver in his hands. His pale hair seemed to burn like white fire, and his pale purple eyes glittered like jewels.

"Do you know what you have done, Craugh?" Sokadir demanded. *"Do you know what you have done?"*

Fear, Wick decided. There was fear in Sokadir's voice. That put the little Librarian ill at ease at once. Why would Sokadir feel vulnerable here in the forest that had been his home for over a thousand years?

"I've reunited the three weapons that allowed the escape at the Battle of Fell's Keep," Craugh said. "And I've come for the true story of what happened there, Sokadir."

"That story is best forgotten."

"It can't be. It never will be," Craugh said. "It's a specter that looms over the fragile peace of the races. The goblinkin are rising again, and their numbers are increasing. Instead of fighting among themselves, humans, dwarves, and elves should once more unite to hold our lands and protect our familes from the goblinkin."

"Families! Faugh! What do you know of families, Craugh? Do you even remember your own mother and father? Brothers or sisters? Can you?"

Wick sneaked a look at Craugh, wondering how the wizard would answer.

"The Battle of Fell's Keep casts a pall over the races," Craugh said. "Each seeks to find fault with the other. There is no trust. Mayhap laying this matter to rest still won't help, but I feel it must be tried."

"We were *betrayed*, Craugh. By one of our *own*!"

"Don't ye say it were Master Oskarr!" Bulokk threatened. "I'll climb that tree if I have to, an' chop ye right out of it!"

For a moment, all was quiet. Then Sokadir spoke again. "No, it wasn't Oskarr. He shed his blood in that battle, and he would have shed it all—if he hadn't been needed to guide the survivors out of there and get us all to safety." He fell silent. "I'm coming down."

"Come ahead," Craugh said. "You'll be with friends."

Sokadir dropped like a falling leaf, sliding from side to side. Then he was on the ground, as silently as the owl that glided over his head. As he strode toward the main campfire, a huge brown bear fell into step behind him. He carried Deathwhisper, still glowing silver, in his hand, but there was no arrow nocked to string.

Bulokk and Quarrel held their weapons out, and everyone drew close, staring at them.

"Magic weapons," Sokadir said in disgust. "Boneslicer, the axe that could cleave any metal with the force of an earthquake. Seaspray, the sword that could summon waves. Deathwhisper, the bow that could strike with the force of a storm." He shook his head. "All of this power from some magical metal wizards and alchemists and blacksmiths forged in Dream."

"I see you didn't bother throwing your own weapon away the first chance you got," Cobner observed unkindly.

"I couldn't," Sokadir said. "I found out what they were truly made for."

"Lord Kharrion hid himself under another name in Dream," Sokadir said as he sat in front of the campfire.

"We figured that out," Wick said. "But how did you know?"

"My son," the elven warder stated quietly. "Qardak. He'd always had an interest in wizardly things. When he was young, he ran away with my brother."

"Larrosh?" Wick asked, finding that interesting but not totally unexpected.

"Yes. My brother has always had a calling for wizard's work as well. From the time he was very young, Larrosh tried to find his way among wizards."

"He was second born," Craugh said softly. "He knew the crown was yours when your father passed away."

Sokadir smiled a little sadly. "But these past thousand years, it's been his instead. Strange, the paths life takes us down, isn't it?"

"Yes," Craugh agreed.

"If the vidrenium wasn't made to create magic weapons," Wick asked, "what was it made for?"

"To create an even greater weapon," Sokadir said. "Do you remember the tales of a dragon named Thalanildim? He was also called the Ravager?"

"I remember him," Craugh said.

From the tone in the wizard's voice, Wick got the feeling that Craugh had really known the dragon. Which would have been impossible for anyone—except, perhaps, Craugh.

"Sixteen hundred years ago and more, before Shengharck claimed the Broken Forge Mountains as his own and made his alliance with Lord Kharrion, Thalanildim made his home here. He was crass and evil, worse even than Shengharck was."

"That's hard to imagine," Cobner said. "I seen Shengharck. Helped put an end to him with the little warrior here." He nodded to Wick.

Sokadir's purple eyes widened in surprise. "You? You're a wizard?"

Wick didn't know how to answer that.

"He's a Librarian," Craugh supplied. "From the Vault of All Known Knowledge."

Sokadir smiled a little at that. "So you built it, did you?"

"We did," Craugh admitted. "There's still a lot of work to be done there, but we saved so much of what we knew."

"Then another attempt can be made to destroy the world at a later date," Sokadir said bitterly. "Lord Kharrion put the fear of books and knowledge in the goblinkin. If they ever find your precious Library, they'll tear it to pieces and burn every book in it."

The prediction sent a surge of fear through Wick. That was his worst nightmare.

"Thalanildim was killed," Craugh said, "fourteen hundred years ago. Four hundred years before the Cataclysm."

"I know," Sokadir replied. "But Lord Kharrion was there in Dream, working on the mysterious magical metal that made these weapons. He was going to use it to raise Thalanildim. When Qardak bound the magic in the three weapons, we played right into Lord Kharrion's hands and didn't know it." He paused and looked at Craugh. "You have, too. By bringing all the weapons here, you've allowed that old spell to once more become possible. You need to get these people out of here as soon as possible, and *never* come back here again."

That set off an immediate response through the assembled ranks of warriors.

"An undead dragon," Brandt mused. "The Unity had problems with the Boneblights and the Embyrs. Can you imagine what might have happened if Lord Kharrion had succeeded?"

"More than that," a mocking voice said. "I can still make it happen."

Wick turned, tracking the voice instantly. There, just beyond the firelight's reach, shadowy figures emerged from the treeline. A huge troll held one of the dwarven pirates in his grasp. As Wick watched, recognizing Tarlis, who had been kind and a good friend aboard *One-Eyed Peggie*, the troll snapped his neck like kindling. Callously, the troll tossed Tarlis's body to the side.

Craugh spoke harshly and pointed his staff. A jagged green lightning bolt leapt from the staff and struck the troll, tearing it into chunks of burnt flesh that flew in all directions.

Arrows flew into the camp, digging into flesh and chopping dwarves down before they could move to defend themselves.

"Scatter!" Cobner growled, grabbing his battle-axe and charging into the mass of shadows. "We're targets standing here against the light!"

The others, the ones who were still alive and not too badly wounded, moved into the darkness to clash with their foes. Metal rang as blade met blade.

A tall man with a lean, hollow face and dead gray eyes stood revealed for a moment. He wore black robes that were covered with darker black sigils that absorbed the light from the campfire.

An arrow whizzed over Wick's head, missing him by inches. If he hadn't ducked low at Cobner's shouted command it would have pierced his skull. Terror vibrated through him. He looked around and spotted Craugh, who threw a green fireball at the other wizard.

The fireball sped across the intervening distance, then smashed against an invisible barrier that glowed red at the impact. The green flames spread over the wizard but didn't touch him. In seconds, the trees all around him and behind him were burning.

Cobner and Hallekk were in the thick of it. As they engaged enemy after enemy, all of them human and goblinkin, Wick realized that the Razor's Kiss were among them. In the next moment, Wick glimpsed Brandt and Ryman Bey exchanging vicious sword blows. As usual when he was in the thick of a fight, Brandt smiled with the joy he felt.

To Wick's left, Volsk, one of the Band of Thieves dwarves, struggled against two Razor's Kiss opponents, barely holding his own against the two swords with his whirling battle-axe.

Unwilling to see his friend go down beneath enemy blades, Wick dashed in and kicked one of the Razor's Kiss thieves in back of the knee. It was a move that Cobner had shown him again and again, emphasizing that he had to get his hips into it. Amazingly, the thief 's knee buckled, but he was adroit. As he went down, he twisted and came around with the knife in his left hand, lunging for Wick's throat.

The little Librarian threw himself backward, but knew instantly he was far too late. He expected to feel the cool bite of the knife across his throat at any instant. His breath froze in his throat.

Then Hallekk stepped in, blocking the blow with his axe handle. He stepped forward and brought a massive hobnailed boot smashing down on the thief 's head, leaving him stretched out unconscious or dead.

"Hit an' get clear," Hallekk said. "Hit an' get clear. Ye're a little fella." He grabbed Wick's arm and yanked him to his feet.

"Thanks," Volsk said, grinning through a mask of blood as he yanked his battle-axe from the head of his other foe. "They had me. Weren't no way out."

Wordlessly, Wick nodded. He got his bearings and headed for the nearest tree. He couldn't fight out in the open. He lacked the necessary size and strength. *And skill*, he reminded himself. *Despite Cobner's best efforts*.

Breath rasping hot and dry against the back of his throat, Wick plastered himself against the tree. Peering around it, he saw the figures locked in combat. The fires blazing in the treetops cast garish shadows over them.

Wick felt sick to his stomach with guilt and fear. His friends were in the middle of the battle, fighting for their lives and perhaps dying, and there was nothing he could do.

Still, defiance he hadn't expected thrived in him. He bent low and picked up two large rocks. He could throw. Picking out his targets, he threw with astonishing accuracy. Both goblinkin dropped to the ground.

Catching movement from the corner of his eye, Wick dropped flat on his back. An axe *thunk*ed into the tree where he'd been.

"Ye're fast, halfer," the goblinkin leered. It put a huge foot on the tree and tried to yank the blade free. "I'll give ye that. But ye won't be as fast when I chop yer legs off."

Wick scrabbled and caught a handful of dirt. Without thinking anything other than, *Idon'twanttodieIdon'twanttodie!*, he threw the dirt into the goblinkin's face. The dirt got into its eyes, nose, and open mouth. It didn't know whether to rub its eyes, sneeze, or spit.

Grabbing the goblinkin's leg, Wick bit his opponent as hard as he could, hoping he didn't end up with a chunk of goblinkin flesh in his mouth because that would have made him sick.

The goblinkin howled in mortal agony and started hopping up and down on his good leg as it tried to shake Wick loose of its other leg. The little Librarian chose that moment to kick his opponent's other leg out from under him. Falling backward, the goblinkin struck its head against the tree. It tried to get up again, acting as though it didn't have full possession of its senses.

Wick released his bite hold and crawled on top of the goblinkin's chest. Even as the goblinkin reached for him, the little Librarian grabbed his opponent's overly large ears and used them has handles to slam the goblinkin's head against the tree again and again and again and—

"I think it's dead," a calm voice said.

Still panicking, Wick managed to stop slamming the goblinkin's head against the tree. Even the bark was smashed and torn. He glanced over and saw Quarrel standing with her back against a nearby tree.

"You never know," Wick said. "These things can be very tricky."

Quarrel glanced at the inert goblinkin. "Trust me on this one."

Pushing himself up on shaking legs, Wick stood. He panted and tried to regain his breath.

"Are we winning?" Wick asked.

Quarrel shook her head. "I don't know." She showed him a long cut on her left arm. Blood dripped everywhere. "I need help getting this stopped."

For a moment, Wick froze. There was too much blood. The cut was deep. *I'm a Librarian. Not a medical doctor.*

"Wick," she said. "Please."

Swiftly, he wrapped her wounded arm, pulling the flesh together as best he was able.

She bit back a cry of pain and slumped against the tree. For a moment he thought she'd passed out. Working as quickly as he could, he knotted the makeshift bandage into place.

Then he noticed the shadow that fell over him, blocking out the moonslight that poured through a clearing in the trees.

"Look out!" Quarrel said, struggling to bring her sword up.

Wick dodged to one side but couldn't avoid the troll's backhand blow that snapped his head sideways. His senses reeled as he flew into the brush. That was probably the only thing that saved his life, because the troll swung a trident after him, trying to skewer him. Desperately, Wick rolled in the brush to keep from getting impaled.

"Forget the halfer," a man's voice commanded. "Get the girl."

"Yes, Master Broghan." The troll reached for Quarrel. She tried to defend herself, but she was weak from loss of blood and could barely lift Seaspray.

The troll batted the sword away and closed a hand over her head.

"Don't harm her." The wizard dressed in black stepped out of the shadows. "Bring her and the sword. We can always use a hostage."

Wick's thoughts spun. If the wizard was here, where was Craugh? Had something happened to him? He didn't want to believe that. The thought scared him and hurt him in ways he didn't expect. He couldn't imagine a world without Craugh in it.

The troll gathered Quarrel and threw her over his shoulder. Then he picked up Seaspray.

"Come on," Kulik Broghan said. "With all of the weapons in close proximity to Thalanildim, we may still be able to activate the spell that Lord Kharrion wove into the vidrenium."

No!

The troll glanced around in a manner that let Wick know he might have given voice to his denial. Then it lumbered after the wizard, going deeper into the forest.

Wick glanced around wildly. Shadowy figures still battled near the burning trees, and he could hear the sounds of others close by.

"Help!" he called. "Cobner!"

"Wick!" Cobner yelled back. "Wick! Hold on! I'll find you!"

But as Wick watched the troll disappear into the shadows, he knew he couldn't let Quarrel be taken without doing *something*. He pushed himself up, lurching after the troll and the wizard as his head spun.

"Wick!" Cobner called. A sound of crashing bodies sounded behind him.

"They've got Quarrel," Wick called. "They've got her sword. They're going to try to activate the spell on Thalanildim."

"Where?"

"I don't know. But it has to be close."

A horse whinnied deeper in the forest. Suddenly afraid that the wizard and the troll would slip away and disappear, Wick sped up, running as quickly and stealthily as he could. He barely kept the troll in sight in the shifting fog that slid and twisted through the Forest of Fangs and Shadows. Every time branches slid across his face he kept remembering the spiders' webs.

Only a short distance up the hill, the Razor's Kiss and goblinkin had left a group of horses. By that time, three other men, including Ryman Bey and Gujhar, had joined Kulik Broghan.

Wick couldn't help wondering how many of his friends now lay dead or were dangerously wounded. He didn't even know if Quarrel was still alive.

This was all a trap, he realized bitterly. *Getting into Kulik Broghan's fortress was far too easy. They expected us to do that*. He wanted to cry out for Craugh or Cobner or Hallekk, someone bigger and stronger who could rescue Quarrel and prevent Kulik Broghan from raising Thalanildim.

"Mount up," Kulik Broghan ordered. "If we can get Thalanildim partially raised, it will tilt the odds drastically in our favor."

By then Wick was close enough to see the shadows shifting through the trees. The horses stamped the ground and their hoofbeats sounded hollow. The acrid sweat stink of them pinched Wick's nose.

He paused at the edge of the clearing where the horses were tethered, dropping down to hide in the brush. The sound of the fighting got closer, catching up to him.

"They're fighting their way in this direction," Ryman Bey said. "Are you sure you killed that wizard?"

"He's as good as dead if he's not dead already," Kulik Broghan declared. "I studied under Lord Kharrion. He taught me a lot about Craugh. Lord Kharrion had a special hatred of him."

Craugh! Wick walled off the immediate deluge of grief that filled him.

"Let me have the sword."

The troll handed the sword to Kulik Broghan. Sparks leaped from the weapon as the wizard touched it, and the blade glowed bright blue. Cursing, he shoved the weapon under his robe to hide it. He kicked his heels against the horse's side and reined it around, charging down the decline in the direction of Darkling Swamp.

Ryman Bey took Quarrel, throwing her across the saddle in front of him, then he urged his horse into motion as well.

Twenty riders in all poured out of the clearing. More than twice that many horses remained until the goblinkin and Razor's Kiss thieves scattered the animals. Four riders thundered for the narrow gap between the trees.

Knowing that he might lose Quarrel, Wick ran, unable to help himself. He angled through the forest toward the gap, hoping to cut the horses off. *You are* not *Taurak Bleiyz*, he reminded himself. *They don't need you! You're expendable!*

But he ran anyway.

Even as fleet of foot as he was, Wick almost missed the horses. The last one passed him just as he reached the gap. Before he knew what he was doing, he leaped and reached for the horse's tail, screaming out behind it. He knotted his fingers in the coarse hair and hoped his arms weren't jerked from their sockets.

He was falling when the horse's speed yanked him forward, dragging him into the animal's flashing rear hooves. He slammed against the horse's legs with bruising force, causing the horse to stumble, then finally fall.

The goblinkin was thrown from the saddle and smashed into a tree with a meaty crunch that left it sagged into a limp collection of broken bones and torn flesh. The horse rolled once, but Wick hung on, not daring to let go his grip.

Wobbly but frightened, the horse pushed itself to its feet. Wobbly but frightened, Wick did the same. He ran two steps forward and threw himself into the saddle as the horse galloped forward again. In the saddle, he stayed low and hung onto the pommel. He bounced precariously, neither foot able to reach a stirrup. Still, it was better than riding bareback. And with his slight weight spread across the animal's back instead of a much heavier goblinkin, the horse ran at full speed with more agility.

In fact, the horse ran too fast. In no time at all, he pulled up next to a Razor's Kiss thief who was was hunkered low over his own saddle. When he saw Wick, the man's face filled with surprise. He drew his sword, straightening his back and falling behind for just a moment, then he was back with a vengeance, urging his mount on to greater speed.

Spotting a low-hanging branch ahead, Wick reined the horse to the right. The thief followed him at once, standing up in the stirrups to take a swing. At that moment, however, both horses ran under the low-hanging branch. The branch took the thief out of the saddle with a loud *thwack*!

Wick rode on. Wisps of fog drifted across the narrow trail the horses raced down. As he drew even with the next rider, a goblinkin, Wick slipped a small knife from his belt that Cobner had given him.

The goblinkin looked over its shoulder, grimaced, and pulled his club out to strike.

Ducking low, Wick thumped his heels against his animal's side. The goblinkin swung the club but it merely whistled over Wick's head. The little Librarian reached out and sliced the saddle's girth strap, dumping the goblinkin at once.

As the horse galloped around the next turn and started the steeper decline there, Wick glimpsed the Darkling Swamp ahead of him. The black surface sat placid and daunting.

15

Lord Kharrion's Wrath

Death waited out in Darkling Swamp, Wick knew. Crocodiles and poison snakes and large snapping turtles. Then there were dryads and banshees that lived in the cypress trees knotted in the center.

Three piers ran out into the water, proof that some—whether elven or human from Calmpoint and Deldal's Mills—fished or hunted there.

Kulik Broghan and Ryman Bey made for the middle one.

Wick turned and looked back the way he'd come, hoping desperately that rescue was just behind him. Instead, there was no one. He tried to rein the horse in, but it was in the grip of sheer terror and wanted to join the others.

"Look!" one of the Razor's Kiss thieves yelled. "It's the halfer!"

Two of them drew bows and nocked back arrows. Two others wheeled their mounts around and rode on an interception course.

Lacking the strength to pull the frightened horse's head around, Wick slid his weight over to the right stirrup, dropping down as one of the arrows whizzed over his head and the other pierced the saddle pommel a scant inch from his hand. He let go the pommel when he was almost on top of the other horses.

As skillfully as he could, Wick hit the ground and rolled, hoping to take away some of the brunt of the landing as well as stay a moving target. The air rushed out of his lungs when he hit, and he lost all control, skidding across the rough ground, losing skin and collecting bruises as he went.

Fortunately, he ended up in brush. There were hundreds of scratches involved, but he could hide almost immediately. Resisting the impulse to lie still until he was certain he was of a piece, he scrambled through the brush and tried not to leave a trail or anything moving behind him.

"I don't know what you hope to do here, halfer," Kulik Broghan said. "You don't have any magic, and you don't have any sword skills that can stand up against the armed men and goblinkin that are here with me."

Wick didn't answer. He was terrified and didn't know what he could do, either. But he hadn't been able to leave Quarrel alone to her fate. He found a safe spot near the water under a tall copse of cypress trees and stood in water up to his knees, hoping that no snakes or crocodiles were nearby.

"You found Boneslicer and Seaspray when we couldn't," Kulik Broghan taunted as he stepped down from his horse and walked to the end of the pier with the sword in his hand. "So we have your cleverness to thank for that."

Don't mention it, Wick thought. *Ever!*

"We had searched those areas for years. I like to think that we would have eventually found them."

Wick took cover and prepared to move. "Why would you want to unleash Lord Kharrion's Wrath now?" He moved, six feet away from where he'd been standing, and listened as arrows cut through the brush where he'd been before.

"Are you still alive?" Kulik Broghan asked.

Wick didn't answer, knowing better than to give the archers another easy target.

"If we'd gotten him," one of the archers said, walking along the ouside of the brush ringing the swamp, "you'd have heard him flopping around in there."

"Unless you got him in the heart and killed him immediately," the other archer said. He circled in the other direction.

"We had the two weapons," Kulik Broghan said as he held Seaspray out to the swamp, "but we couldn't do what Craugh managed to do in tracking Sokadir down. Nor could we have brought Sokadir out to us the way Craugh did. We knew he would trust Craugh enough to come forward. All we had to do was remain hidden long enough for that to happen. Then we could make our move. As we have done."

Wick knelt in the water and felt a snake slide through the water next to his leg.

"As to why I am doing it," the wizard went on, "it's to unite the goblinkin once more. After he'd destroyed Dream the first time in his search for the vidrenium, Lord Kharrion learned that Oskarr had come into possession of the enchanted ore only after the Battle of Fell's Keep. When he saw the weapons being used there, he knew what had occurred. So he brought in a traitor to act against the defenders there, made them all sick so there was hope that those weapons would fall into his possession. We took Seaspray, but we missed Boneslicer and Deathwhisper."

Behind Kulik Broghan, Quarrel tried to push herself to her feet. In the pale moonslight, Wick saw that the bandage he'd put on her arm had soaked through with blood. He felt torn as he looked on, feeling the need to do something, but not seeing his way clear to doing anything.

"Now," the wizard said, "everything is within our grasp again." He shouted powerful, terrible Words.

In the middle of the swamp, fierce bubbling took place and a sulfurous stench rent the air, boiling over the normal fecund stink of the swamp. Incredibly, Kulik Broghan droned on, and *something* rose out in the middle of the Darkling Swamp.

Wick thought back over all the references he'd read to Thalanildim. After his adventure with Shengharck when he had returned to the Vault of All Known Knowledge, Wick had read a lot about dragons. Much had been written about Thalanildim, but he had never learned where the great dragon's final battle had taken place. Nor had he ever learned who had finally destroyed Thalanildim.

But now the remains of the great dragon dragged themselves up out of the muck and the mire. Wick had no doubt that what he was seeing was a dragon, and it was the biggest dragon he had ever seen. It was also the most fearsome. Shengharck had been more than a hundred feet long from nose to tail, but Thalanildim was twice that.

The dead dragon stood on its hind legs and towered above the tallest trees in the swamp. Mud and dead plants clung to its body, which was malformed and mostly skeletal. Water and muck dripped through the holes of itself where flesh and dragon scales were missing. In life, Thalanildim had been beautiful. Its scales had been deep ermine with a bronze belly and gold-tipped claws. Now it was mud brown and black as though scorched by a horrible fire.

Thalanildim kept the bat wings closed about itself, but Wick saw several holes through them, as if rats had been at it while it had slept in death. Its head was shaped like a pickaxe, the jaws, the narrow end, and the horned head covered in broken horns.

"Who are you that calls Thalanildim?" the dragon demanded in a cold, empty voice. The moonslight showed the empty sockets where its eyes had been.

"I am Kulik Broghan, a wizard." The man stood at the end of the pier and held Seaspray in his sparking grasp. The sparks reflected in the dark, troubled water.

"You have no right to disturb me." The dragon eyed him with its hollow gaze.

Ryman Bey, guildmaster of the Razor's Kiss, stepped back.

"I come offering a gift." Kulik Broghan held up the sword, still showering sparks.

"What gift?"

"Would you," the wizard asked, "like to live again? To wreak your vengeance on humans, dwarves, and elves as you once did?"

"My time is over. I was killed. By a human." The dragon cocked its head to the side. "He was also a wizard. His name was Craugh."

Fourteen hundred years old, Wick thought in disbelief. *How has a human, even a wizard, lived so long?*

"Craugh," Kulik Broghan stated, "still lives. He's here in this place."

The dragon unfolded its wings. It curled up one claw at the end of a foreleg. "I would have my revenge, human, no matter what the price."

"Then agree to my binding, and to serve me," Kulik Broghan said, "and I can grant you your vengeance."

Bowing, the dragon said, "I submit, my liege, and acknowledge your sovereign power over me." Then it straightened, standing tall and formidable again. "Now give me what I seek."

Horrified, Wick watched as Kulik Broghan spoke more Words and—*twisted*—Seaspray in his grip. Metal screamed as he wrenched it from the shape Master Oskarr had beaten it into a thousand years ago in his Cinder Clouds Islands forge. The hilt crunched and folded and bent, and the blade stretched and wrapped around itself.

"No!" Quarrel cried out, pushing herself weakly forward. "Don't! Please!"

But Kulik Broghan didn't halt his cruel ministrations. In only a short time, Seaspray had been crushed into a ball of metal.

"There," he cried, proud of what he had wrought. "This is only part of what was created to bring you renewed life, but it'll be enough for now. There are two other pieces. You'll have to claim them." He held the metal ball up.

Thalanildim staggered forward through the swamp, sloshing up tall waves of muddy water and muck. The undead dragon bent down to take the metal ball.

"My own dragonheart was destroyed," the fearsome creature said. "Craugh saw it shattered to pieces, never to be formed again."

"Then you should shatter him," Kulik Broghan stated, smiling.

"Yes," Thalanildim said, fitting the metal ball into the center of its hollow chest. Dark purple light suddenly filled the undead dragon's body. Some of the dead scales folded back into place and looked near indestructible again, but there were still many gaping holes. *"Yeeeesssssssss!"* it cried joyously. It curled its foreclaws into fists. "I have missed this feeling! For years I have lain in the bottom of this swamp, no longer able to go, no longer able to enjoy the savagery of the hunt! Now . . . now I am renewed!"

The Razor's Kiss thieves, including Ryman Bey, as well as the goblinkin drew back from the undead thing.

Thalanildim opened its beak and screamed, and the Forest of Fangs and Shadows shivered in fear of the terrible noise.

"No!" Quarrel shouted, pushing past Kulik Broghan and reaching toward the dragon. "I will have that sword!"

Looking at the misshapen ball magically suspended in the dragon's chest, Wick didn't believe that even Master Oskarr (if he were alive) would be able to return the sword to its original shape. But as Quarrel reached for it, the metal ball quivered and tried to pull loose from the mysterious force holding it prisoner.

Swinging its head around, Thalanildim glared at Quarrel. "Foolish human," it snarled, lifting one of its clawed feet to smash down on her.

Quarrel dodged to one side, leaping into the swamp as the massive foot came down. Kulik Broghan stepped back, narrowly avoiding the foot and the claws as they smashed through the pier and reduced the end of it to a collection of broken planks.

Then a blazing green lightning bolt exploded against the dragon's chest, rocking it back on its heels.

Glancing to the left, Wick saw Craugh, Brandt, and Hallekk riding horses, followed by others. Evidently they'd been able to gather some of the stampeded mounts and get control of them.

Then Kulik Broghan cast a wall of invisible force that bowled over the three lead horses, toppling Craugh and the others from their mounts. The horses in the rear leaped over the downed animals and rushed on.

Wick looked to where Quarrel had gone under the dark water and didn't see her. He couldn't help wondering if the dragon's stomp had injured her. Before he knew it, he was in motion, running rapidly through the swamp. Thankfully, his dweller balance and agility stood him in good stead as he ran across the slick, soft bottom. When a log in front of him opened its eyes, then its great cavernous mouth, he leaped over it, barely avoiding the crocodile's snapping teeth.

He landed on the other side, moving as fast as he could, his heart thundering in his chest and his ears. He thought only of Quarrel, not knowing how many of his friends were already dead, knowing that Cobner had been suspiciously absent.

"Craugh!" the dragon screamed.

Wick wasn't certain if the undead creature recognized Craugh or the wizard's power. He leaped again, this time over the splintered remains of the pier. A shadow drifted over his head and he glanced up to see a giant foot descending toward him. He threw himself forward again, trying in vain to get out of the way, knowing that he couldn't get the course change he needed on the slippery mud.

I'm going to die! Squished flatter than a sheet of parchment! I hope it doesn't't—

Then Quarrel leaped up from the water, coming straight at him in a dive, looping her uninjured arm around his head and shoulders. Together, they splashed into the water and the foot missed crushing them by inches.

Quarrel caught Wick by the shirt front and pulled him from the swamp. "Get up!" she yelled. Terror had widened her eyes, but she was still functioning. "We have to get my sword!"

We? Wick thought, watching her charge after the dragon as it stalked toward shore with steps that shook the earth and quivered through the water. *We are not dragon slayers. Well, there was the one, but that was—*

Then another lightning bolt blazed from Craugh's staff and staggered Thalanildim back on its heels. This time the undead dragon went over and down, falling on its back into the swamp.

"Wick! Come on!" Quarrel caught hold of the dragon's side where the bones were exposed, finding easy hand- and footholds as she pulled herself on top of the creature.

No! Wick thought, cowering where he stood.

On the shore, Craugh battled with Kulik Broghan, who called to the dragon. Mystic bolts of green and purple shot between the two wizards, ripping away the shadows and crackling across the shields each had in place.

Sokadir and his bear were among the goblinkin then. The elven warder rode the bear and shot Deathwhisper, ripping goblinkin and thieves apart when he hit them.

"Wick!" Quarrel was in the center of the dragon's chest, pulling hard on the metal ball that had been Seaspray and now gave the dragon unlife. "Help me! My arm is too weak to get a proper hold! We can do this!"

Frozen, definitely not wanting to get any closer to the dragon, Wick watched her pulling at the metal ball.

"Wick, *please*!"

Sighing, knowing he was probably rushing to his doom, he ran to the dragon's side, grabbed a rib and climbed up. He joined Quarrel at the chest, then hesitantly took hold of the metal ball. Power vibrated through his arms and he released it at once.

"It won't hurt you," Quarrel told him. "Take hold with me." She maintained her hold and that gave him hope.

Wick knelt and latched onto the metal ball, forcing himself to hang on this time. Grudgingly, the metal ball shifted, almost pulling loose.

Then Thalanildim sat up and screamed again. Wick and Quarrel hung on.

"Inside its chest," Quarrel said, ducking into the cavity and standing on bone.

"I'll kill you," the dragon threatened as it got to its feet. It tried to reach for them, but Craugh hit it again with another lightning bolt, staggering it again and nearly knocking it over. Recovering, the dragon spread its wings and vaulted into the air.

Wick glanced out the chest cavity and saw the ground fall away from them as Craugh threw another lightning bolt that missed. Kulik Broghan lay stretched out on the ground, a smoldering mass at the swamp's edge.

"It's f-f-f-flying!" Wick shrilled. He couldn't believe it. He turned to Quarrel. "It c-c-can't f-f-f-fly! It's w-w-wings are f-f-full of h-h-h-holes!"

"I've always been told that dragons fly just as much from magic as from the hot gases inside them," Quarrel said as she took a fresh hold on the metal ball. "I guess this proves maybe there's more to the magic theory."

Wick decided, even as he hung far above the earth, that the subject bore substantial investigation. If he lived.

"But it won't live if we can free Seaspray from it," Quarrel said.

"True," Wick said, "but it might not fly, either. Do you want to fall?"

Without warning, a fire dawned in the dragon's belly, a great furnace coming to life. The heat was almost hot enough to blister them.

Wick looked toward the ground, which suddenly shifted as the dragon heeled over and sailed perpendicular. If he hadn't been quick, he wouldn't have grabbed onto a rib and been able to hang from it so that he didn't fall.

Quarrel held on with her uninjured arm and one leg. "Get Seaspray," she said.

It was all Wick could do to hold his position. The fire in the dragon's belly boiled free and erupted out its throat and sprayed toward Craugh, who held up his staff and formed an invisible dome barrier that kept out the flames and the worst of the heat.

Sokadir fired Deathwhisper and the ruby shafts struck the dragon three times in quick succession, hitting the chest twice near Wick and smashing through one of the wings. Fiery pits sizzled in the dragon scale. Roaring in pain, Thalanildim heeled over on its side.

Craugh attacked again with another lightning bolt as the dragon flew low. Evidently it wasn't tracking who was who, because Thalanildim breathed fire again and cooked three goblinkin hiding in the swamp, causing the water to boil up in clouds of steam.

More of Deathwhisper's magical bolts hammered the dragon, causing it to vibrate, but not appearing to do too much harm. When Thalanildim heeled over again, it caught Quarrel reaching for the metal ball. Losing her grip, she tumbled free and fell before Wick could help her.

Frozen in fear, holding onto one of the dragon's ribs, Wick watched her flail as she plummeted toward the swamp.

"Get Seaspray!" she yelled. Then she dropped into the black water.

Wick knew that the fall might have killed her on impact, and that made him even more afraid. But he knew he didn't have a choice. Either Thalanildim would kill his friends, or it would die and he would fall anyway. Grimly, he leaped for the metal ball. Wrapping both arms around it, he put his feet against one of the ribs and pushed.

Thalanildim screamed in pain and faltered in flight. It hammered at its chest like it was having indigestion.

Then, miraculously, the metal ball pulled free of the dragon. Although he wanted to try to hold onto it, Wick instinctively released it and grabbed for the nearest rib. He missed. Then he fell.

Down and down he tumbled, not sure how high up he'd been. The only good thing was that he had managed to fall free of the dragon while over the swamp. The metal ball fell ahead of him, dropping faster than he was.

Below the metal ball, an arm thrust out of the black water, coming out of the swamp up to the shoulder. It was a woman's arm, supple and lean.

As Wick watched, the metal ball glowed cool blue, then—in the space of a heartbeat—it unfolded and reshaped and became a sword again. The hilt slapped naturally into the waiting hand, as if it had been designed to do that very thing.

The image of Quarrel's arm (for that was, of course, who it was) was something Wick knew he would remember forever. Then Quarrel's head and shoulders crested as she treaded water, gasping for air.

In the next minute, Wick dropped into the water. He held his breath as he went under, shifting so that he went under feet first. As soon as he touched the muddy bottom (thinking of snakes and crocodiles and other horrible things that might be crawling, slithering, or swimming through the depths), he pushed with both feet and swam for the surface.

Thalanildim had already come around to attack them, breathing fire and obviously intent on getting Seaspray back. Evidently some of the power that the metal had awakened within the dragon yet lingered. The fire in its belly blazed again, burning far outside the dragon's ravaged body till it looked like a comet falling from the sky. It crashed into the swamp, throwing a tidal wave of muck in all directions.

"Behind me," Quarrel commanded. Despite her injury, she held the sword in both hands as if she was taking strength from it.

Wick slid in behind her, knowing that she wouldn't offer much protection when the dragon's breath struck them. It was far too late to run.

Then Sokadir was there, firing bright arrow after arrow into the dragon and breaking its forward momentum. Thalanildim tried to stand its ground, digging its claws into the muck and screaming in anger.

Holding Seaspray high, Quarrel slammed the flat of the blade against the swamp. Immediately a dark wall of water rose before her and cascaded into the dragon, knocking it down onto its back.

Steam boiled up, filling the black sky with a huge, hot fog that nearly obscured Wick's sight. As he watched, Thalanildim's fire extinguished except for a few fleeting coals.

Bulokk ran through the water, carrying Boneslicer high. He was in waist-high water when he swung the axe and chopped off Thalanildim's head as the dragon tried in vain to get to its feet. A final death shivered through the dragon's body, shaking it to pieces that scattered over the swamp.

It never moved again.

Looking back to shore, Wick discovered that no goblinkin or Razor's Kiss thieves remained alive or willing to fight. He threw up twice, saw that it attracted turtles, fish, and something with lethal-looking tentacles, and he ran for the shore.

"Little warrior!" Cobner met Wick in a huge bear hug as soon as he reached the shore. "You're alive!"

"I am," Wick agreed, hugging the big dwarf back fiercely and not minding that he couldn't quite catch his breath. "And so are you."

Then Cobner held Wick at arm's length as if he were a child and Cobner was the proud father. "You've done went and killed your second dragon!"

"Actually," Wick said, "it was already dead."

"Well, it was looking right lively there for a time." Cobner put Wick on the ground and beamed. "Looks like I'm a dragon behind you."

"Believe me," Wick said, "the next one we find, you can have all to yourself."

Cobner roared with laughter.

"Did we lose anyone?" Wick asked.

Cobner sobered some then. "Tarlis. The pirate from *One-Eyed Peggie*. But no one else, thank the Old Ones. We've been blessed this night, little warrior."

"We were," Craugh said, coming over to join them. The wizard stood on shaky legs, but he stood. One side of his face was bruised and lacerated and looked like it would need a few stitches, but he appeared to otherwise be in good health. "You brought us this far, Wick." The wizard clapped the little Librarian on the shoulder.

"And he even ripped the heart out of an undead dragon to do it," Cobner added proudly. "I told him them lessons I've been giving him on how to fight would stand him in good stead. He's becoming a regular champion hero."

Nodding toward Bulokk and Quarrel, who were walking out of the swamp, the dwarf helping the human, Wick said, "There are the real heroes. If they'd given up on their destinies, those weapons would have never been found. Or they wouldn't have had the ties Craugh needed to use to find Sokadir."

Alysta came and sat on the ground near them, wrapping her tail around her paws. "Where is Sokadir?"

All of them looked around, but the elven warder had disappeared into the night.

A Note From Grandmagister Edgewick Lamplighter

We spent days in the Forest of Fangs and Shadow looking for Sokadir, but we never found him again. He had completely disappeared.

Craugh tried to use the connection between the three weapons, but none of the visions worked again. Later, he supposed that it was because there was actually a fourth component of the spell: Thalanildim itself. After all, Lord Kharrion had helped design the vidrenium in Dream, and it had been crafted with the dragon in mind.

We traveled back through the Forest of Fangs and Shadows largely without incident. We decided not to go back through Laceleaves sprawl and went instead toward Darbrit's Landing.

Unfortunately, though we had laid to rest the threat of Lord Kharrion's Wrath, we were no closer to the solution of who betrayed the defenders at the Battle of Fell's Keep. We found one of the abandoned sprawls (the one where you're obviously reading this journal, my apprentice) and I wrote this journal.

We stayed here for several days, healing from our injuries and burying poor Tarlis. We also hoped that Sokadir would return, but he didn't. While I was here, though, I went back through my research notes, something I always do when I don't find a proper solution to a problem I've not solved—and something I hope I've taught you to do.

While I was doing that, I deduced who had to be the one who betrayed the defenders at the Battle of Fell's Keep. In the end, there was only one person it could be. I knew that it had to be someone versed in wizardry. Someone who was at the Battle of Fell's Keep. And someone, as it turned out, who had knowledge of what was being created in Dream. This was the person who went to the Cinder Clouds Islands and managed to steal the bow reinforcements Master Oskarr had made. Someone who could be invisible when he wanted.

This person, as it turns out, was also at Dream under a ficticious name. He was an elf, and he called himself Banir and claimed he was from Silverleaves Glen. But what gave him away was that one of the journal keepers whose work survived Dream's destruction was a very vivid writer. He wrote down descriptions of everything. Including this imposter's very extraordinary physical feature.

Banir the elf had mismatched eyes. One was purple, but the other was dark brown. I thought that—

Afterword

"Grandmagister . . . Juhg, isn't it?"

Startled, Juhg looked up from his reading. Although he hadn't yet finished Grandmagister Lamplighter's final postscript, he knew where his mentor had been going with his deductions. There had been only one place to go, only one person that all the specifics fit.

Juhg stared at the empty space in front of him, not too terribly surprised to find the voice apparently came from empty air.

"Prince Larrosh," Juhg said tiredly. He blinked against the bright morning sunlight, surprised that the dawn had come without him knowing. But he had been totally engrossed in translating the book.

"Ah, you know me." Larrosh swept off his cloak of invisibility and touched Juhg's chin with the tip of his longsword. "That is Grandmagister Lamplighter's book?"

Juhg saw no reason to lie. Larrosh already knew what was *in* the book. He just obviously hadn't known *where* it was.

"After Craugh came here a few months ago, intent on finding Sokadir again after so many years, I thought perhaps Grandmagister Lamplighter had put everything together," Larrosh said.

"There isn't much," Juhg said, "that gets by Grandmagister Lamplighter."

Larrosh laughed. "I did. Once." He lifted the cloak and rendered himself invisible again. "That's how I got by your men below, taking out the guards one by one till my warriors could take them all prisoner." He revealed himself again and gestured with the longsword to the door. "Why don't we join them?"

Juhg started to close the journal and put it away.

'I'll take that," Larrosh said, and snatched it from him.

"Your warriors are with you?" Juhg went to the door and started down the rope ladder.

"Of course. What use would a prince be without his warriors?"

"Do they know you betrayed your brother and are responsible for the deaths of your nephews?"

"Go ahead and tell them," Larrosh challenged. "They won't believe you. Sokadir is a myth to them. I've been their prince for the last thousand years. What are you going to offer them as proof? A book written so that they can't read it?"

Juhg didn't say anything. Some of his dismay lifted when he saw Raisho and the others were still alive, though tied securely and sat in place like children. To his surprise, Craugh was also there.

"Craugh," Juhg called.

The wizard looked up. His hands were tied behind him and a strange glowing necklace hung at his chest. One eye was swelled shut and his face was heavily marked by a beating. Since some of the bruises were faded yellow with age, Juhg knew that the beatings had been going on for a while. He couldn't believe that he would ever see the wizard so . . . helpless.

"It's my fault, Juhg," Craugh said. "I made the mistake of underestimating him." He nodded toward the necklace. "He's made me helpless."

Larrosh grinned. "I kidnapped him from your ship using a spell similar to the one Grandmagister Lamplighter used to get the weapons from Kulik Broghan's all those years ago. Mirrors are wonderful, deceitful things. You can tell yourself what you see in there is the truth, or that it's lying to you. It's really up to you what you believe." He shrugged. "If I'd wanted to, I could have set fire to your ship or holed her and sent you to the bottom. My bog beasts almost had you in Shark's Maw Cove."

"I'll know how to ward against such a thing next time," Craugh vowed.

Larrosh spun on him. "There won't be a *next* time. This ends here. Now. I have the book that was hidden in this place, and I have the books you found in the other places."

"Then what's to become of us?" Juhg asked.

Larrosh looked at him. "You came here to murder the prince of Laceleaves. You'll be killed, of course."

"What ye did at the Battle of Fell's Keep was despicable," Raisho said. "Ye deserve to be 'anged."

"And who will hang me?" Larrosh taunted. He shook his head. "What I did at the Battle of Fell's Keep was to protect my people. If I hadn't made the deal with Lord Kharrion, if I hadn't helped him in Dream and again in the Painted Canyon, he would have let his goblinkin hordes tear Laceleaves Glen apart. I protected them."

"By betraying those heroes," Juhg said. Anger burned through him. He'd been a slave for a time, and he knew firsthand how cruel and unjust the world could be.

"When you can't save everyone, you take care of your family and your people first," Larrosh said.

"You thought Lord Kharrion was going to win."

"Lord Kharrion *should* have won. What happened when the Unity beat him was an aberration. Craugh should never have been able to do what he did."

"You sacrificed your own nephews," Juhg said. "You weren't saving your family first. You thought you were saving yourself."

Larrosh looked a little uneasy in that moment. "They wouldn't listen. Sokadir wouldn't listen."

"Worse than that," Craugh said hoarsely. "You allowed Sokadir to believe his own son betrayed him and those defenders at the Battle of Fell's Keep."

"I didn't—"

"That's what you did!" a loud voice accused.

Drawn by the voice, Juhg looked up and saw Sokadir kneeling high in the tree above them. The elven warder's face was impassive, as though carved of stone, but his purple eyes gleamed with fire.

"You told me Qardak's binding of the weapons to strengthen our wards failed," Sokadir said. "You told me it was because he had been tainted by Lord Kharrion while he'd been studying at Dream. But it was you who had been tainted, brother."

"The goblinkin would have destroyed our homeland," Larrosh argued. "What I did, I did to save our home."

The elven warders started talking among themselves in frantic voices. From what Juhg understood, most of them had never before seen the absentee prince.

"You betrayed men who were heroes," Sokadir said. "You branded one of the bravest dwarves I had ever known a traitor. You killed my *sons*!"

"How," Juhg asked, "did you get Deathwhisper?"

"My son. Qardak. He told me he had the bow reinforcements made for me. I didn't know they were from Master Oskarr's forge until I saw his weapon and Seaspray. Then I saw his mark on the weapons his warriors carried, and I knew he spoke the truth when he told me he'd made them." Sokadir's voice broke. "I couldn't believe my son was a thief. Then Qardak told me that the bow's parts were made of the mystic metal he'd worked on in Dream, and that Master Oskarr must have stolen that."

"That metal was lost, not stolen," Juhg said, "when Dream was destroyed. Master Oskarr never knew what he had. He only knew he'd traded mermen for it."

"I've had enough of this," Larrosh snarled. "Everything you're talking about, it's a thousand years old. It doesn't matter now."

"It matters now," Juhg said, "because the lies about the Battle of Fell's Keep still manage to haunt the relationship between dwarves, elves, and humans. At a time when we should be uniting and pooling our resources, we're remaining apart." That was one of the things about Greydawn Moors that he truly loved in that moment. Nowhere else, even though it had been threatened before the Vault of All Known Knowledge had been destroyed, did the peoples of the world live together in such harmony. "We've waited a thousand years for the truth about that battle. The lies that were woven that day still bind our future and threaten the lives of every human, dwarf, elf, and dweller that lives." He looked at the elven warriors surrounding them. "If we don't pull together, you'll all be overrun by the goblinkin at some point."

"Don't listen to him! He's lying! That's all outsiders ever do!" Larrosh turned to the guards. "Kill the assassins! Execute them all!" He drew his own sword.

"Stay your hands!" Sokadir thundered. "I *am* the prince of Laceleaves Glen, and it is *my* order you will obey!"

For a moment, many of the younger guards looked undecided. Then the eldest among them took control and told them to stand down.

"Kill them, I said!" Larrosh shrilled. He rushed at Craugh, his blade lifted to pierce the old wizard's throat.

Juhg launched himself without thinking, staying low and grabbing the elf 's feet. Larrosh tripped and sprawled, coming around instantly to try to slit Juhg's throat. Juhg dodged back, once, twice, then rolled to his feet and stood ready, breathing in, determined to try one of the Kritkov dwarven grappling techniques he'd read about and taught to some of Varrowyn's warriors at the Vault of All Known Knowledge.

Movement drew his attention overhead and he watched as Sokadir dropped gracefully through the branches until he landed on the ground before Juhg.

"No," Sokadir said. "You'll not cause anyone else's death."

"Then by blood right, I challenge you for the right to rule. Right here. Right now."

Without a word, Sokadir handed Deathwhisper to Juhg, then drew his own longsword and fighting knife. He stood and waited. "You don't want to do this, brother," he said softly. "I will banish you, but I won't take your life. Even after all you've done."

Larrosh laughed bitterly. "You won't take my life?" He cursed and started circling. "Do you know where I *should* be? Ruling at Lord Kharrion's side, is where I *should* be. He was going to make me a king."

"Of goblinkin?" Raisho snorted. "One day they would 'ave rose up an' et ye. Mayhap fed ye yer own tripe afore they did."

"Don't do this," Sokadir whispered.

"Why? Are you afraid?"

"I don't want to kill you."

"Well, I *want* to kill you!" Larrosh lifted his hand and purple embers gathered around the ring he wore.

Without warning, the heavy necklace Craugh had worn sailed through the air and landed around Larrosh's neck. The purple embers died and faded away.

"Well," Craugh said, standing and dusting his hands off. "I had no further need of that. You'll find, Larrosh, that I'm not as ill-informed as I've let you believe."

Panic and anger filled Larrosh's brown eye and purple eye then. He grabbed the necklace and tried to pull it off but it wouldn't budge. "When I am prince," he told the elven guard, "kill the wizard first." He turned and attacked Sokadir with sword and knife, cutting hard and fast.

Although Juhg had read books on bladework and seen several swordfights, none of them were anything like the lightning display that ensued. Afterwards, he thought there were seven moves in all, perhaps nine, strike, riposte, and counter. But at the end, Sokadir plunged his sword through his brother's heart and slashed Larrosh's throat with his knife.

Larrosh stood in wide-eyed shock for a moment, but he was already dead. Then he fell and slid off Sokadir's blade.

Tears streamed down Sokadir's cheeks as he turned to face the guards. "I am your prince once again. Free those men and make a litter for my brother."

Days later, after Larrosh had been given a sky burial and the stories had all been finally told and made sense of while Craugh mended from his wounds, Sokadir escorted Juhg, the wizard, Raisho, and his crew back to Darbrit's Landing where *Moonsdreamer* still sat safely at anchor.

Prince Sokadir had agreed to go back to Greydawn Moors to tell the story of what had happened at the Battle of Fell's Keep after he'd spent time going among his people again. Juhg had already decided to put the Novices to work making copies of the book he would write on the way back to Greydawn Moors that told the entire history of the search for the truth, and of the truth itself. As those copies were made, they would be placed in the Libraries he was building. He also planned to enlist readers to read the stories out loud to the public.

Gradually, the story would be told, and it would serve two functions. The truth would be known, and others might be made curious to learn to read so they might read it for themselves.

That, he thought, was going to be the hardest part: making sure what he wrote and drew was compelling enough to keep those readers turning the pages. Still, it was about honor and betrayal, mixed with wizardry and mystery, and those were always favorites.

"Do you think it will matter?" Sokadir asked as Raisho gave the order to prepare to sail. Going down the Steadfast River would be much easier than coming up it.

"We'll be telling the truth," Juhg said, "about something that has affected the life of everyone living out there today. It'll matter. The truth always does. That's one of the things that Grandmagister Lamplighter always taught me. The truth is stronger than the strongest man. Stronger than the best wizardly spell."

Craugh harrumphed at that, but Juhg ignored him. Despite his displeasure, Juhg knew the wizard recognized the truth as well.

"Lord Kharrion was the greatest evil the world has ever known," Juhg went on. "But misassumptions, lies, and cover-ups cast as great an evil as evil itself. For a thousand years, evil has lived on in the shadow of itself, in all the fears and whispered gossip of what took place at the Battle of Fell's Keep. It has kept good people from each other's sides during their time of need." He looked at Sokadir. "It kept you from your people for a thousand years."

Sokadir nodded.

"You can't replace that time," Juhg stated quietly.

"No," the elf prince agreed. "But your Grandmagister's efforts to get at the truth have given me back my son in ways that I had thought forever lost to me." He held his hand out to Juhg, a rare honor among elves because they didn't like touching other races. "I give you my word, Grandmagister Juhg, that this truth you have uncovered—even though it is hurtful—will be told throughout the Forest of Fangs and Shadows. To every trade caravan that comes nearby, and to all the surrounding towns and villages."

"The truth is everything in the end," Juhg said. "It is the greatest power in the world to make all people equal. If everyone knows what the truth is, no one can use lies to separate those people and turn them against one another."

And he believed that, because he was only repeating the last thing Grandmagister Lamplighter had written to him in the final journal before asking him to find Sokadir and tell him the truth.

Sokadir took his leave, vanishing once more into the forest with his warriors at his heels.

Looking out at the sun setting ahead of them, turning the sky red and purple, Juhg thought about Grandmagister Lamplighter and all that his master had risked to come this far. A sense of completion filled Juhg, knowing he'd had a hand in one of Grandmagister Lamplighter's greatest works.

But still, it wasn't the same. Grandmagister Lamplighter's absence gave a hollowness to the victory.

"I miss him, too," Craugh said. "But I know he's out there somewhere, having the adventure of his life."

"I know," Juhg said. He looked at the wizard. "I was afraid there for a while, though, that I had lost you."

Craugh laughed. "Over that little amount of blood you found on the cabin floor with the word BEWARE written in it?"

"Yes."

"Trust me," Craugh said, "the day I am killed, you'll be able to paint this ship in blood. Not all of it mine."

Juhg frowned. "That's not exactly a restful thought."

"Perhaps not, Grandmagister, but it is the truth."

"I suppose it is. Perhaps more restful thinking requires wine. I know Raisho keeps a stash of it aboard."

They went together, wizard and Librarian, as Raisho and his men got *Moonsdreamer* once more underway. For a while, Juhg swapped stories of Grandmagister Lamplighter with Craugh as the wizard drank the wine. But, eventually as he'd known it would, his work called him.

He pulled out his journal, a quill, and a bottle of ink, and quietly in the ship's galley, Juhg set to work with the love that he'd been taught by his mentor.